Also by Andi Watson

Glister
Princess Decomposia and Count Spatula

KERRY

and the Knight of the Forest

Cover art, text, and interior illustrations copyright © 2020 by Andi Watson

All rights reserved. Published in the United States by RH Graphic, an imprint of Random House Children's Books, a division of Penguin Random House LLC, New York.

RH Graphic with the book design is a trademark of Penguin Random House LLC.

Visit us on the Web! RHKidsGraphic.com • @RHKidsGraphic

Educators and librarians, for a variety of teaching tools, visit us at RHTeachersLibrarians.com

Library of Congress Cataloging-in-Publication Data
Names: Watson, Andi, author.
Title: Kerry and the knight of the forest / Andi Watson.
Description: First edition. | New York : RH Graphic, [2020] | Audience: Ages 8–12 | Audience: Grades 4–6 | Summary: "Kerry gets lost on his way home and has to navigate through a fantastical forest to find his way out, only most of the creatures in the forest are not there to help him"—Provided by publisher.
Identifiers: LCCN 2019025827 | ISBN 978-1-9848-9330-7 (library binding) | ISBN 978-0-593-12523-6 (hardcover) | ISBN 978-1-9848-9329-1 (paperback) | ISBN 978-1-9848-9331-4 (ebook)
Subjects: LCSH: Graphic novels. | CYAC: Graphic novels. | Lost children—Fiction. | Forests and forestry—Fiction. | Fantasy.
Classification: LCC PZ7.7.W375 Ke 2020 | DDC 741.5/973—dc23

Designed by Patrick Crotty

MANUFACTURED IN CHINA
10 9 8 7 6 5 4 3 2 1
First Edition

A comic on every bookshelf.

To my Family

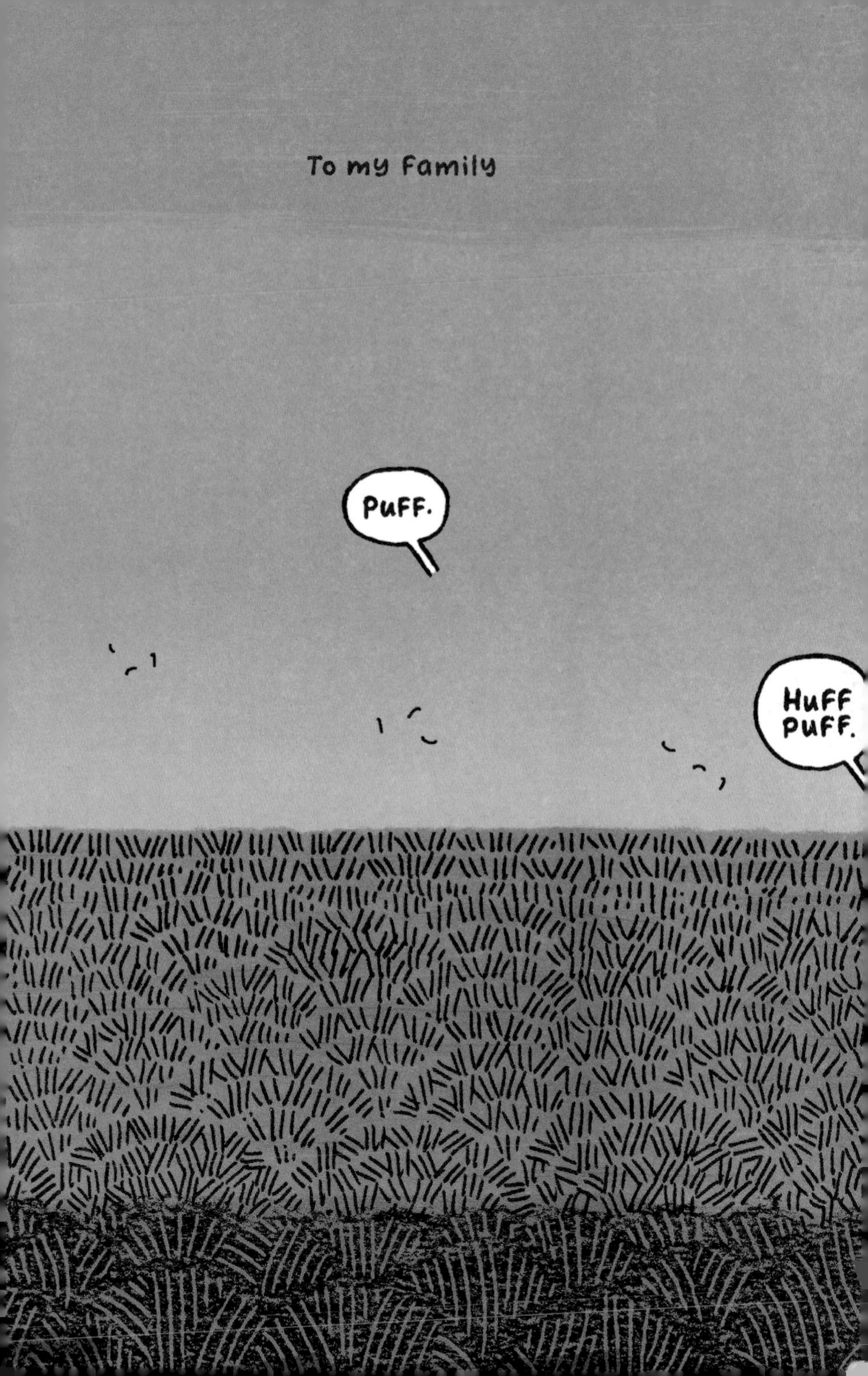
PUFF.
HUFF
PUFF.

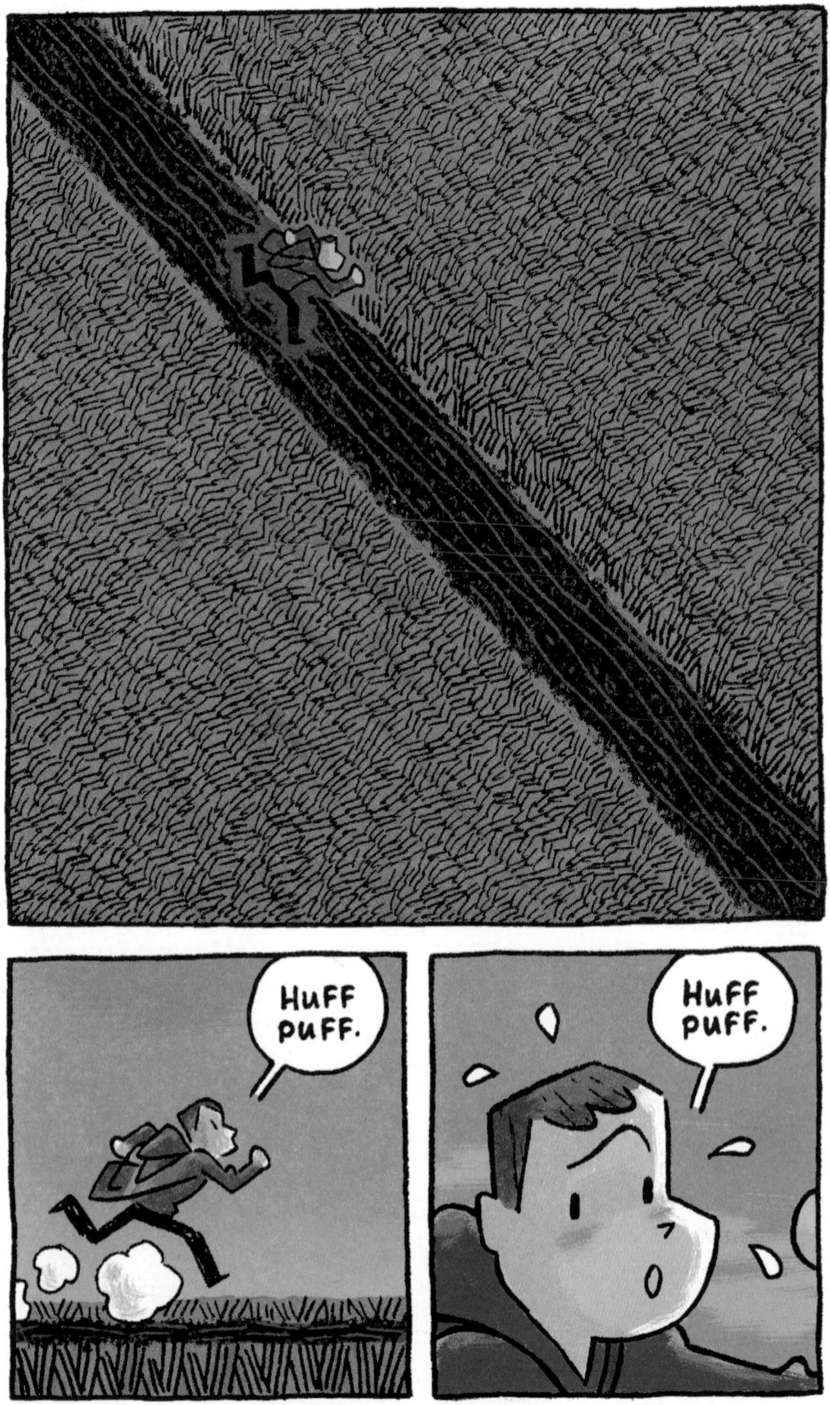
HUFF PUFF.
HUFF PUFF.

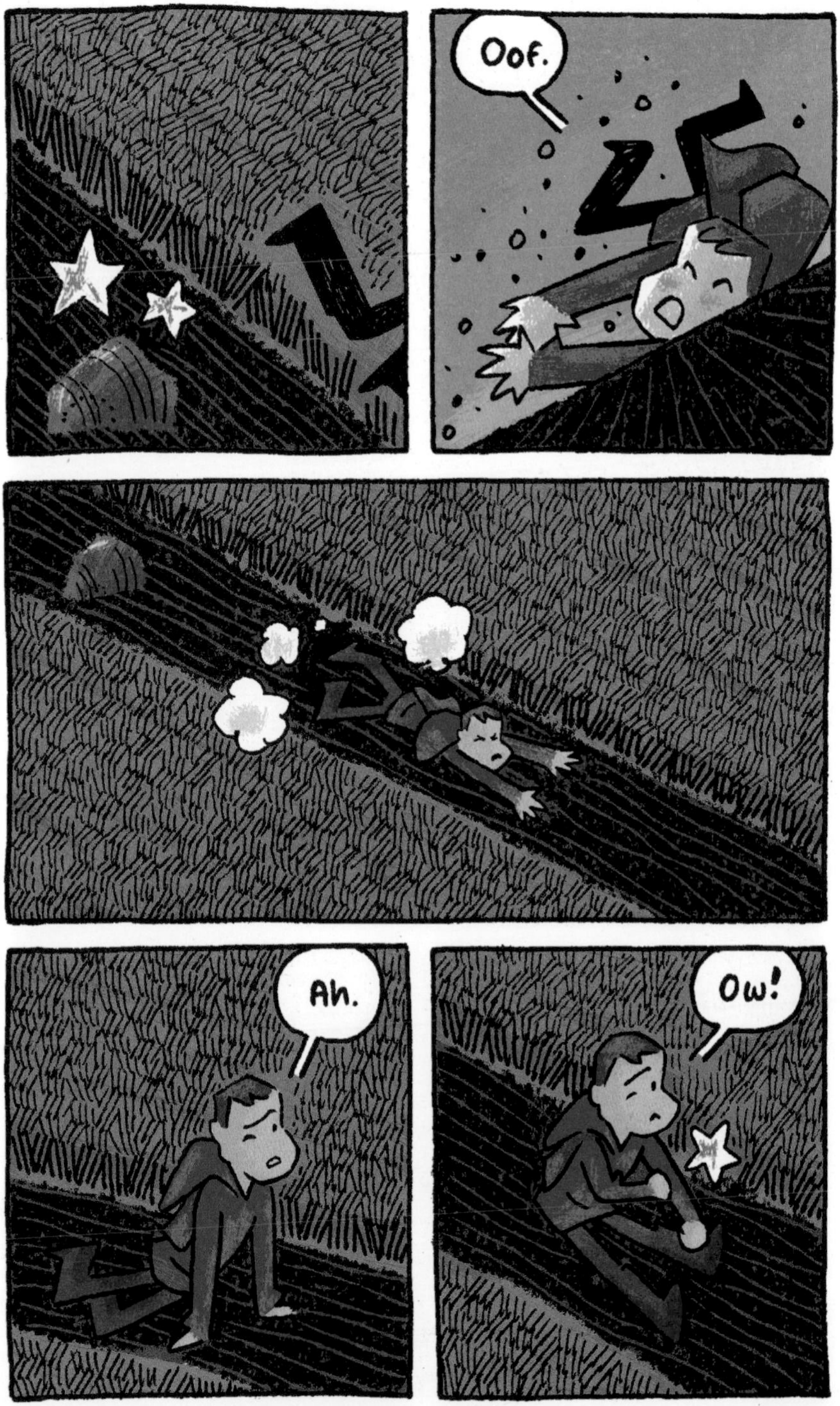
Oof.
Ah.
Ow!

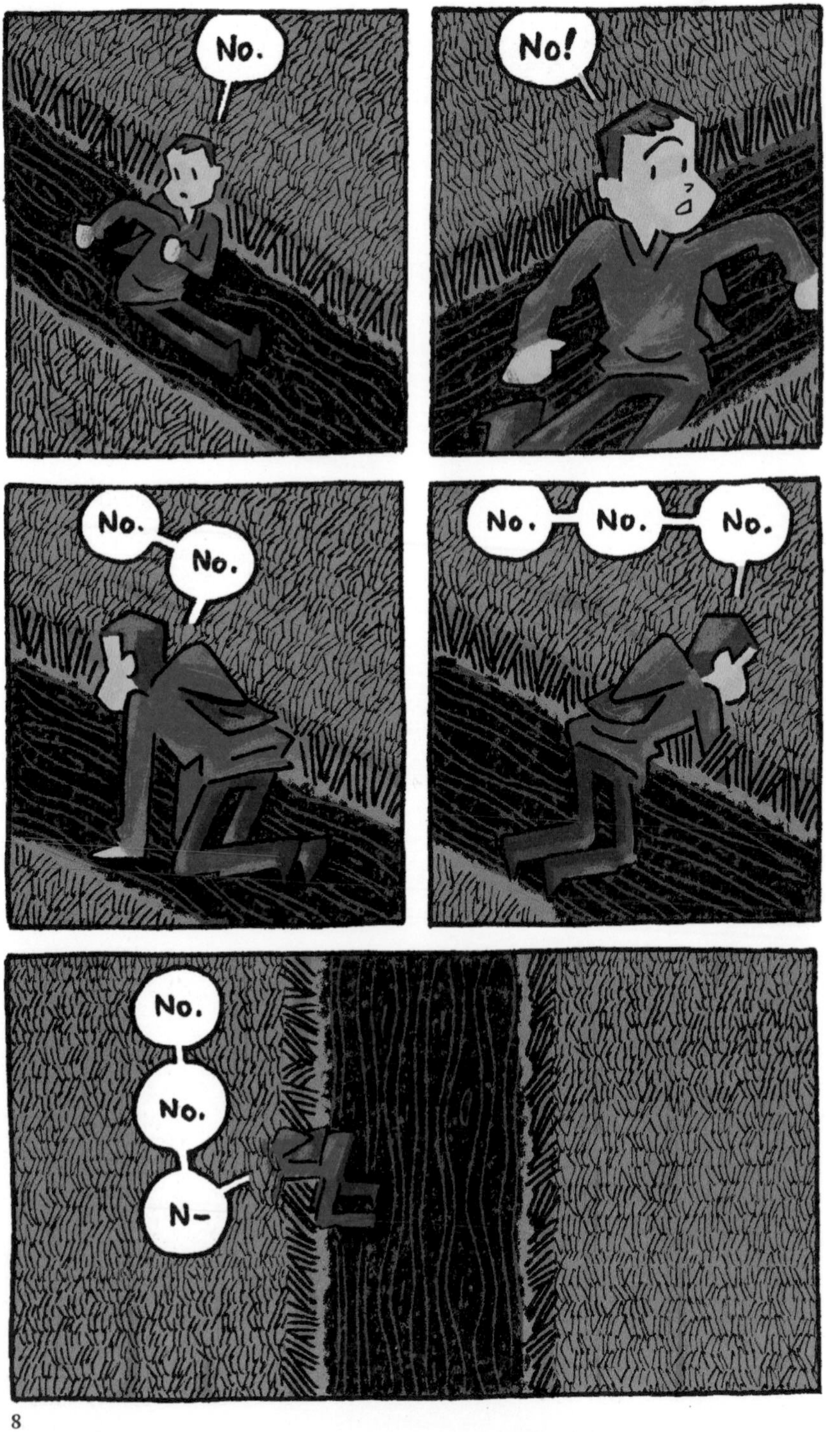
No.
No!
No.
No.
No.
No.
No.
No.
No.
N-

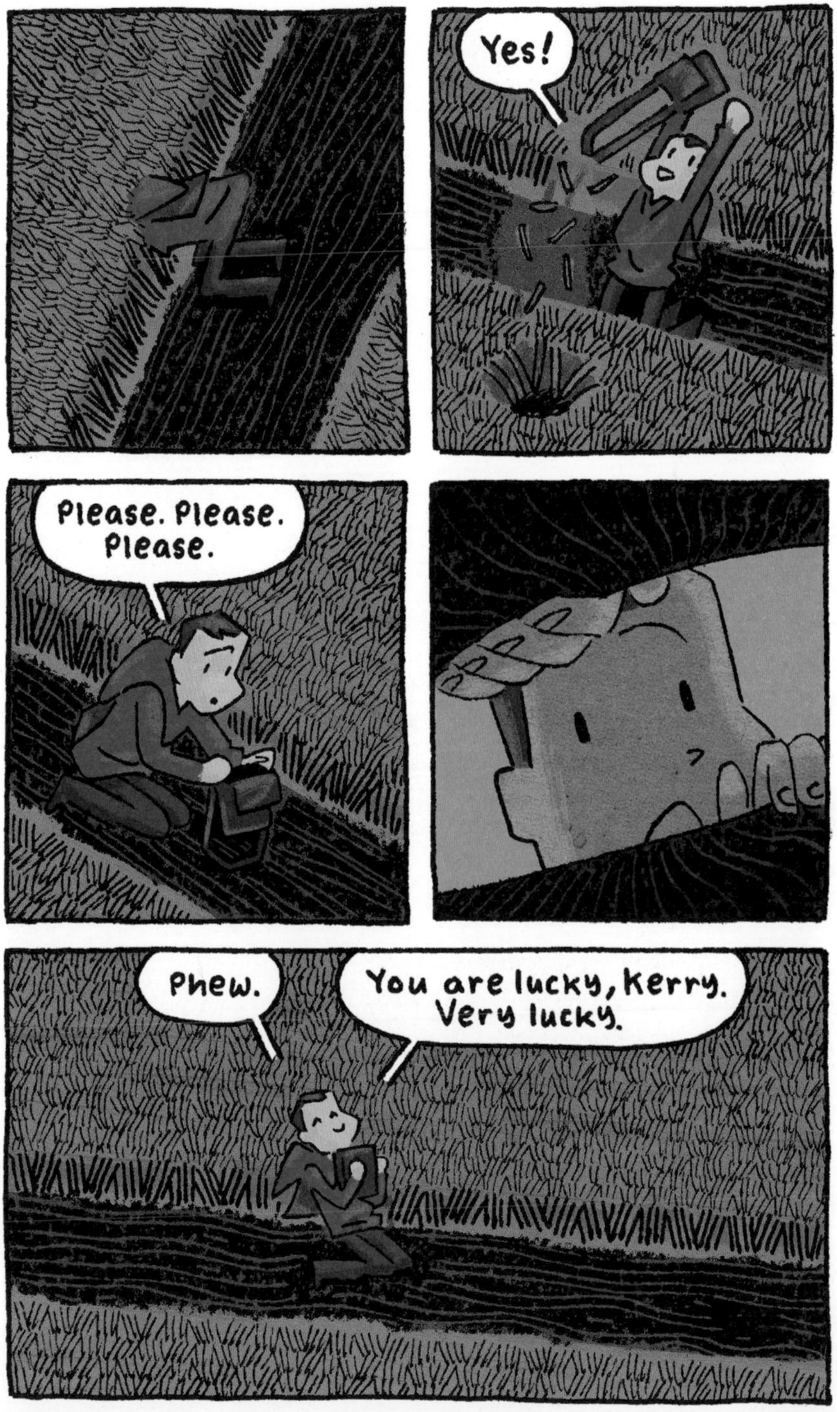
Yes!
Please. Please. Please.
Phew.
You are lucky, Kerry. Very lucky.

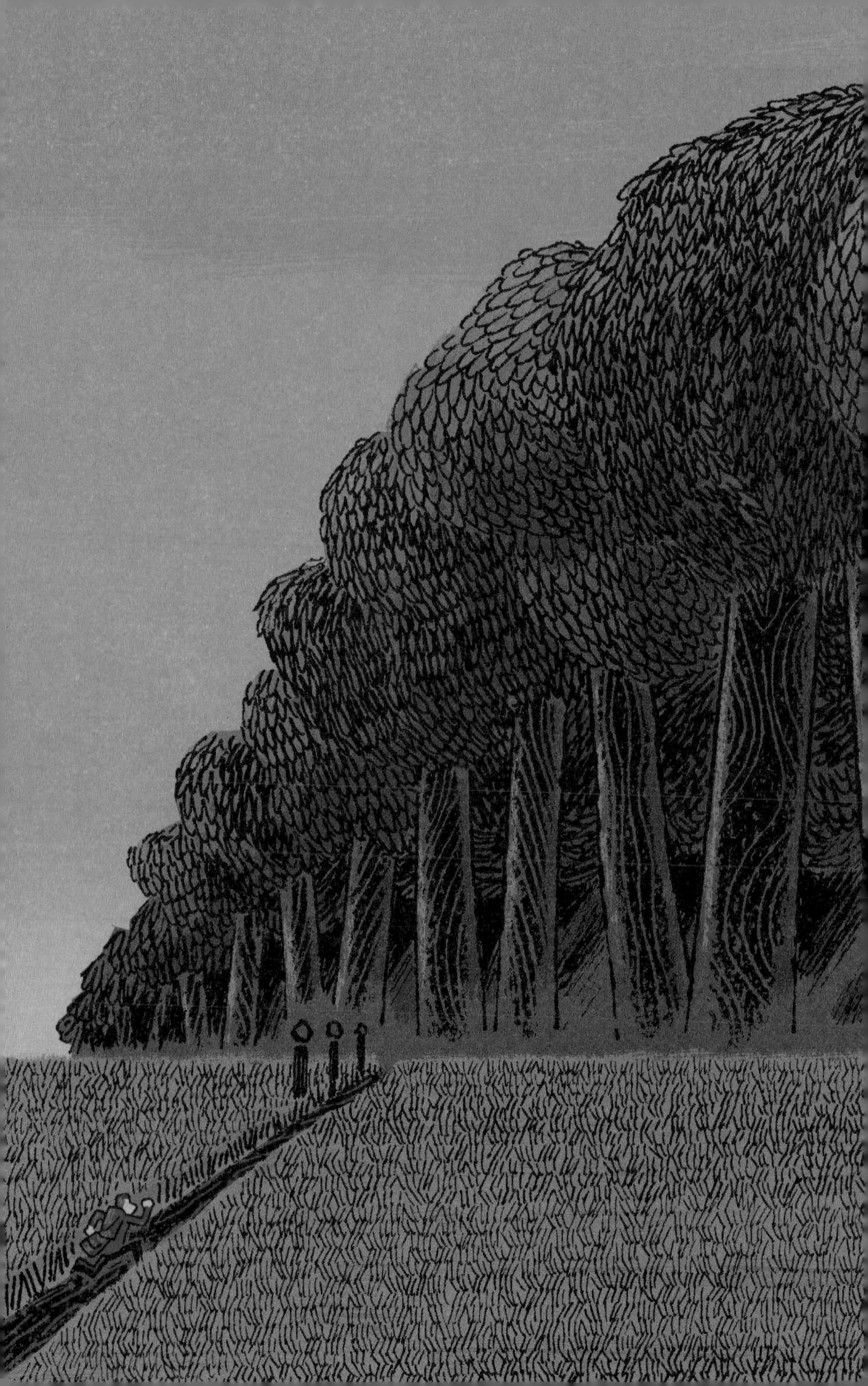

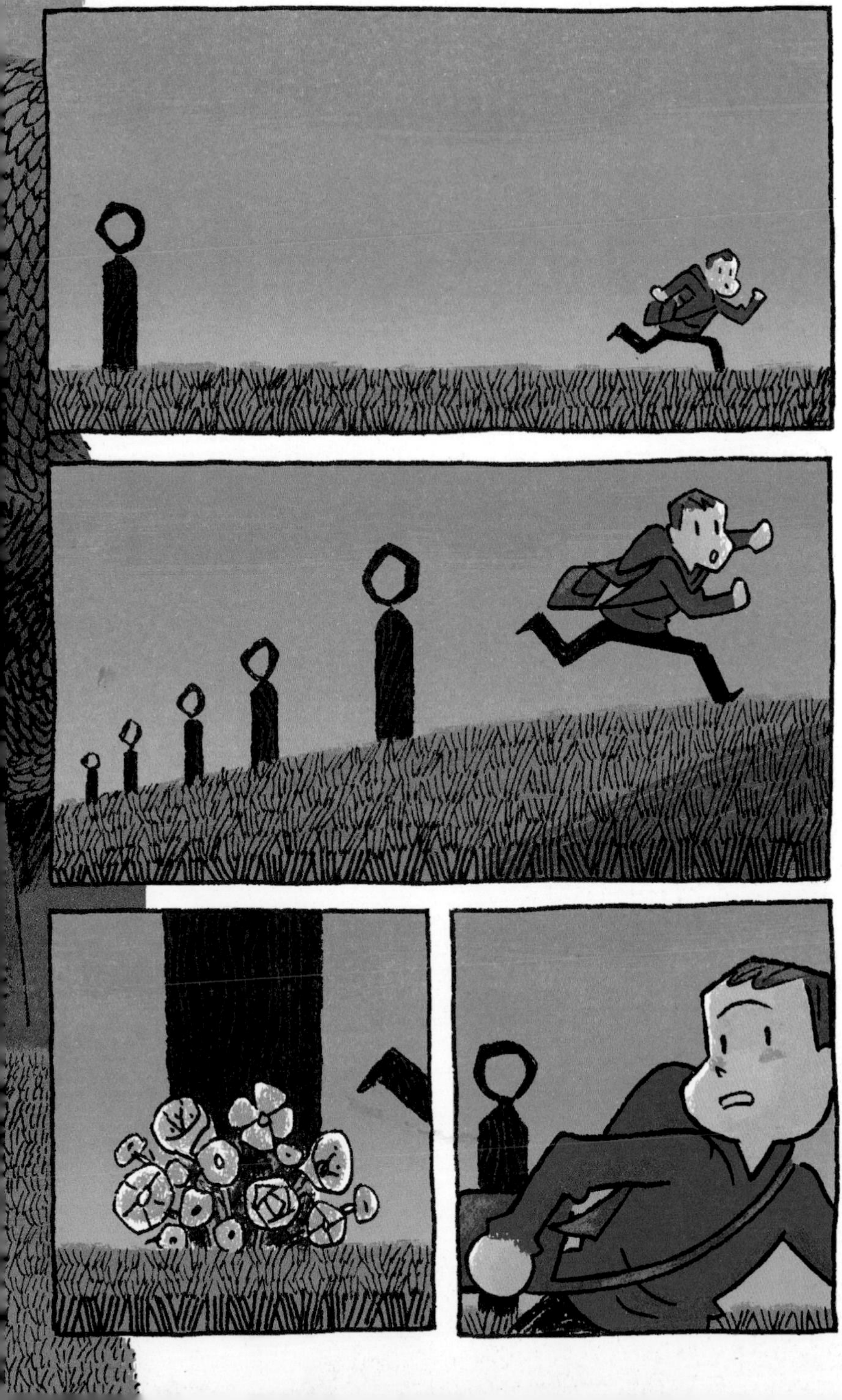

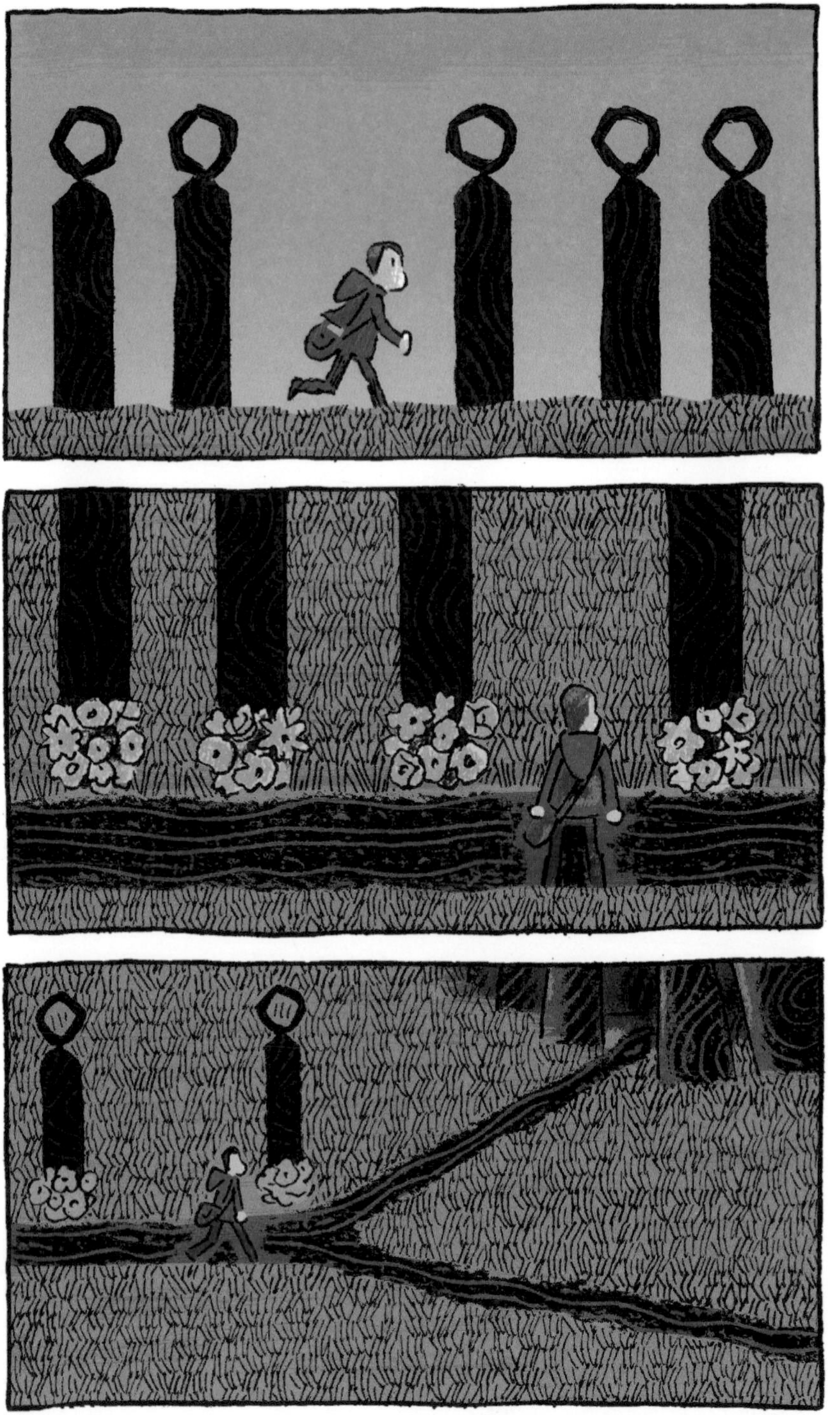

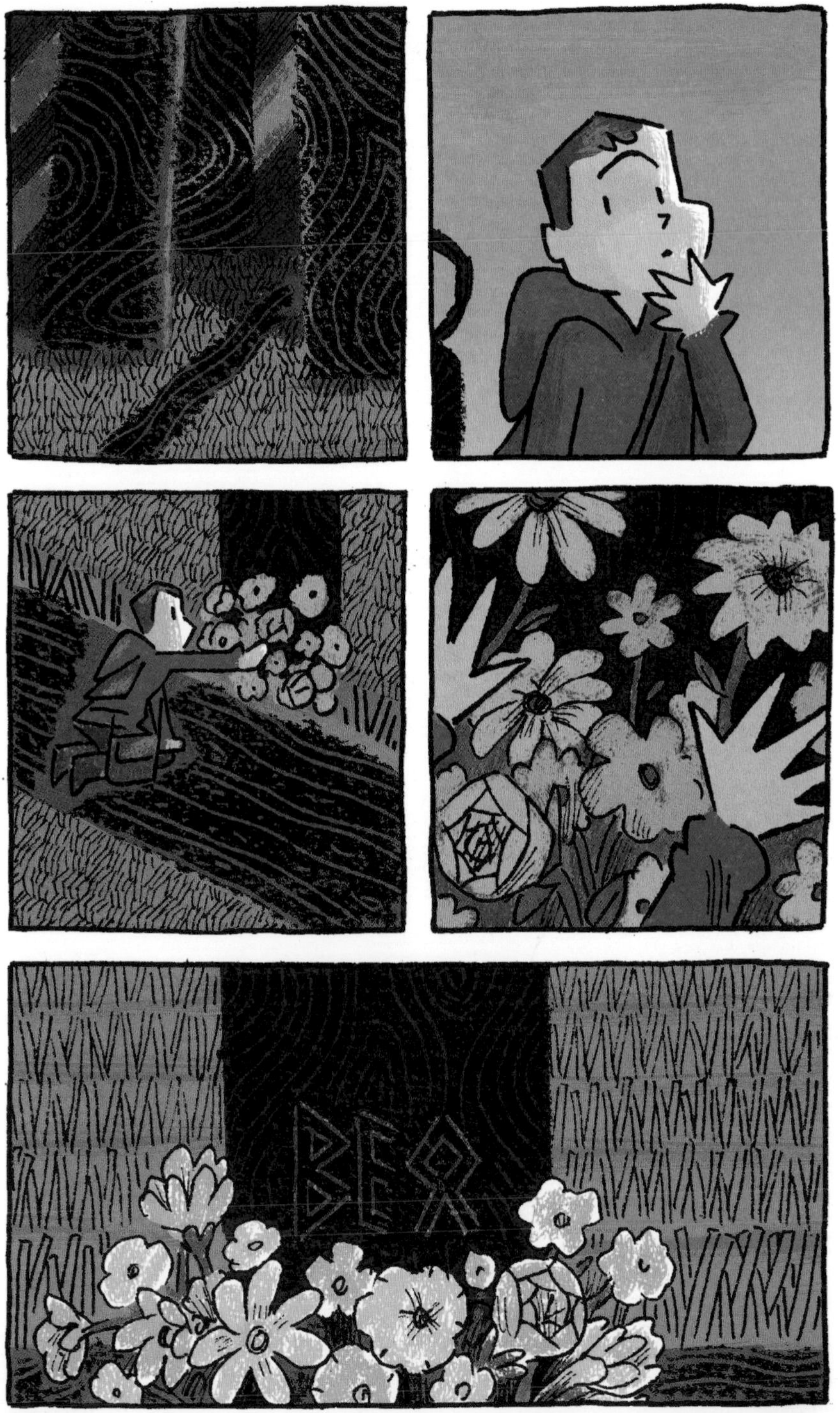

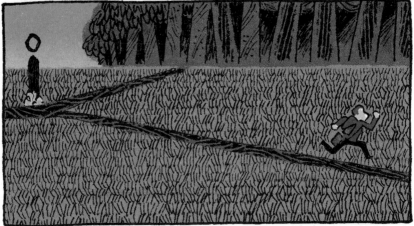

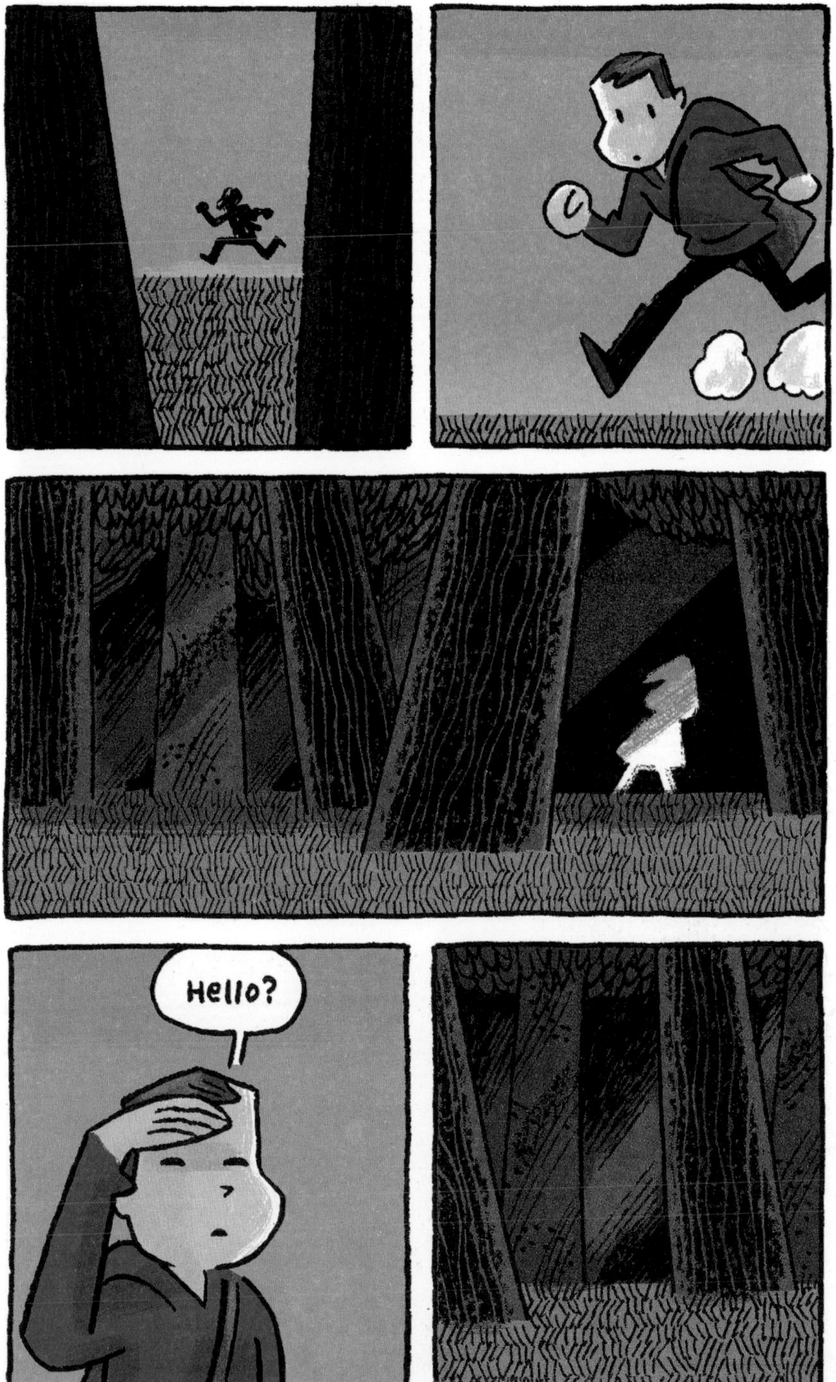
Hello?

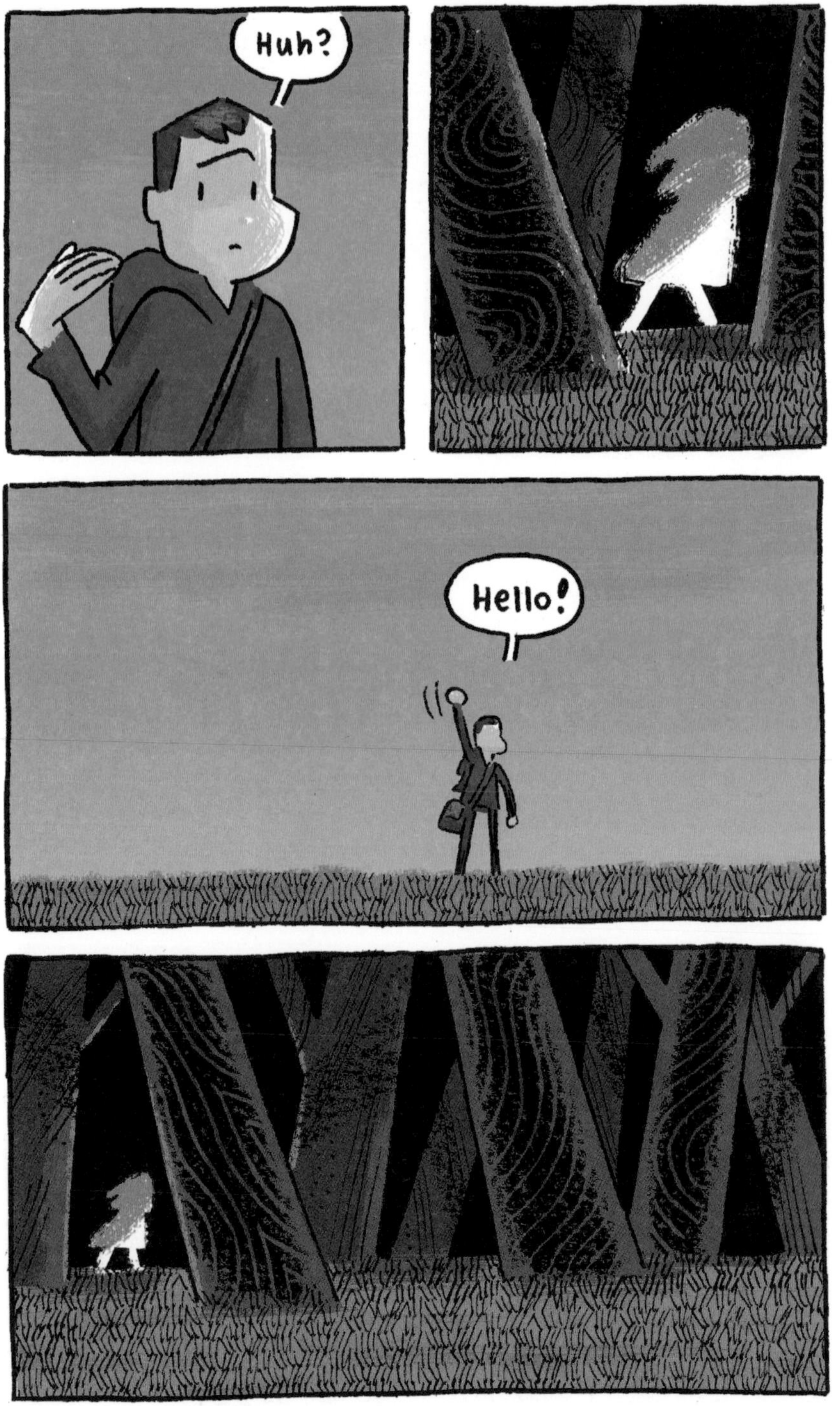
Huh?
Hello!

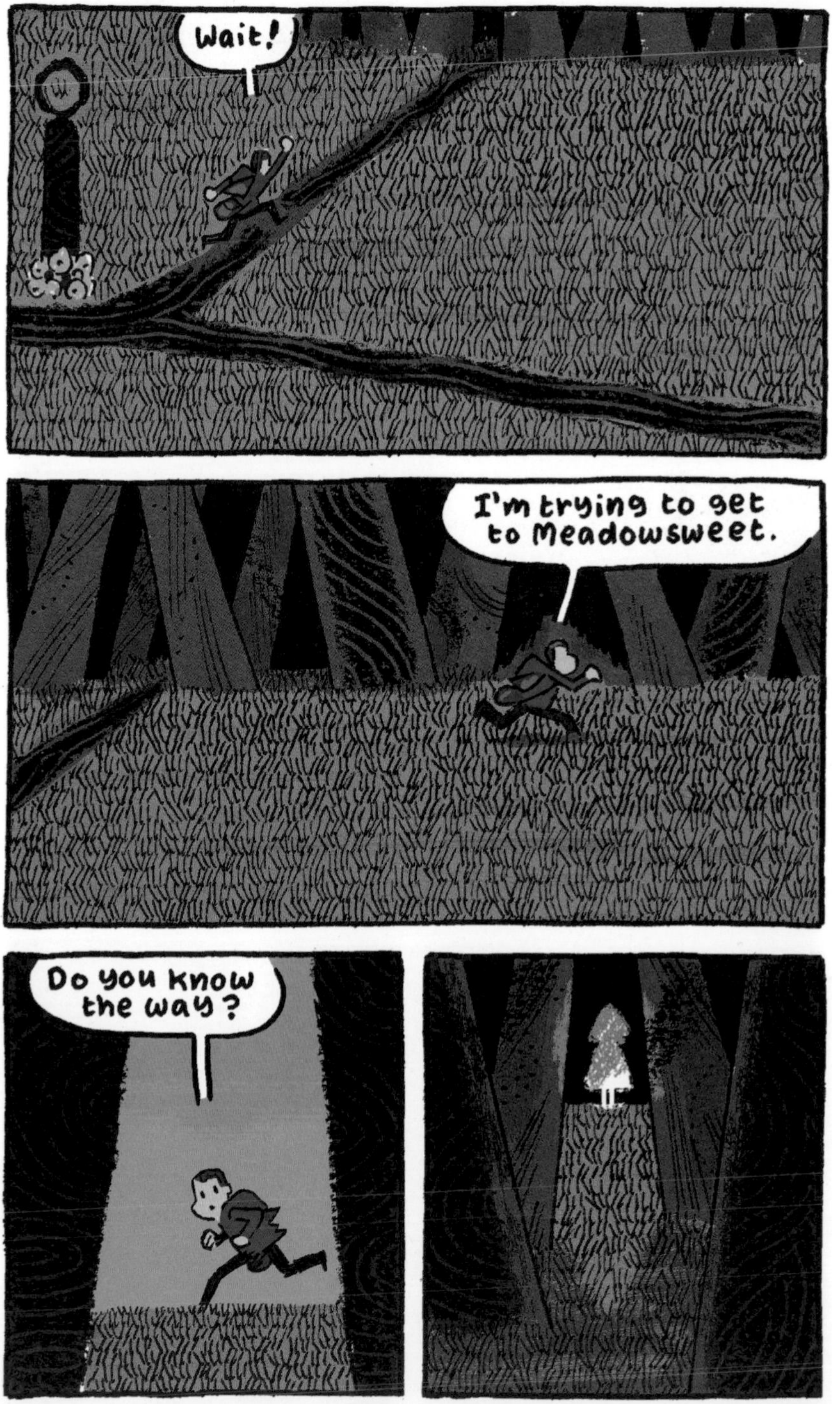
Wait!
I'm trying to get to Meadowsweet.
Do you know the way?

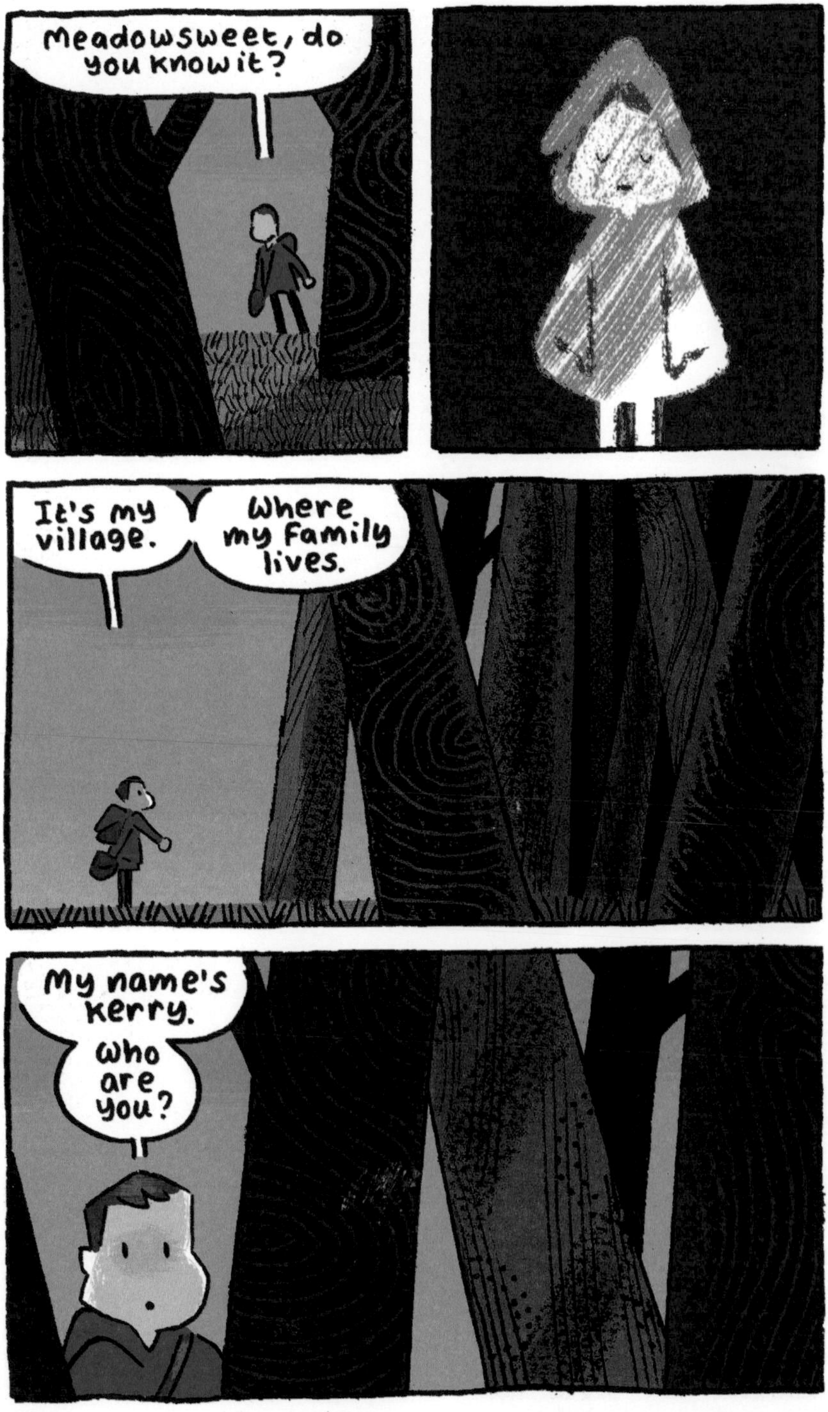

Meadowsweet, do you know it?
It's my village.
Where my family lives.
My name's kerry.
Who are you?

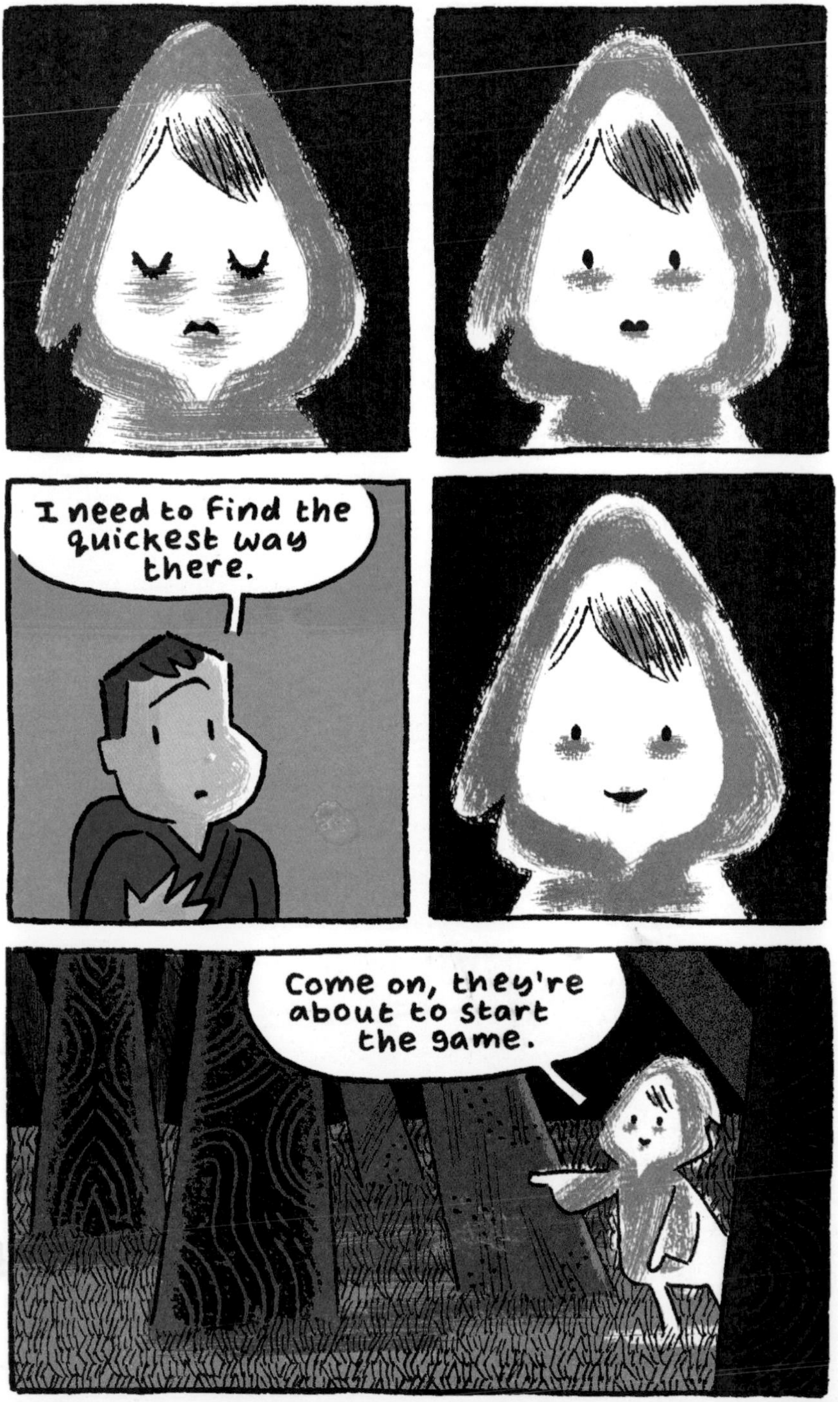
I need to find the quickest way there.
Come on, they're about to start the game.

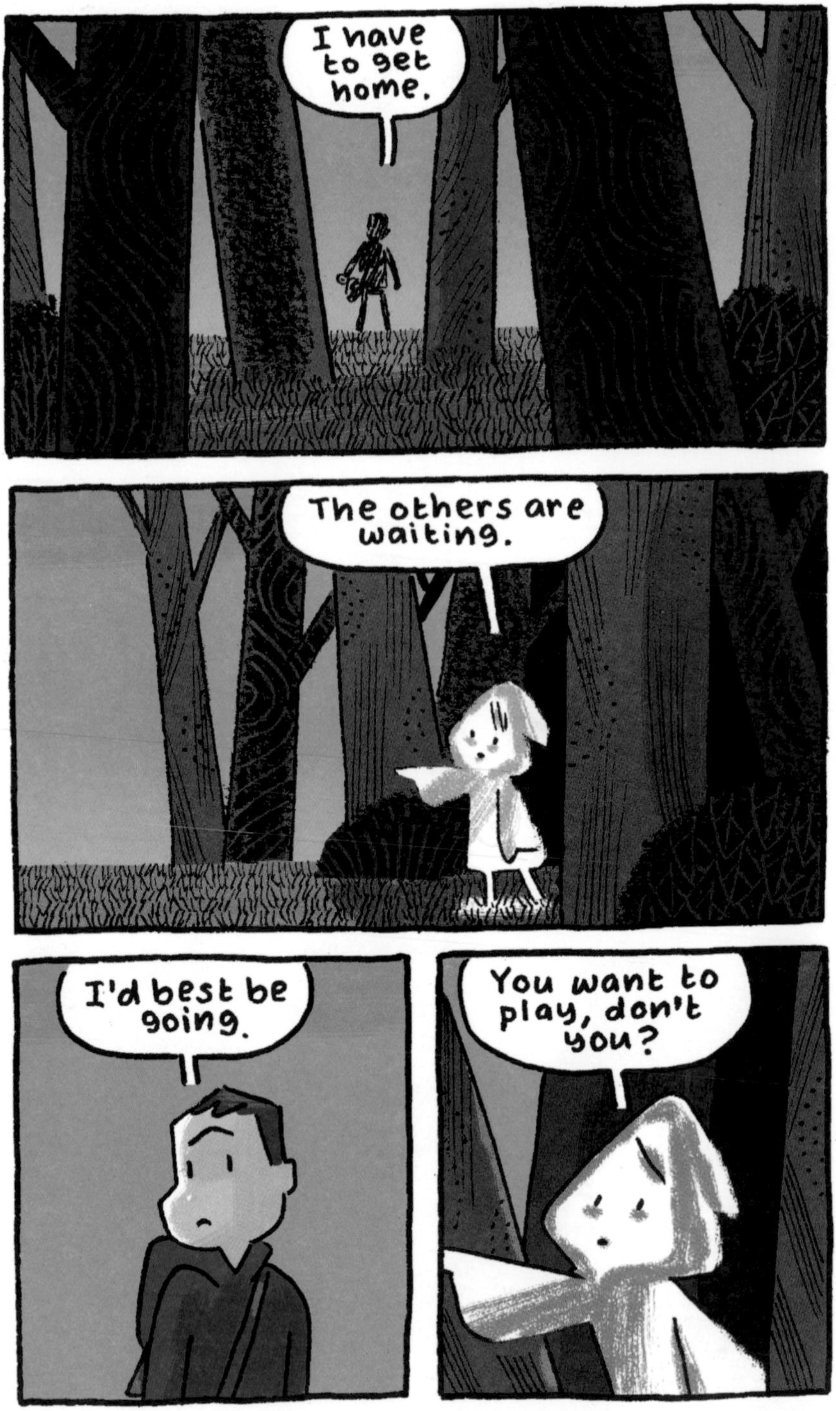
I have to get home.
The others are waiting.
I'd best be going.
You want to play, don't you?

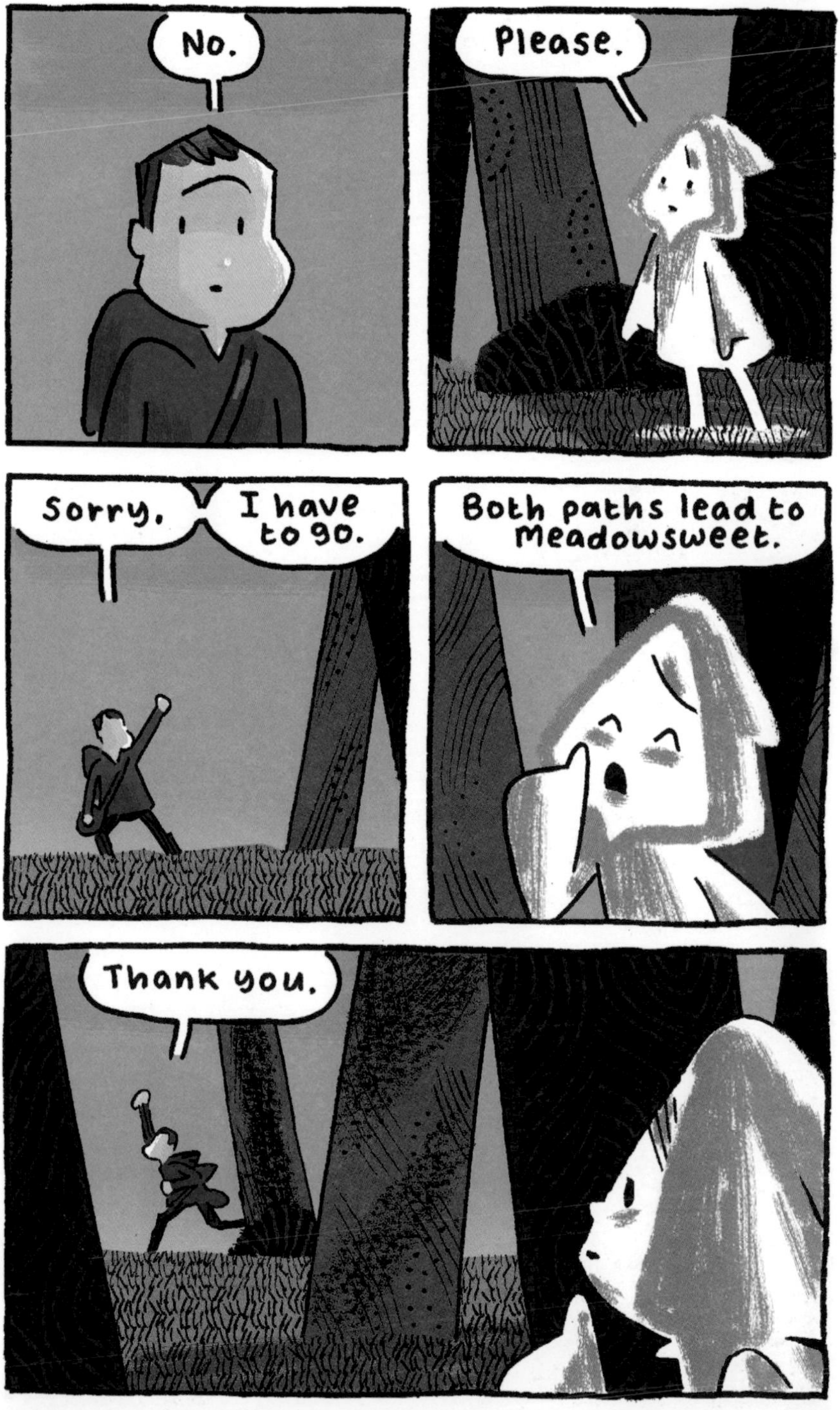
No.
Please.
Sorry.
I have to go.
Both paths lead to Meadowsweet.
Thank you.

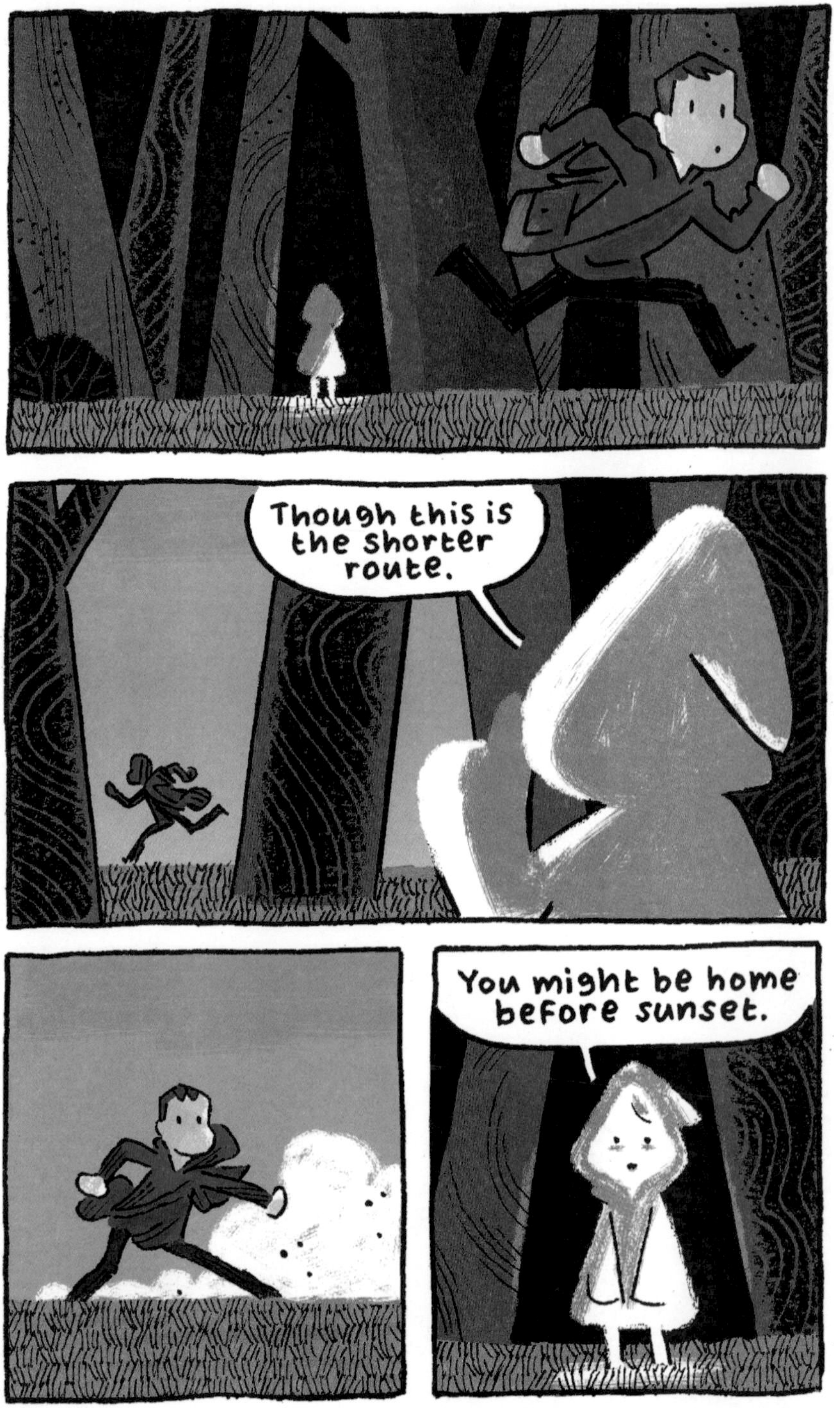
Though this is the shorter route.
You might be home before sunset.

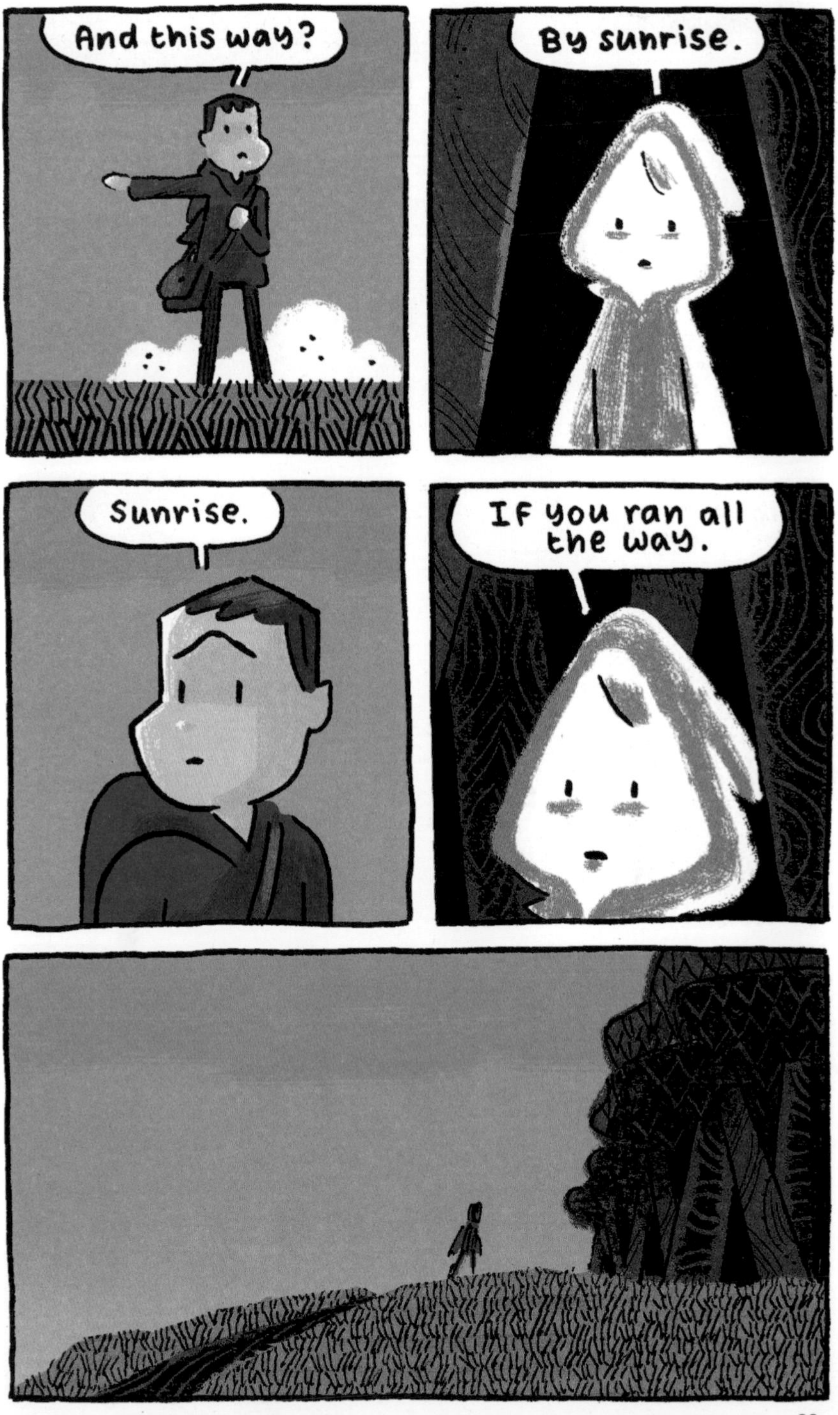
And this way?
By sunrise.
Sunrise.
If you ran all the way.

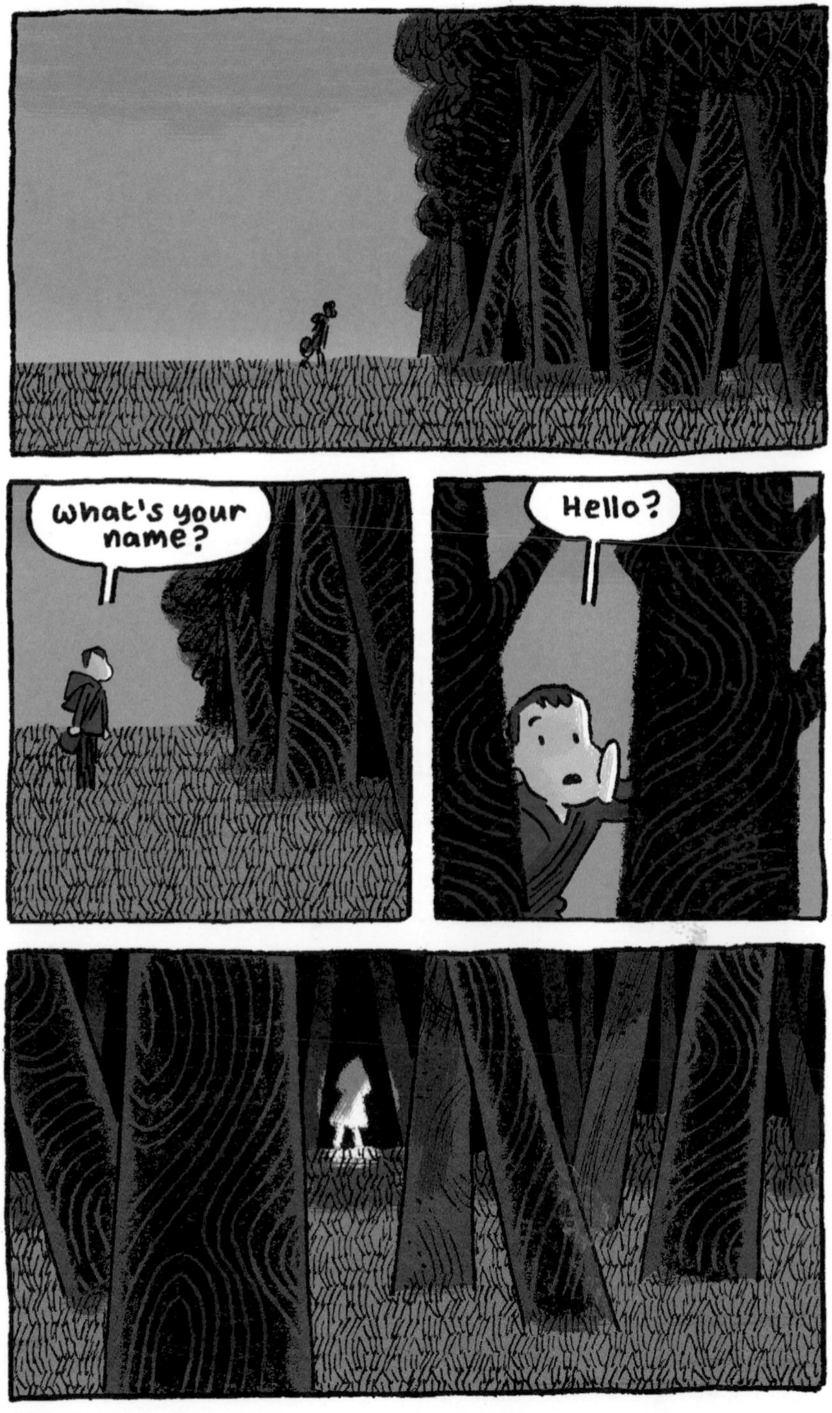
What's your name?
Hello?

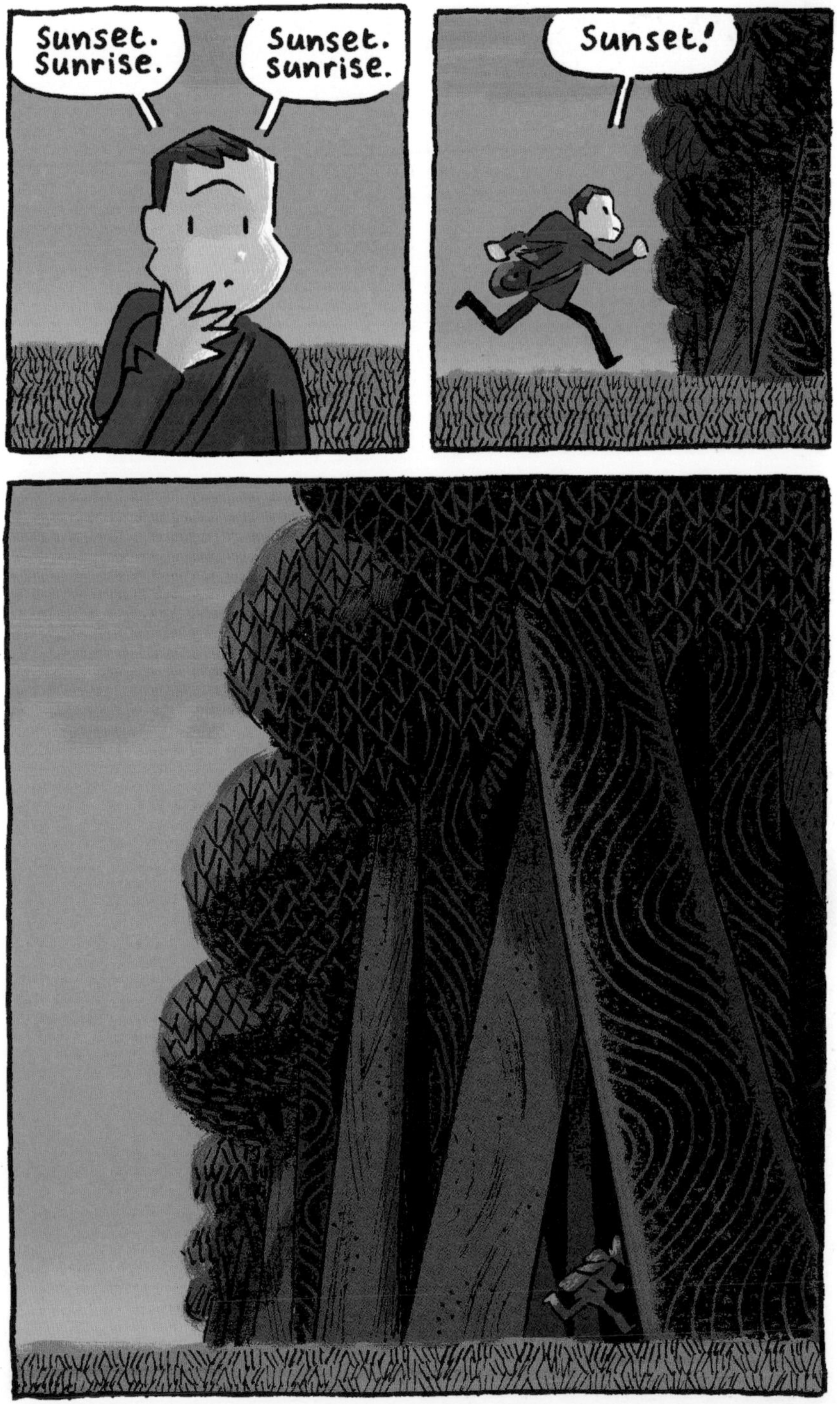
Sunset. Sunrise.
Sunset. Sunrise.
Sunset!

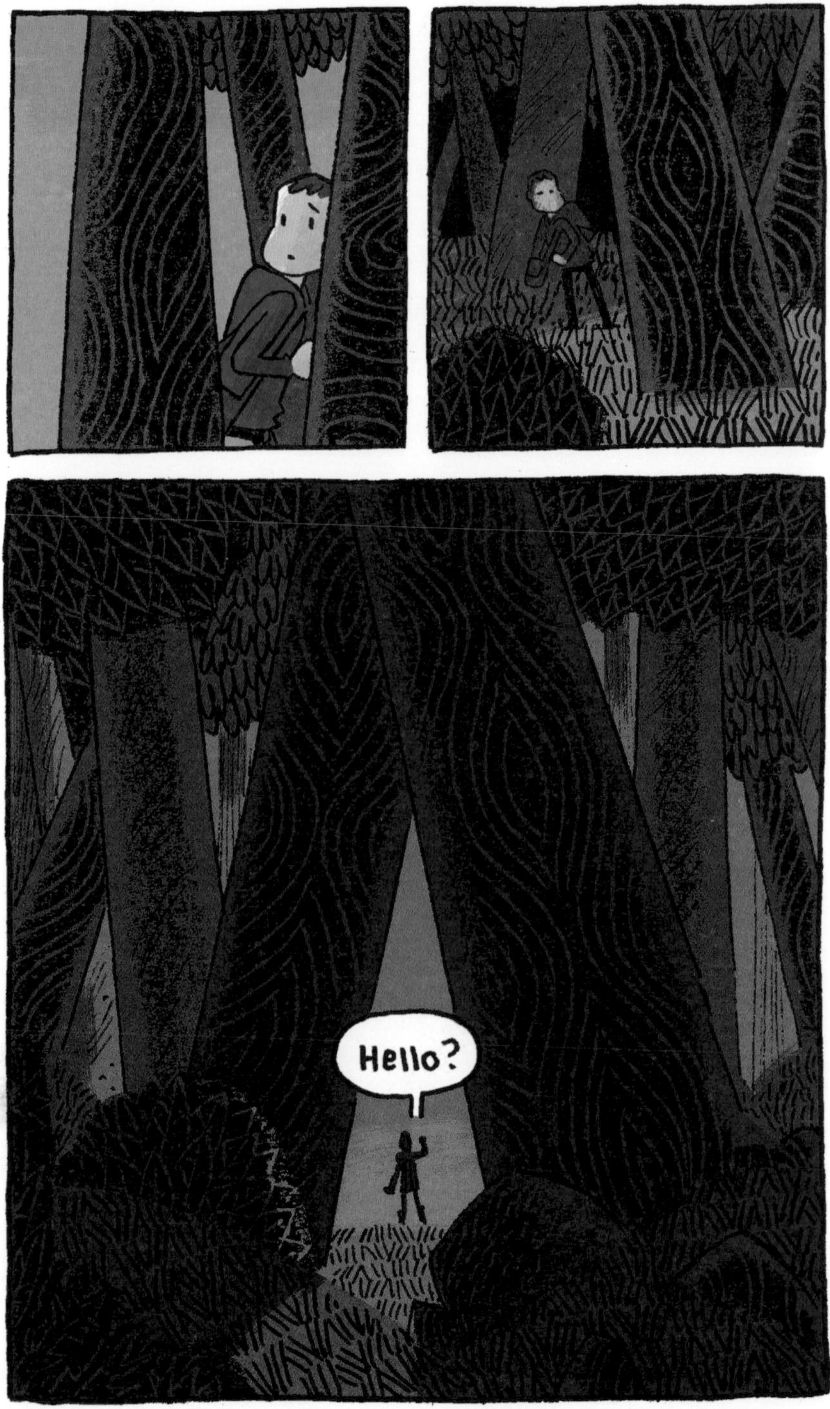
Hello?

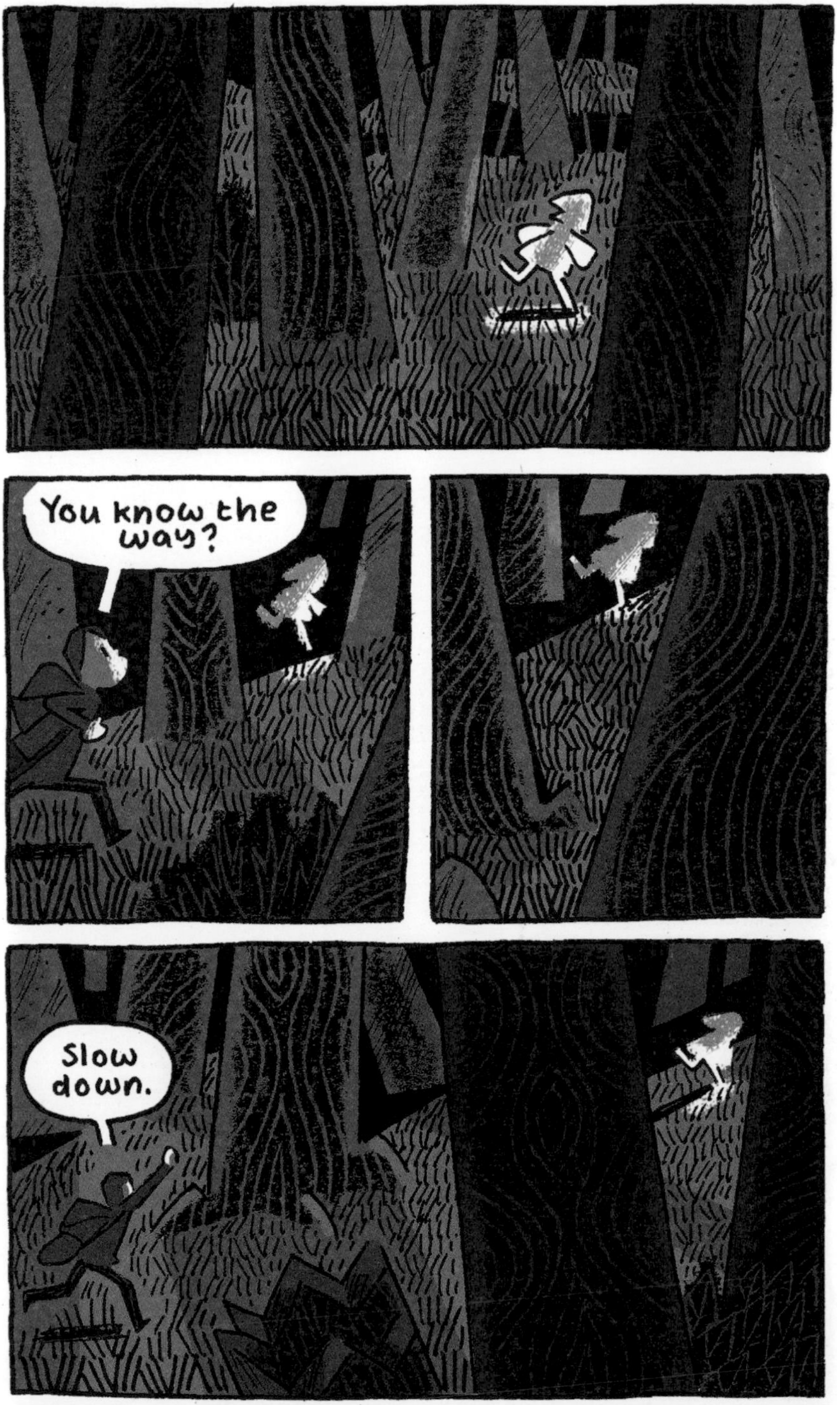
You know the way?
Slow down.

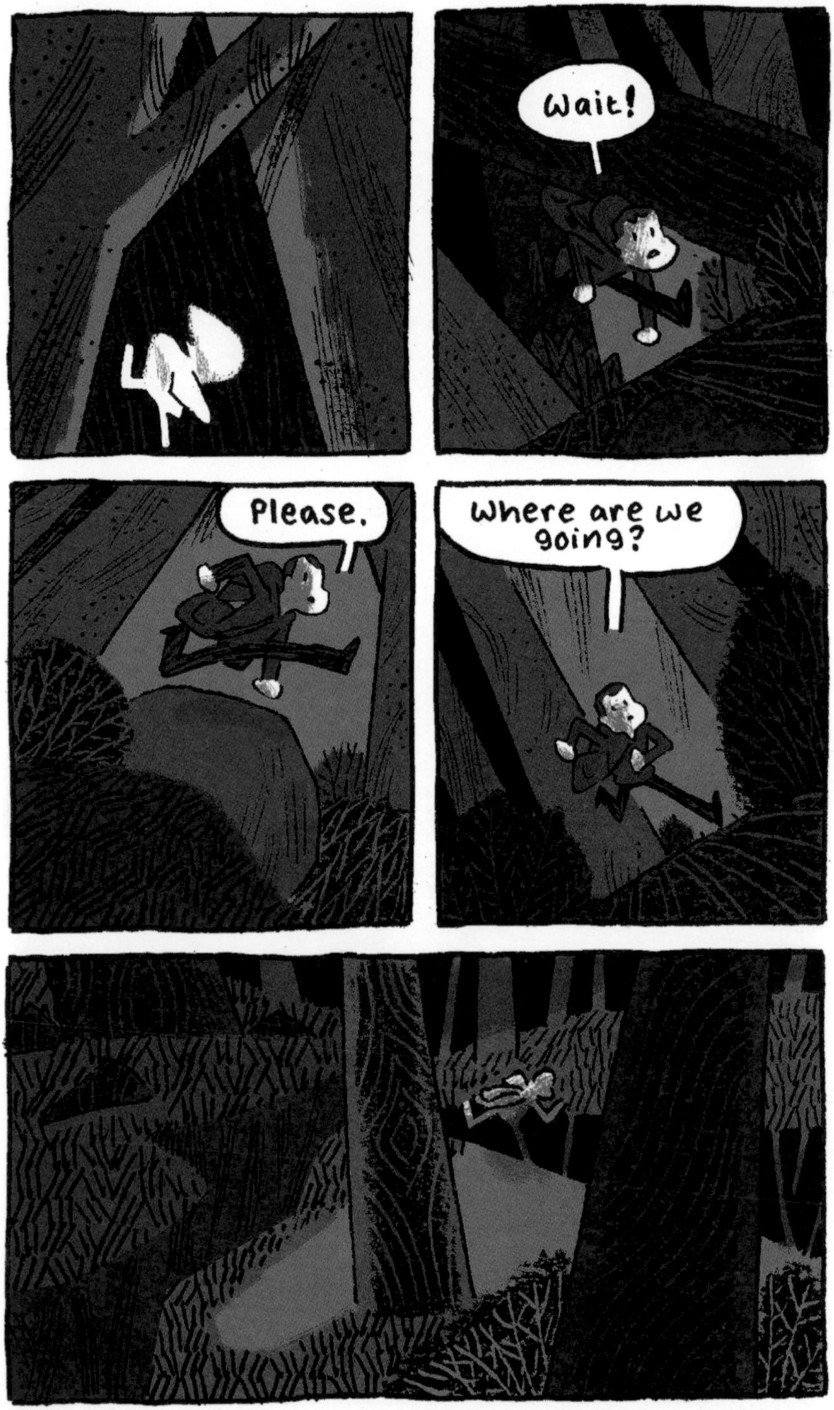
Wait!
Please.
Where are we going?

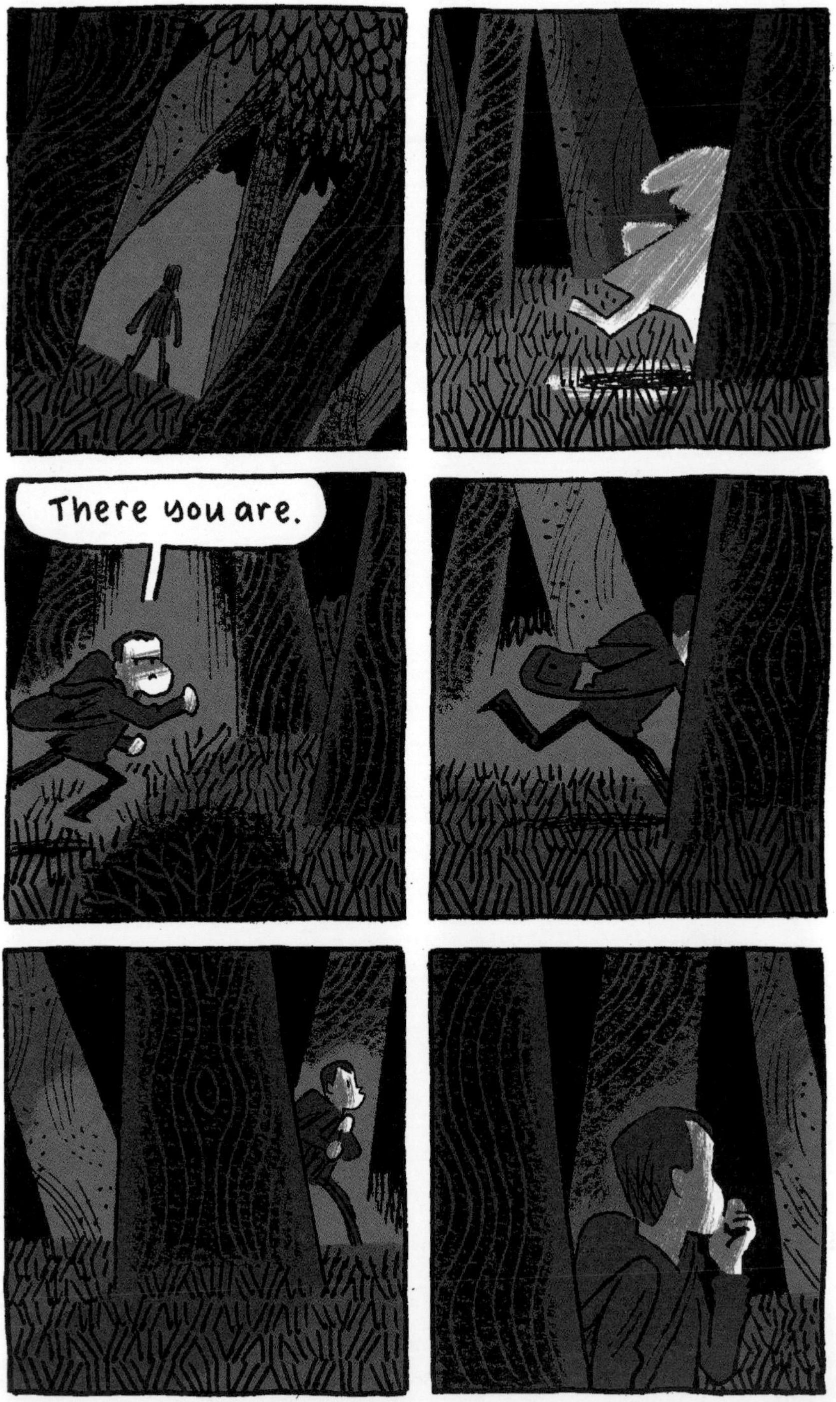
There you are.

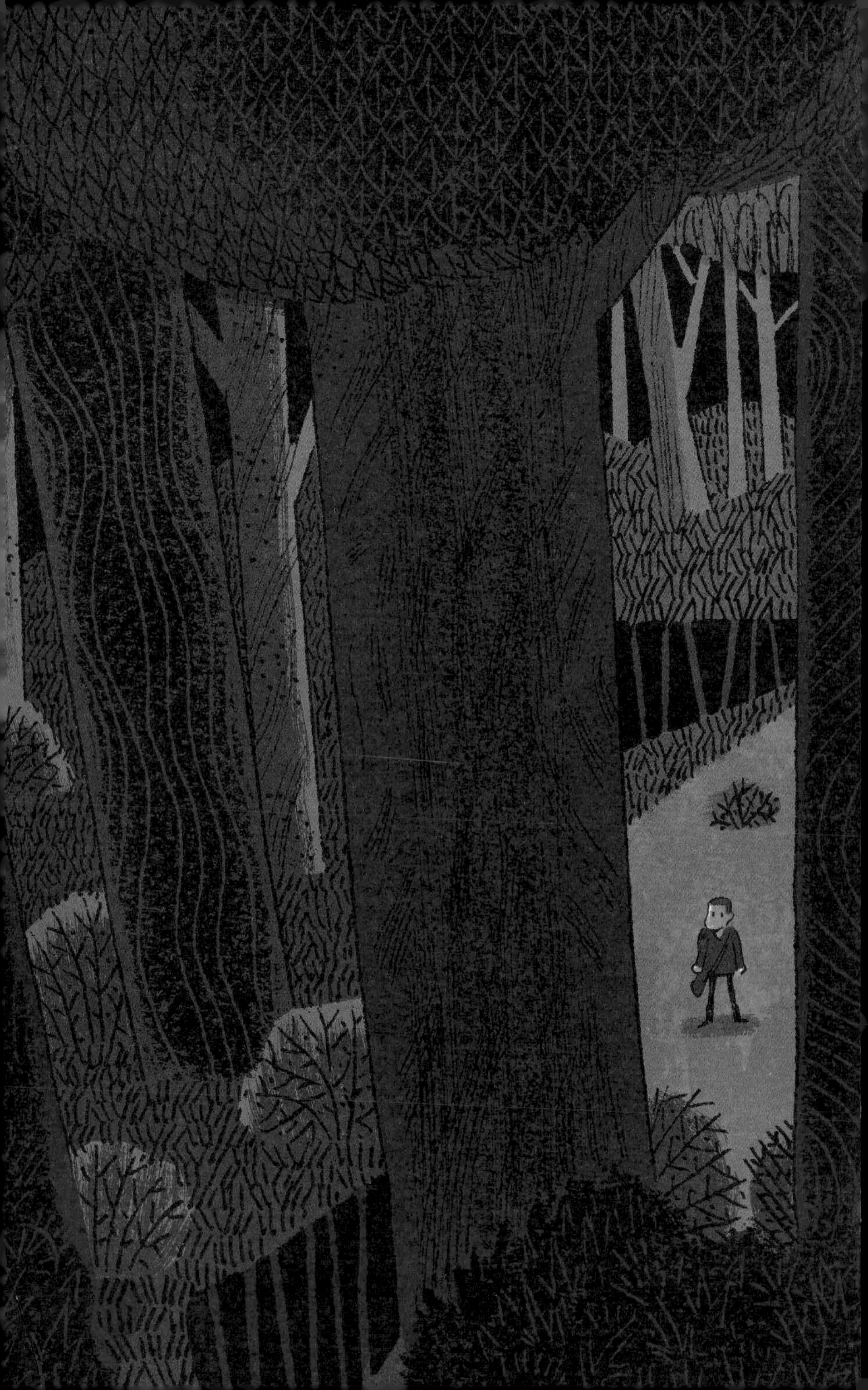

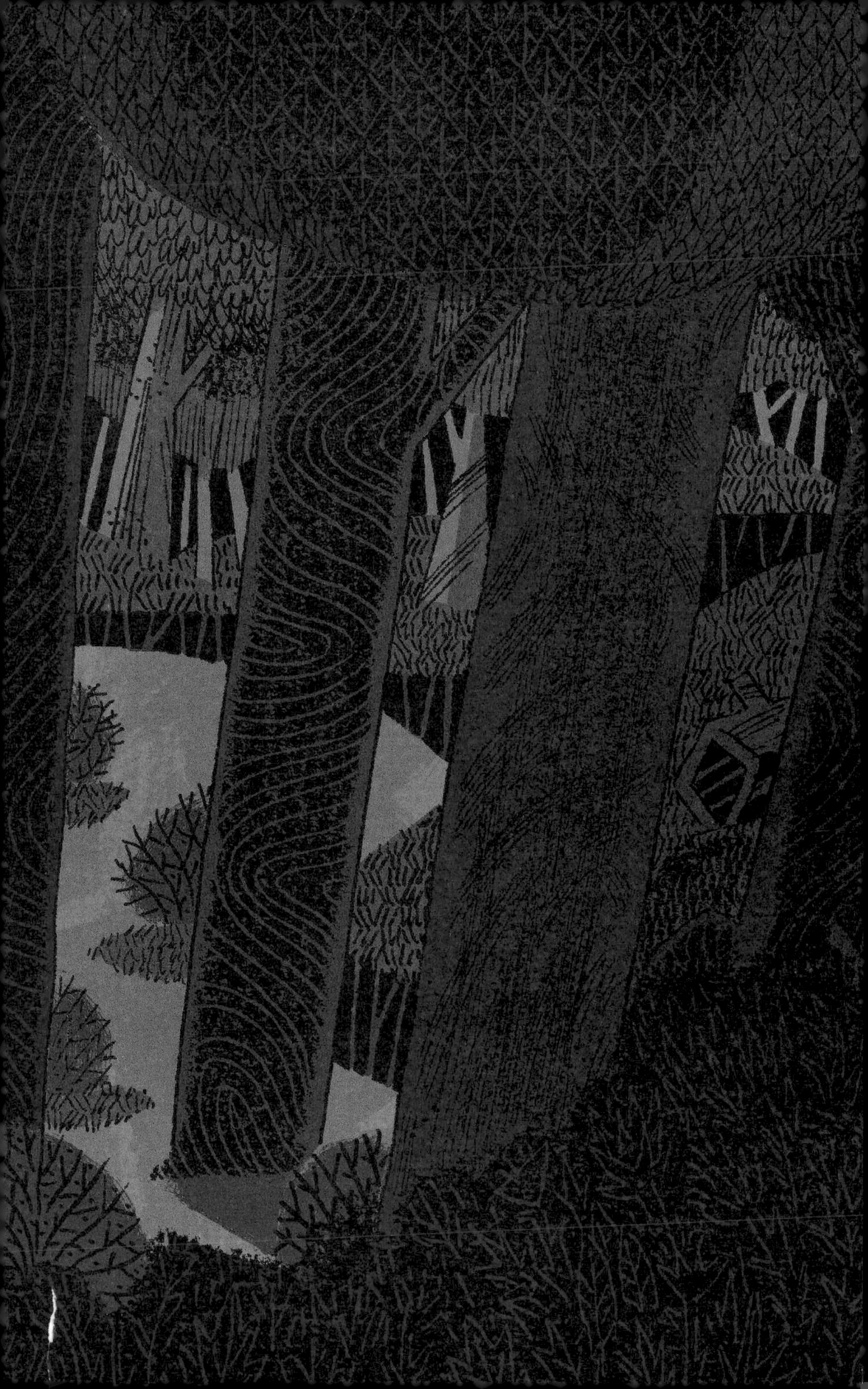

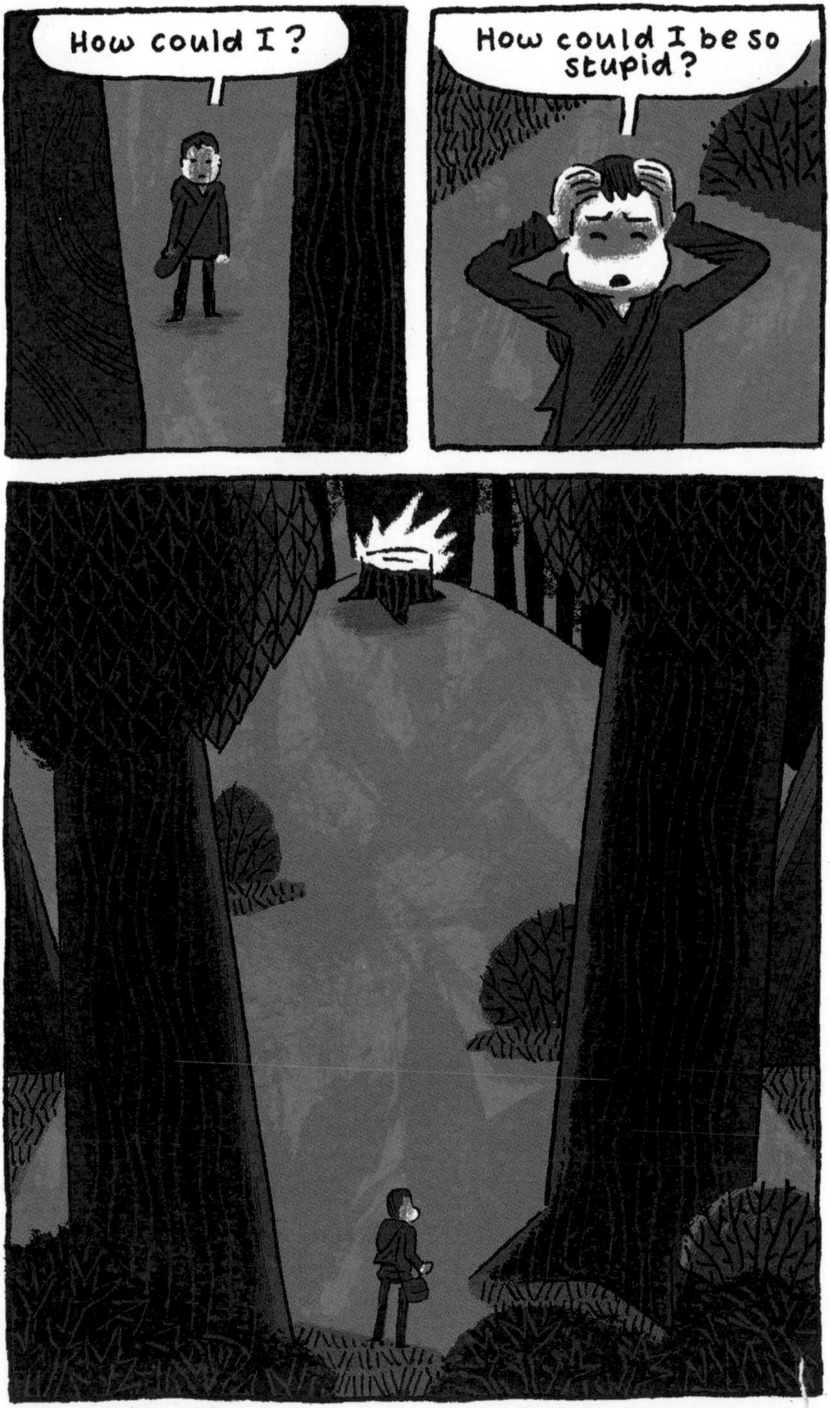
How could I?
How could I be so stupid?

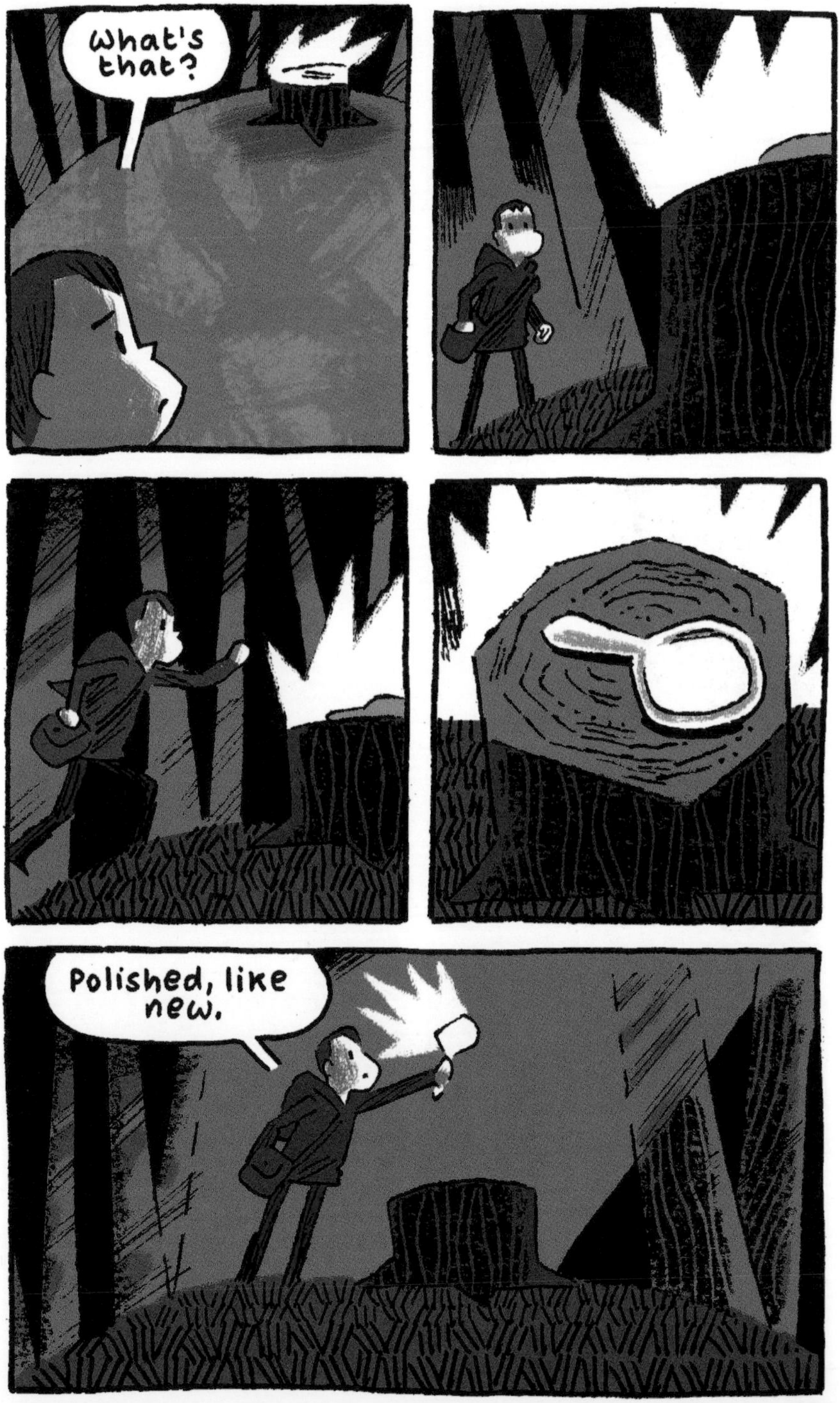
What's that?
Polished, like new.

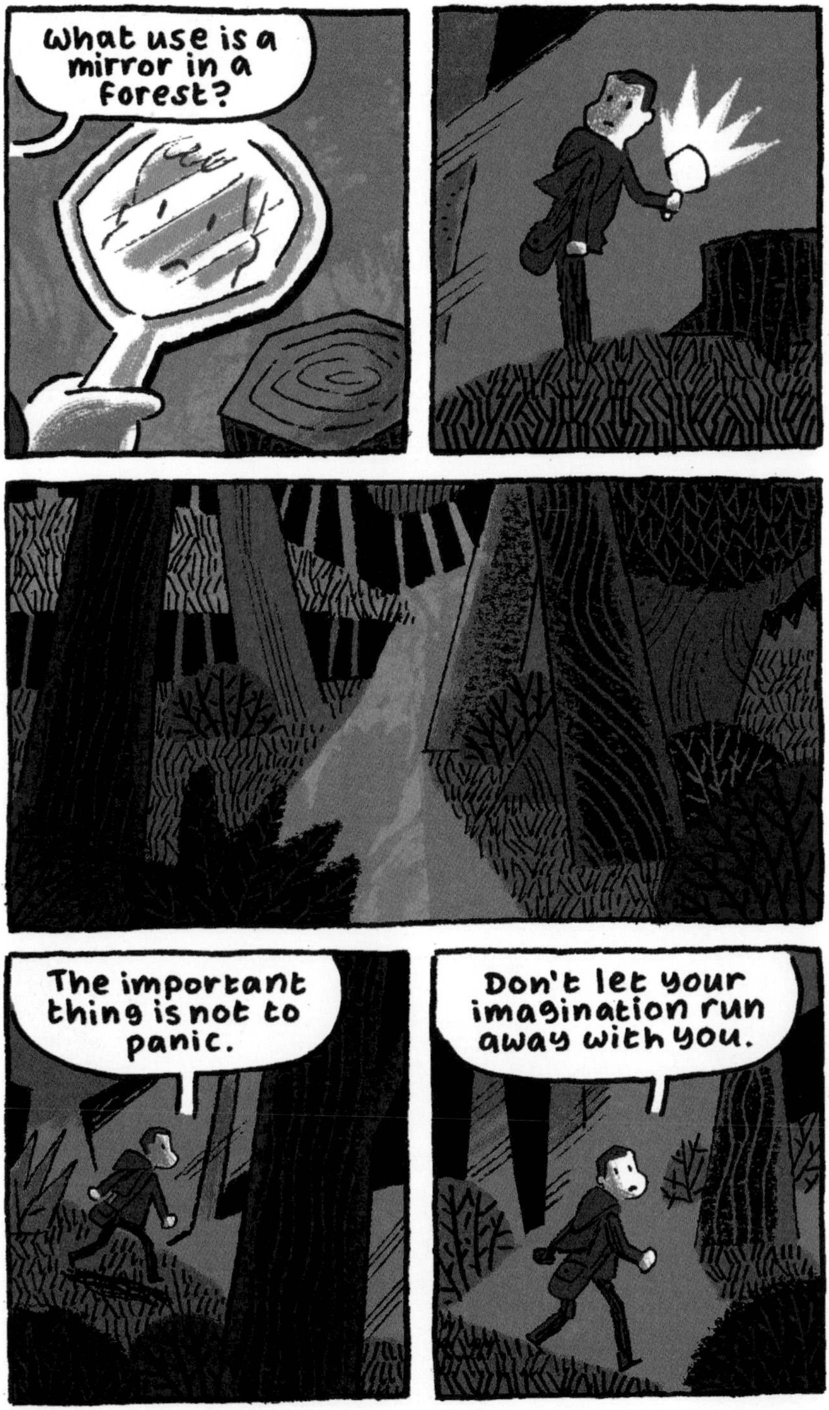
What use is a mirror in a forest?
The important thing is not to panic.
Don't let your imagination run away with you.

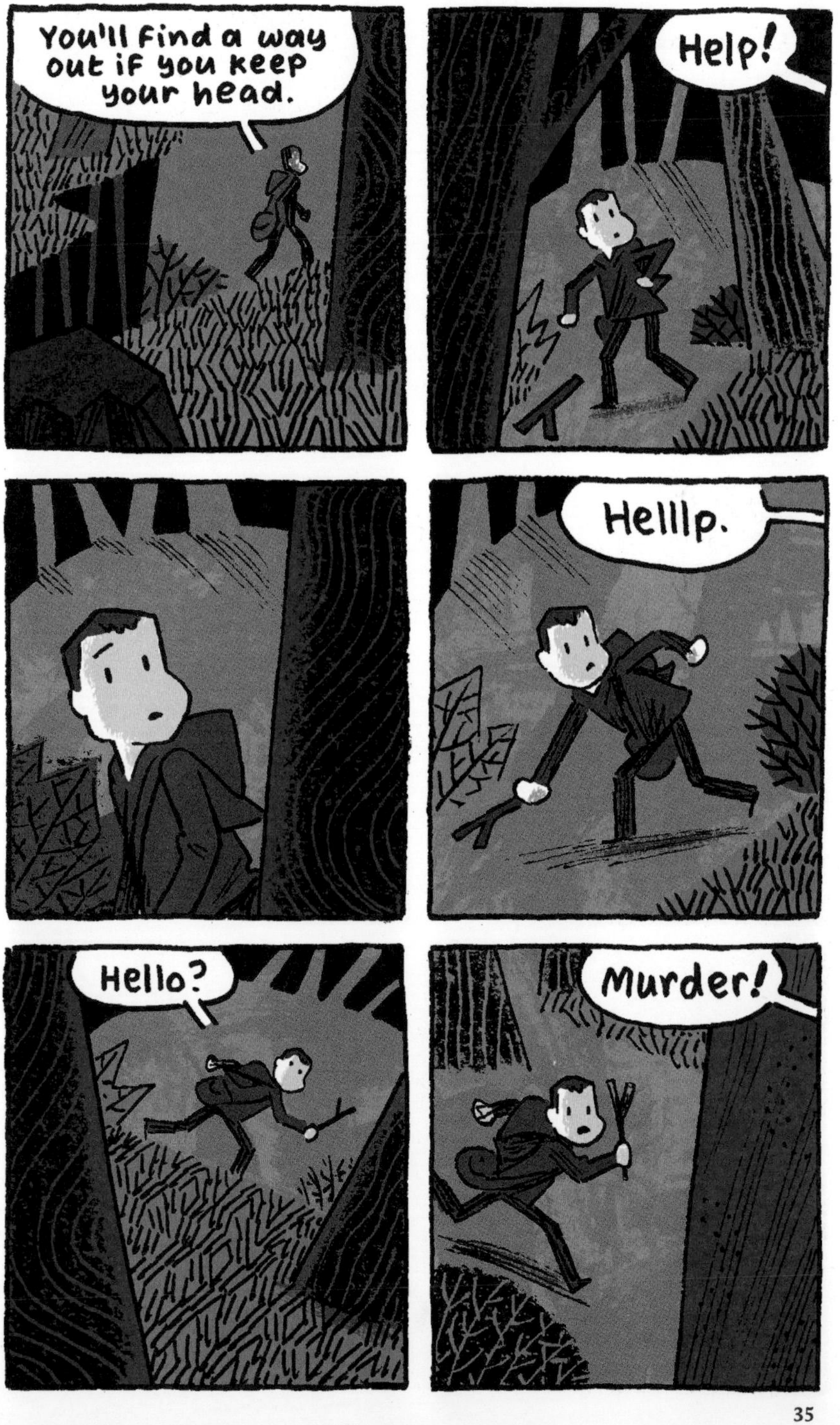
You'll find a way out if you keep your head.
Help!
Helllp.
Hello?
Murder!

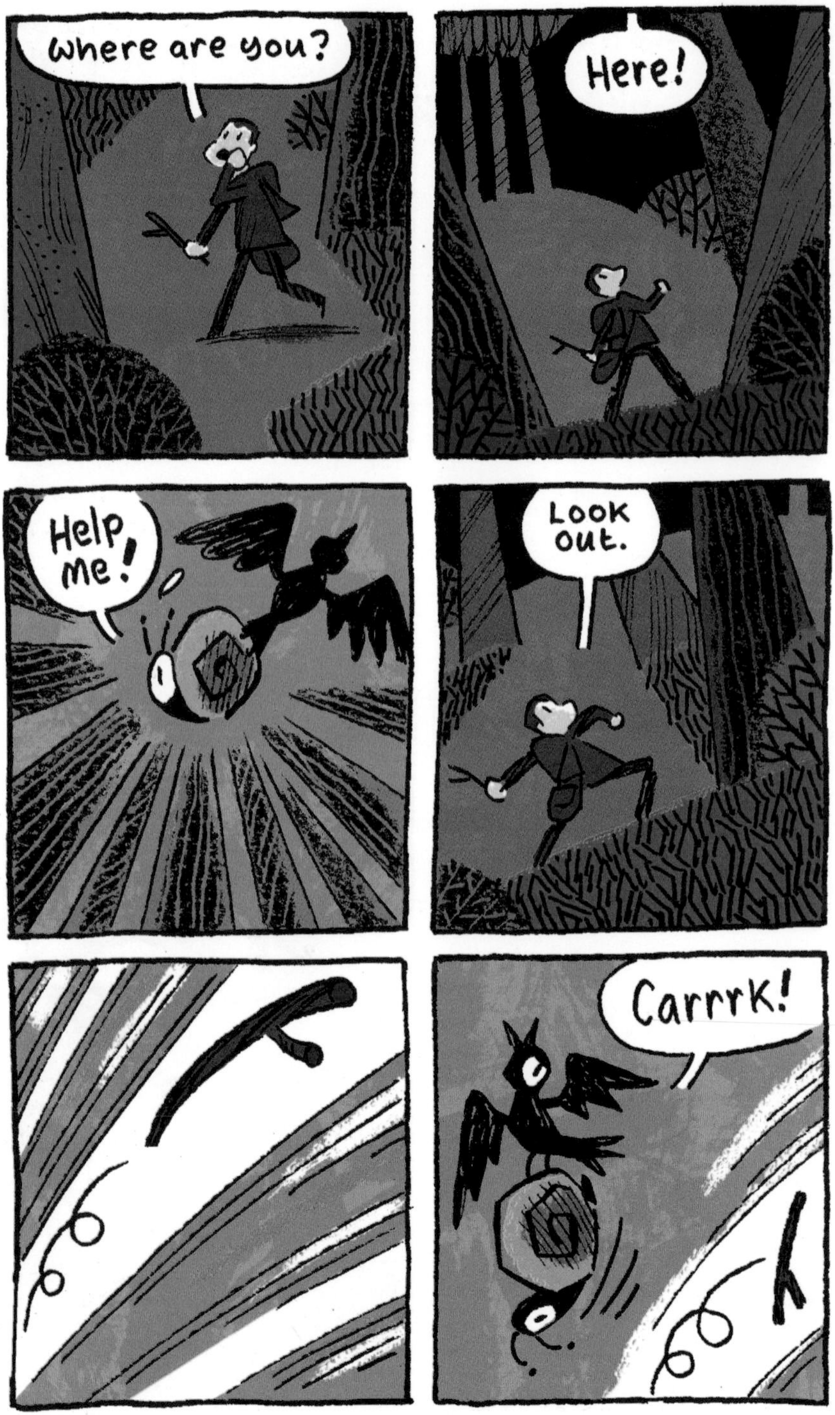
where are you?
Here!
Help me!
Look out.
Carrrk!

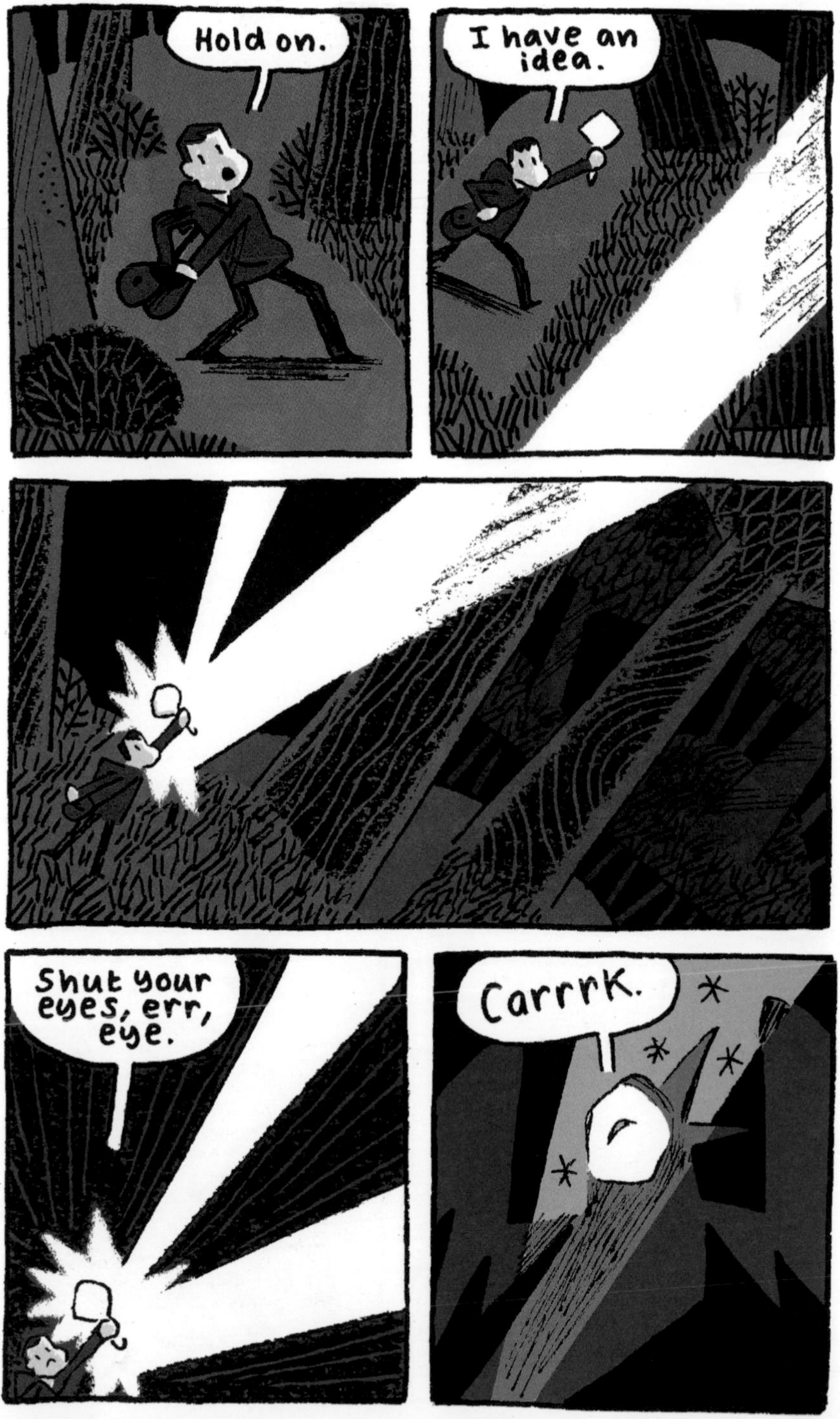
Hold on.
I have an idea.
Shut your eyes, err, eye.
Carrrk.

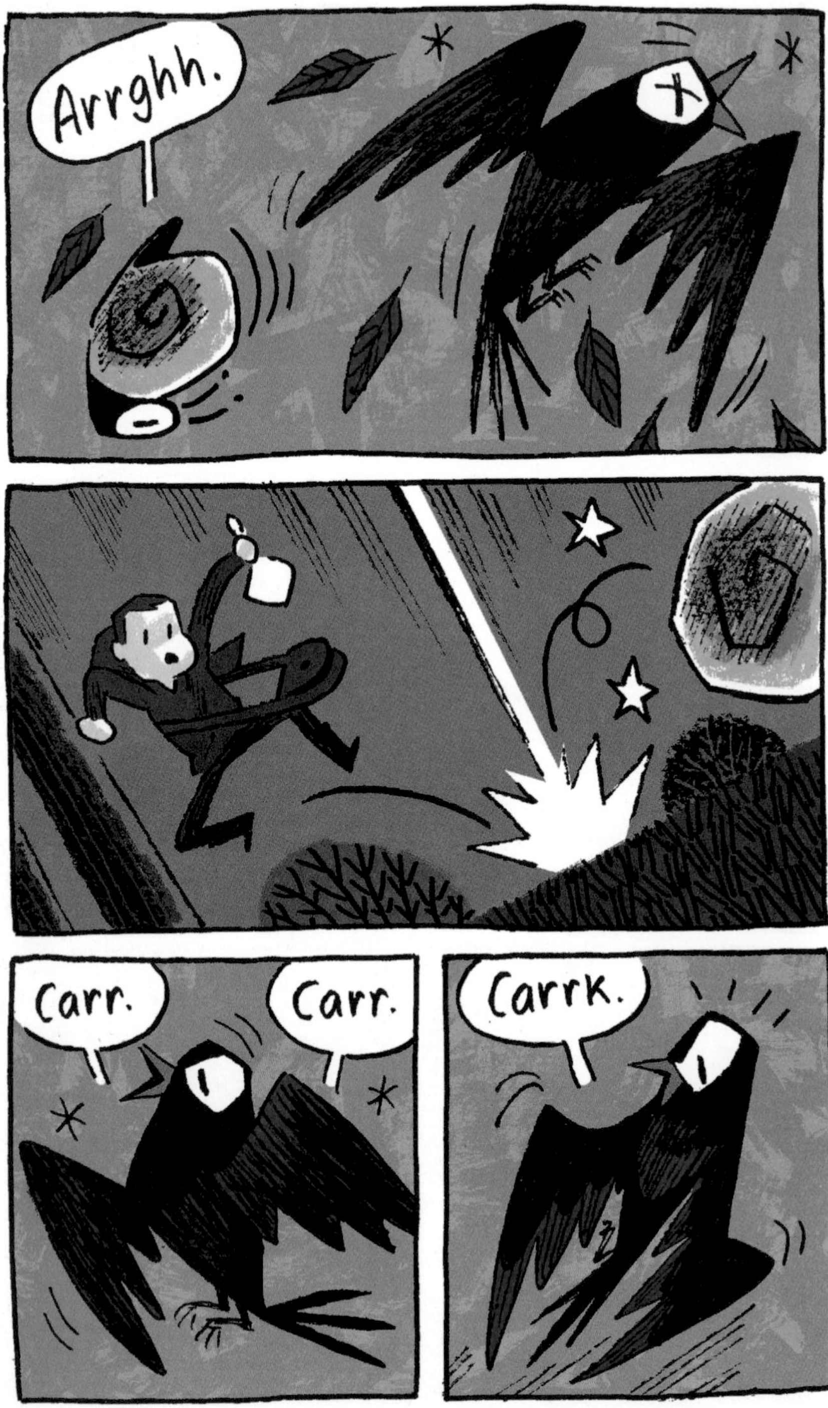
Arrghh.
Carr.
Carr.
Carrk.

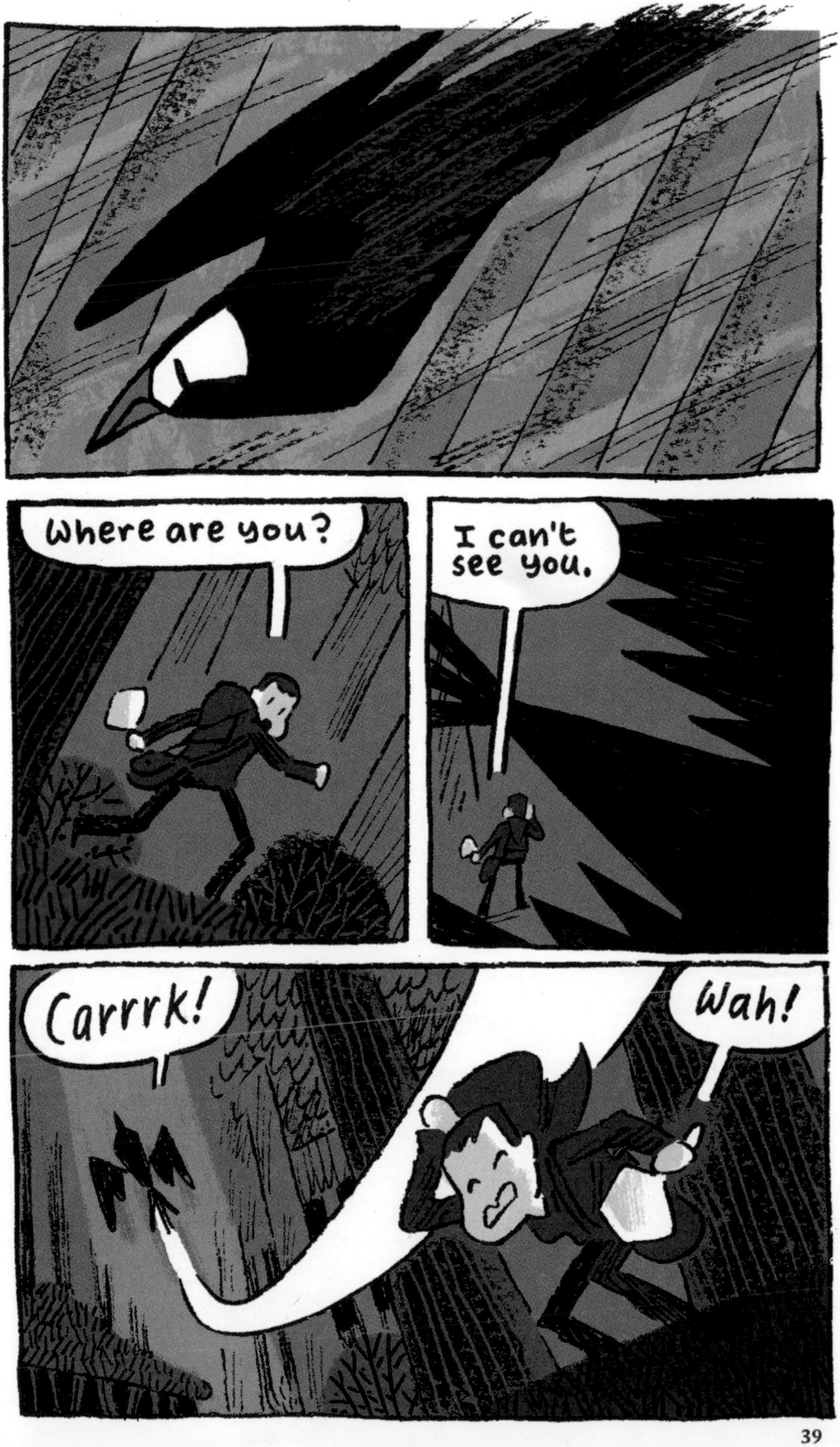
Where are you?
I can't see you.
Carrrk!
Wah!

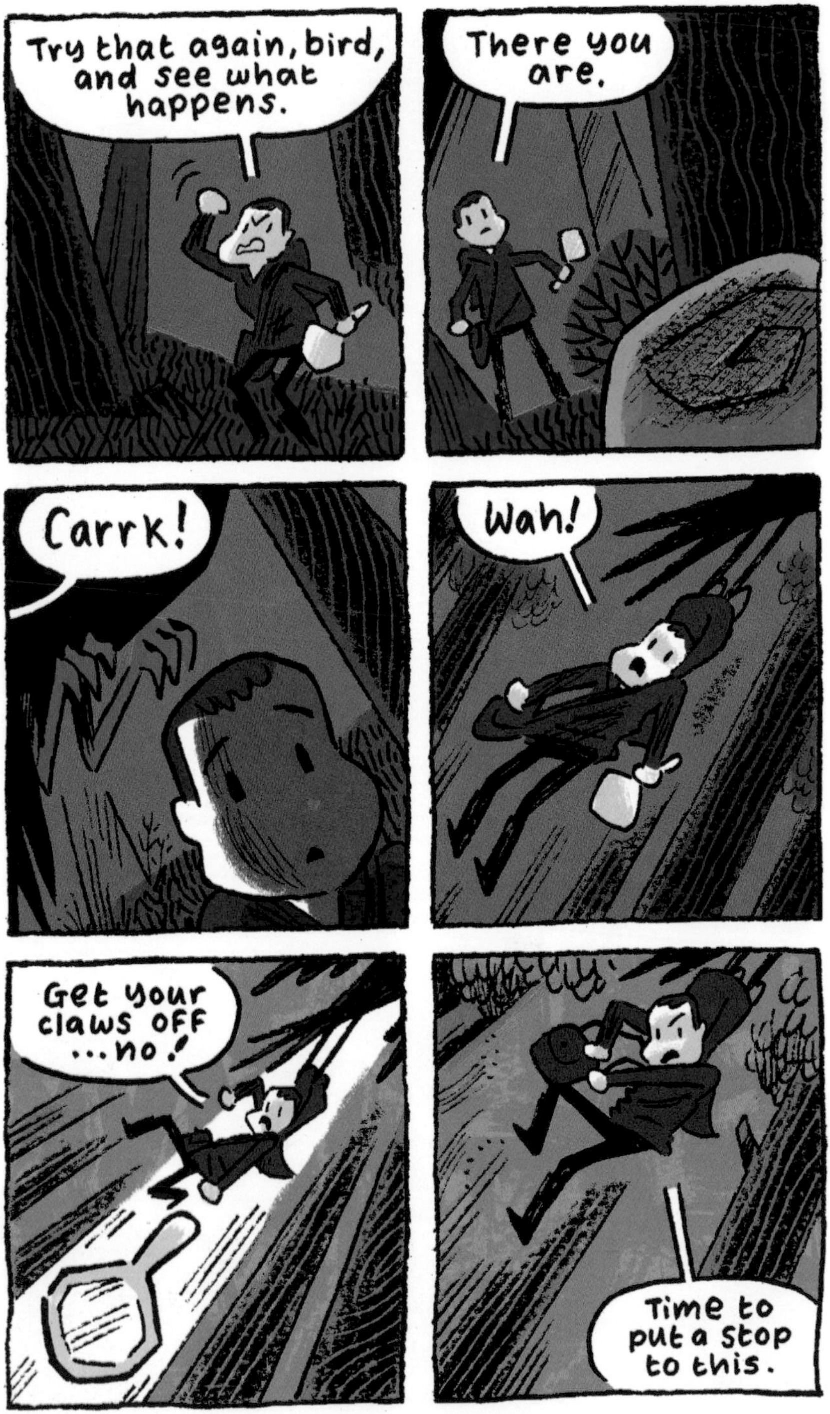
Try that again, bird, and see what happens.
There you are.
Carrk!
Wah!
Get your claws off ...no!
Time to put a stop to this.

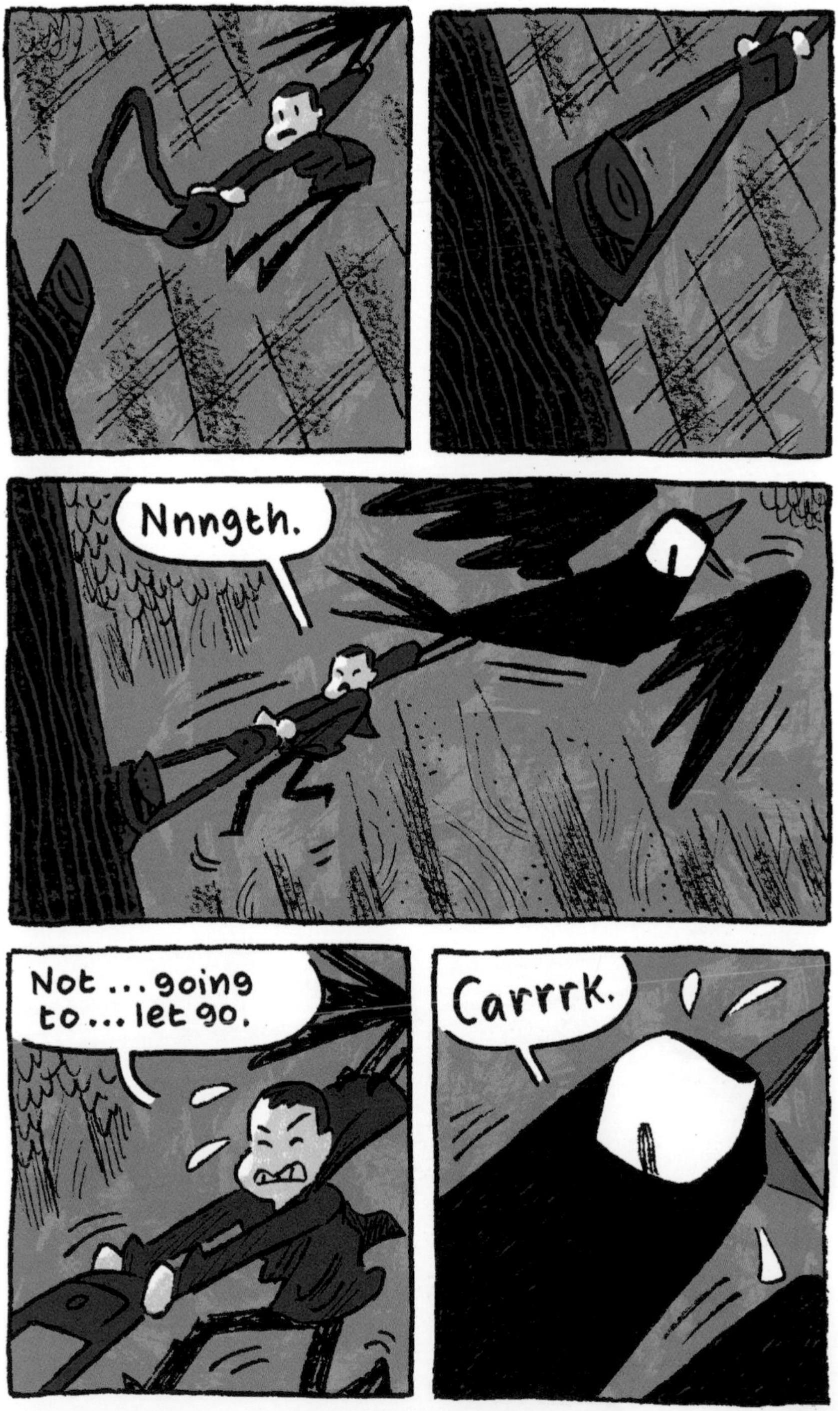
Nnngth.
Not ... going to ... let go.
Carrrk.

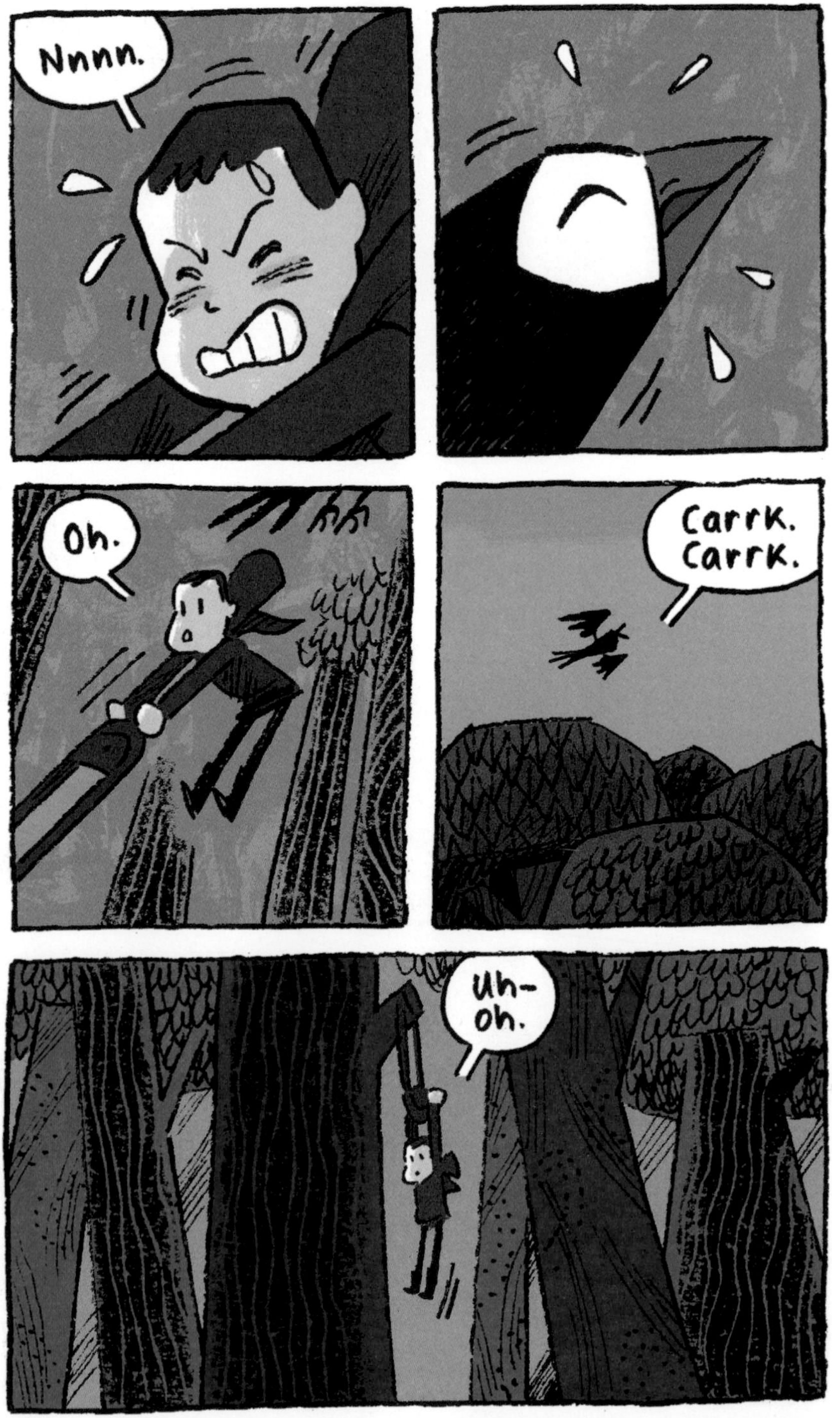
Nnnn.
Oh.
Carrk. Carrk.
Uh-oh.

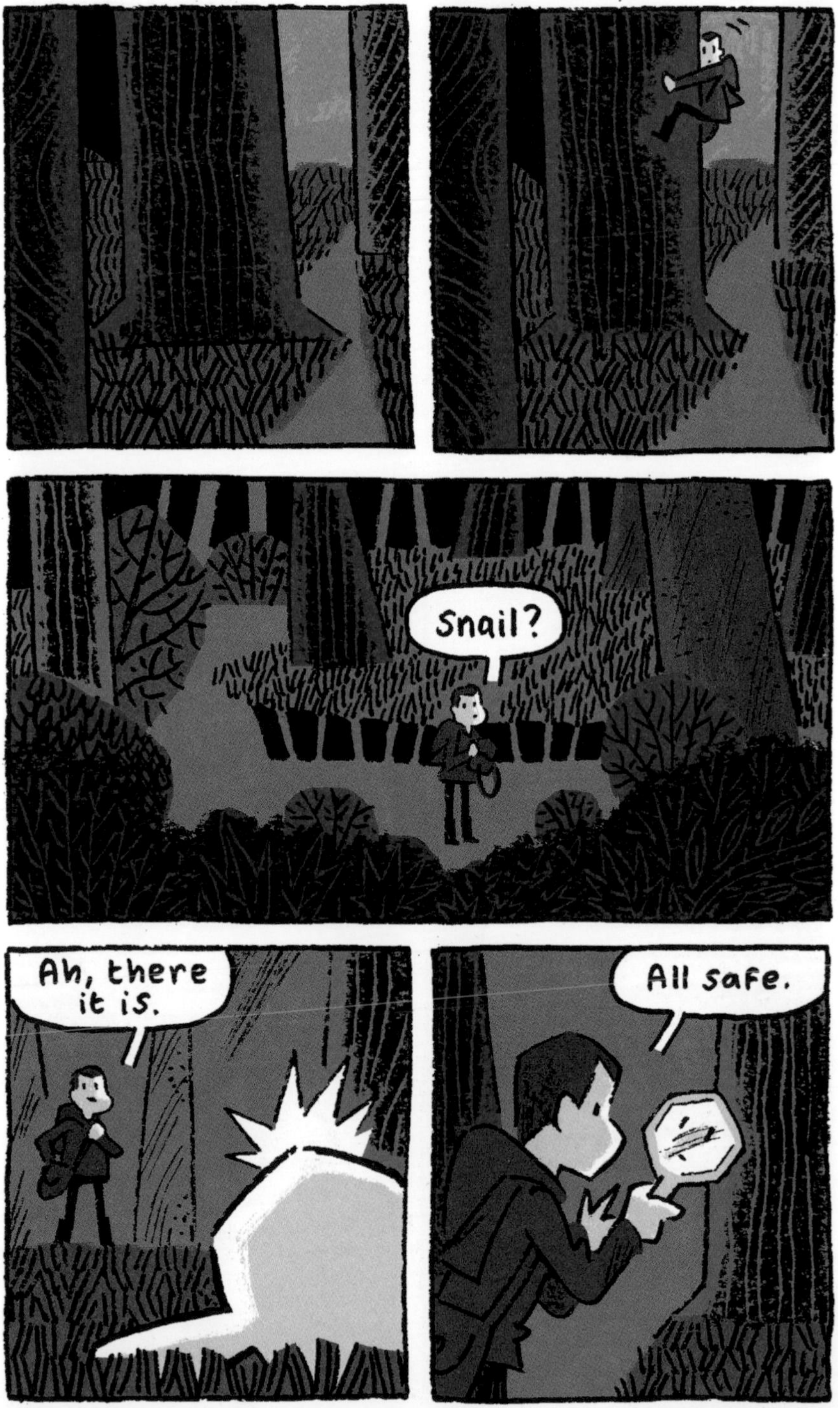
Snail?
Ah, there it is.
All safe.

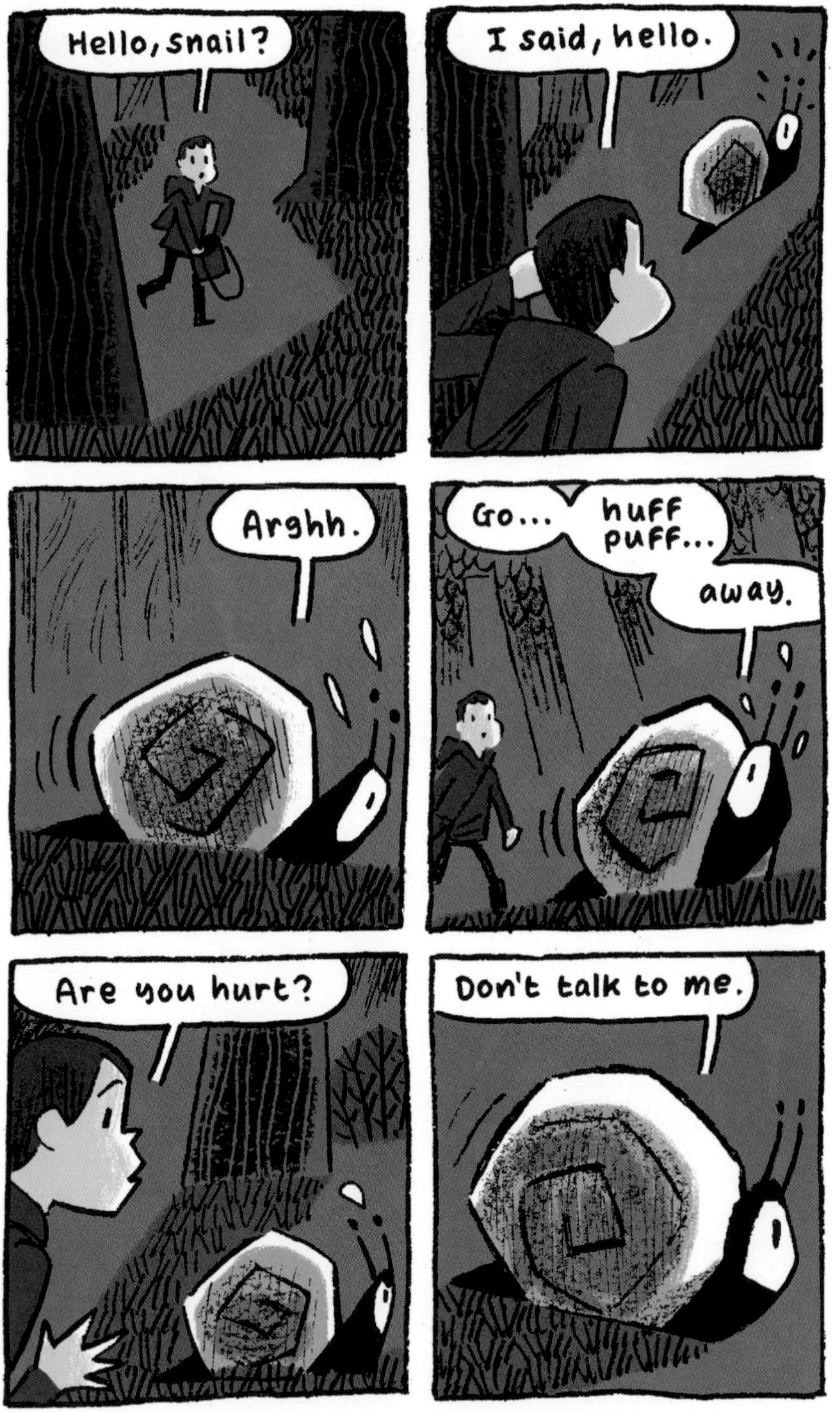
Hello, snail?
I said, hello.
Arghh.
Go...
huff puff...
away.
Are you hurt?
Don't talk to me.

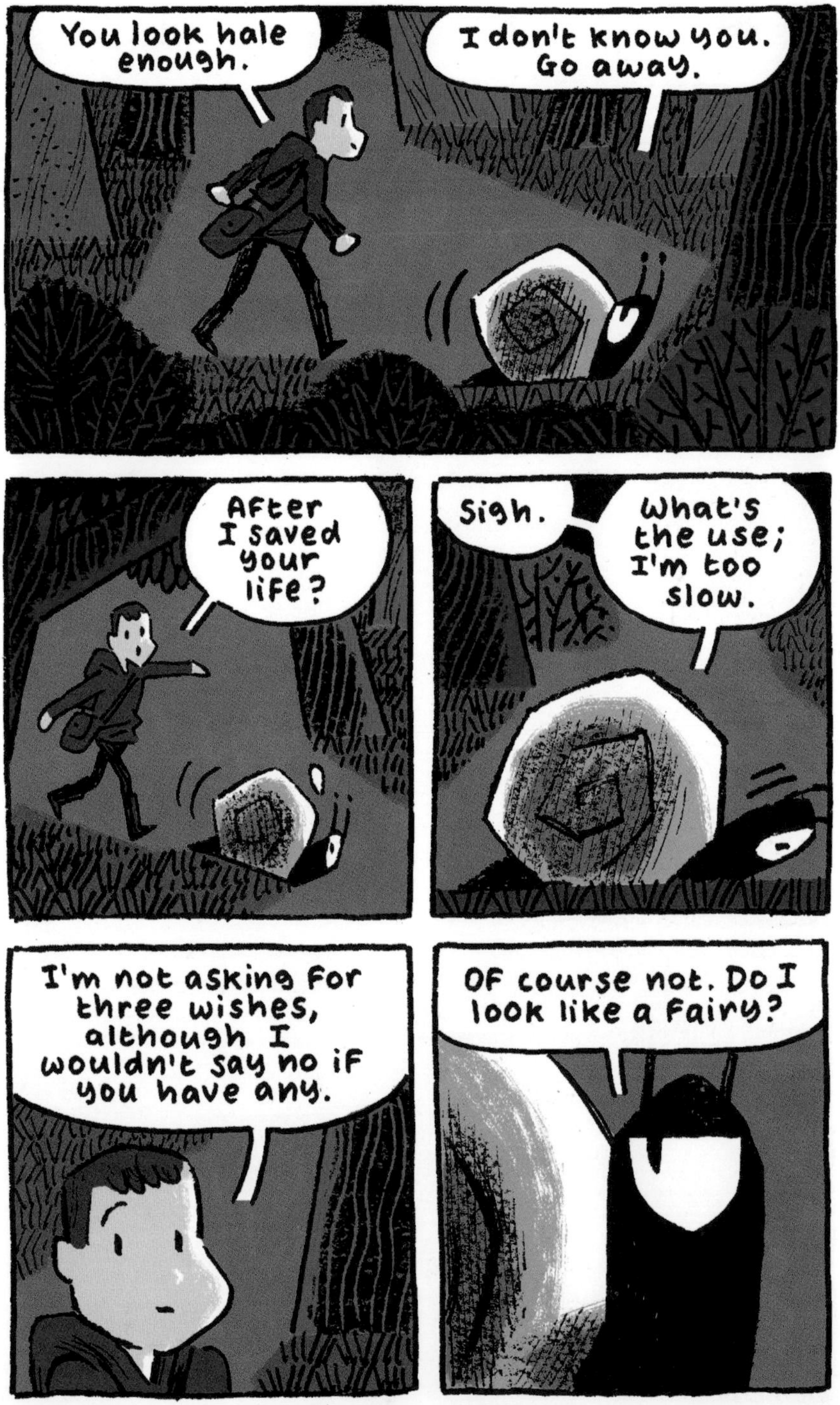
You look hale enough.
I don't know you. Go away.
After I saved your life?
Sigh.
What's the use; I'm too slow.
I'm not asking for three wishes, although I wouldn't say no if you have any.
Of course not. Do I look like a fairy?

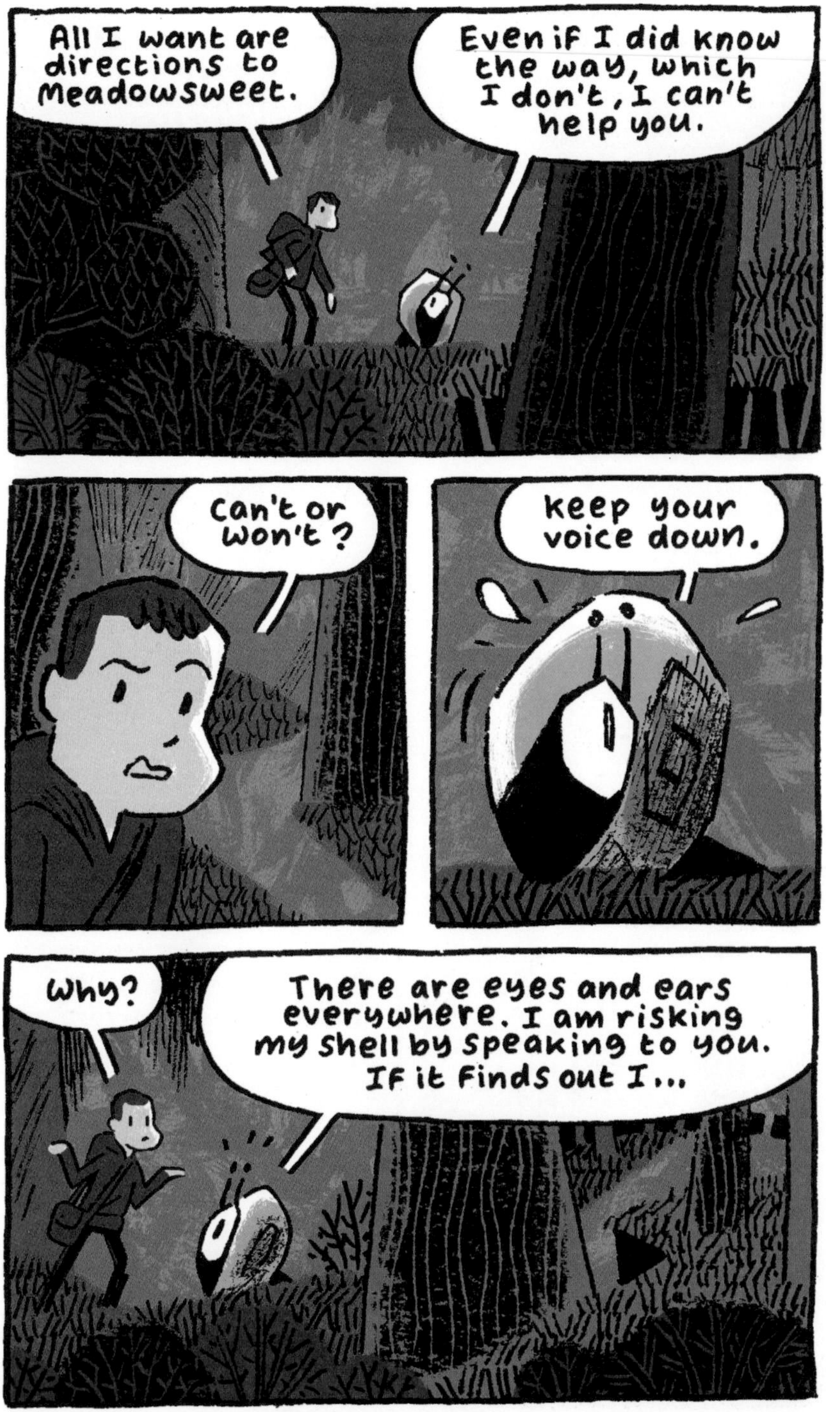
All I want are directions to Meadowsweet.
Even if I did know the way, which I don't, I can't help you.
Can't or won't?
Keep your voice down.
Why?
There are eyes and ears everywhere. I am risking my shell by speaking to you. If it finds out I...

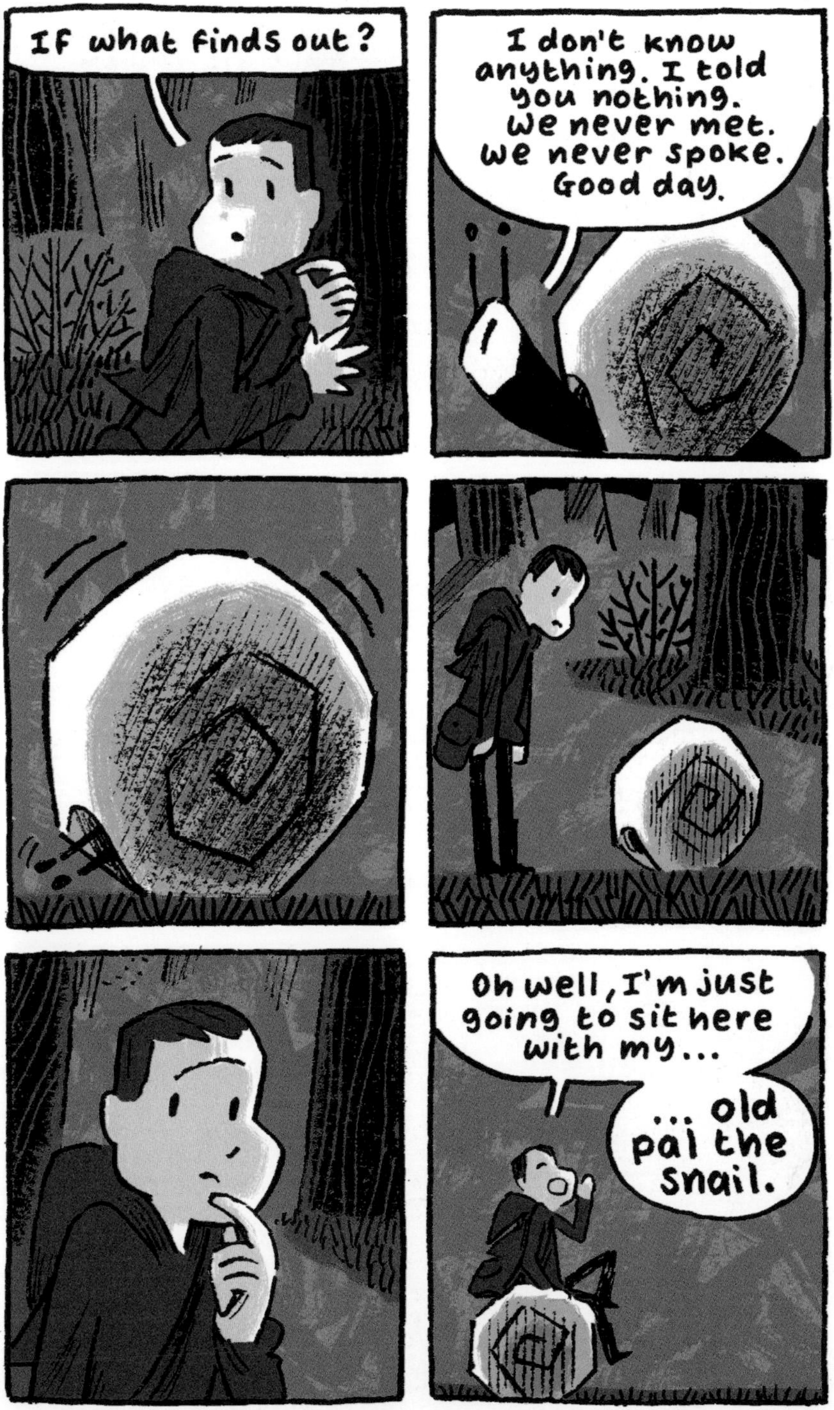
If what finds out?
I don't know anything. I told you nothing. We never met. We never spoke. Good day.
Oh well, I'm just going to sit here with my...
... old pal the snail.

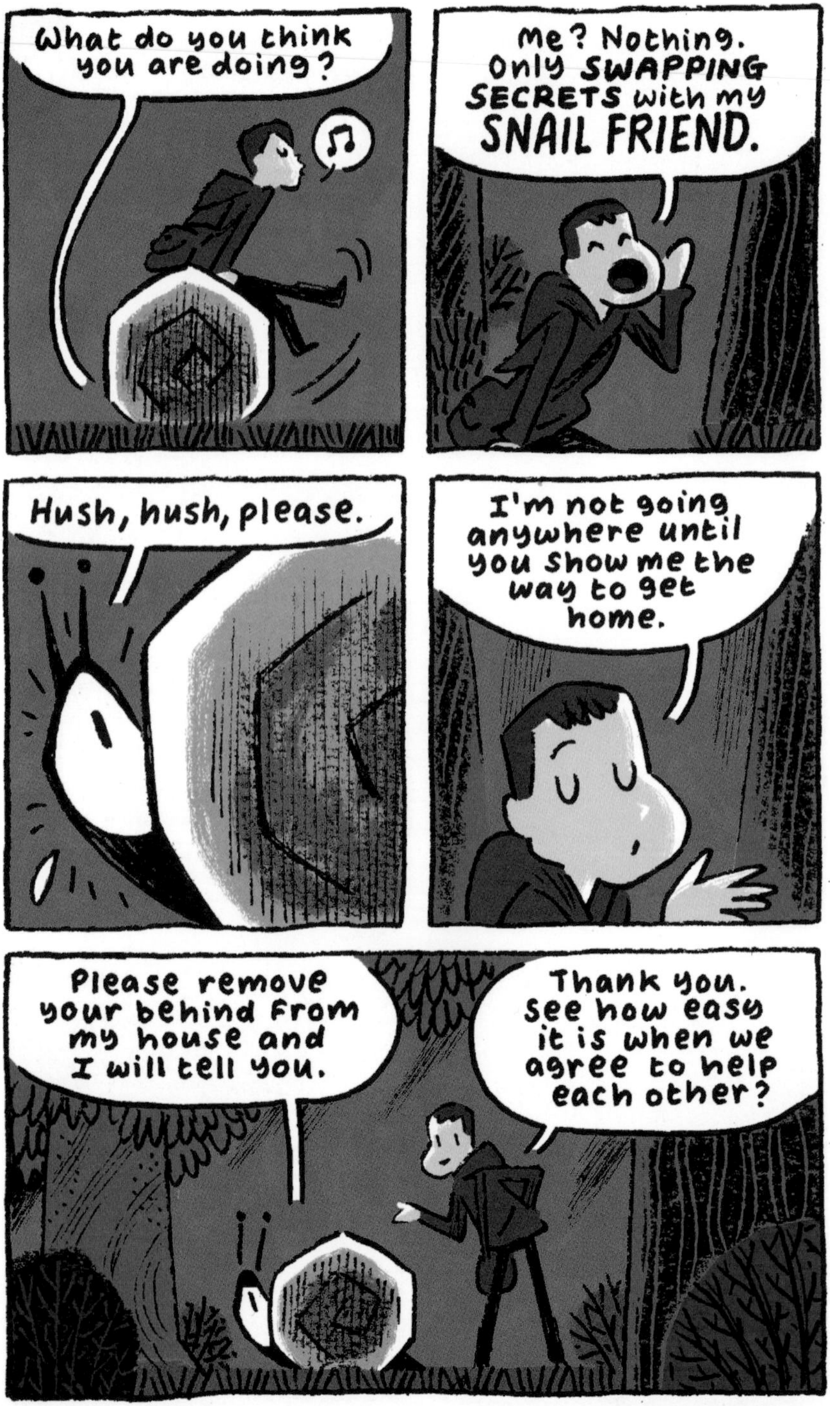
What do you think you are doing?
Me? Nothing. Only SWAPPING SECRETS with my SNAIL FRIEND.
Hush, hush, please.
I'm not going anywhere until you show me the way to get home.
Please remove your behind from my house and I will tell you.
Thank you. See how easy it is when we agree to help each other?

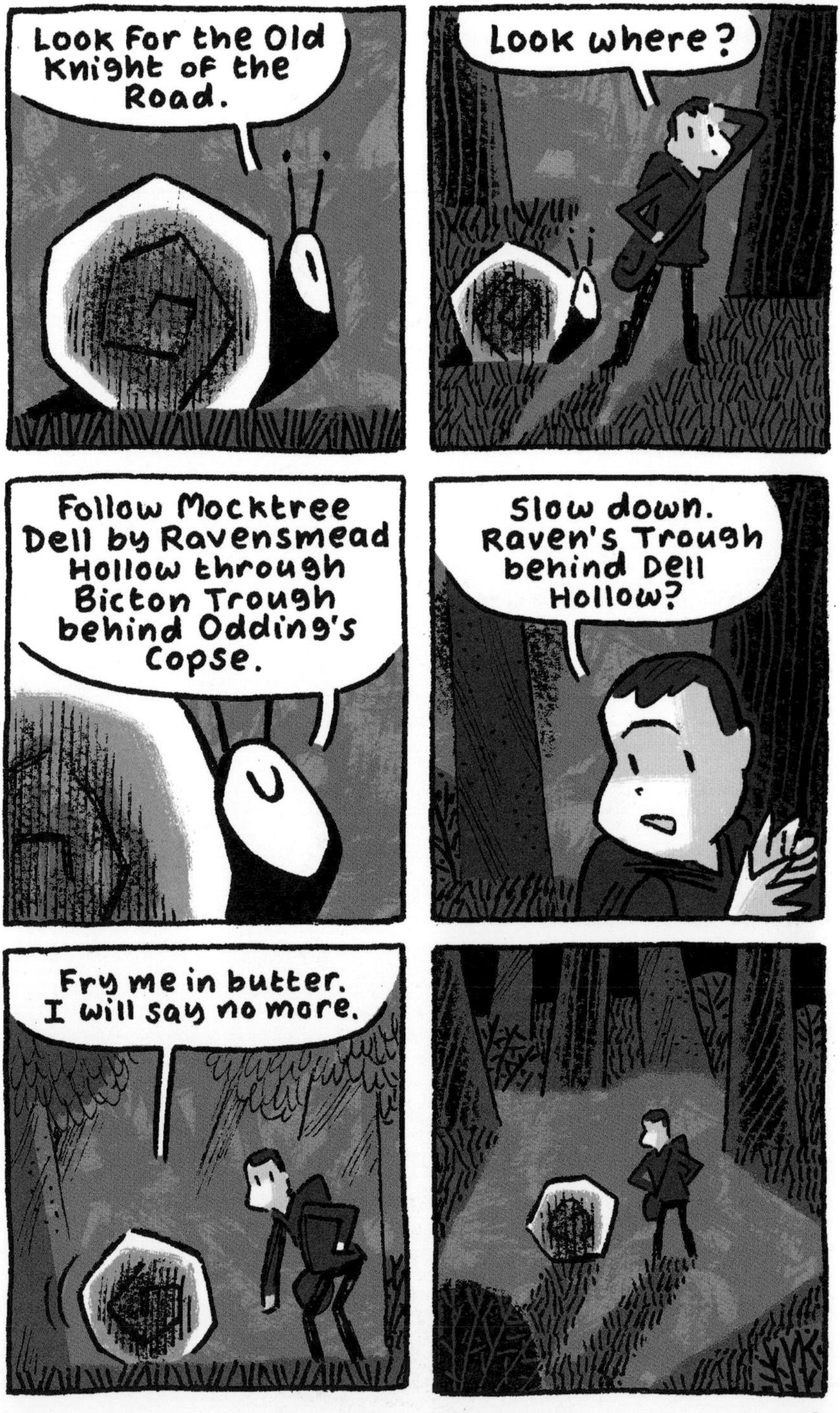
Look for the Old Knight of the Road.
Look where?
Follow Mocktree Dell by Ravensmead Hollow through Bicton Trough behind Odding's Copse.
Slow down. Raven's Trough behind Dell Hollow?
Fry me in butter. I will say no more.

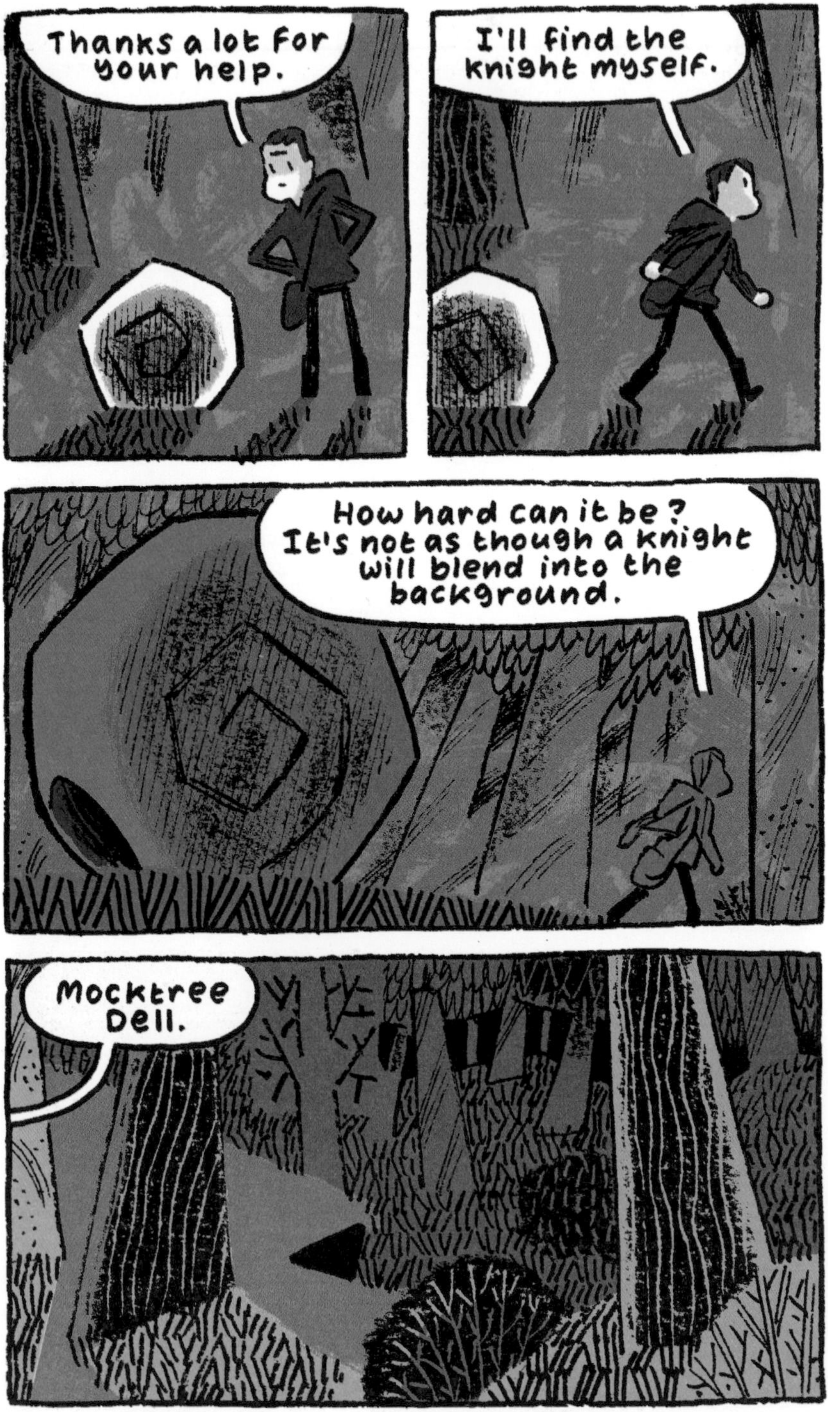
Thanks a lot for your help.
I'll find the knight myself.
How hard can it be? It's not as though a knight will blend into the background.
Mocktree Dell.

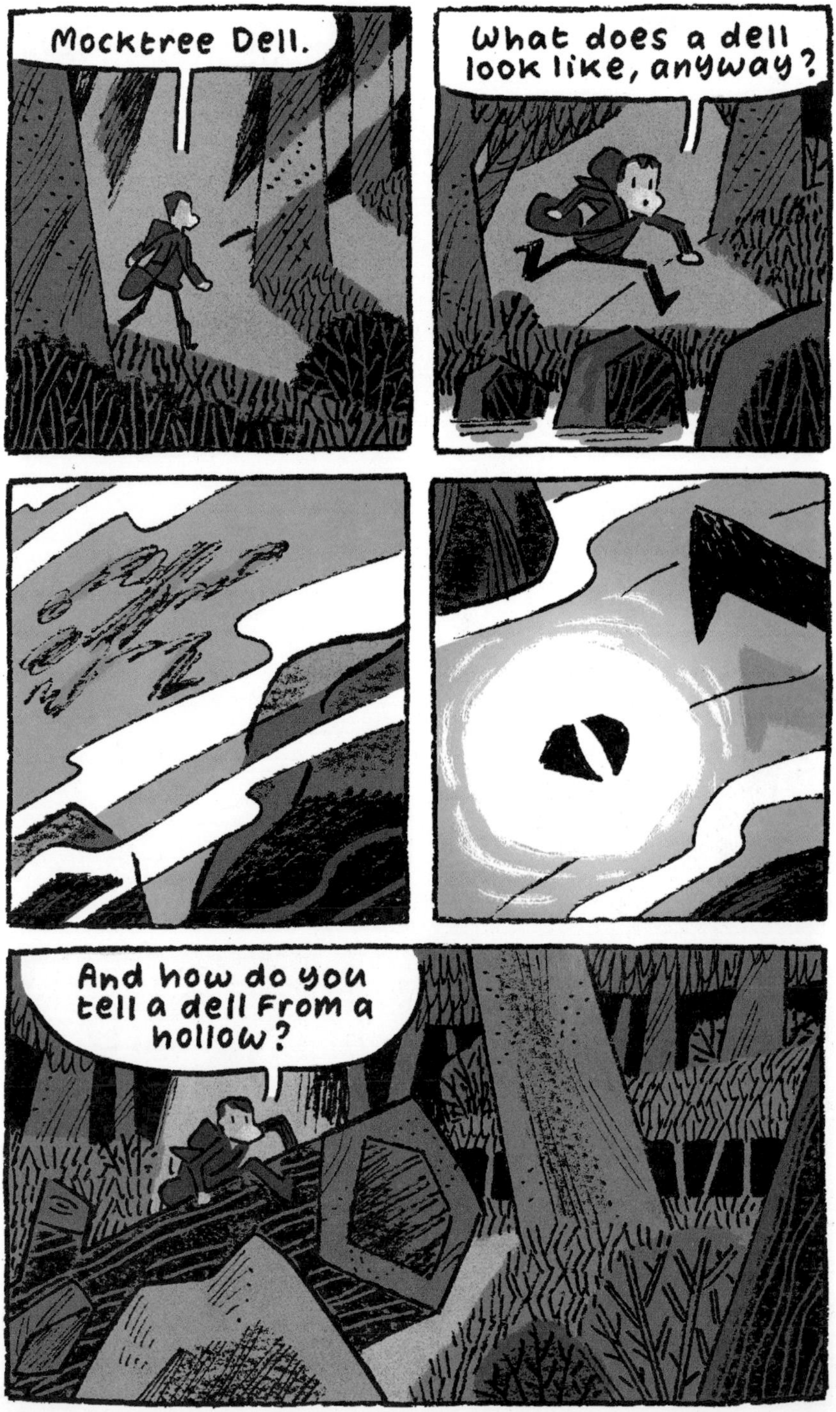
Mocktree Dell.
What does a dell look like, anyway?
And how do you tell a dell from a hollow?

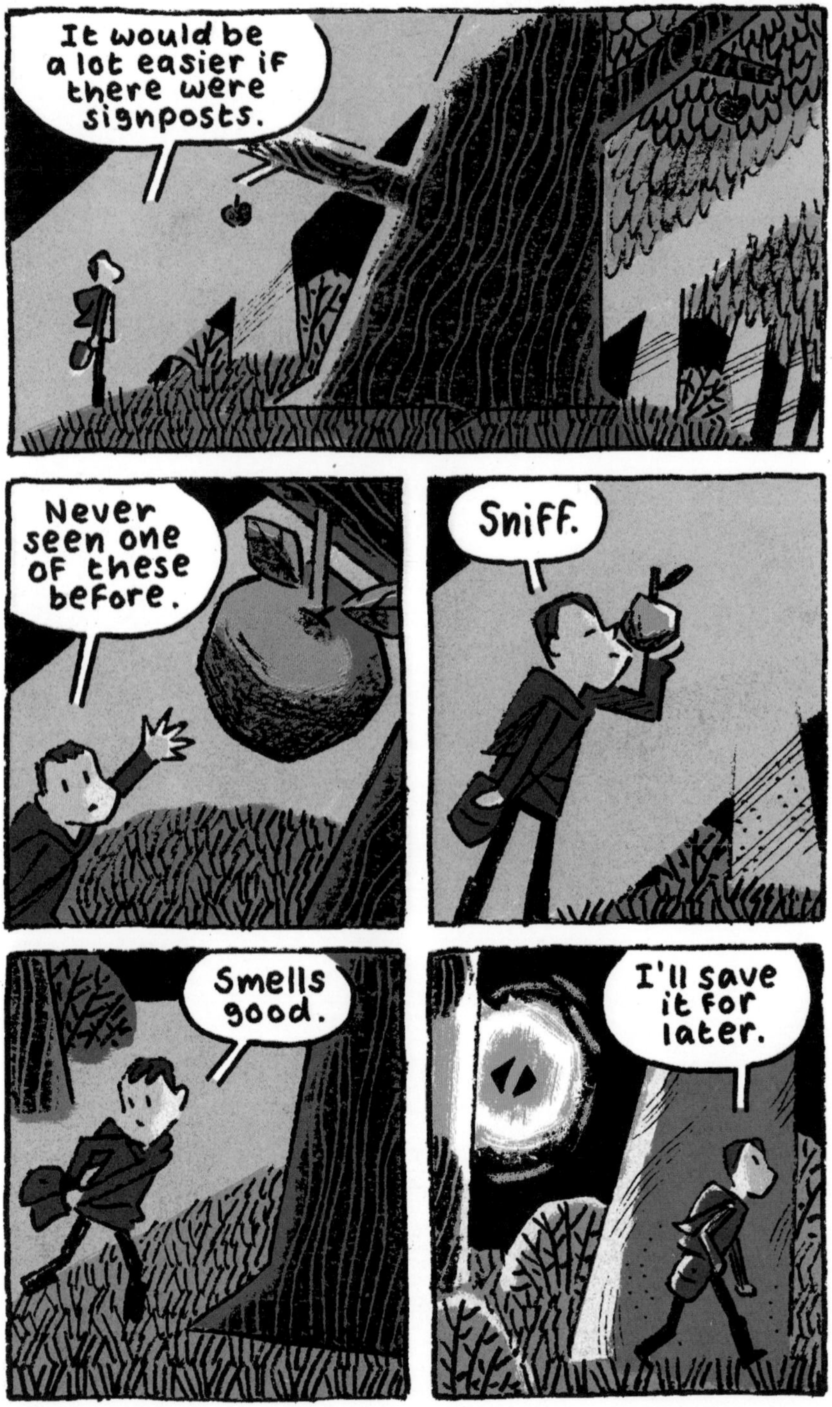
It would be a lot easier if there were signposts.
Never seen one of these before.
Sniff.
Smells good.
I'll save it for later.

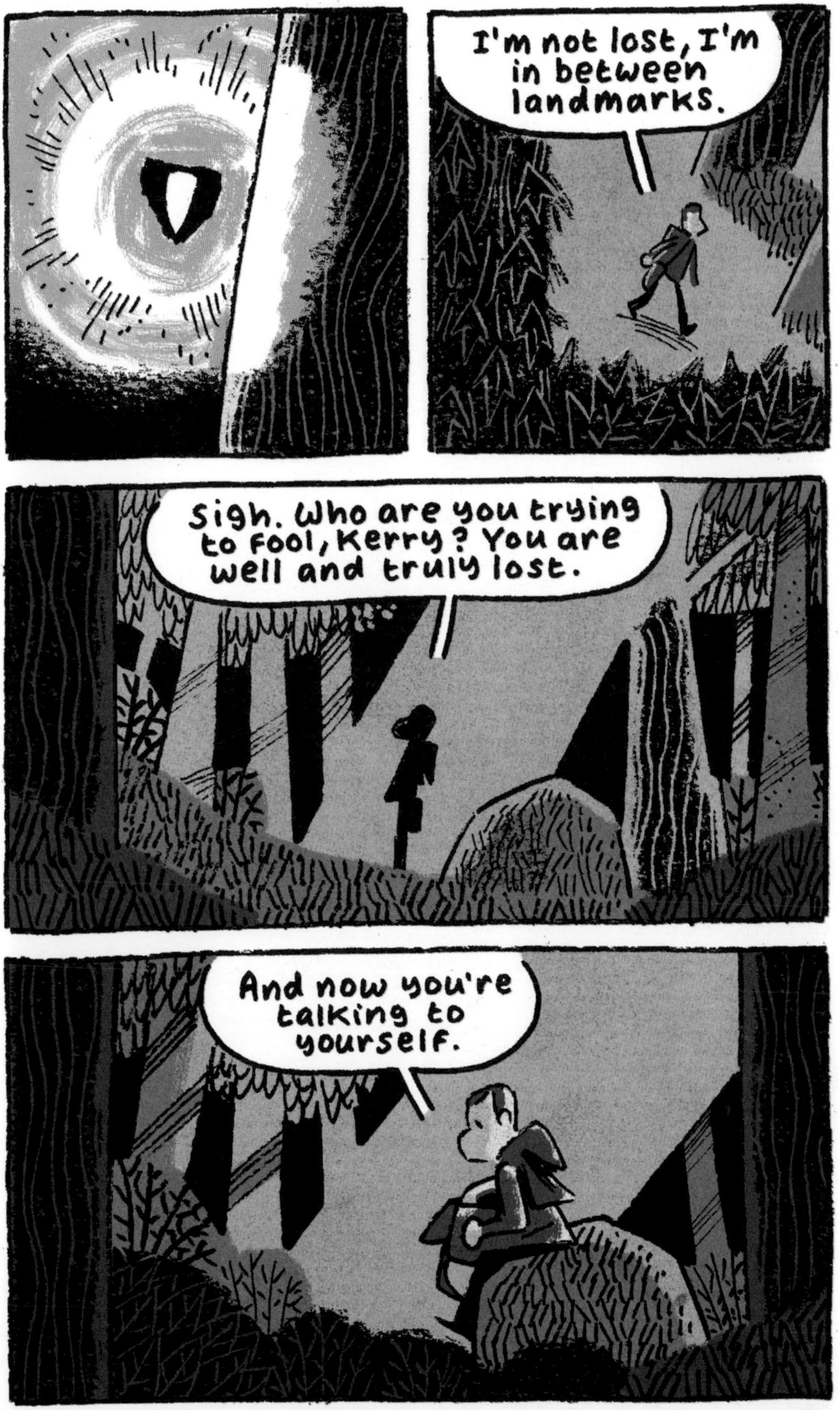
I'm not lost, I'm in between landmarks.
Sigh. Who are you trying to fool, Kerry? You are well and truly lost.
And now you're talking to yourself.

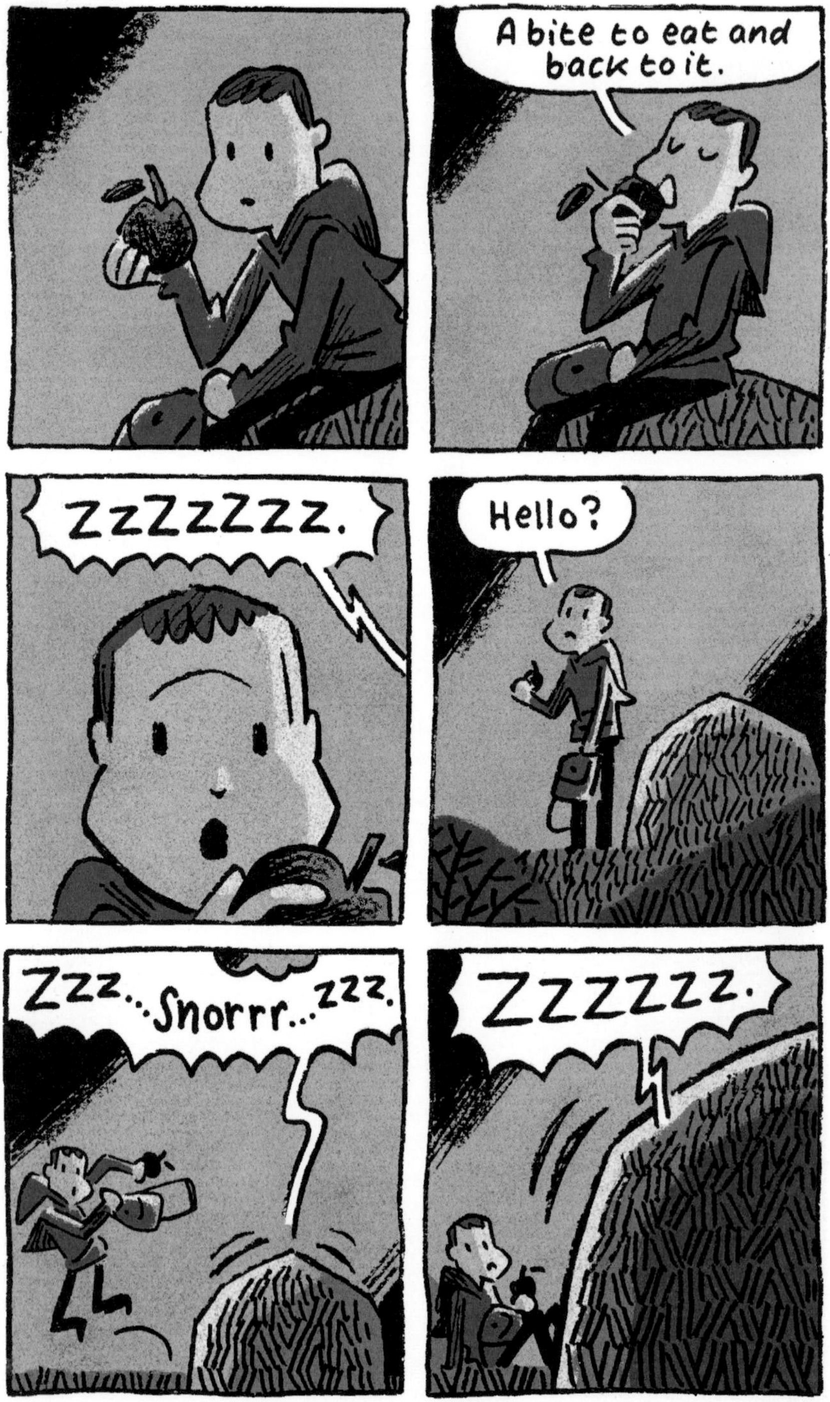
A bite to eat and back to it.
ZzZzZzz.
Hello?
Zzz...Snorrr...zzz.
ZZZZZZ.

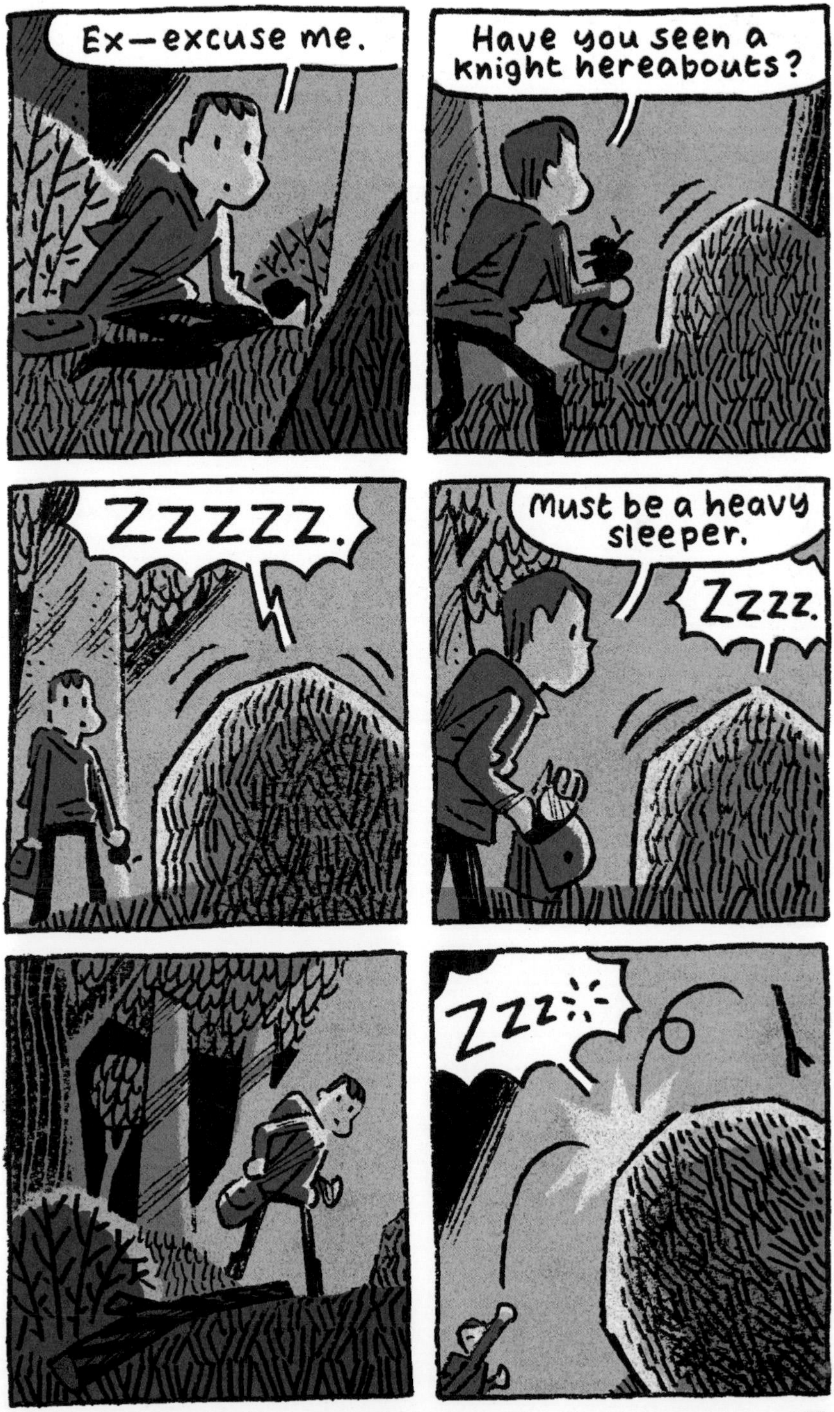
Ex—excuse me.
Have you seen a knight hereabouts?
ZZZZZ.
Must be a heavy sleeper.
Zzzz.
Zzz

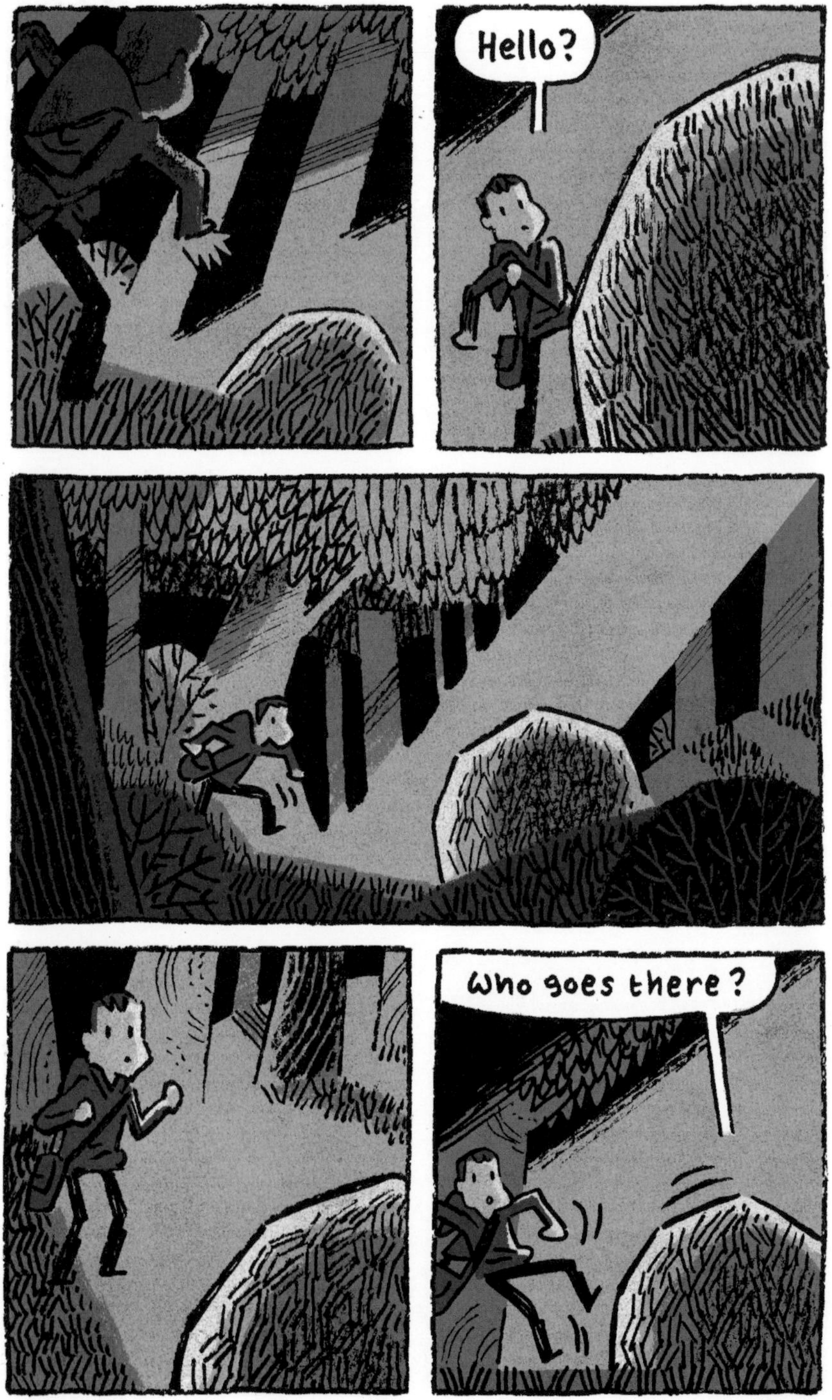
Hello?
Who goes there?

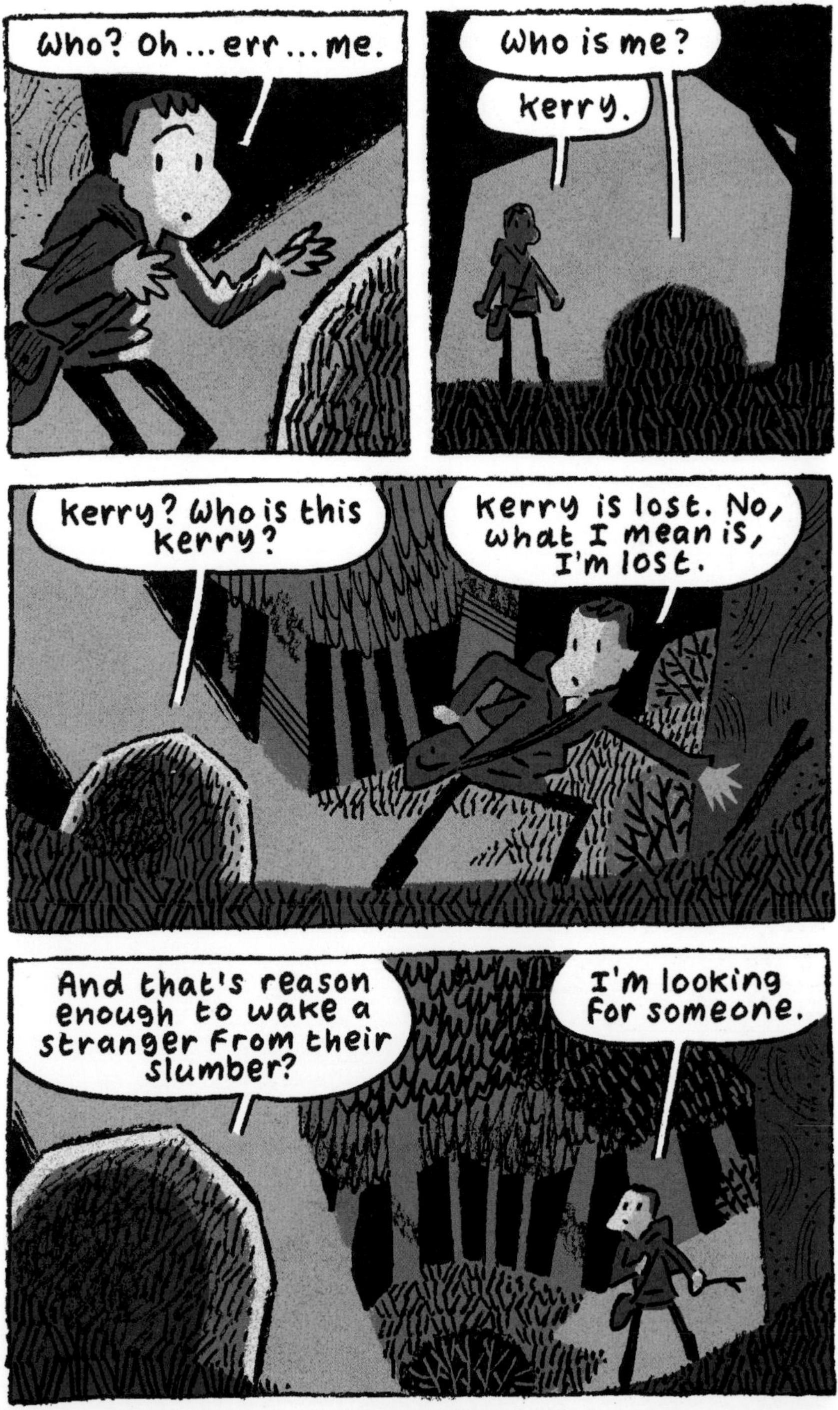
Who? Oh... err... me.
Who is me?
Kerry.
Kerry? Who is this Kerry?
Kerry is lost. No, what I mean is, I'm lost.
And that's reason enough to wake a stranger from their slumber?
I'm looking for someone.

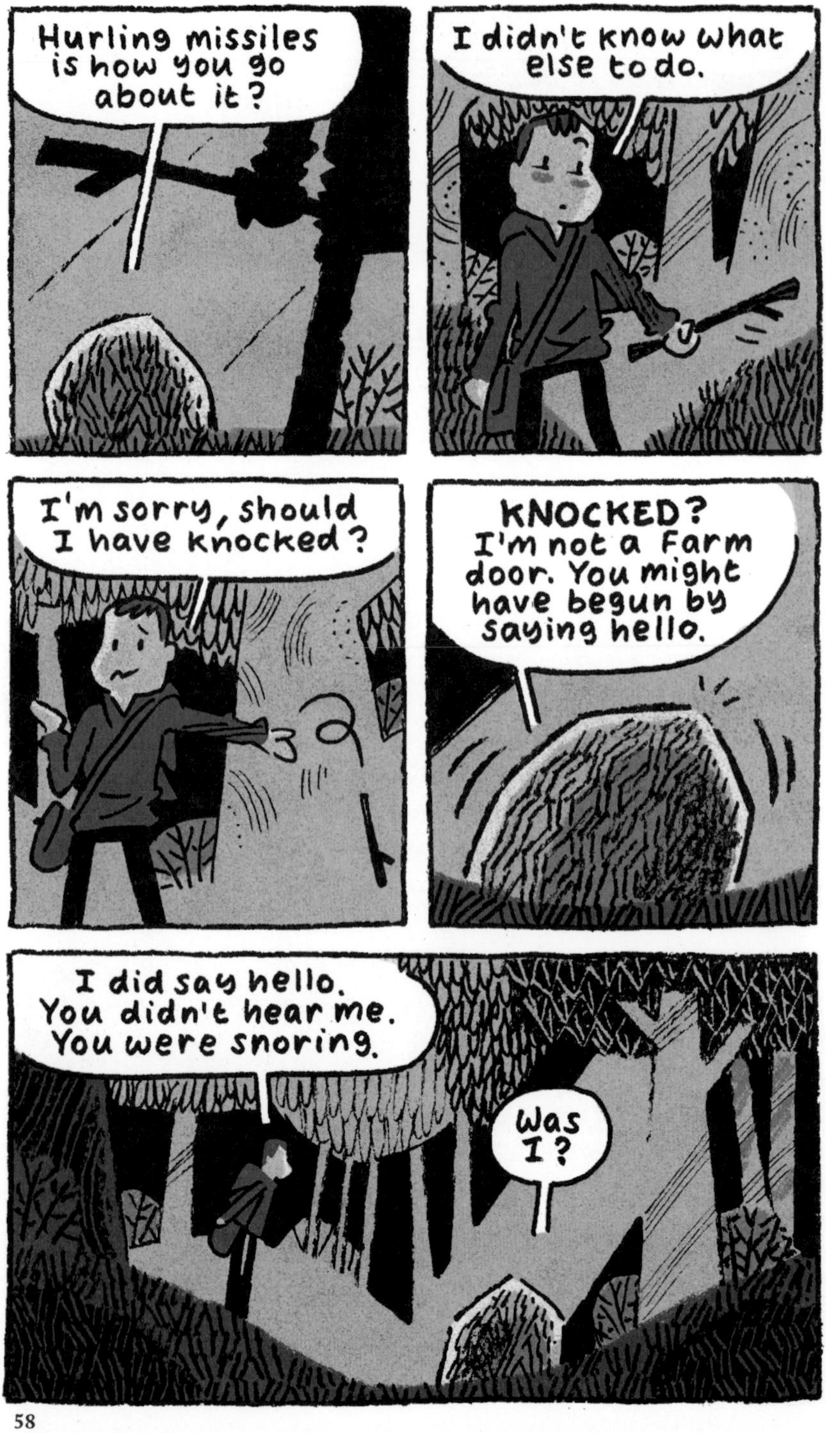
Hurling missiles is how you go about it?
I didn't know what else to do.
I'm sorry, should I have knocked?
KNOCKED? I'm not a farm door. You might have begun by saying hello.
I did say hello. You didn't hear me. You were snoring.
Was I?

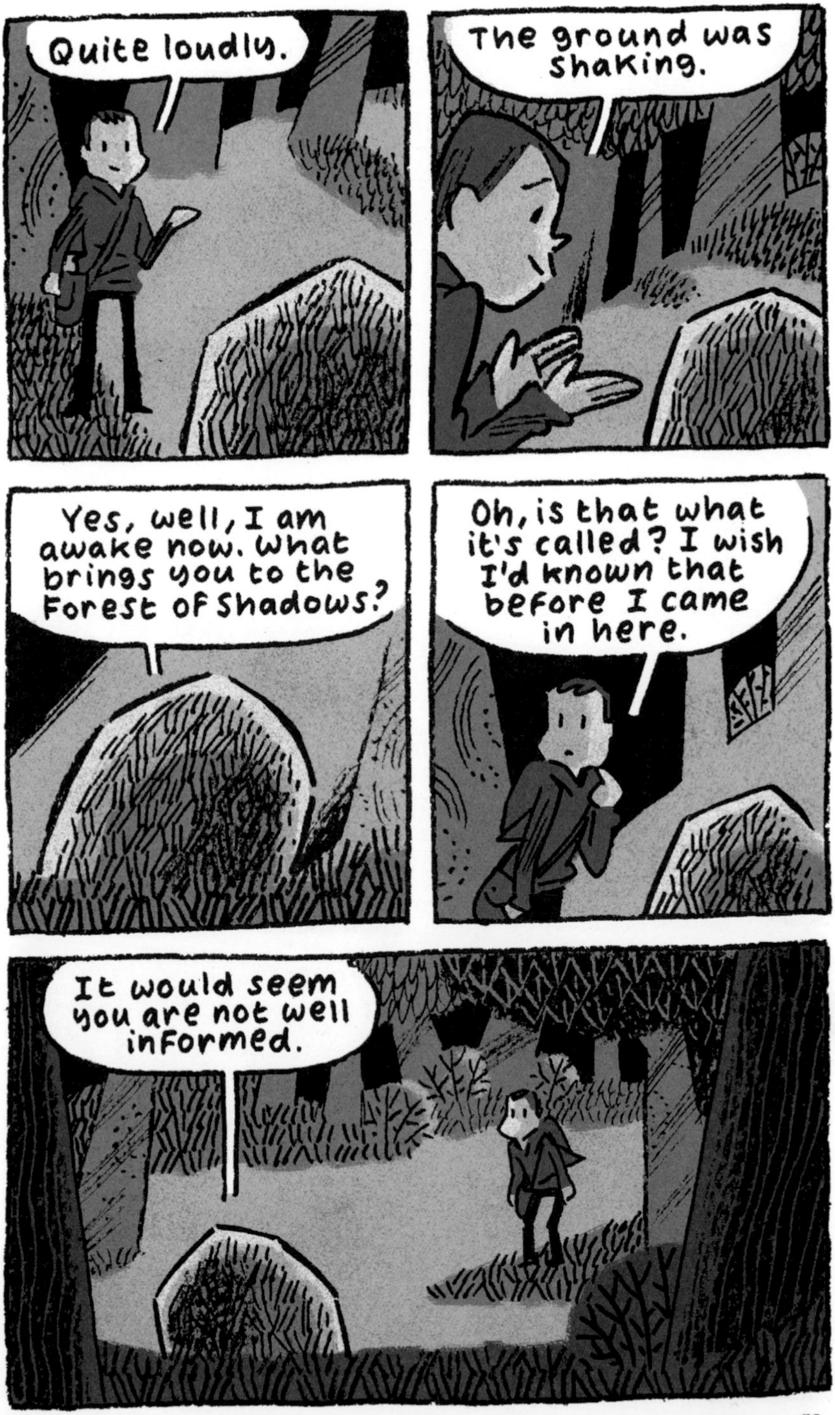
Quite loudly.
The ground was shaking.
Yes, well, I am awake now. What brings you to the Forest of Shadows?
Oh, is that what it's called? I wish I'd known that before I came in here.
It would seem you are not well informed.

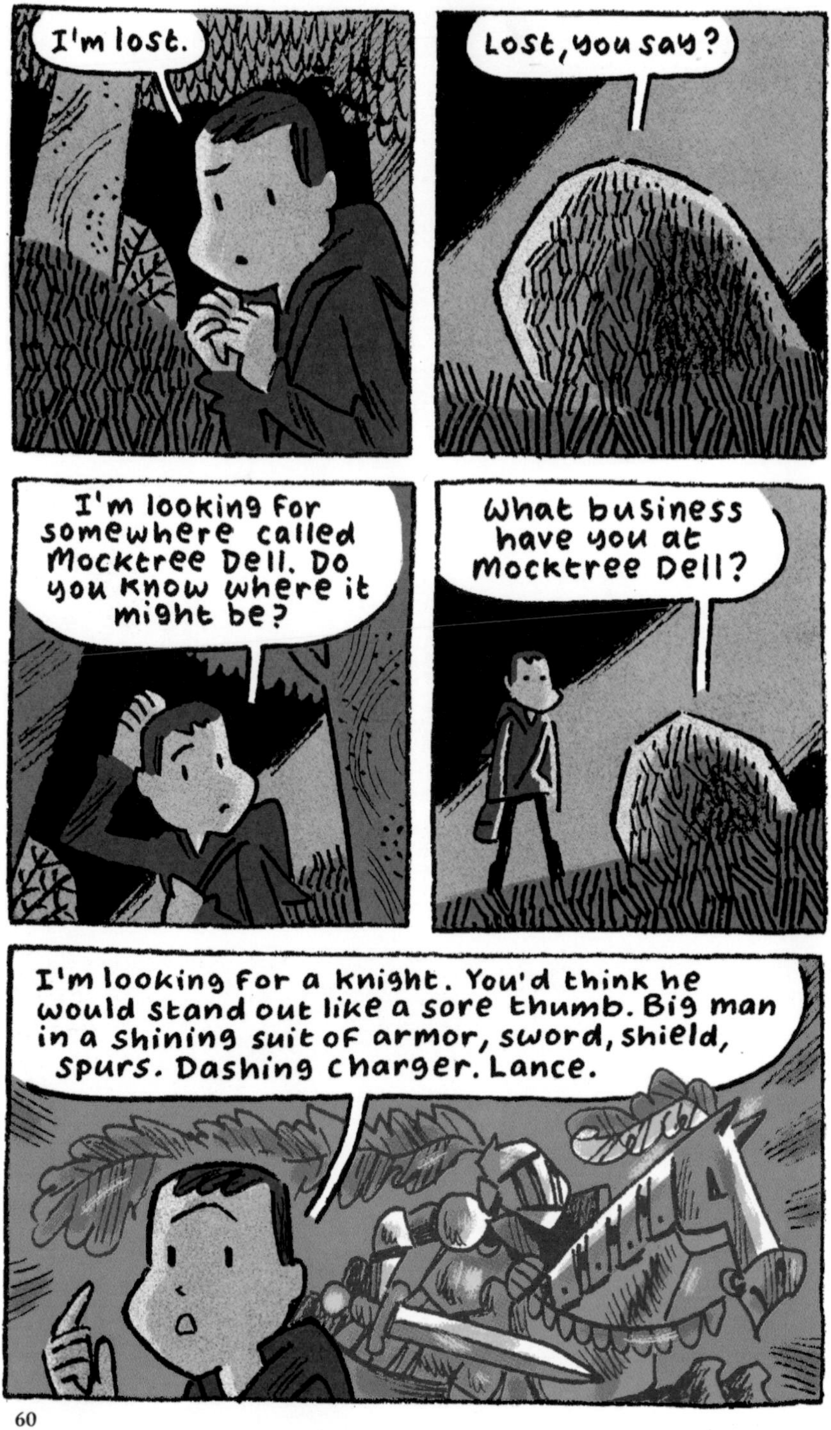
I'm lost.
Lost, you say?
I'm looking for somewhere called Mocktree Dell. Do you know where it might be?
What business have you at Mocktree Dell?
I'm looking for a knight. You'd think he would stand out like a sore thumb. Big man in a shining suit of armor, sword, shield, spurs. Dashing charger. Lance.

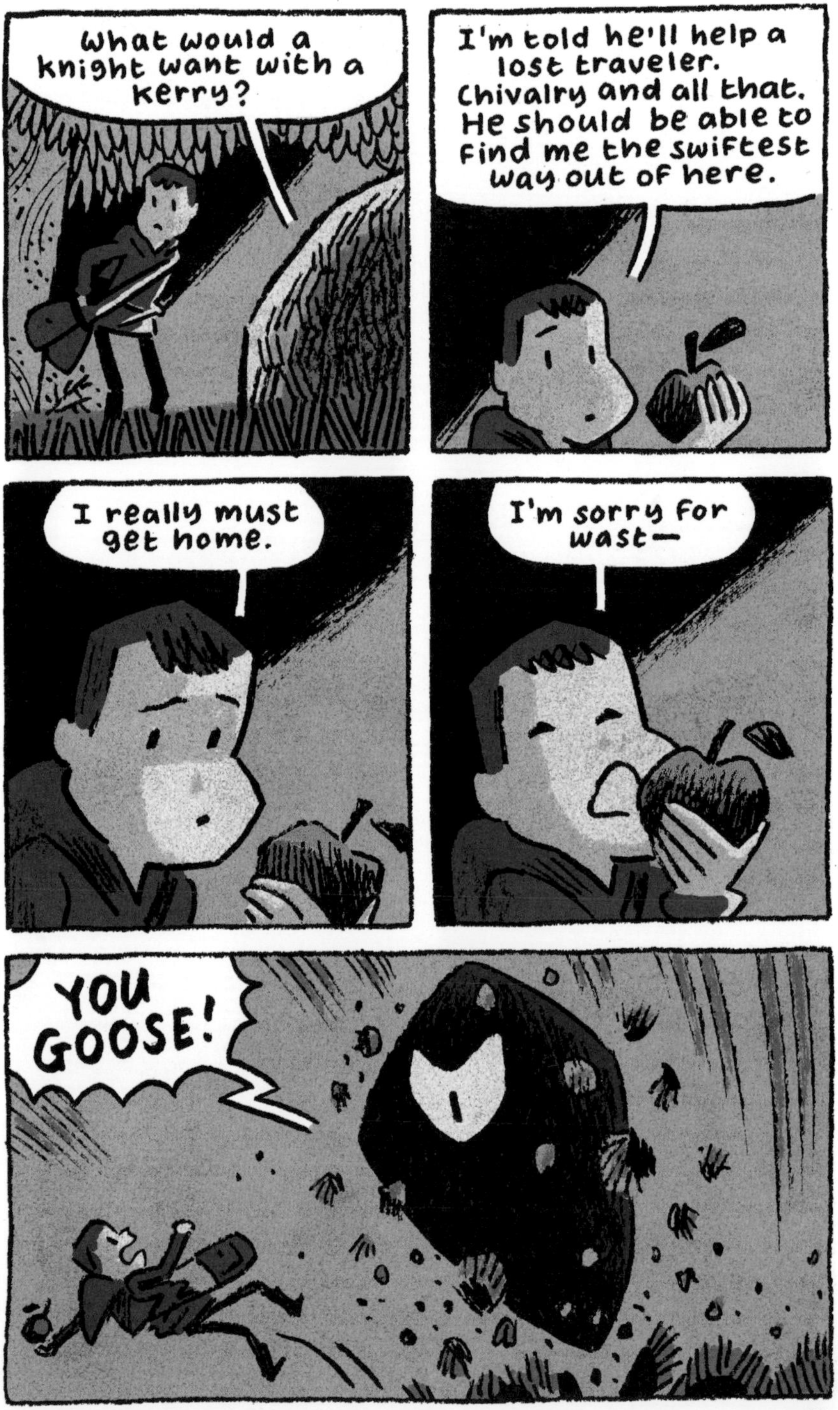
What would a knight want with a kerry?
I'm told he'll help a lost traveler. Chivalry and all that. He should be able to find me the swiftest way out of here.
I really must get home.
I'm sorry for wast—
YOU GOOSE!

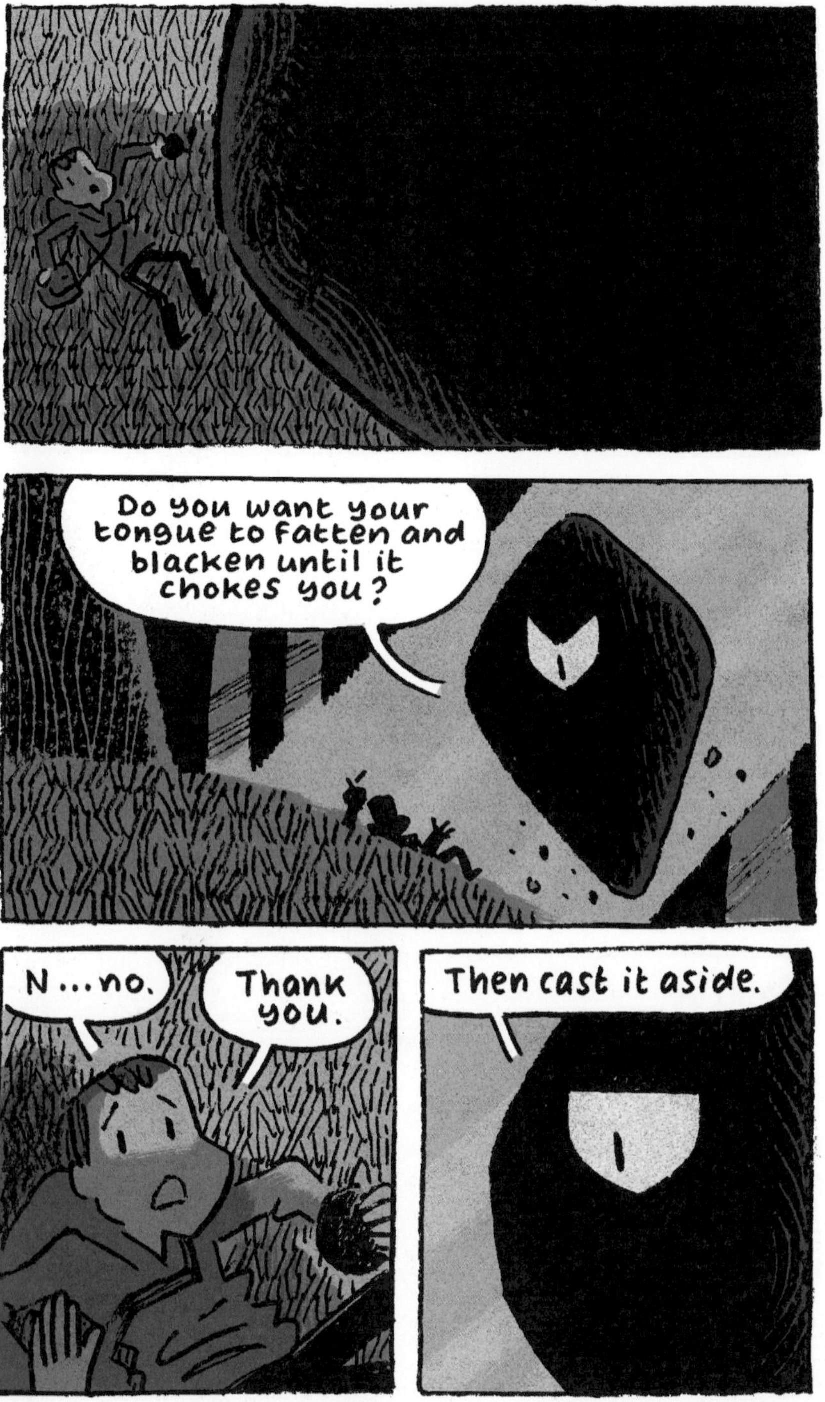
Do you want your tongue to fatten and blacken until it chokes you?
N...no.
Thank you.
Then cast it aside.

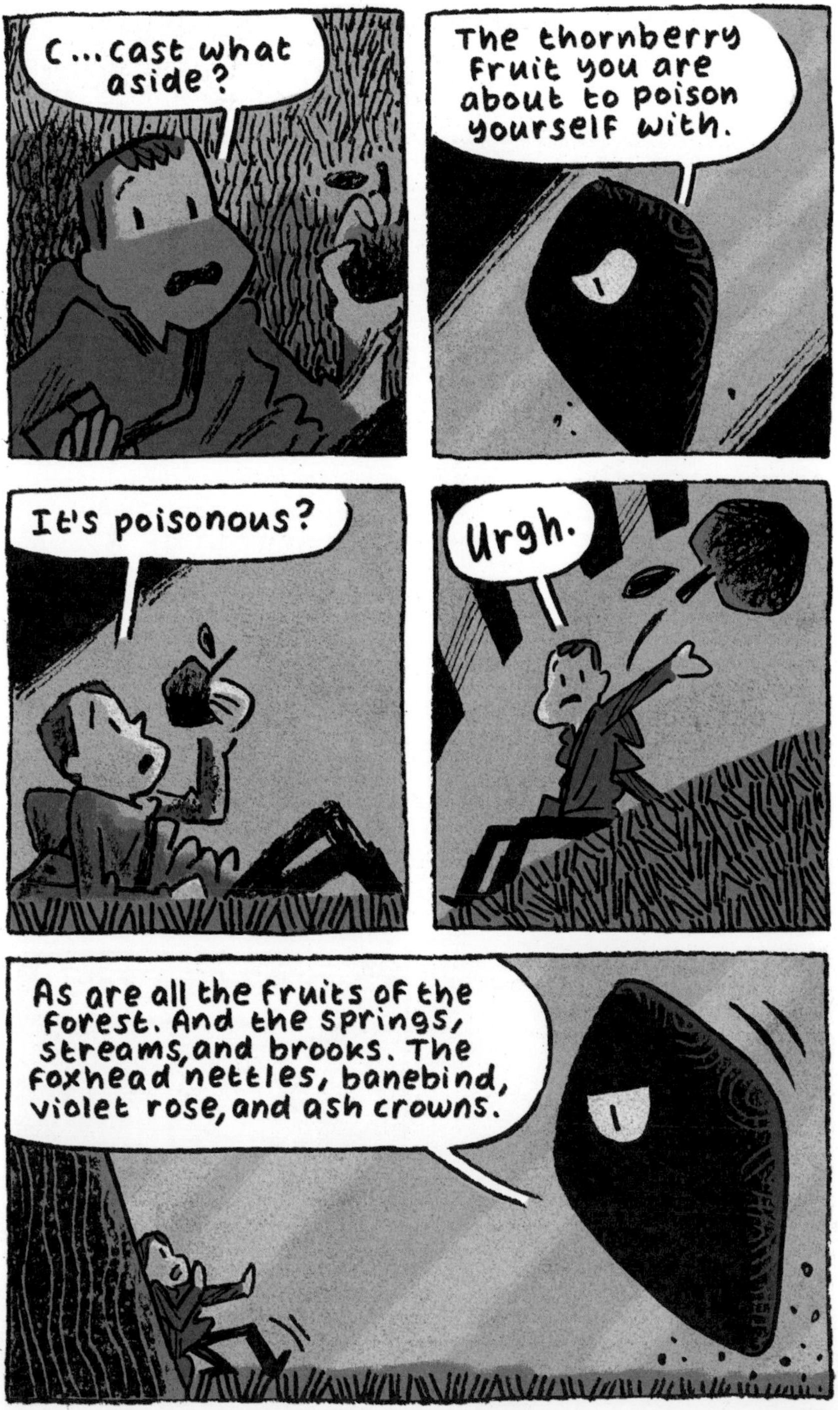

C...cast what aside?
The thornberry fruit you are about to poison yourself with.
It's poisonous?
Urgh.
As are all the fruits of the forest. And the springs, streams, and brooks. The foxhead nettles, banebind, violet rose, and ash crowns.

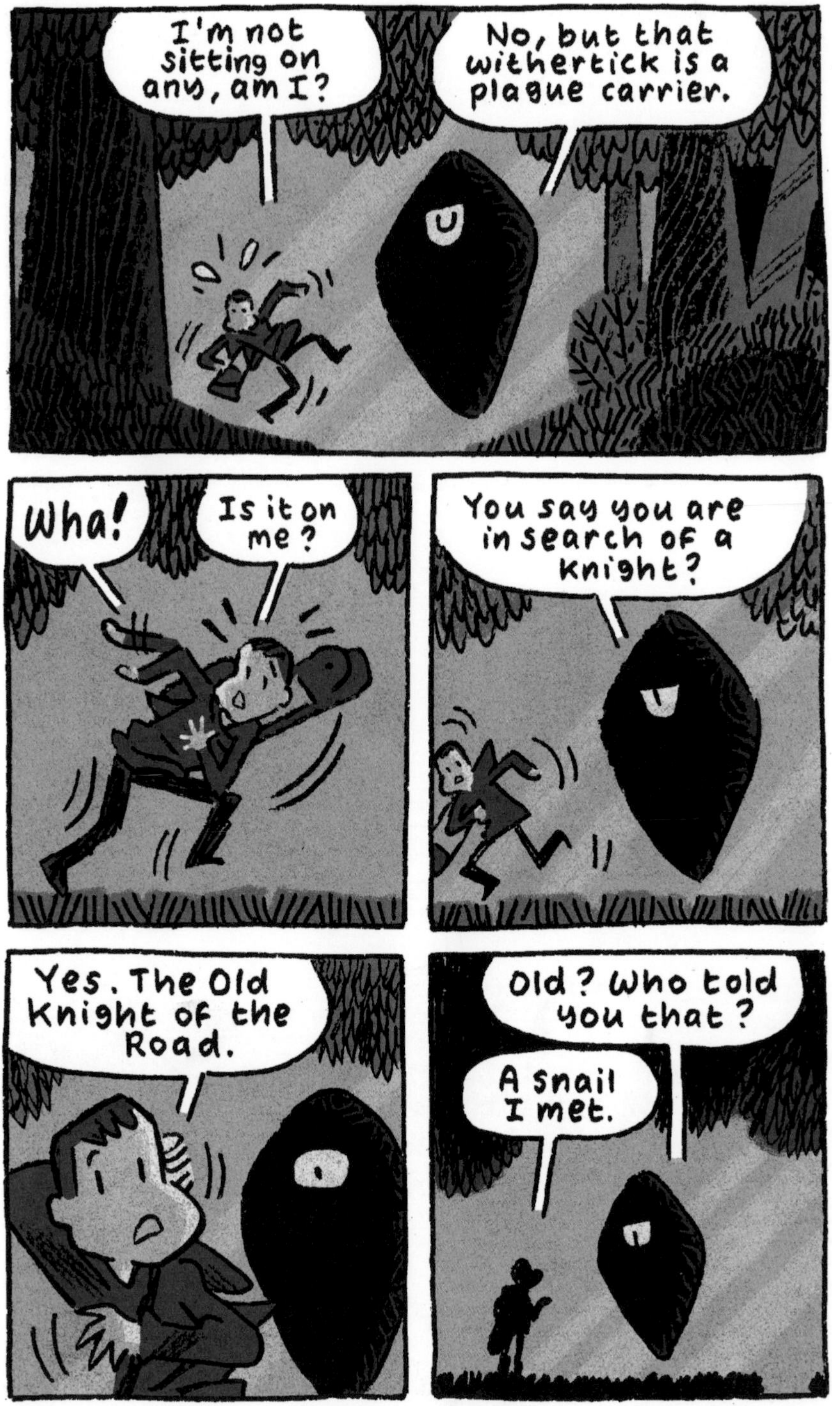
I'm not sitting on any, am I?
No, but that withertick is a plague carrier.
Wha!
Is it on me?
You say you are in search of a knight?
Yes. The Old Knight of the Road.
Old? Who told you that?
A snail I met.

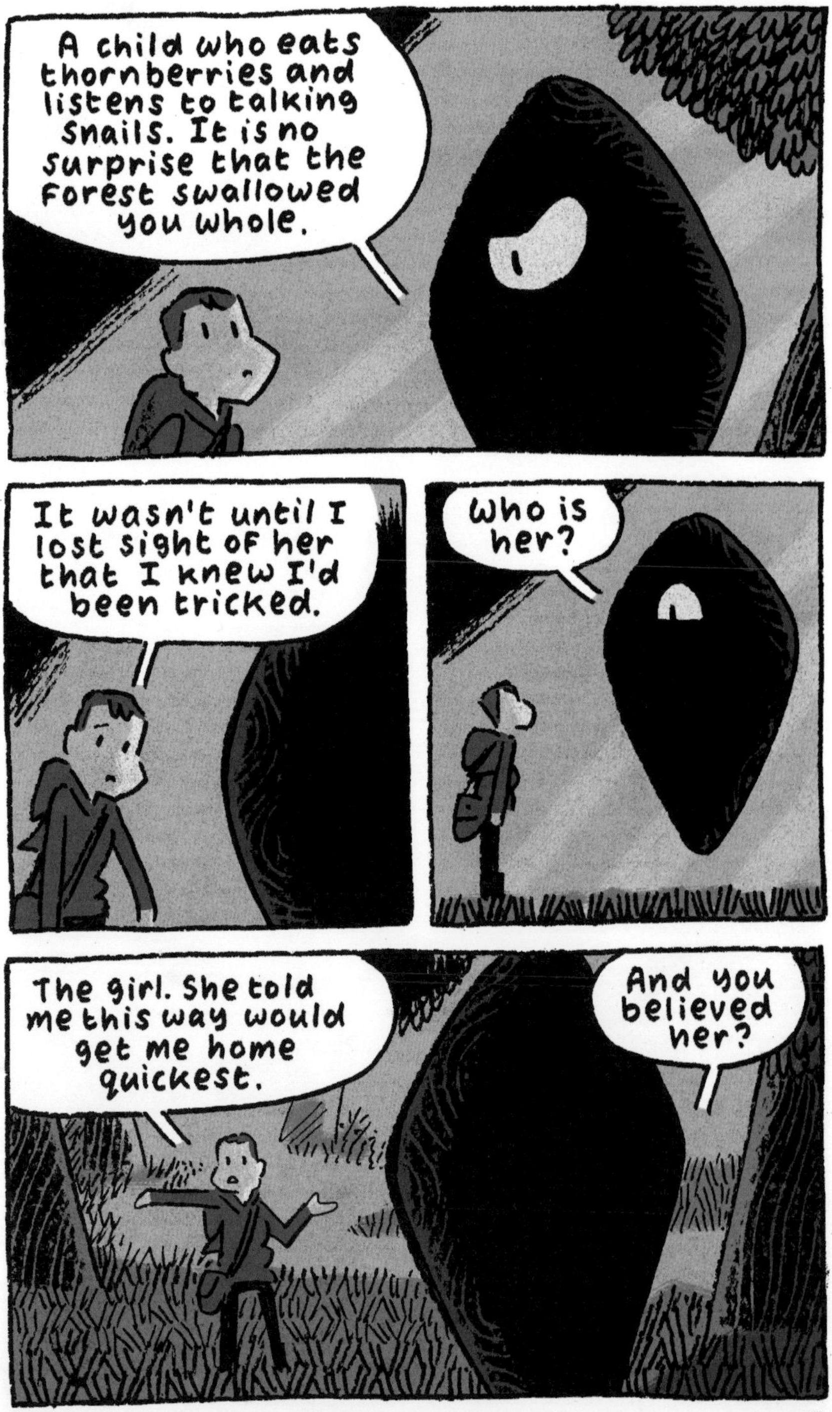
A child who eats thornberries and listens to talking snails. It is no surprise that the forest swallowed you whole.
It wasn't until I lost sight of her that I knew I'd been tricked.
Who is her?
The girl. She told me this way would get me home quickest.
And you believed her?

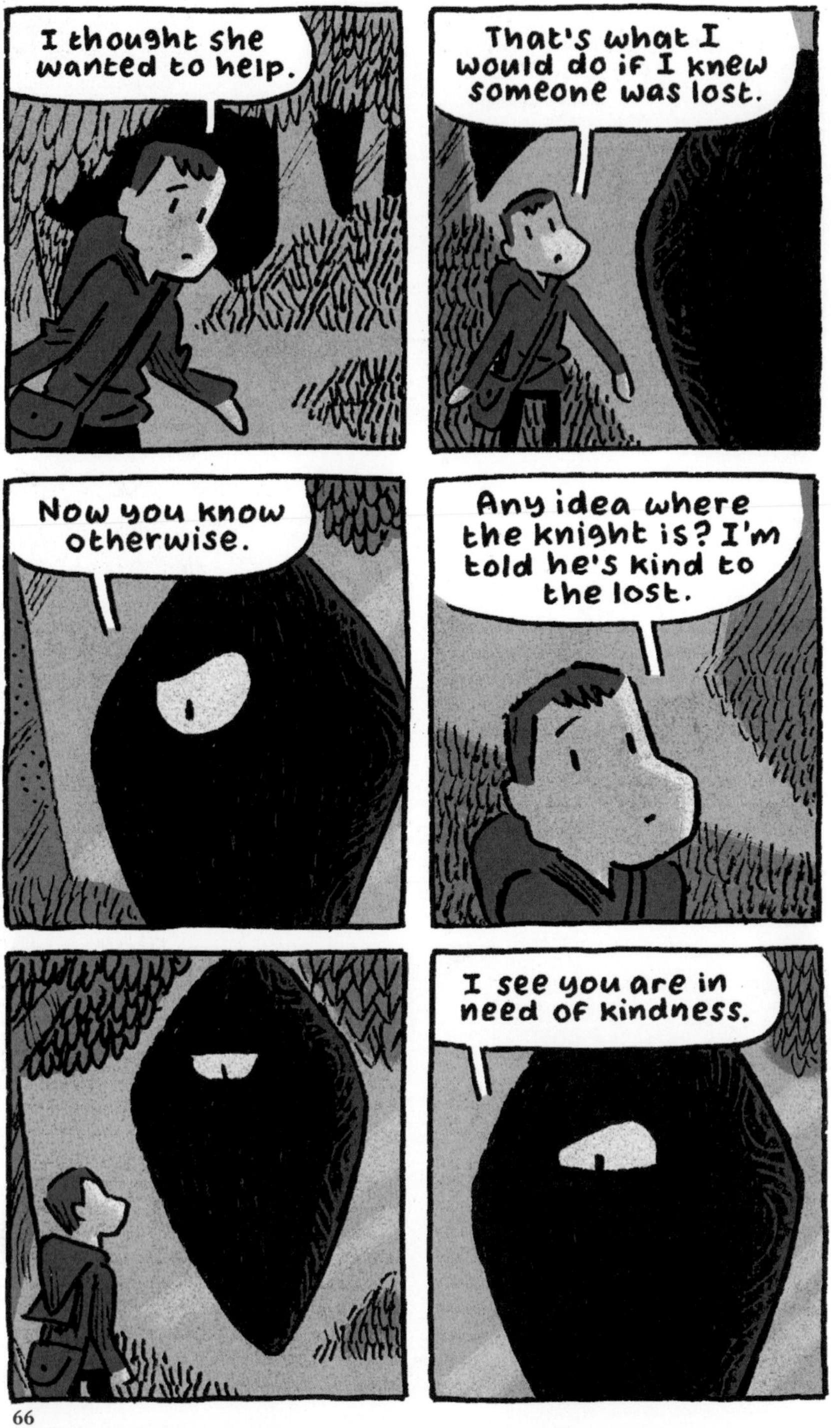
I thought she wanted to help.
That's what I would do if I knew someone was lost.
Now you know otherwise.
Any idea where the knight is? I'm told he's kind to the lost.
I see you are in need of kindness.

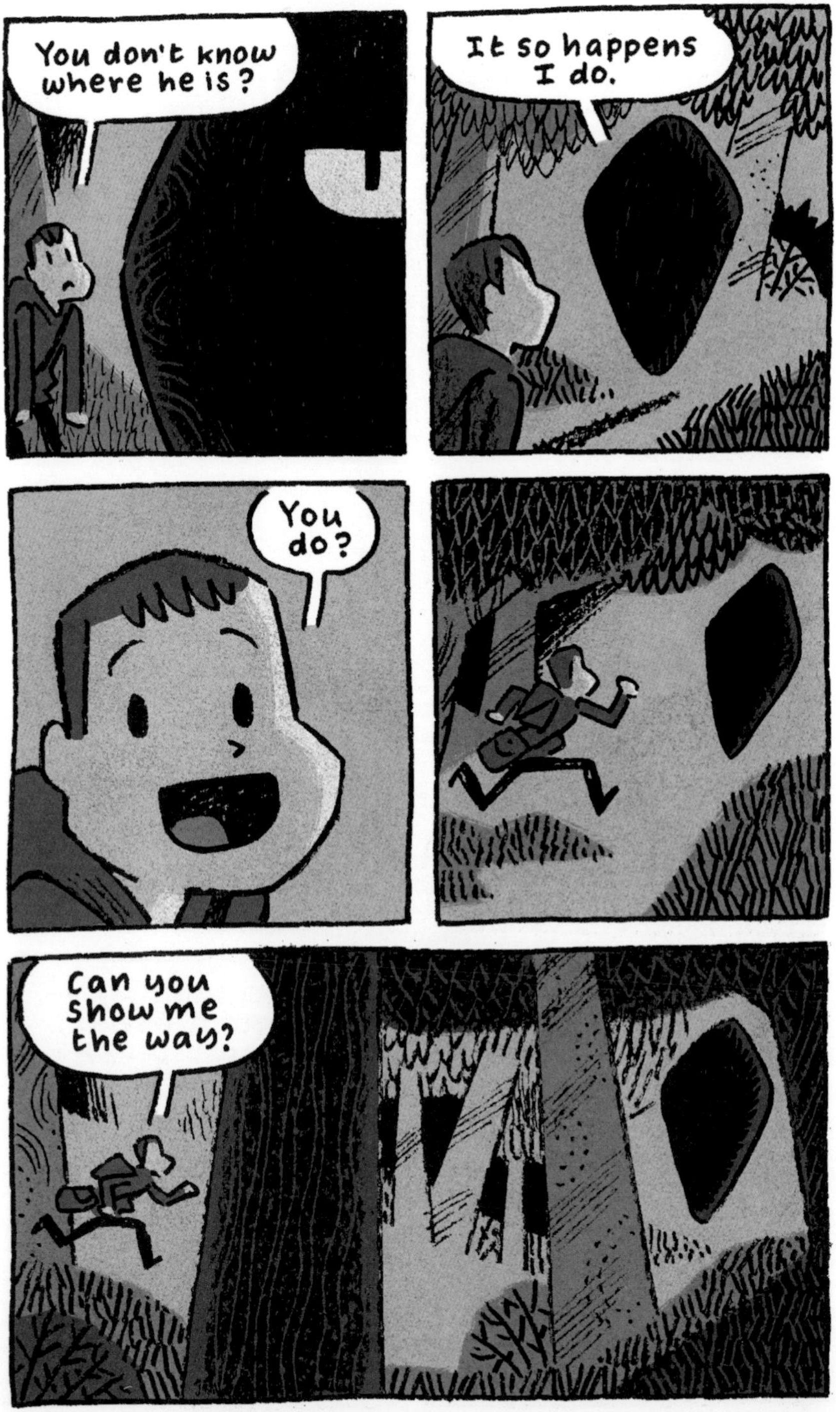
You don't know where he is?
It so happens I do.
You do?
Can you show me the way?

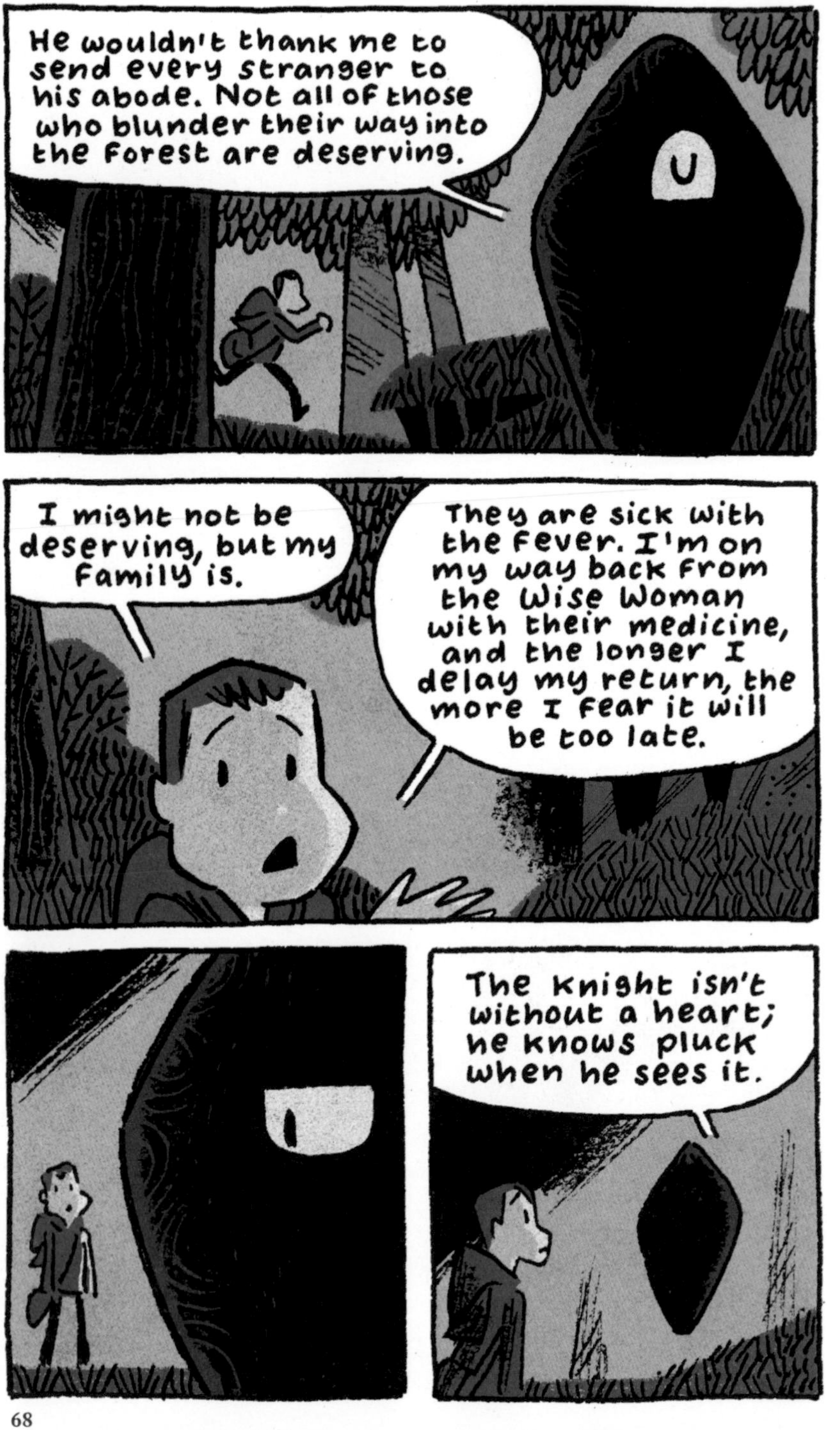
He wouldn't thank me to send every stranger to his abode. Not all of those who blunder their way into the forest are deserving.
I might not be deserving, but my family is.
They are sick with the fever. I'm on my way back from the Wise Woman with their medicine, and the longer I delay my return, the more I fear it will be too late.
The Knight isn't without a heart; he knows pluck when he sees it.

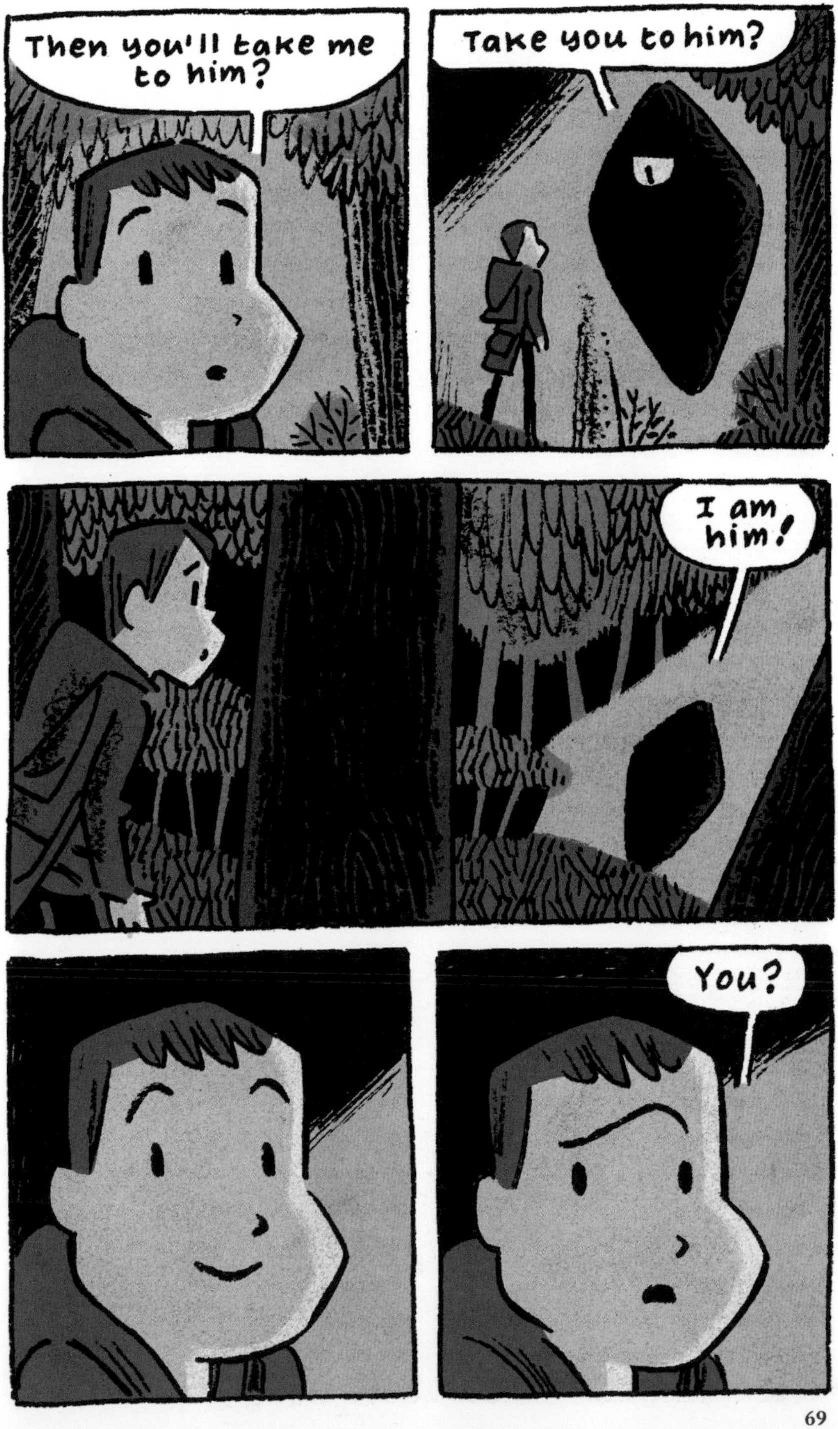
Then you'll take me to him?
Take you to him?
I am him!
You?

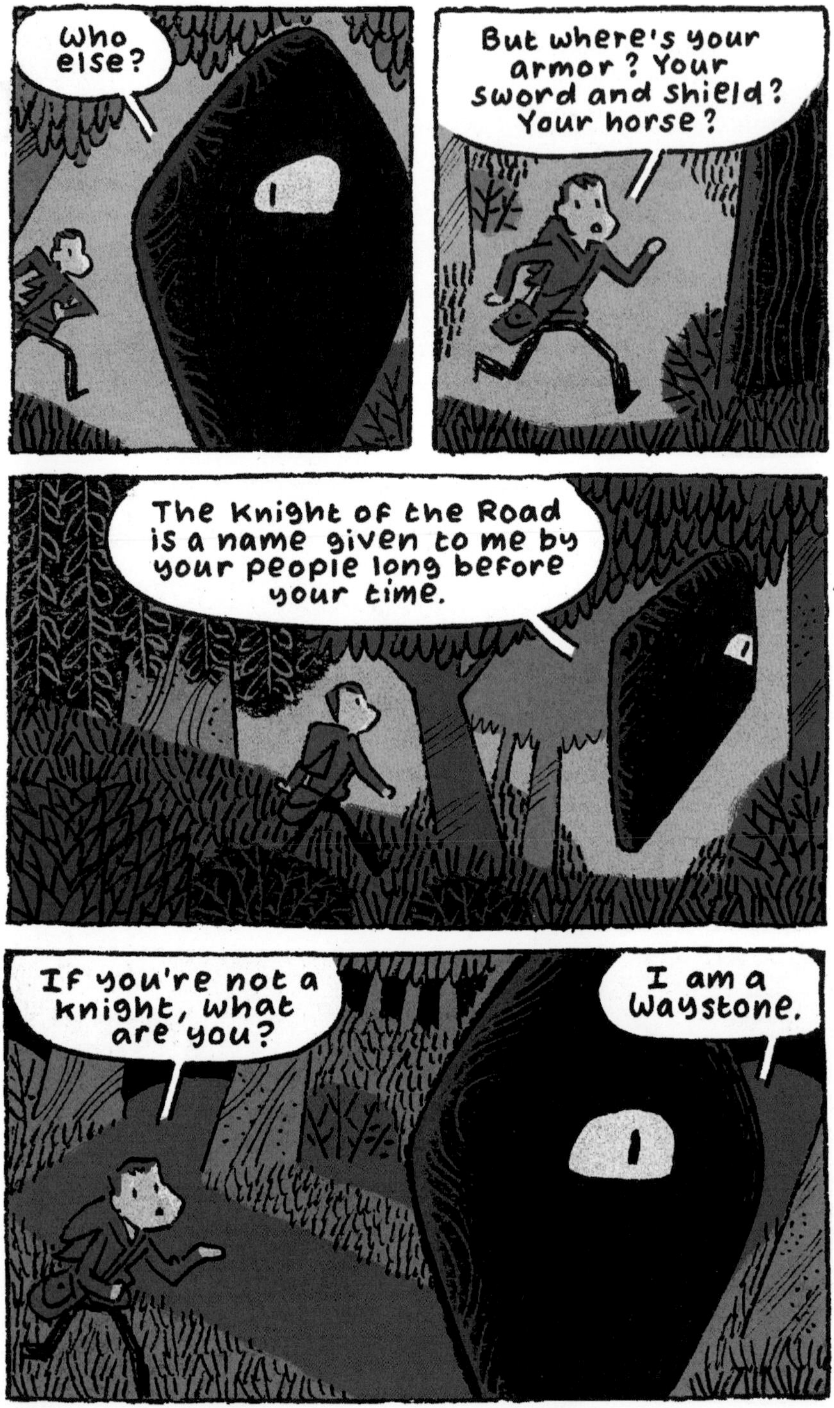
Who else?
But where's your armor? Your sword and shield? Your horse?
The Knight of the Road is a name given to me by your people long before your time.
If you're not a knight, what are you?
I am a Waystone.

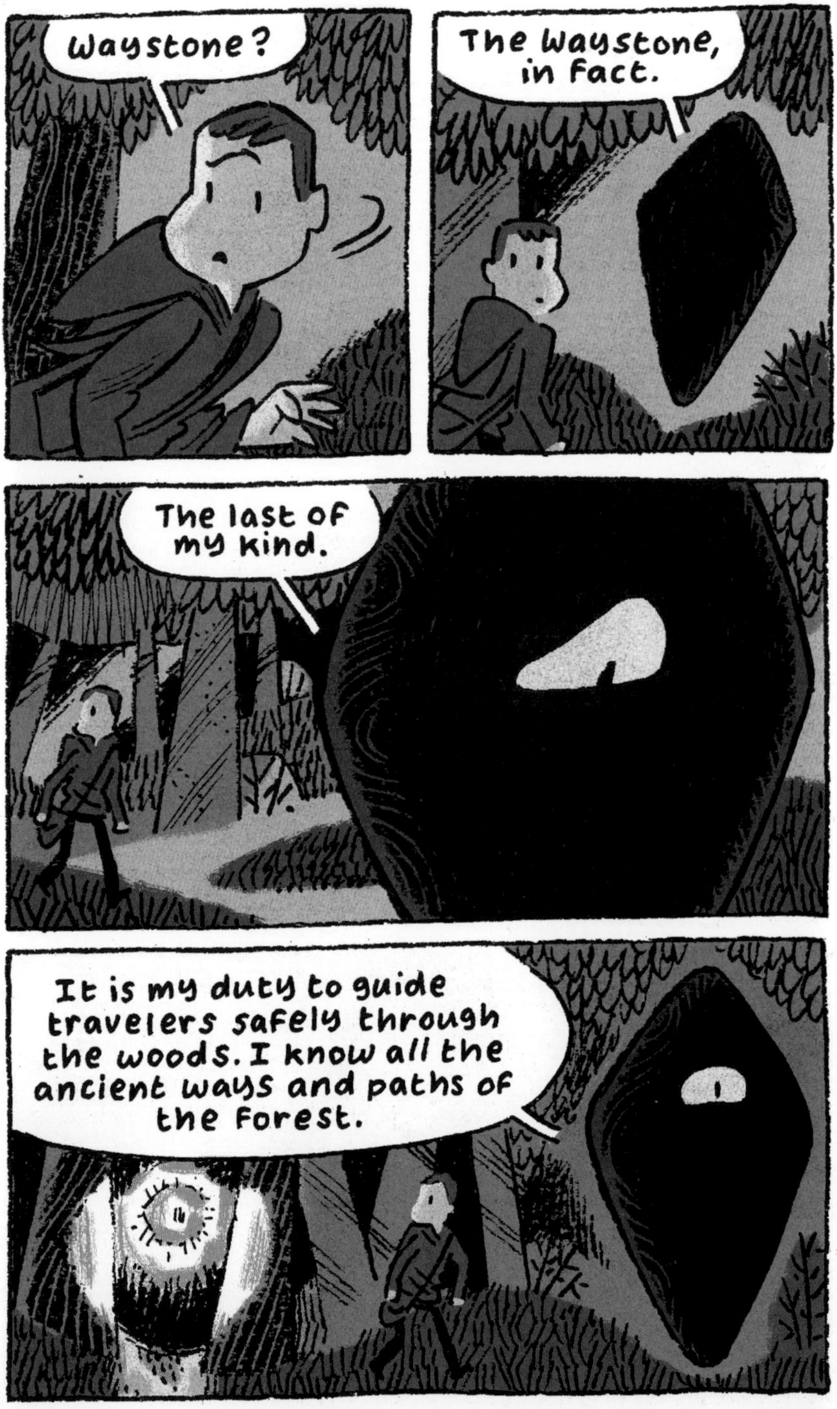
Waystone?
The Waystone, in fact.
The last of my kind.
It is my duty to guide travelers safely through the woods. I know all the ancient ways and paths of the forest.

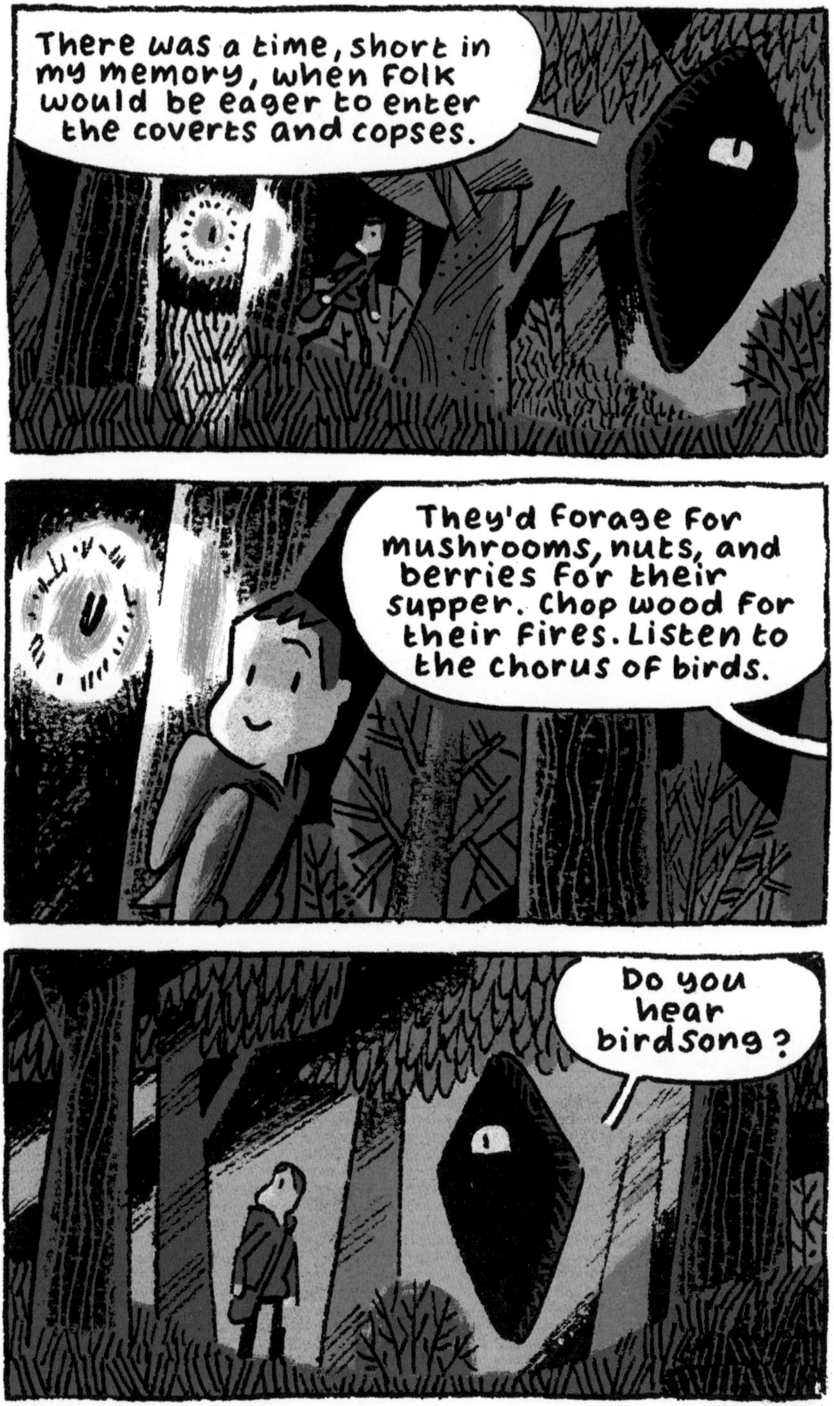
There was a time, short in my memory, when folk would be eager to enter the coverts and copses.
They'd forage for mushrooms, nuts, and berries for their supper. Chop wood for their fires. Listen to the chorus of birds.
Do you hear birdsong?

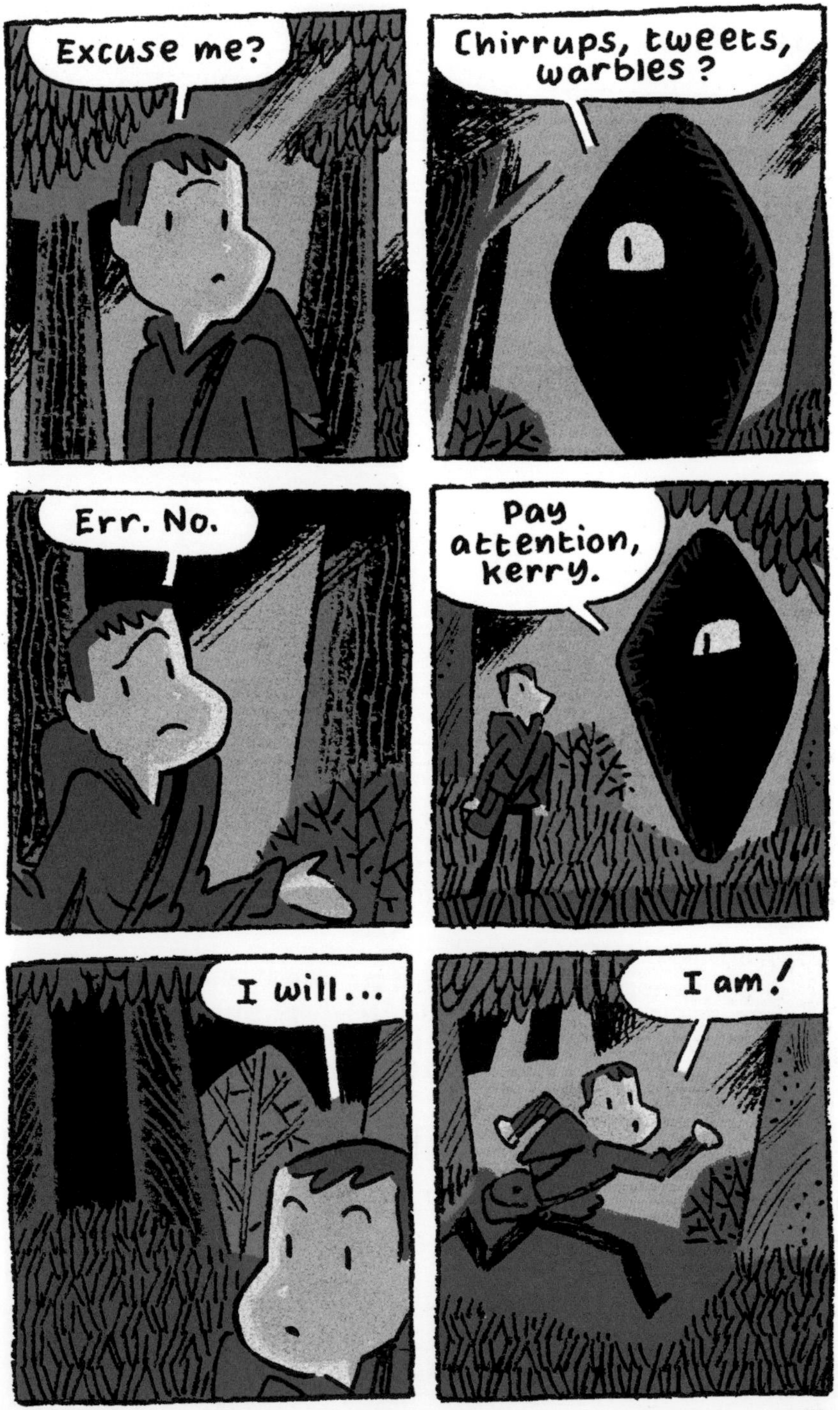
Excuse me?
Chirrups, tweets, warbles?
Err. No.
Pay attention, kerry.
I will...
I am!

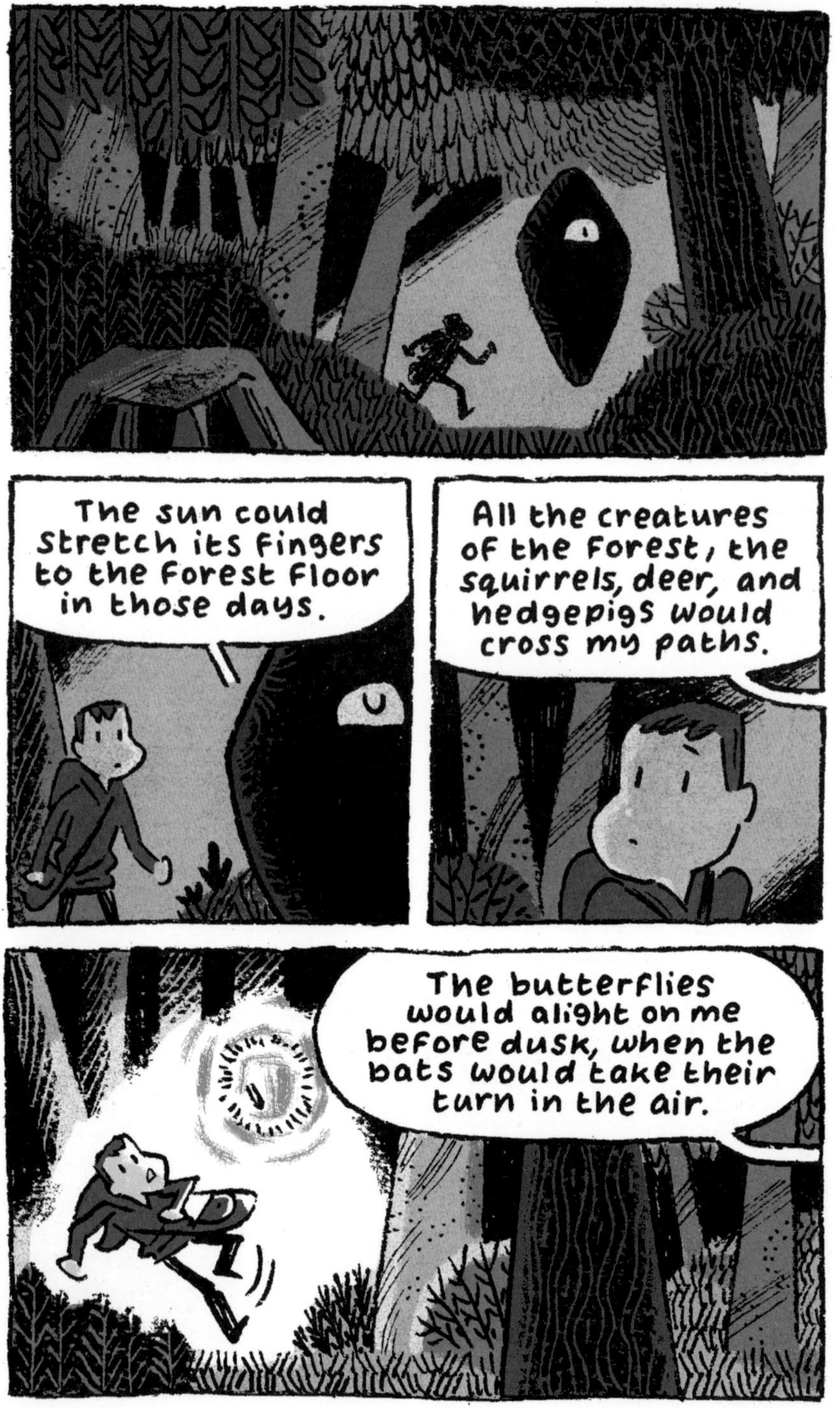
The sun could stretch its fingers to the forest floor in those days.
All the creatures of the forest, the squirrels, deer, and hedgepigs would cross my paths.
The butterflies would alight on me before dusk, when the bats would take their turn in the air.

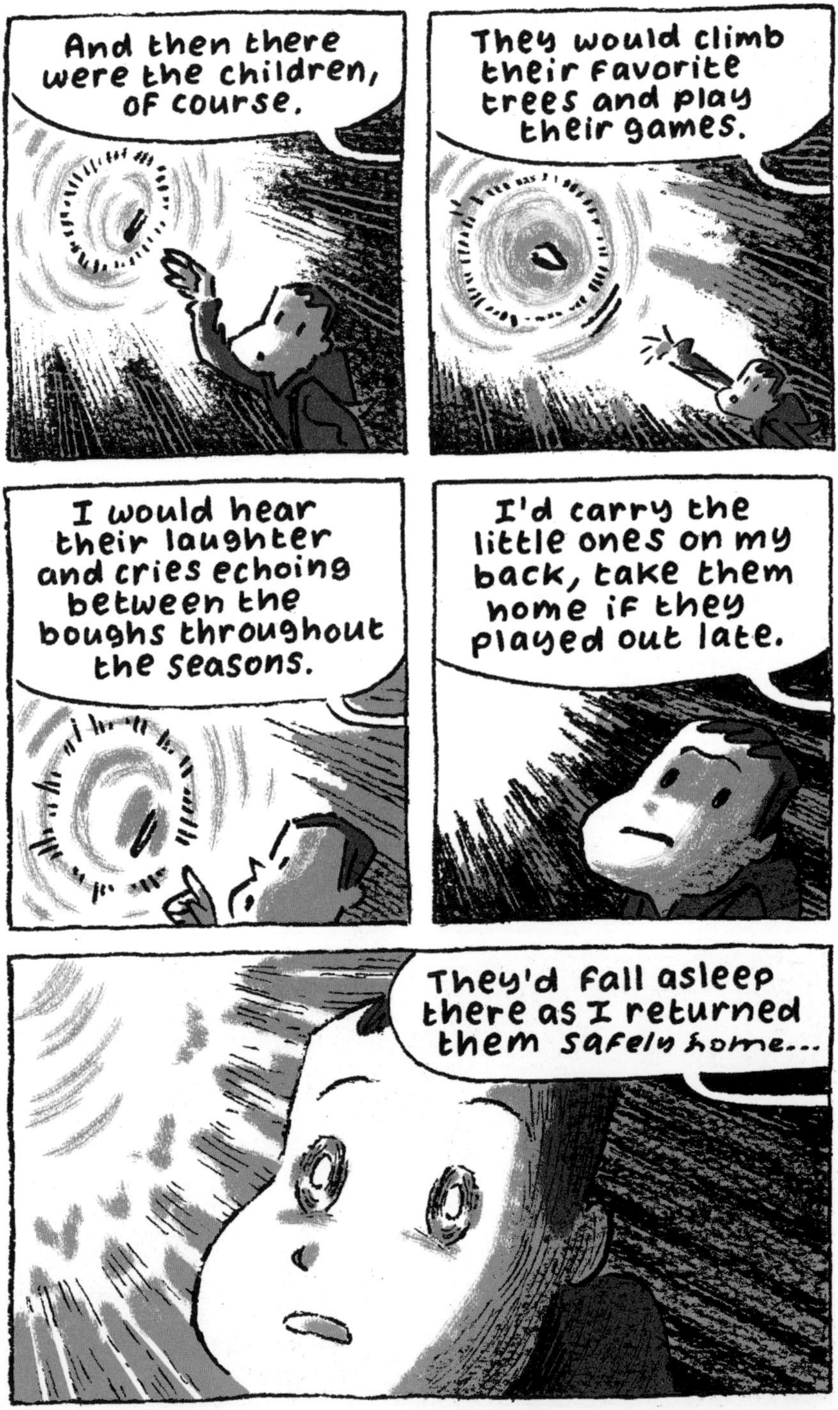
And then there were the children, of course.
They would climb their favorite trees and play their games.
I would hear their laughter and cries echoing between the boughs throughout the seasons.
I'd carry the little ones on my back, take them home if they played out late.
They'd fall asleep there as I returned them safely home...

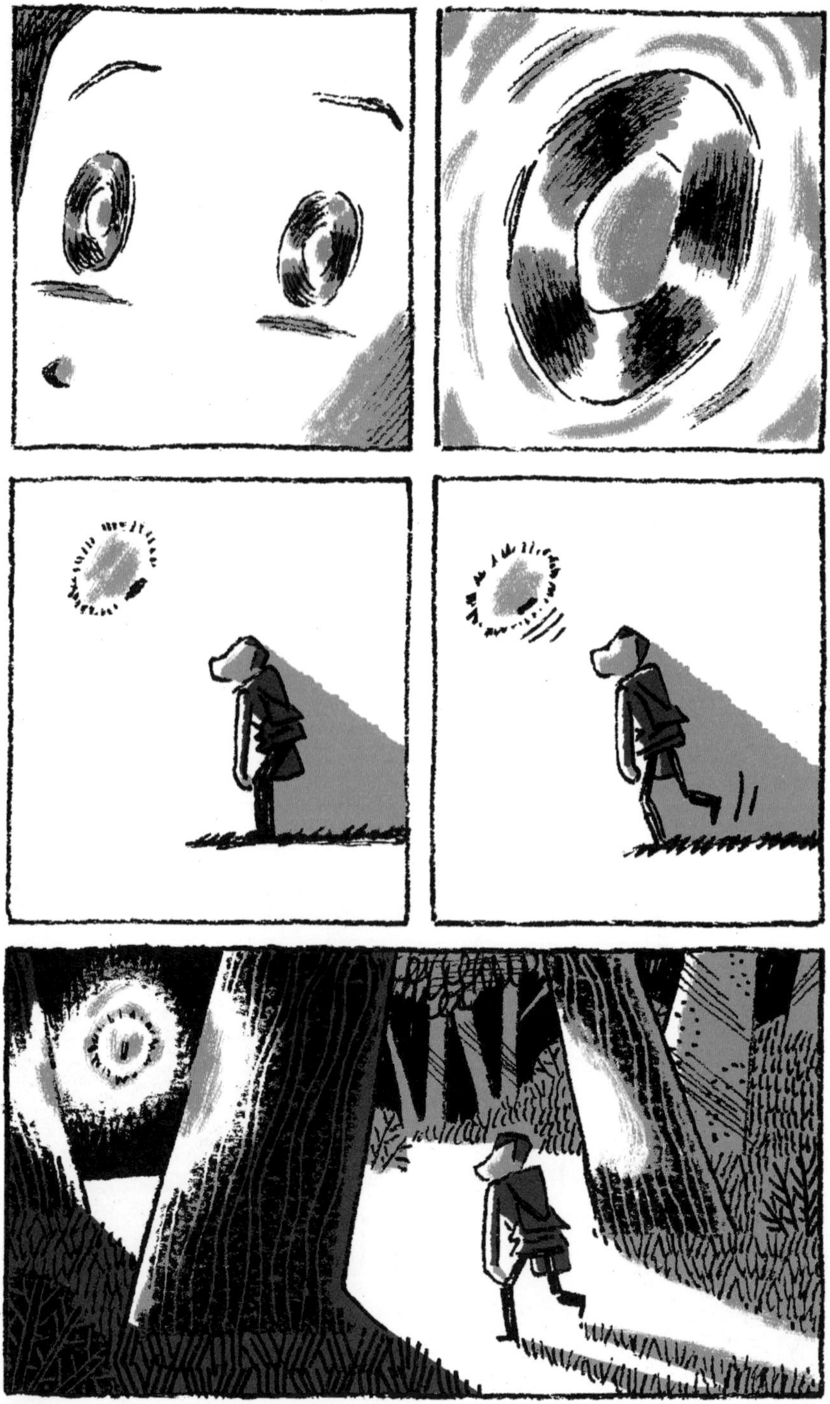

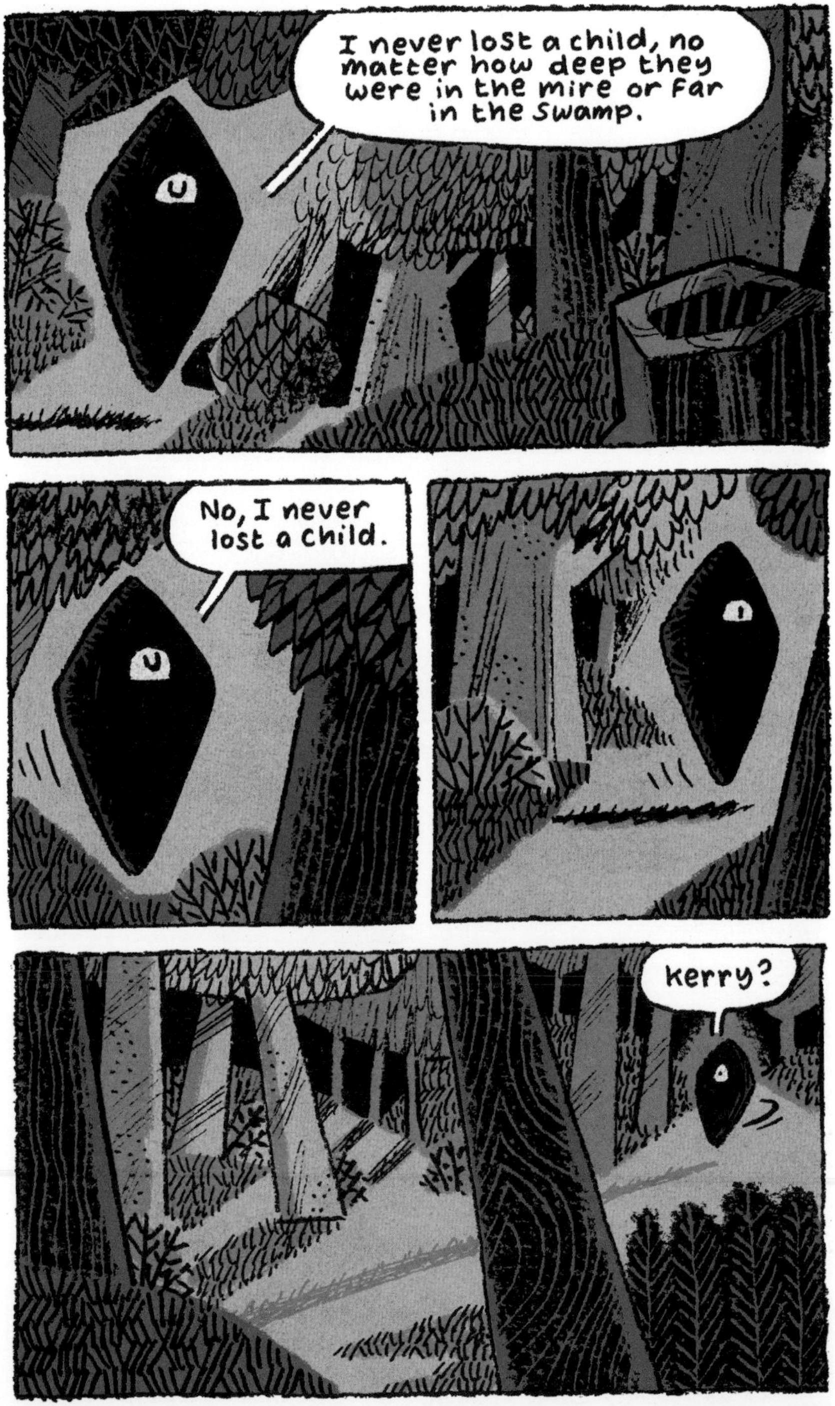
I never lost a child, no matter how deep they were in the mire or far in the Swamp.
No, I never lost a child.
Kerry?

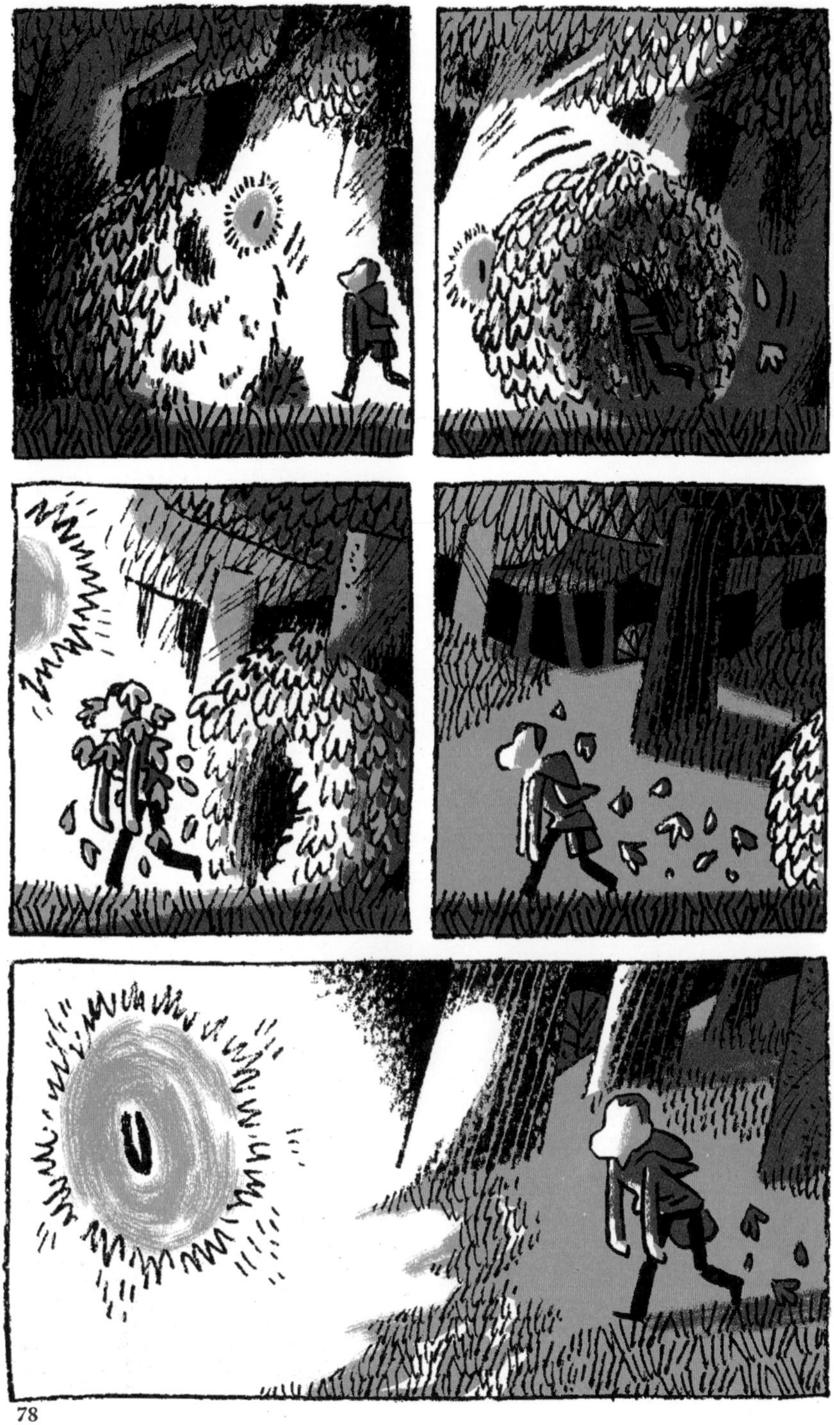

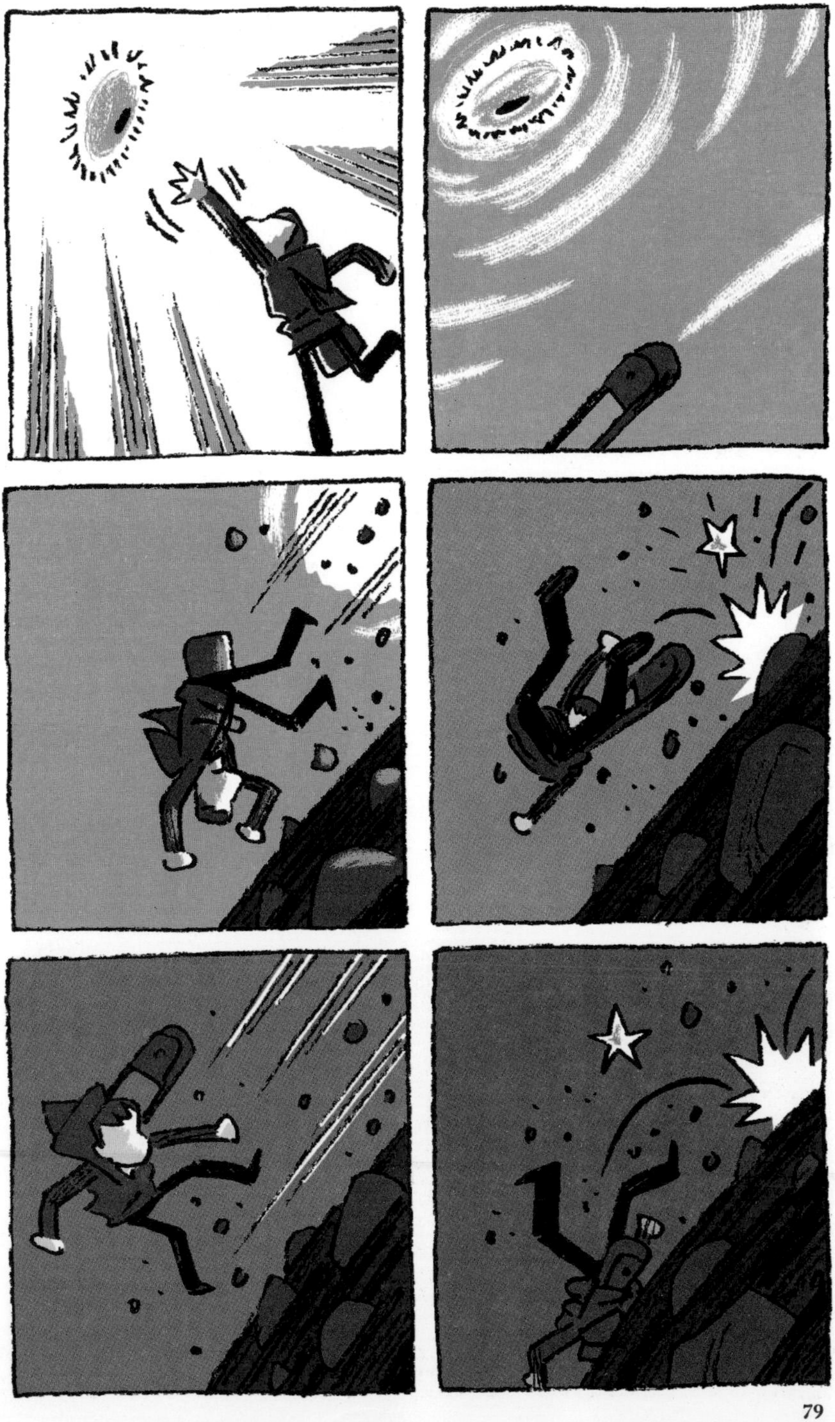

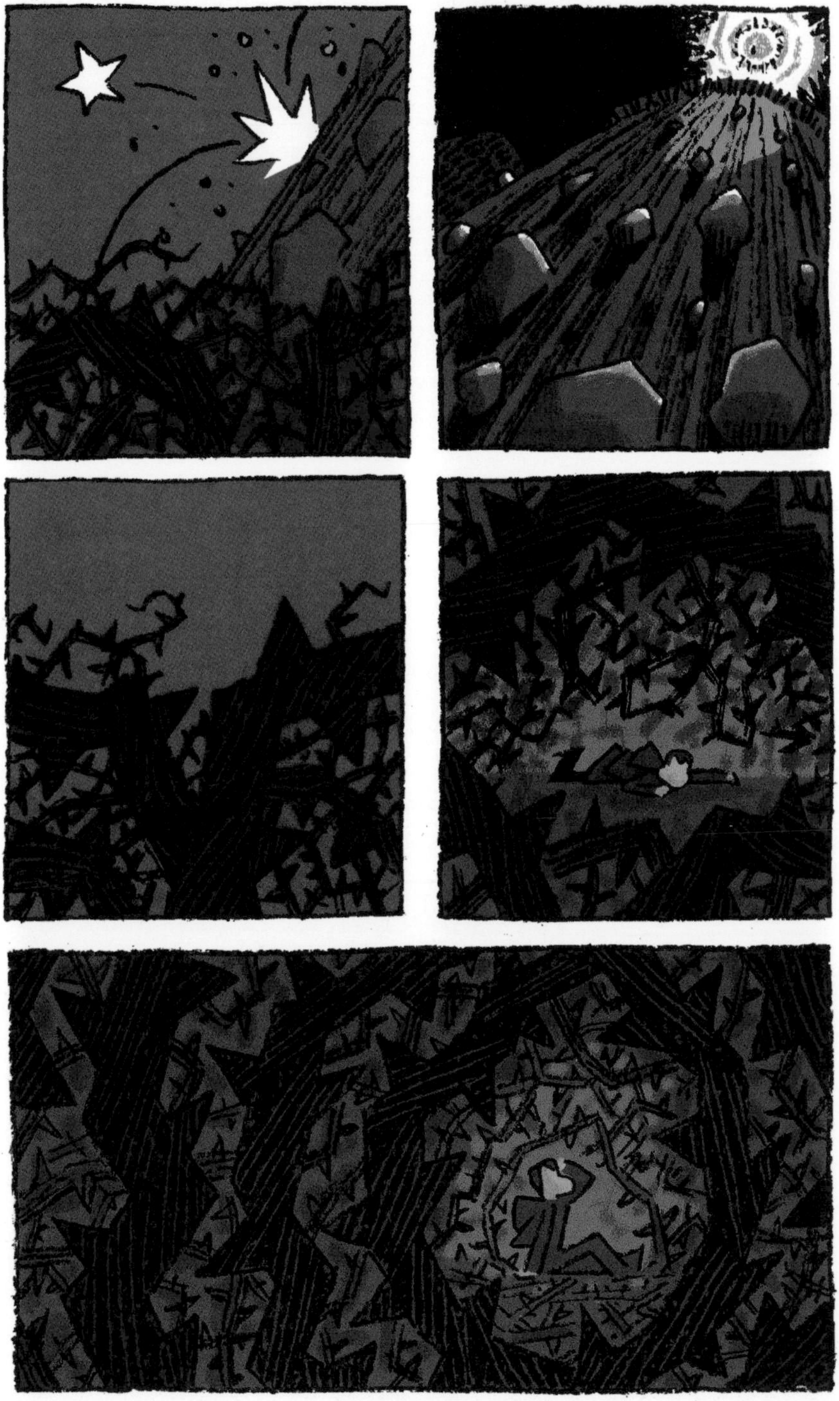

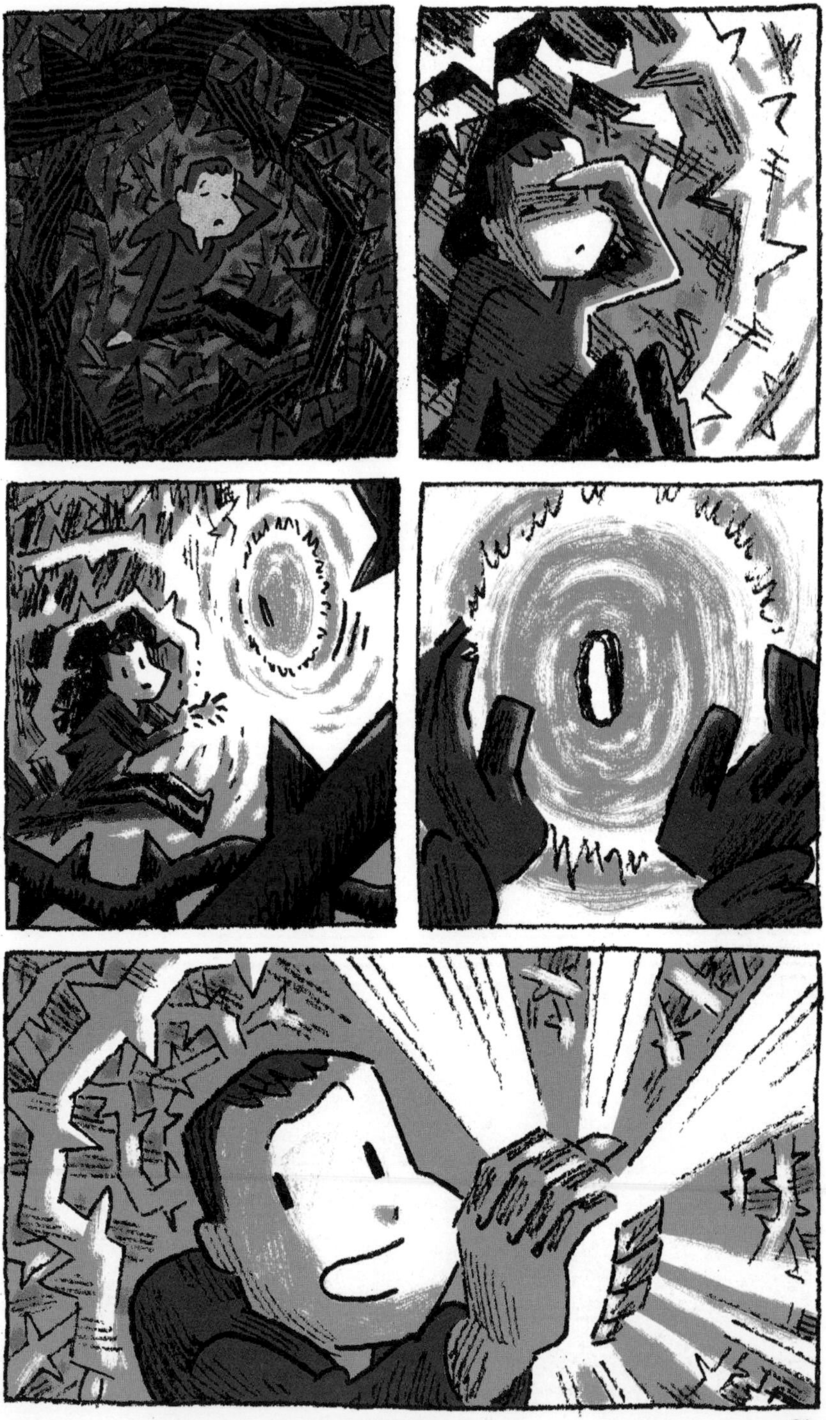

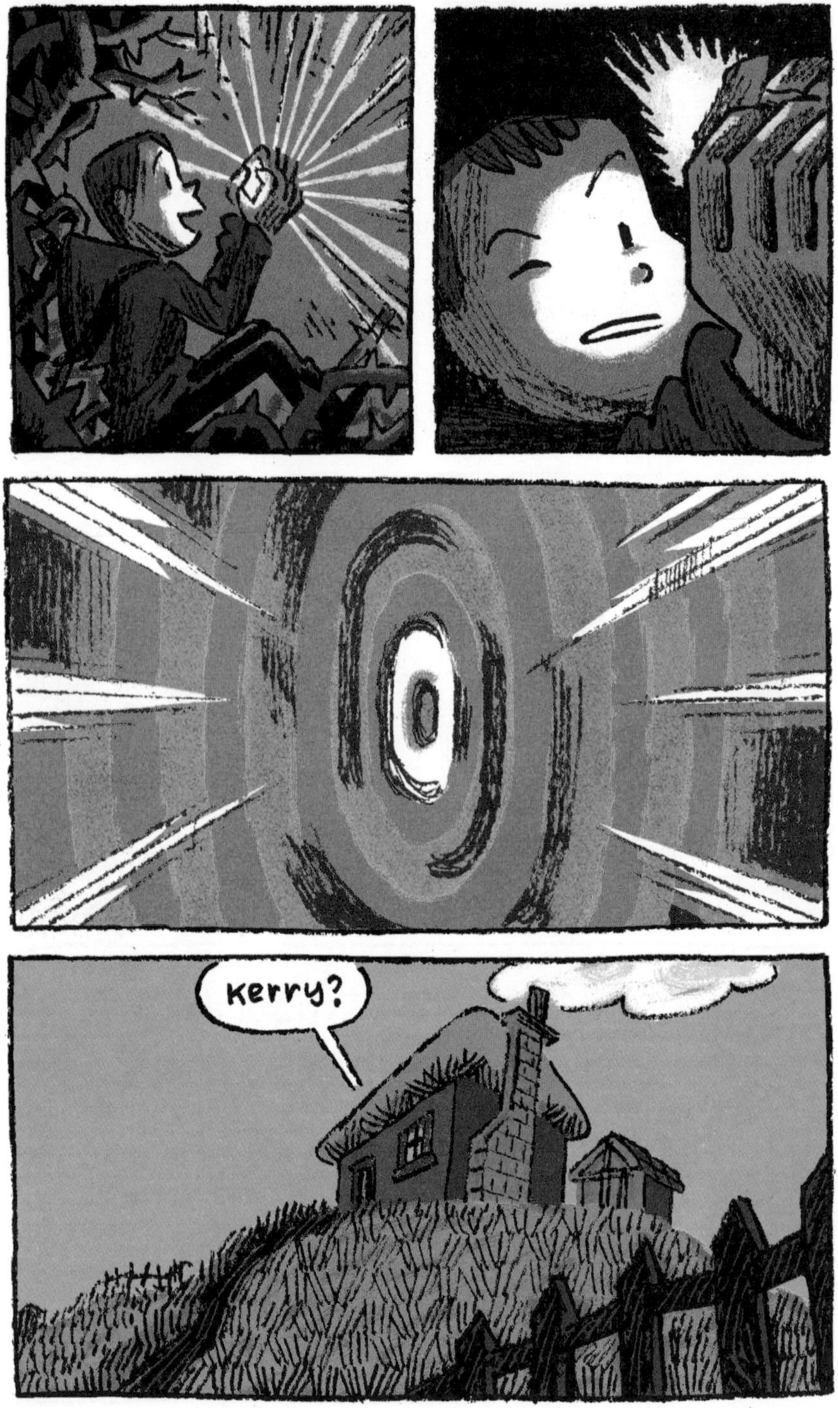
kerry?

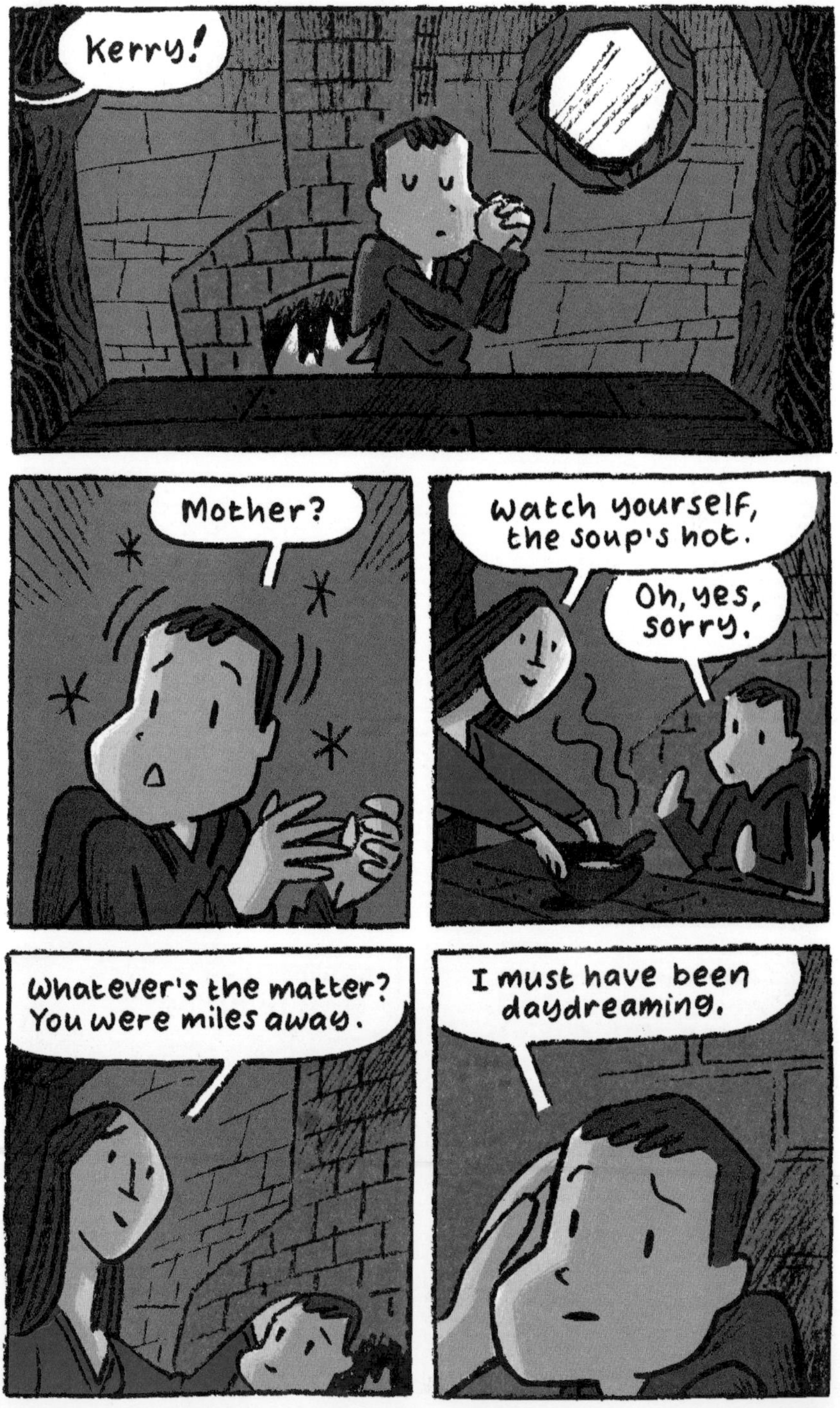
Kerry!
Mother?
Watch yourself, the soup's hot.
Oh, yes, sorry.
Whatever's the matter? You were miles away.
I must have been daydreaming.

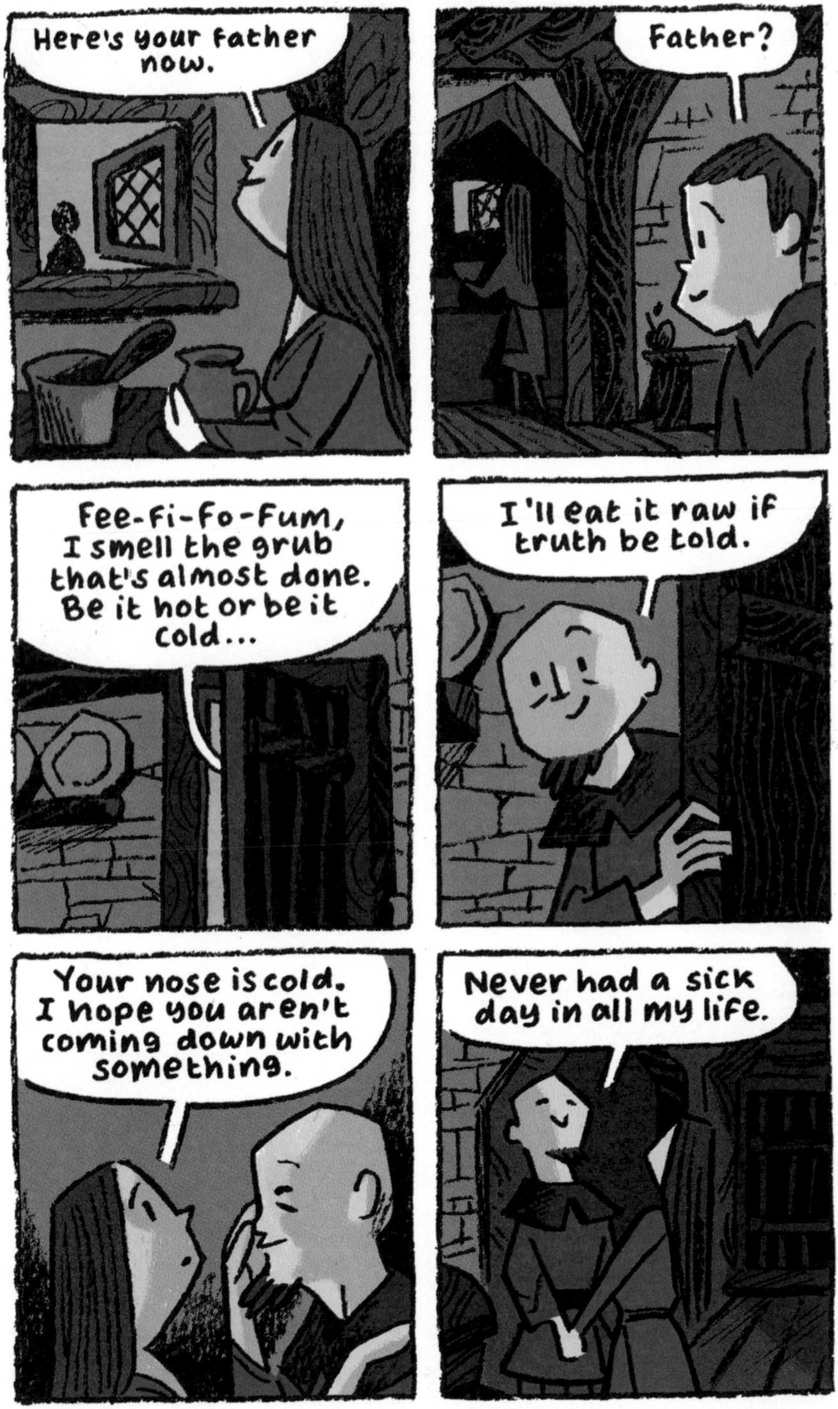
Here's your father now.
Father?
Fee-Fi-Fo-Fum, I smell the grub that's almost done. Be it hot or be it cold...
I'll eat it raw if truth be told.
Your nose is cold. I hope you aren't coming down with something.
Never had a sick day in all my life.

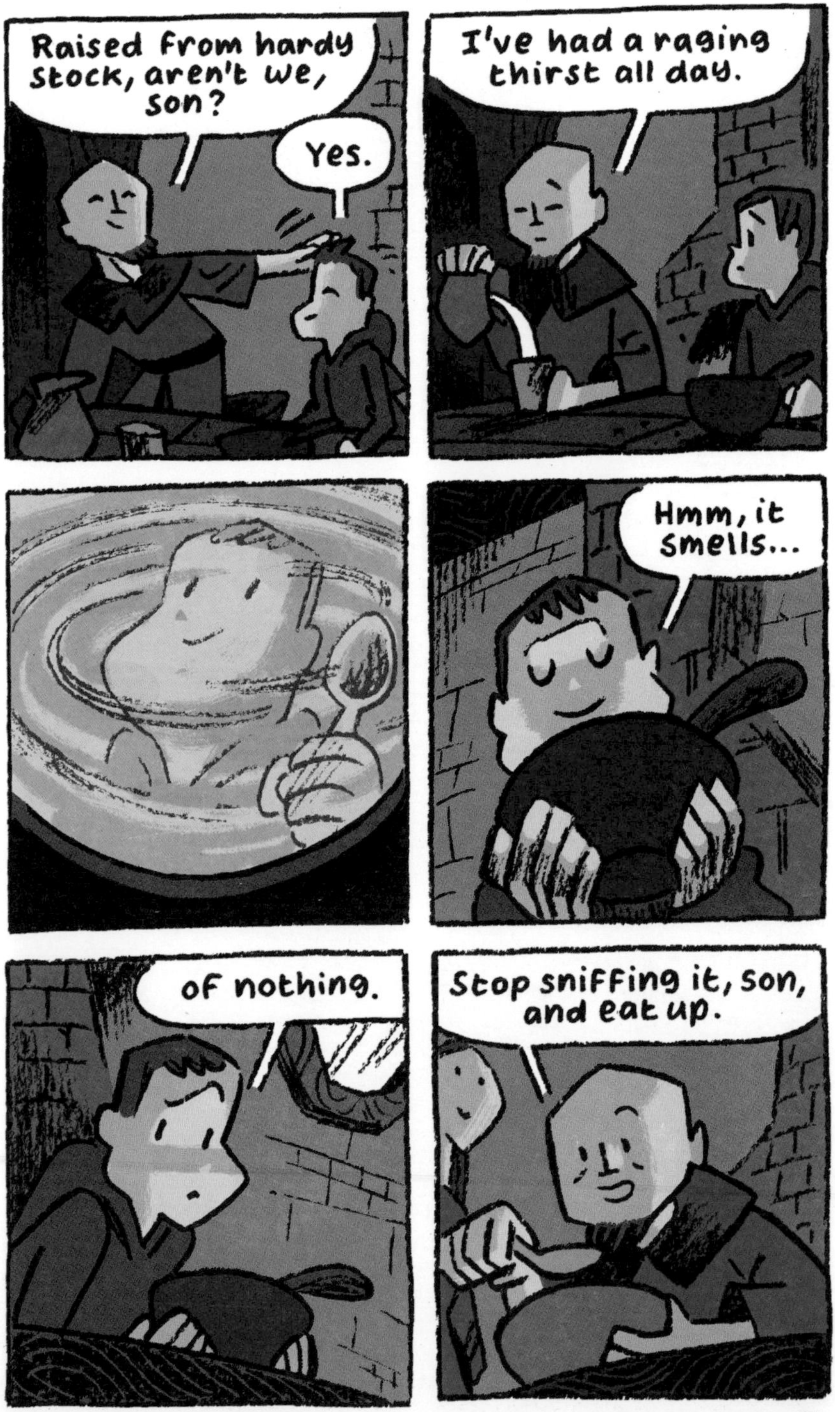
Raised from hardy stock, aren't we, son?
Yes.
I've had a raging thirst all day.
Hmm, it smells...
of nothing.
Stop sniffing it, son, and eat up.

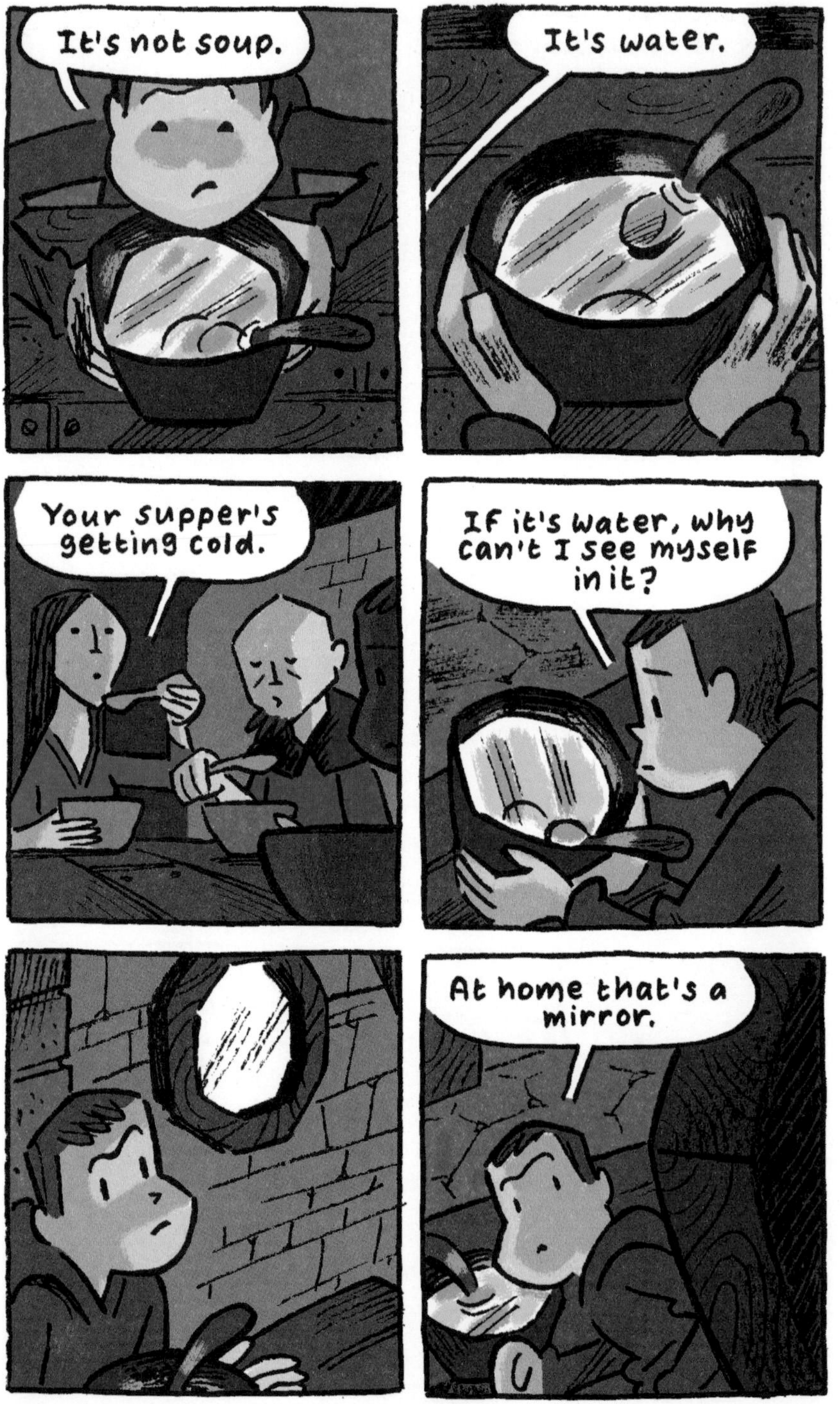
It's not soup.
It's water.
Your supper's getting cold.
If it's water, why can't I see myself in it?
At home that's a mirror.

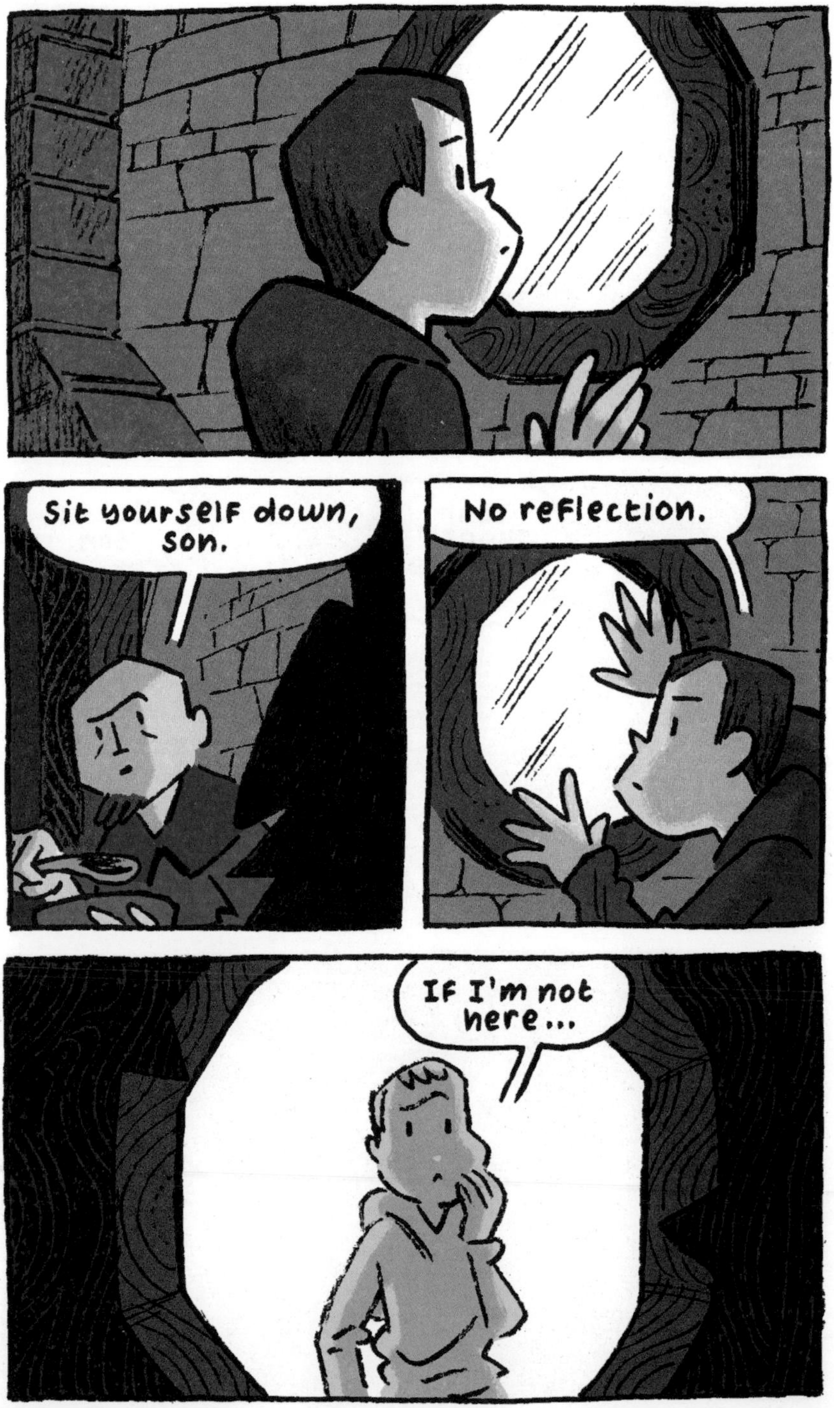

Sit yourself down, son.
No reflection.
If I'm not here...

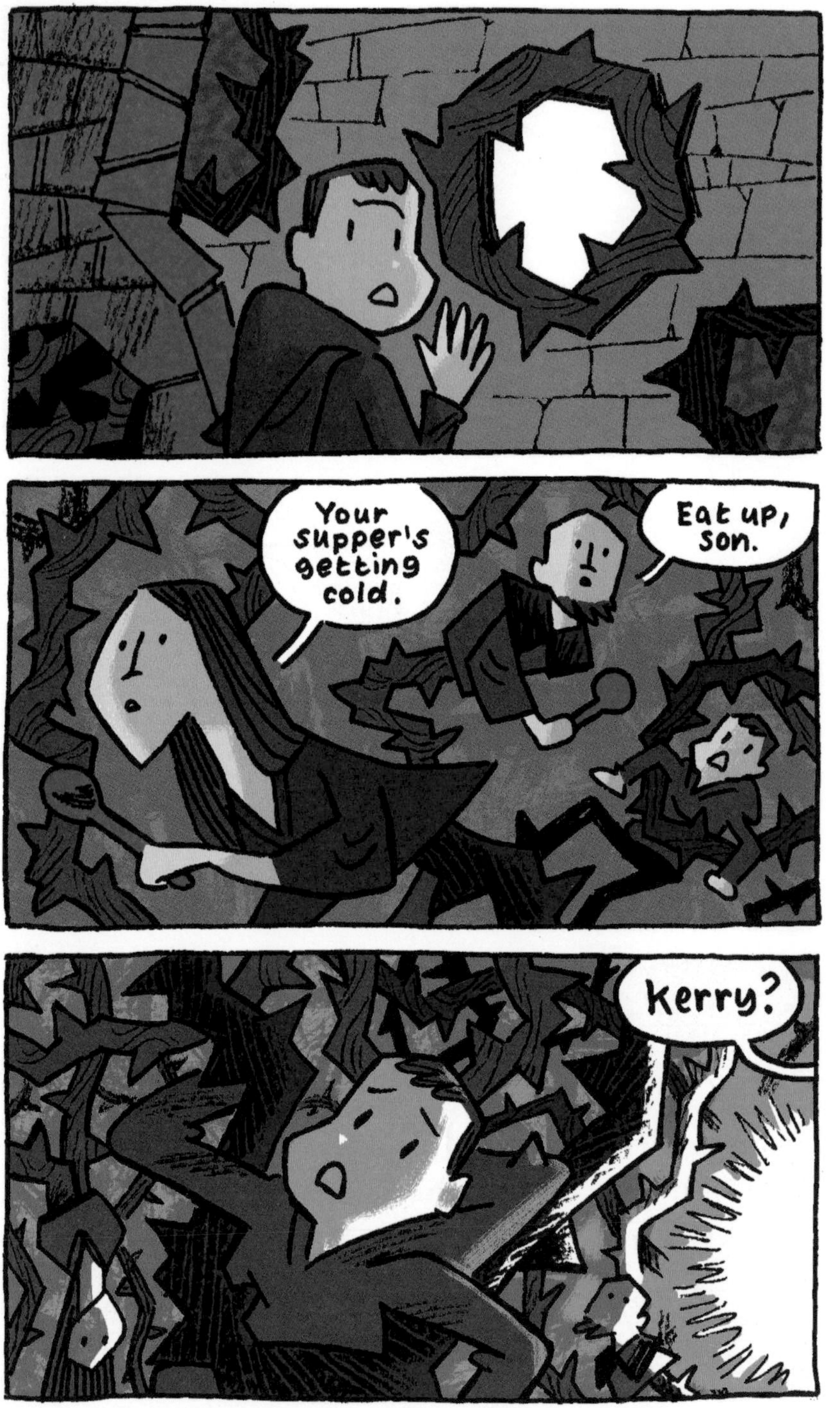
Your supper's getting cold.
Eat up, son.
Kerry?

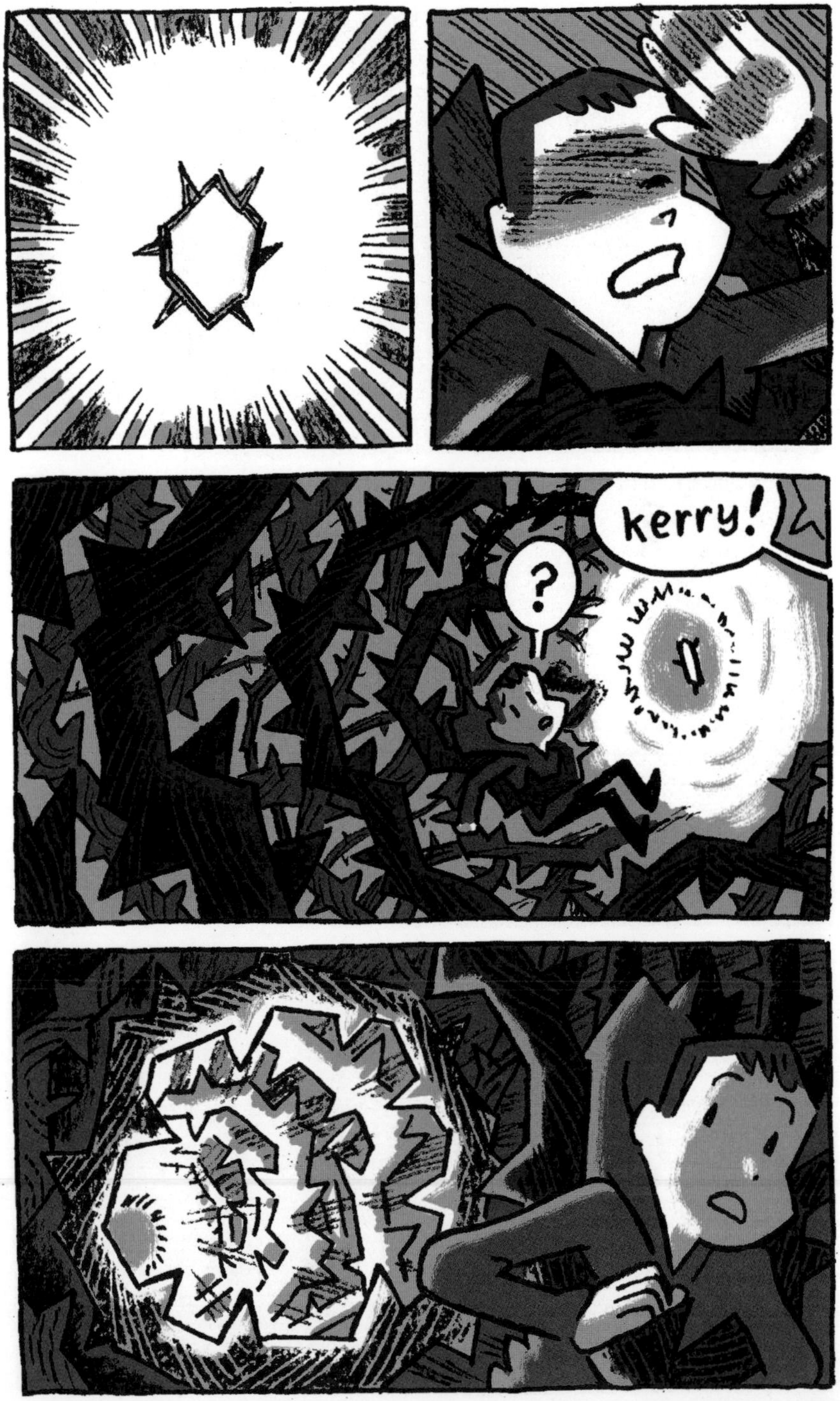
?
kerry!

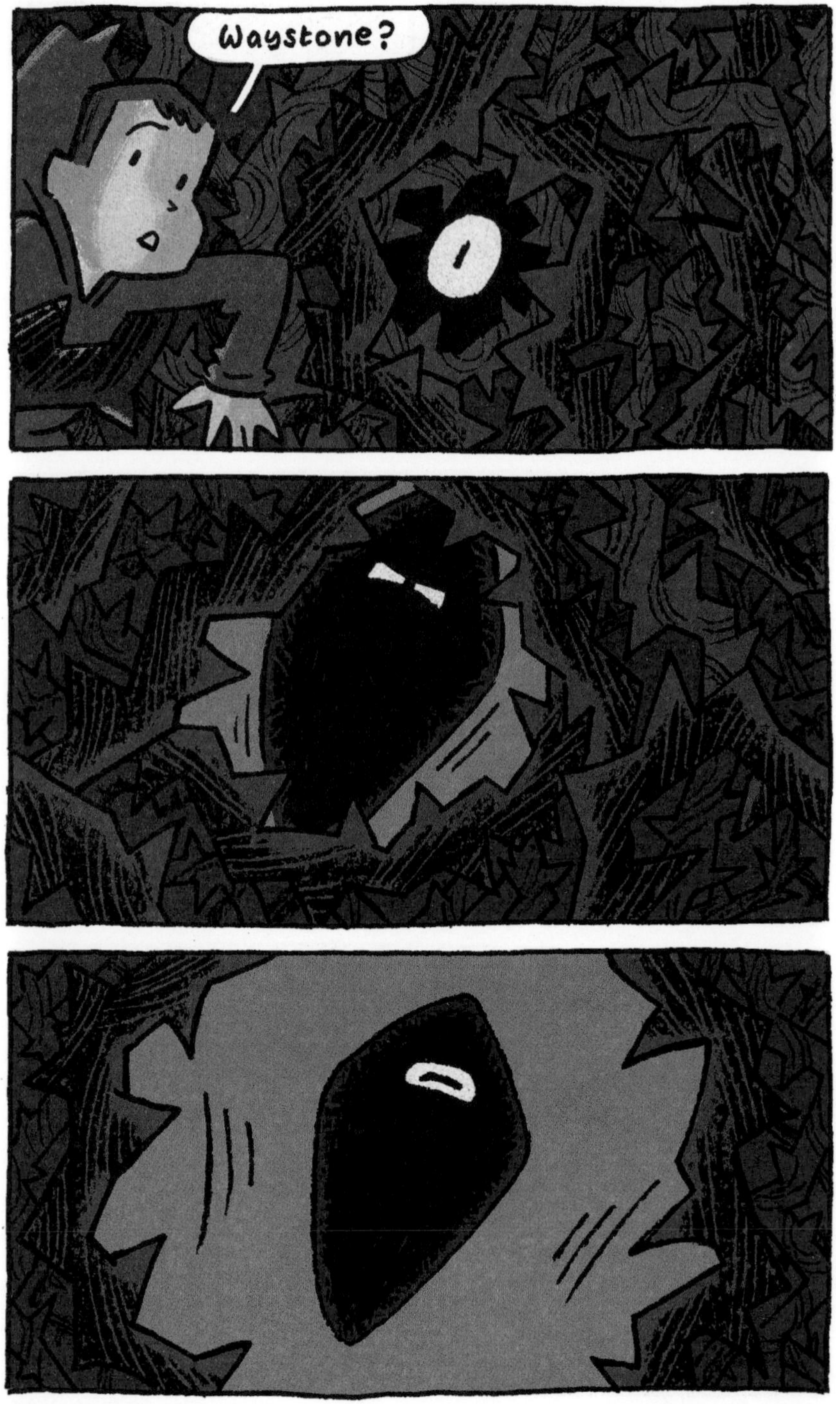
Waystone?

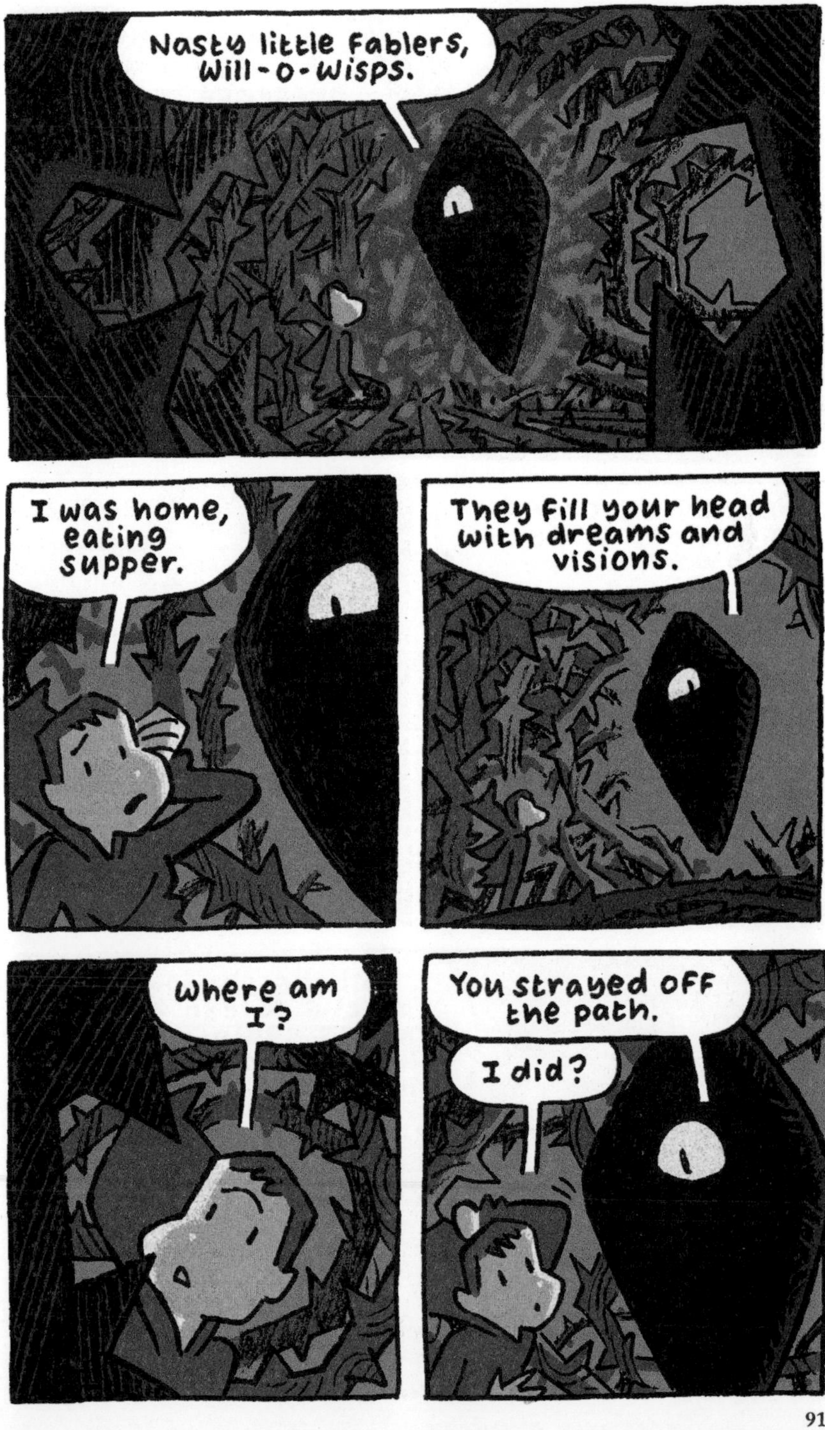
Nasty little Fablers, Will-O-Wisps.
I was home, eating supper.
They fill your head with dreams and visions.
Where am I?
You strayed off the path.
I did?

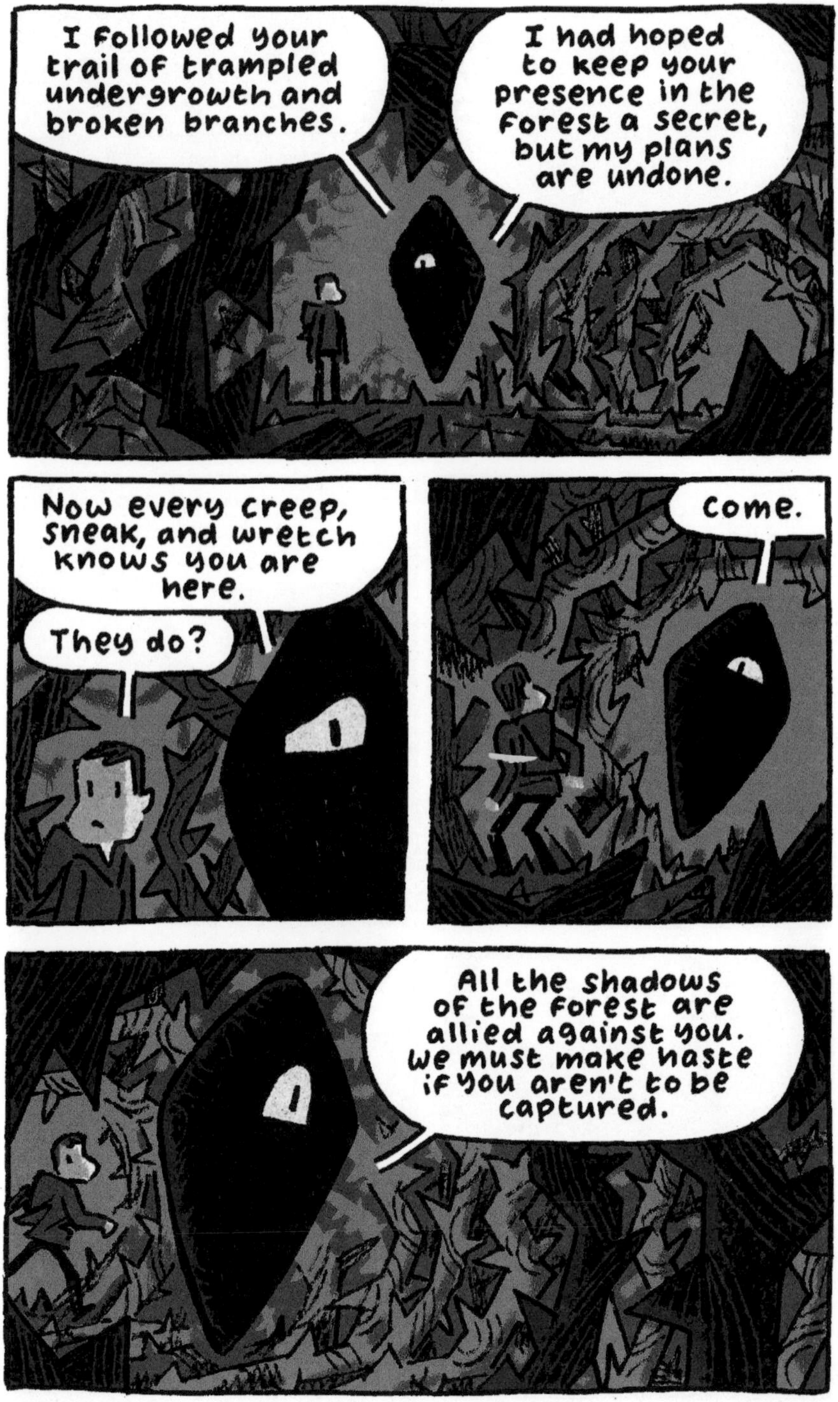

I followed your trail of trampled undergrowth and broken branches.
I had hoped to keep your presence in the forest a secret, but my plans are undone.
Now every creep, sneak, and wretch knows you are here.
They do?
Come.
All the shadows of the forest are allied against you. We must make haste if you aren't to be captured.

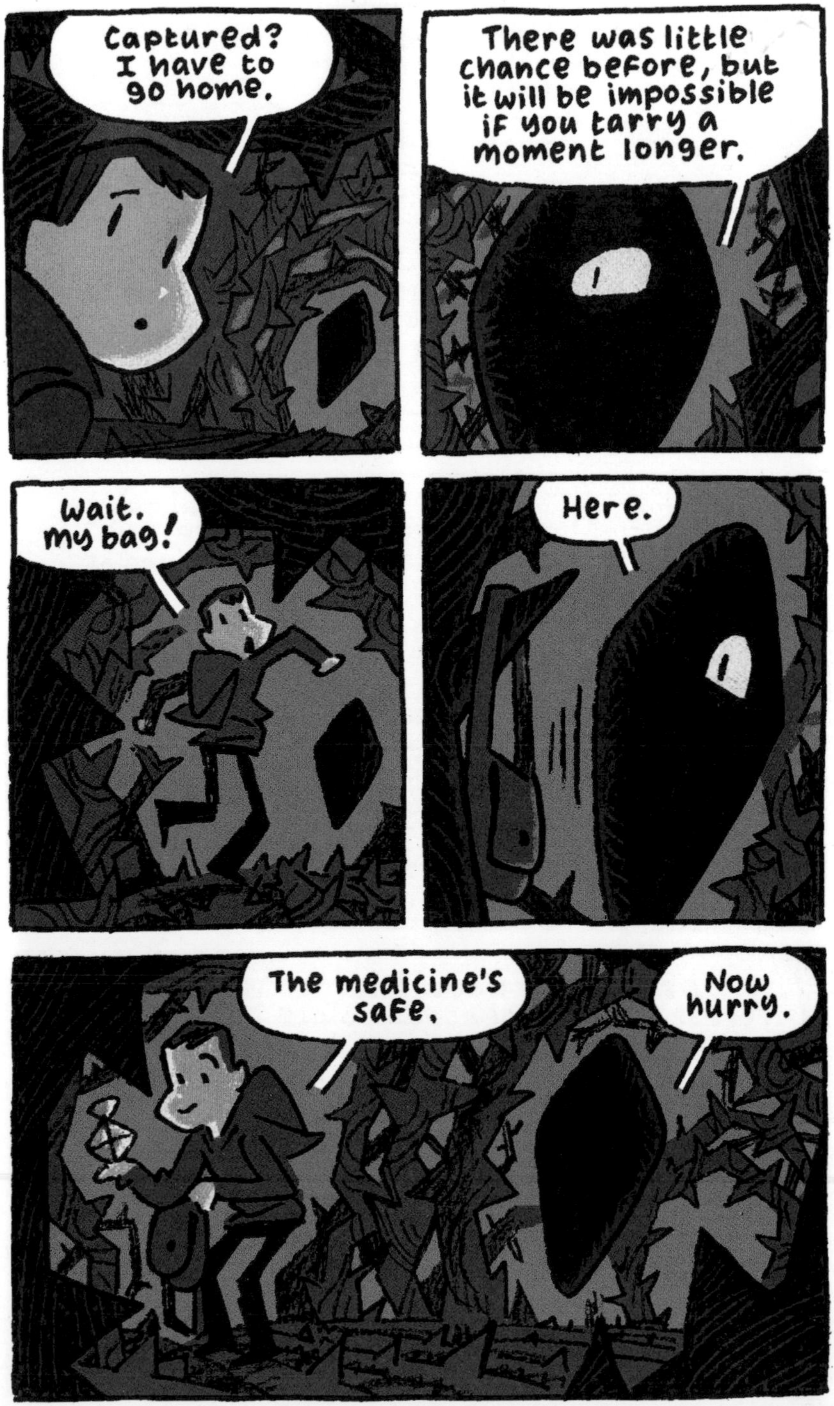
Captured? I have to go home.
There was little chance before, but it will be impossible if you tarry a moment longer.
Wait. my bag!
Here.
The medicine's safe.
Now hurry.

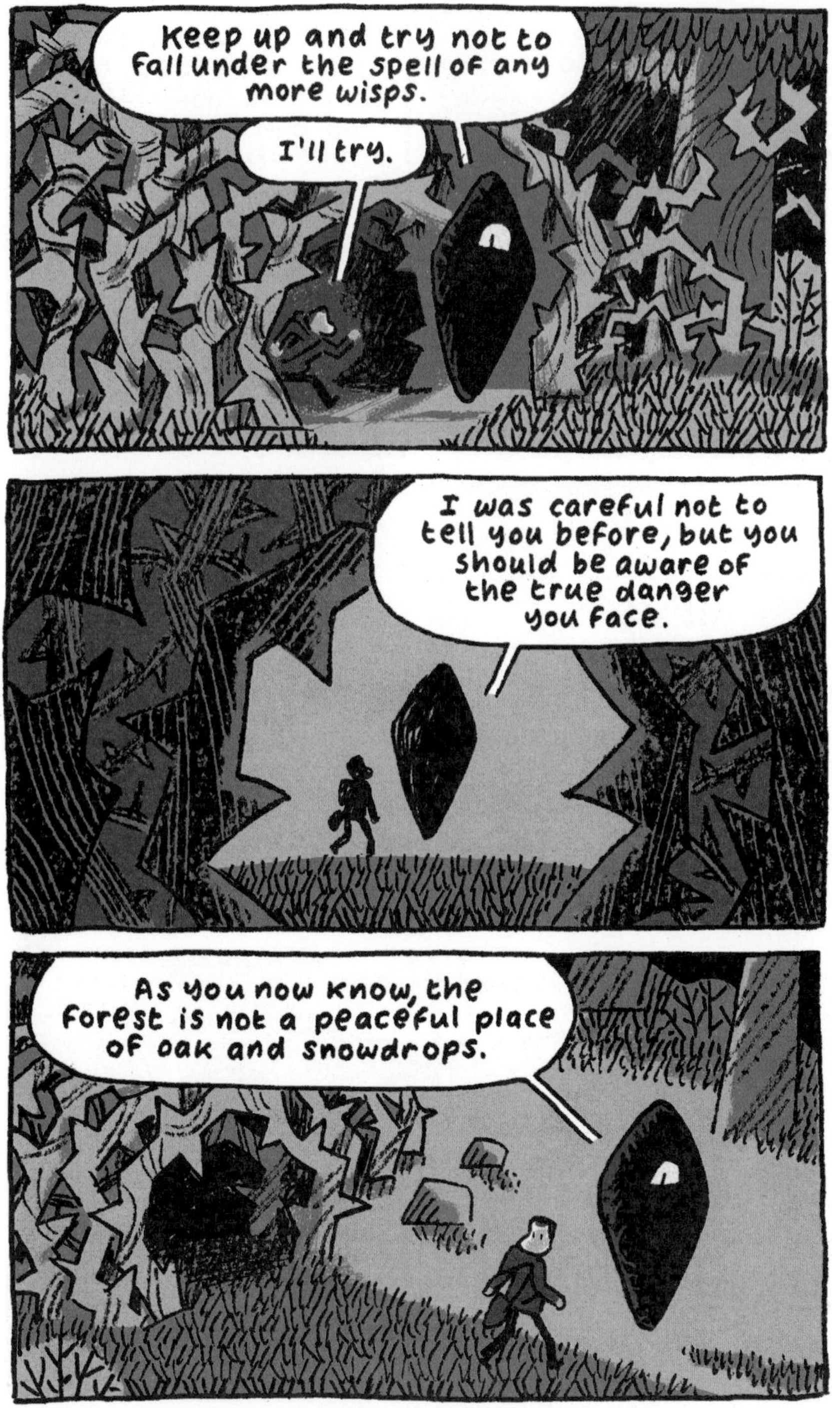
Keep up and try not to fall under the spell of any more wisps.
I'll try.
I was careful not to tell you before, but you should be aware of the true danger you face.
As you now know, the forest is not a peaceful place of oak and snowdrops.

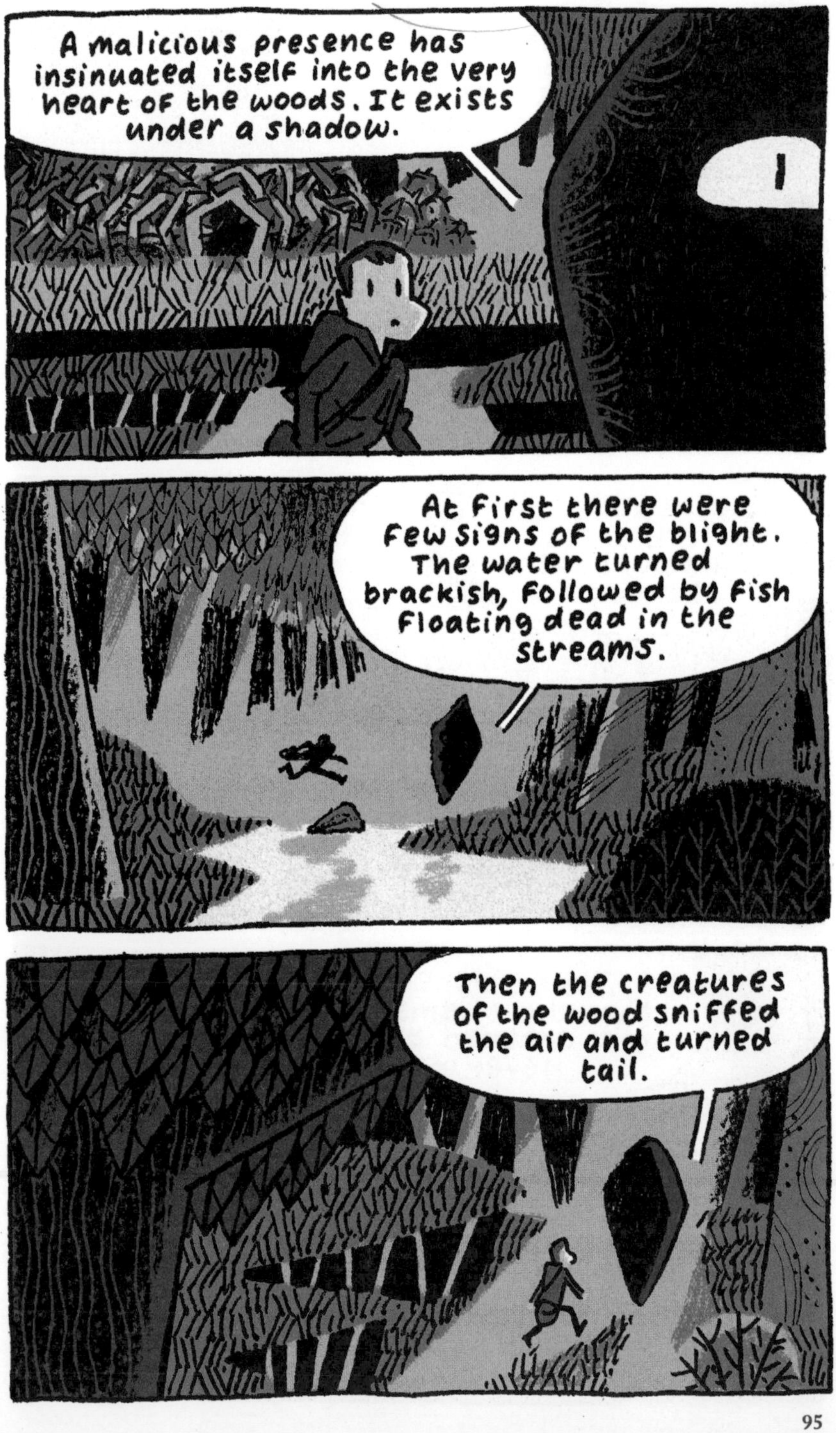
A malicious presence has insinuated itself into the very heart of the woods. It exists under a shadow.
At first there were few signs of the blight. The water turned brackish, followed by fish floating dead in the streams.
Then the creatures of the wood sniffed the air and turned tail.

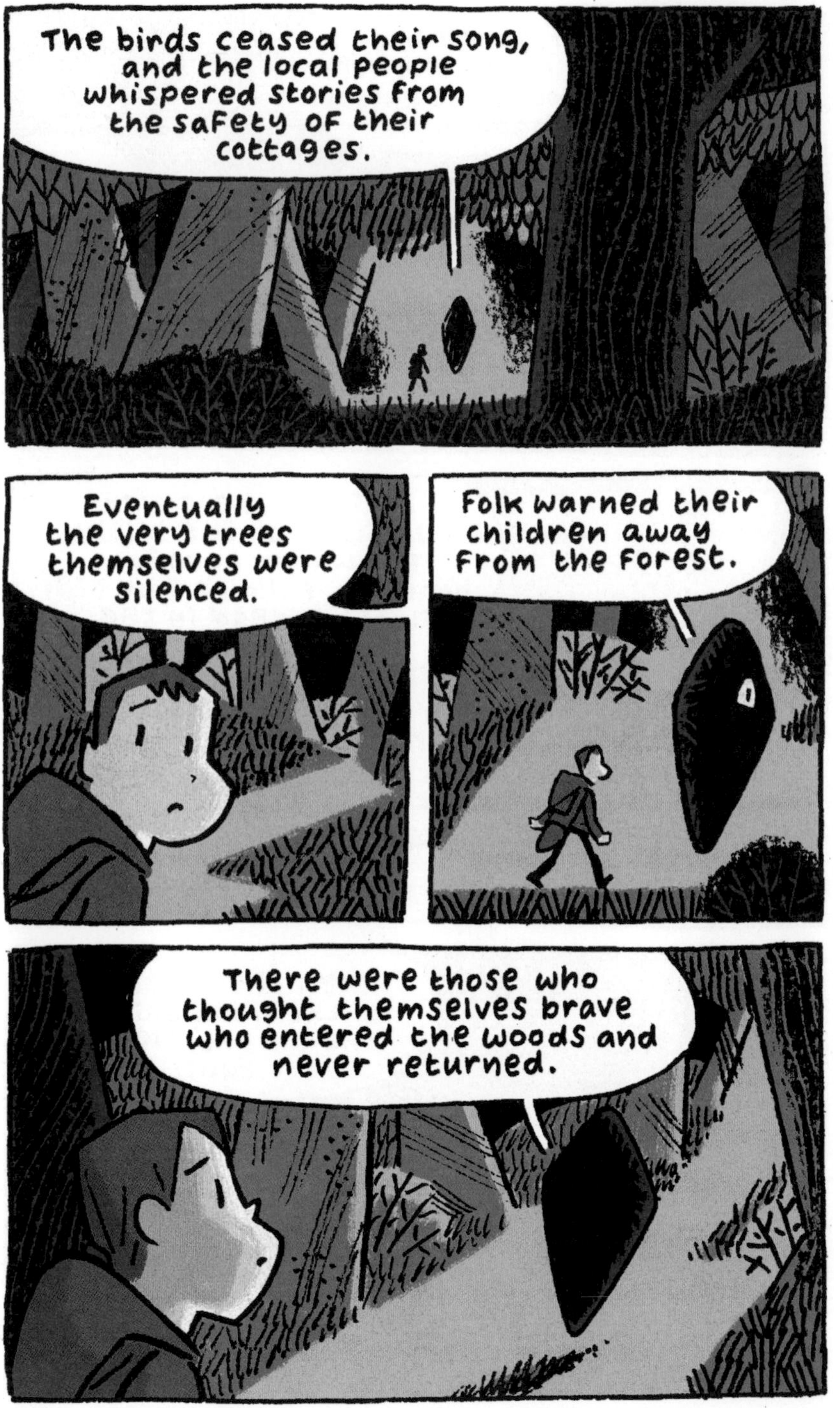
The birds ceased their song, and the local people whispered stories from the safety of their cottages.
Eventually the very trees themselves were silenced.
Folk warned their children away from the forest.
There were those who thought themselves brave who entered the woods and never returned.

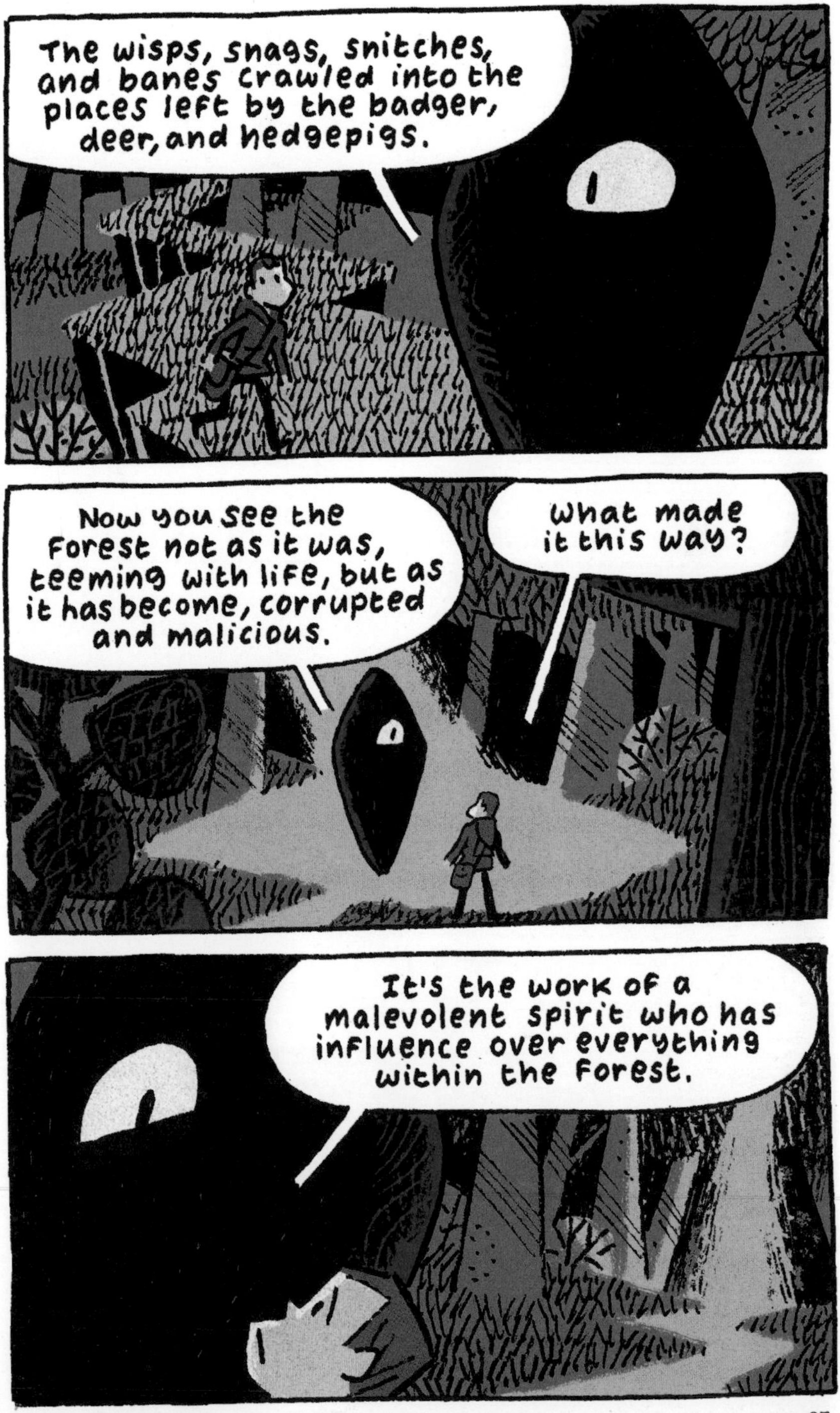
The wisps, snags, snitches, and banes crawled into the places left by the badger, deer, and hedgepigs.
Now you see the forest not as it was, teeming with life, but as it has become, corrupted and malicious.
What made it this way?
It's the work of a malevolent spirit who has influence over everything within the forest.

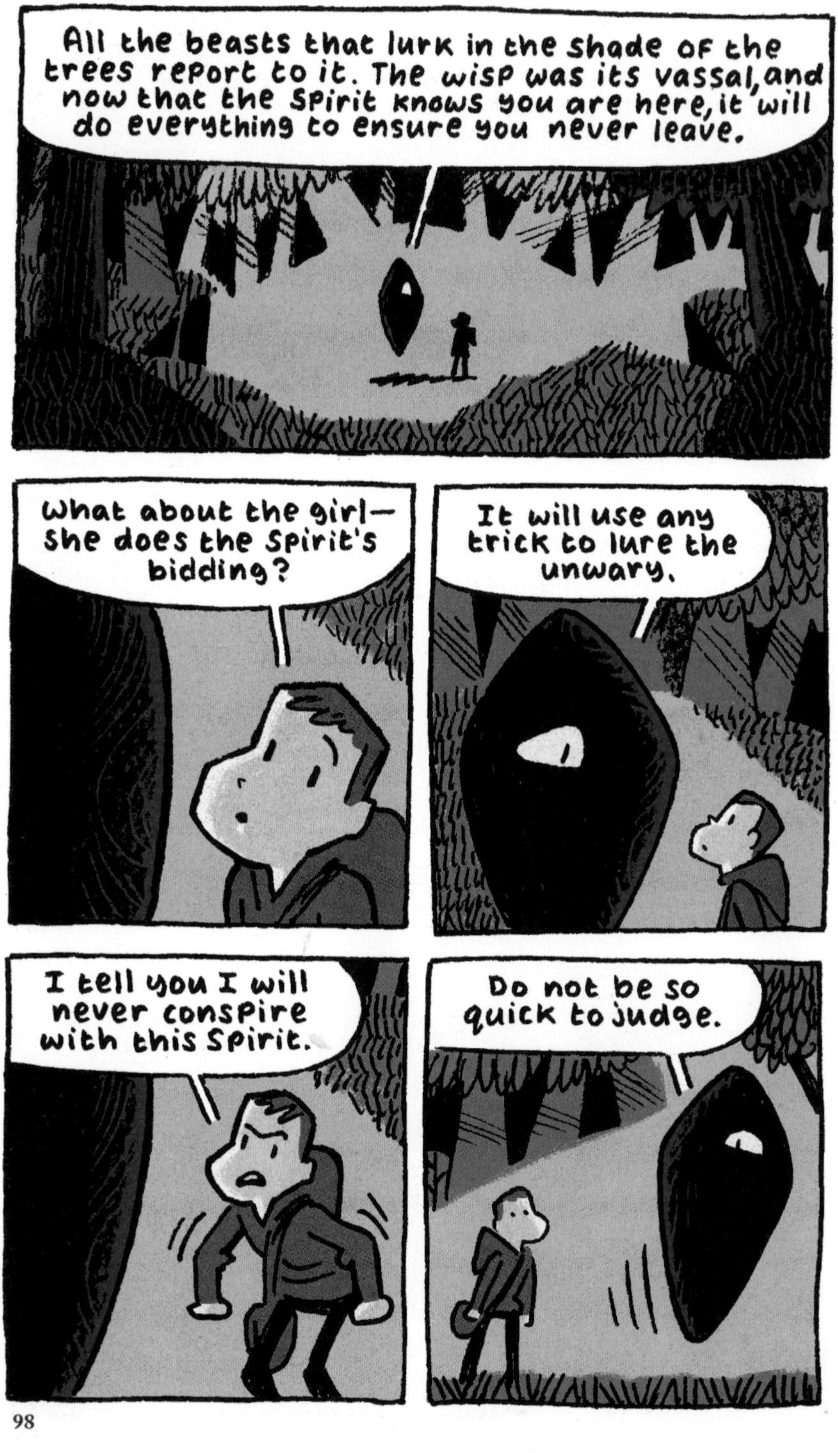
All the beasts that lurk in the shade of the trees report to it. The wisp was its vassal, and now that the Spirit knows you are here, it will do everything to ensure you never leave.
What about the girl— she does the Spirit's bidding?
It will use any trick to lure the unwary.
I tell you I will never conspire with this Spirit.
Do not be so quick to judge.

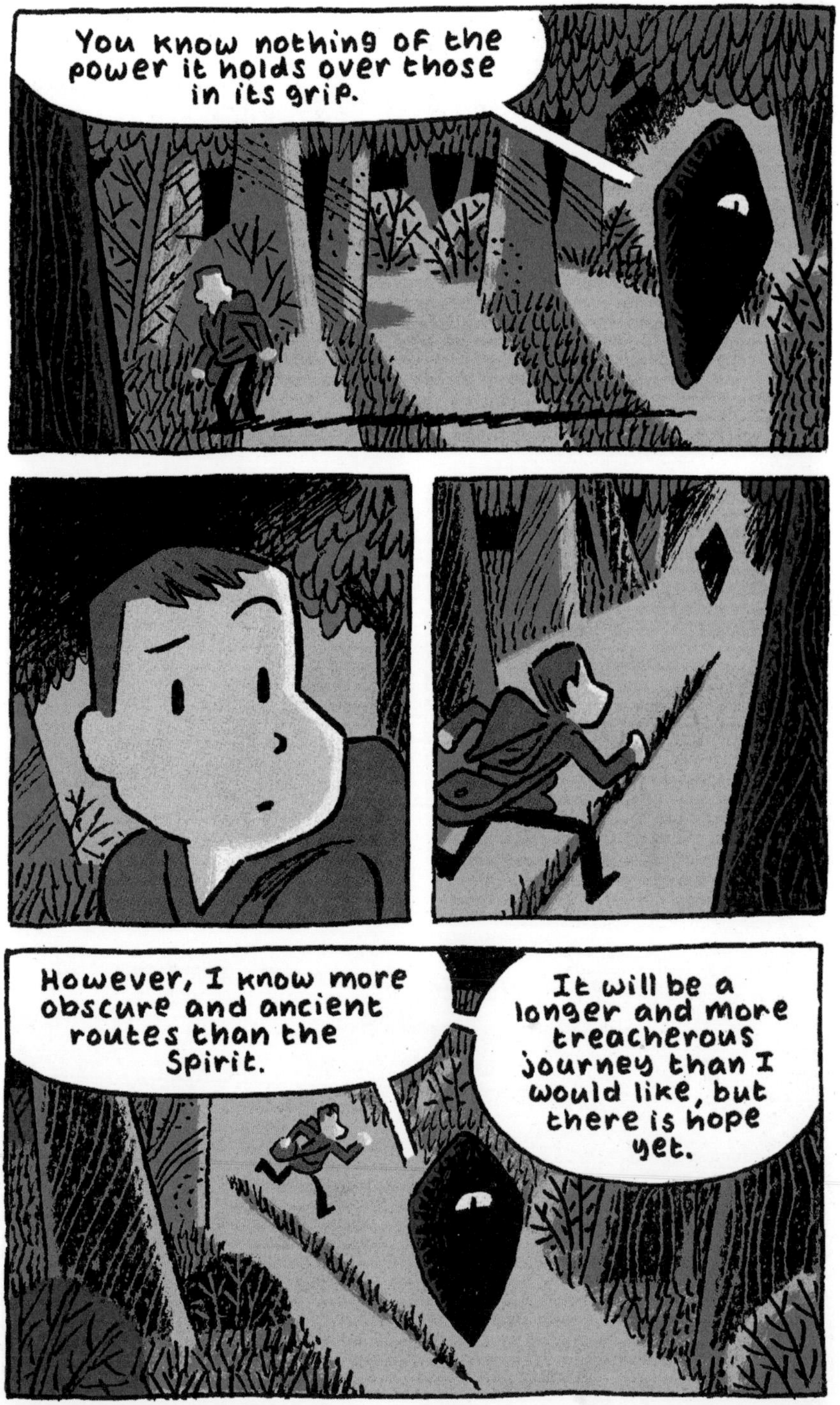

You know nothing of the power it holds over those in its grip.
However, I know more obscure and ancient routes than the Spirit.
It will be a longer and more treacherous journey than I would like, but there is hope yet.

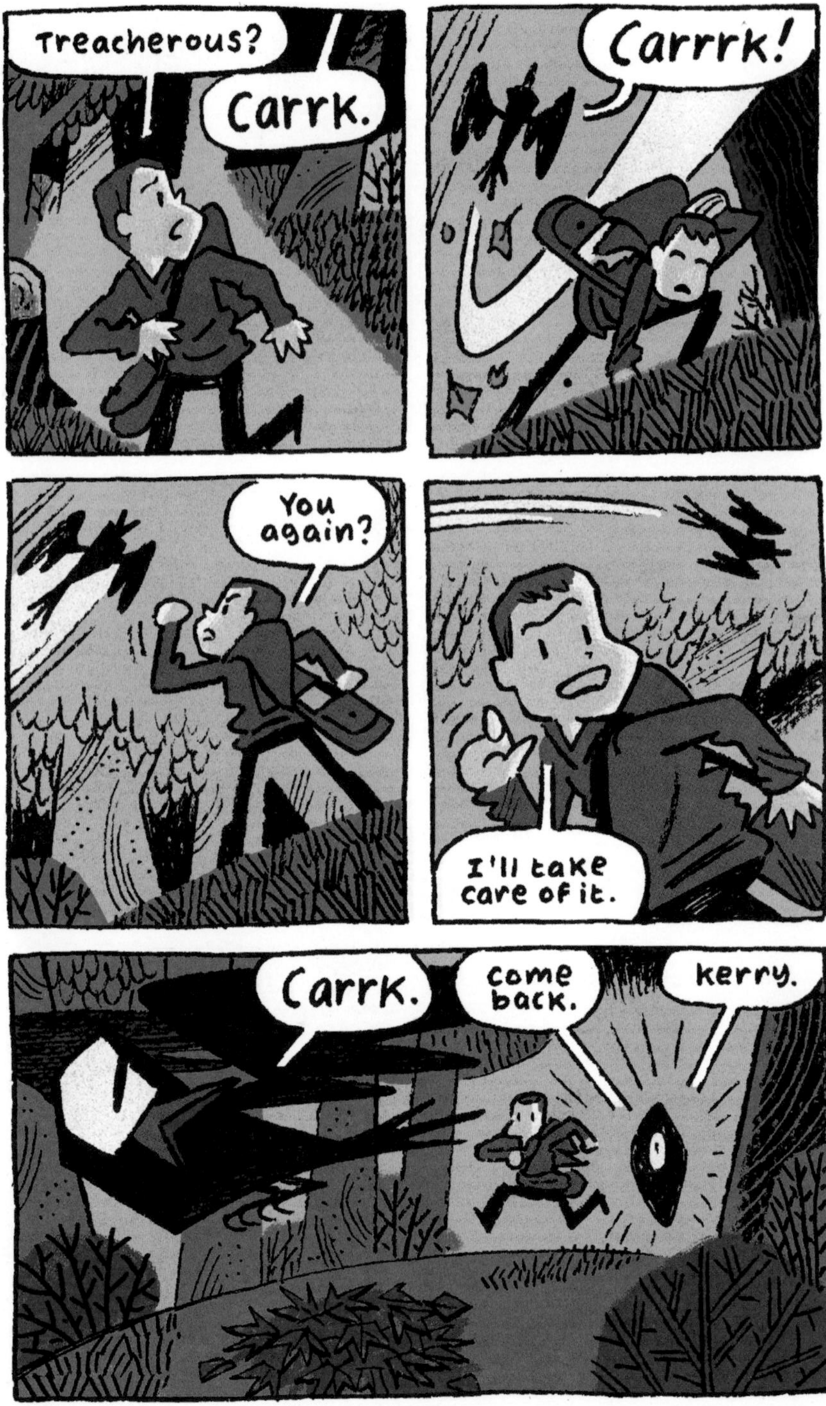
Treacherous?
Carrk.
Carrrk!
You again?
I'll take care of it.
Carrk.
come back.
kerry.

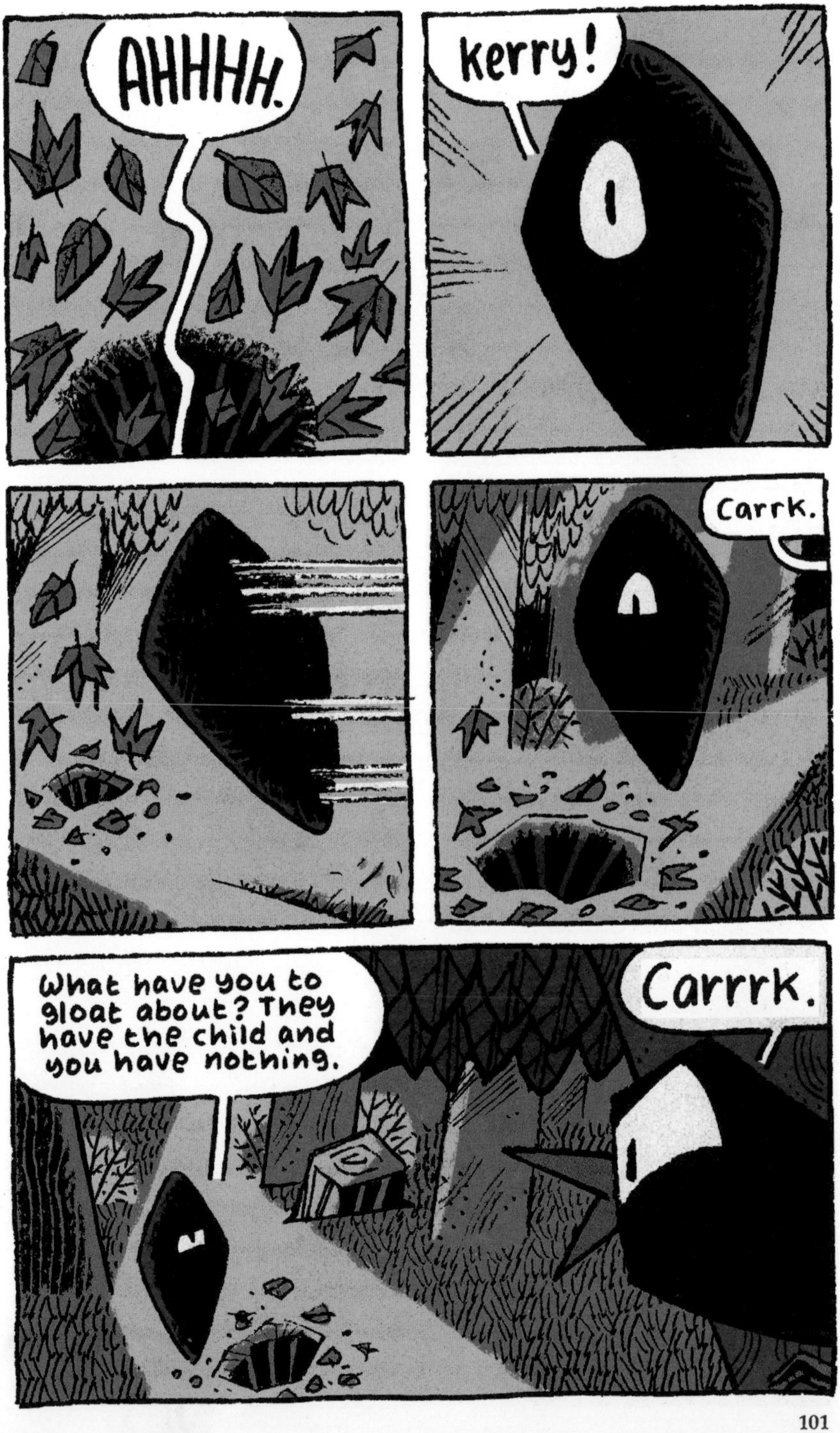
AHHHH.
Kerry!
Carrk.
What have you to gloat about? They have the child and you have nothing.
Carrrk.

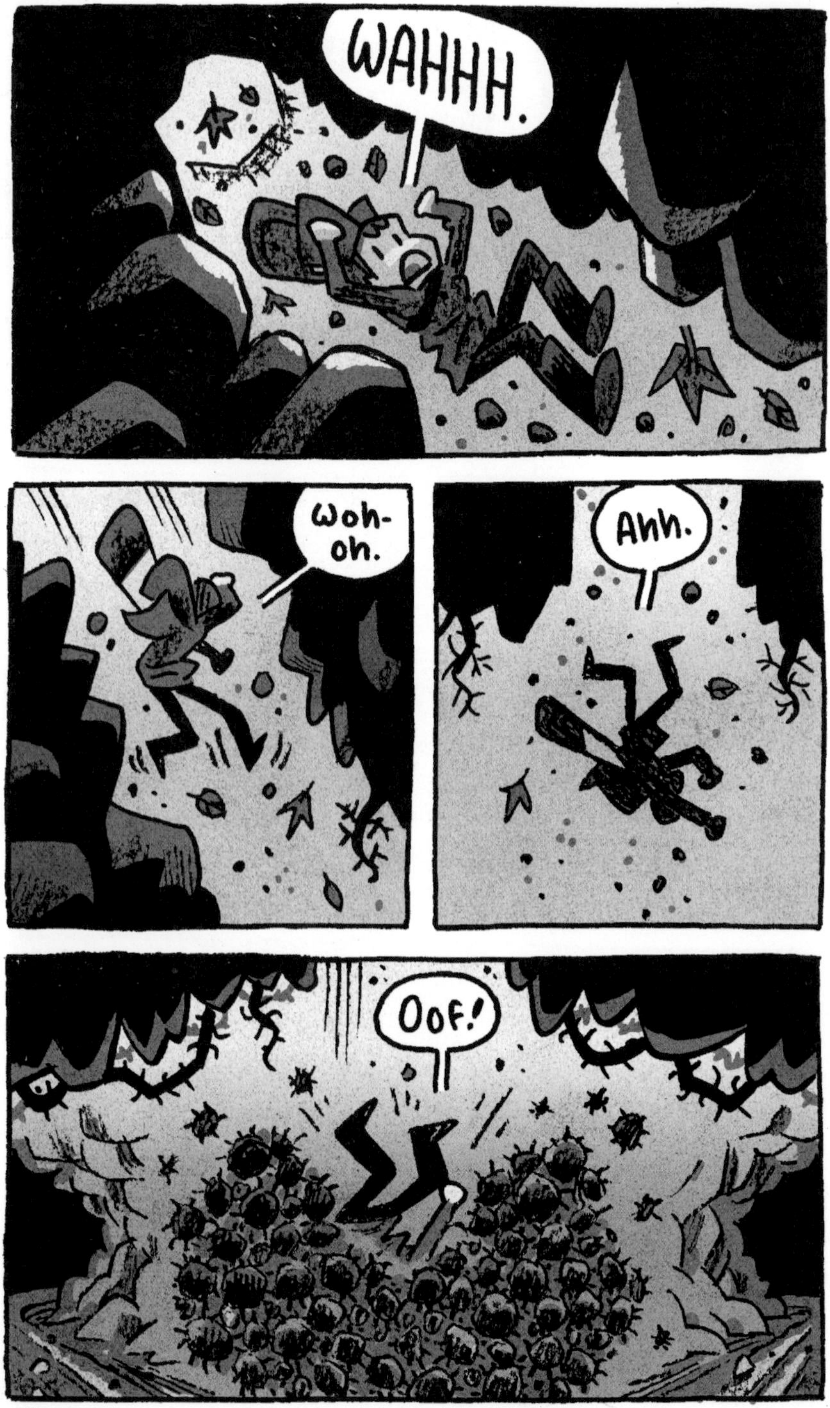
WAHHH.
Woh-oh.
Ahh.
Oof!

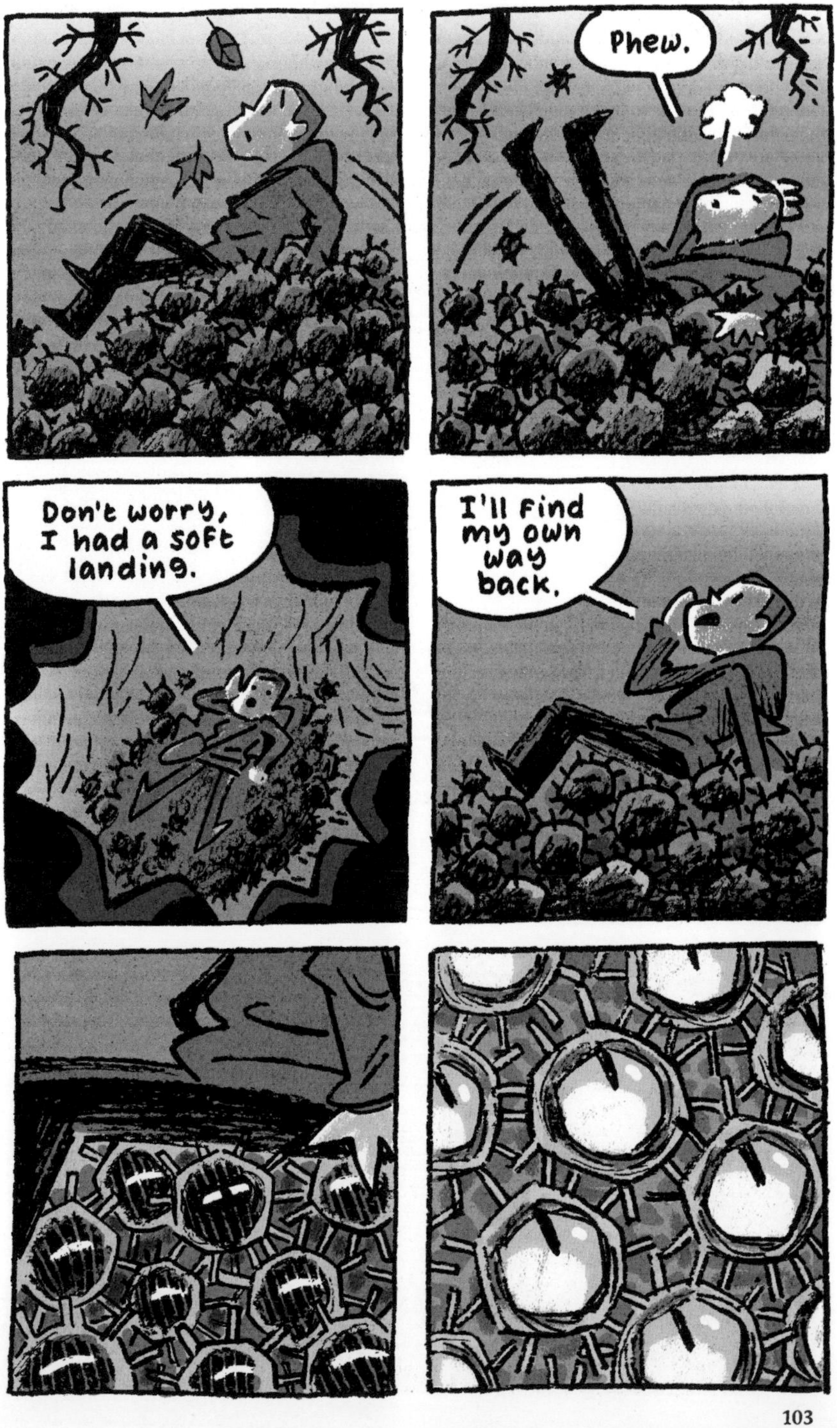
Phew.
Don't worry, I had a soft landing.
I'll find my own way back.

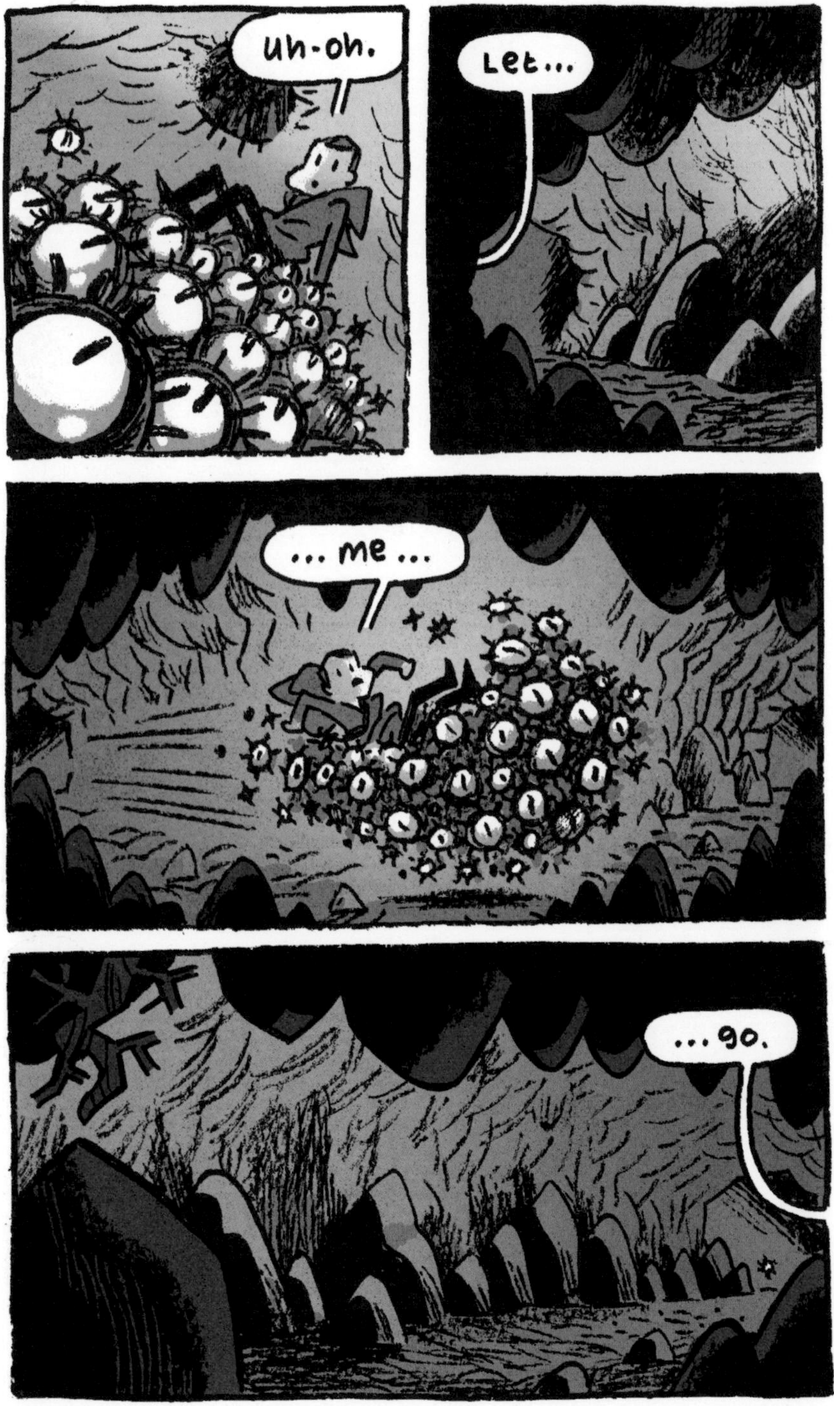
uh-oh.
Let...
... me ...
... go.

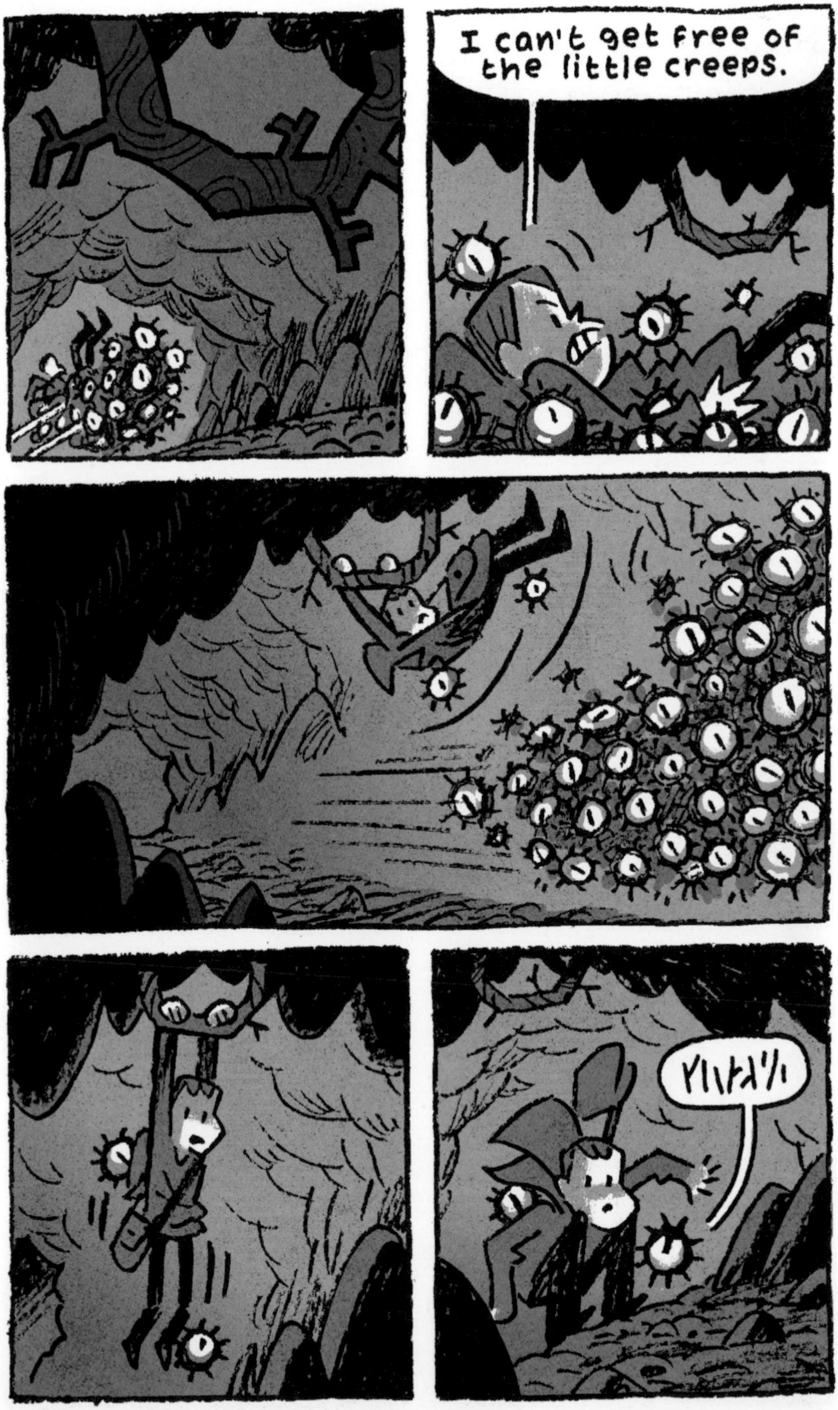
I can't get free of
the little creeps.

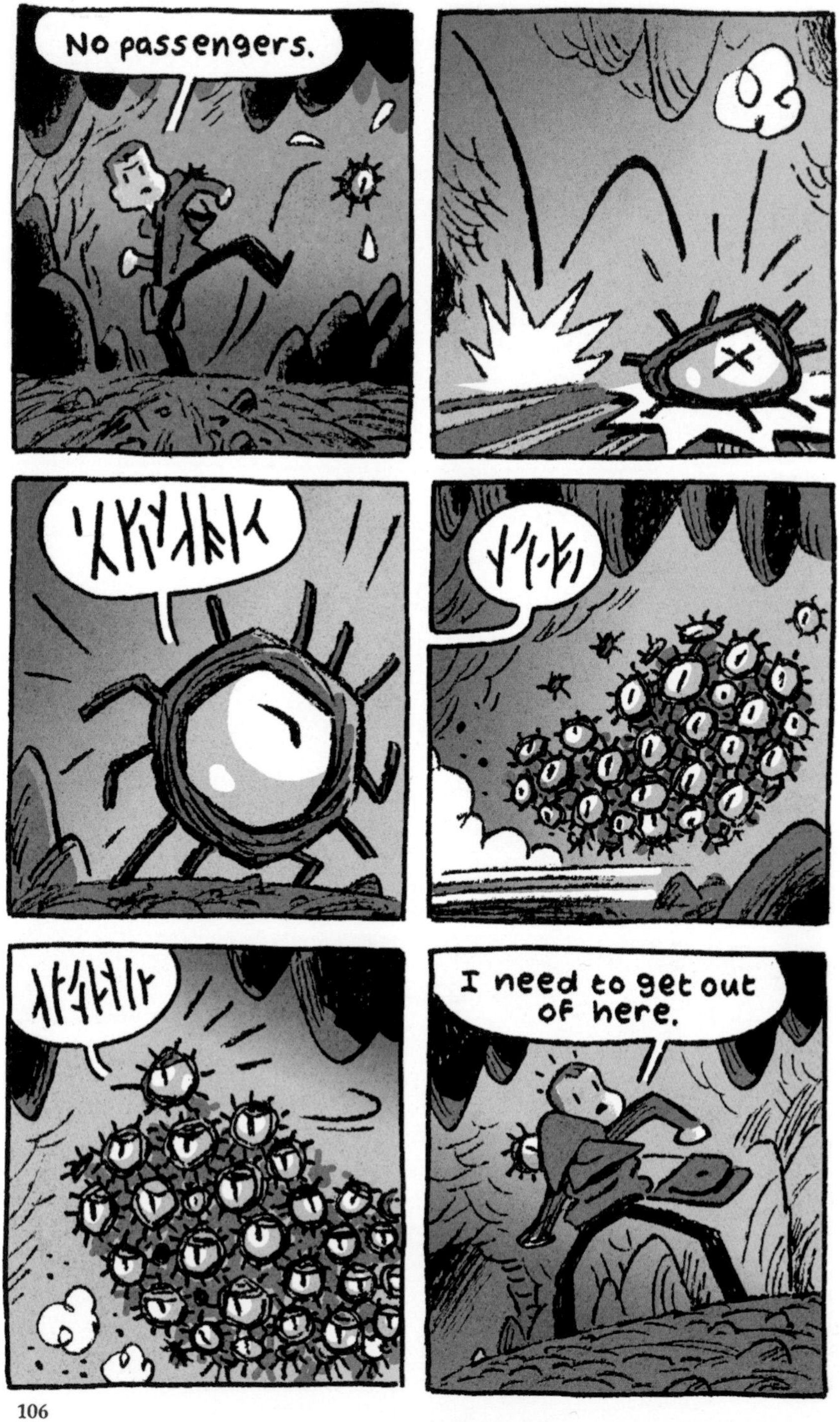
No passengers.
I need to get out of here.

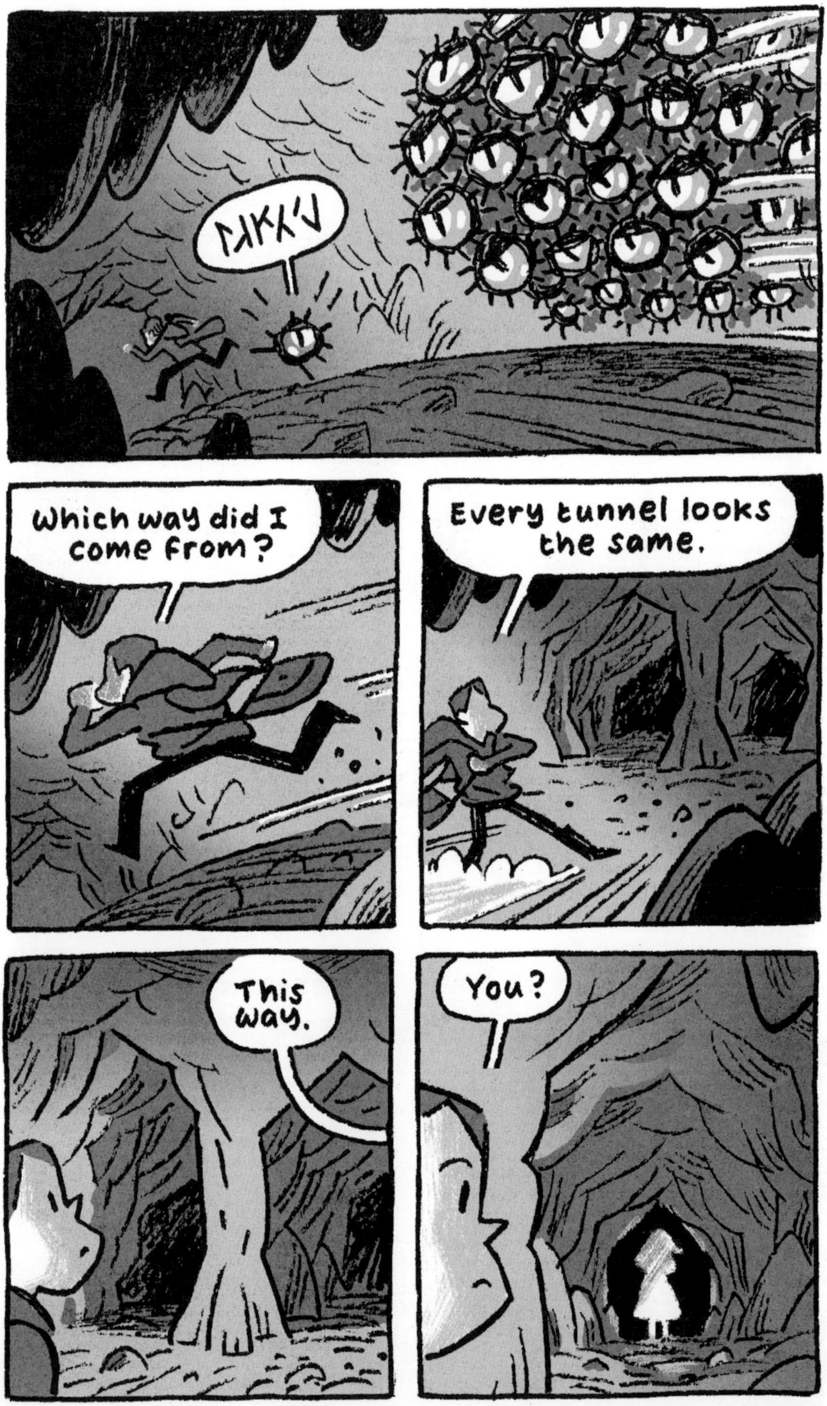
Which way did I come from?
Every tunnel looks the same.
This way.
You?

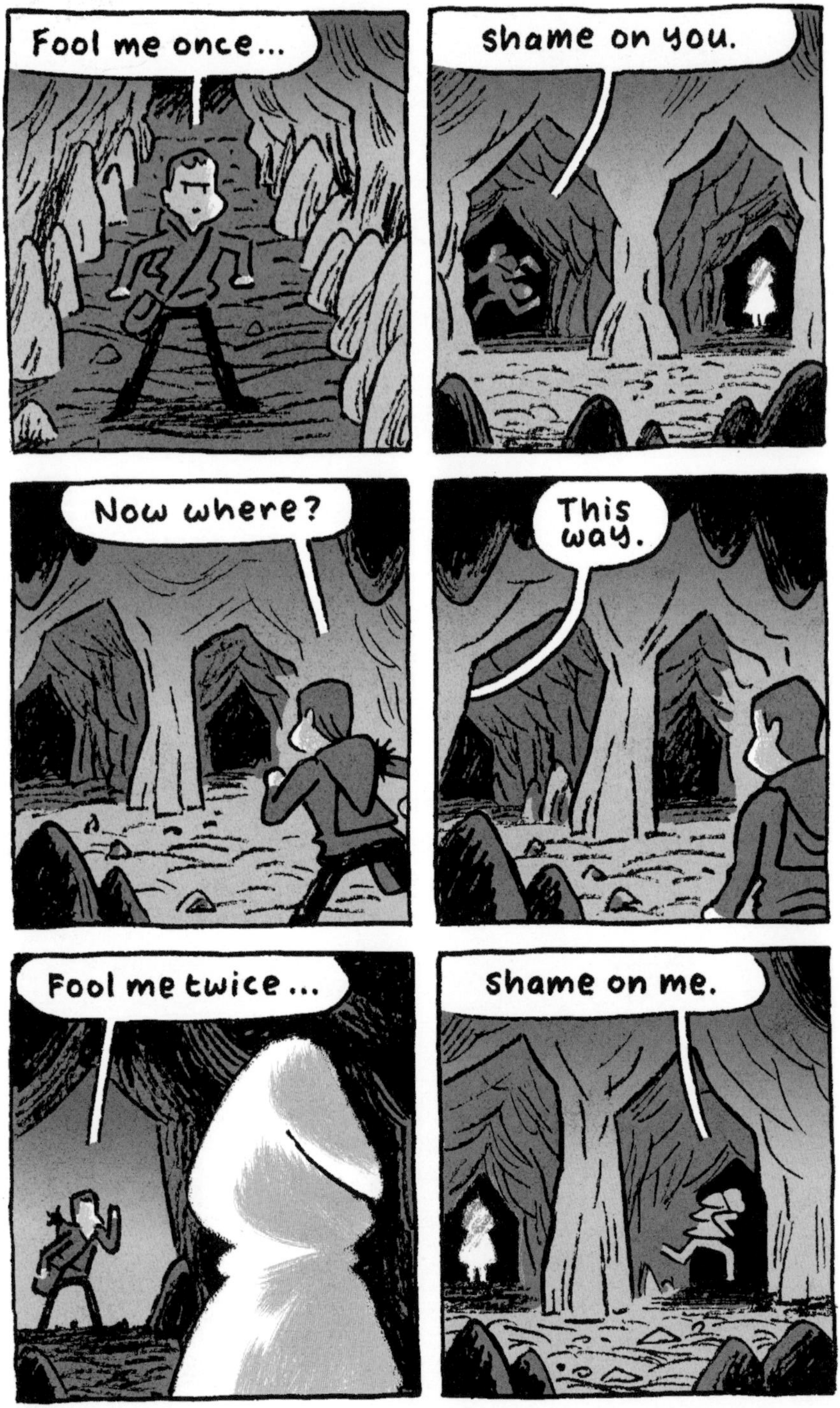
Fool me once...
shame on you.
Now where?
This way.
Fool me twice...
Shame on me.

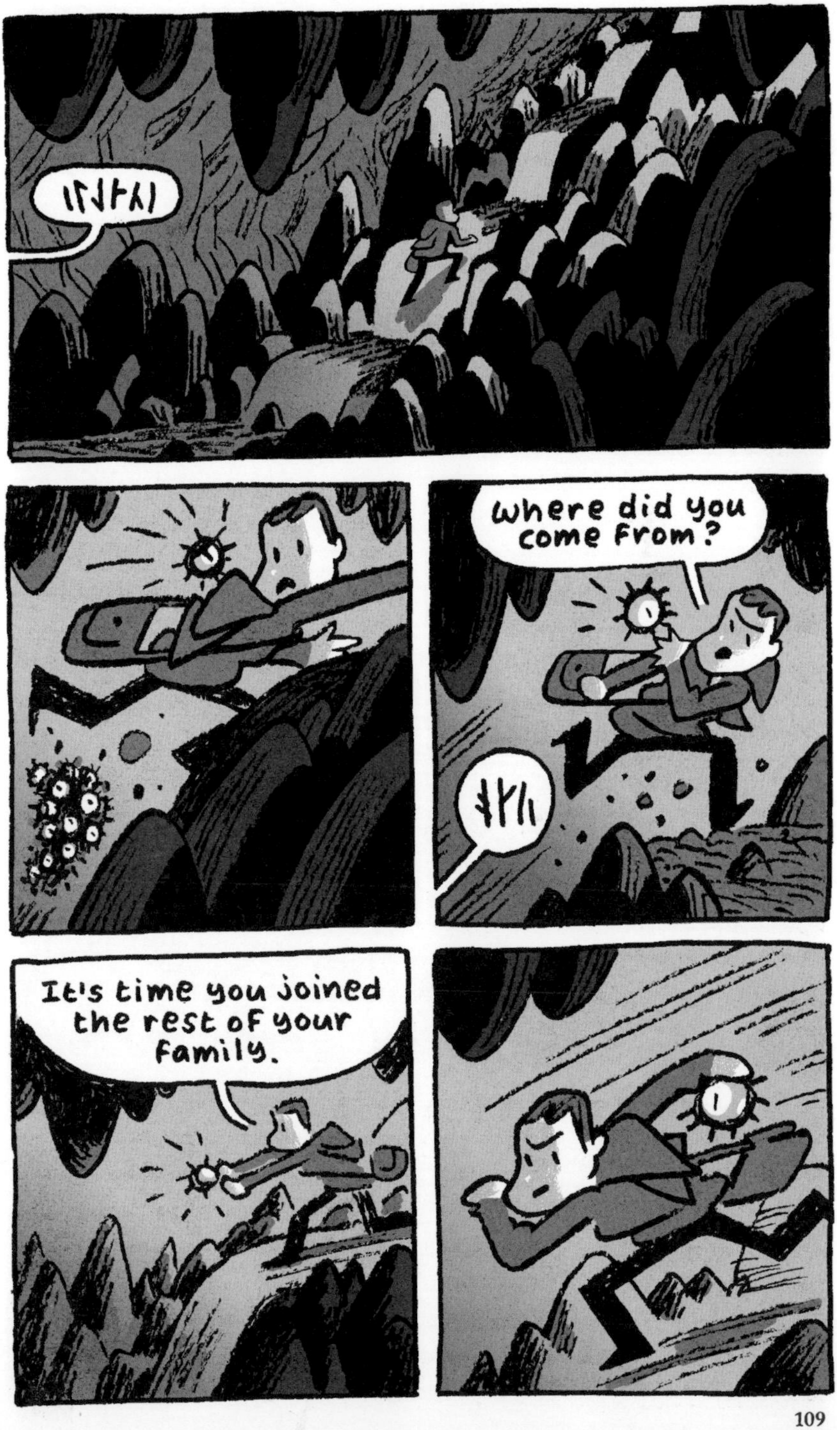
Where did you come from?
It's time you joined the rest of your family.

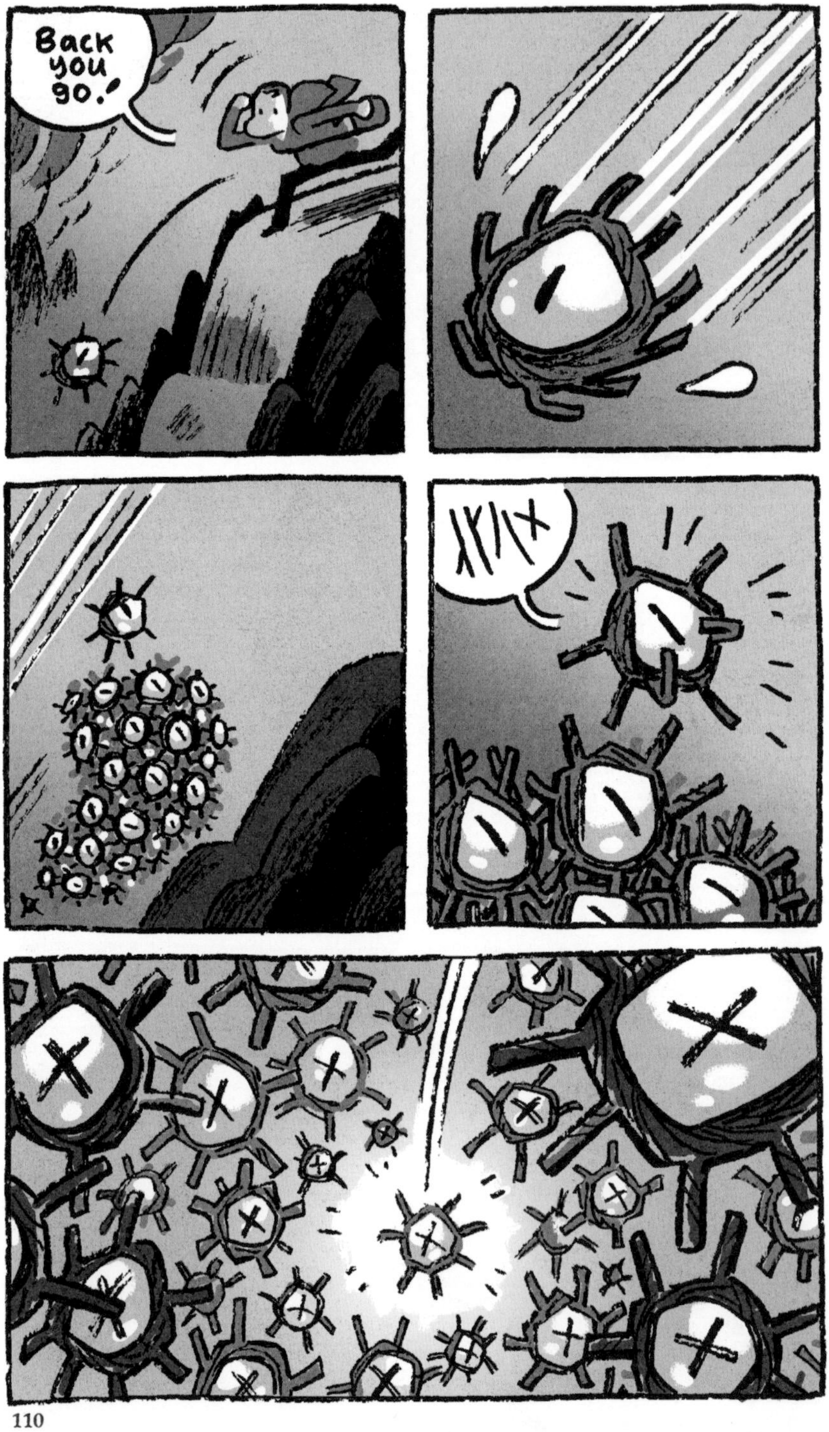
Back you go!

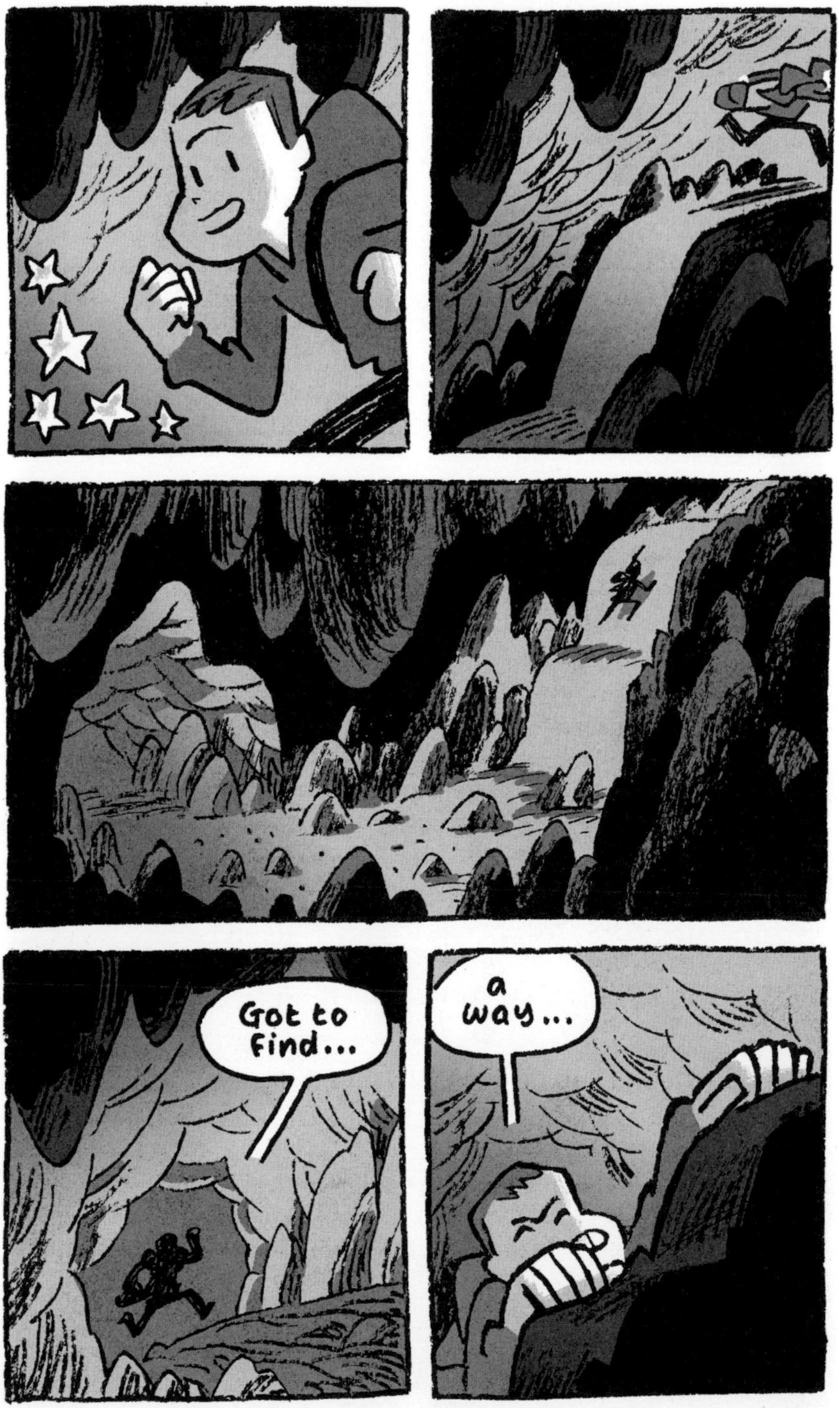
Got to find...
a way...

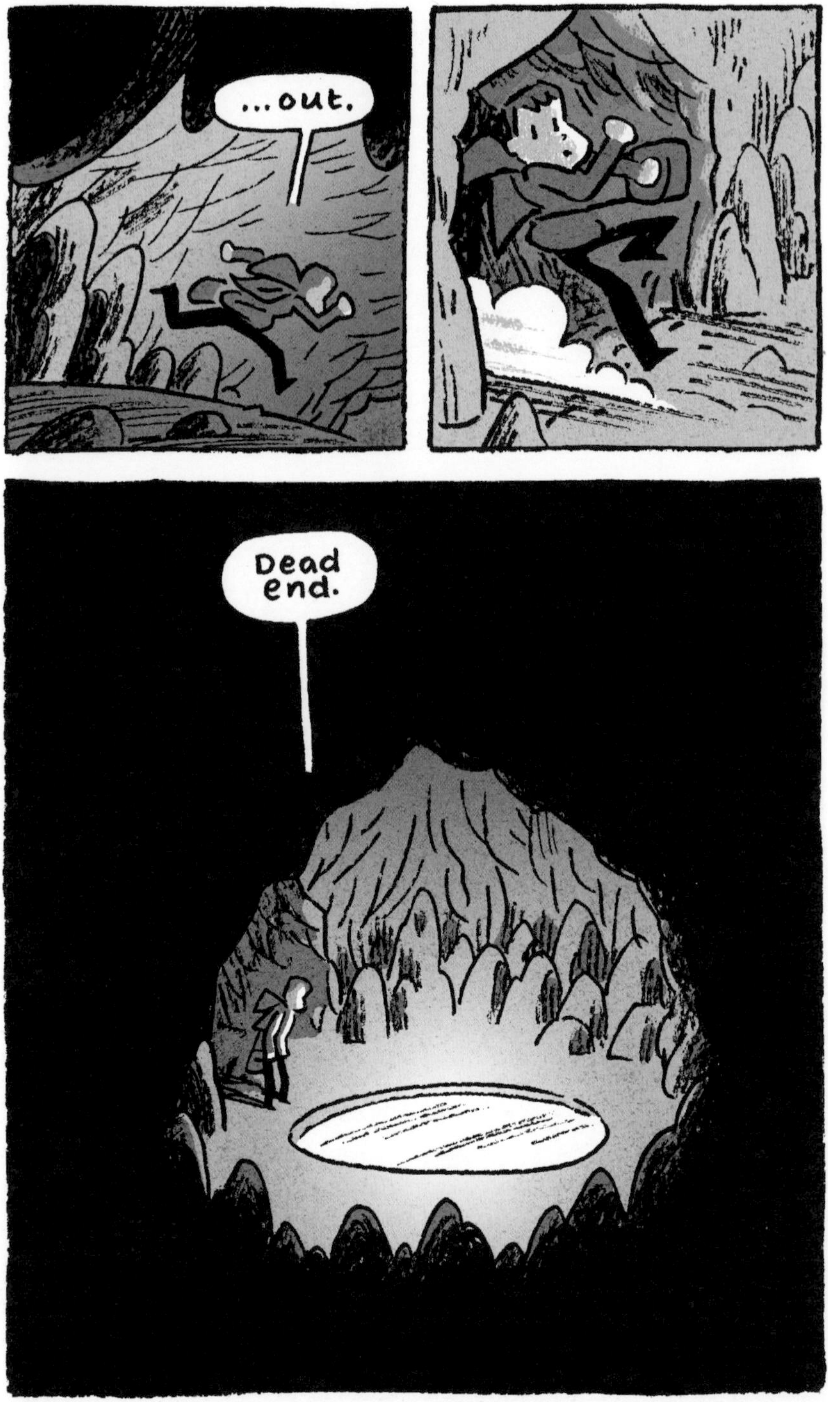
...out.
Dead end.

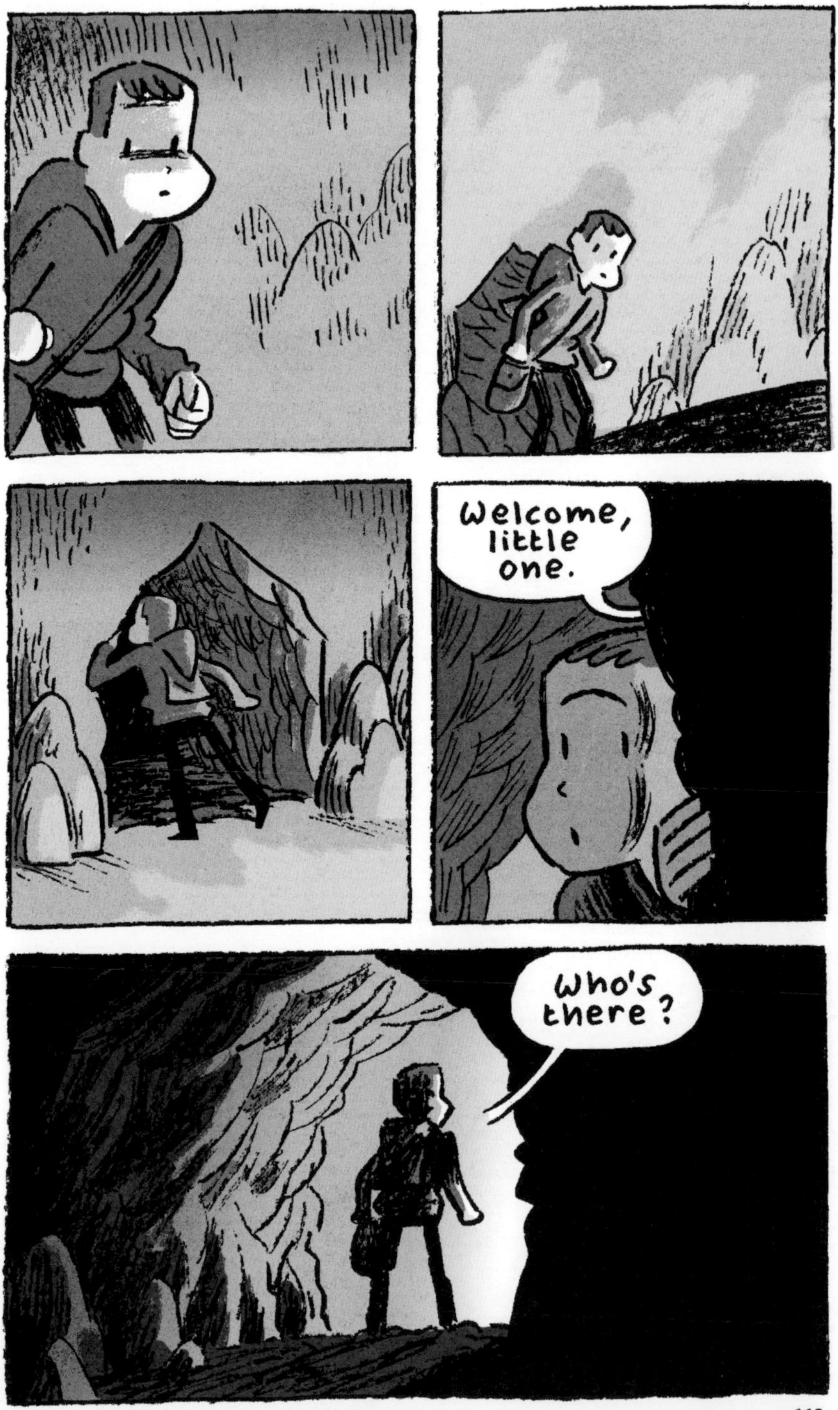
Welcome, little one.
Who's there?

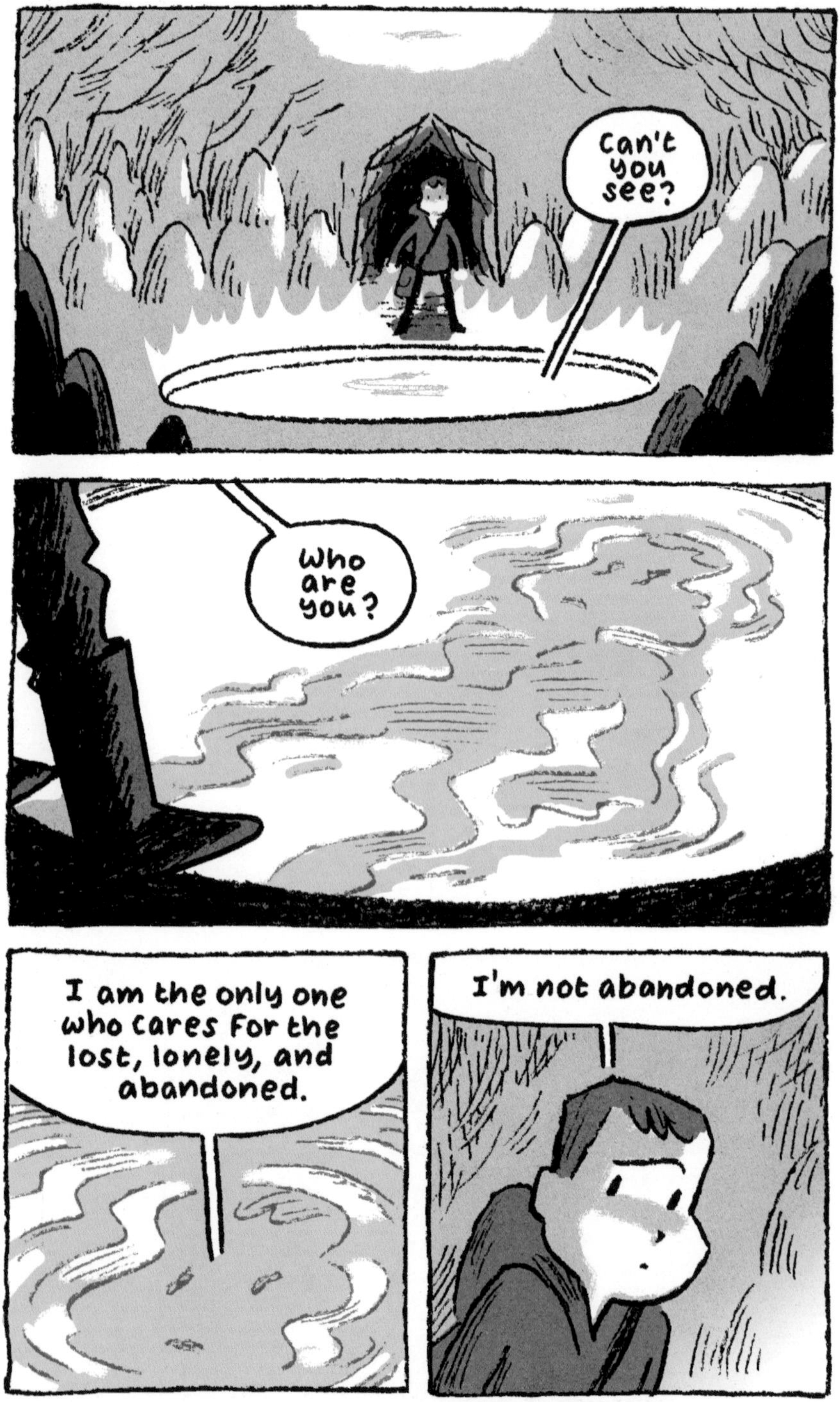
Can't you see?
Who are you?
I am the only one who cares for the lost, lonely, and abandoned.
I'm not abandoned.

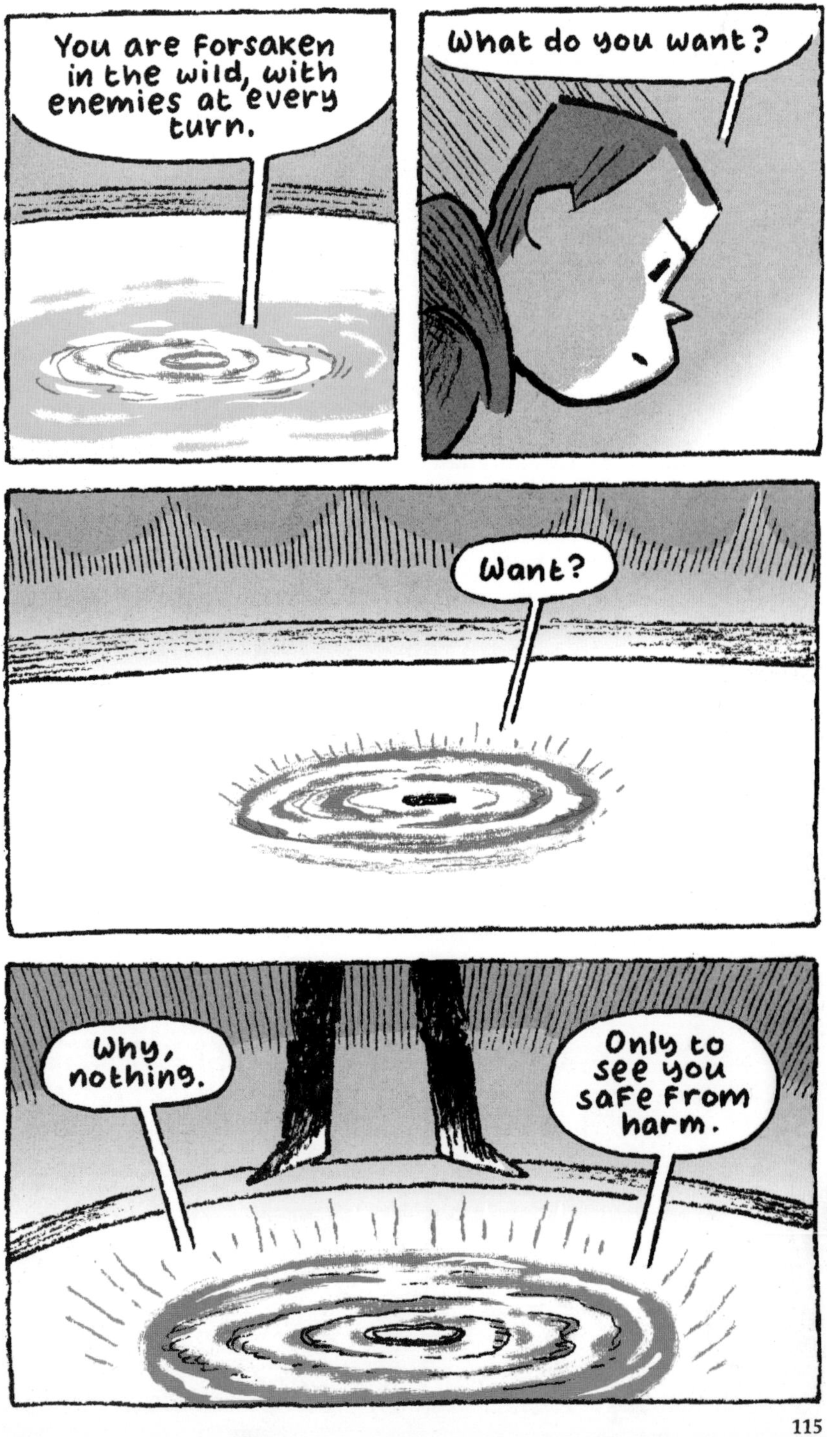
You are forsaken in the wild, with enemies at every turn.
What do you want?
Want?
Why, nothing.
Only to see you safe from harm.

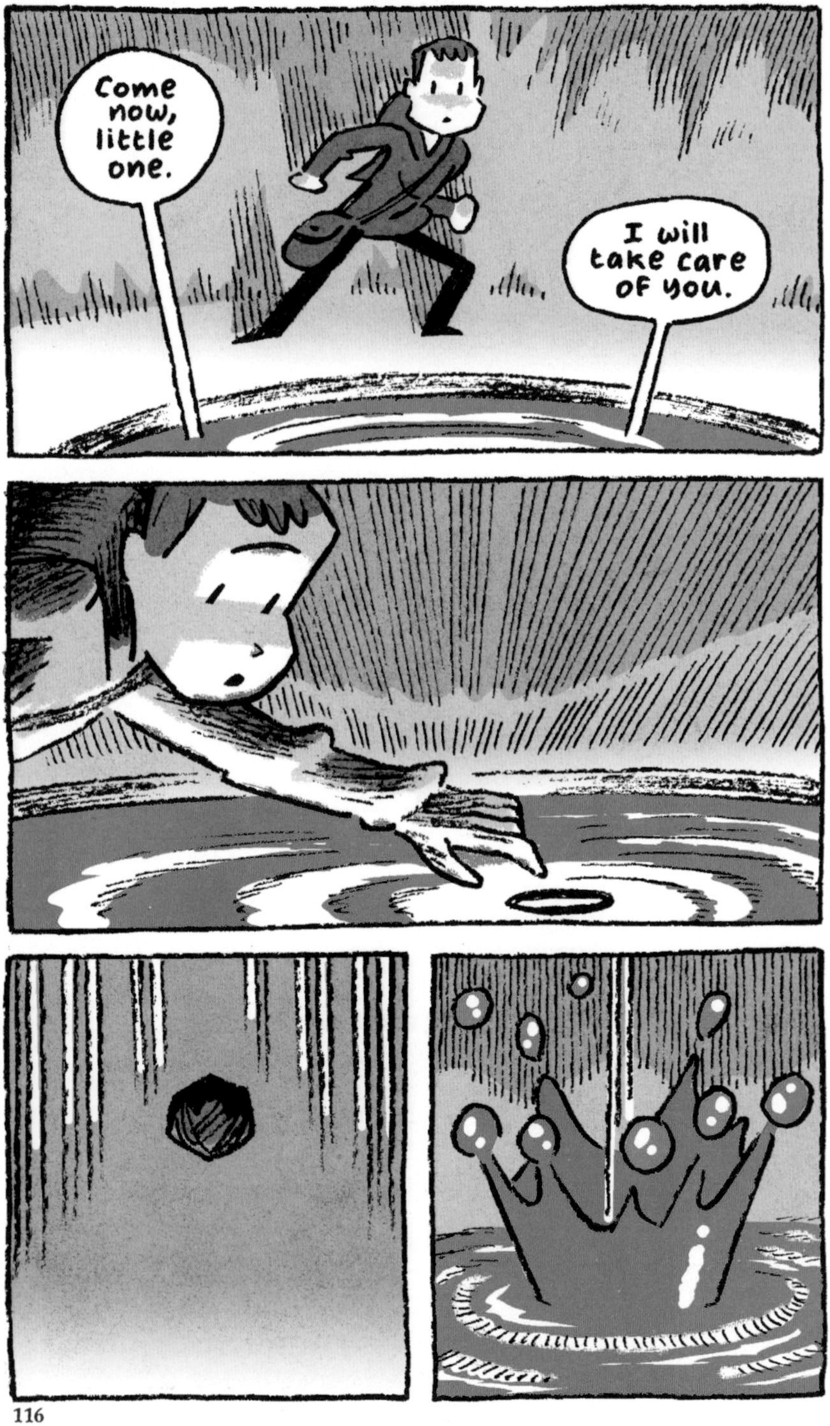
Come now, little one.
I will take care of you.

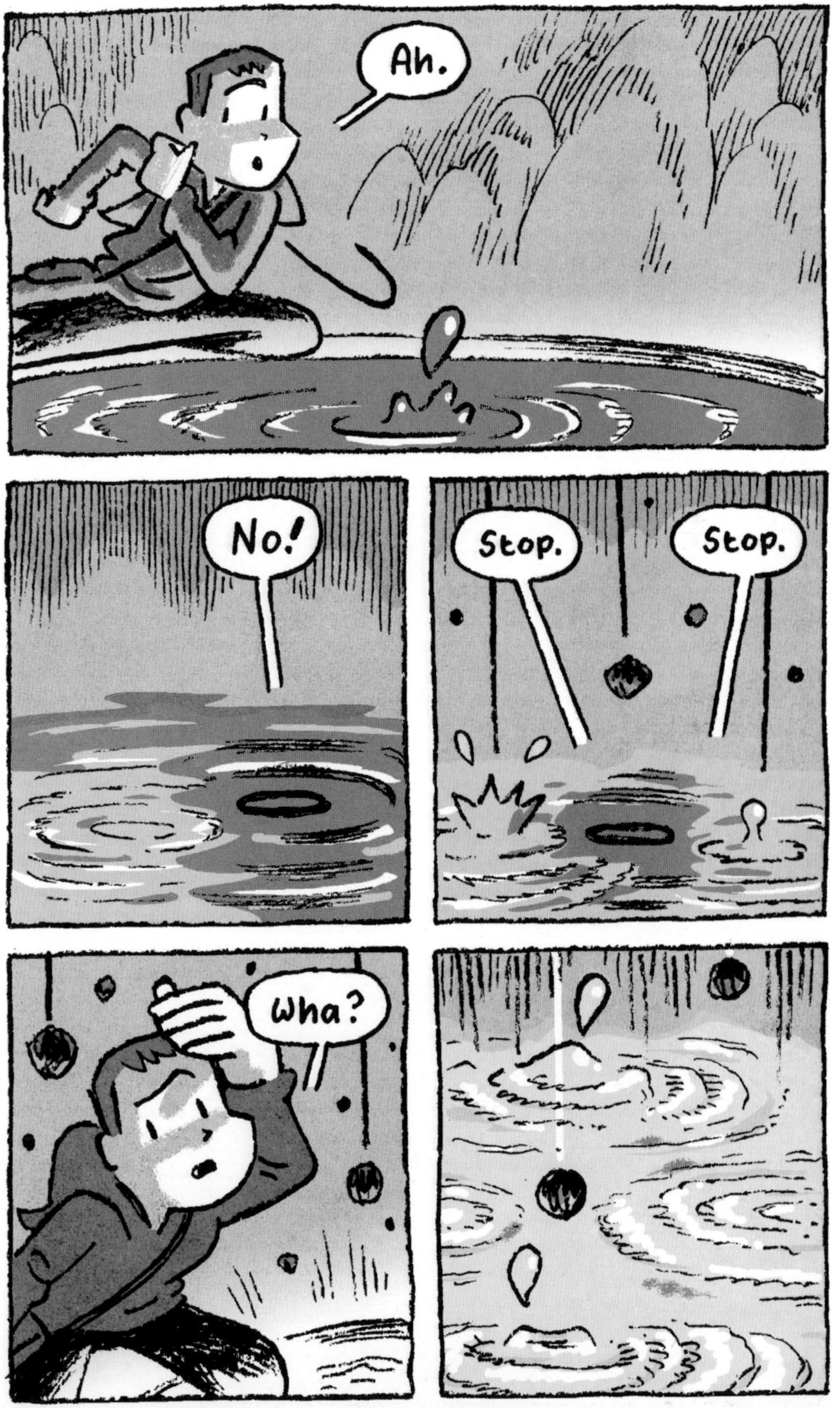
Ah.
No!
Stop.
Stop.
Wha?

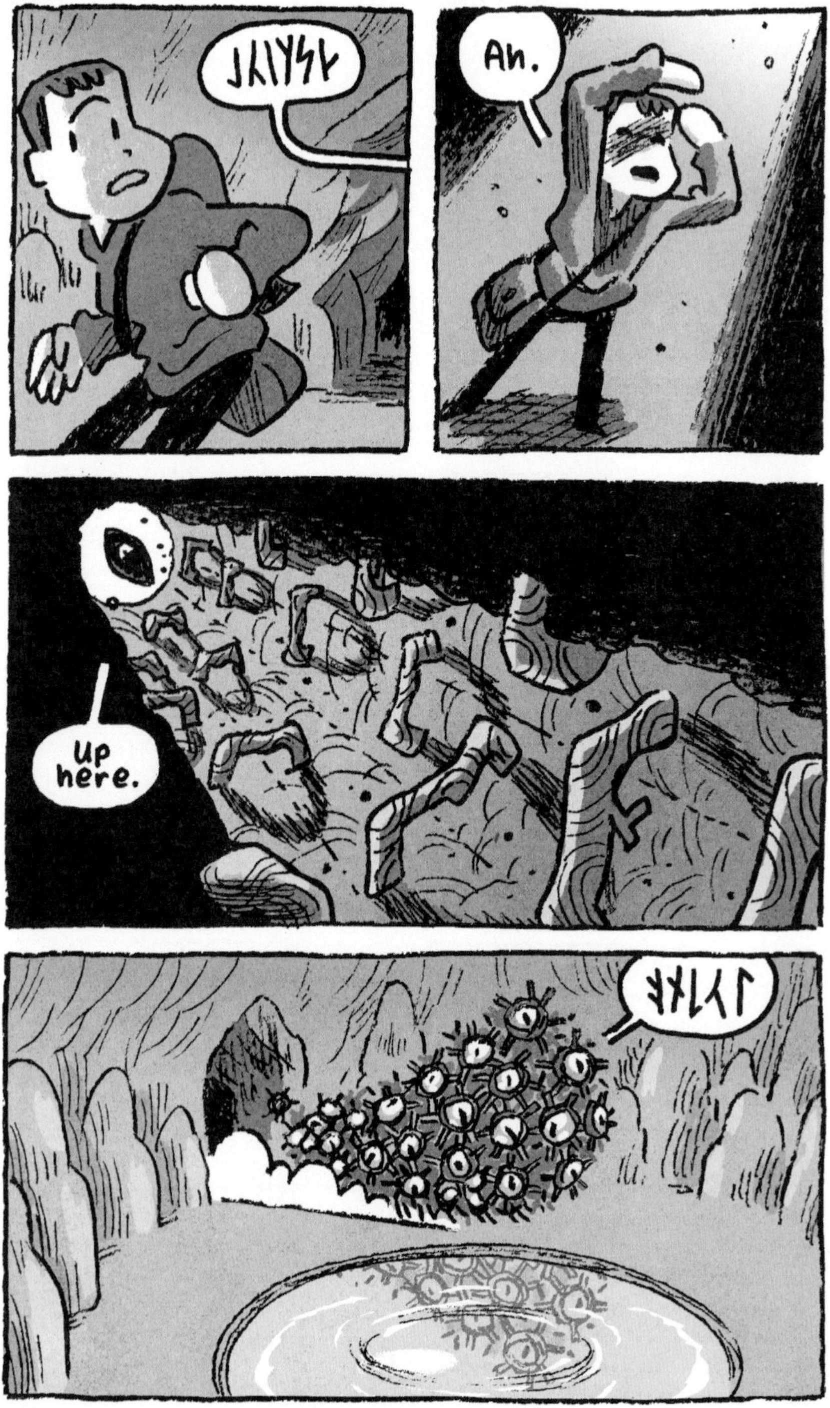
Ah.
Up here.

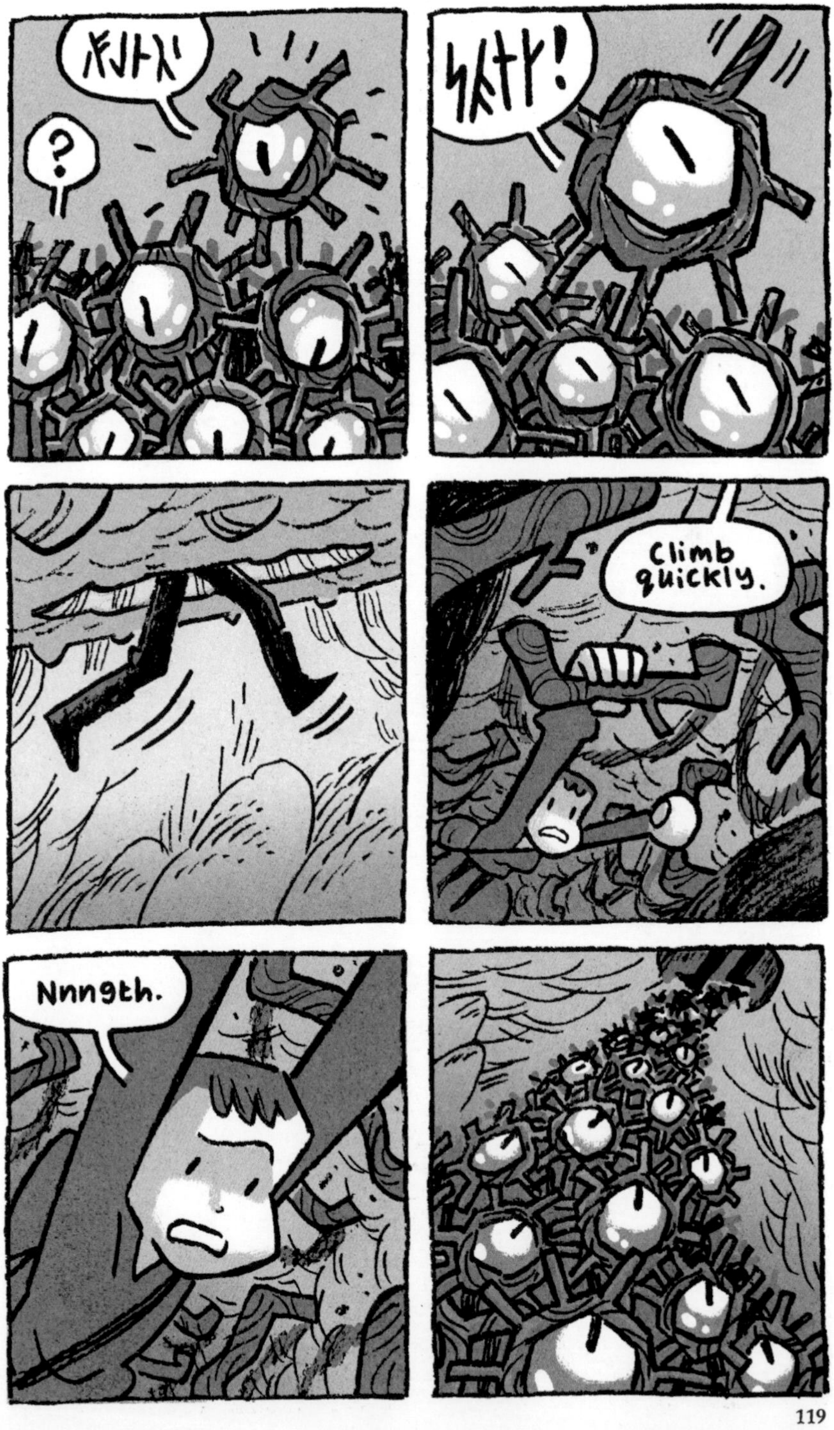
?
Climb quickly.
Nnngth.

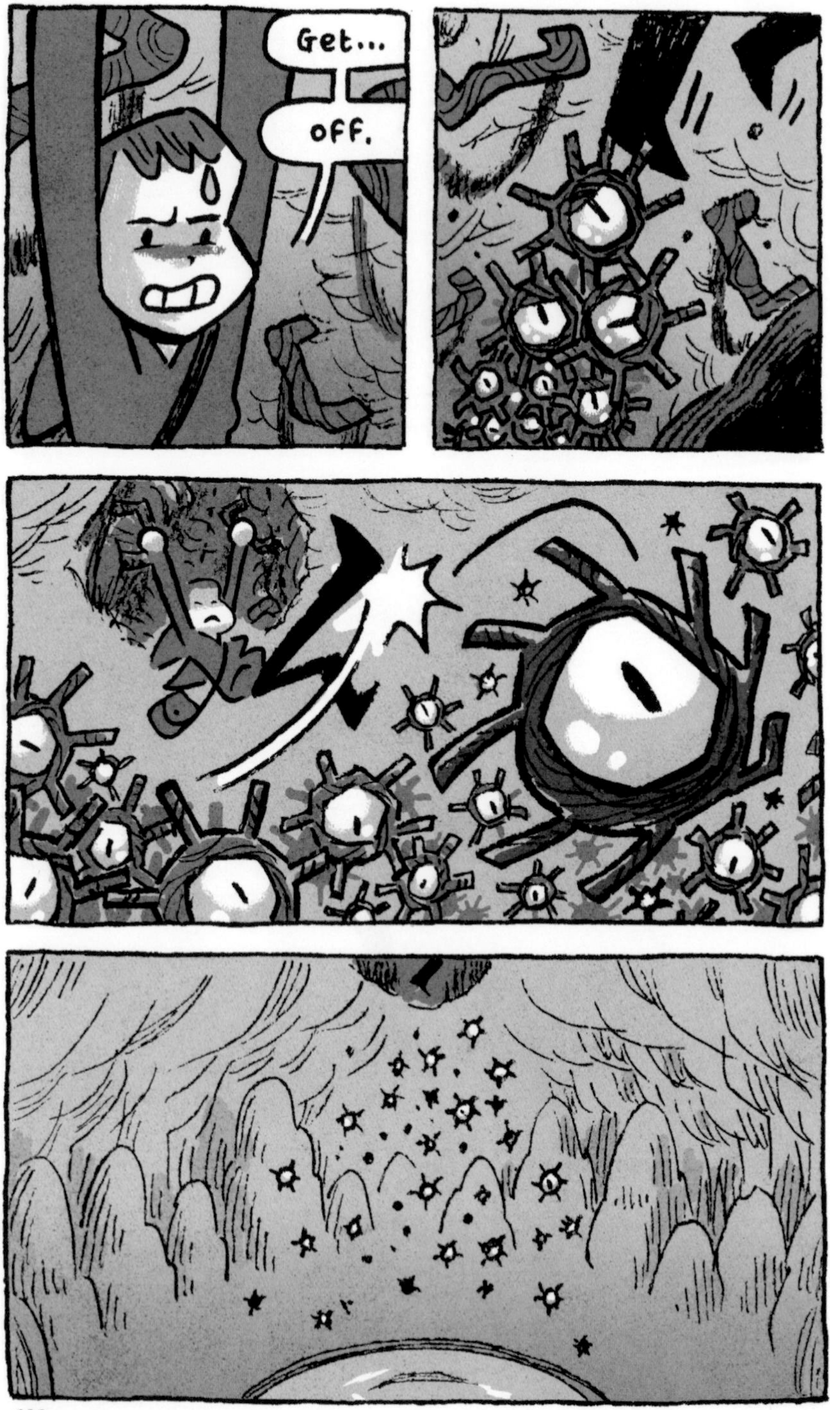
Get...
off.

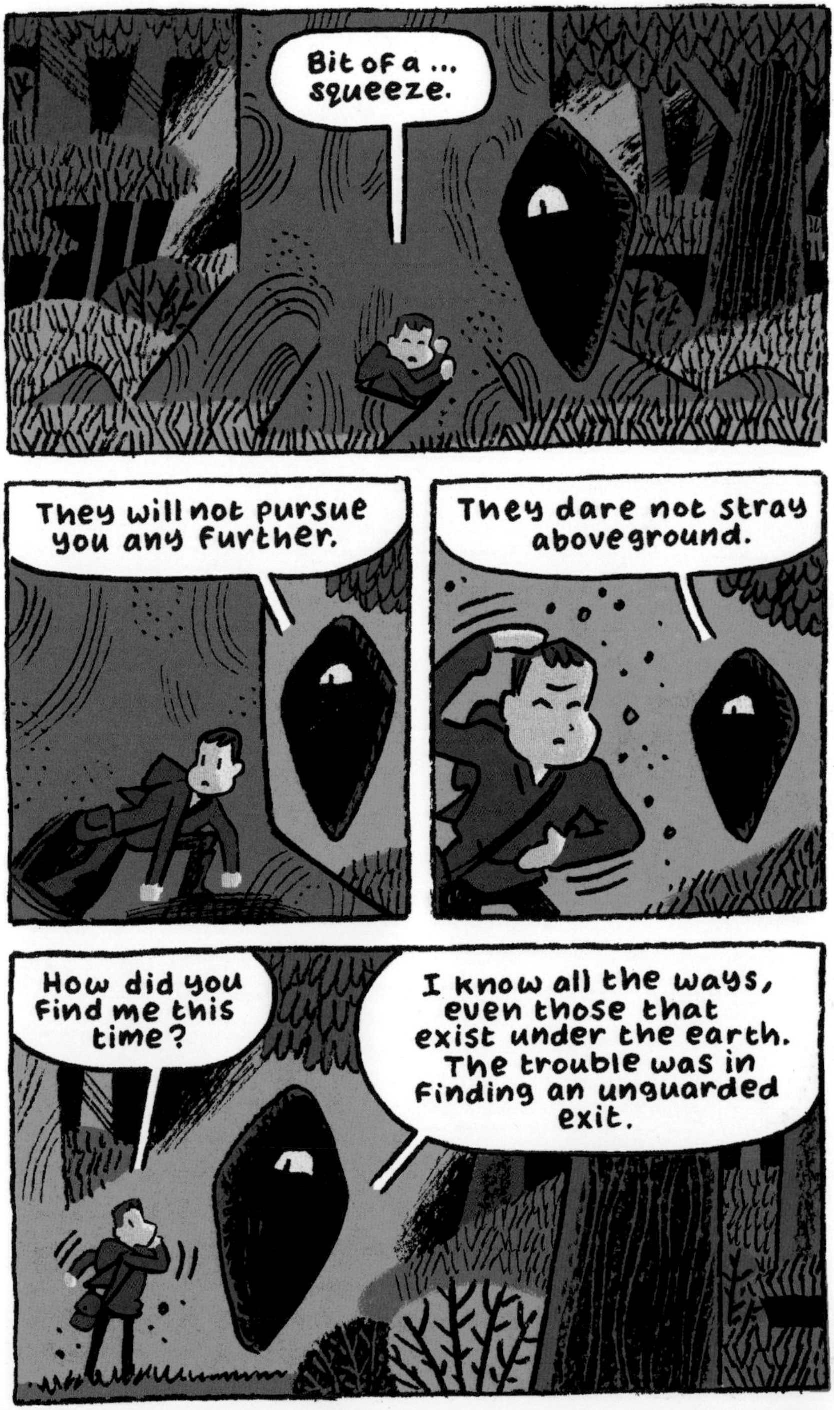
Bit of a ... squeeze.
They will not pursue you any further.
They dare not stray aboveground.
How did you find me this time?
I know all the ways, even those that exist under the earth. The trouble was in finding an unguarded exit.

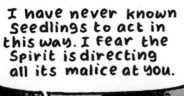

I have never known seedlings to act in this way. I fear the Spirit is directing all its malice at you.

Perhaps so.

Henceforth we must be more wary.

Hold on, there's some —

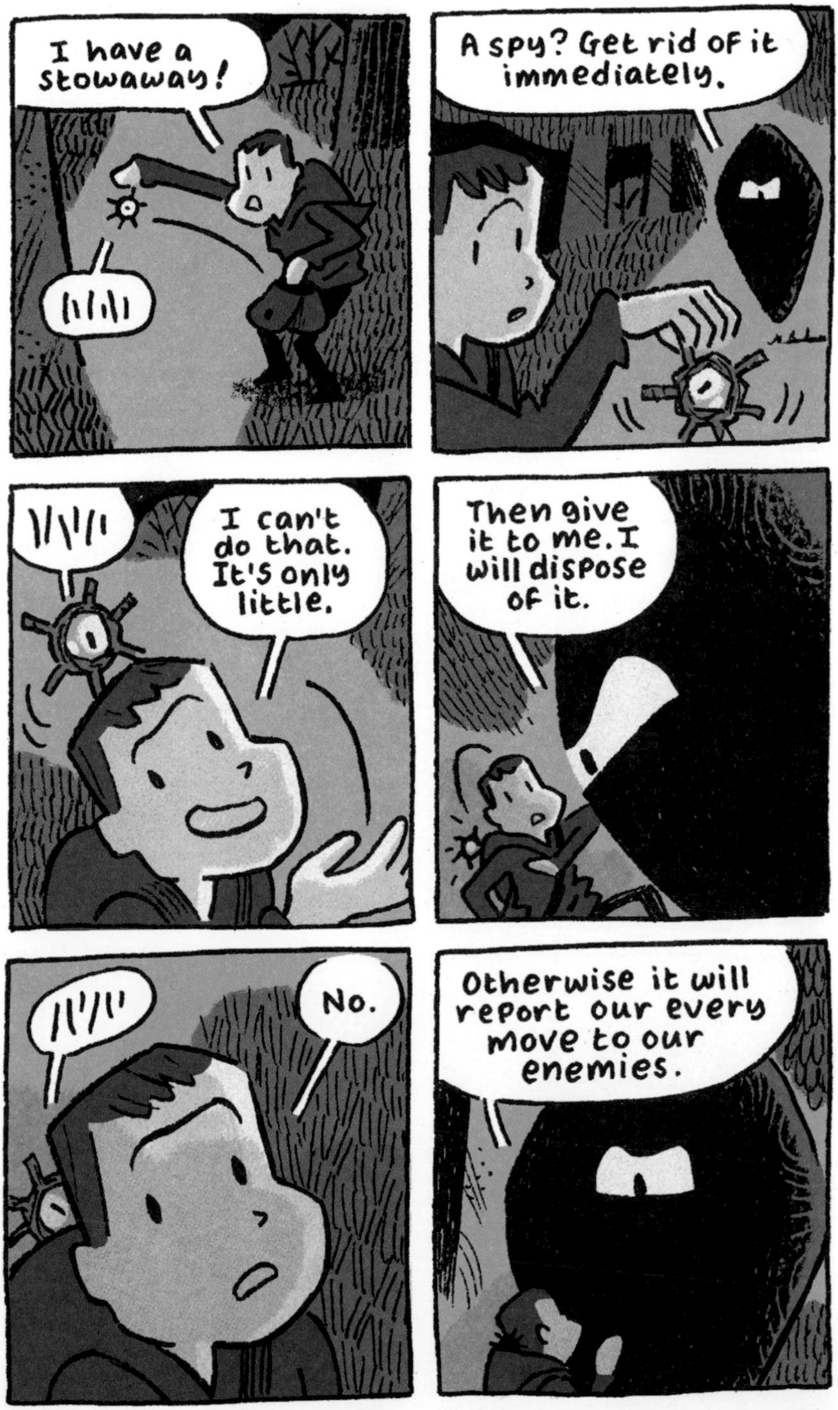
I have a stowaway!
A spy? Get rid of it immediately.
I can't do that. It's only little.
Then give it to me. I will dispose of it.
No.
Otherwise it will report our every move to our enemies.

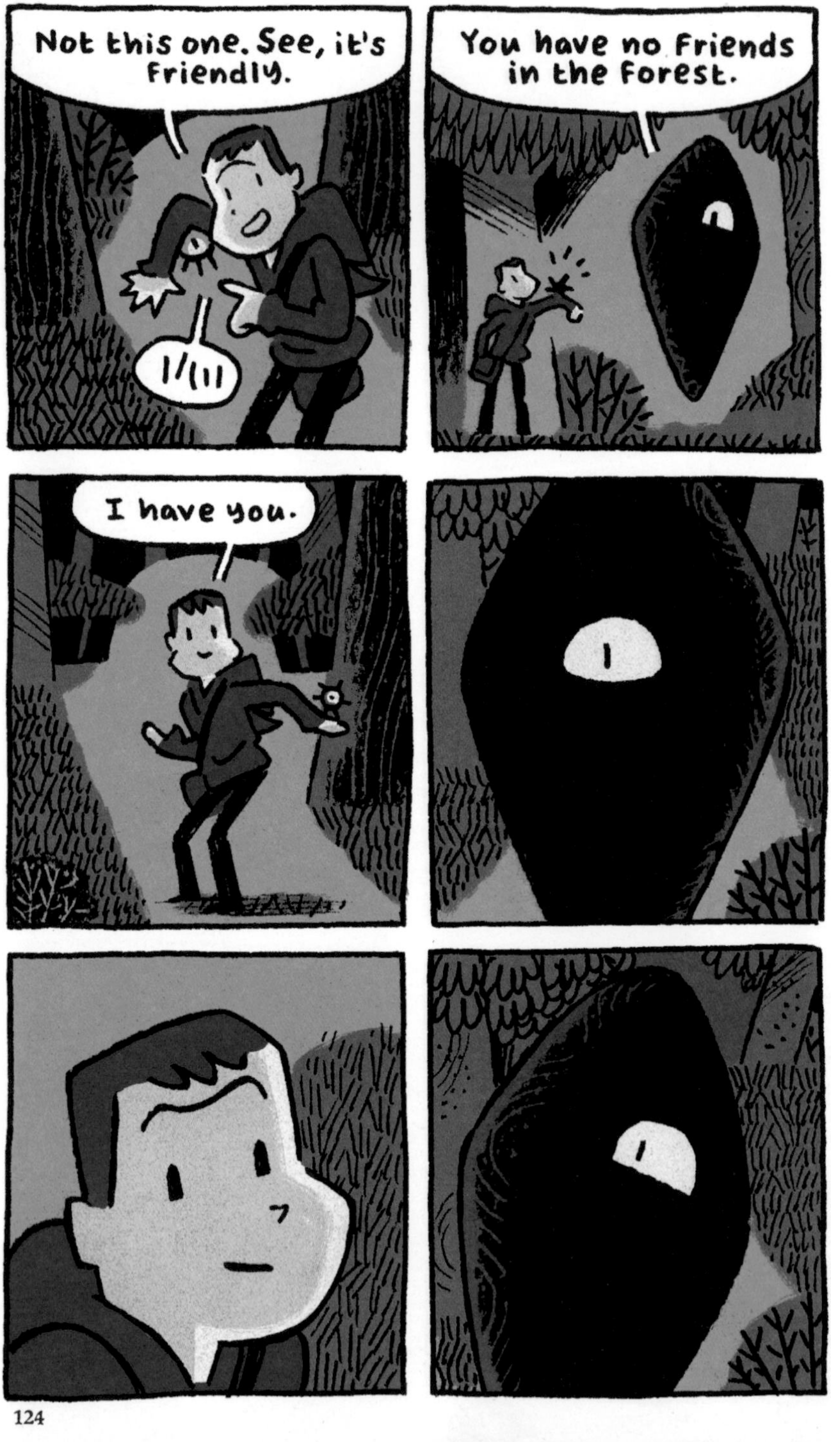
Not this one. See, it's friendly.
You have no friends in the forest.
I have you.

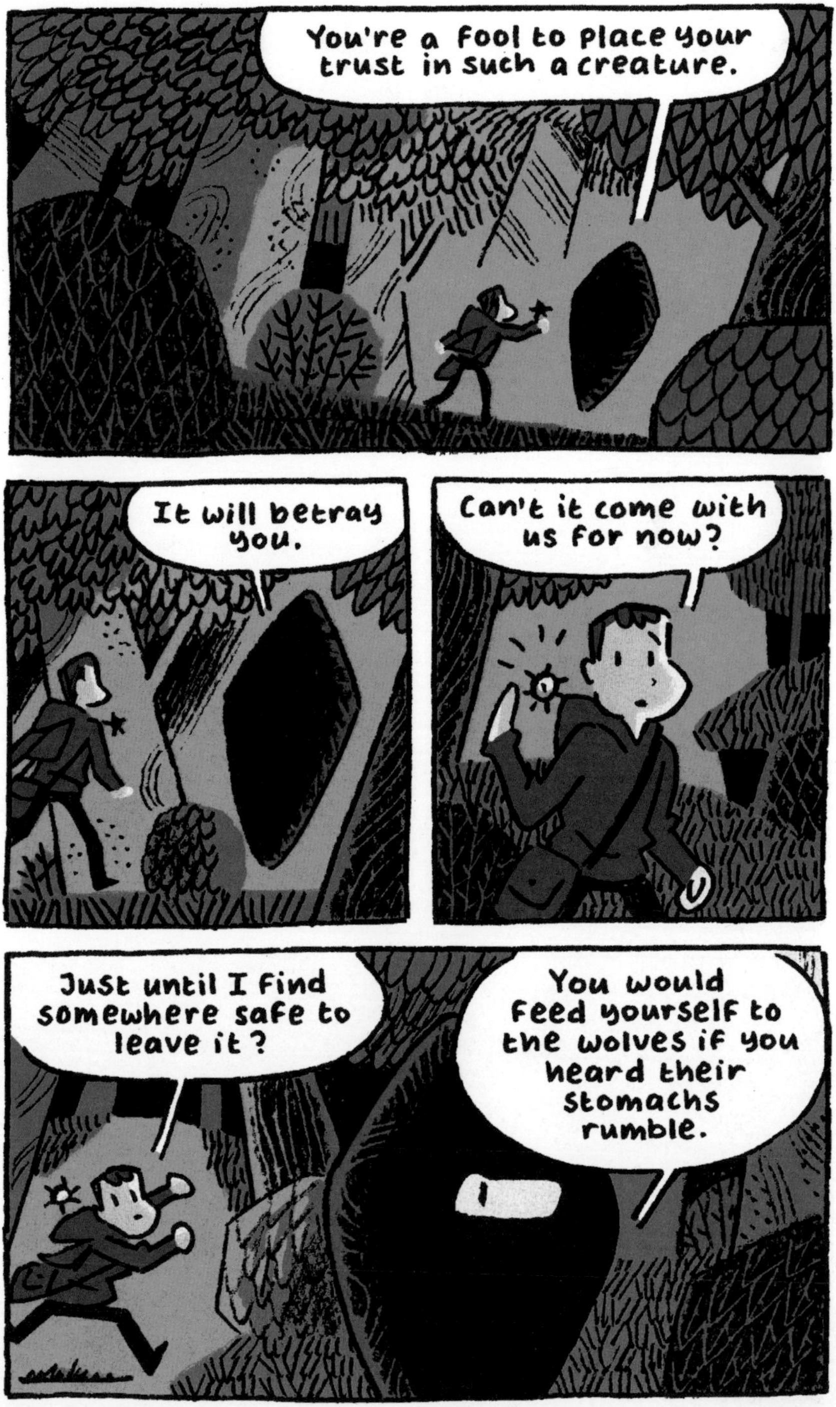
You're a fool to place your trust in such a creature.
It will betray you.
Can't it come with us for now?
Just until I find somewhere safe to leave it?
You would feed yourself to the wolves if you heard their stomachs rumble.

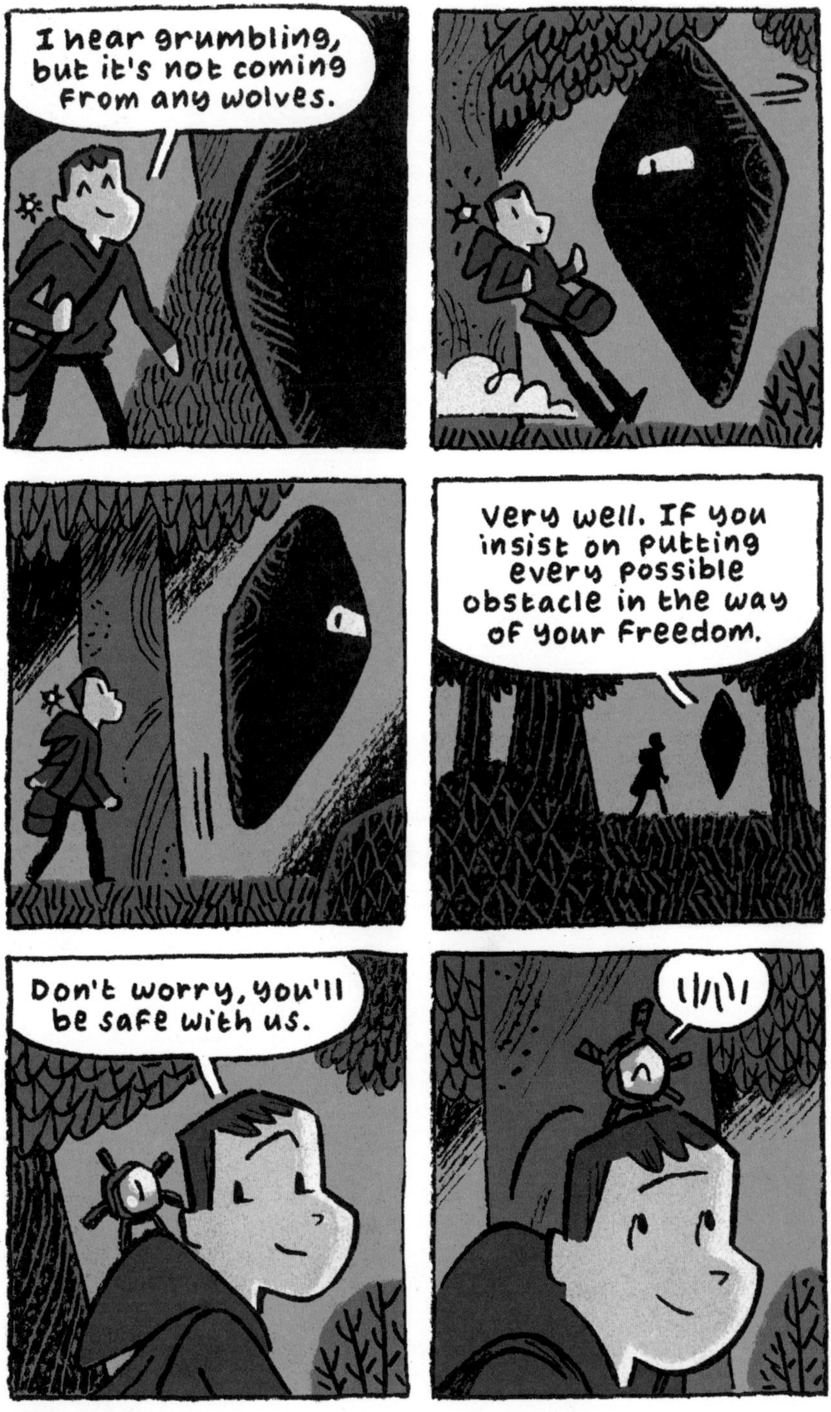
I hear grumbling, but it's not coming from any wolves.
Very well. If you insist on putting every possible obstacle in the way of your freedom.
Don't worry, you'll be safe with us.
|/|\|

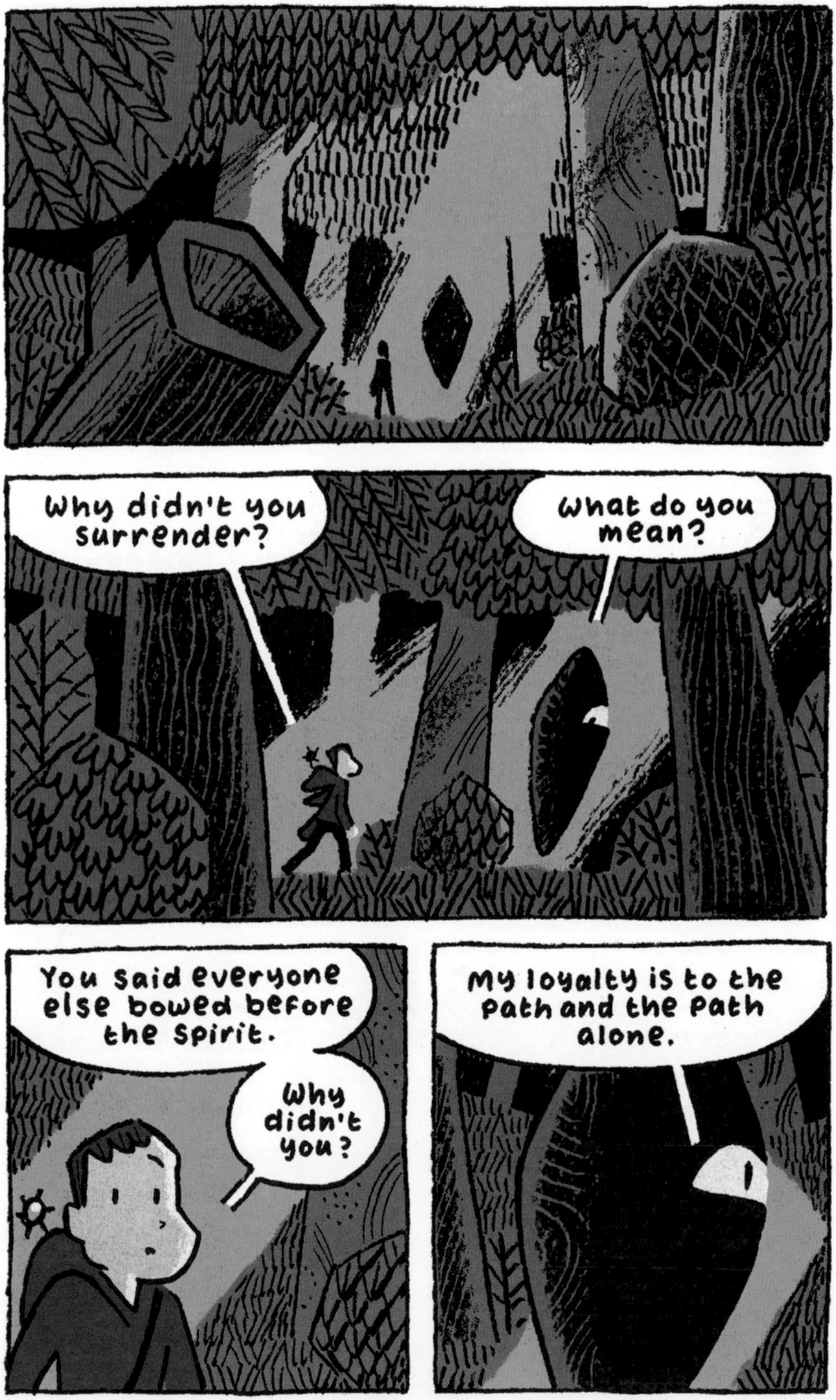
Why didn't you surrender?
What do you mean?
You said everyone else bowed before the spirit.
Why didn't you?
My loyalty is to the path and the path alone.

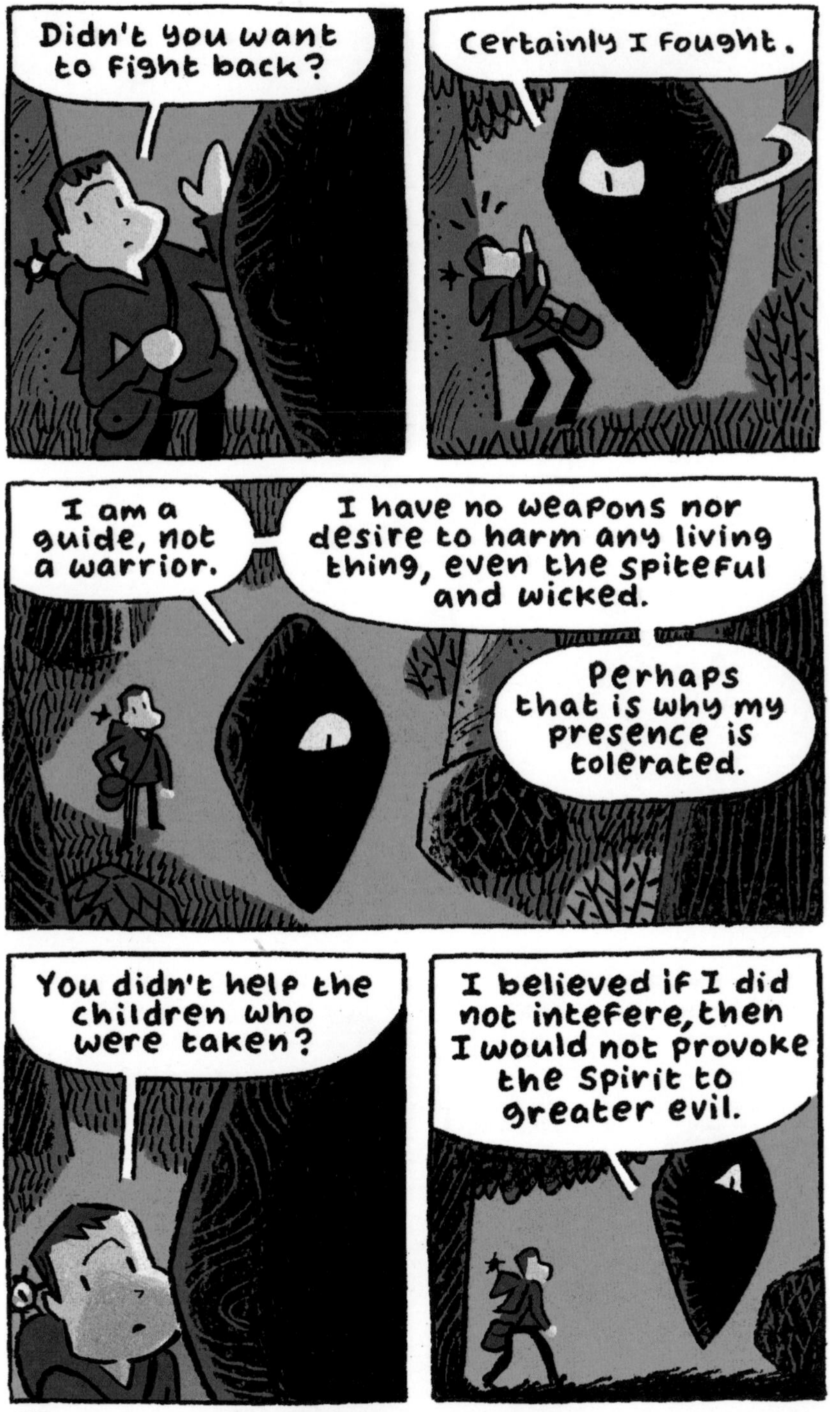

Didn't you want to fight back?
Certainly I fought.
I am a guide, not a warrior.
I have no weapons nor desire to harm any living thing, even the spiteful and wicked.
Perhaps that is why my presence is tolerated.
You didn't help the children who were taken?
I believed if I did not intefere, then I would not provoke the Spirit to greater evil.

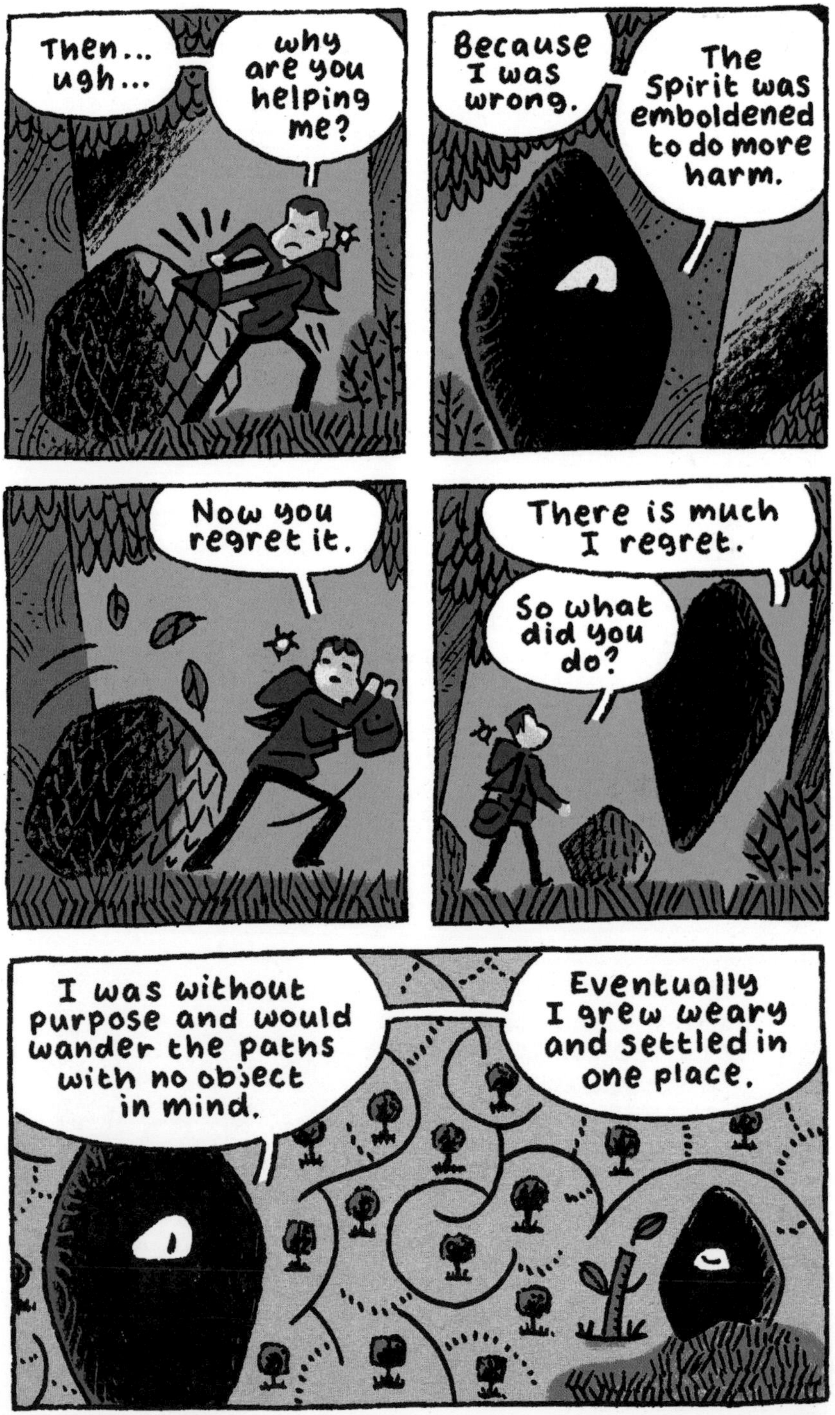
Then... ugh...
why are you helping me?
Because I was wrong.
The Spirit was emboldened to do more harm.
Now you regret it.
There is much I regret.
So what did you do?
I was without purpose and would wander the paths with no object in mind.
Eventually I grew weary and settled in one place.

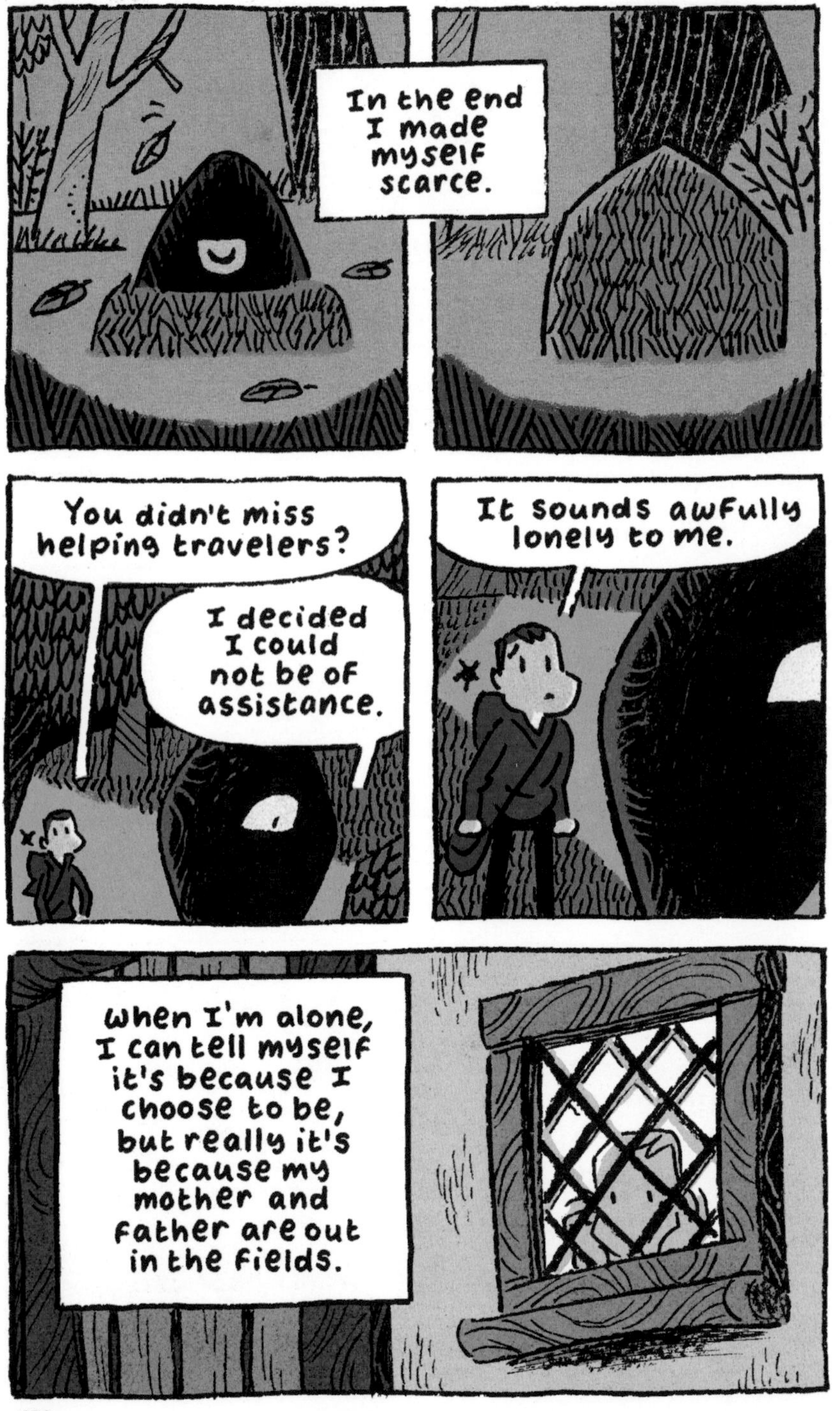

In the end I made myself scarce.
You didn't miss helping travelers?
I decided I could not be of assistance.
It sounds awfully lonely to me.
When I'm alone, I can tell myself it's because I choose to be, but really it's because my mother and father are out in the fields.

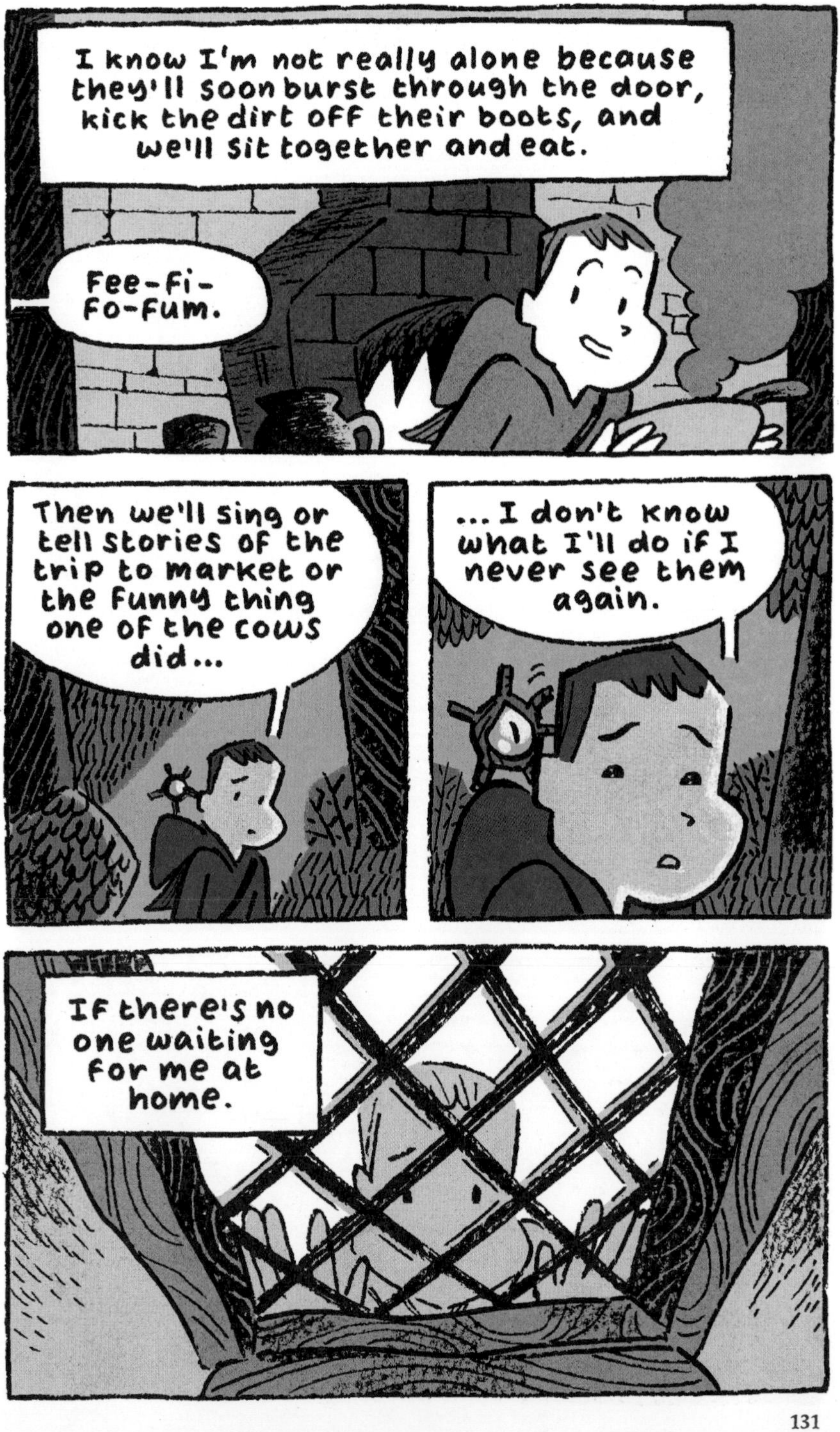
I know I'm not really alone because they'll soon burst through the door, kick the dirt off their boots, and we'll sit together and eat.
Fee-Fi-Fo-Fum.
Then we'll sing or tell stories of the trip to market or the funny thing one of the cows did...
...I don't know what I'll do if I never see them again.
If there's no one waiting for me at home.

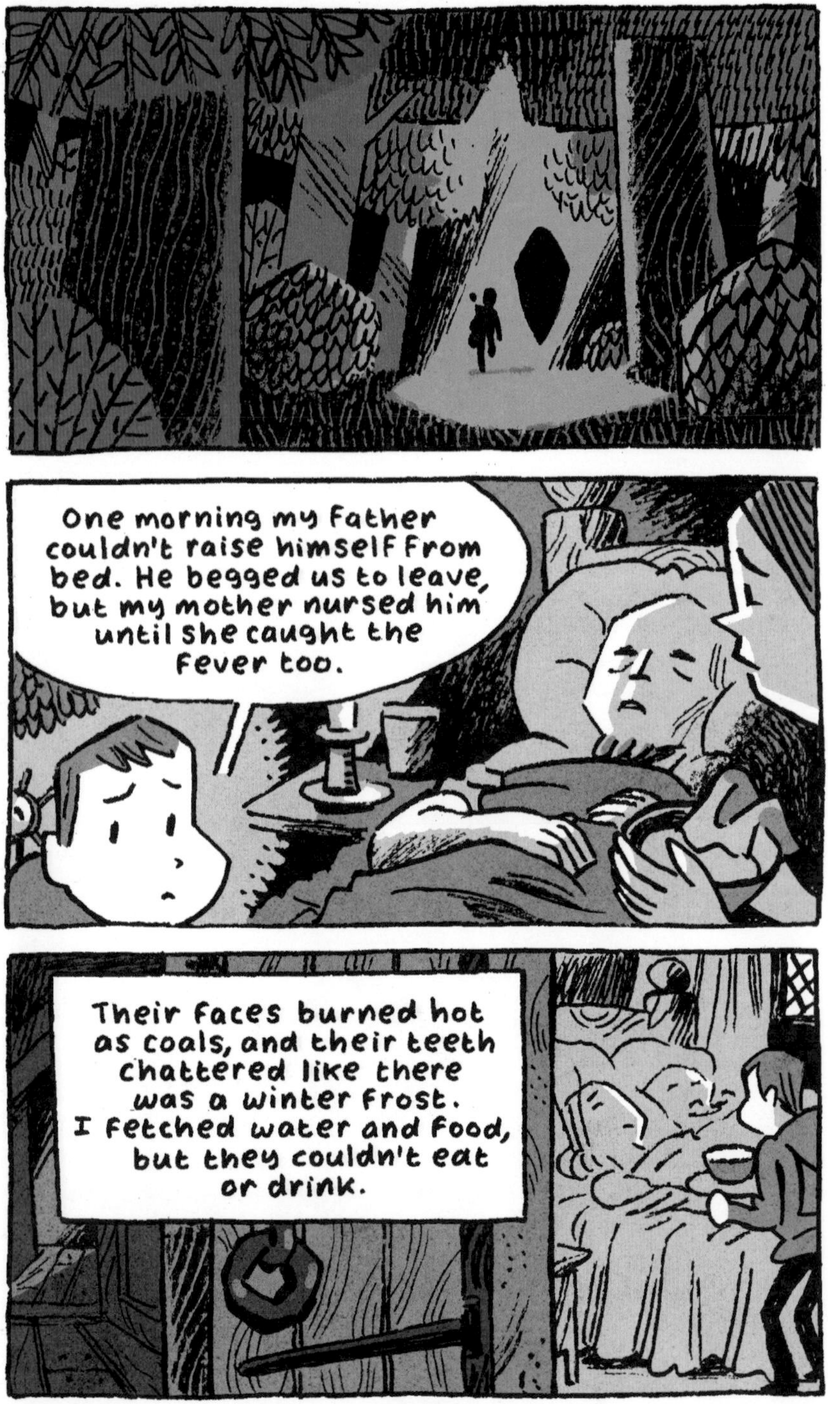
One morning my father couldn't raise himself from bed. He begged us to leave, but my mother nursed him until she caught the fever too.
Their faces burned hot as coals, and their teeth chattered like there was a winter frost. I fetched water and food, but they couldn't eat or drink.

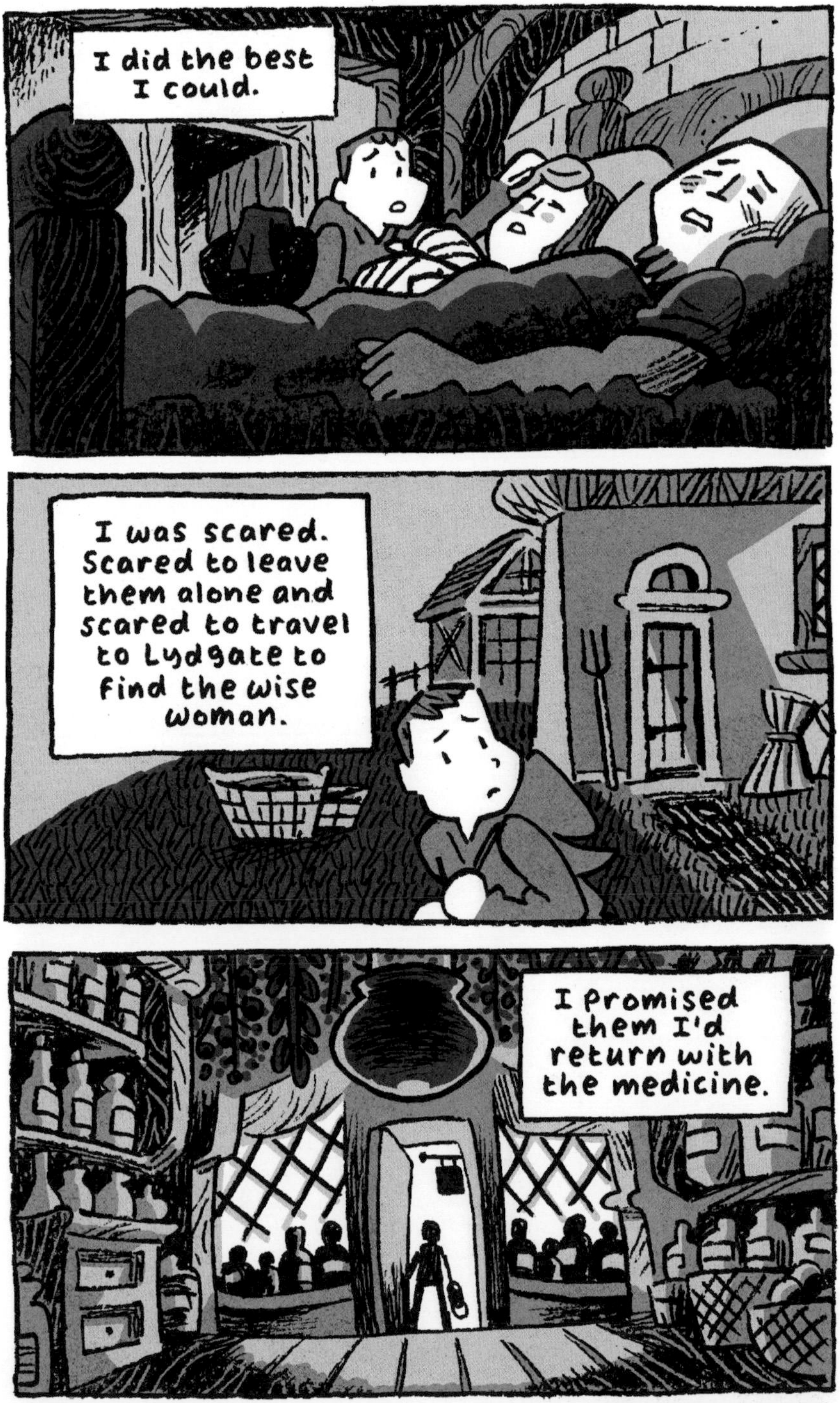
I did the best I could.
I was scared. Scared to leave them alone and scared to travel to Lydgate to find the wise woman.
I promised them I'd return with the medicine.

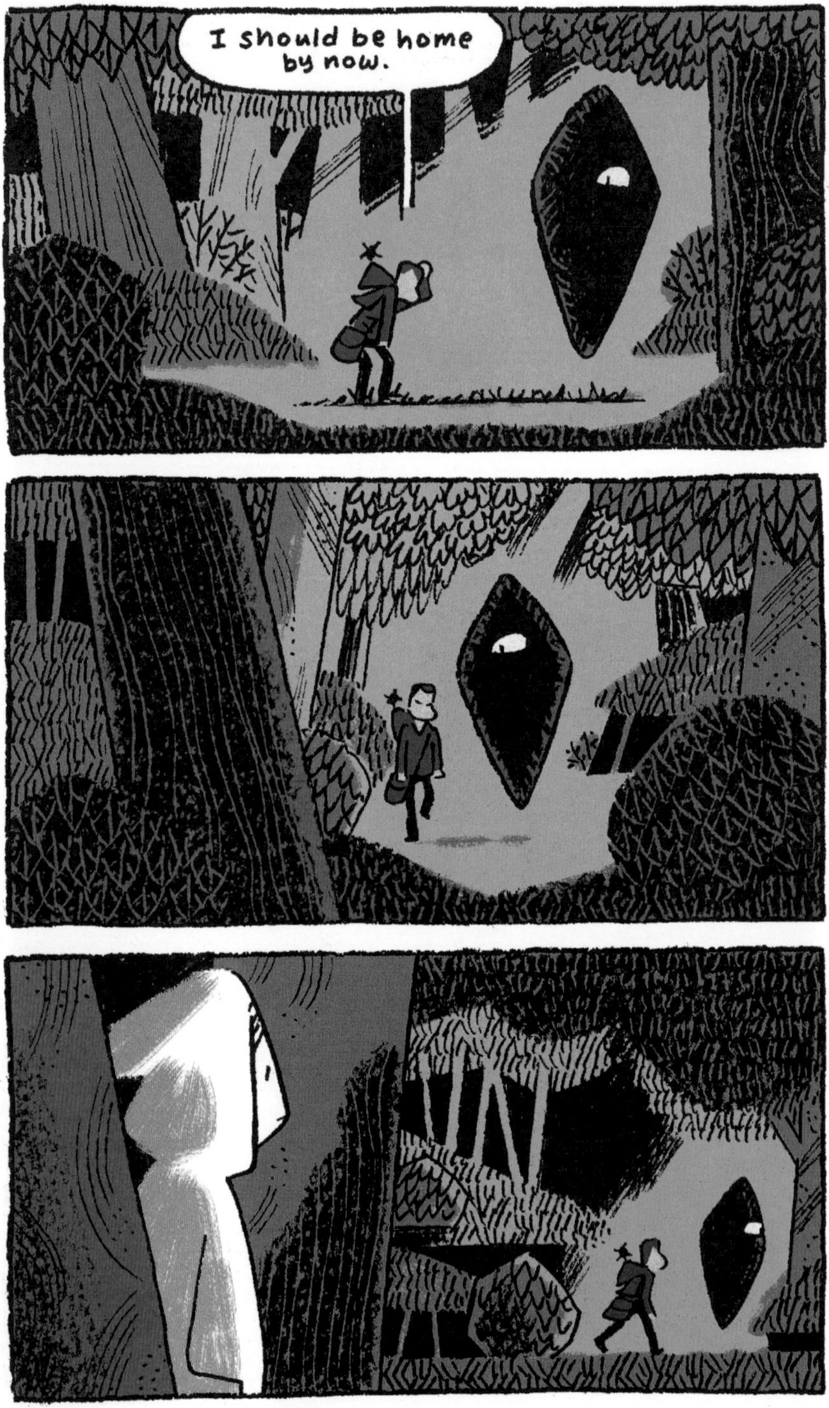
I should be home by now.

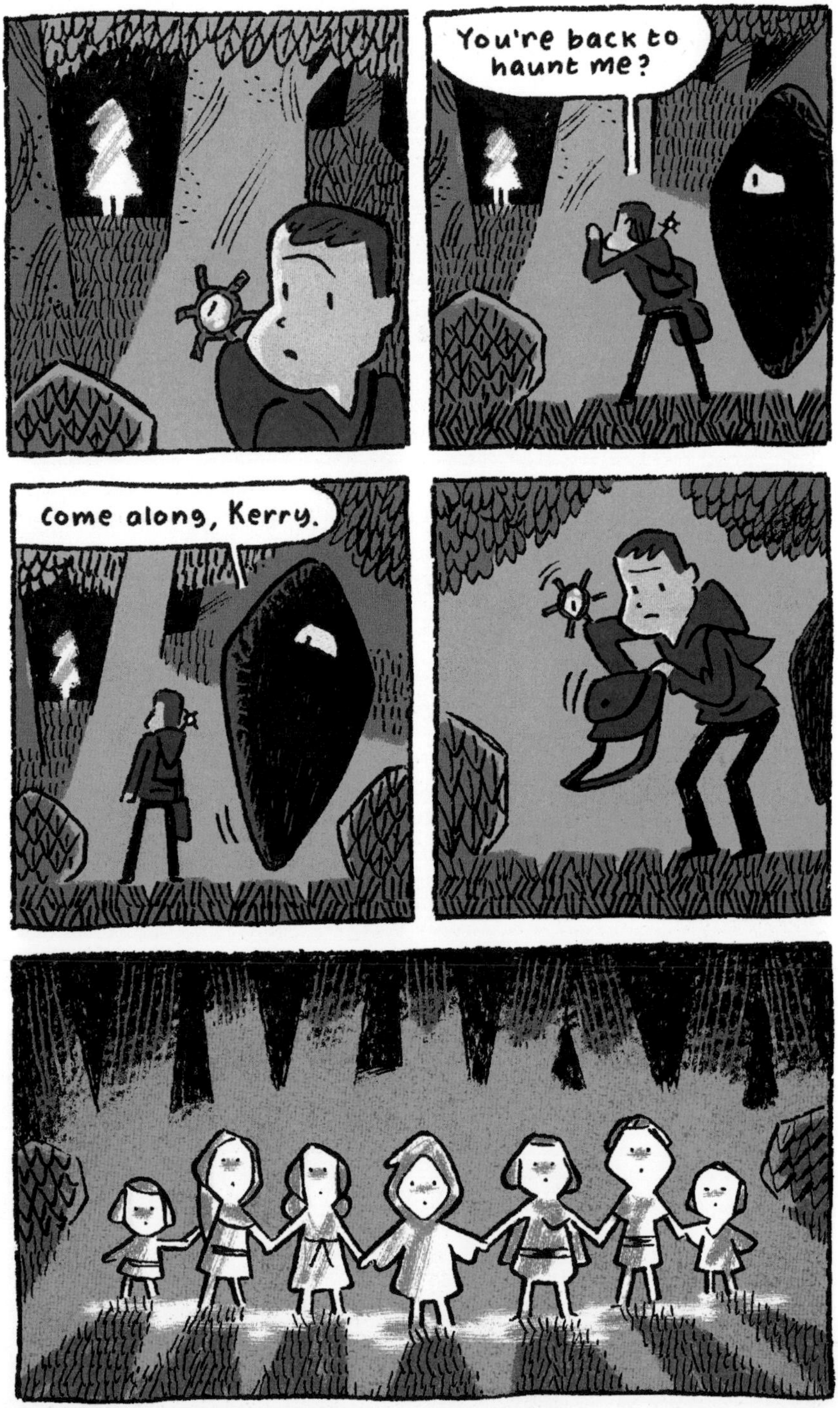
You're back to haunt me?
Come along, Kerry.

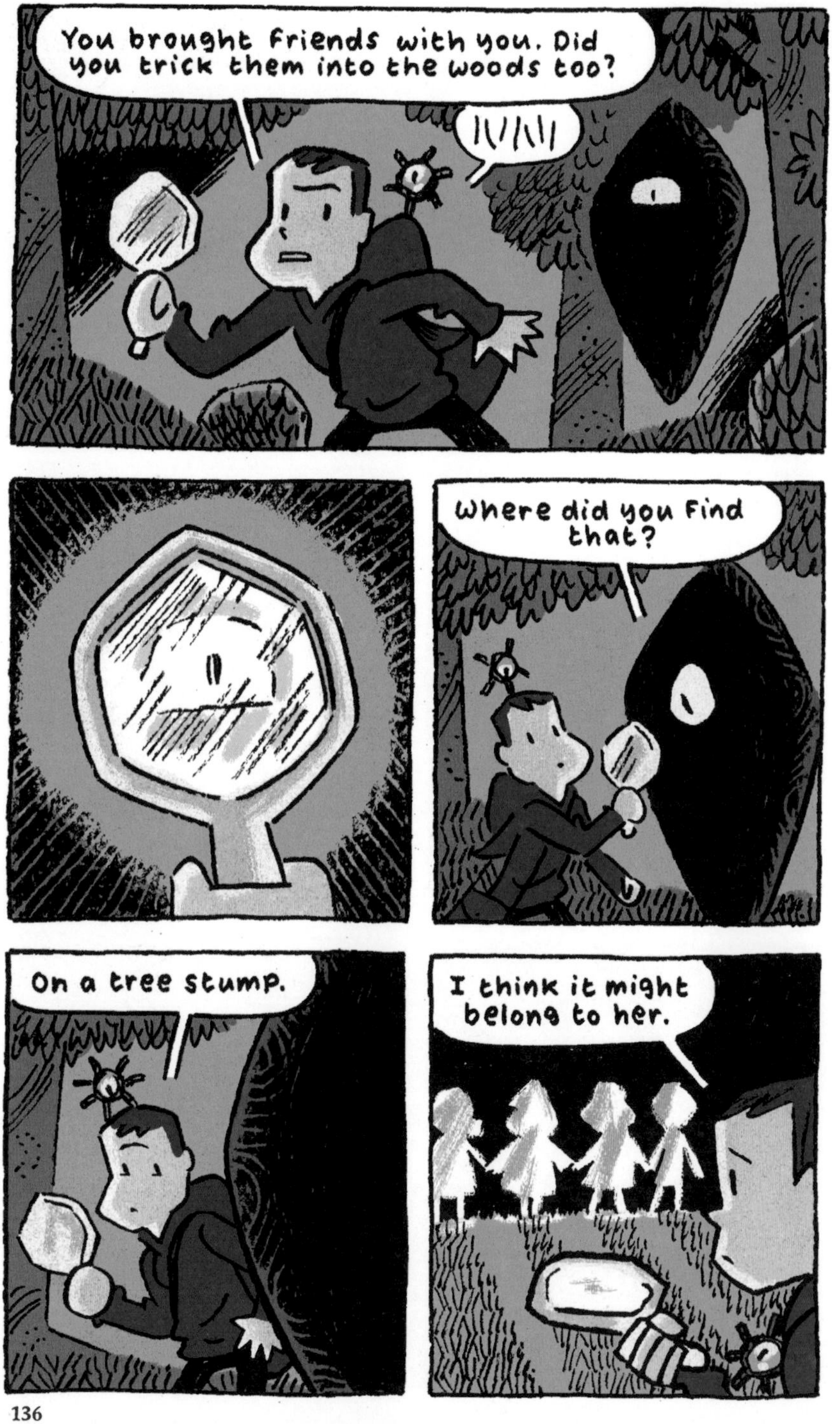
You brought friends with you. Did you trick them into the woods too?
Where did you find that?
On a tree stump.
I think it might belong to her.

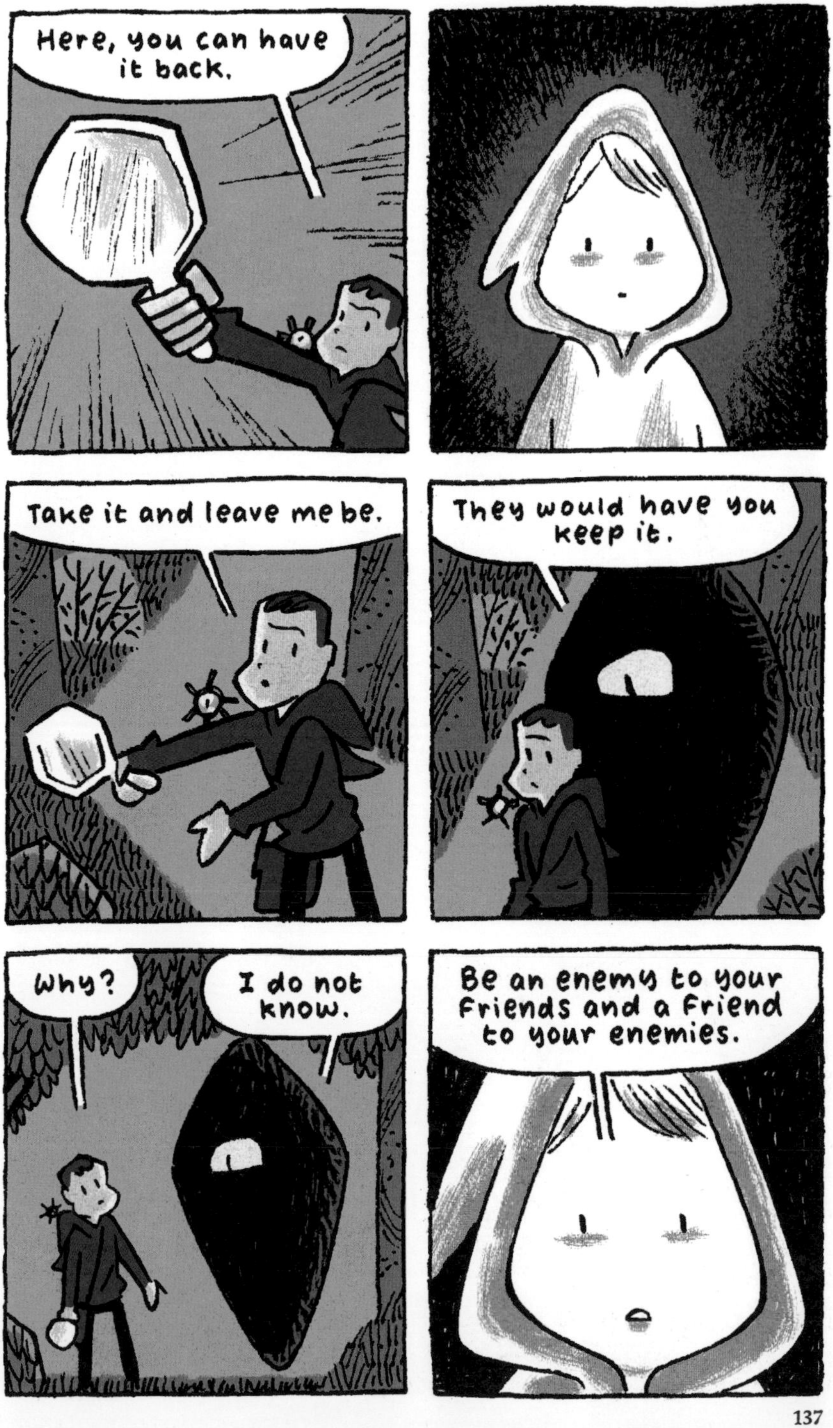
Here, you can have it back.
Take it and leave me be.
They would have you keep it.
Why?
I do not know.
Be an enemy to your friends and a friend to your enemies.

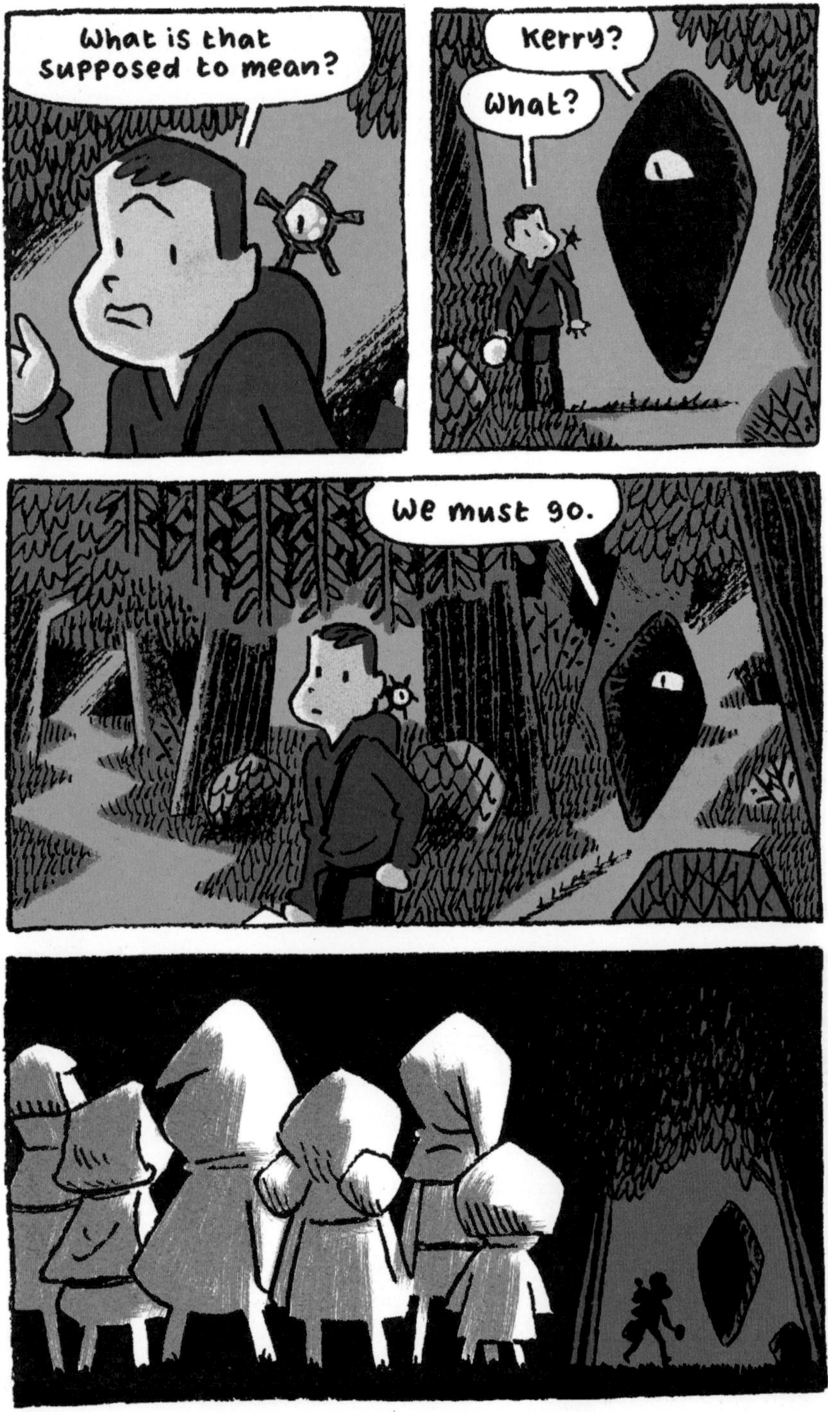
What is that supposed to mean?
Kerry?
What?
We must go.

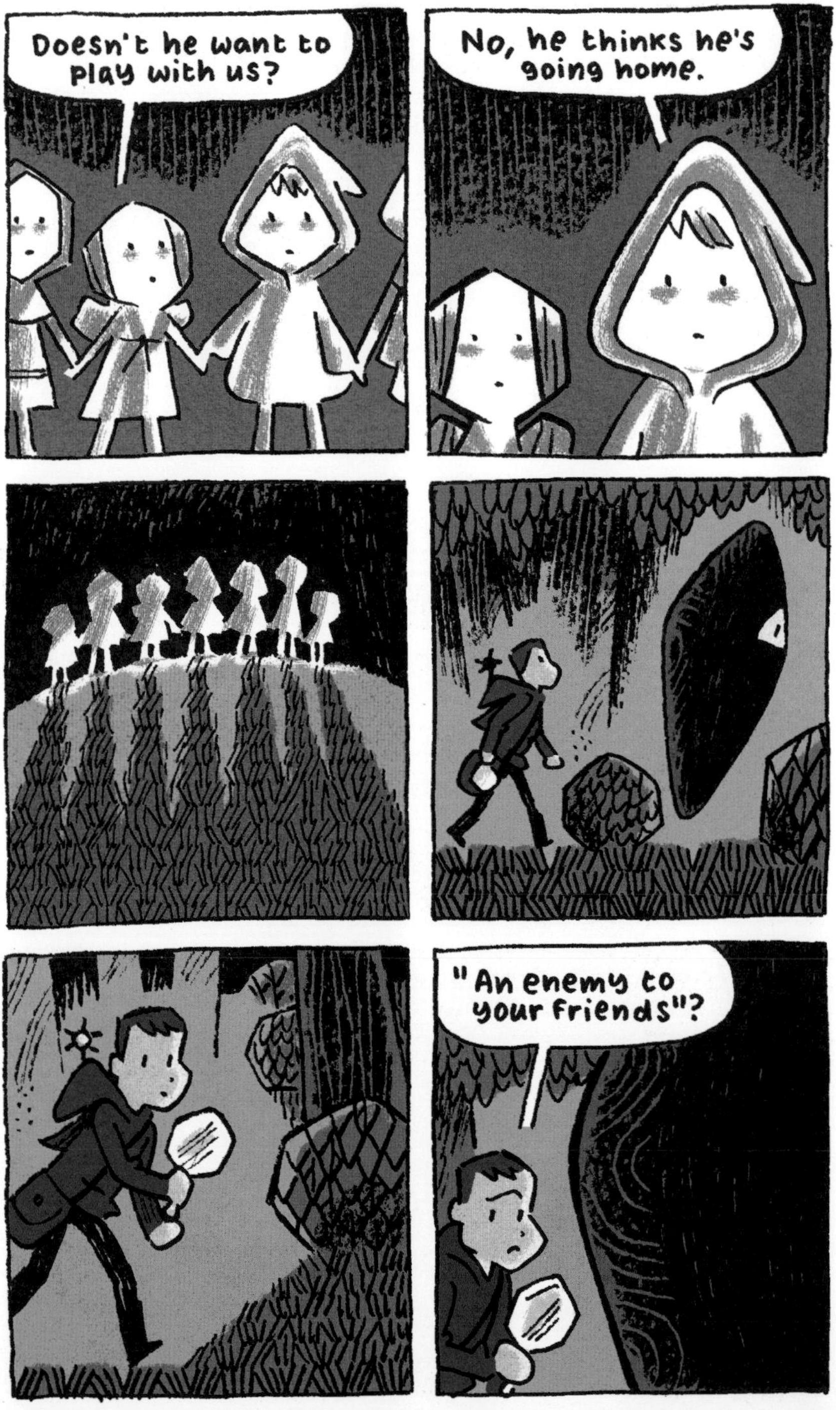
Doesn't he want to play with us?
No, he thinks he's going home.
"An enemy to your friends"?

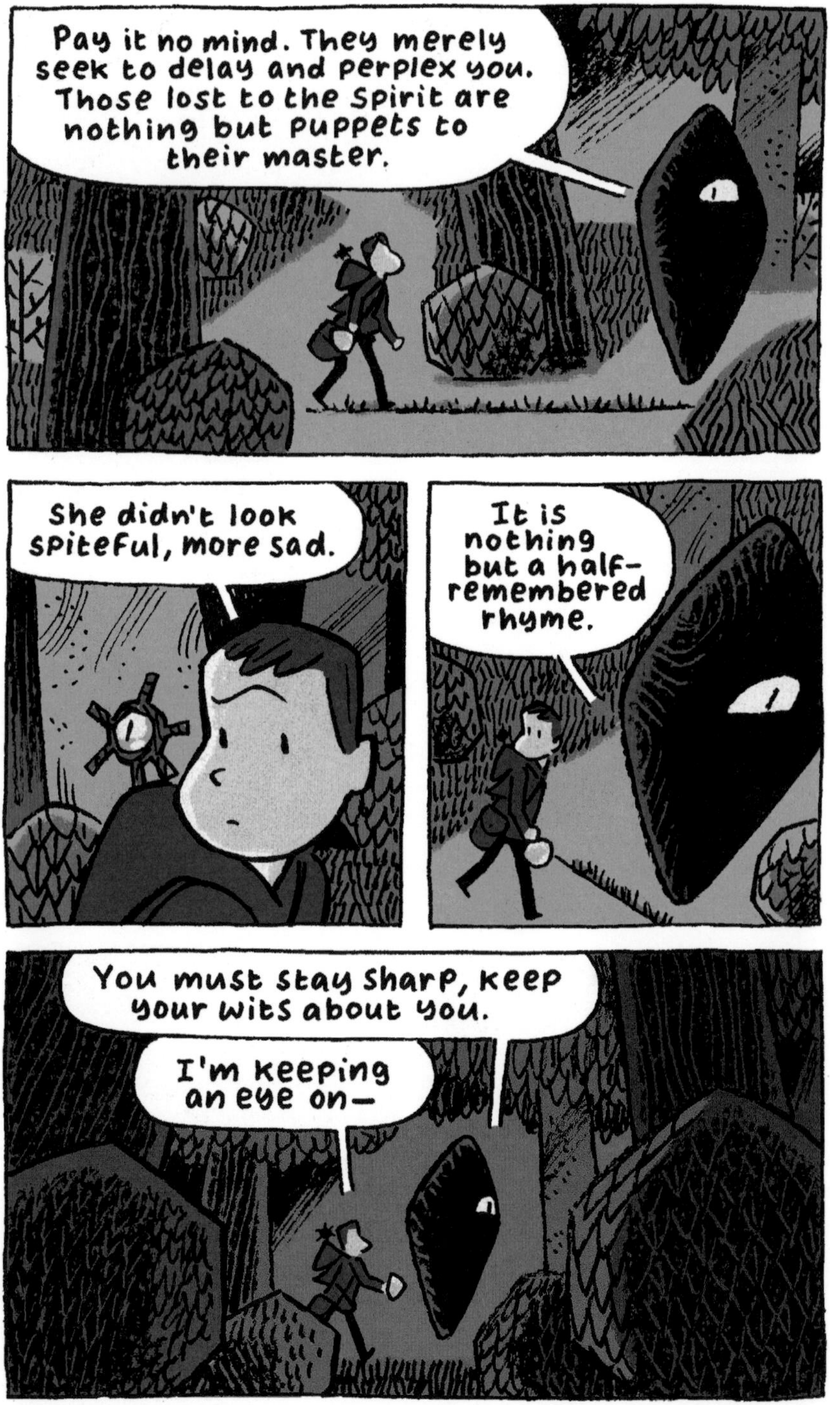
Pay it no mind. They merely seek to delay and perplex you. Those lost to the Spirit are nothing but puppets to their master.
She didn't look spiteful, more sad.
It is nothing but a half-remembered rhyme.
You must stay sharp, keep your wits about you.
I'm keeping an eye on—

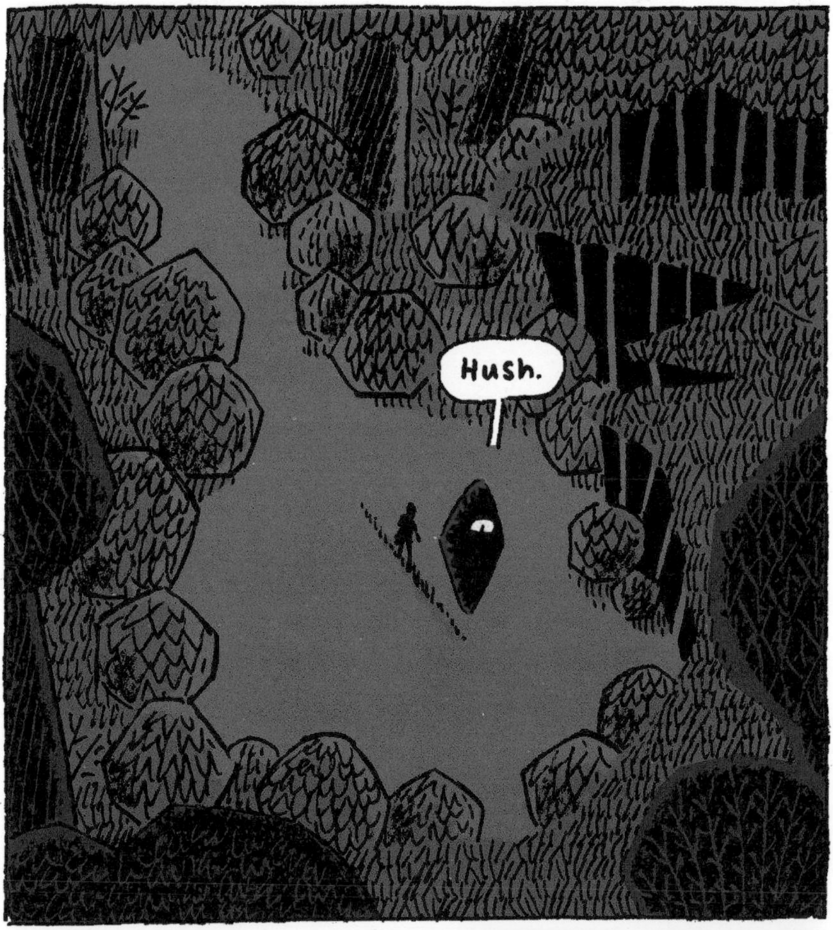
Hush.

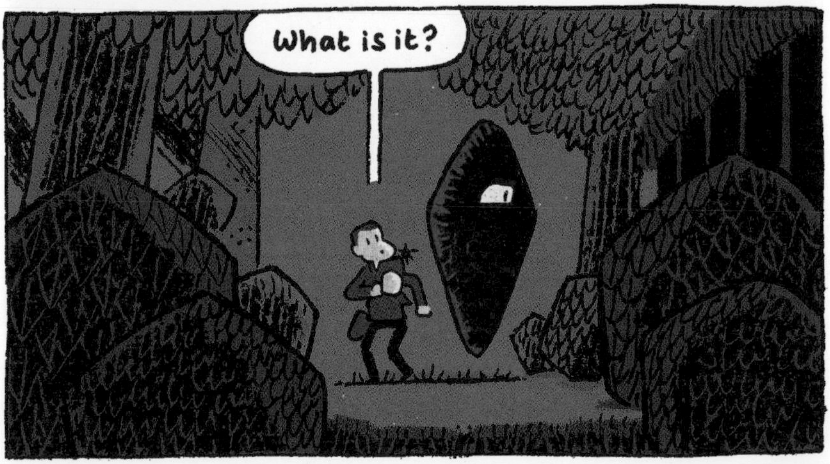
What is it?

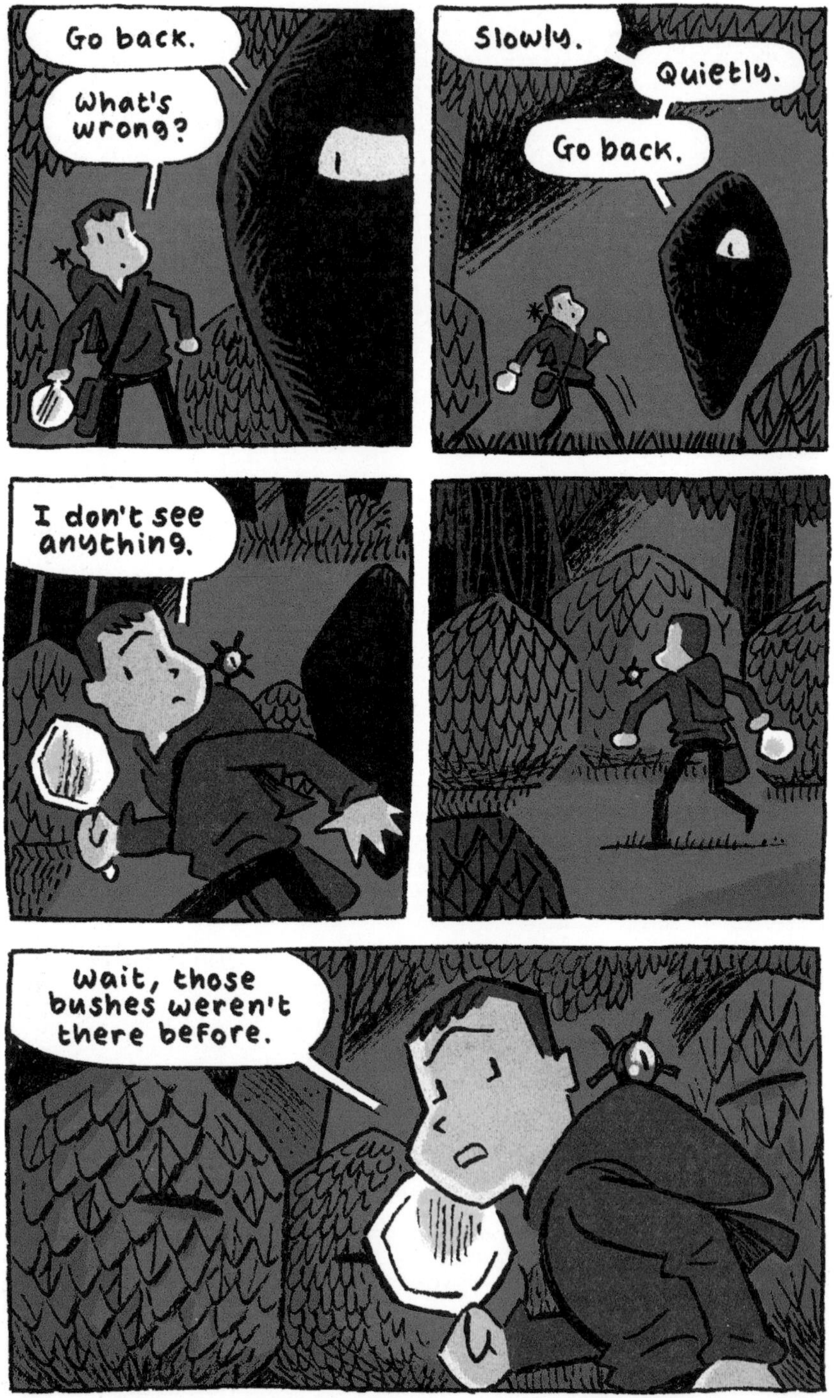
Go back.
What's wrong?
Slowly.
Quietly.
Go back.
I don't see anything.
Wait, those bushes weren't there before.

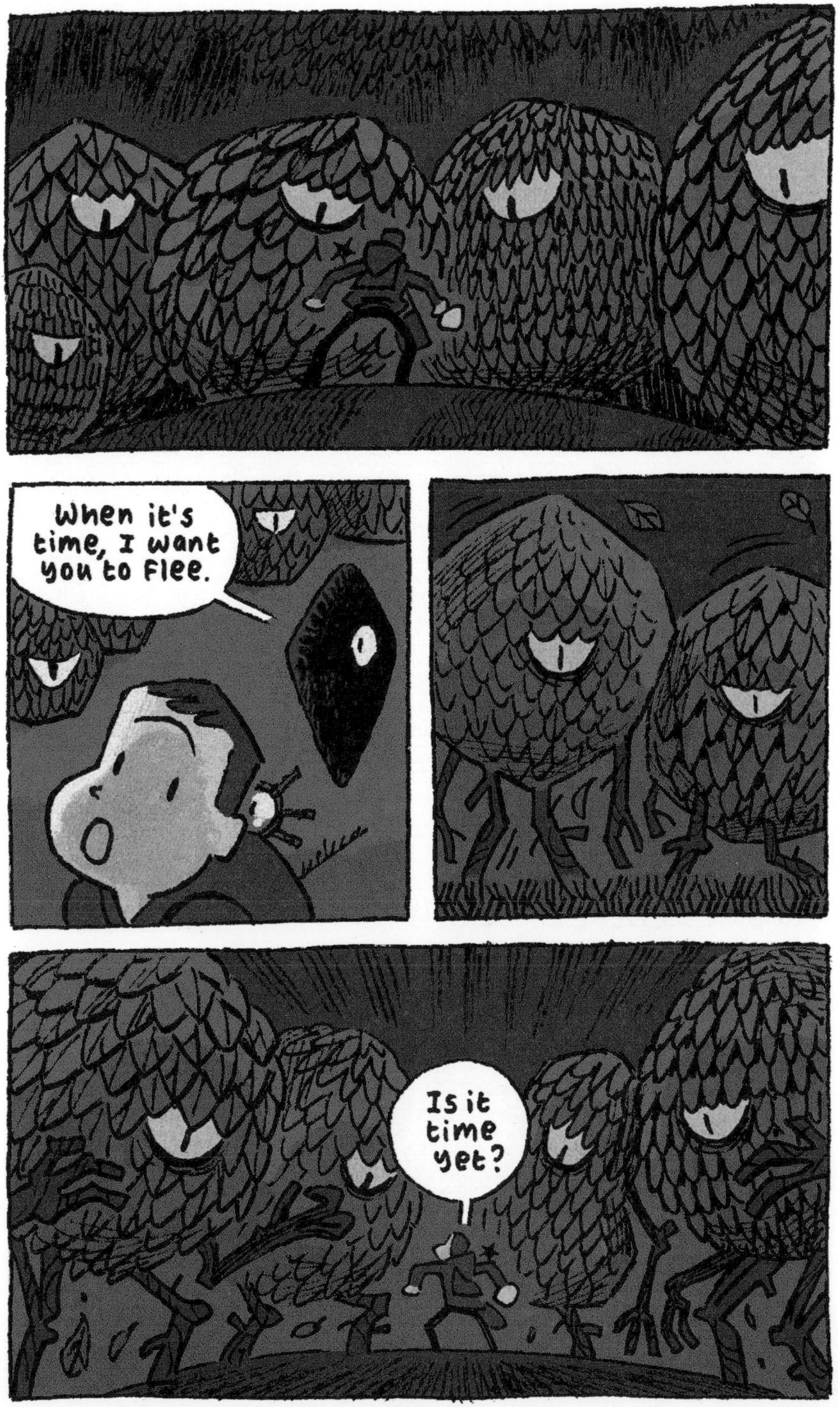
When it's time, I want you to flee.
Is it time yet?

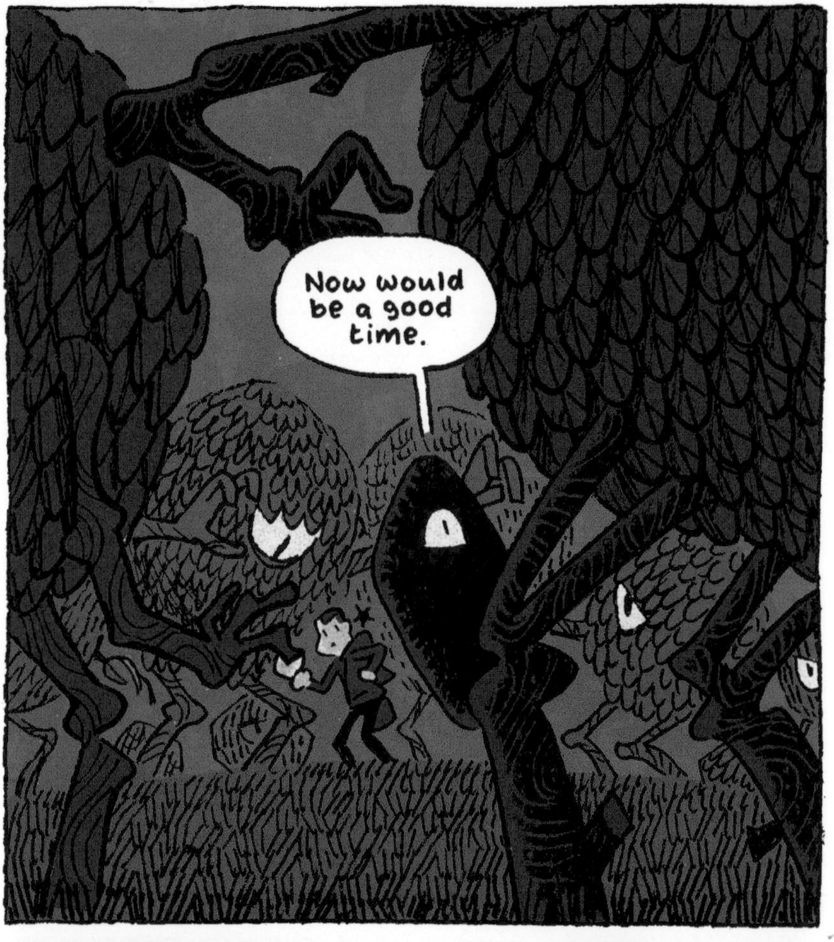
Now would be a good time.

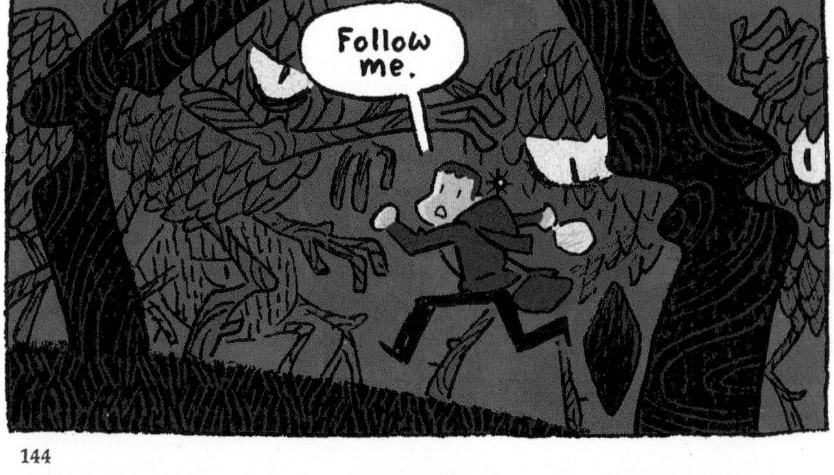
Follow me.

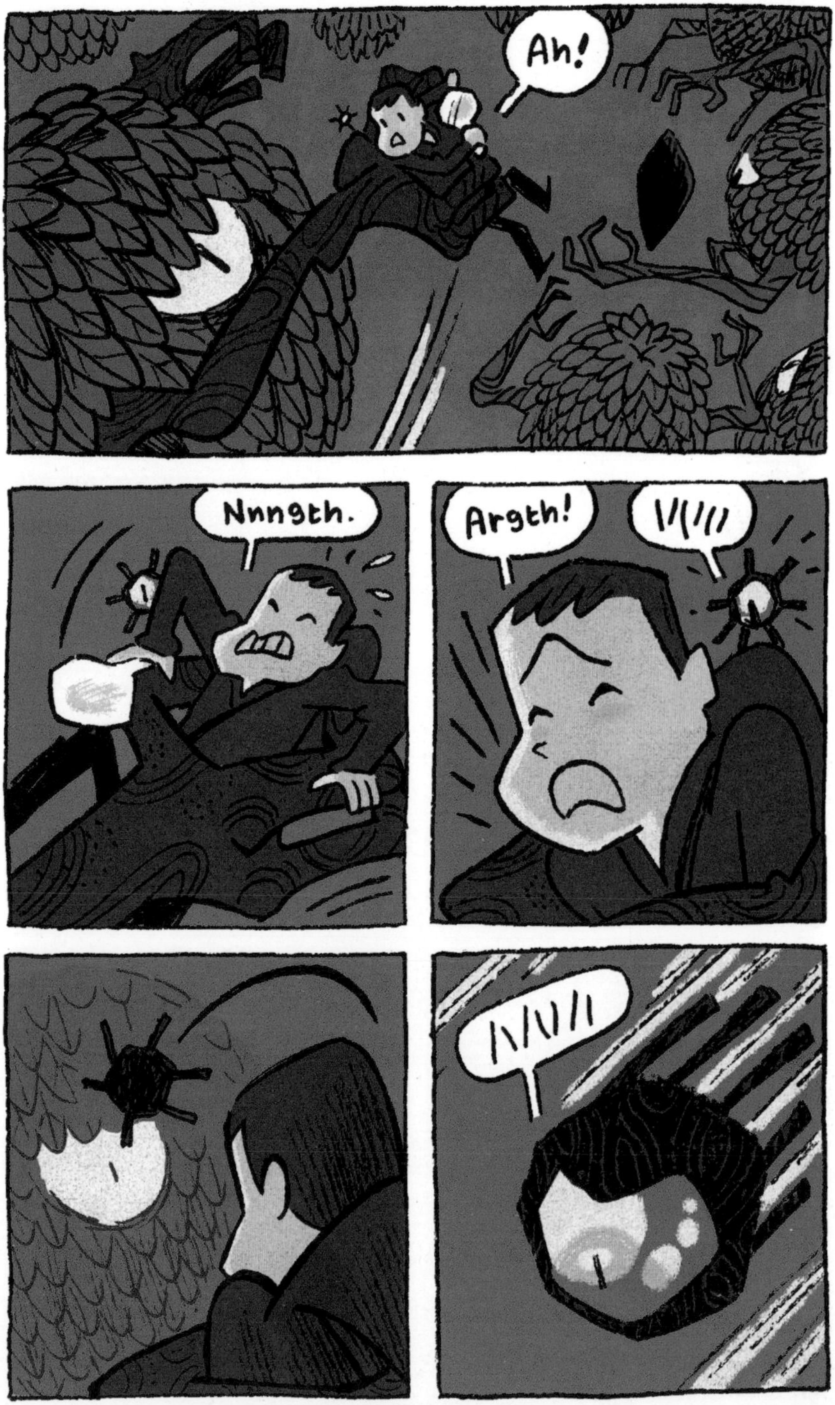
Ah!
Nnngth.
Argth!

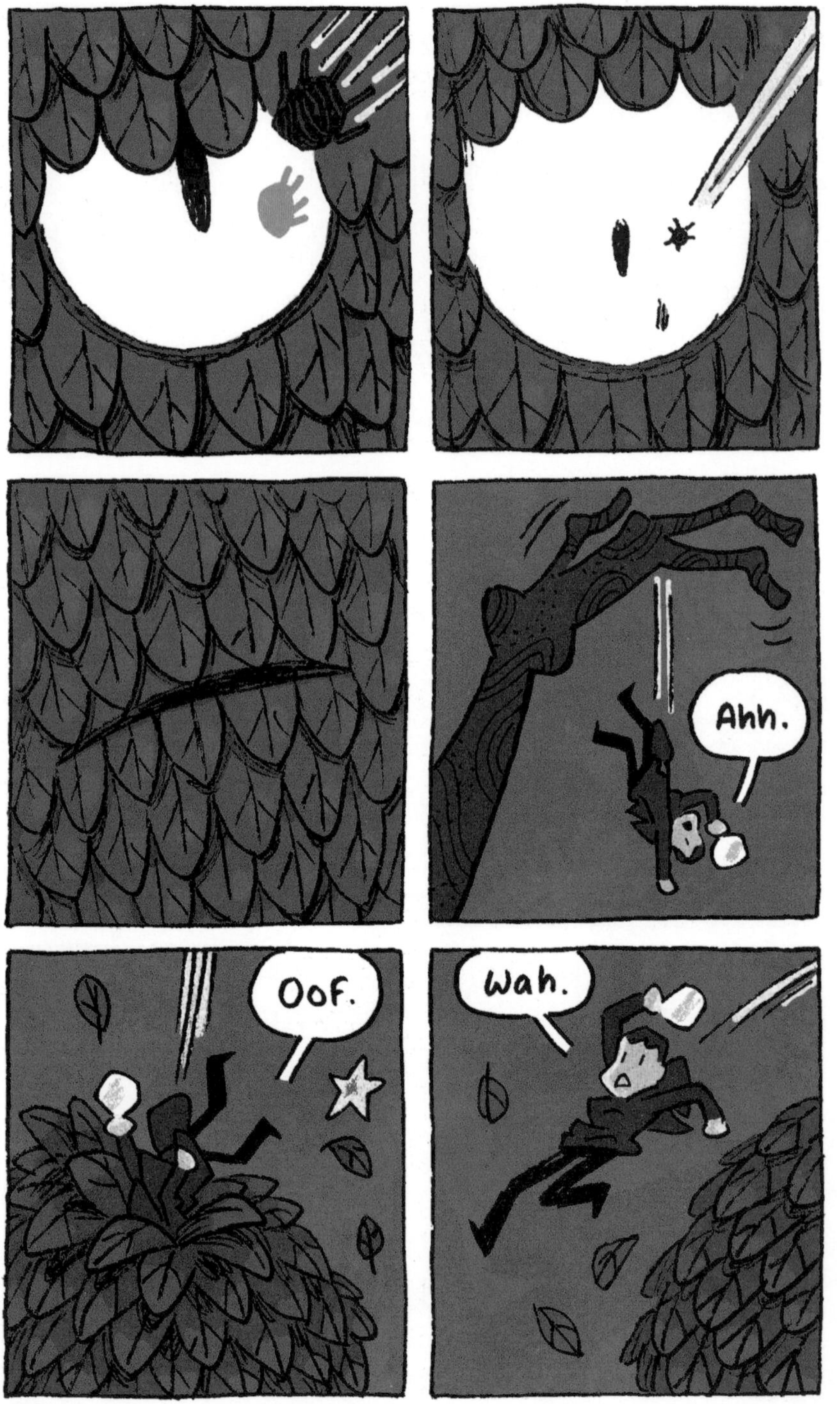
Ahh.
Oof.
Wah.

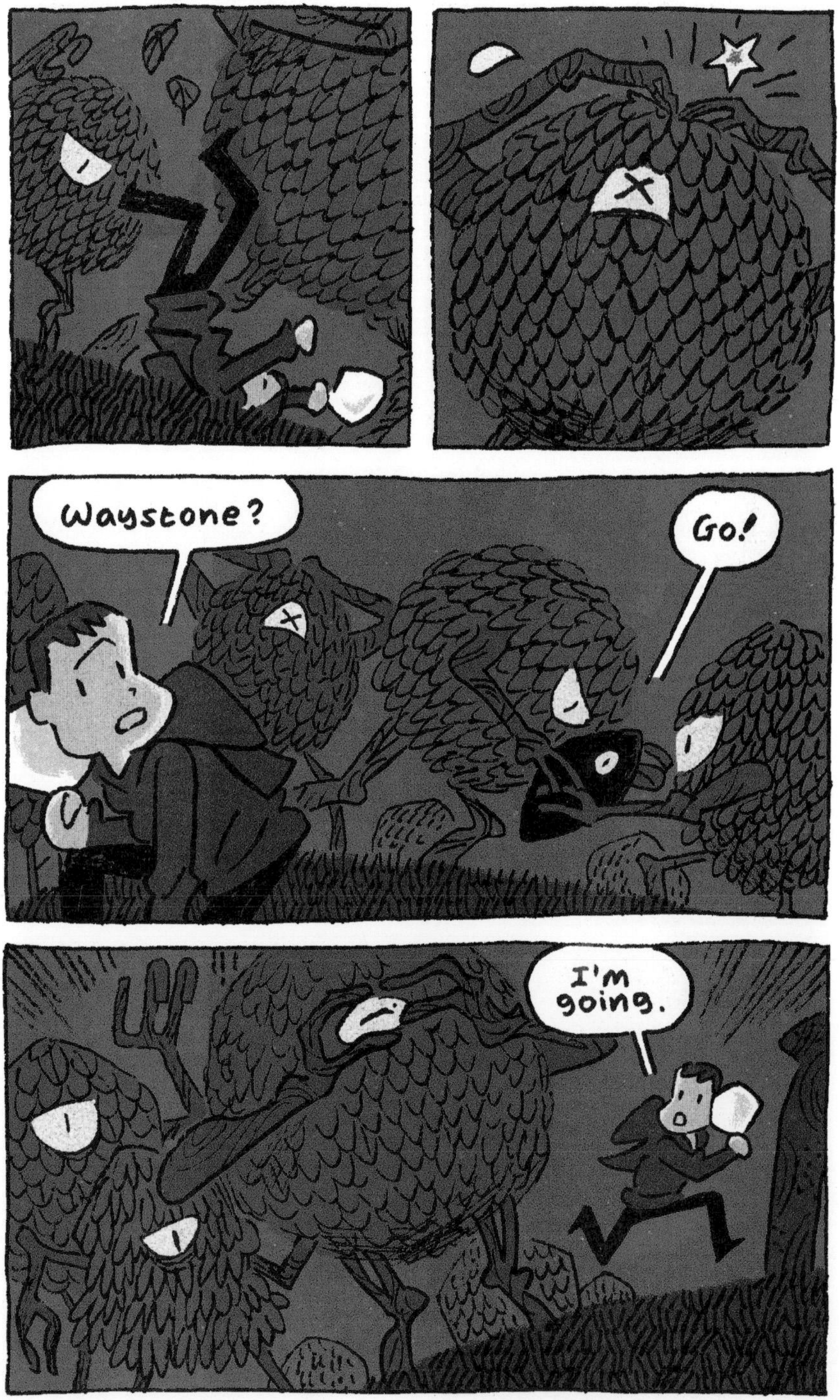
Waystone?
Go!
I'm going.

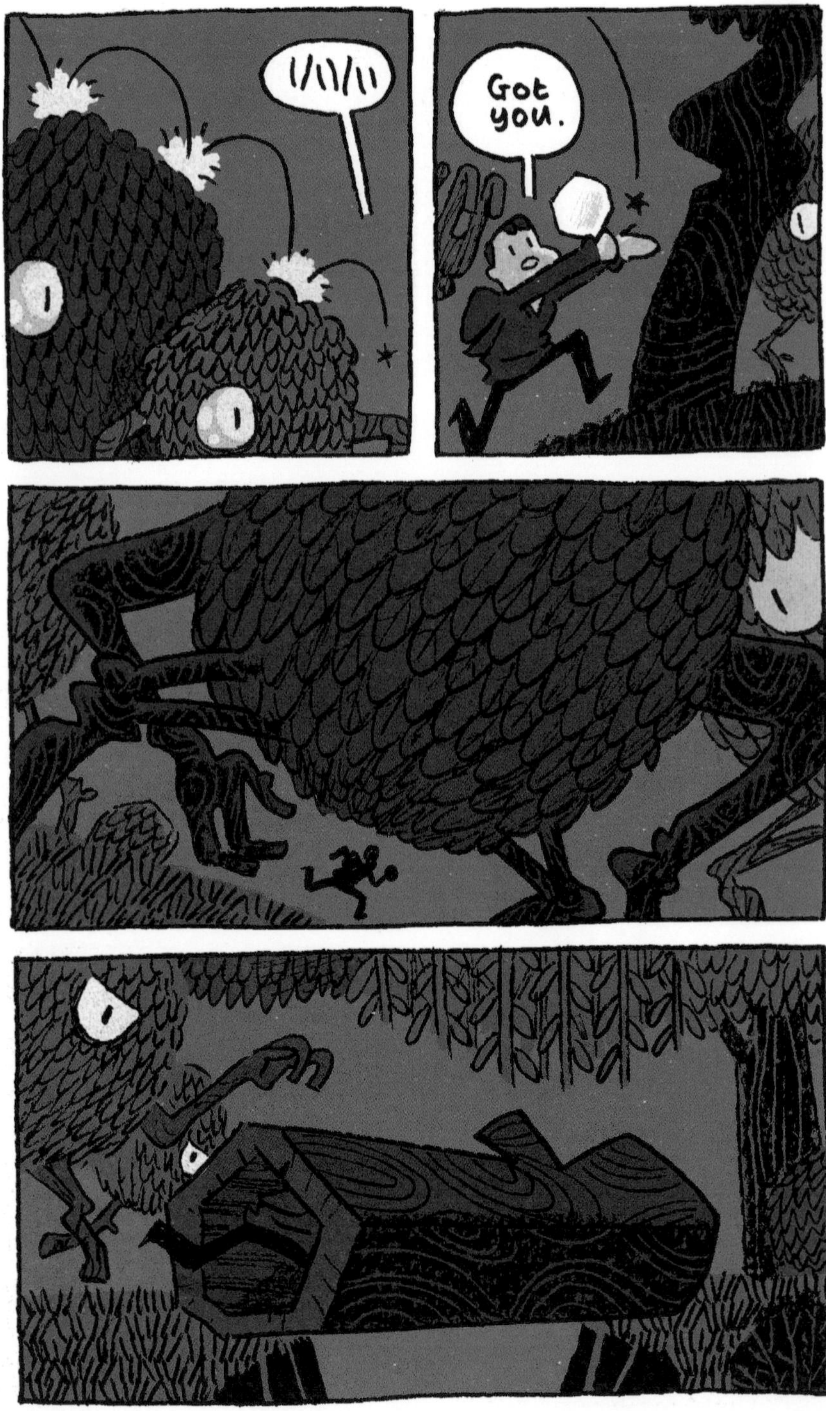
Got you.

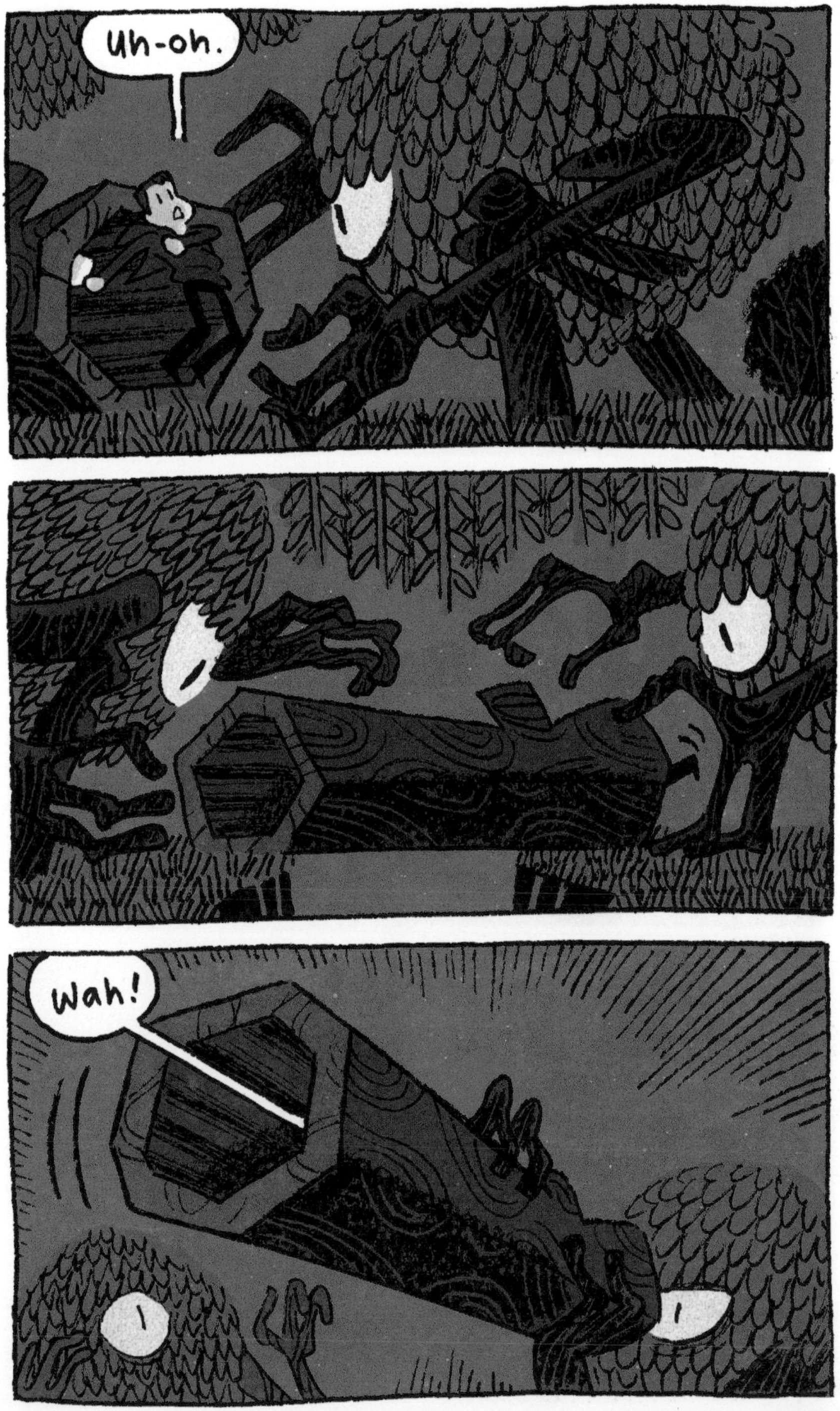
Uh-oh.
Wah!

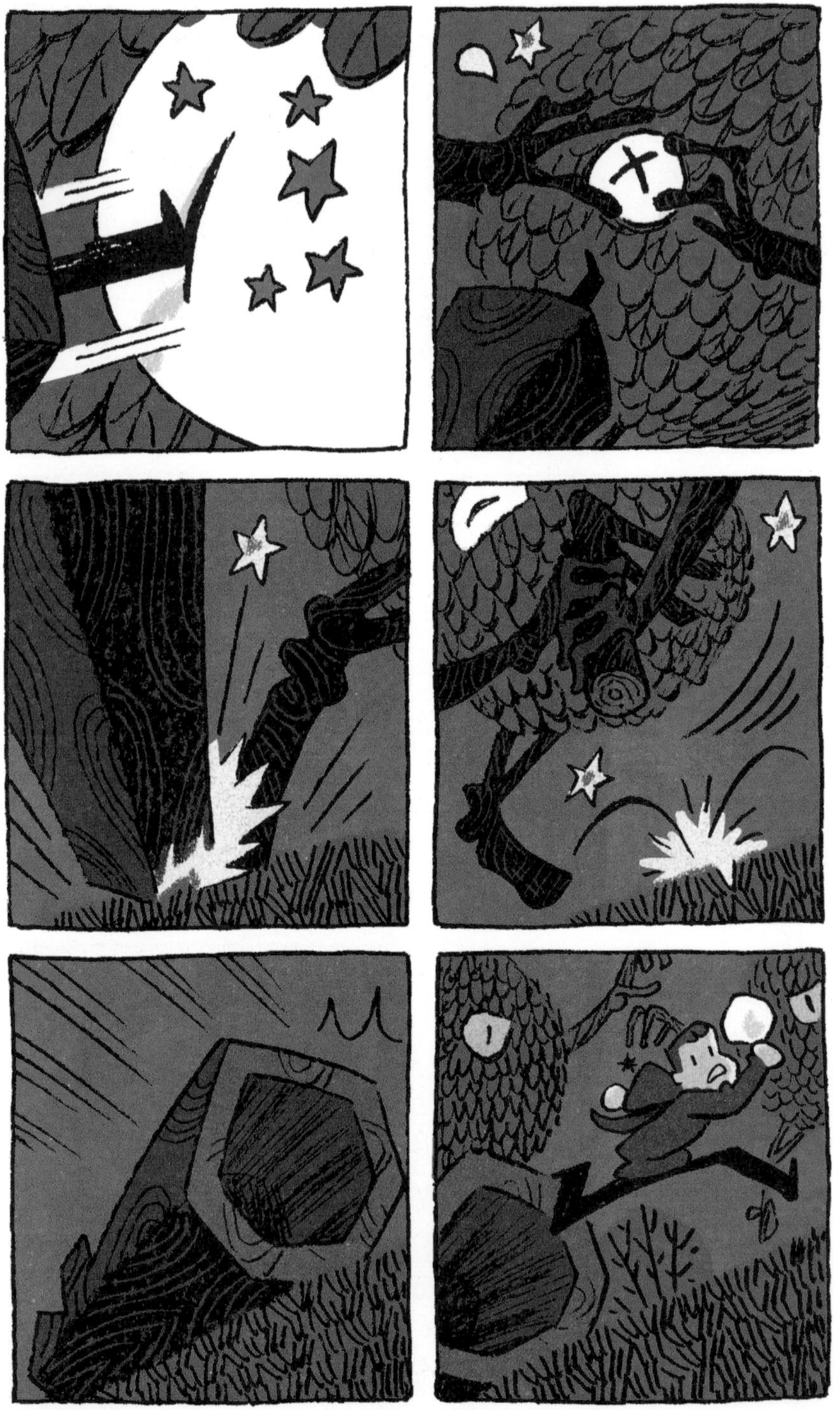

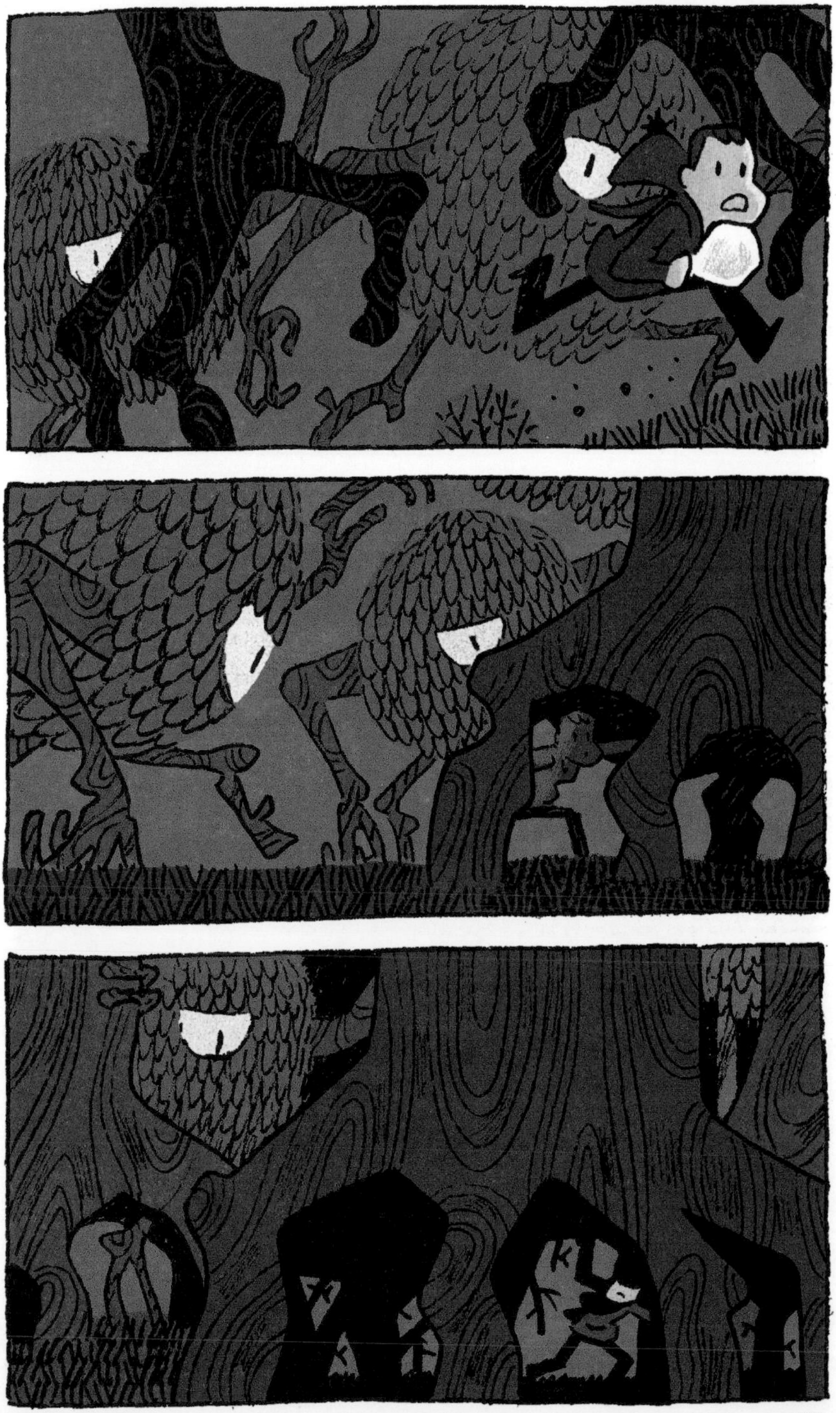

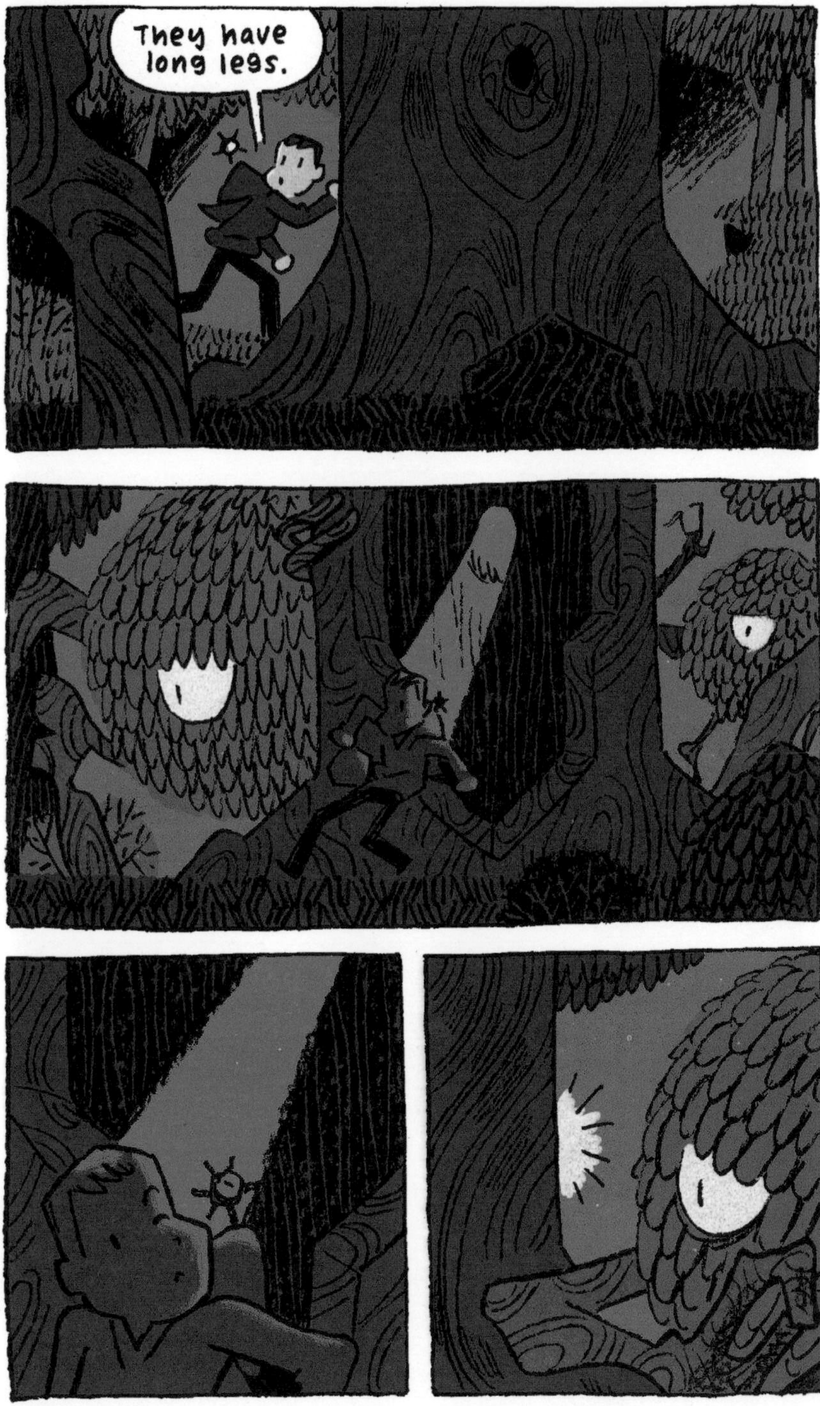
They have long legs.

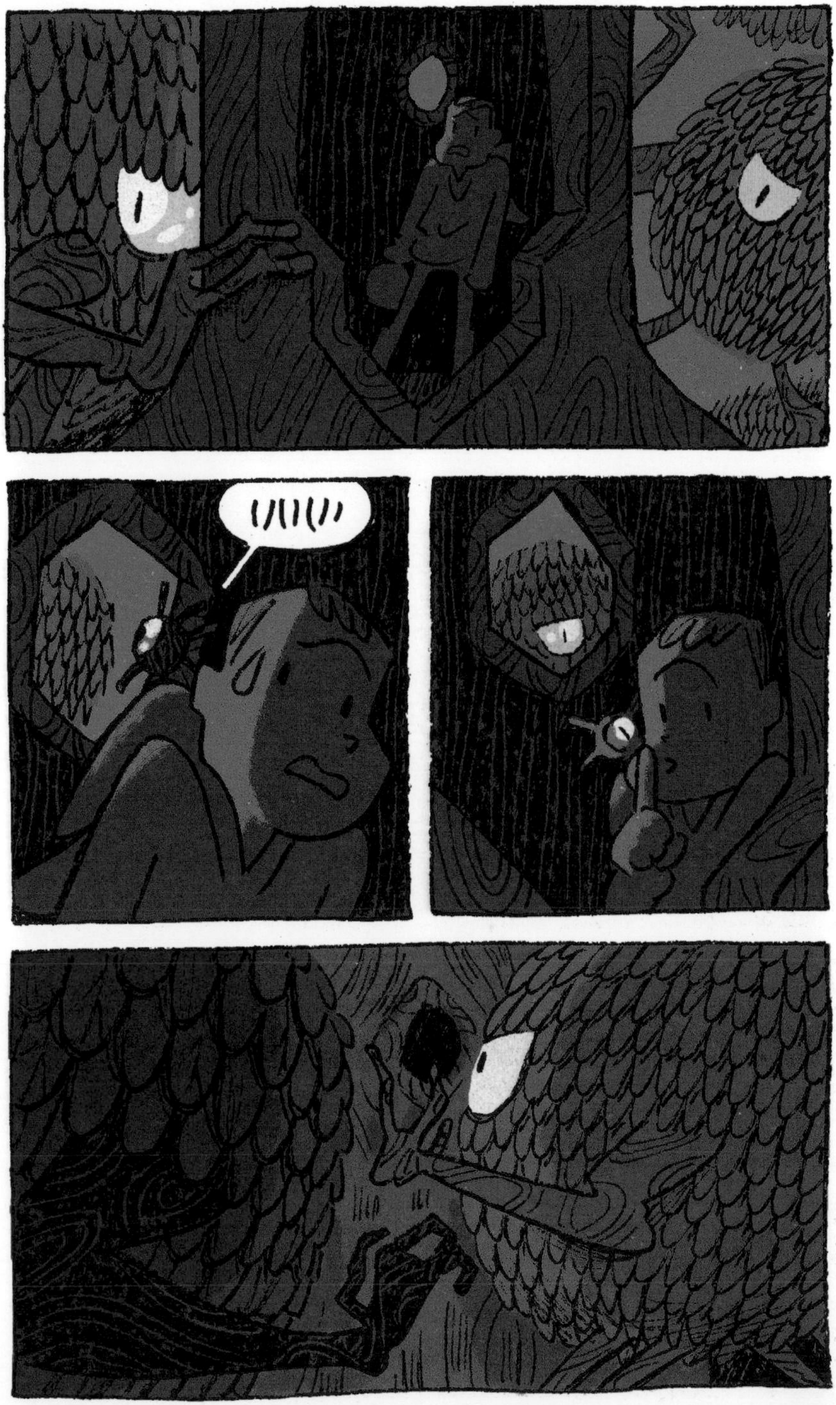

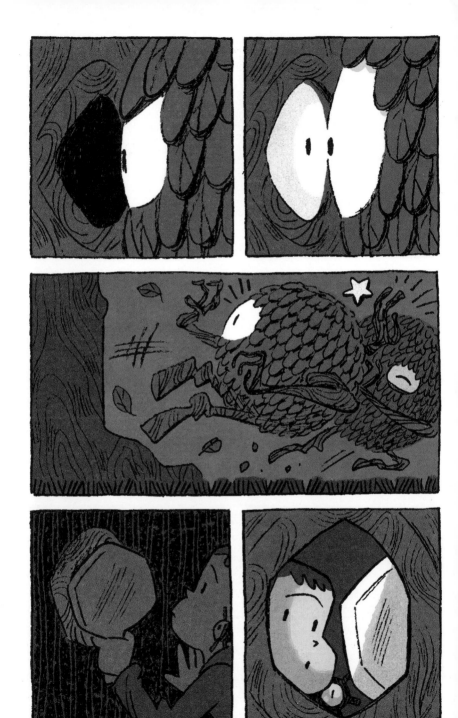

154

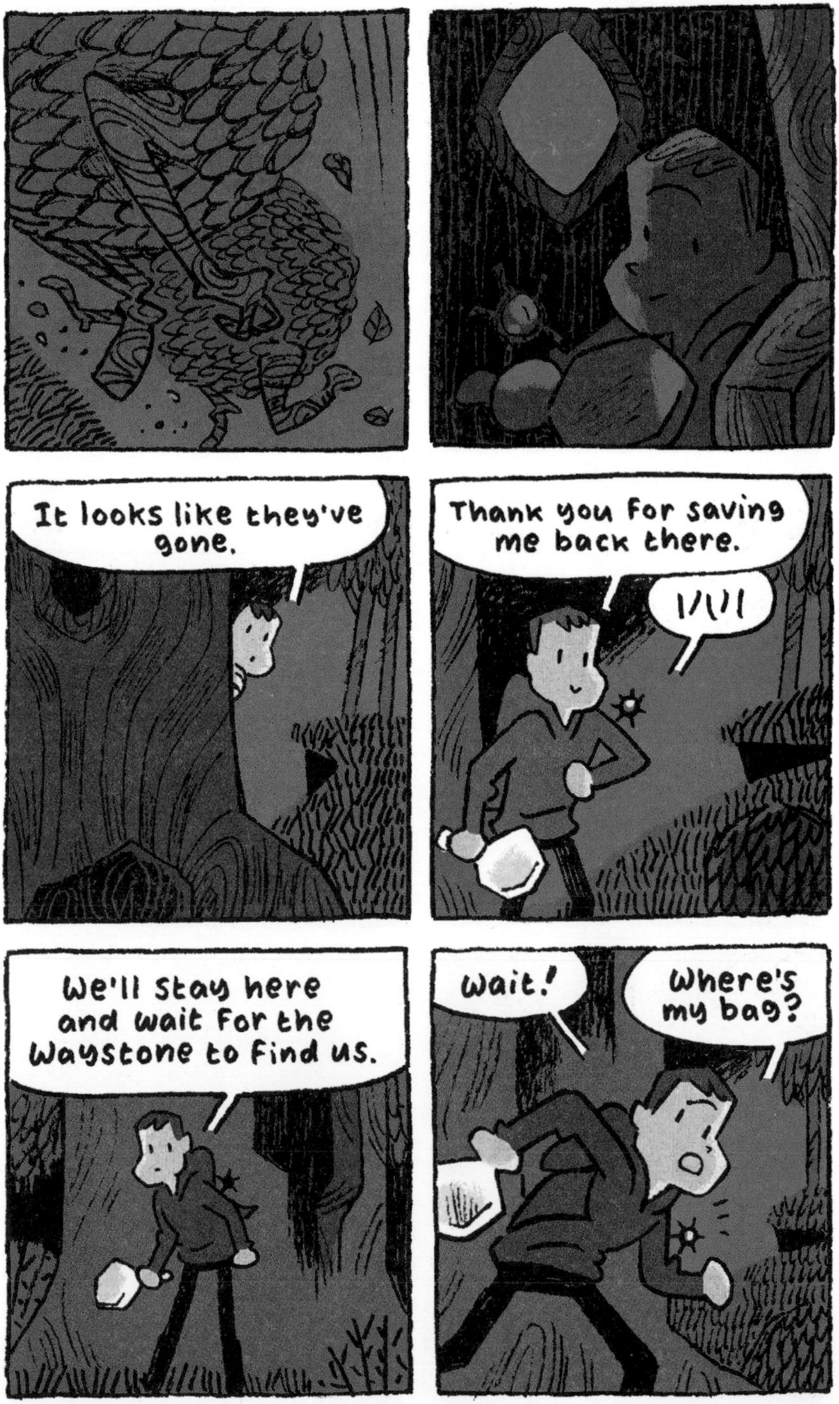
It looks like they've gone.
Thank you for saving me back there.
!/\/!
We'll stay here and wait for the Waystone to find us.
Wait!
Where's my bag?

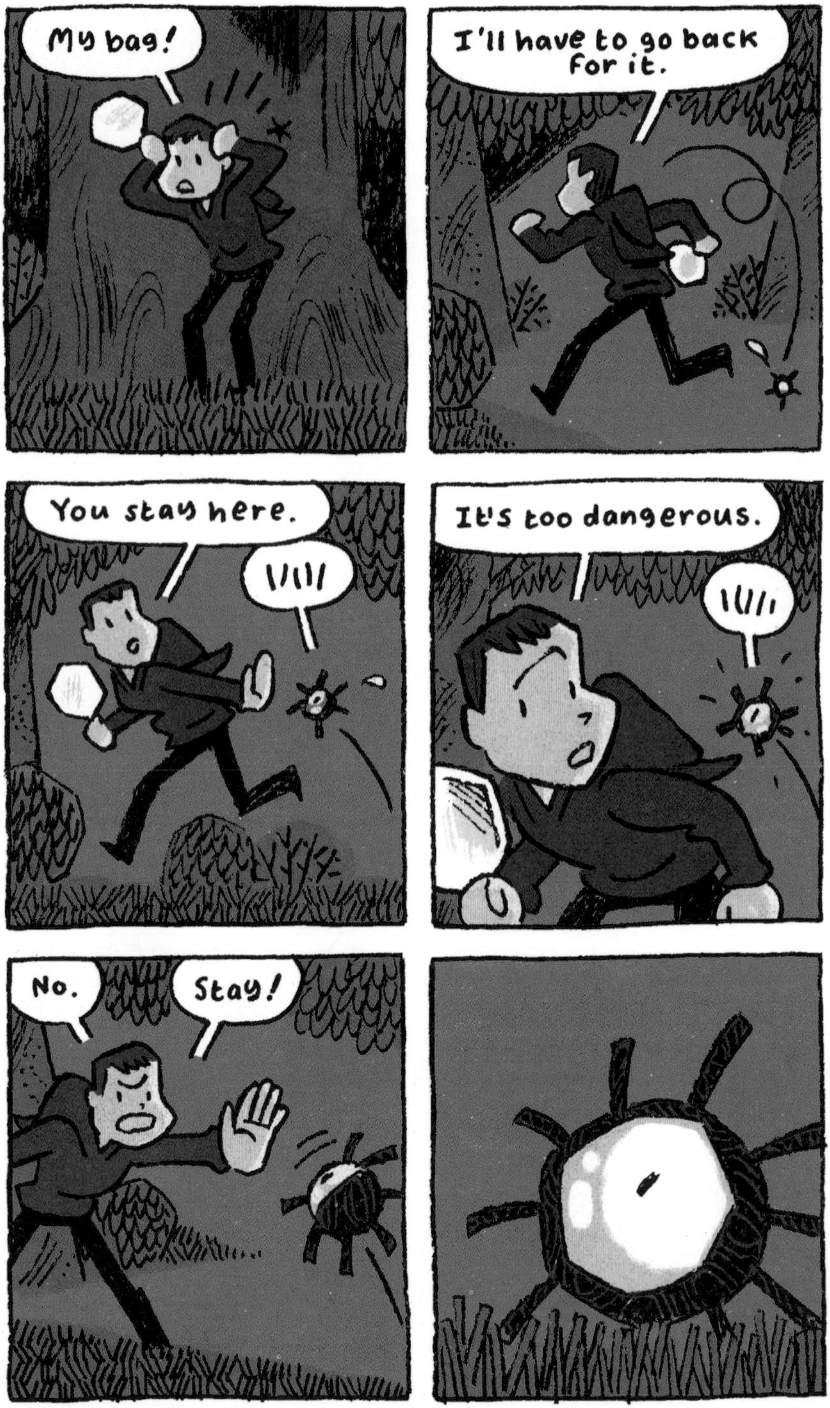
My bag!
I'll have to go back for it.
You stay here.
\/\\/
It's too dangerous.
\\//\
No.
Stay!

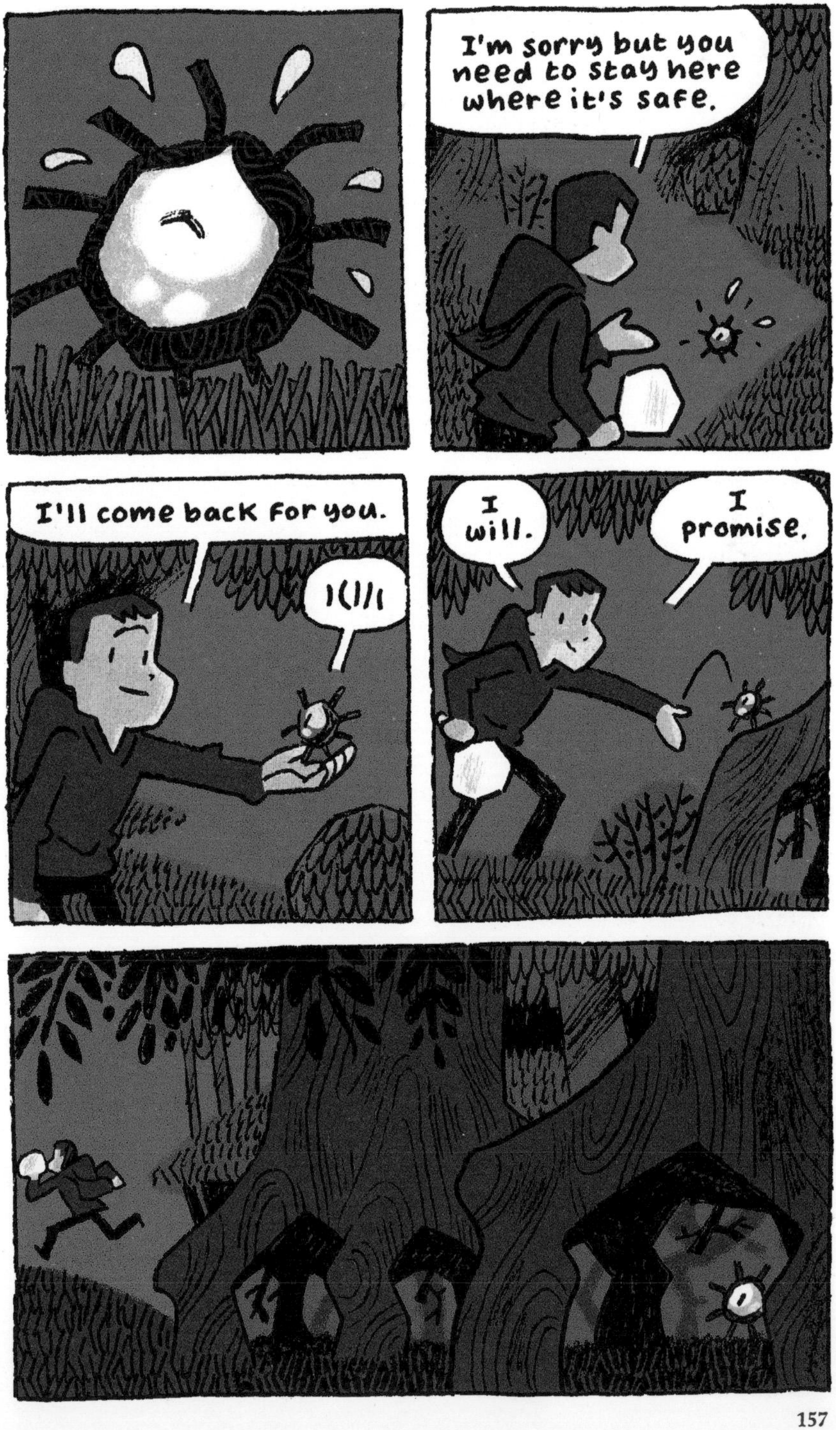
I'm sorry but you need to stay here where it's safe.
I'll come back for you.
I will.
I promise.

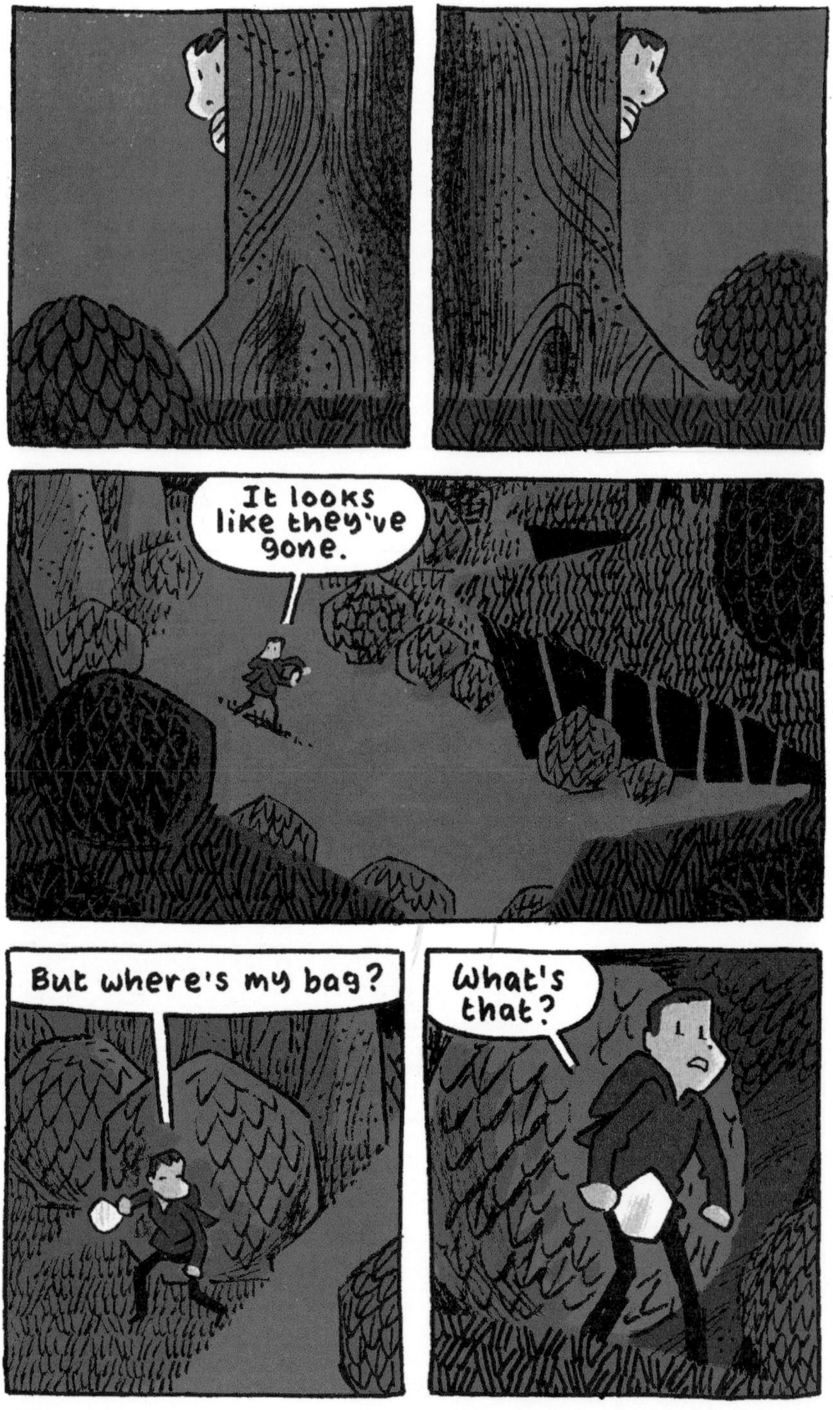
It looks like they've gone.
But where's my bag?
What's that?

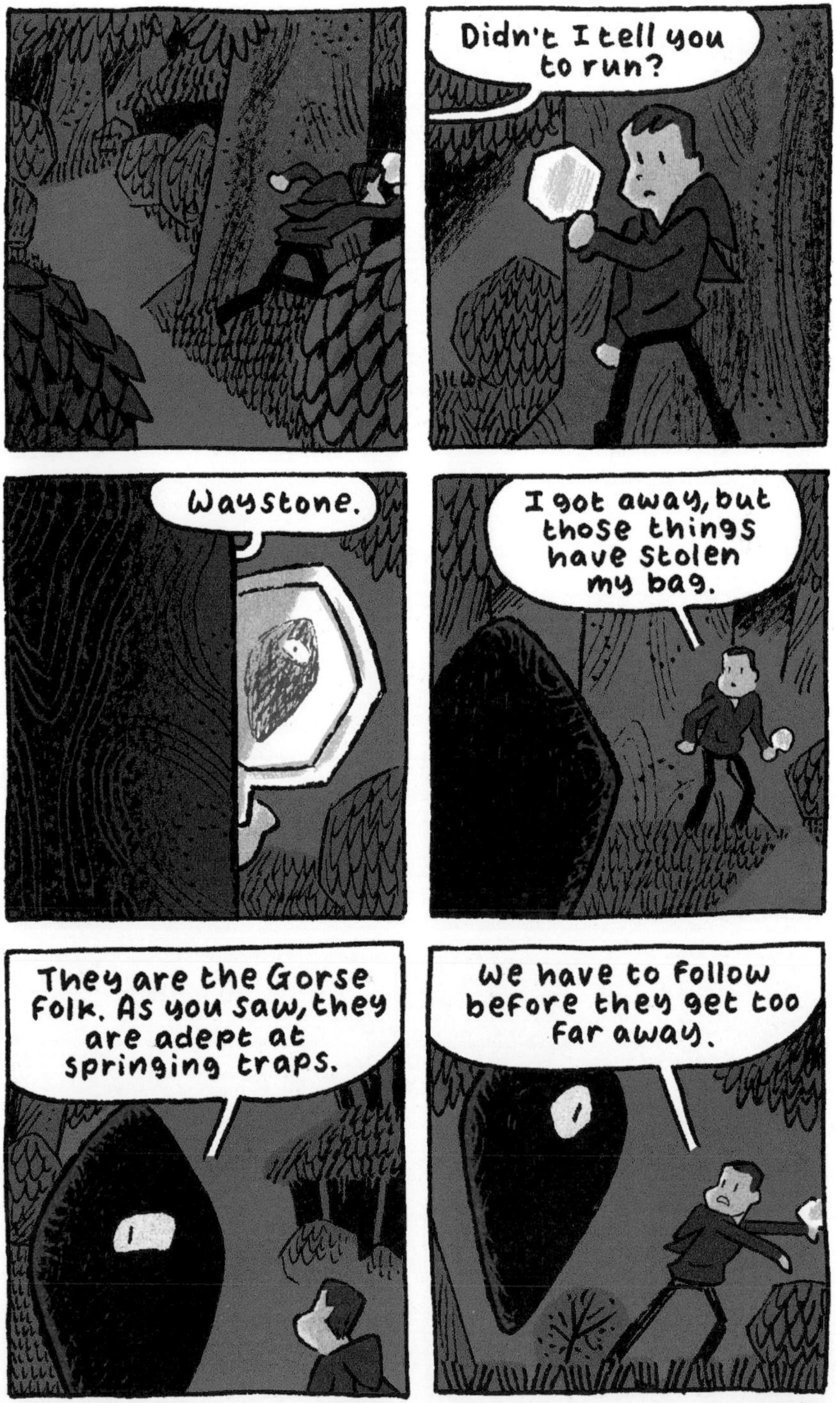
Didn't I tell you to run?
Waystone.
I got away, but those things have stolen my bag.
They are the Gorse Folk. As you saw, they are adept at springing traps.
We have to follow before they get too far away.

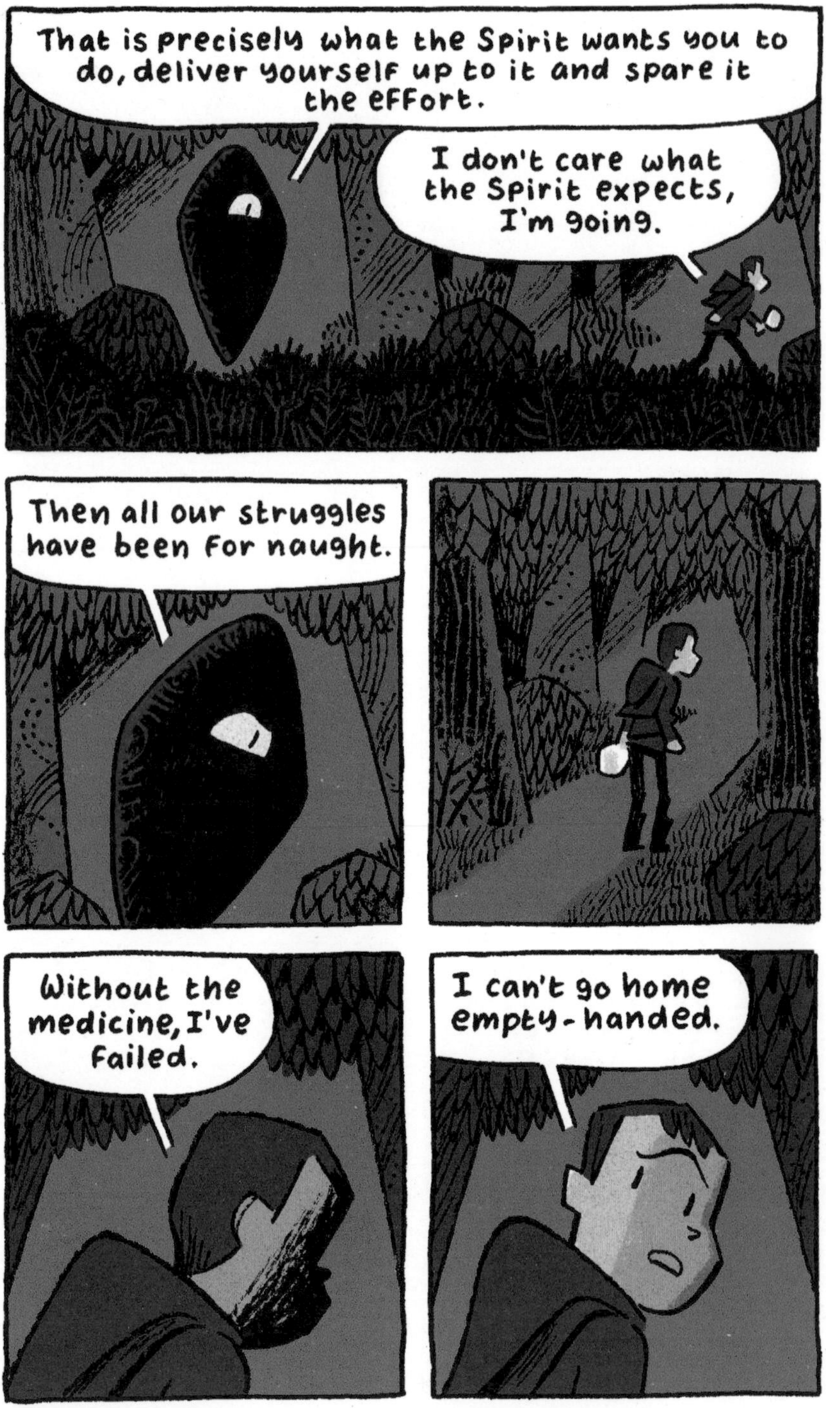
That is precisely what the Spirit wants you to do, deliver yourself up to it and spare it the effort.
I don't care what the Spirit expects, I'm going.
Then all our struggles have been for naught.
Without the medicine, I've failed.
I can't go home empty-handed.

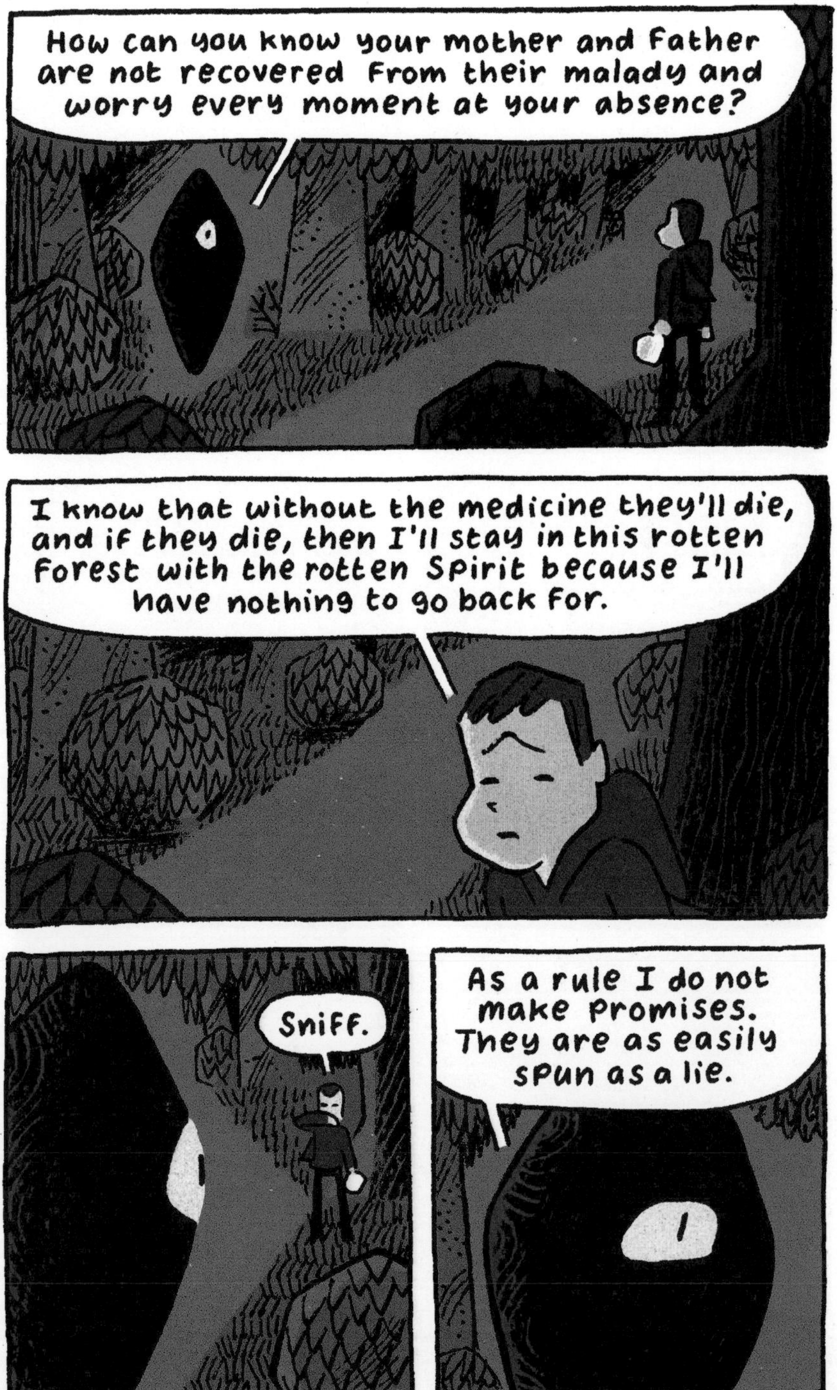
How can you know your mother and father are not recovered from their malady and worry every moment at your absence?
I know that without the medicine they'll die, and if they die, then I'll stay in this rotten forest with the rotten spirit because I'll have nothing to go back for.
Sniff.
As a rule I do not make promises. They are as easily spun as a lie.

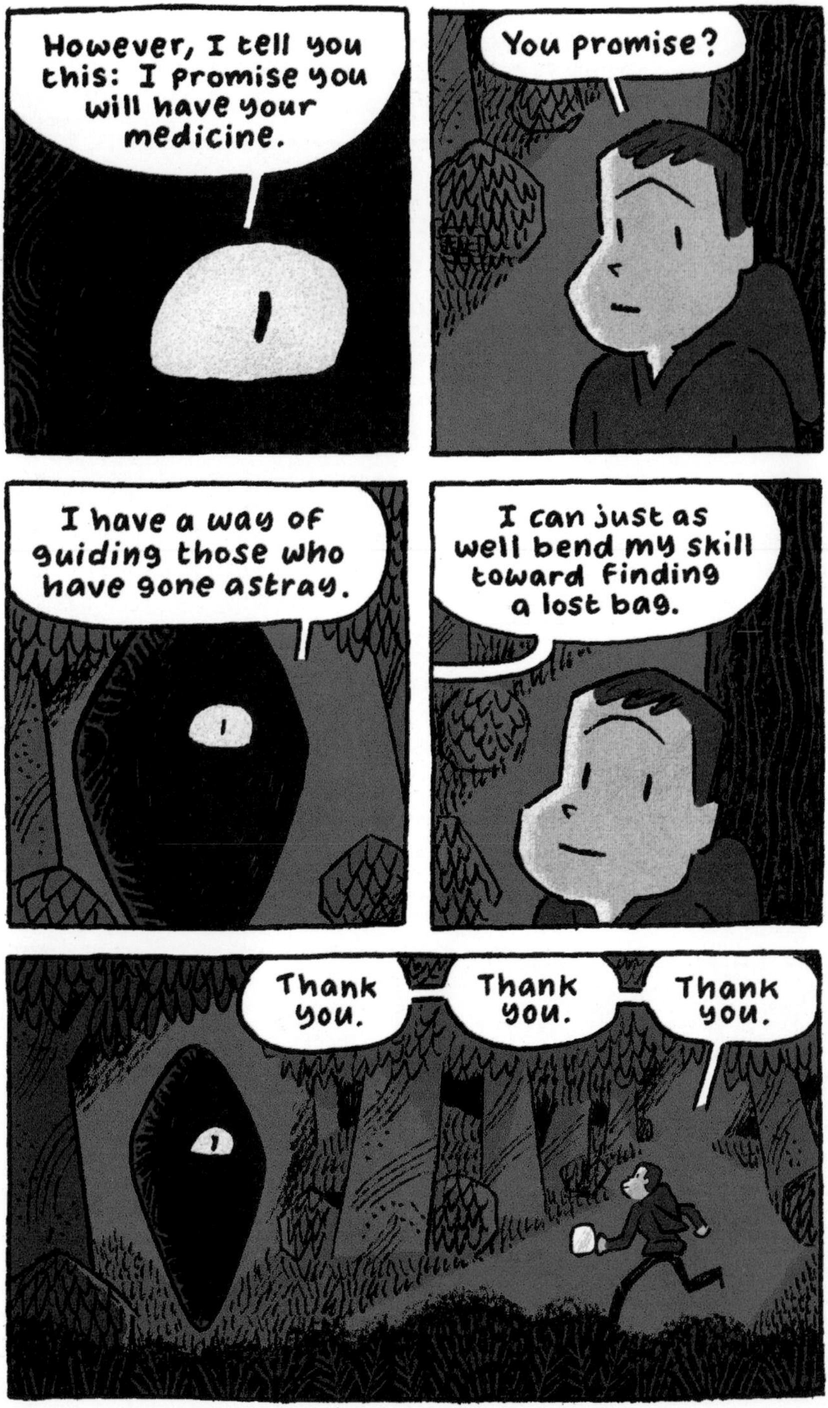
However, I tell you this: I promise you will have your medicine.
You promise?
I have a way of guiding those who have gone astray.
I can just as well bend my skill toward finding a lost bag.
Thank you.
Thank you.
Thank you.

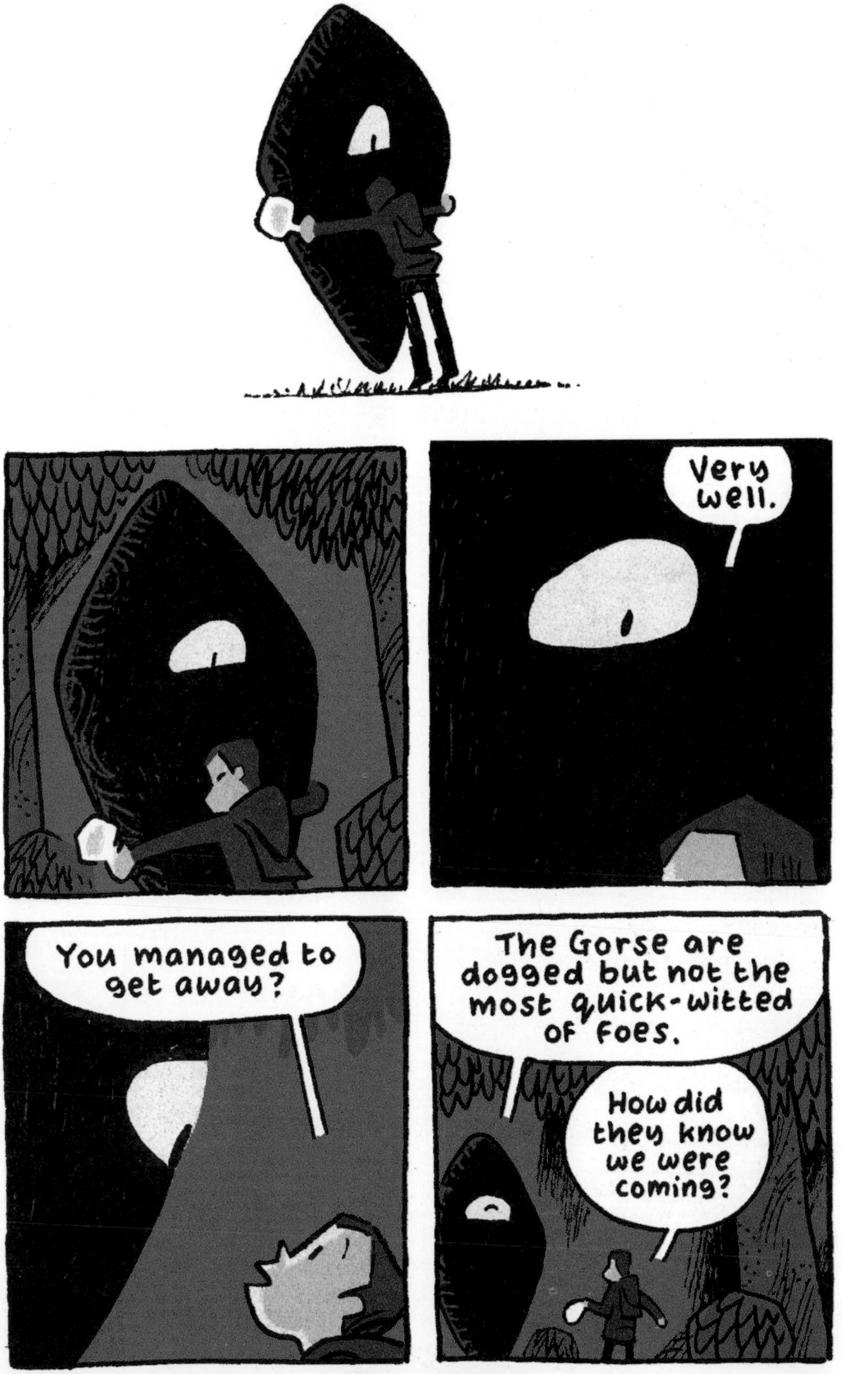
Very well.
You managed to get away?
The Gorse are dogged but not the most quick-witted of foes.
How did they know we were coming?

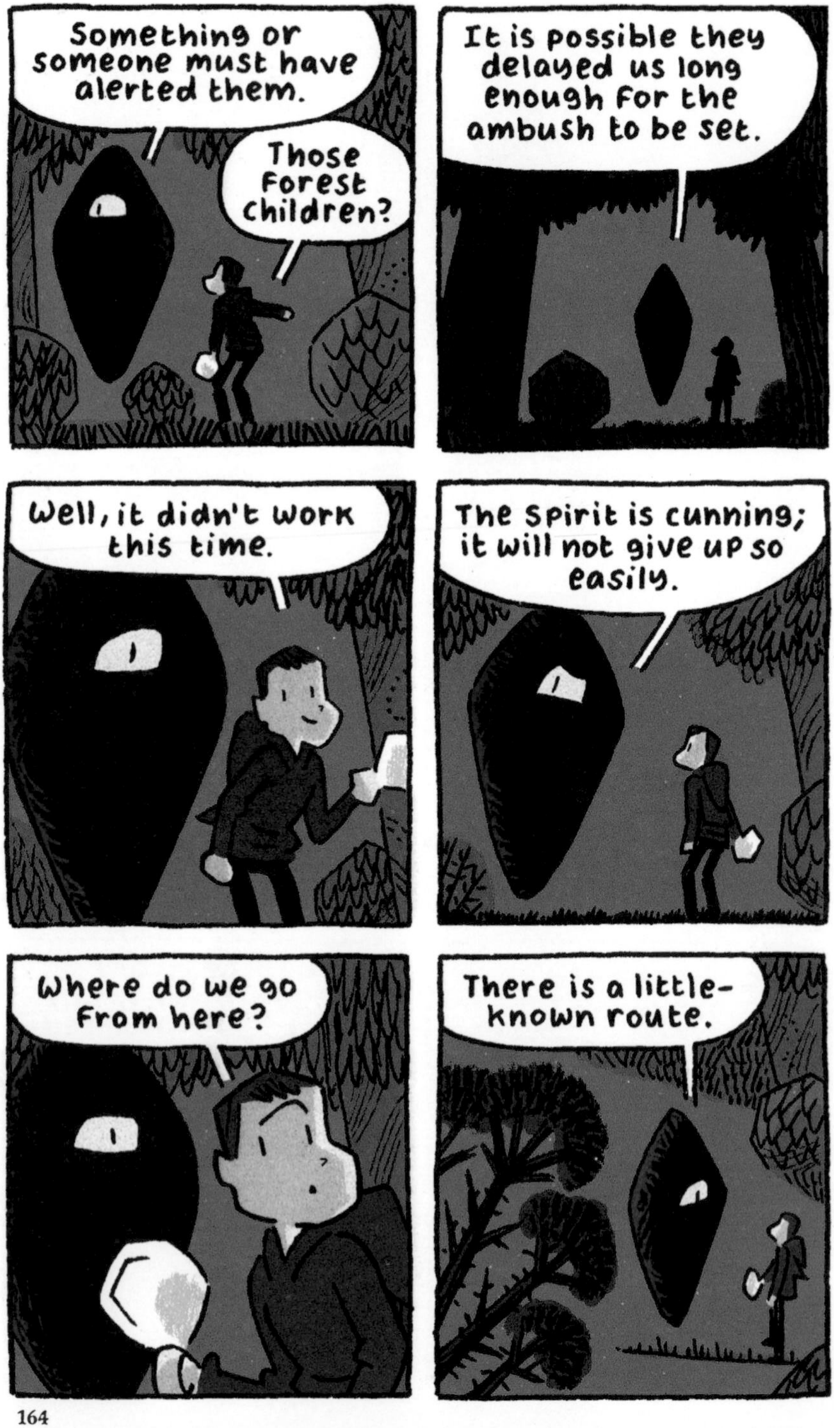
Something or someone must have alerted them.
Those forest children?
It is possible they delayed us long enough for the ambush to be set.
Well, it didn't work this time.
The spirit is cunning; it will not give up so easily.
Where do we go from here?
There is a little-known route.

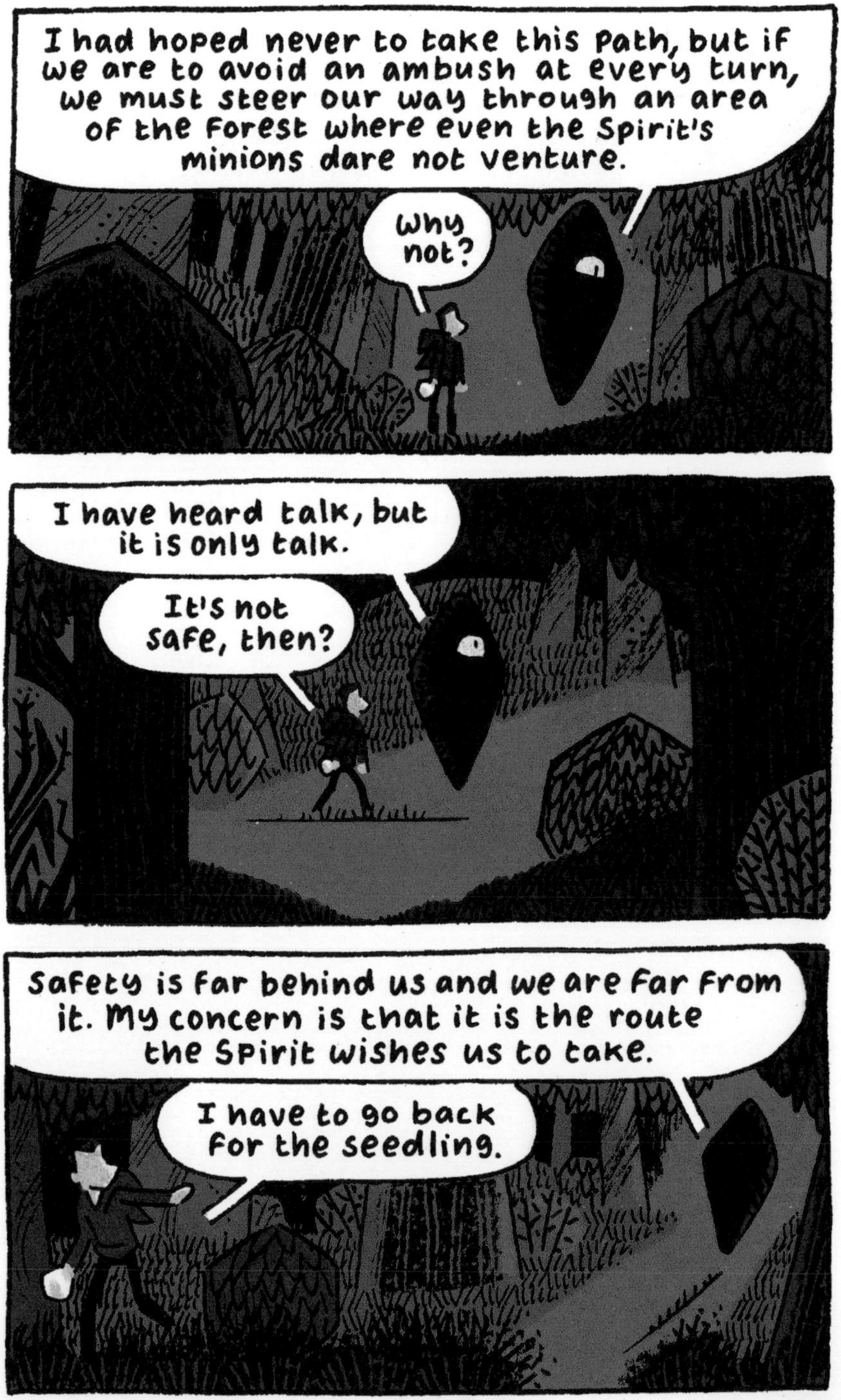
I had hoped never to take this path, but if we are to avoid an ambush at every turn, we must steer our way through an area of the forest where even the Spirit's minions dare not venture.
Why not?
I have heard talk, but it is only talk.
It's not safe, then?
Safety is far behind us and we are far from it. My concern is that it is the route the Spirit wishes us to take.
I have to go back for the seedling.

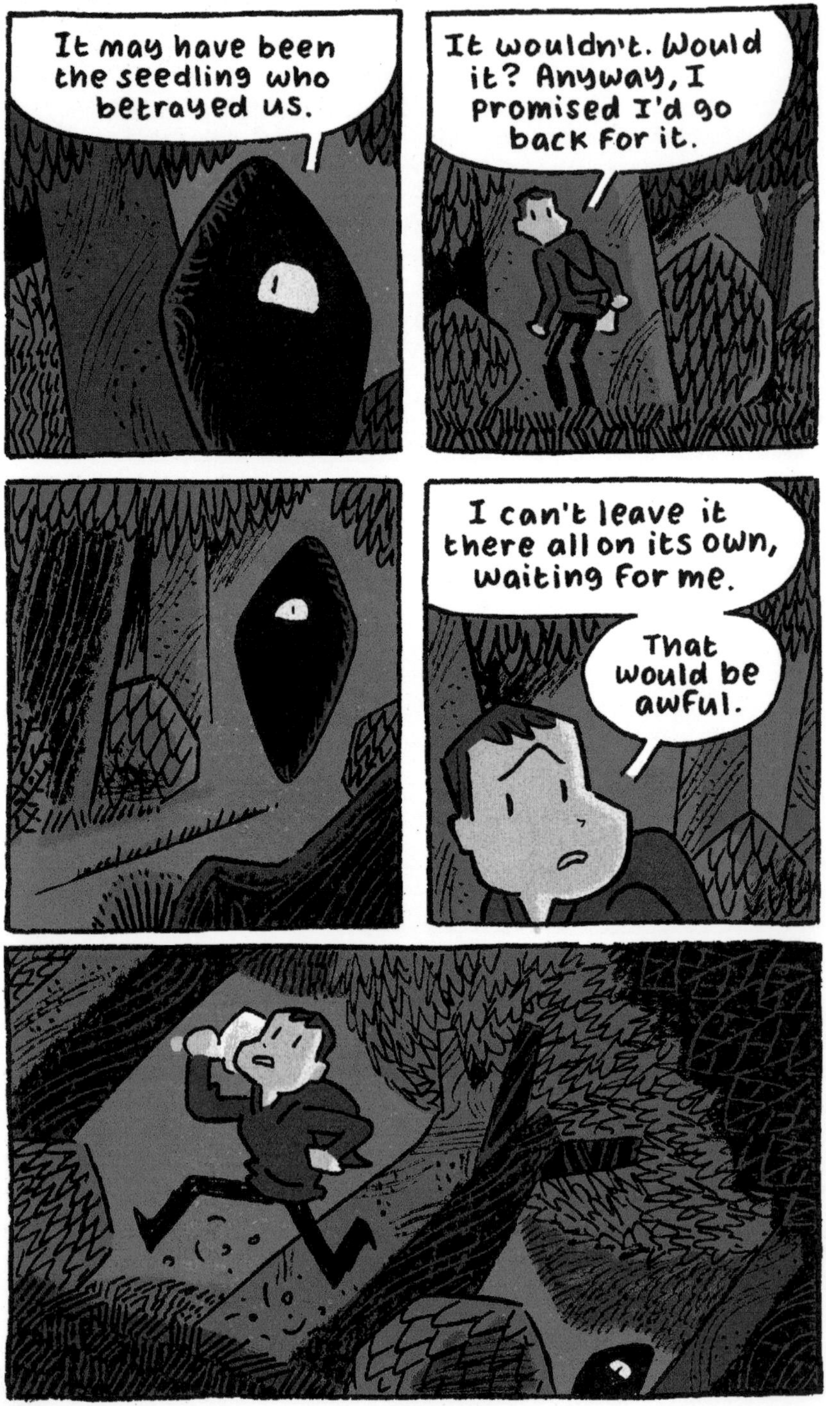
It may have been the seedling who betrayed us.
It wouldn't. Would it? Anyway, I promised I'd go back for it.
I can't leave it there all on its own, waiting for me.
That would be awful.

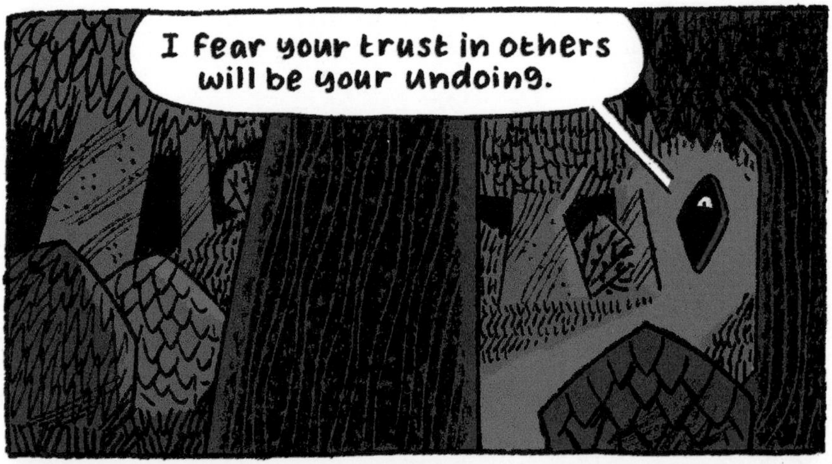
I fear your trust in others will be your undoing.

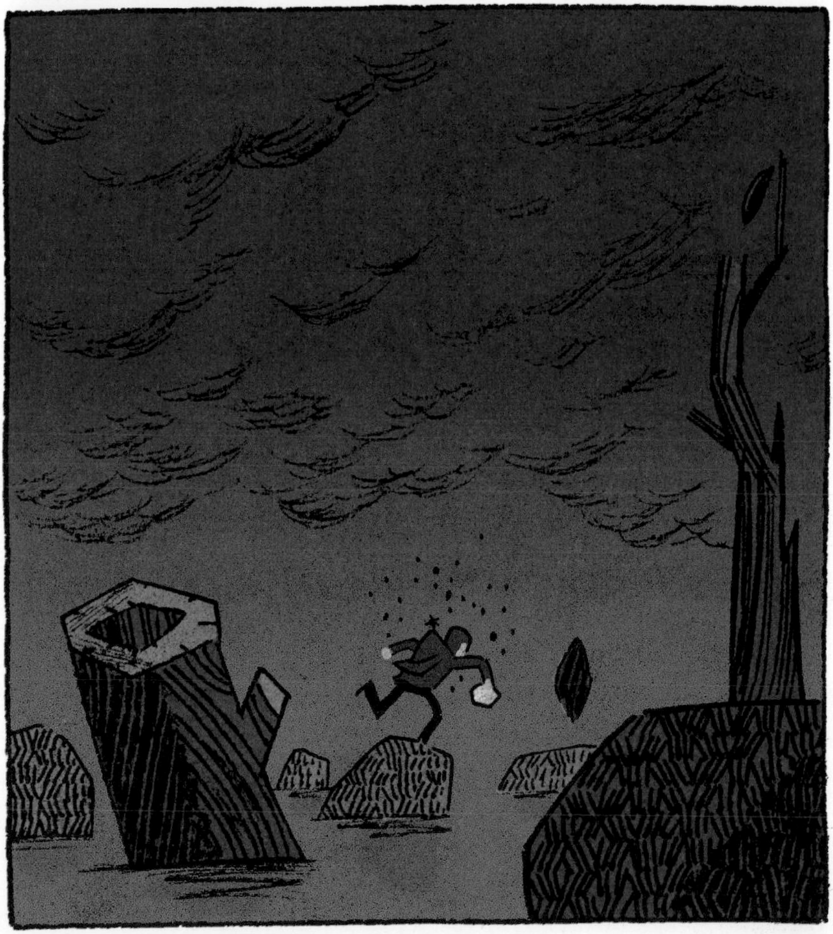

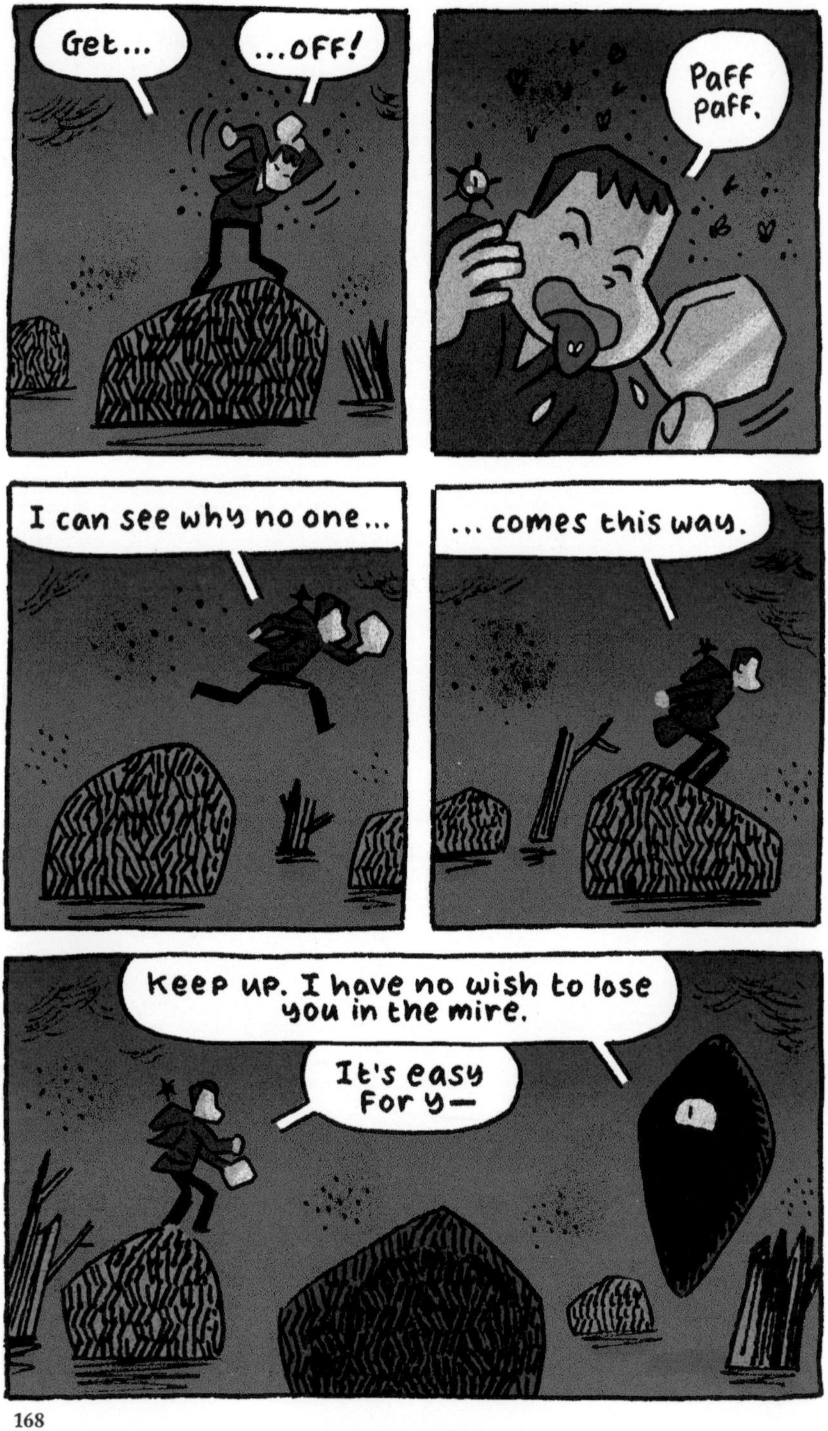
Get...
...OFF!
Paff paff.
I can see why no one...
... comes this way.
Keep up. I have no wish to lose you in the mire.
It's easy for y—

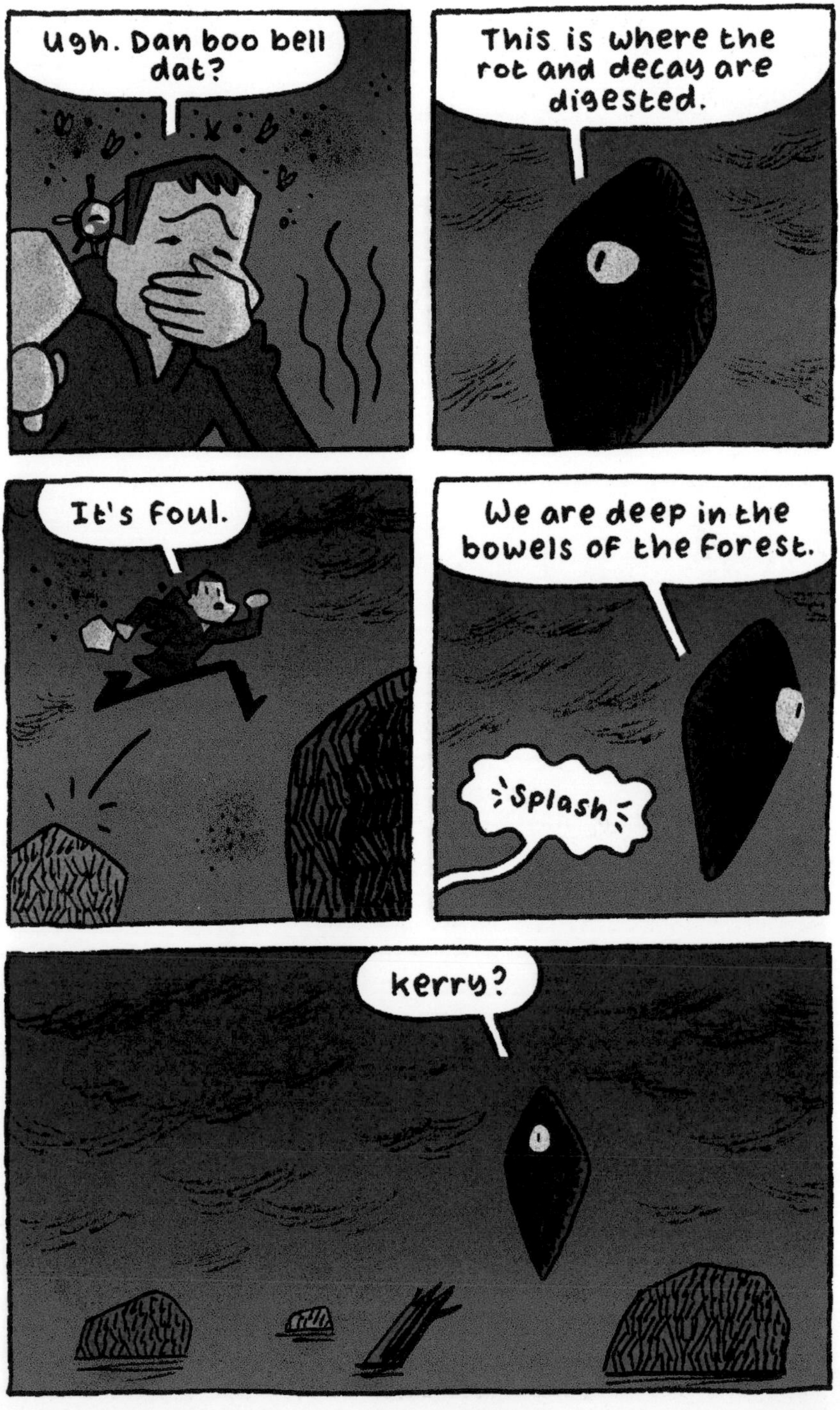
Ugh. Dan boo bell dat?
This is where the rot and decay are digested.
It's foul.
We are deep in the bowels of the forest.
Splash
kerry?

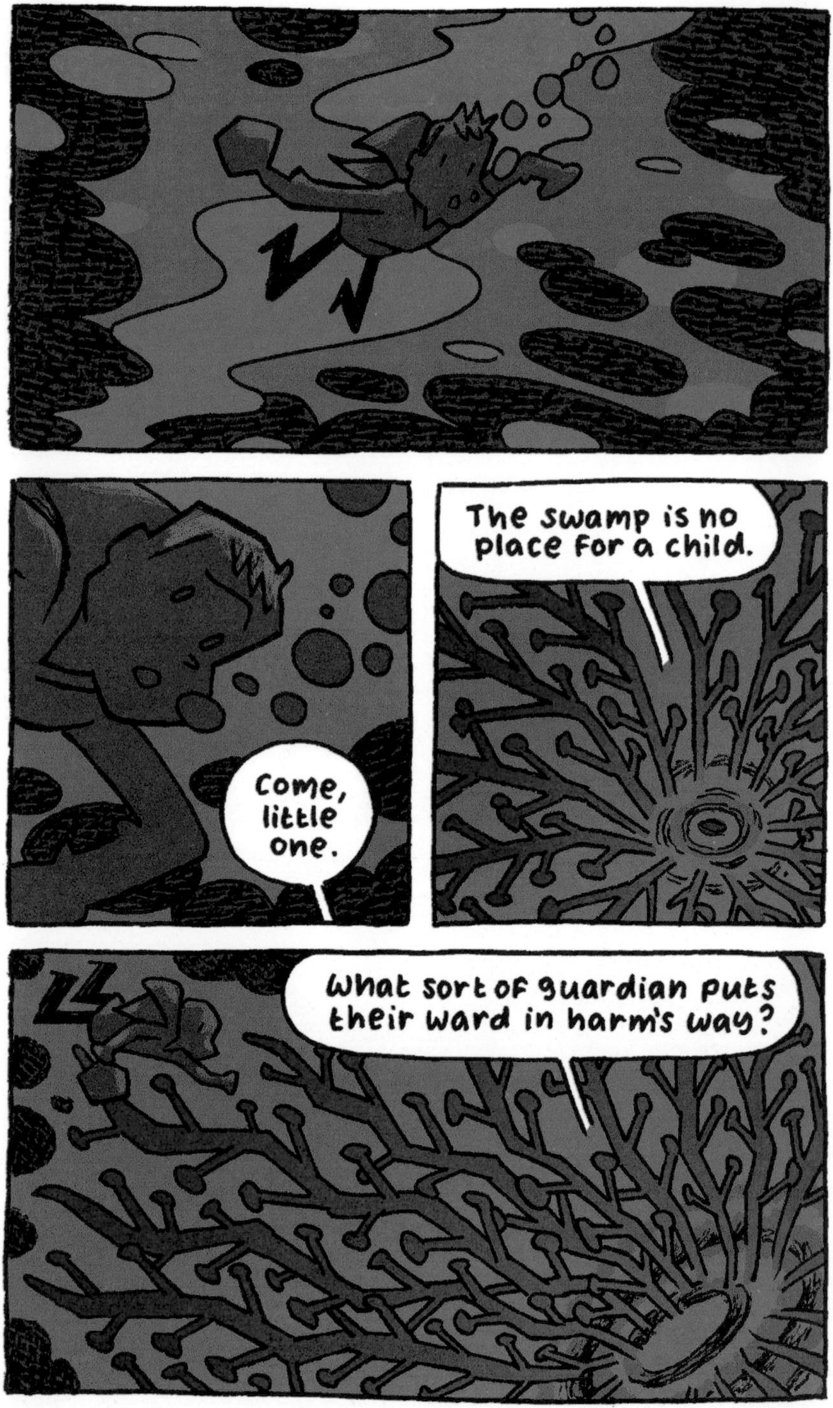
Come, little one.
The swamp is no place for a child.
What sort of guardian puts their ward in harm's way?

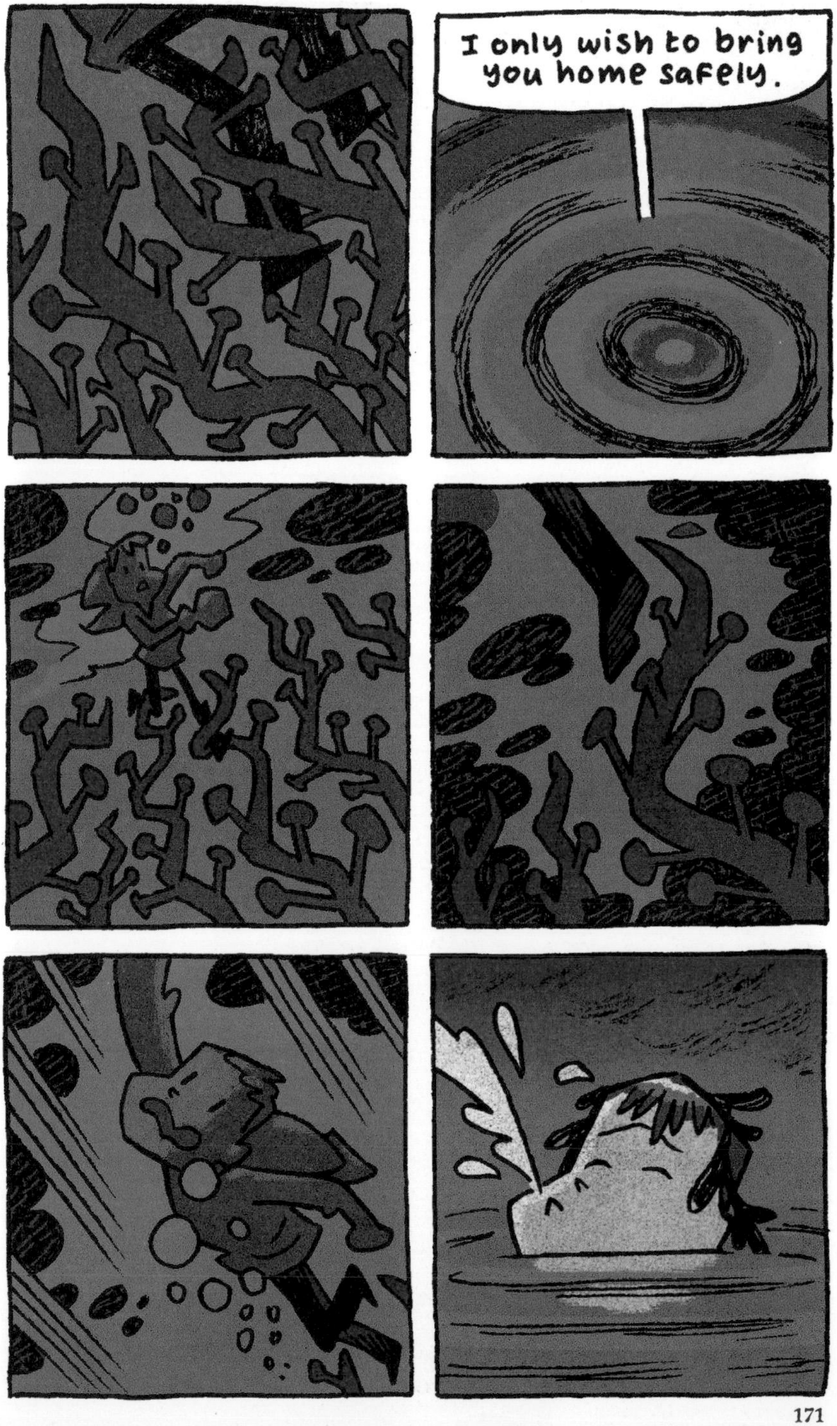
I only wish to bring you home safely.

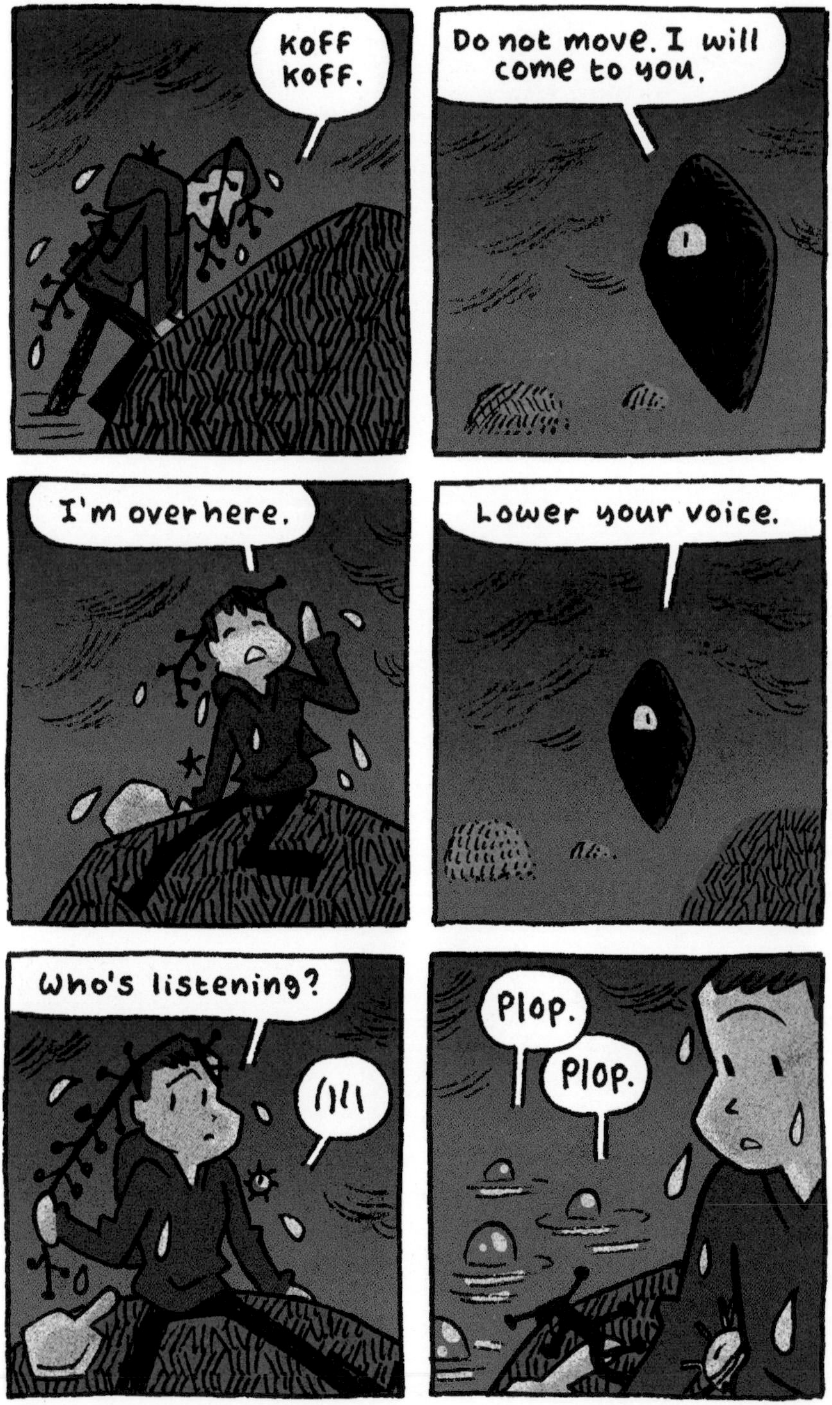
KOFF
KOFF.
Do not move. I will come to you.
I'm over here.
Lower your voice.
Who's listening?
Plop.
Plop.

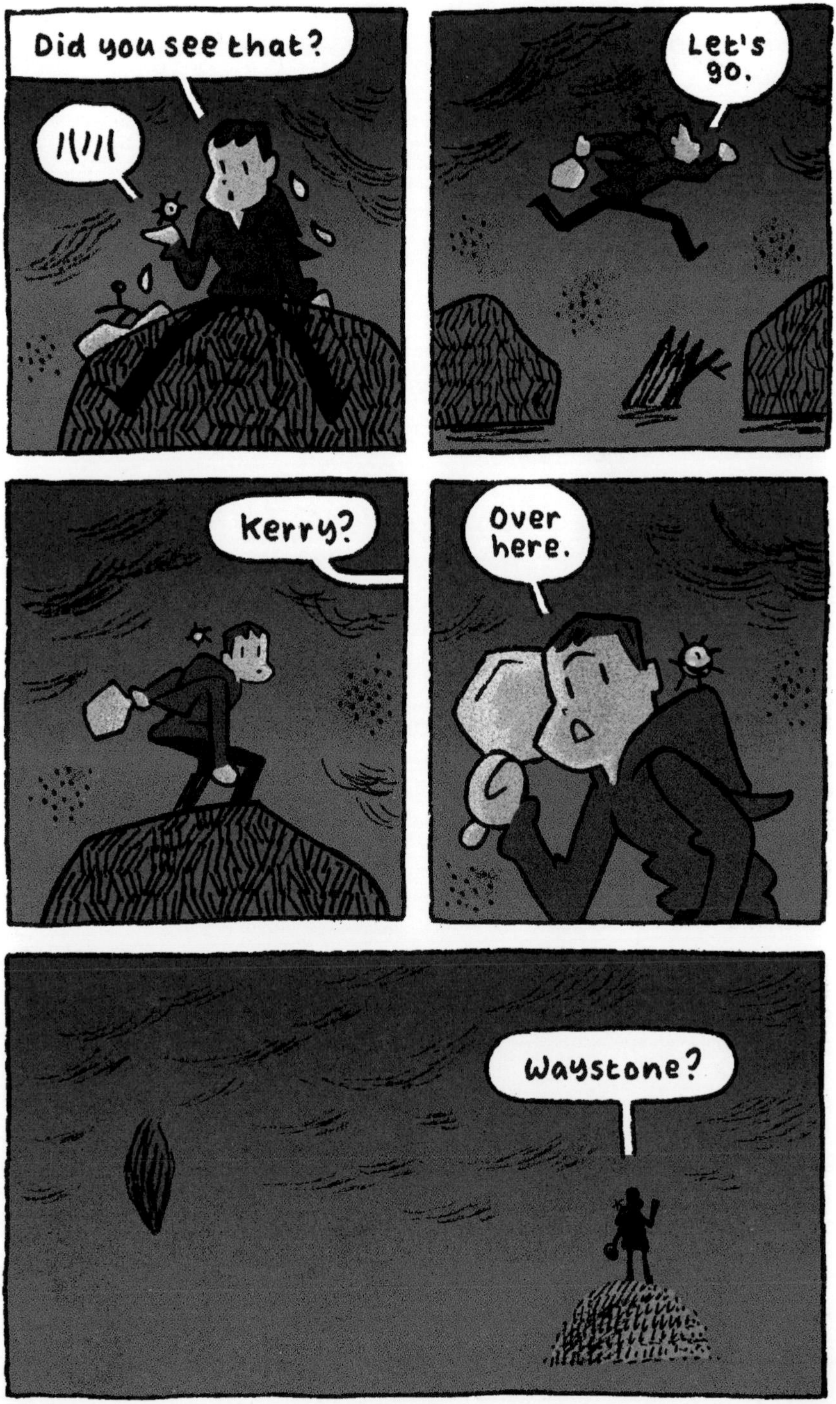
Did you see that?
!\!!/!
Let's go.
Kerry?
Over here.
Waystone?

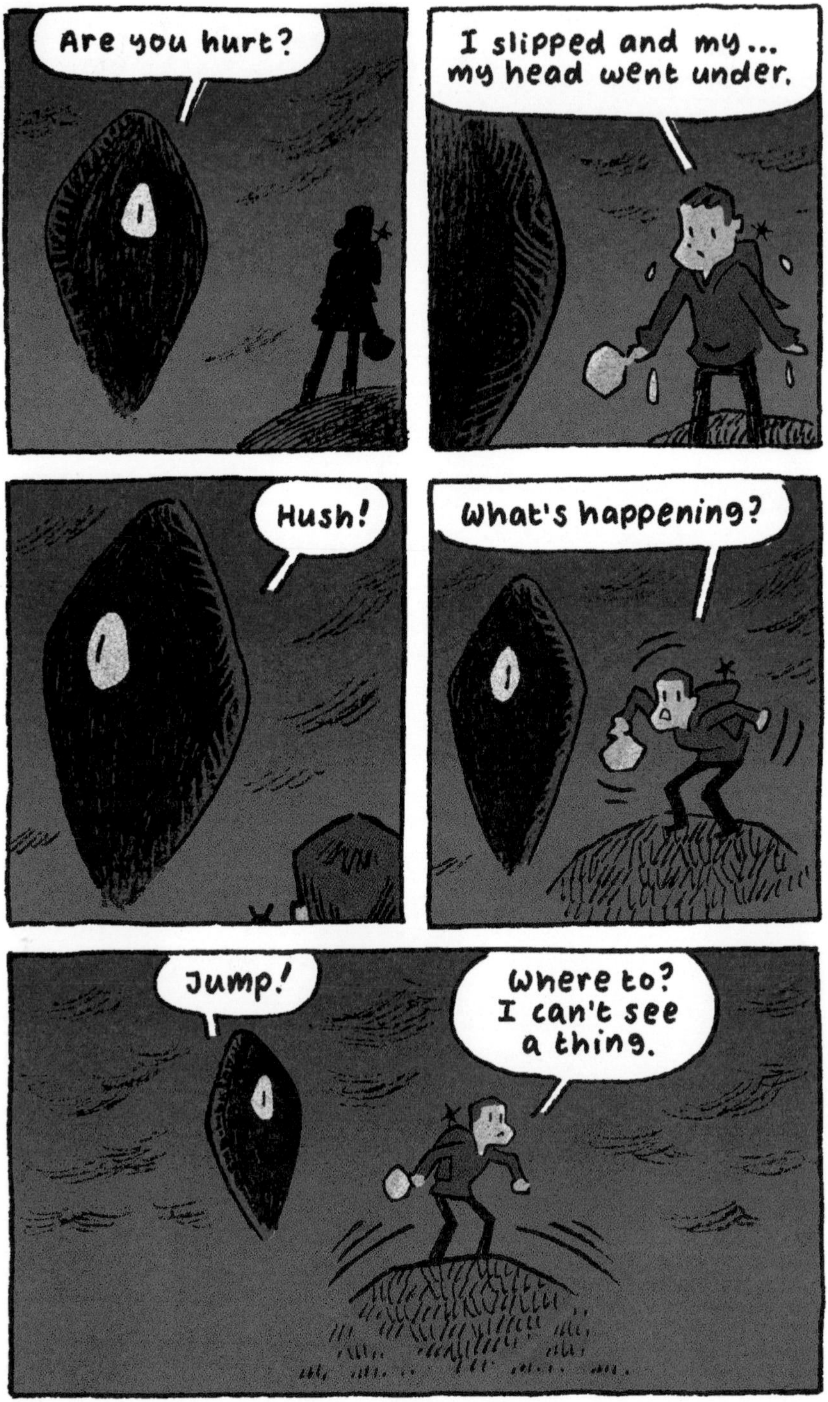
Are you hurt?
I slipped and my... my head went under.
Hush!
What's happening?
Jump!
Where to? I can't see a thing.

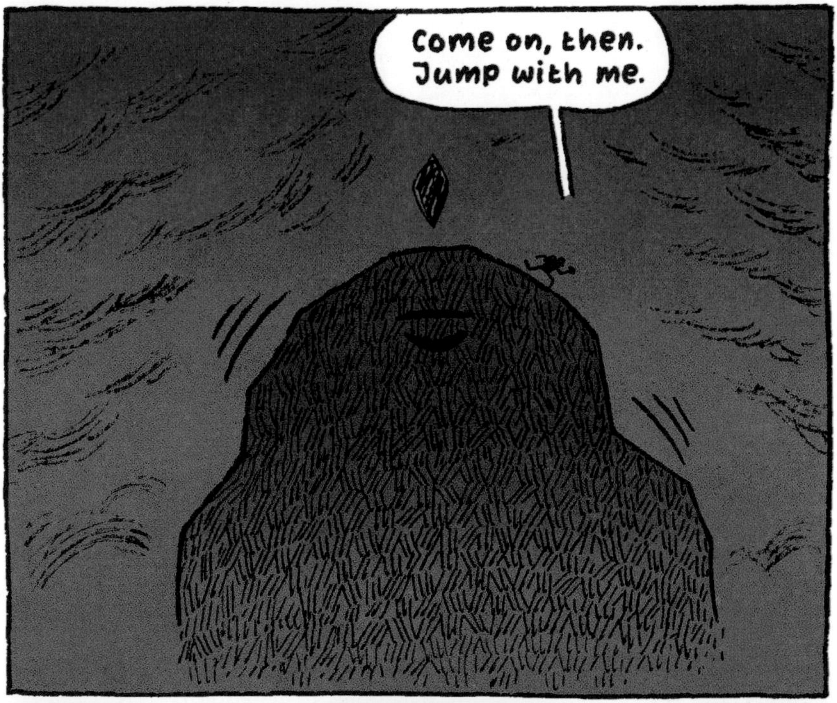
Come on, then. Jump with me.

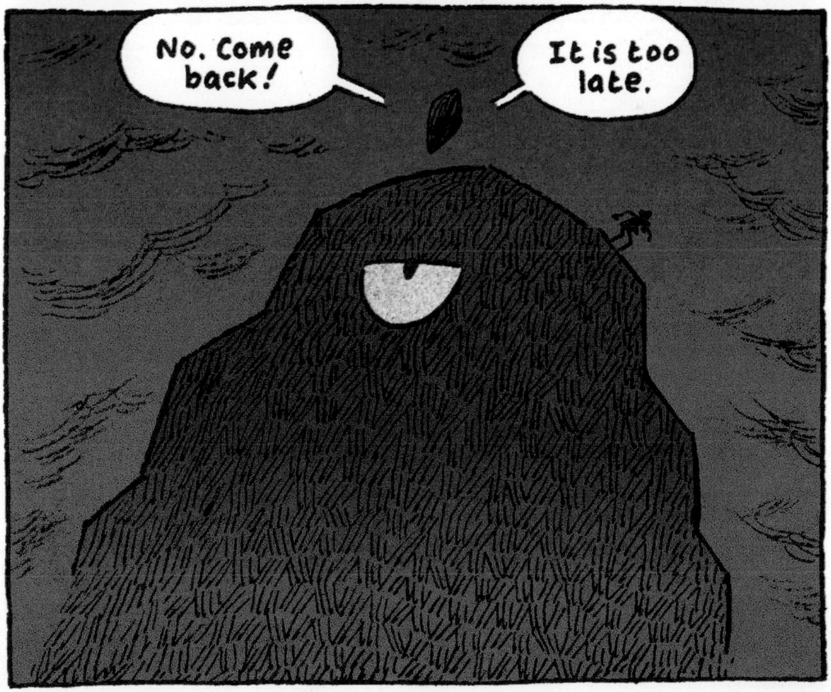
No. Come back!
It is too late.

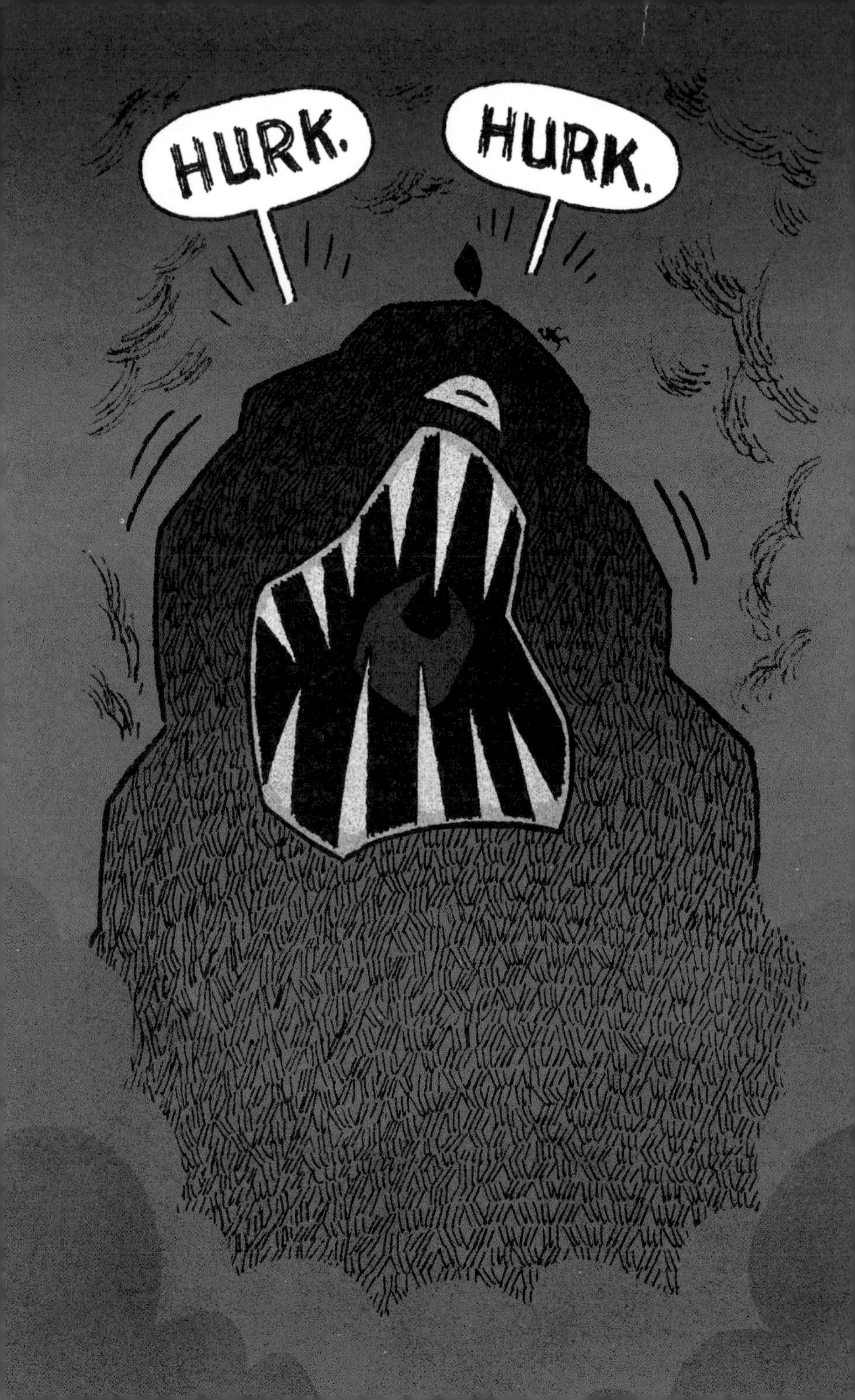
HURK.
HURK.

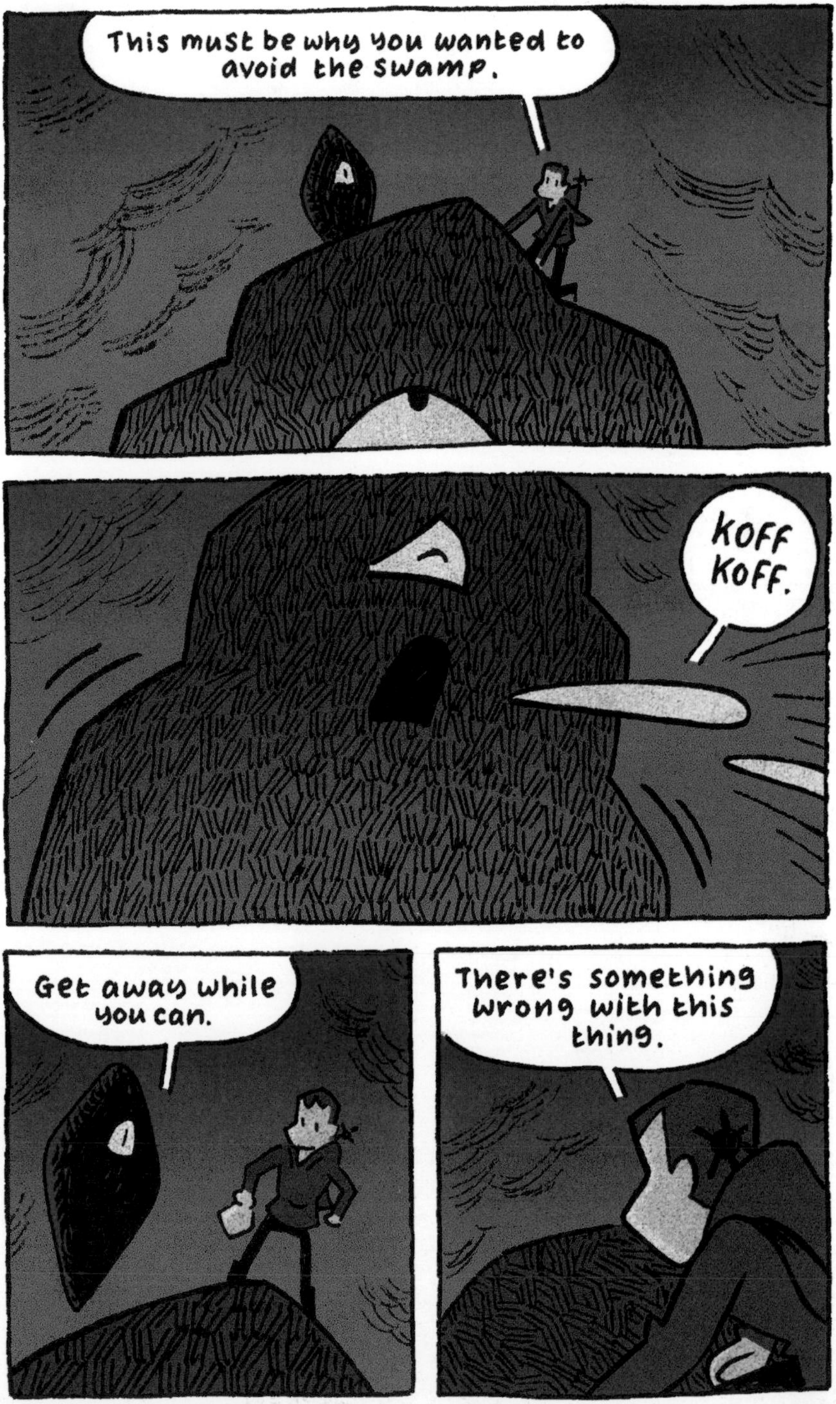
This must be why you wanted to avoid the swamp.
KOFF KOFF.
Get away while you can.
There's something wrong with this thing.

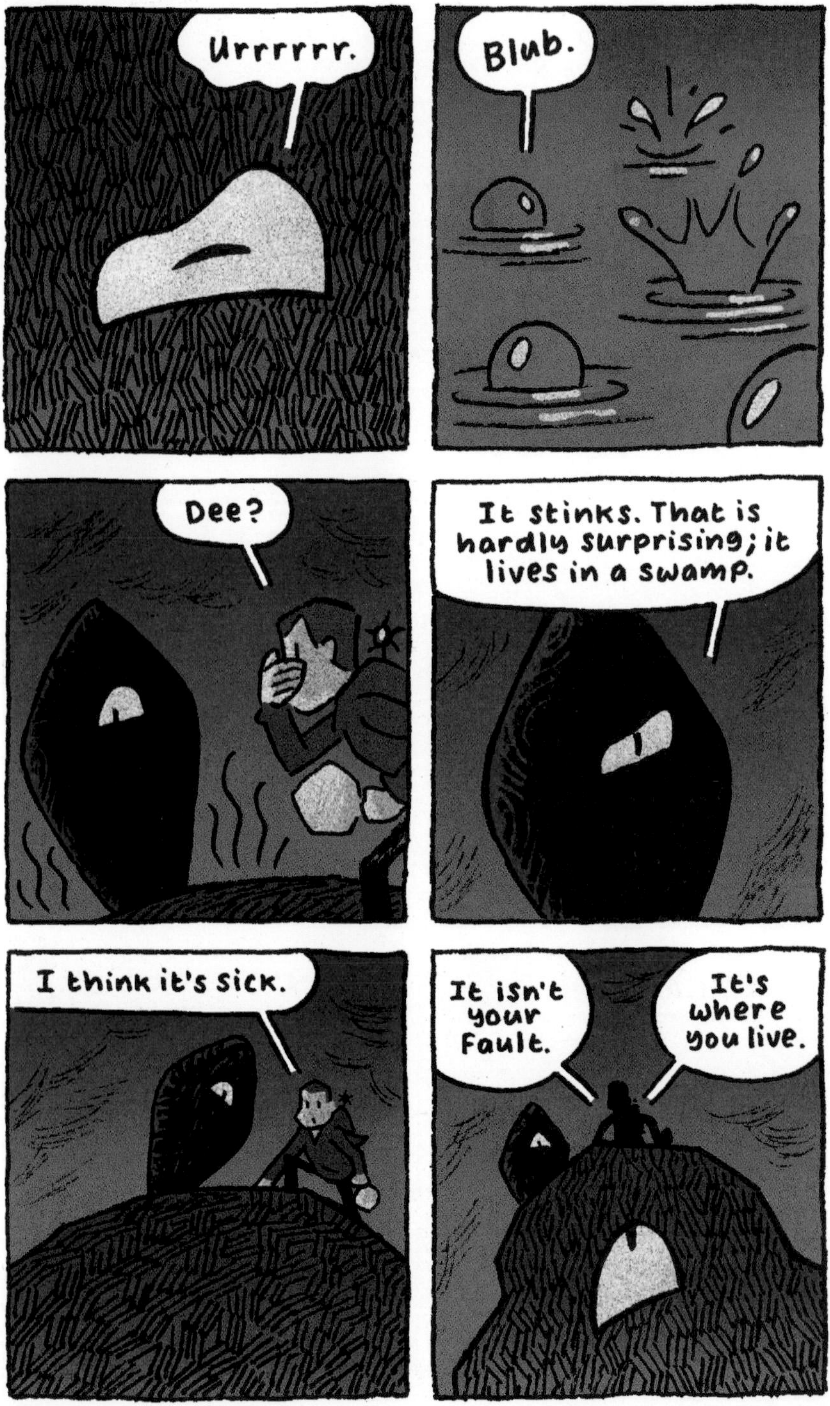
Urrrrrr.
Blub.
Dee?
It stinks. That is hardly surprising; it lives in a swamp.
I think it's sick.
It isn't your fault.
It's where you live.

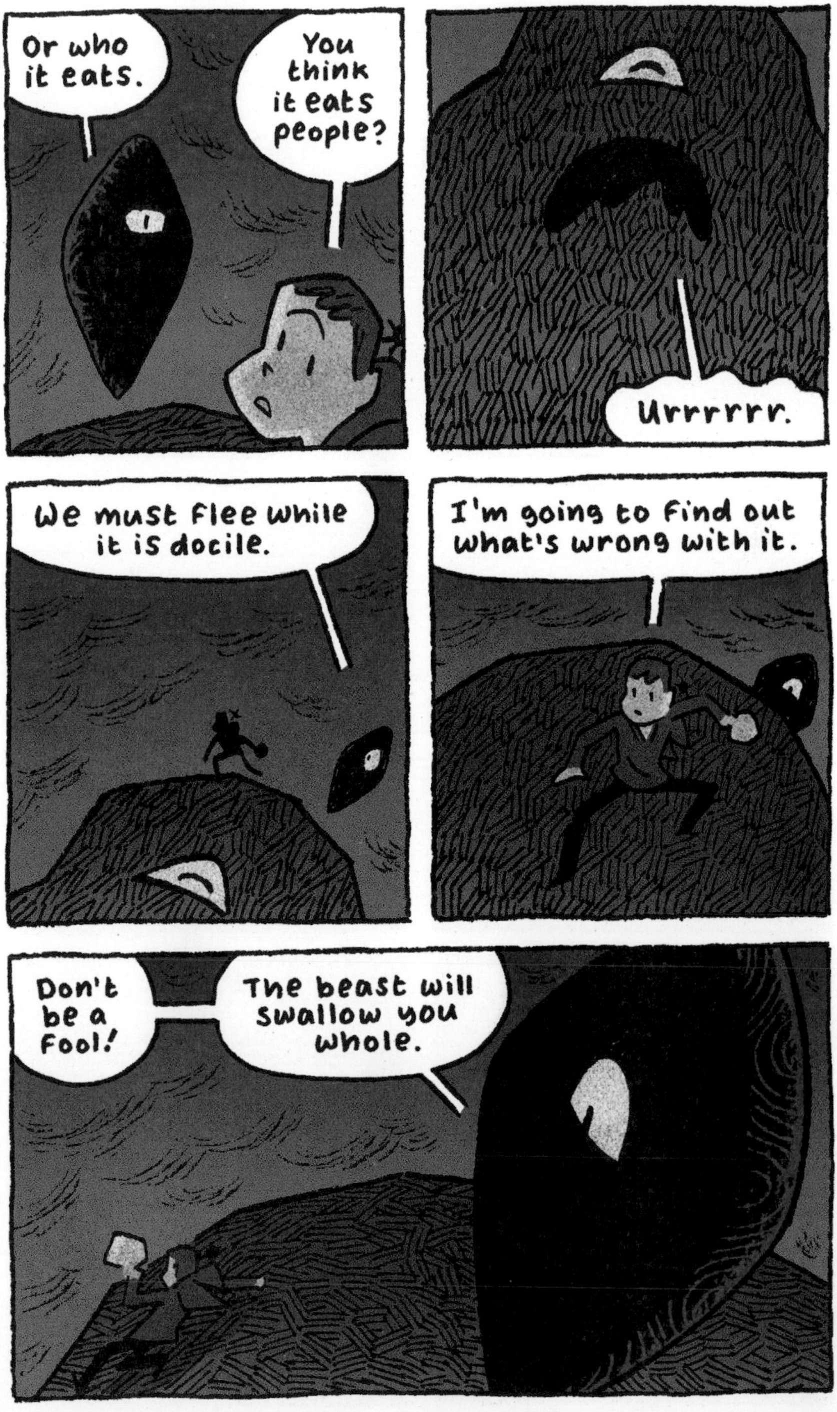
Or who it eats.
You think it eats people?
Urrrrrr.
We must flee while it is docile.
I'm going to find out what's wrong with it.
Don't be a fool!
The beast will swallow you whole.

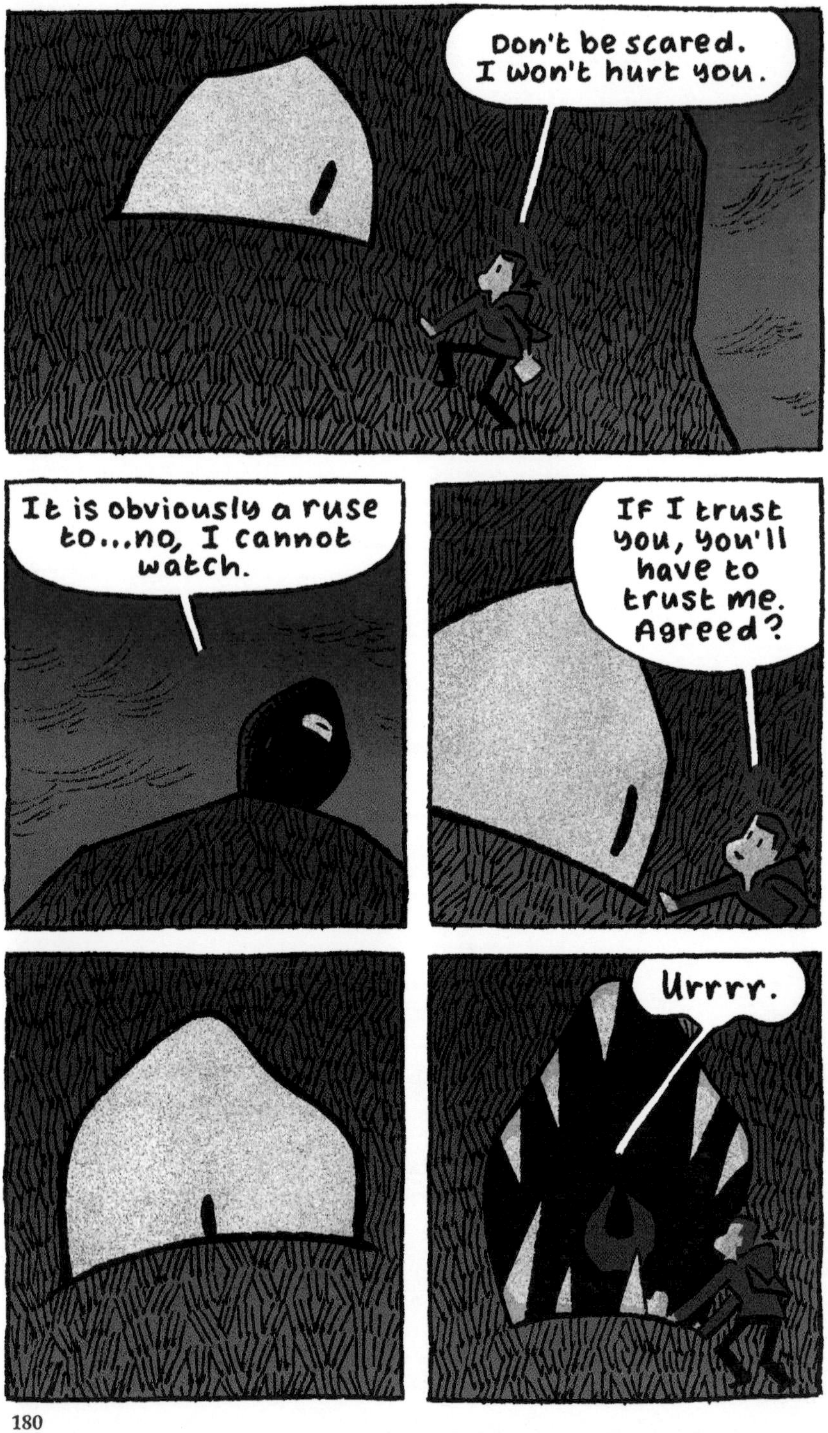
Don't be scared. I won't hurt you.
It is obviously a ruse to...no, I cannot watch.
If I trust you, you'll have to trust me. Agreed?
Urrrr.

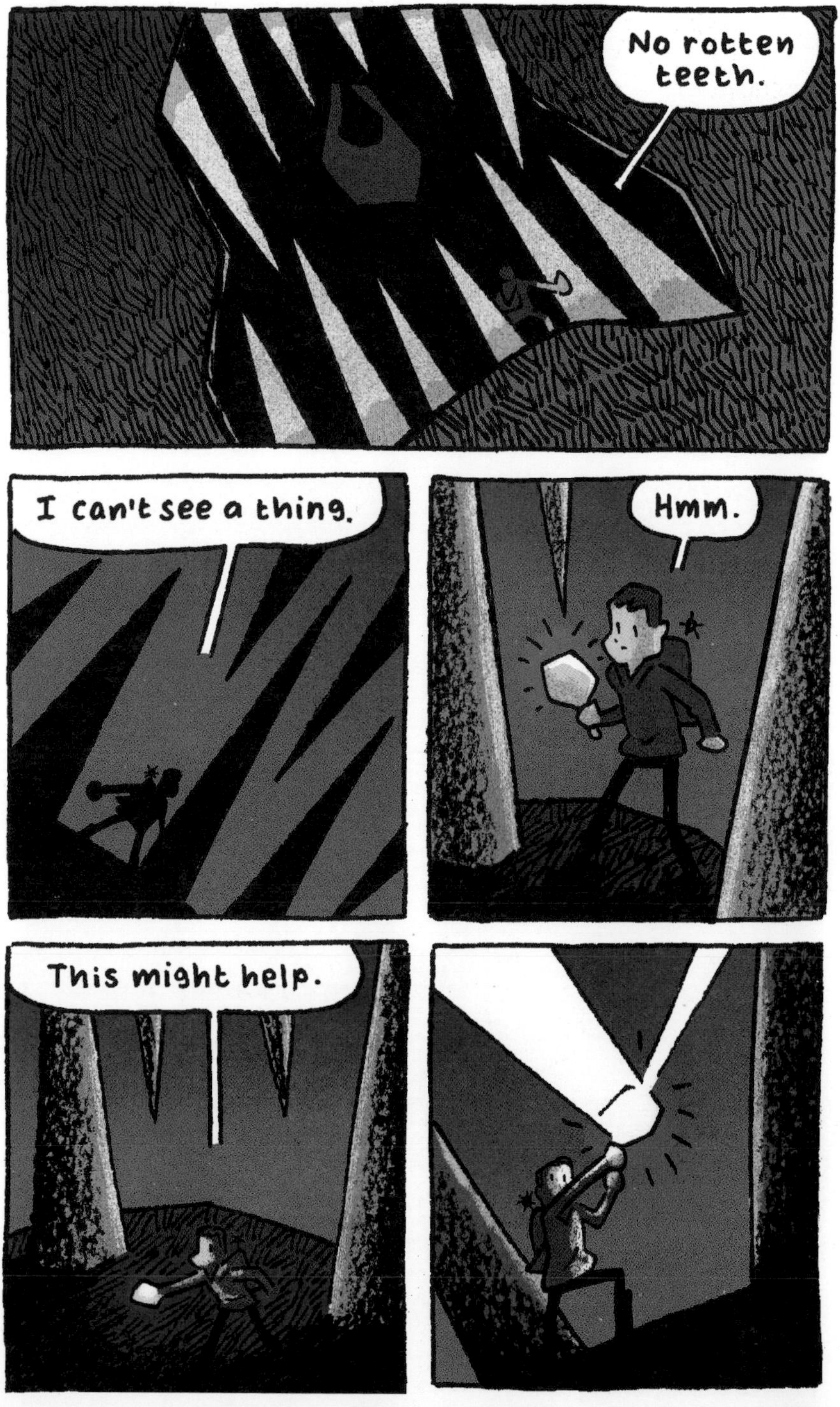
No rotten teeth.
I can't see a thing.
Hmm.
This might help.

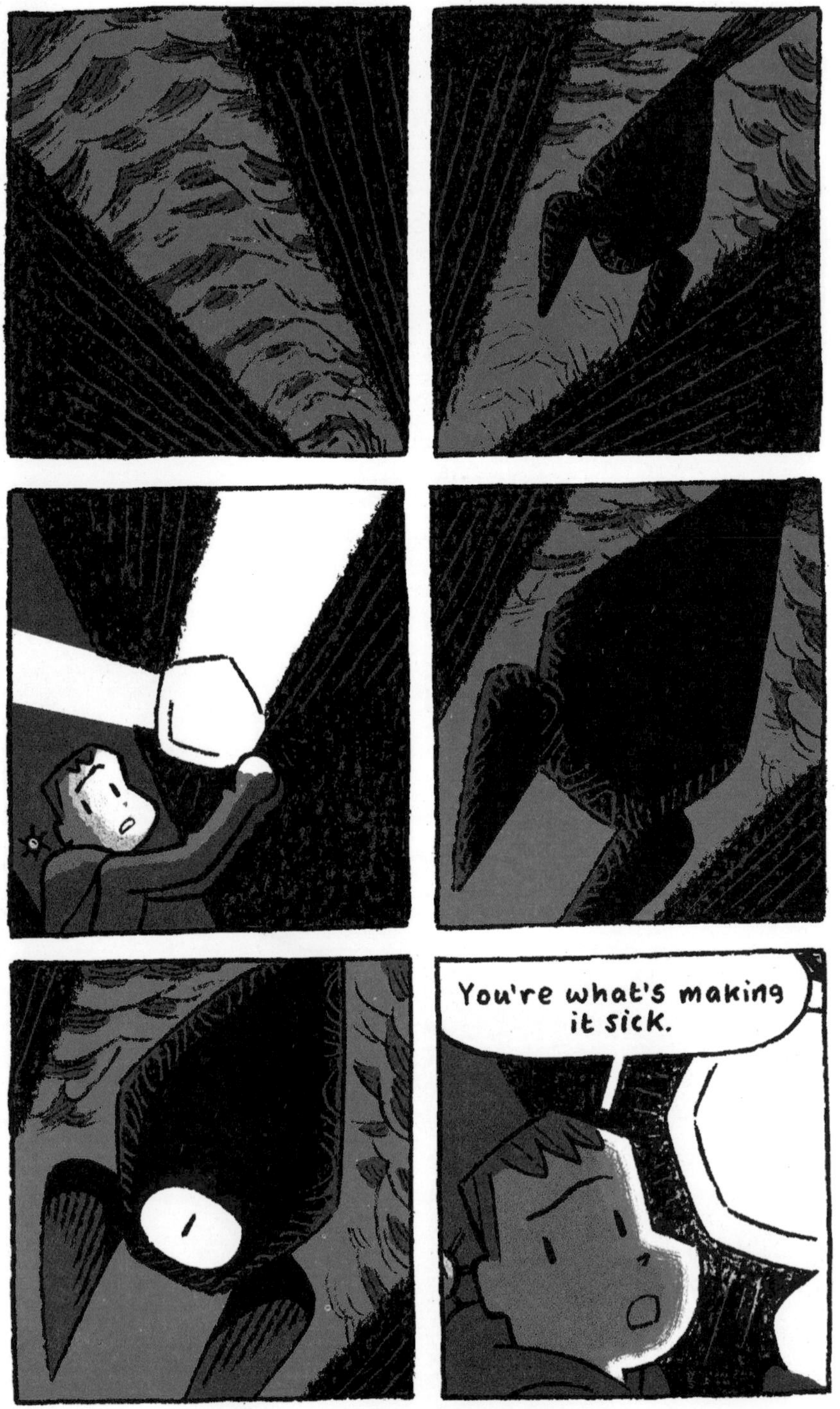
You're what's making it sick.

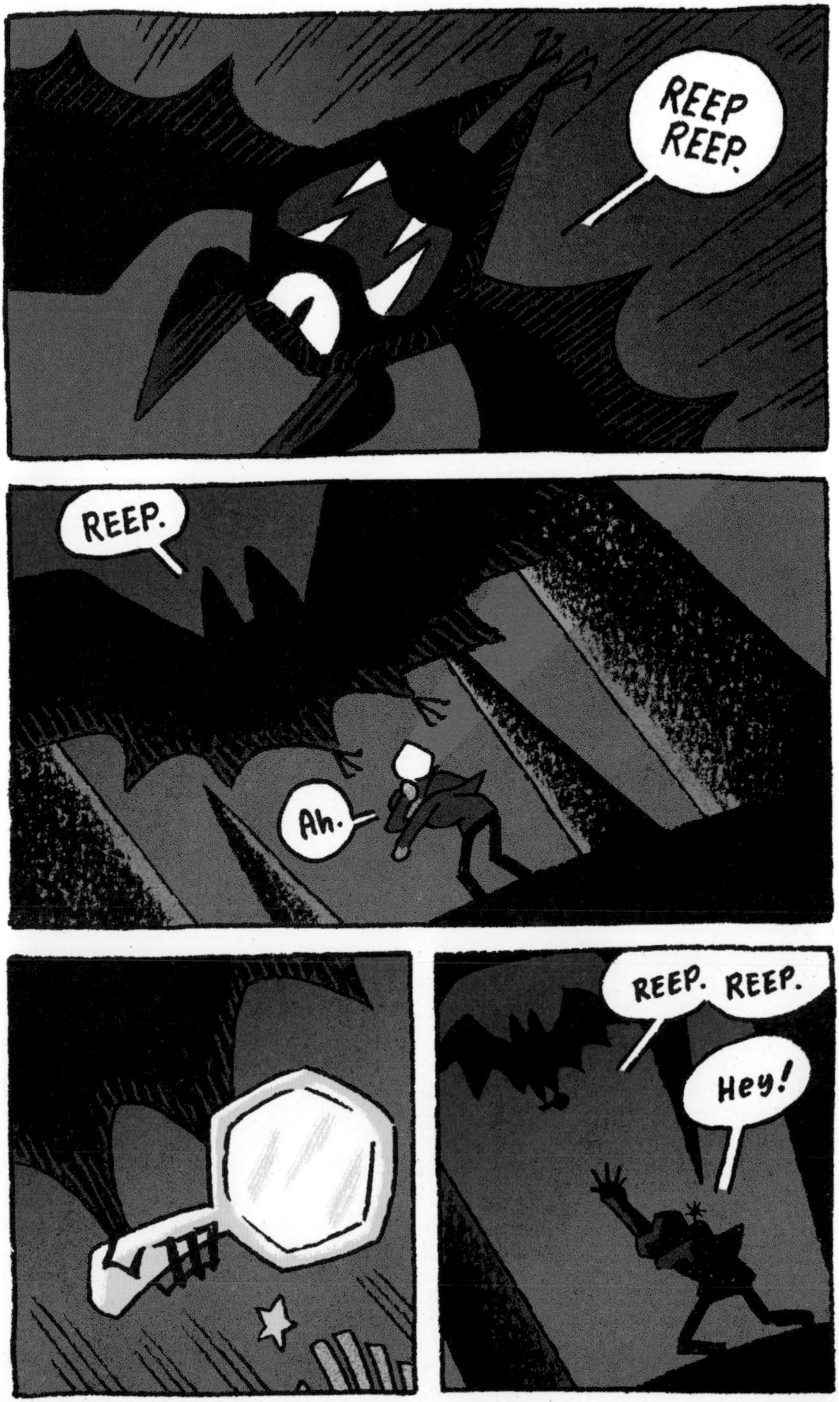
REEP REEP.
REEP.
Ah.
REEP. REEP.
Hey!

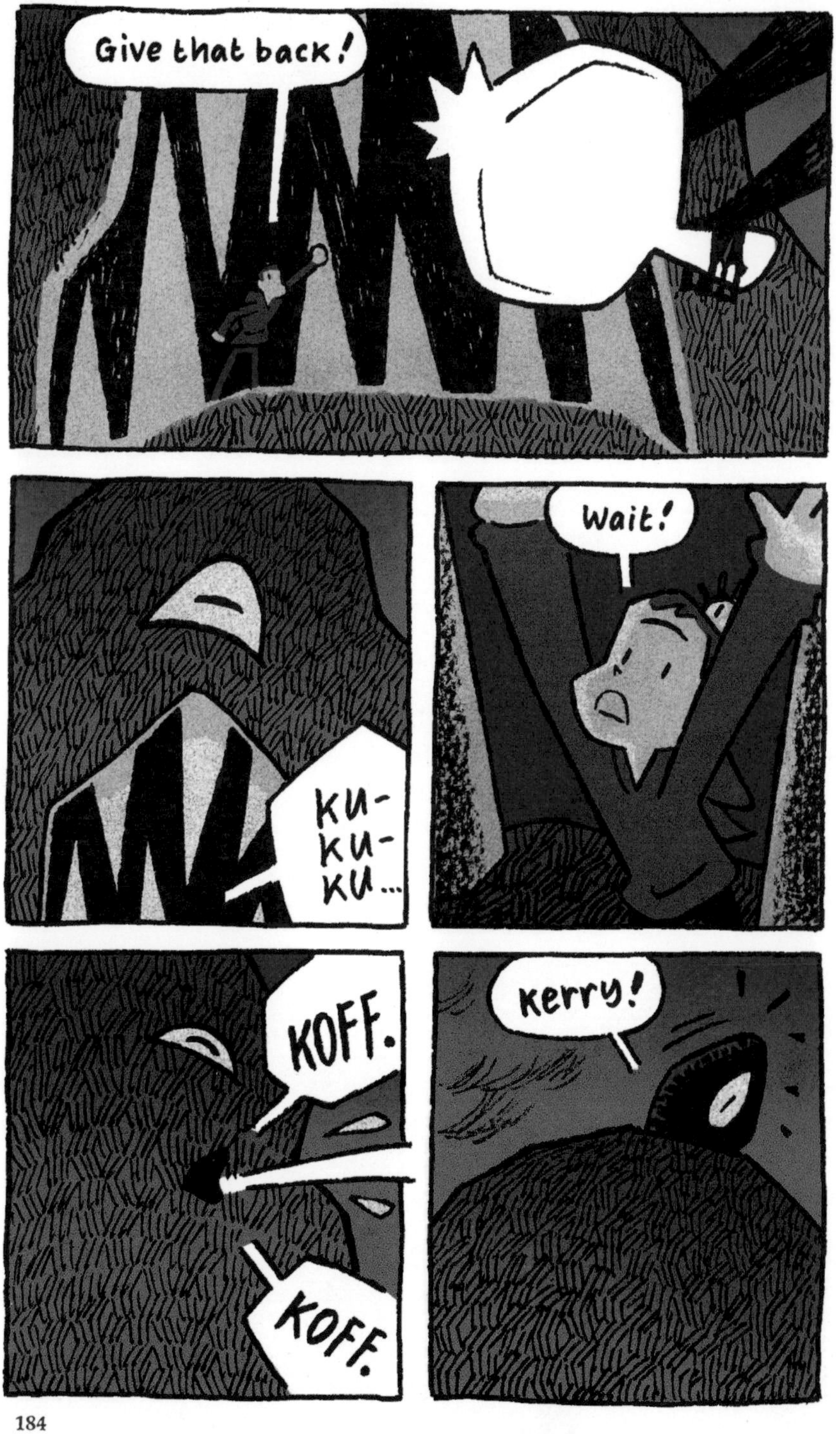
Give that back!
KU-KU-KU...
Wait!
KOFF.
KOFF.
Kerry!

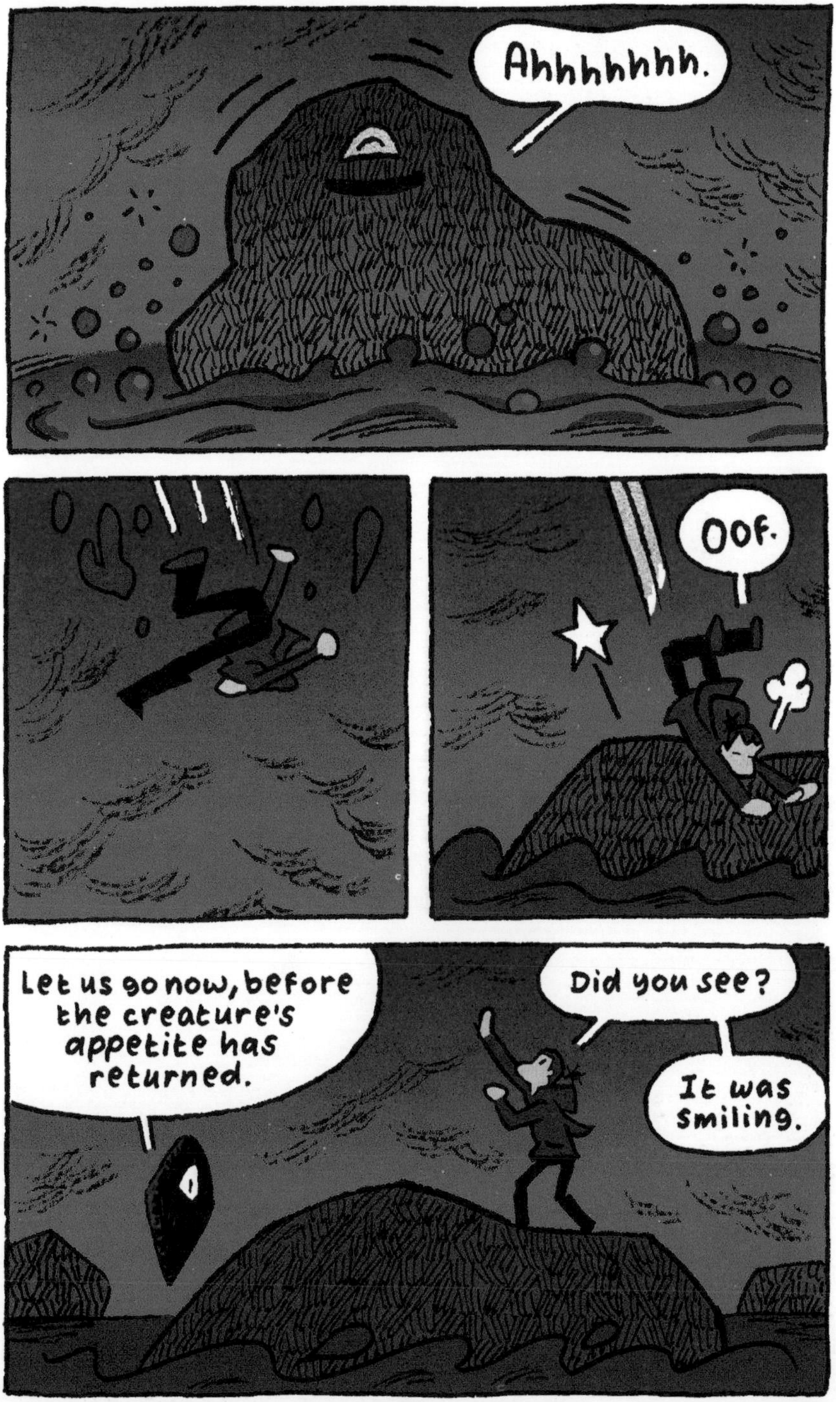
Ahhhhhhh.
OOF.
Let us go now, before the creature's appetite has returned.
Did you see?
It was smiling.

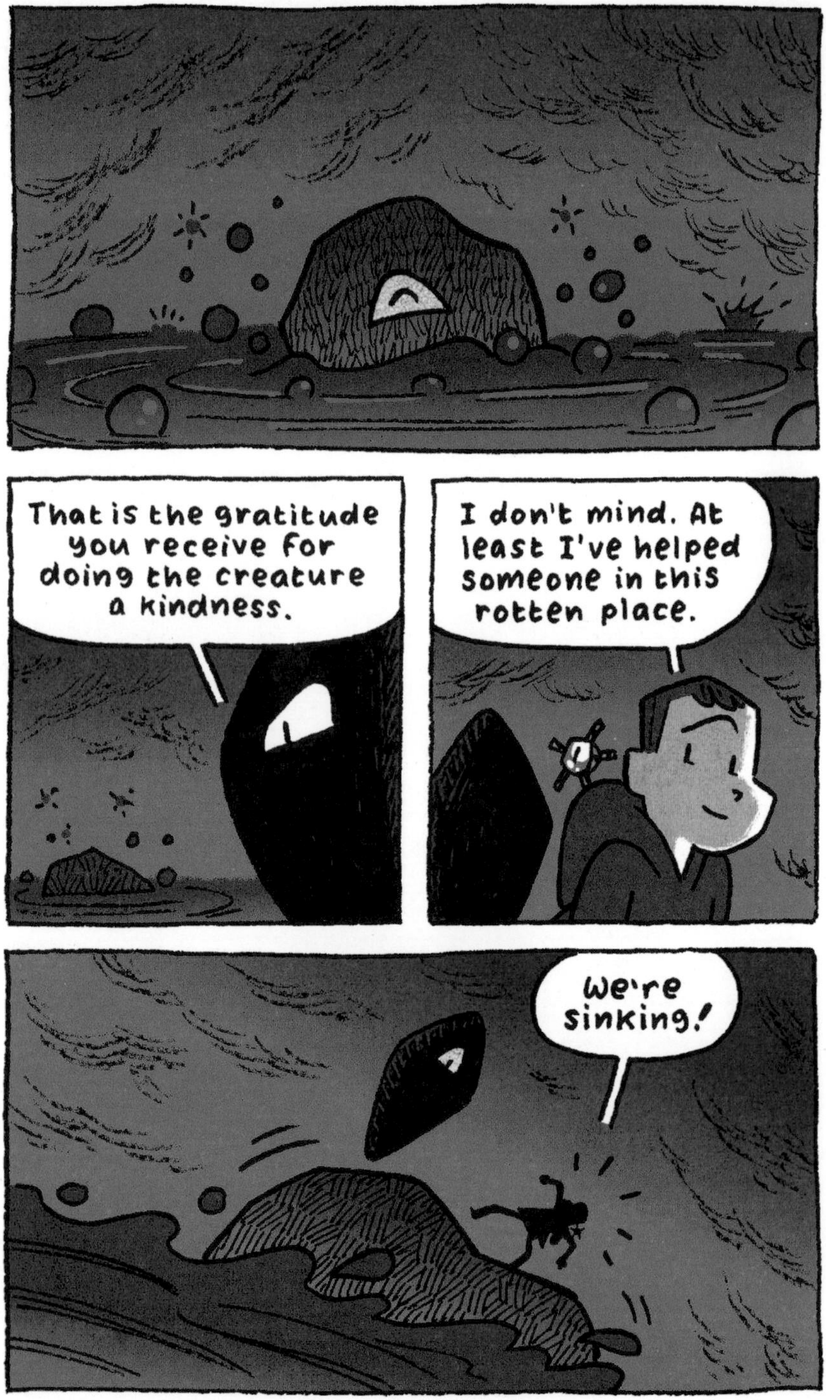
That is the gratitude you receive for doing the creature a kindness.
I don't mind. At least I've helped someone in this rotten place.
We're sinking!

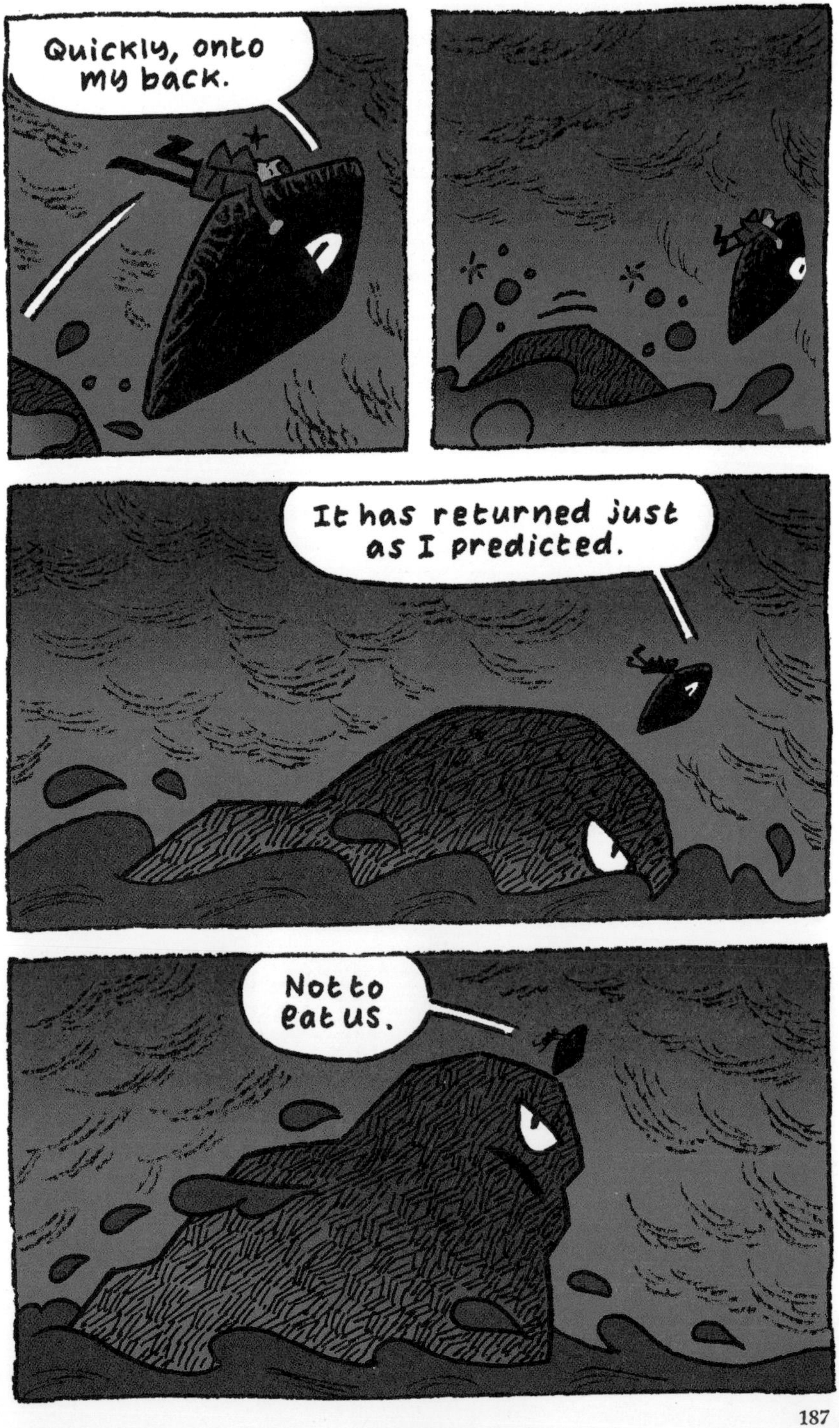
Quickly, onto my back.
It has returned just as I predicted.
Not to eat us.

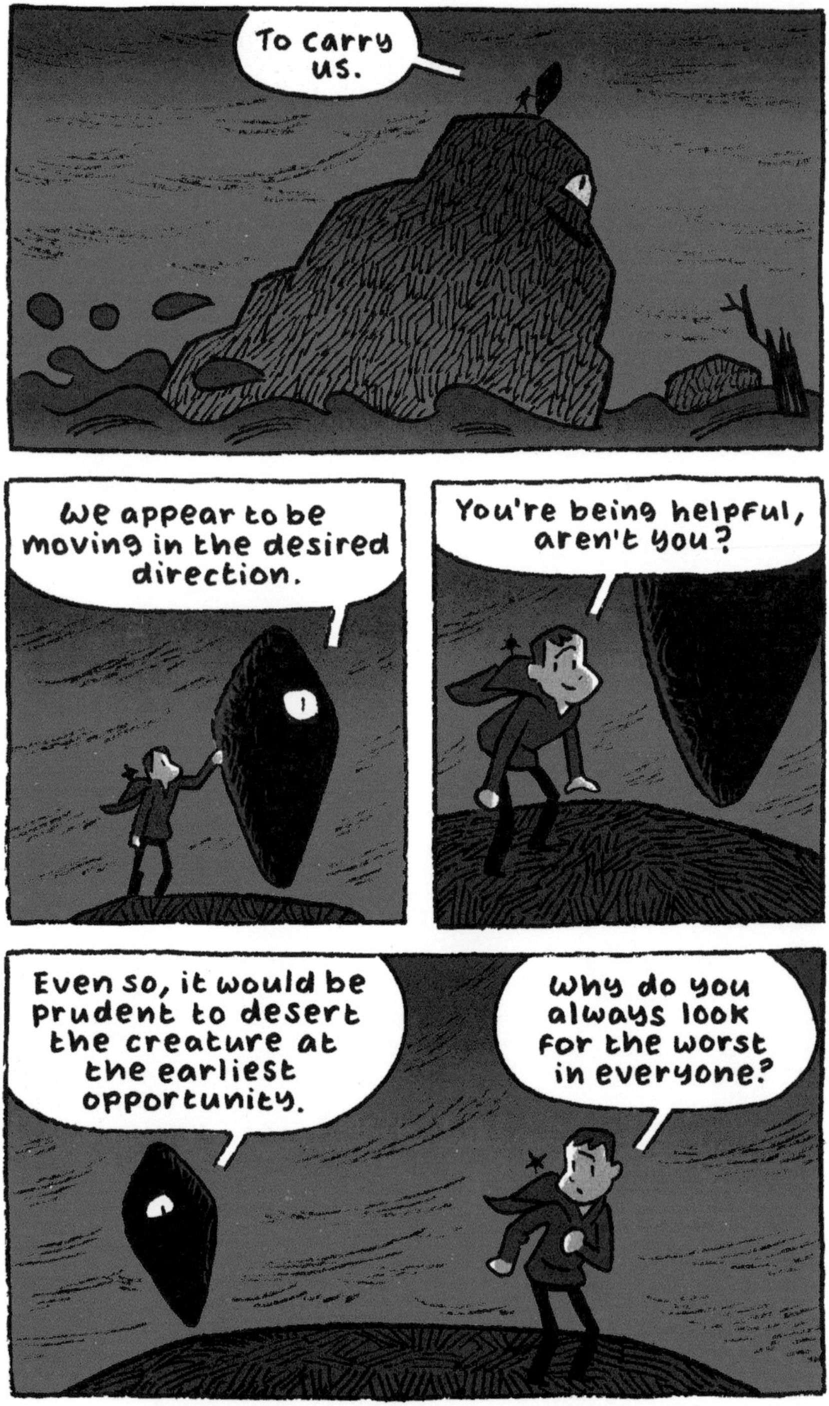
To carry us.
We appear to be moving in the desired direction.
You're being helpful, aren't you?
Even so, it would be prudent to desert the creature at the earliest opportunity.
Why do you always look for the worst in everyone?

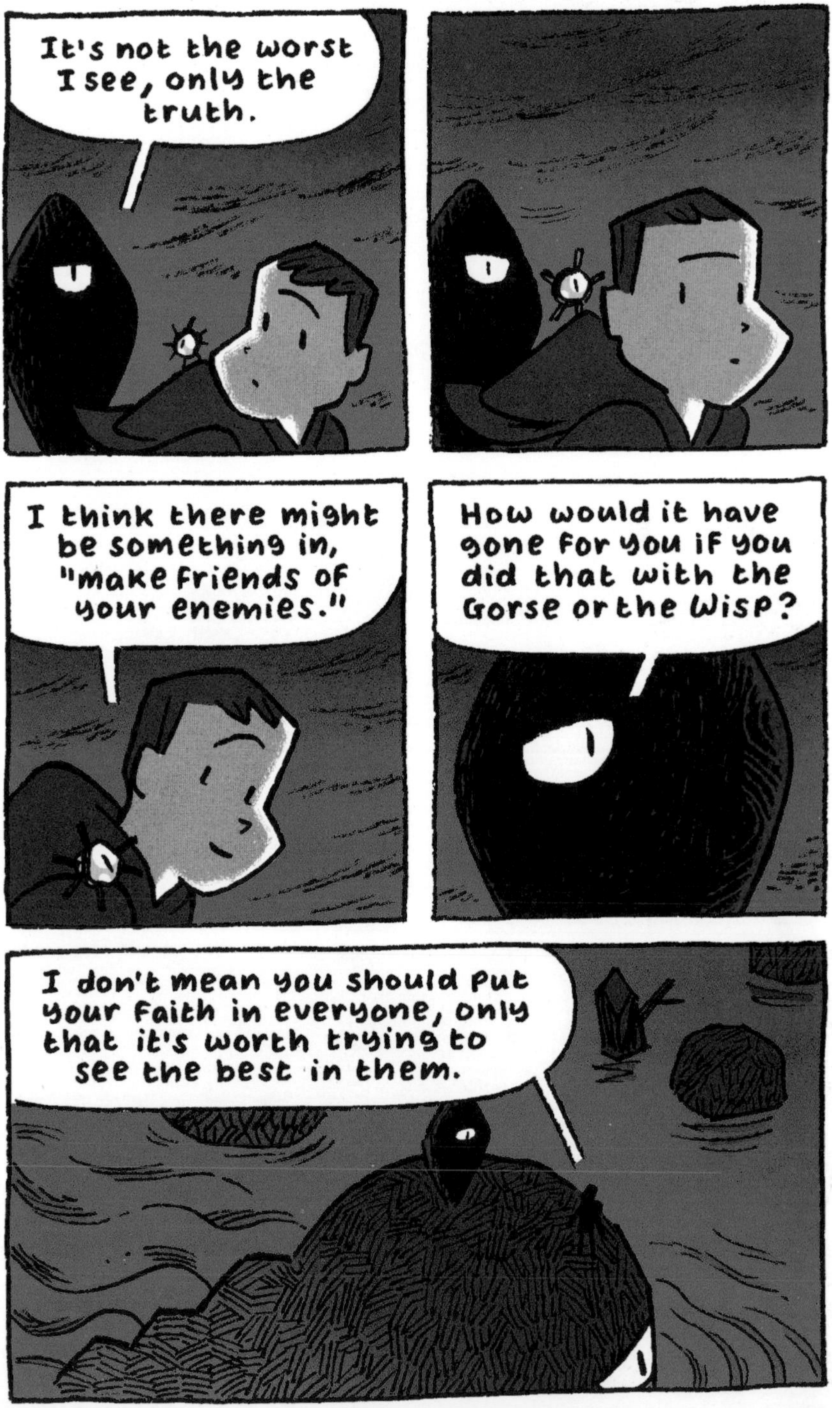
It's not the worst I see, only the truth.
I think there might be something in, "make friends of your enemies."
How would it have gone for you if you did that with the Gorse or the Wisp?
I don't mean you should put your faith in everyone, only that it's worth trying to see the best in them.

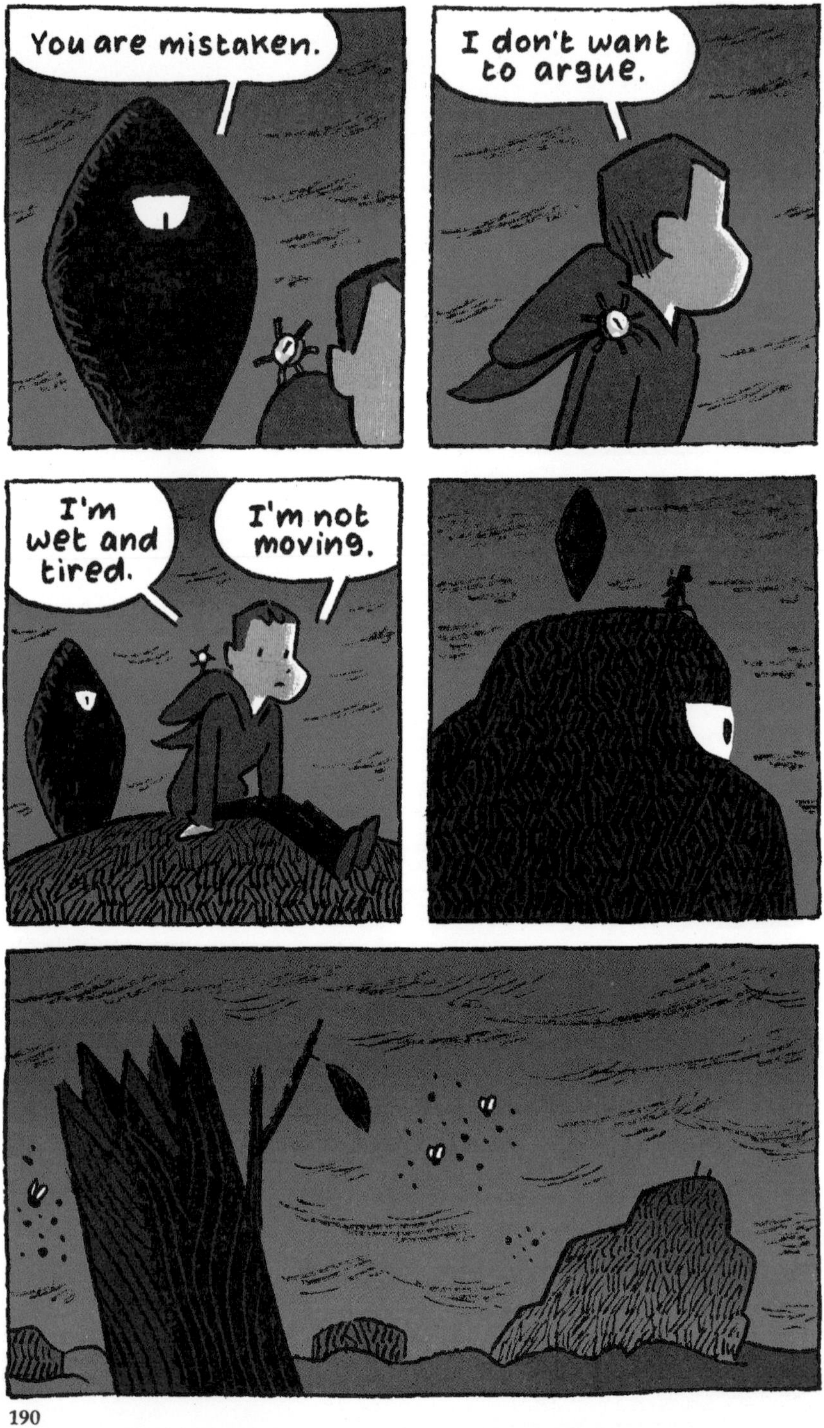
You are mistaken.
I don't want to argue.
I'm wet and tired.
I'm not moving.

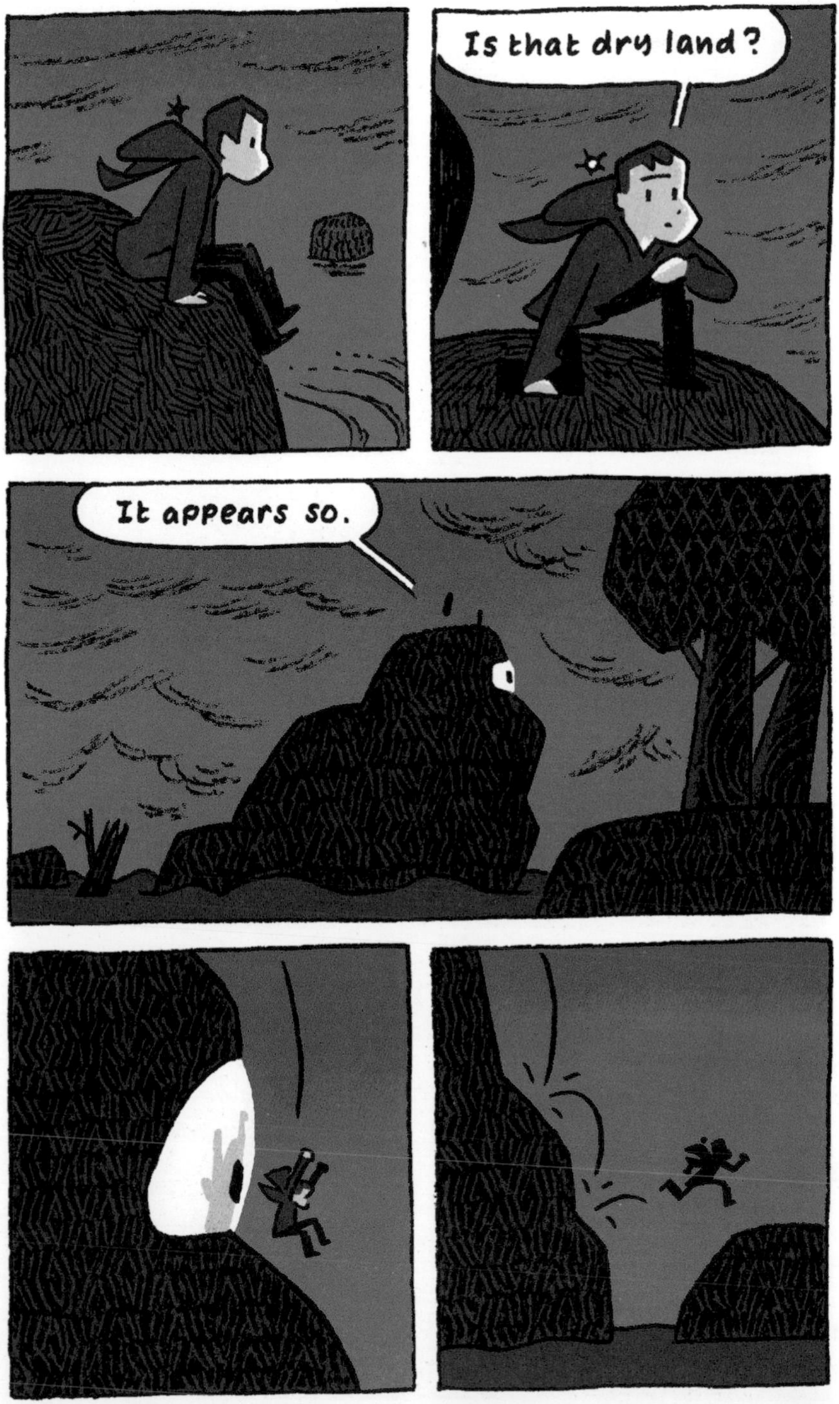
Is that dry land?
It appears so.

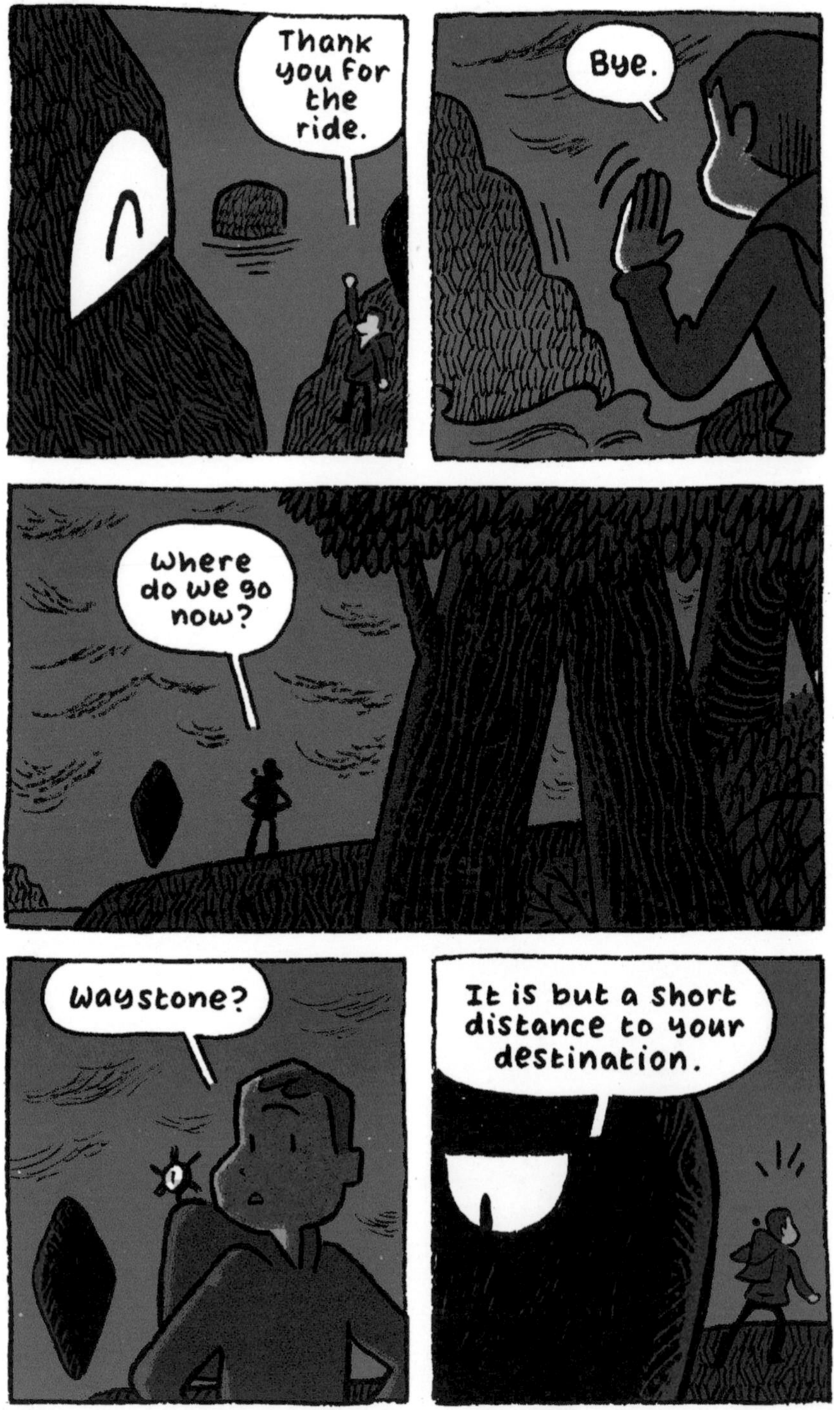
Thank you for the ride.
Bye.
Where do we go now?
Waystone?
It is but a short distance to your destination.

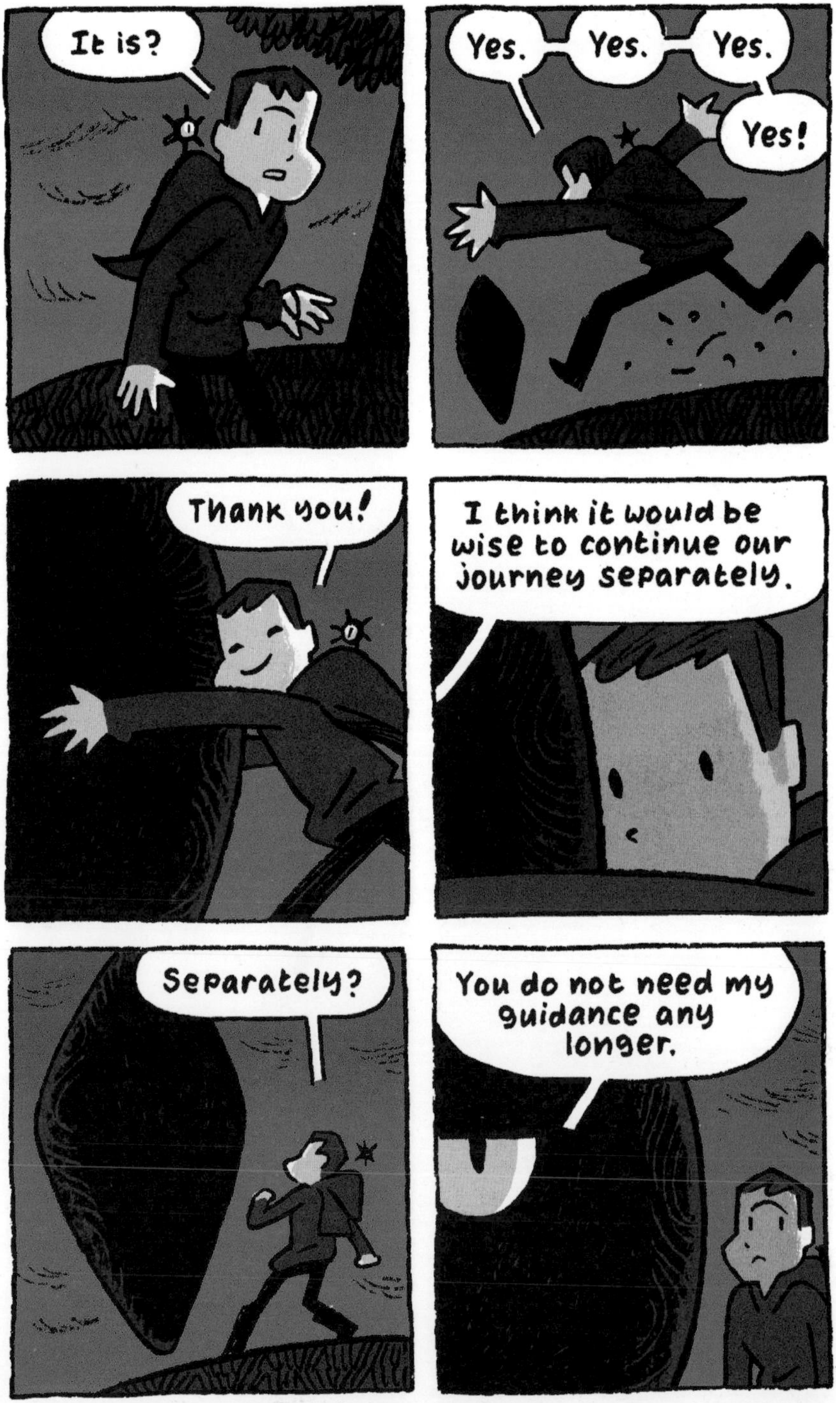
It is?
Yes.
Yes.
Yes.
Yes!
Thank you!
I think it would be wise to continue our journey separately.
Separately?
You do not need my guidance any longer.

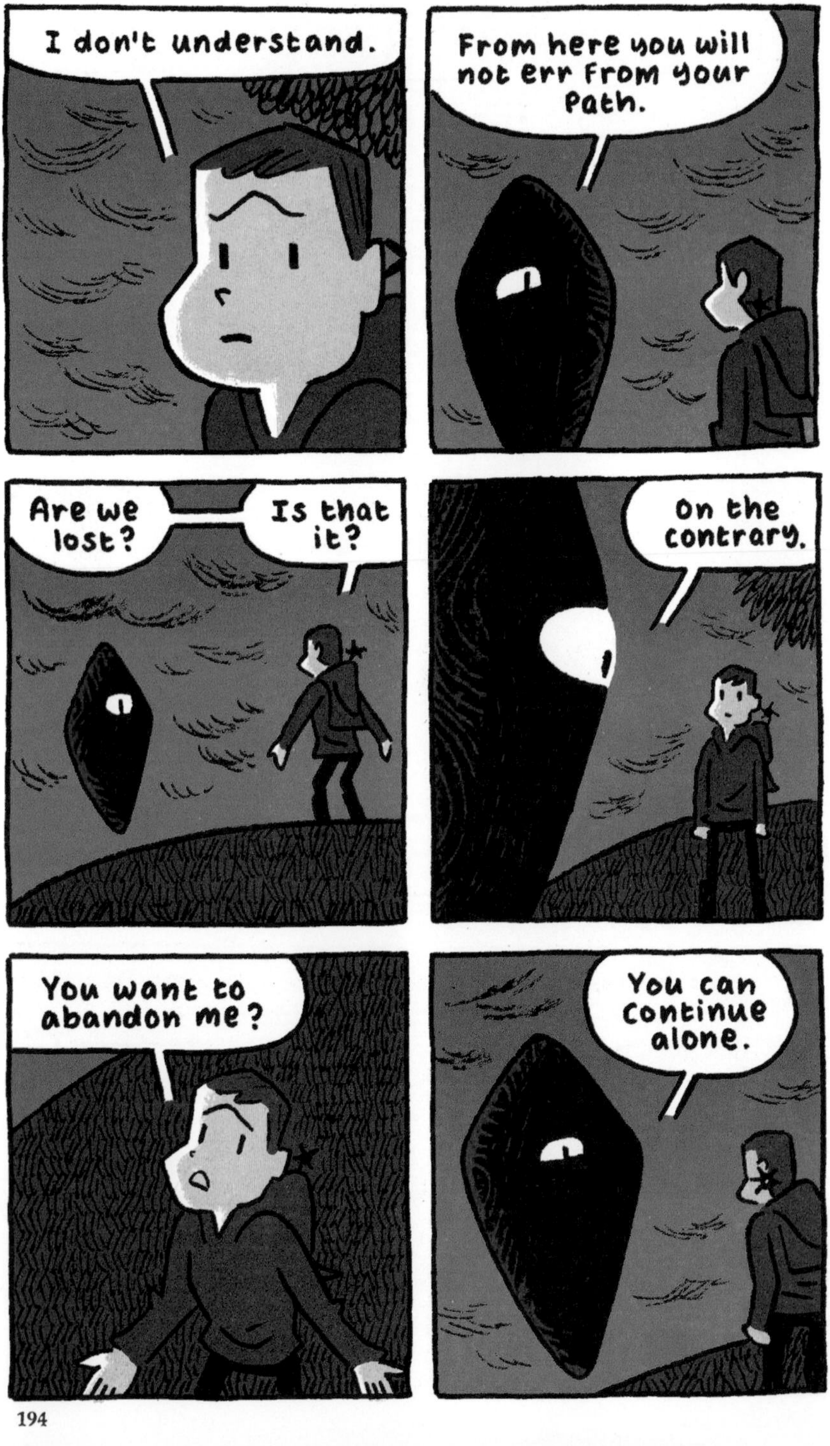
I don't understand.
From here you will not err from your path.
Are we lost?
Is that it?
On the contrary.
You want to abandon me?
You can continue alone.

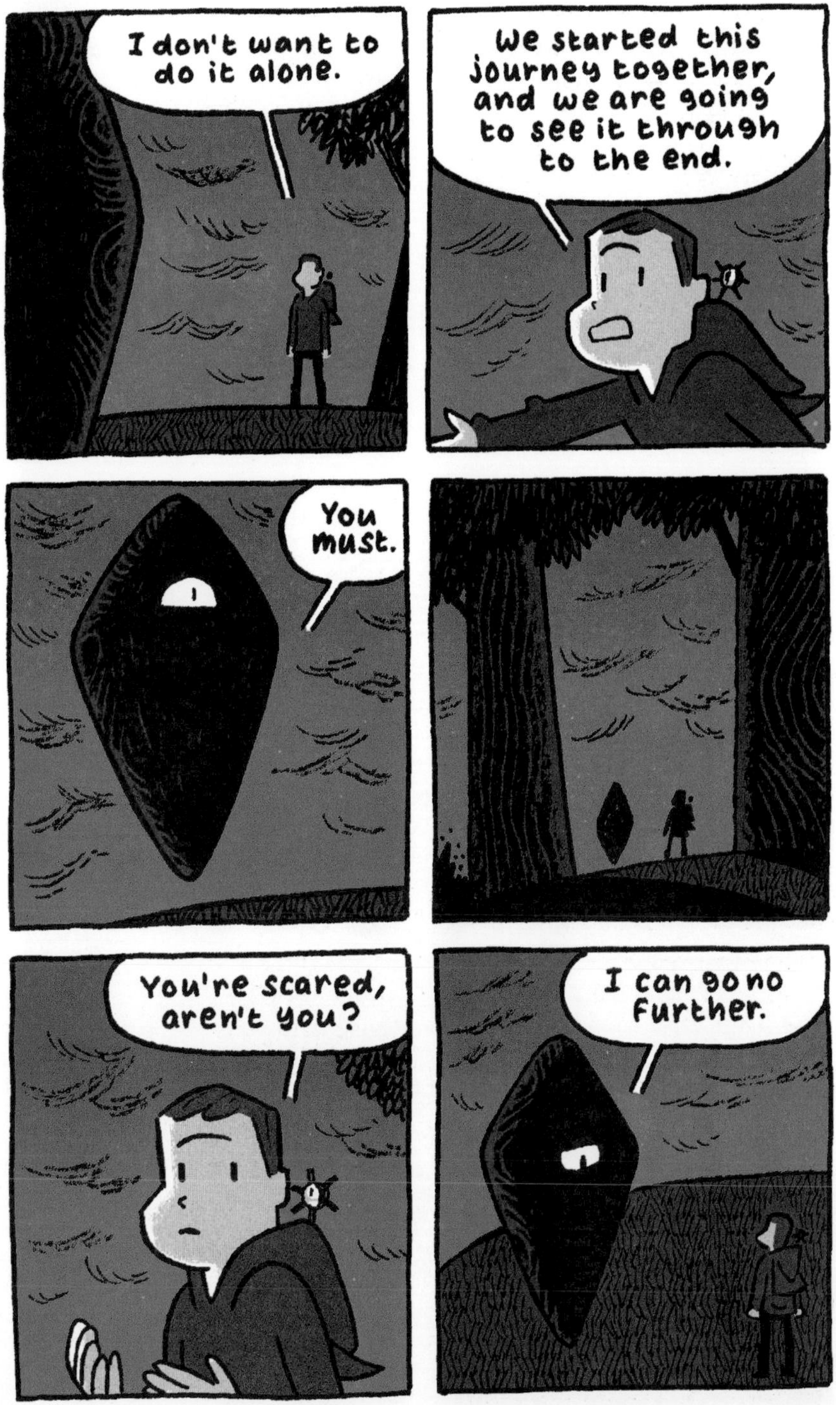
I don't want to do it alone.
We started this journey together, and we are going to see it through to the end.
You must.
You're scared, aren't you?
I can go no further.

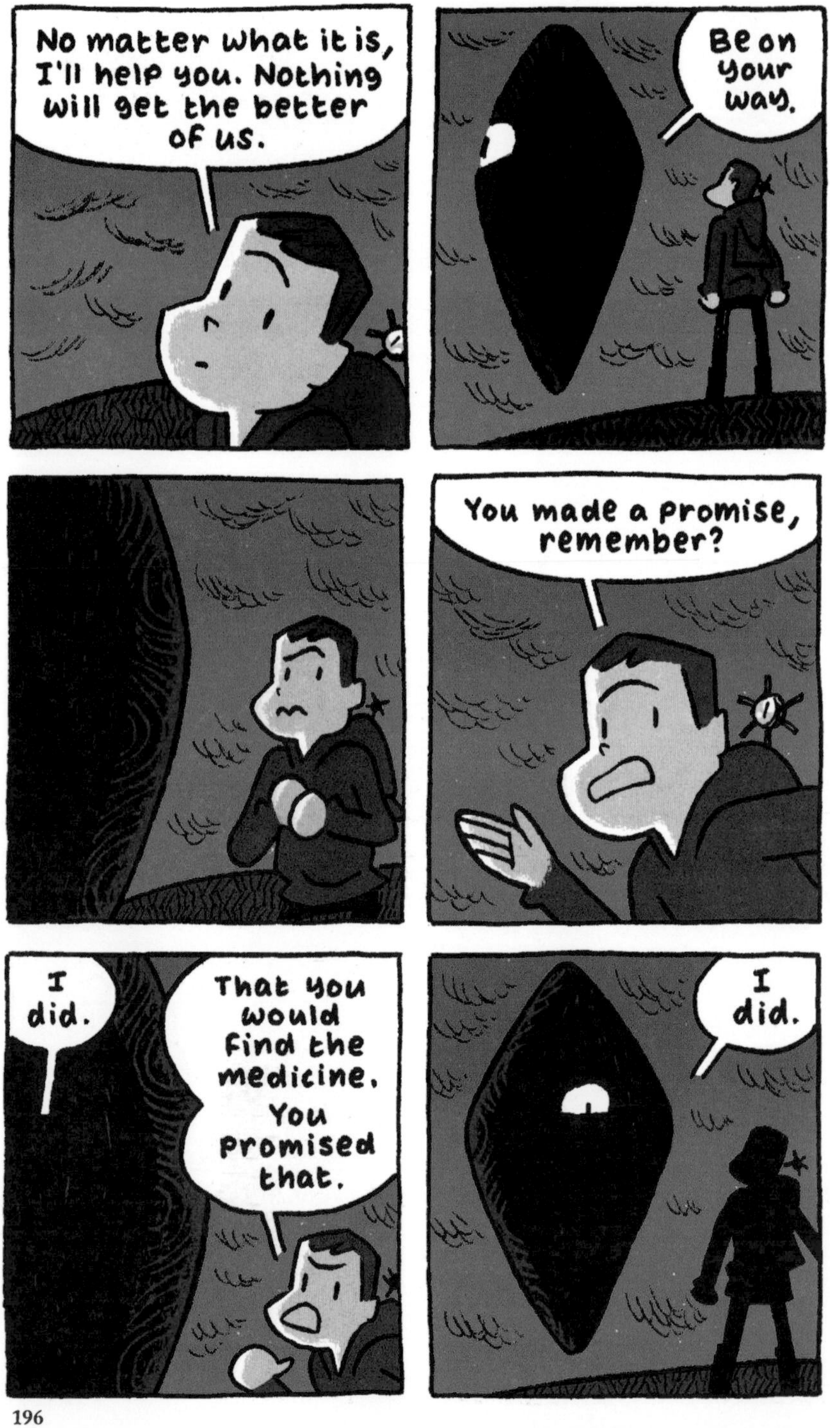
No matter what it is, I'll help you. Nothing will get the better of us.
Be on your way.
You made a promise, remember?
I did.
That you would find the medicine.
You promised that.
I did.

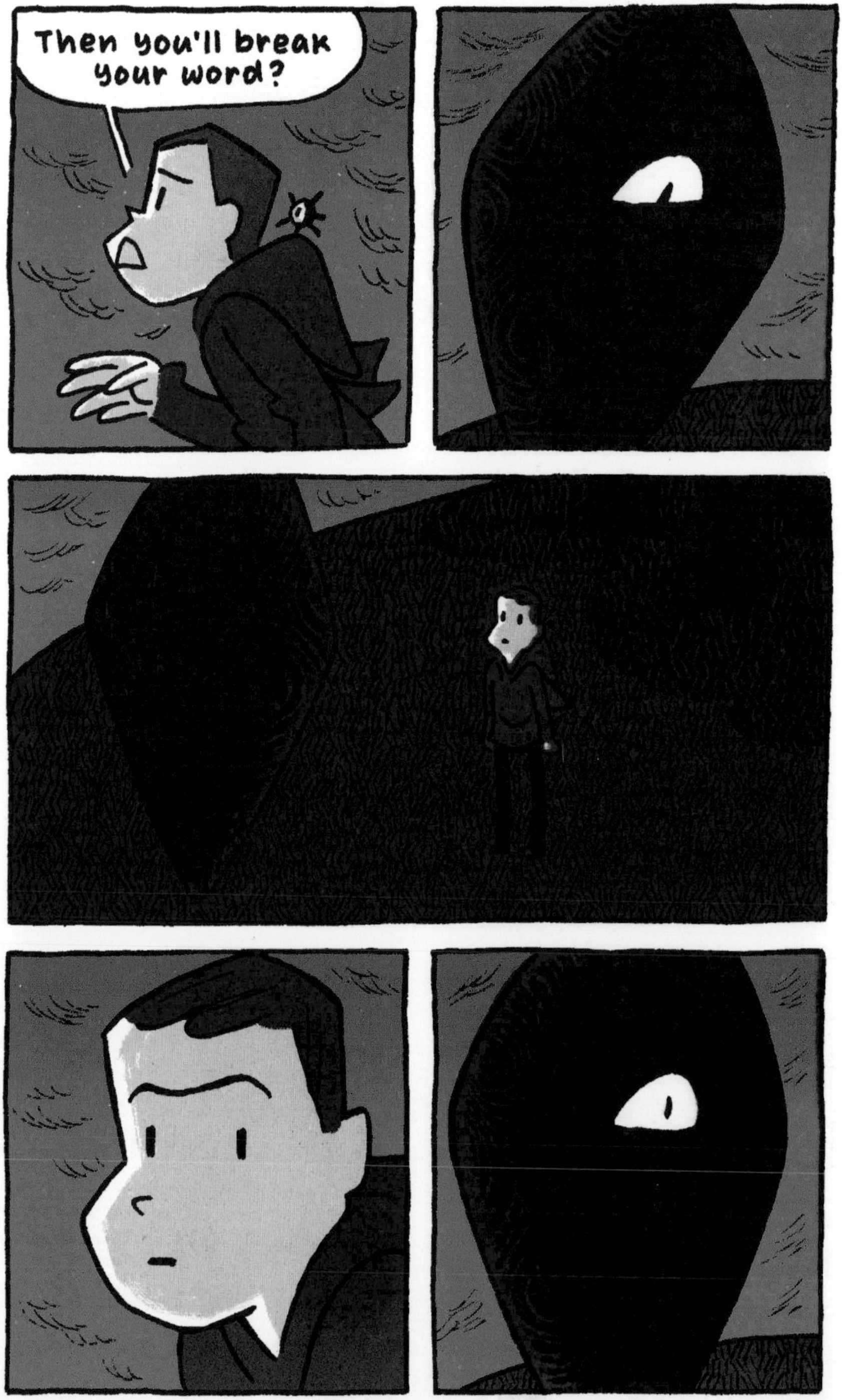
Then you'll break your word?

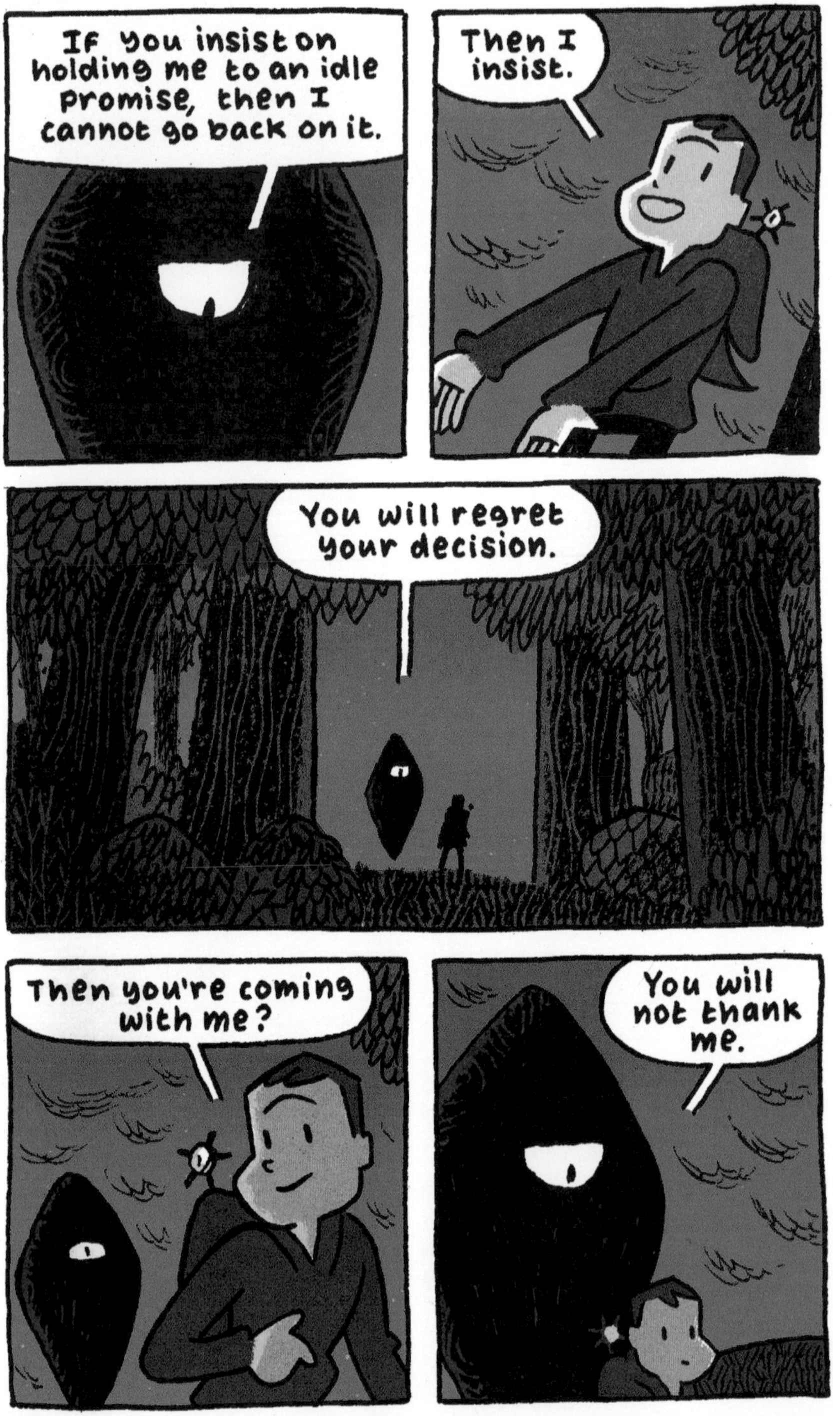
If you insist on holding me to an idle promise, then I cannot go back on it.
Then I insist.
You will regret your decision.
Then you're coming with me?
You will not thank me.

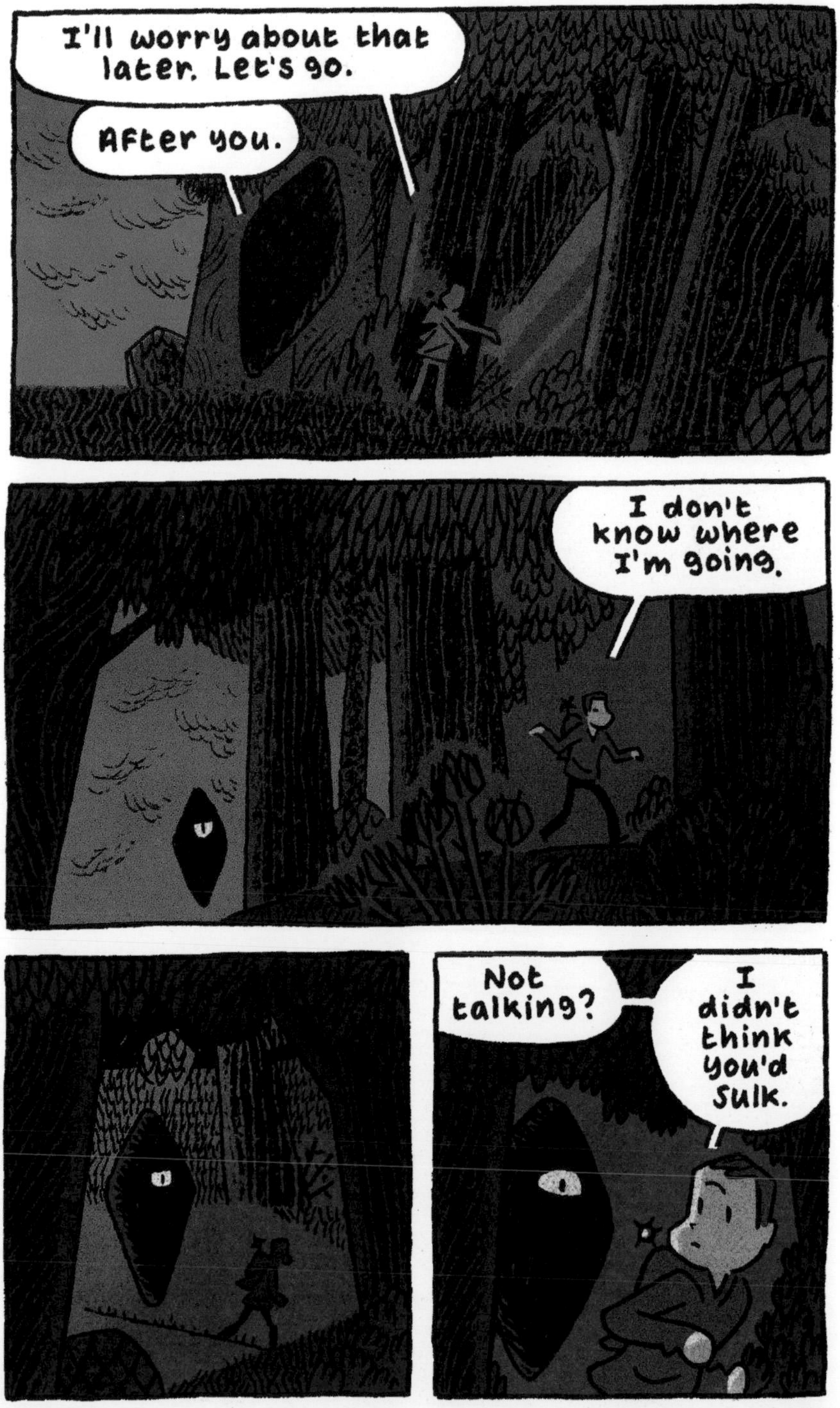
I'll worry about that later. Let's go.
After you.
I don't know where I'm going.
Not talking?
I didn't think you'd sulk.

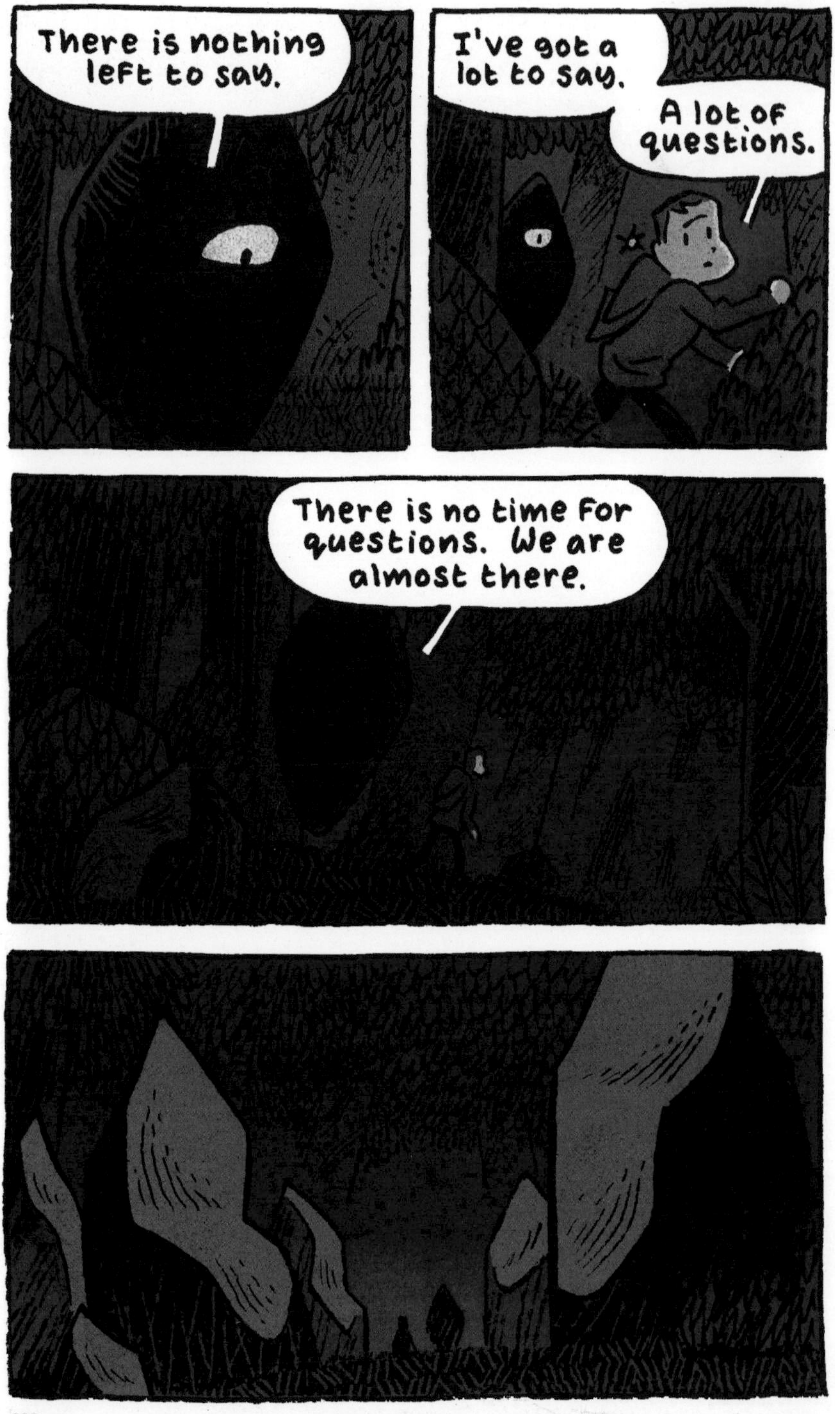
There is nothing left to say.
I've got a lot to say.
A lot of questions.
There is no time for questions. We are almost there.

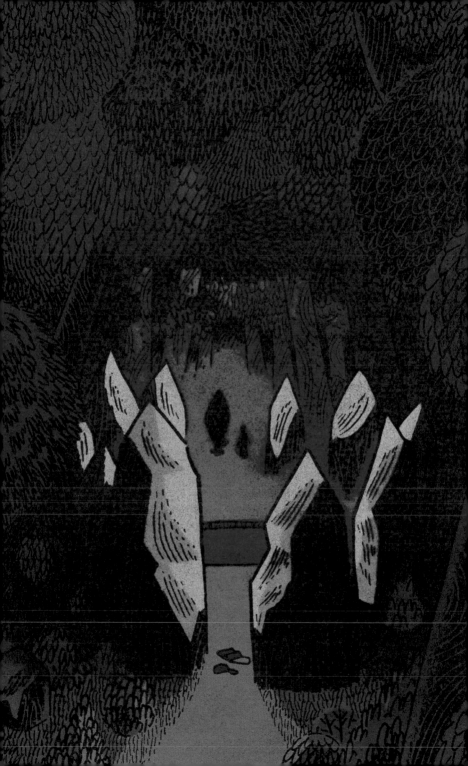

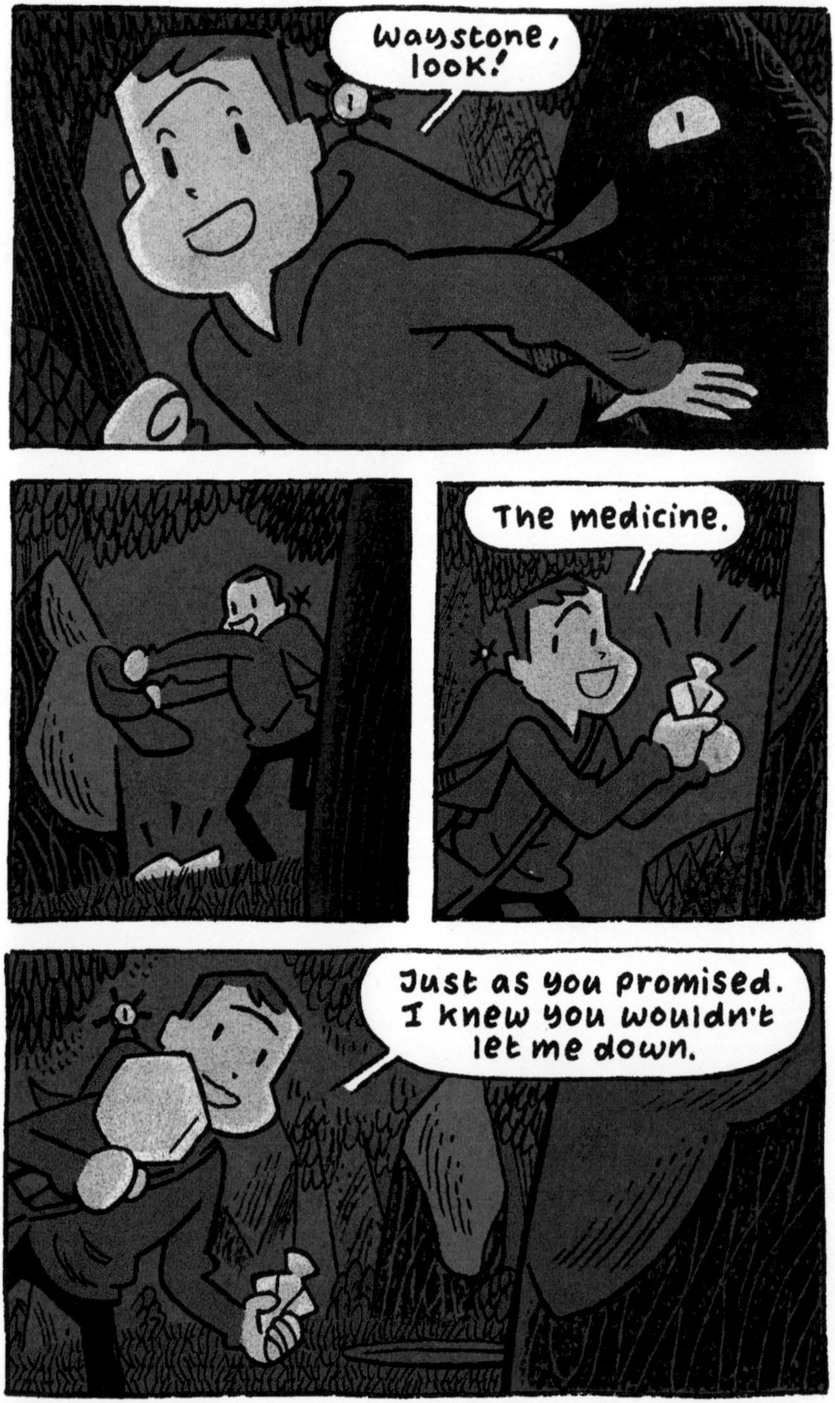
Waystone, look!
The medicine.
Just as you promised. I knew you wouldn't let me down.

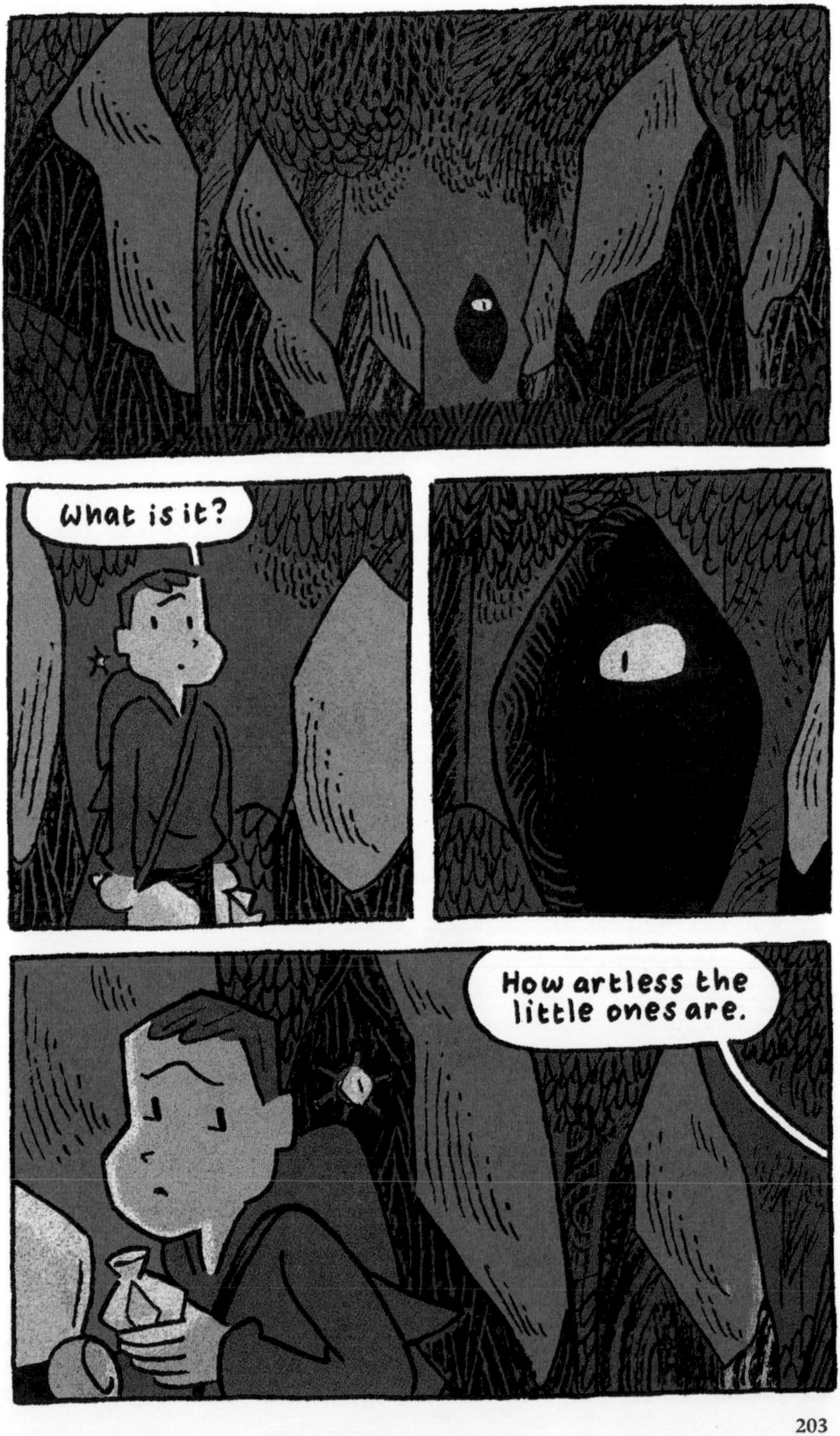
What is it?
How artless the little ones are.

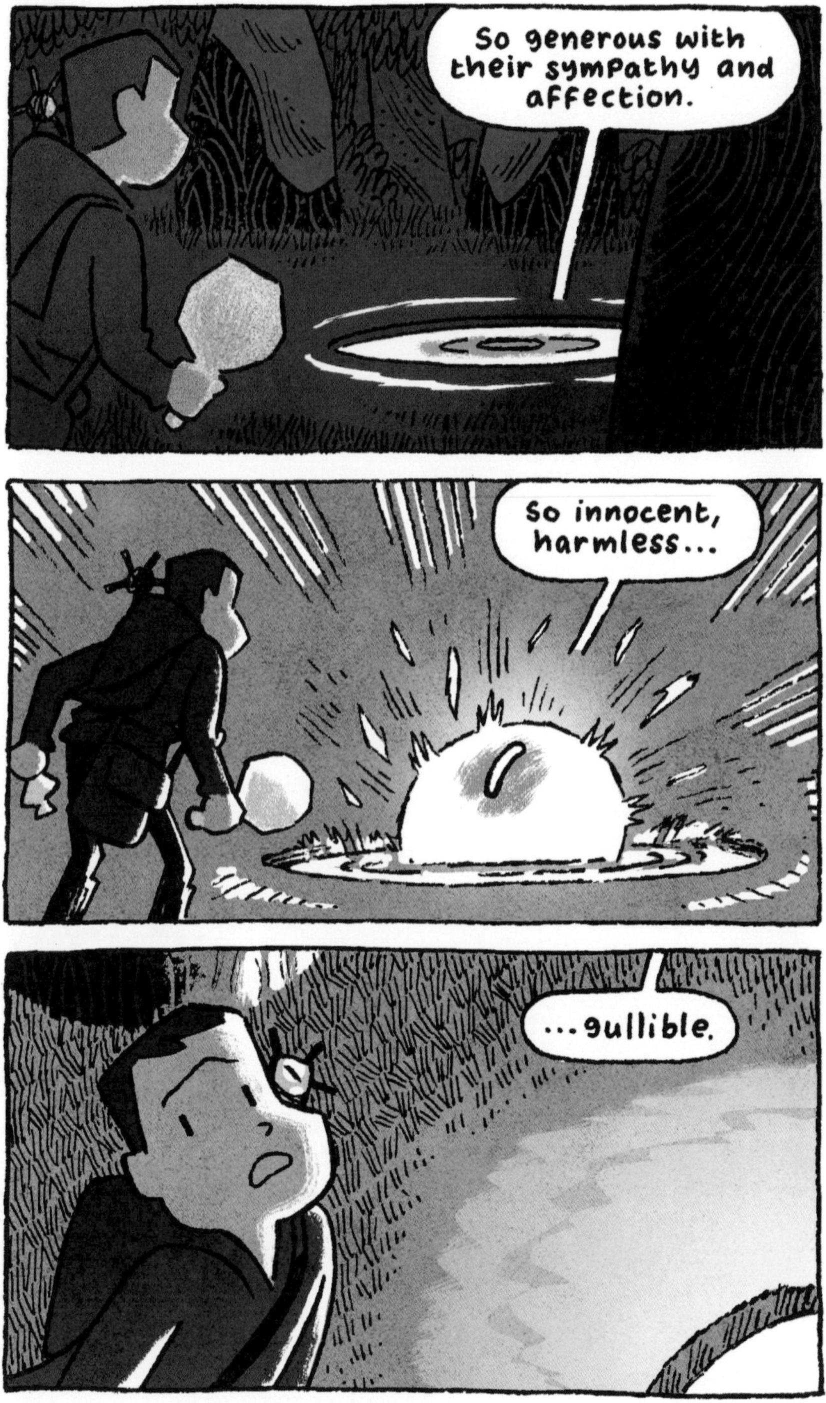
So generous with their sympathy and affection.
So innocent, harmless...
...gullible.

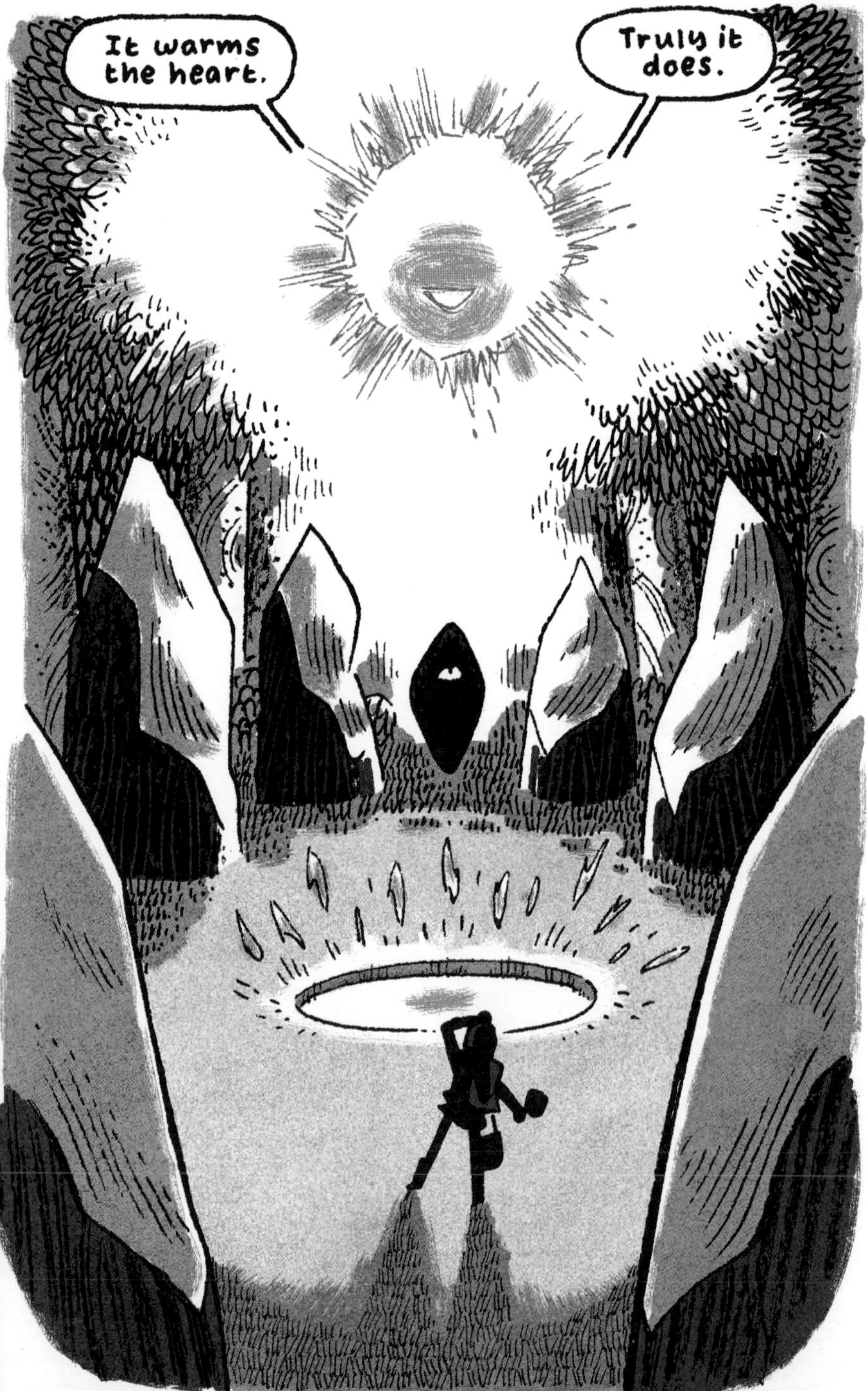
It warms the heart.
Truly it does.

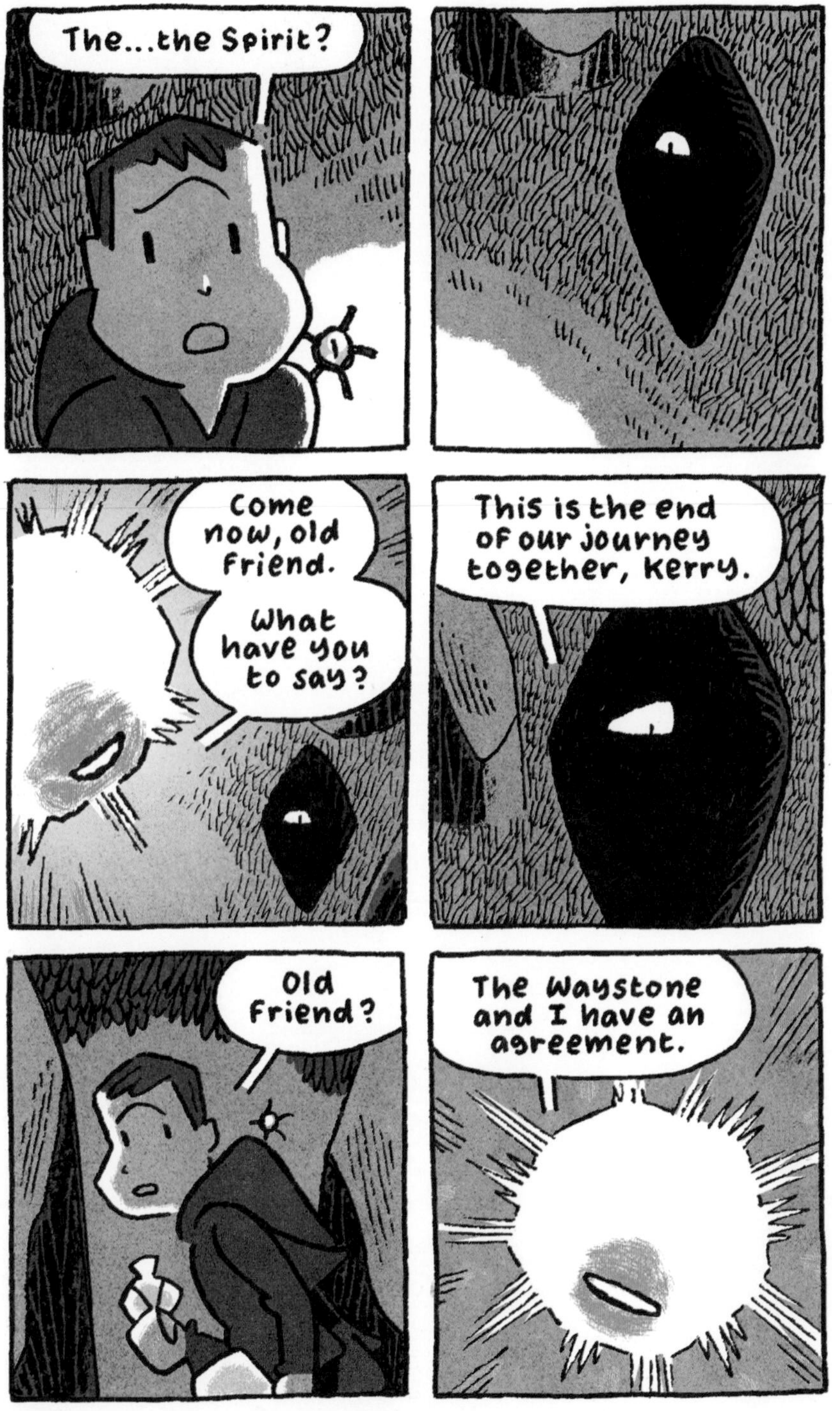
The...the Spirit?
Come now, old friend.
What have you to say?
This is the end of our journey together, Kerry.
Old friend?
The Waystone and I have an agreement.

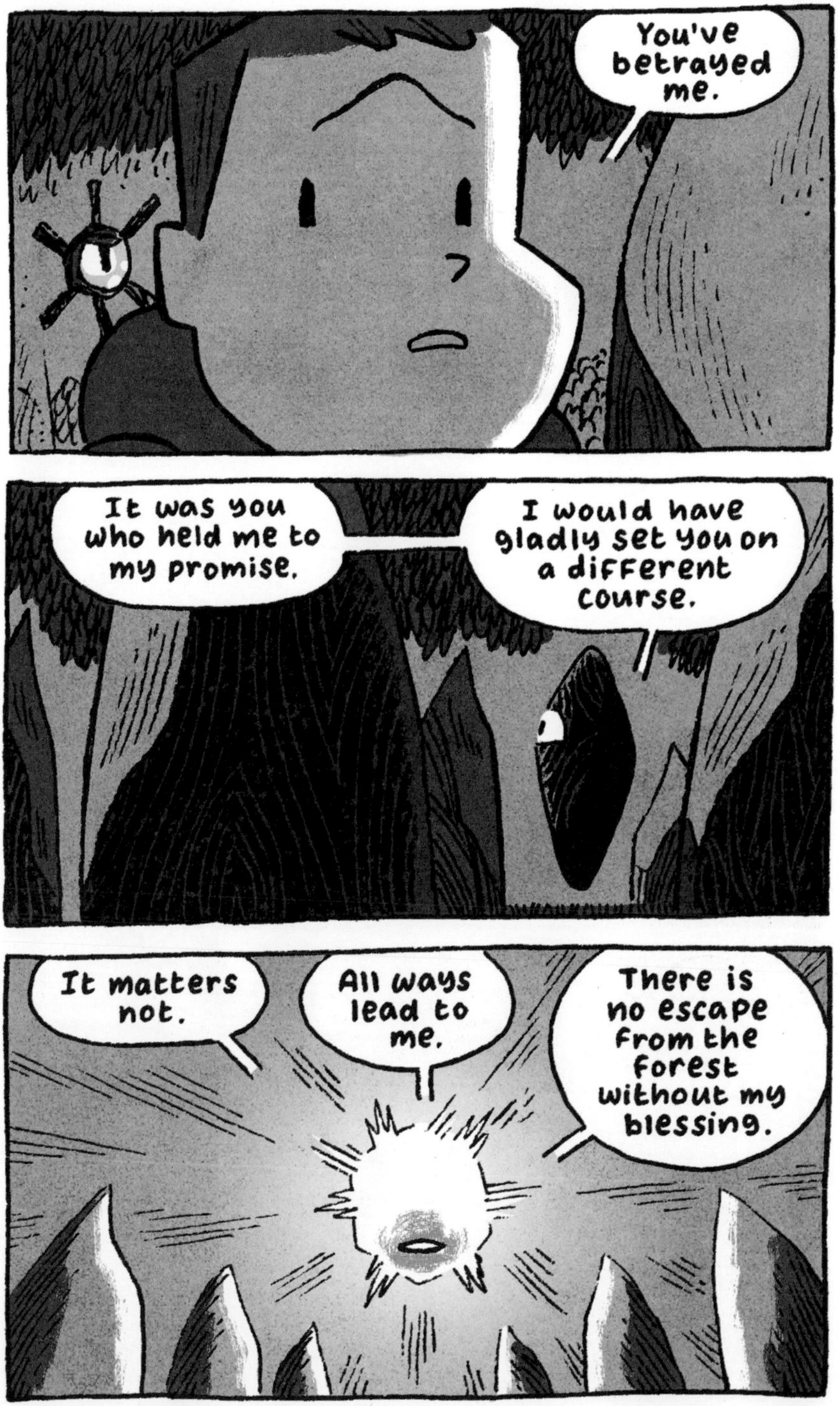
You've betrayed me.
It was you who held me to my promise.
I would have gladly set you on a different course.
It matters not.
All ways lead to me.
There is no escape from the forest without my blessing.

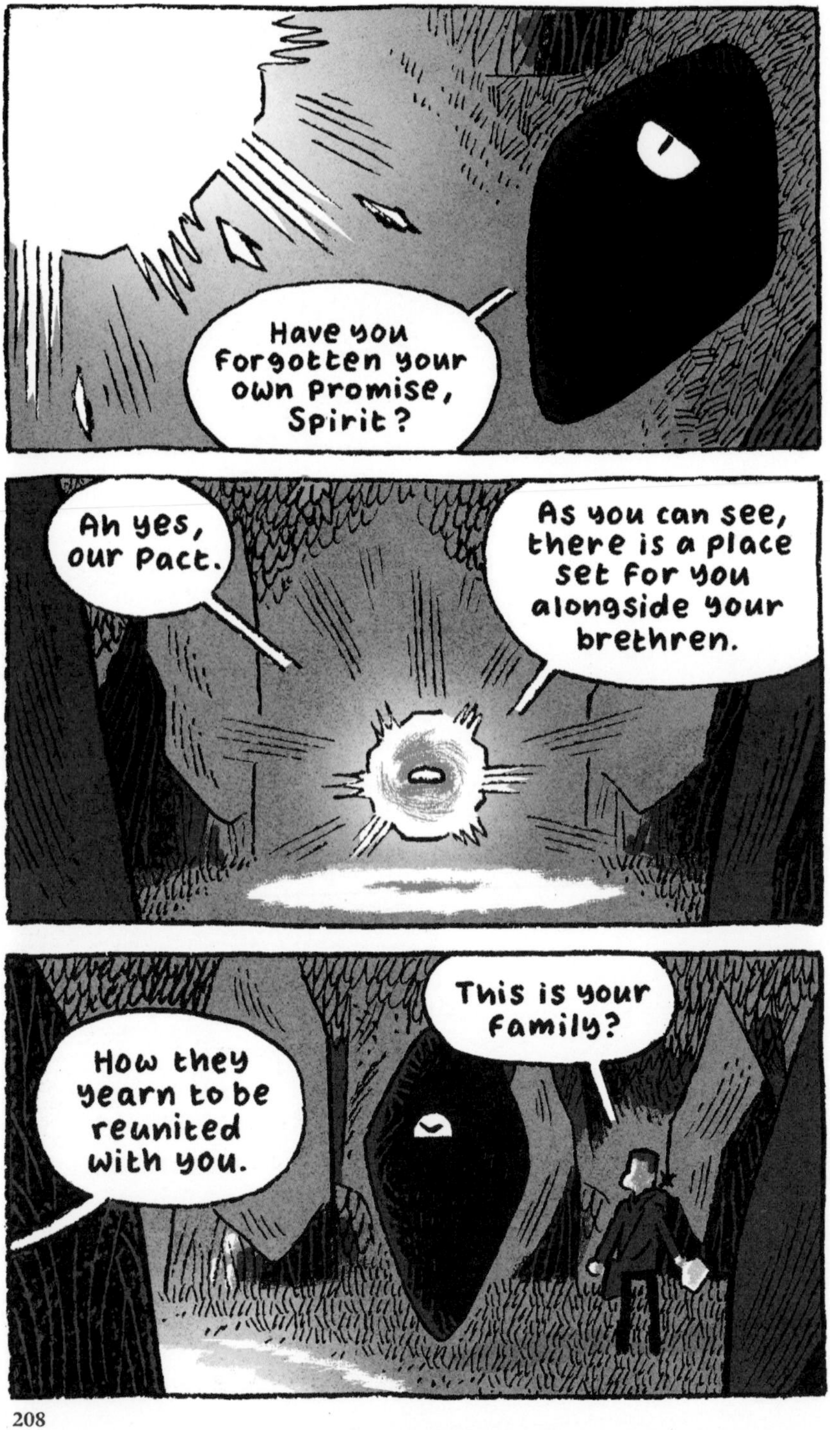
Have you forgotten your own promise, Spirit?
Ah yes, our Pact.
As you can see, there is a place set for you alongside your brethren.
This is your family?
How they yearn to be reunited with you.

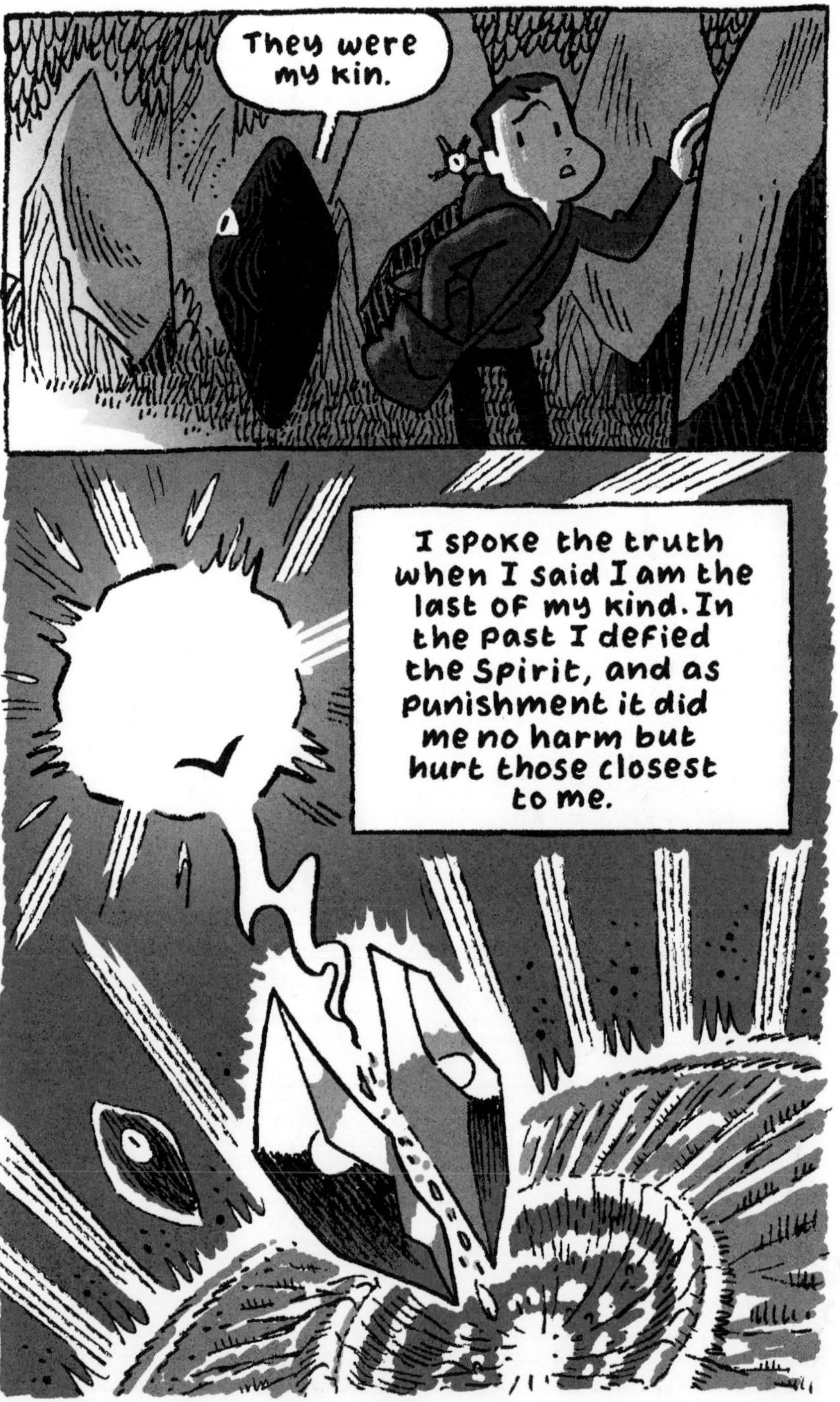
They were my kin.
I spoke the truth when I said I am the last of my kind. In the past I defied the Spirit, and as punishment it did me no harm but hurt those closest to me.

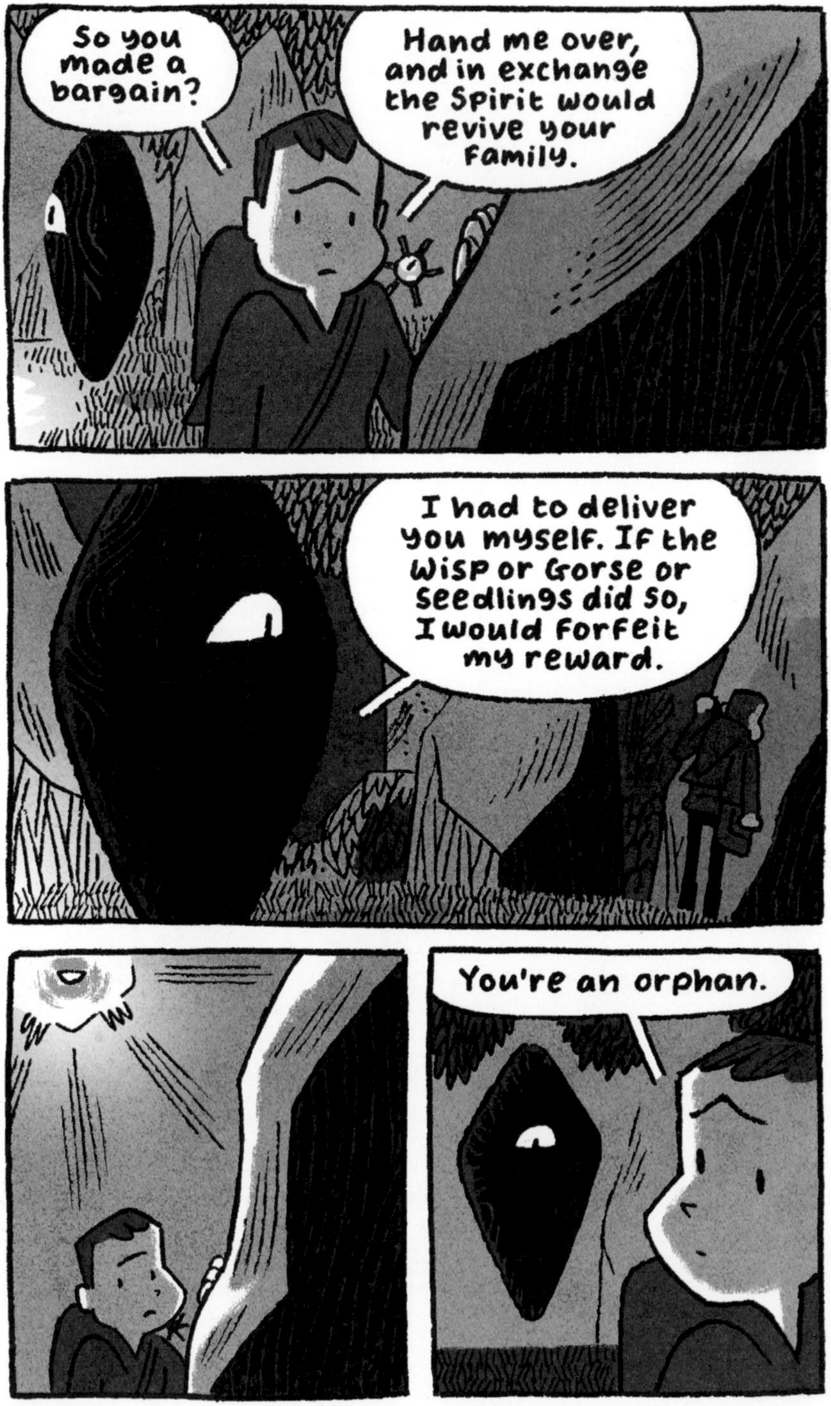
So you made a bargain?
Hand me over, and in exchange the Spirit would revive your family.
I had to deliver you myself. If the Wisp or Gorse or seedlings did so, I would forfeit my reward.
You're an orphan.

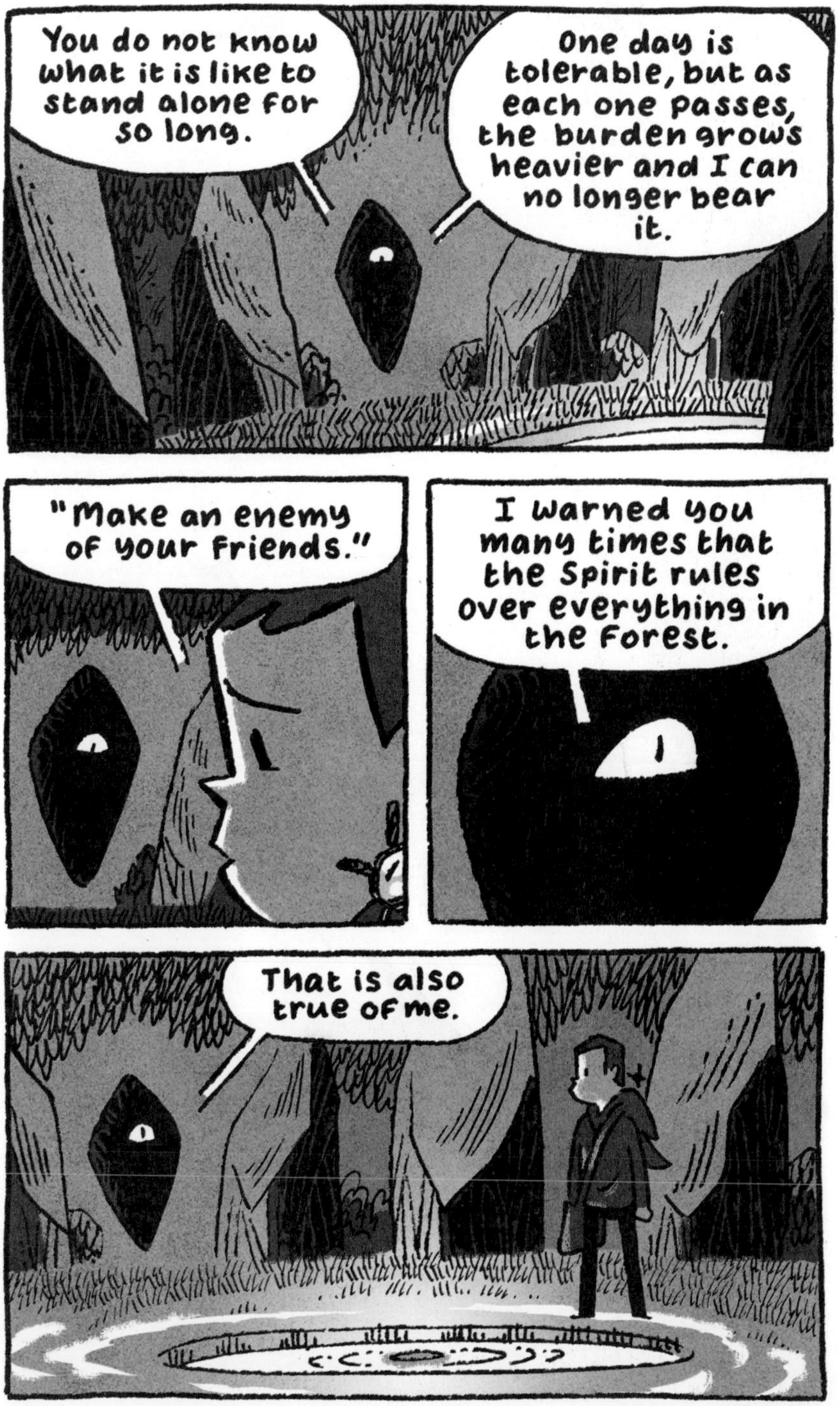
You do not know what it is like to stand alone for so long.
One day is tolerable, but as each one passes, the burden grows heavier and I can no longer bear it.
"Make an enemy of your friends."
I warned you many times that the Spirit rules over everything in the Forest.
That is also true of me.

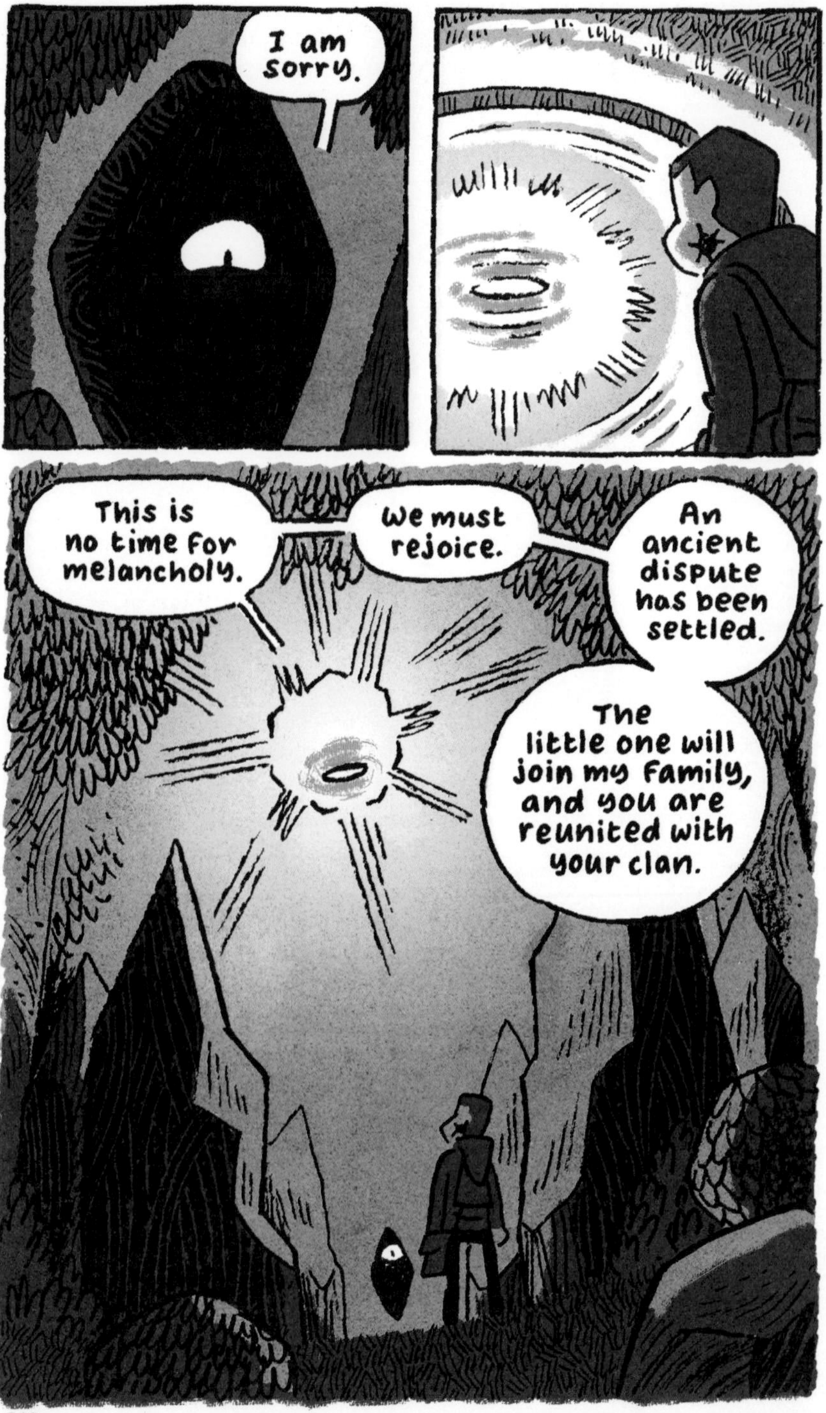
I am sorry.
This is no time for melancholy.
We must rejoice.
An ancient dispute has been settled.
The little one will join my family, and you are reunited with your clan.

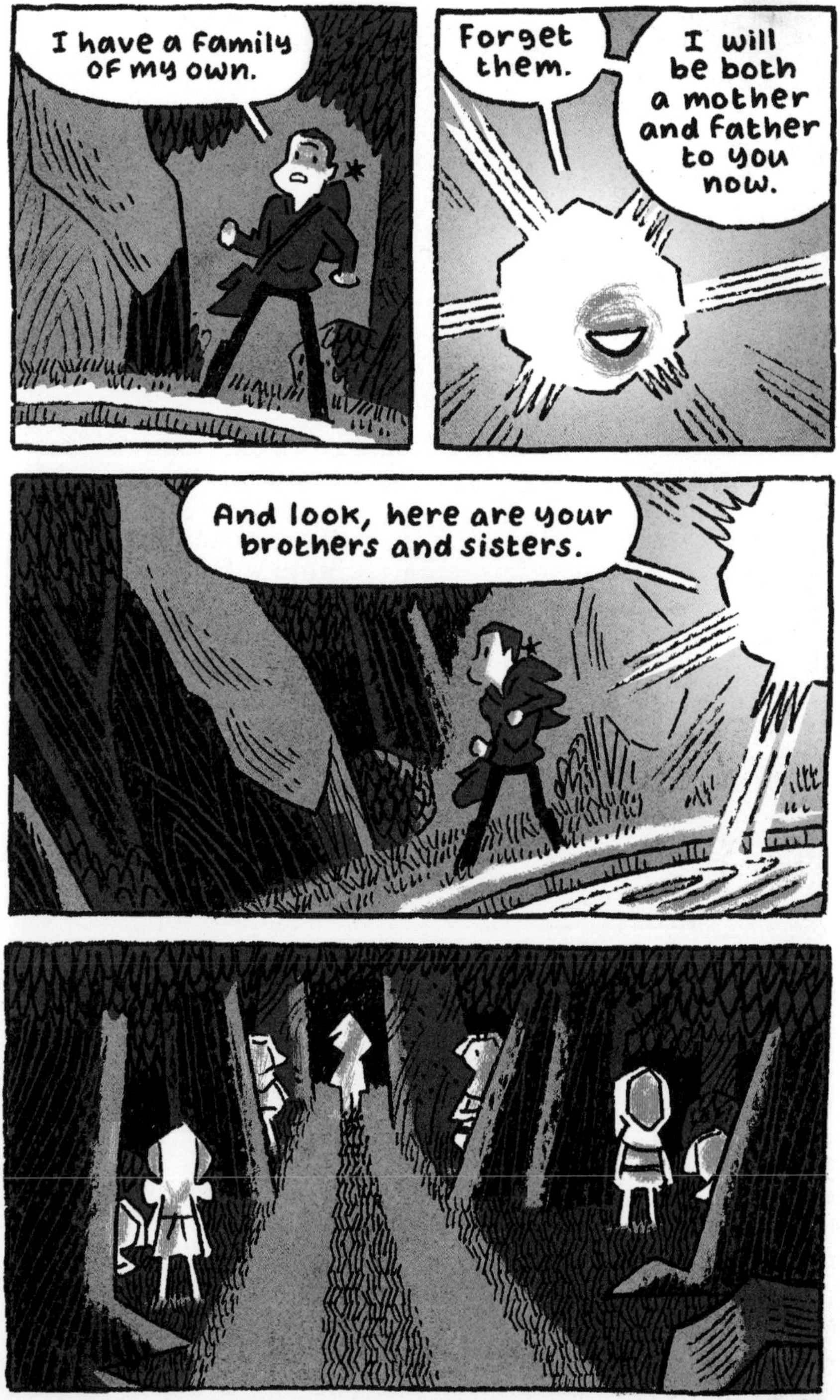
I have a family of my own.
Forget them.
I will be both a mother and father to you now.
And look, here are your brothers and sisters.

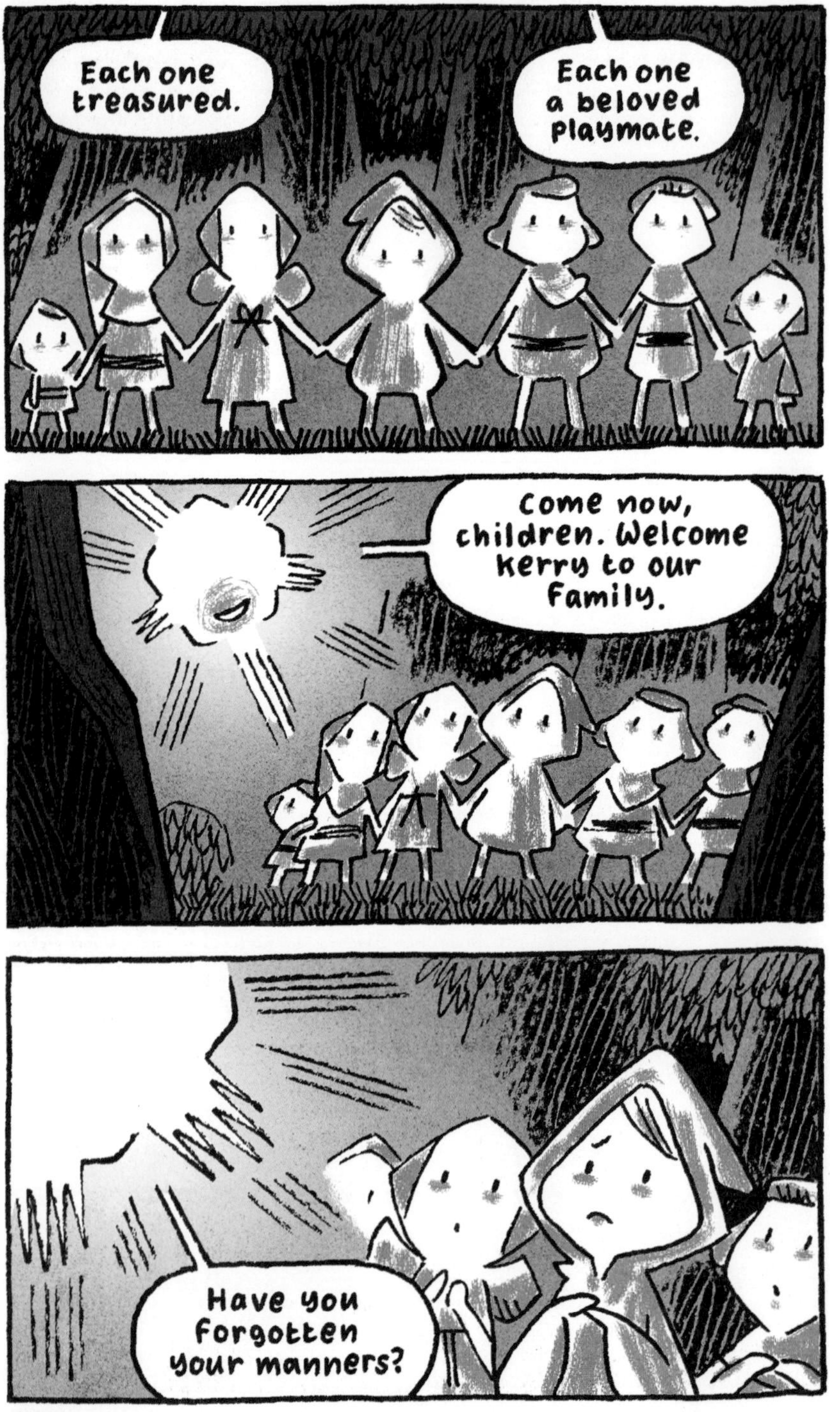
Each one treasured.
Each one a beloved playmate.
Come now, children. Welcome Kerry to our family.
Have you forgotten your manners?

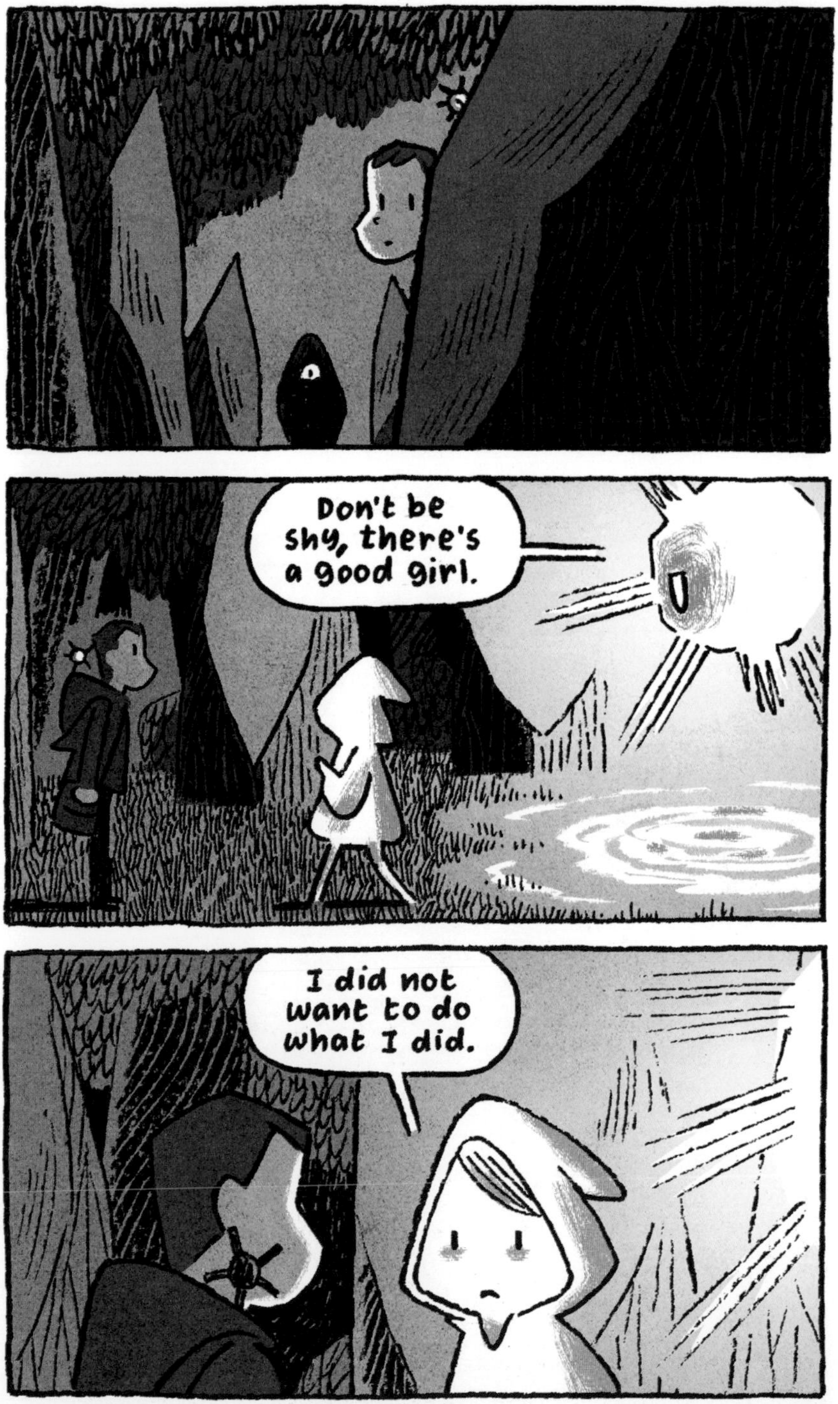
Don't be shy, there's a good girl.
I did not want to do what I did.

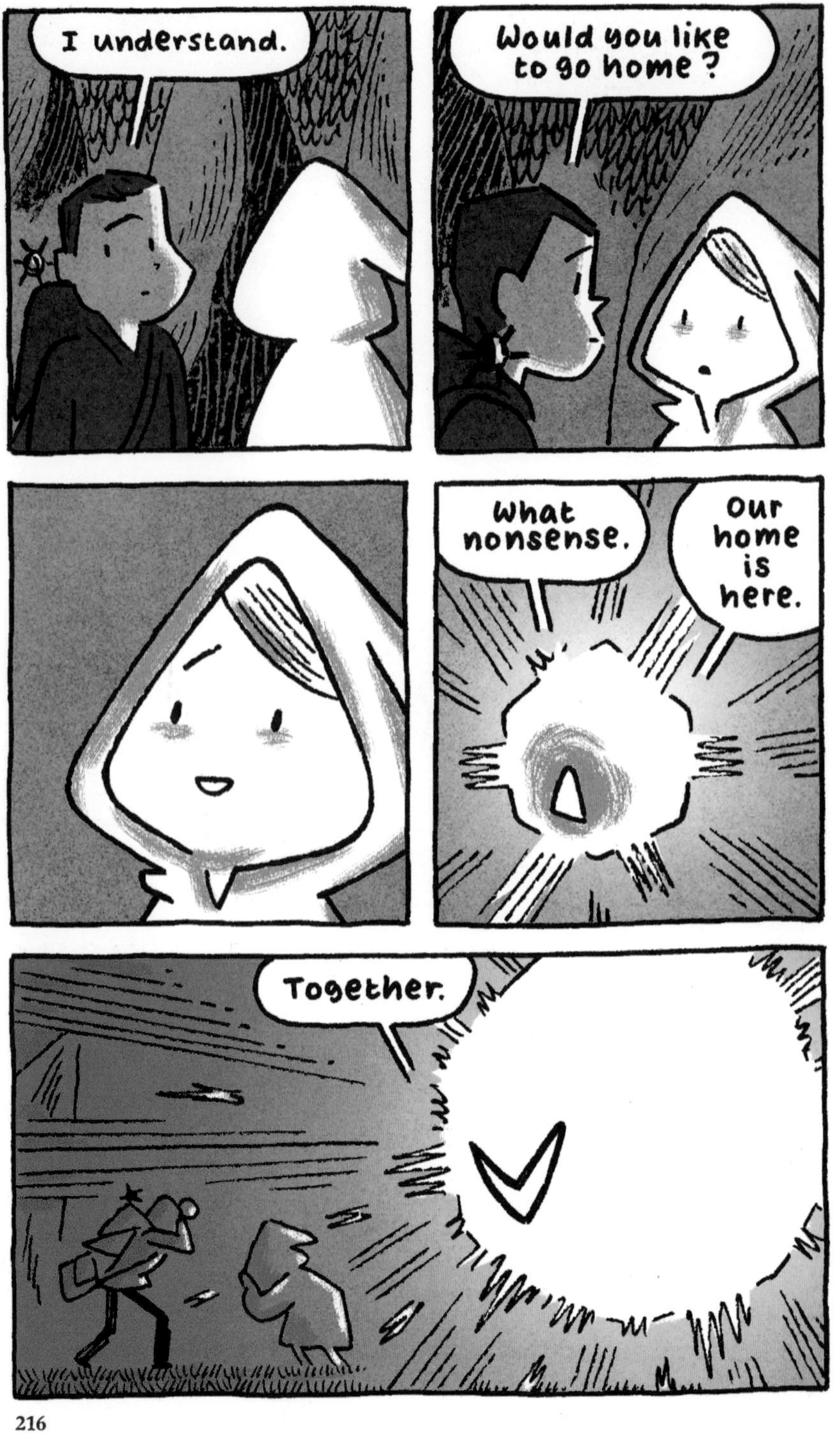
I understand.
Would you like to go home?
What nonsense.
Our home is here.
Together.

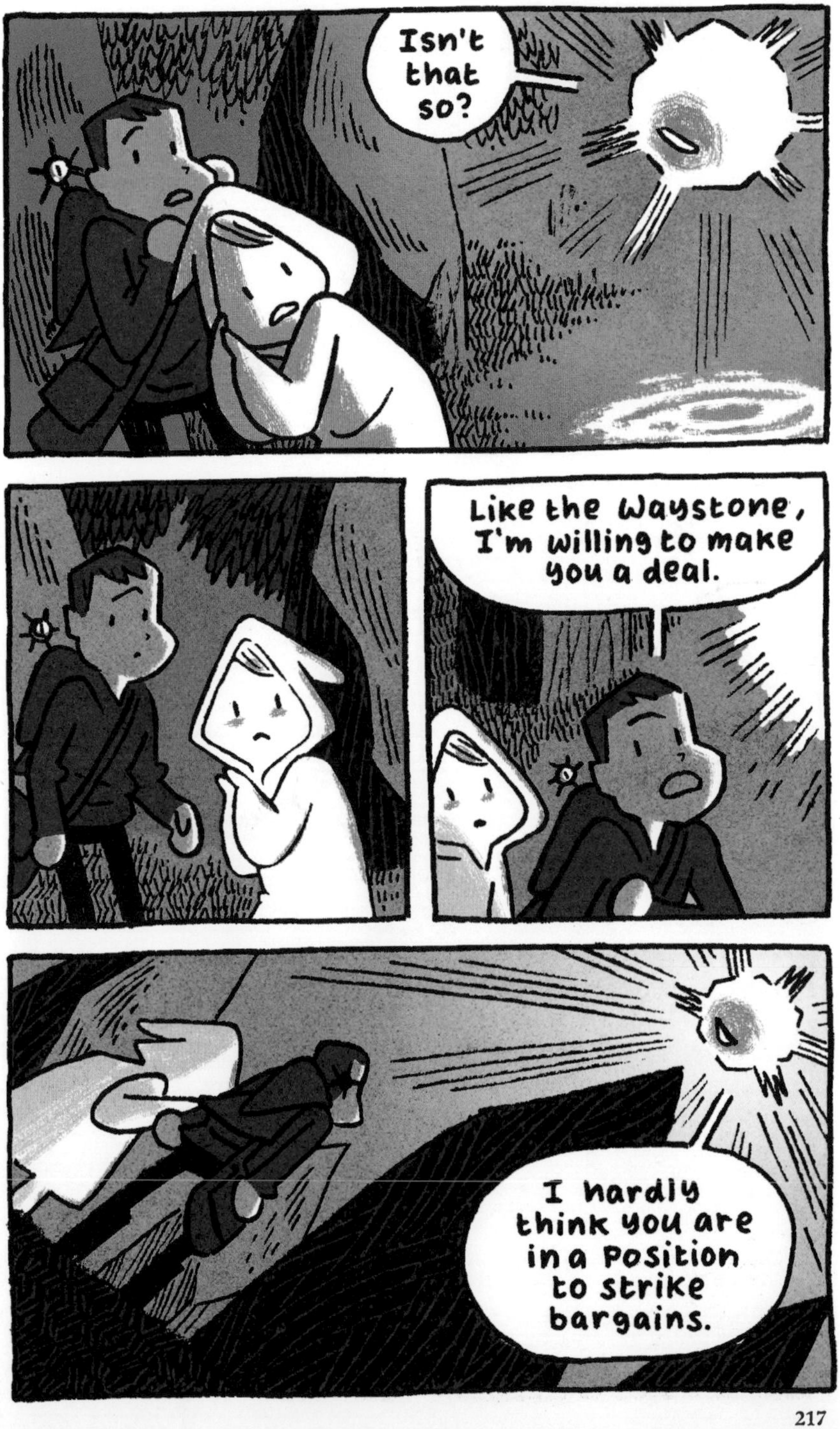
Isn't that so?
Like the Waystone, I'm willing to make you a deal.
I hardly think you are in a position to strike bargains.

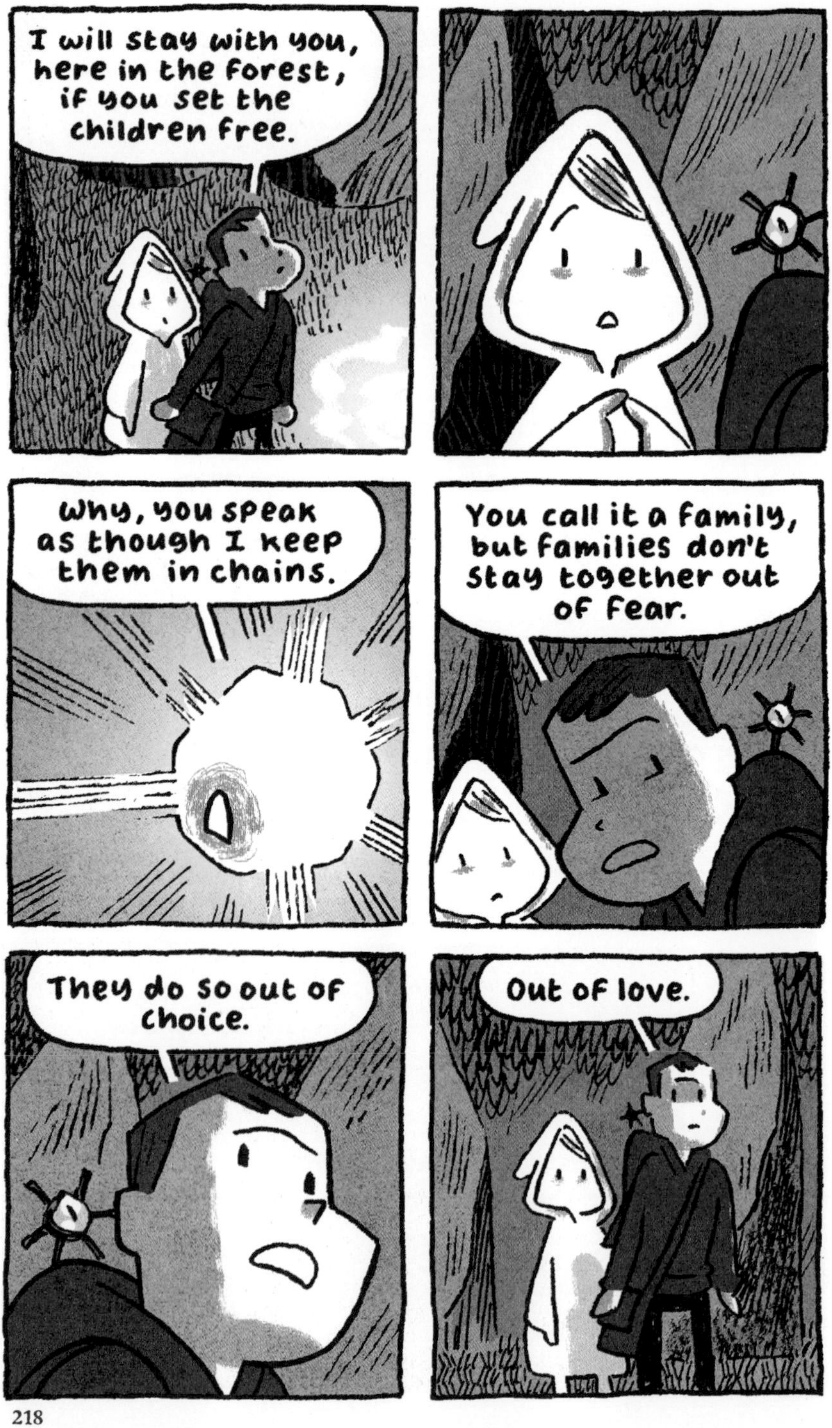
I will stay with you, here in the forest, if you set the children free.
Why, you speak as though I keep them in chains.
You call it a family, but families don't stay together out of fear.
They do so out of choice.
Out of love.

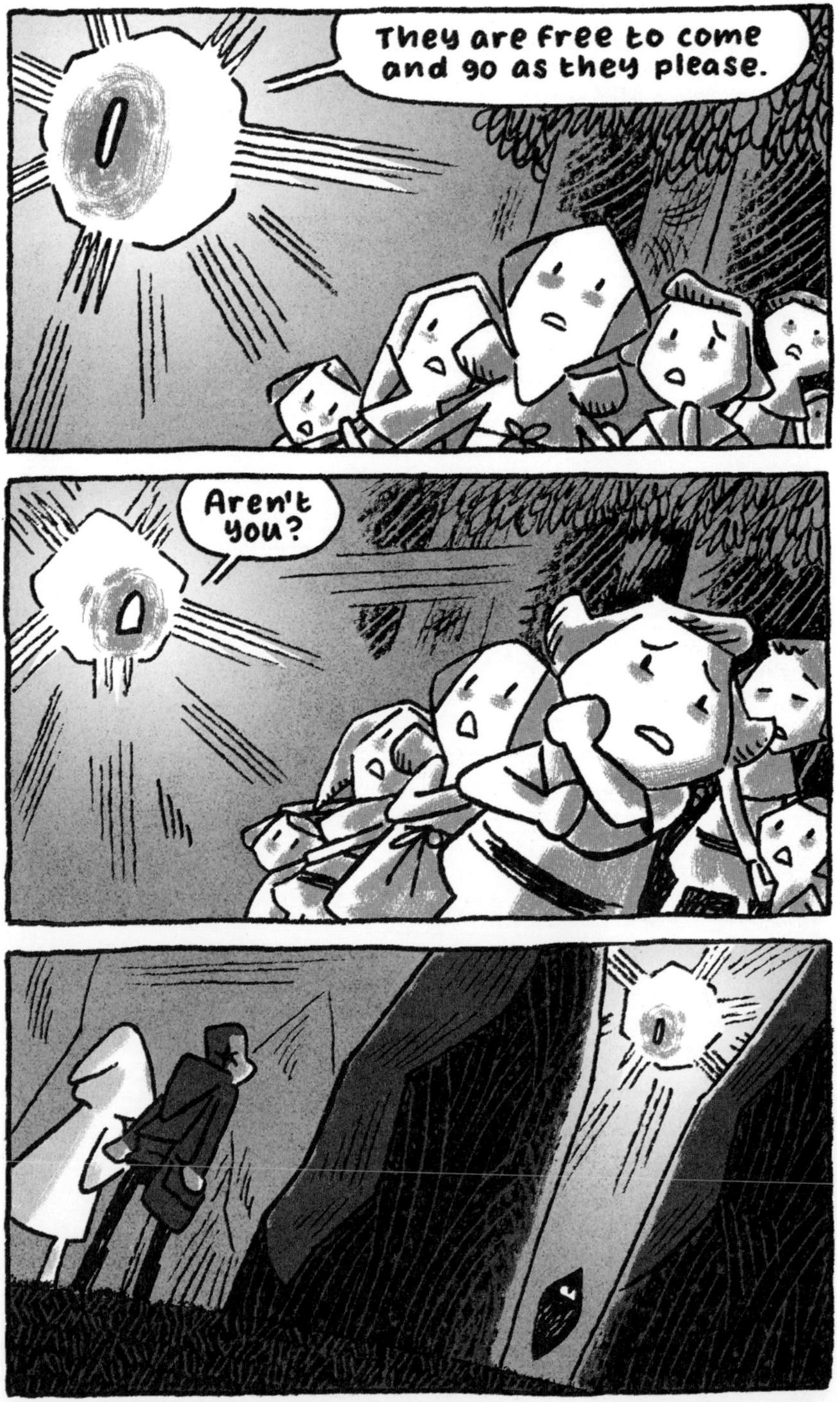
They are free to come and go as they please.
Aren't you?

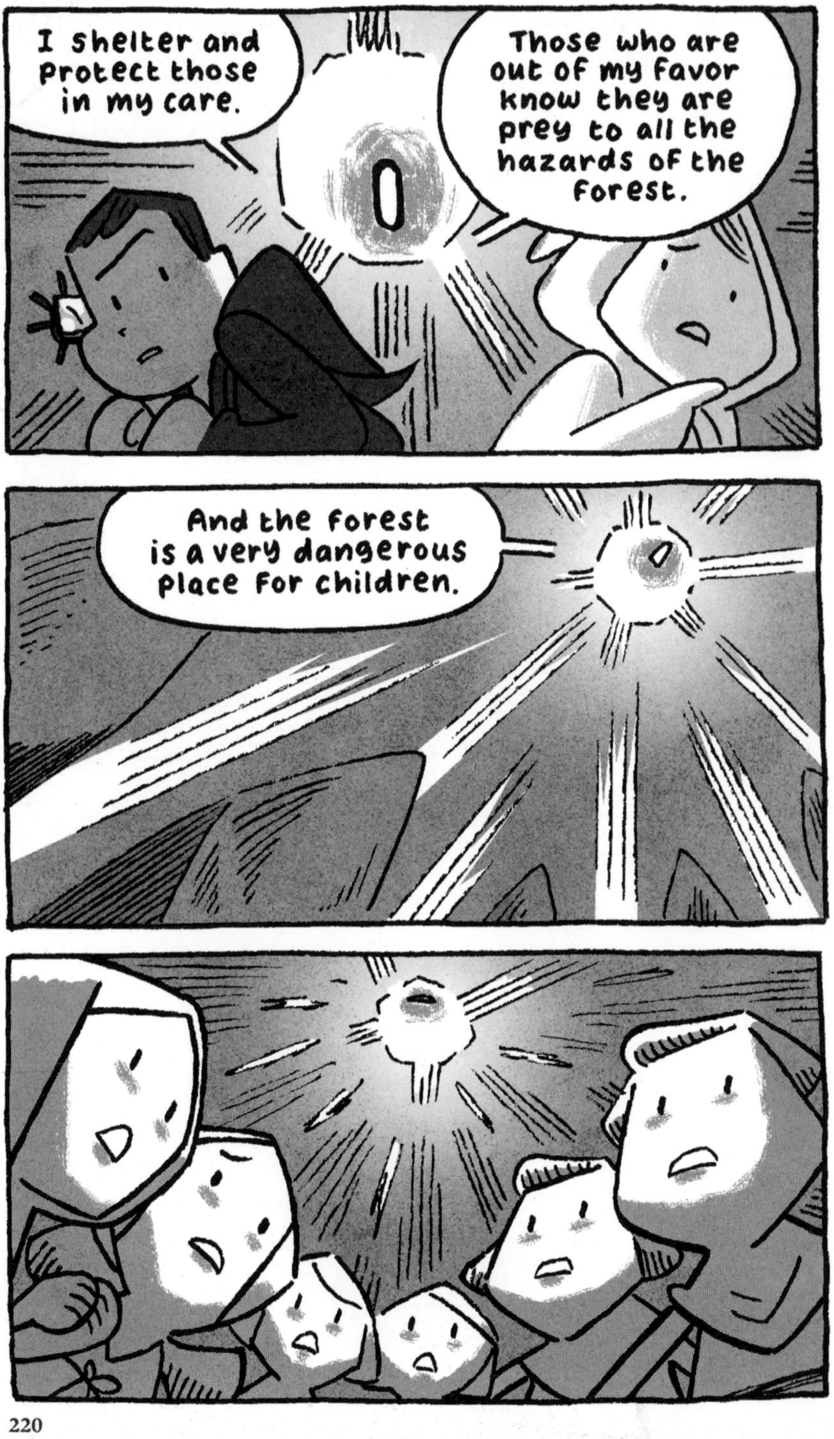
I shelter and protect those in my care.
Those who are out of my favor know they are prey to all the hazards of the forest.
And the forest is a very dangerous place for children.

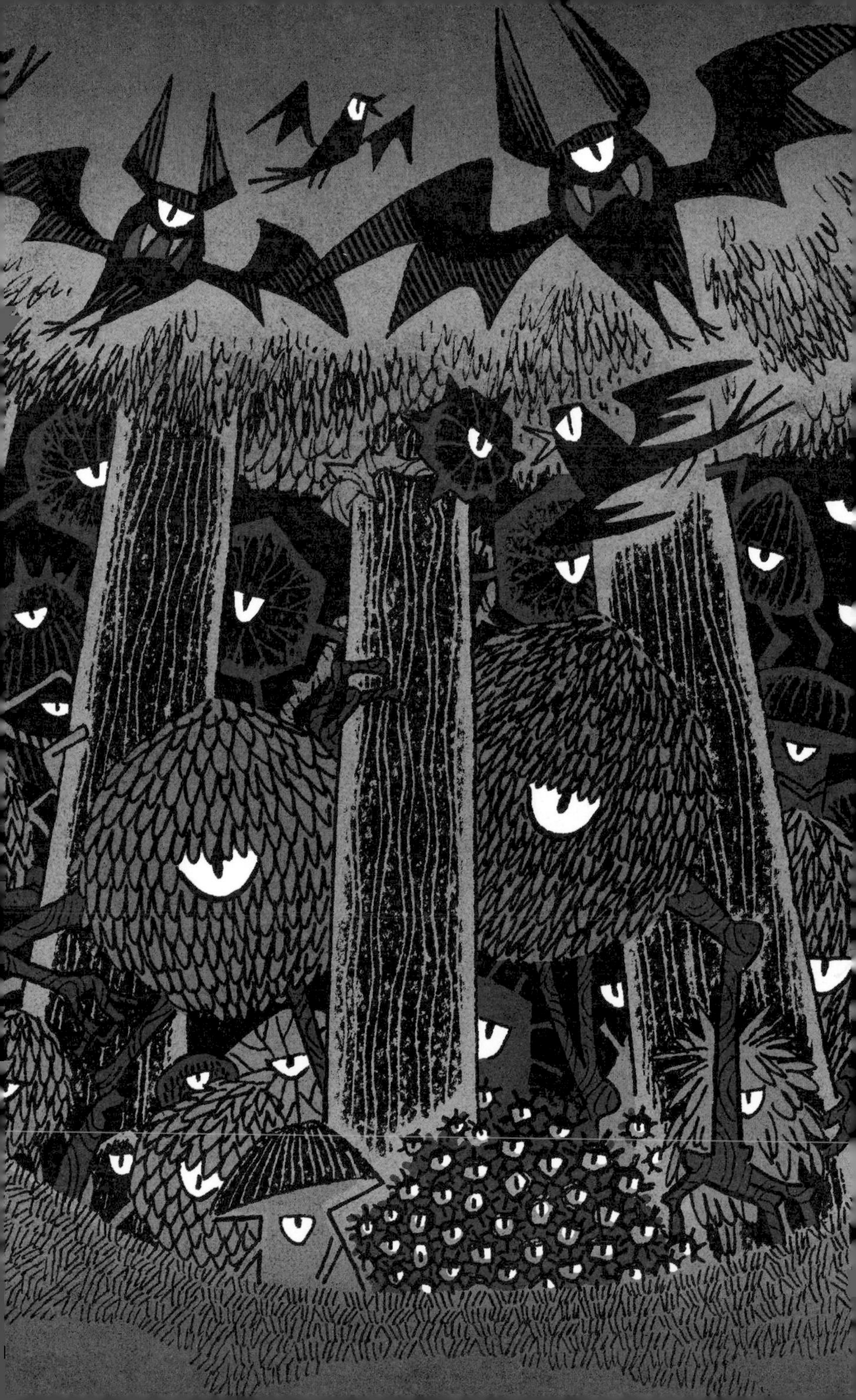

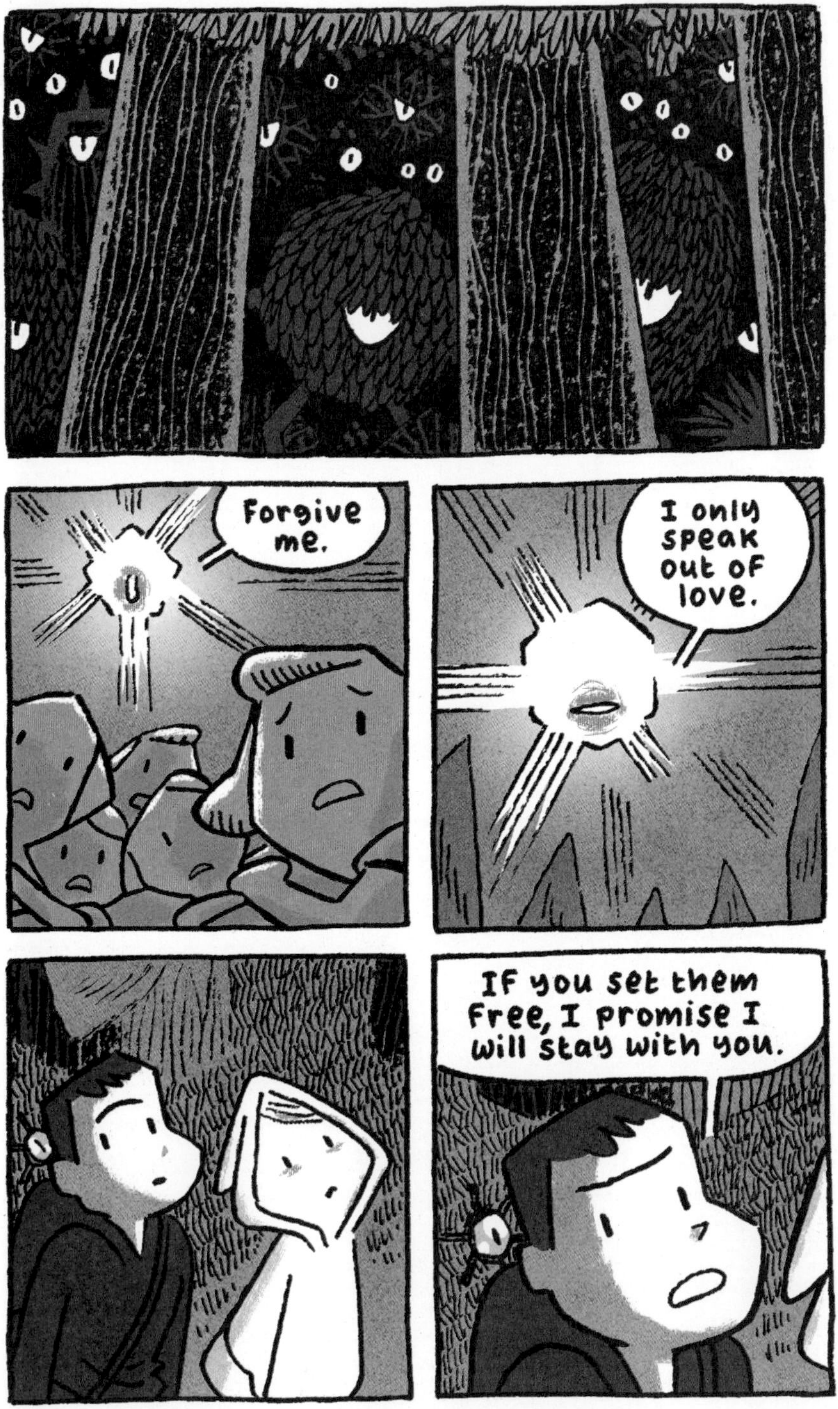
Forgive me.
I only speak out of love.
If you set them free, I promise I will stay with you.

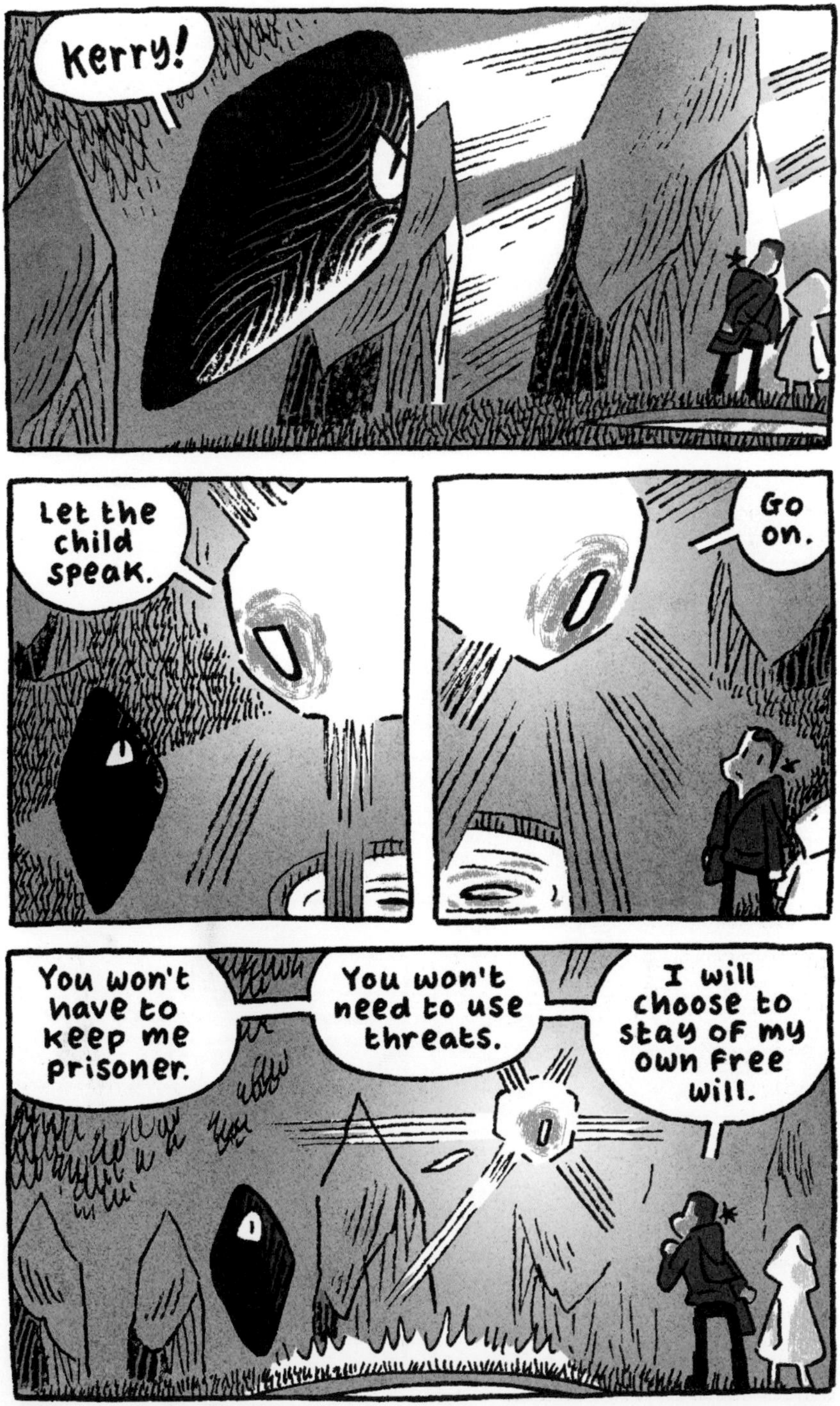
Kerry!
Let the child speak.
Go on.
You won't have to keep me prisoner.
You won't need to use threats.
I will choose to stay of my own free will.

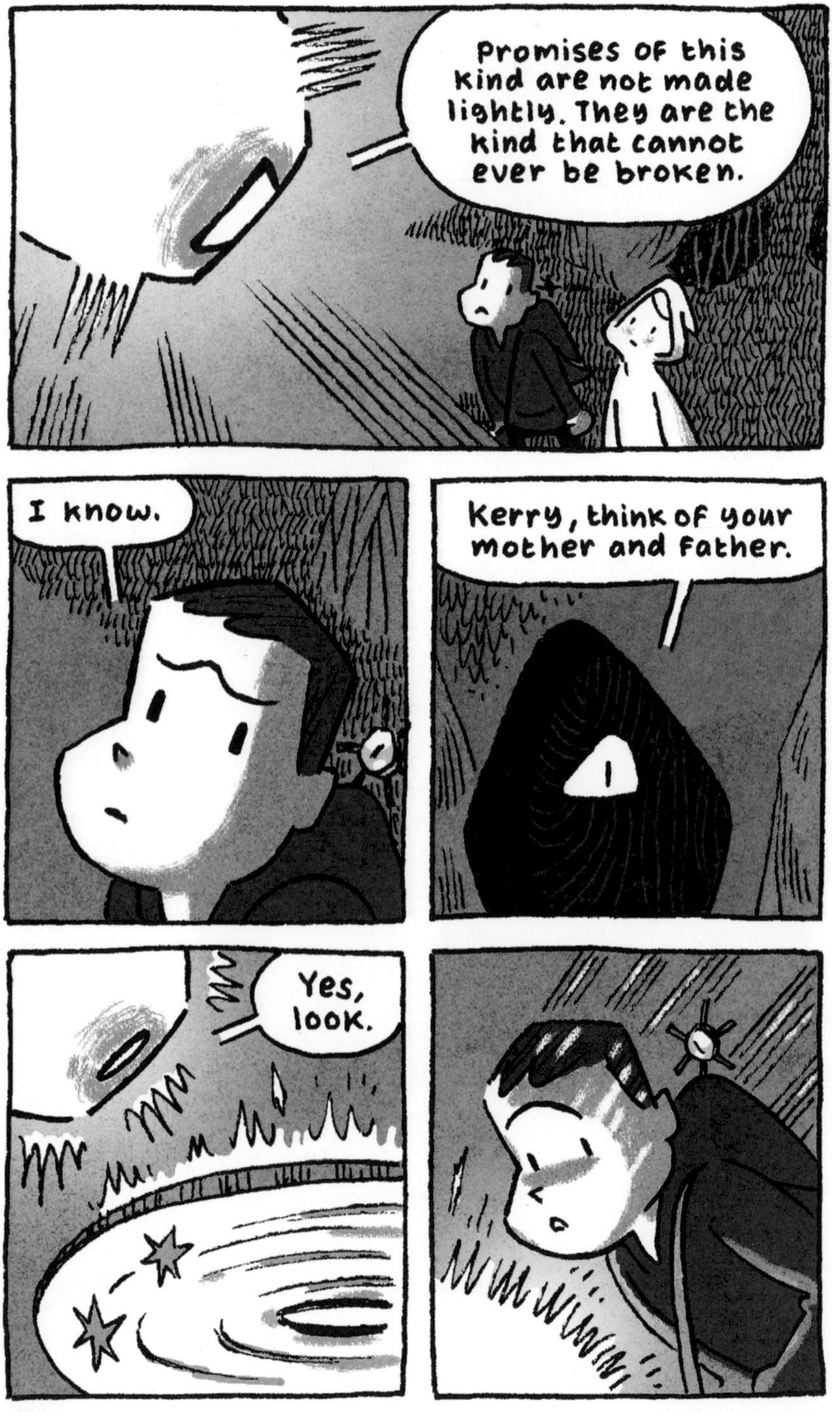
Promises of this kind are not made lightly. They are the kind that cannot ever be broken.
I know.
Kerry, think of your mother and father.
Yes, look.

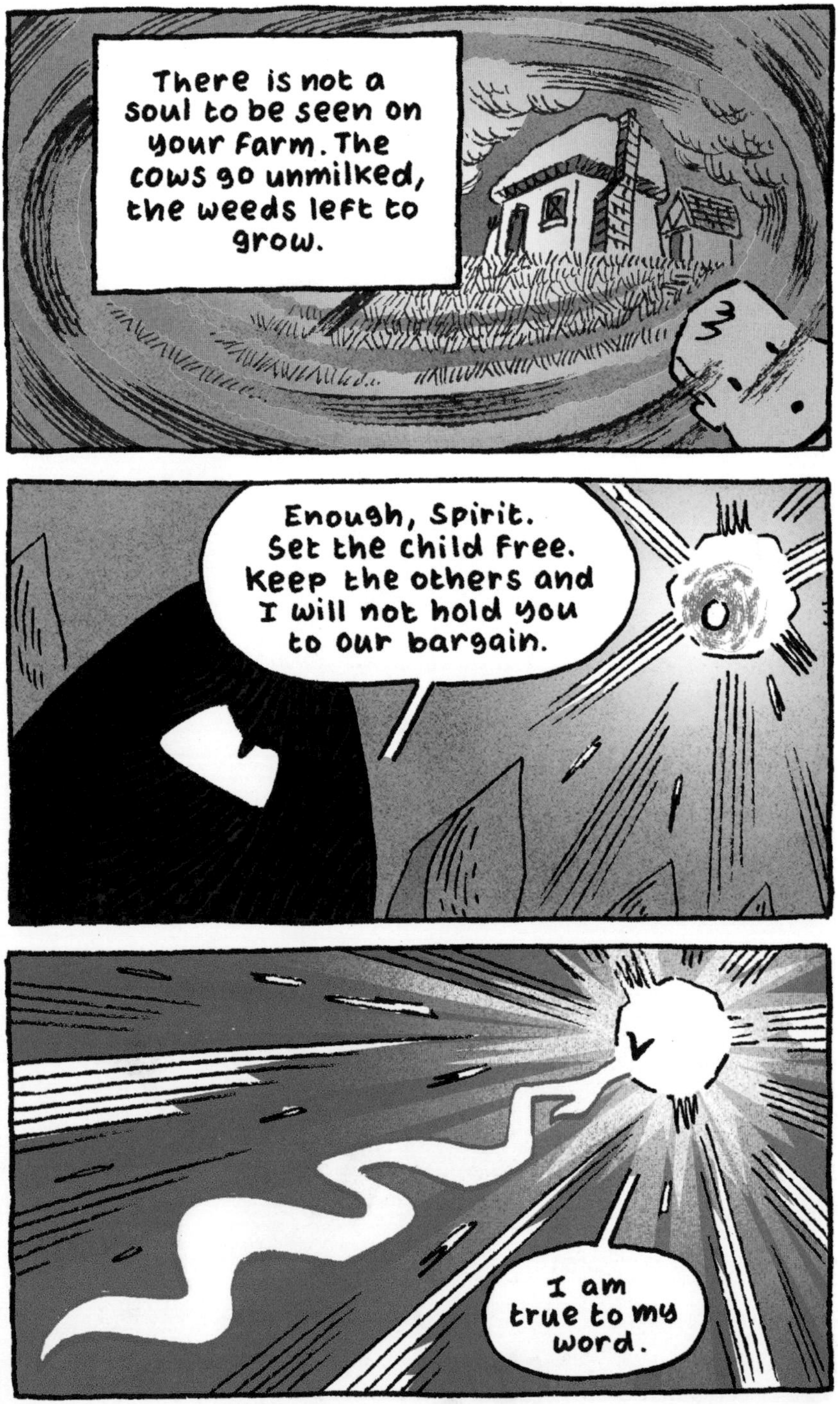
There is not a soul to be seen on your farm. The cows go unmilked, the weeds left to grow.
Enough, Spirit. Set the child free. Keep the others and I will not hold you to our bargain.
I am true to my word.

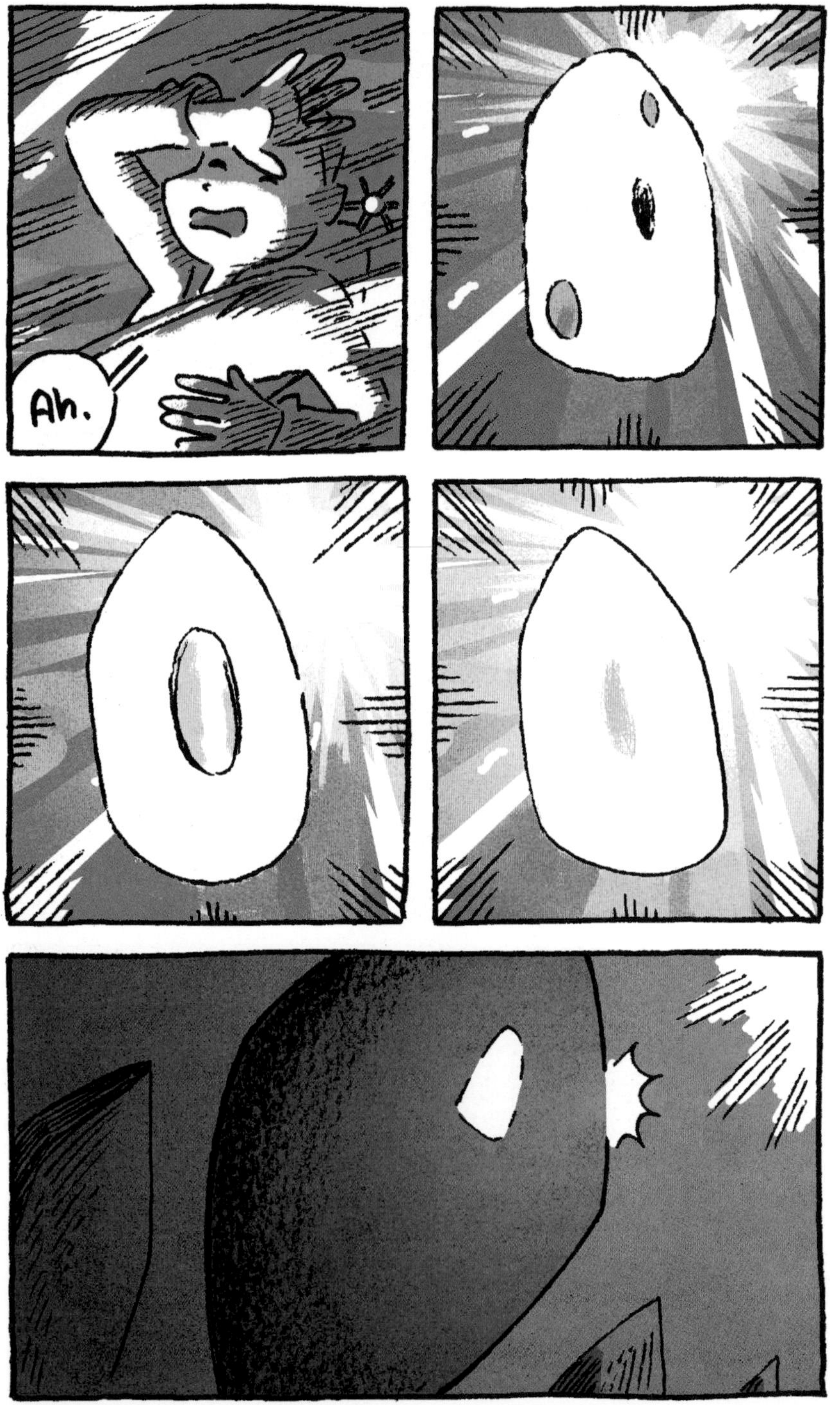
Ah.

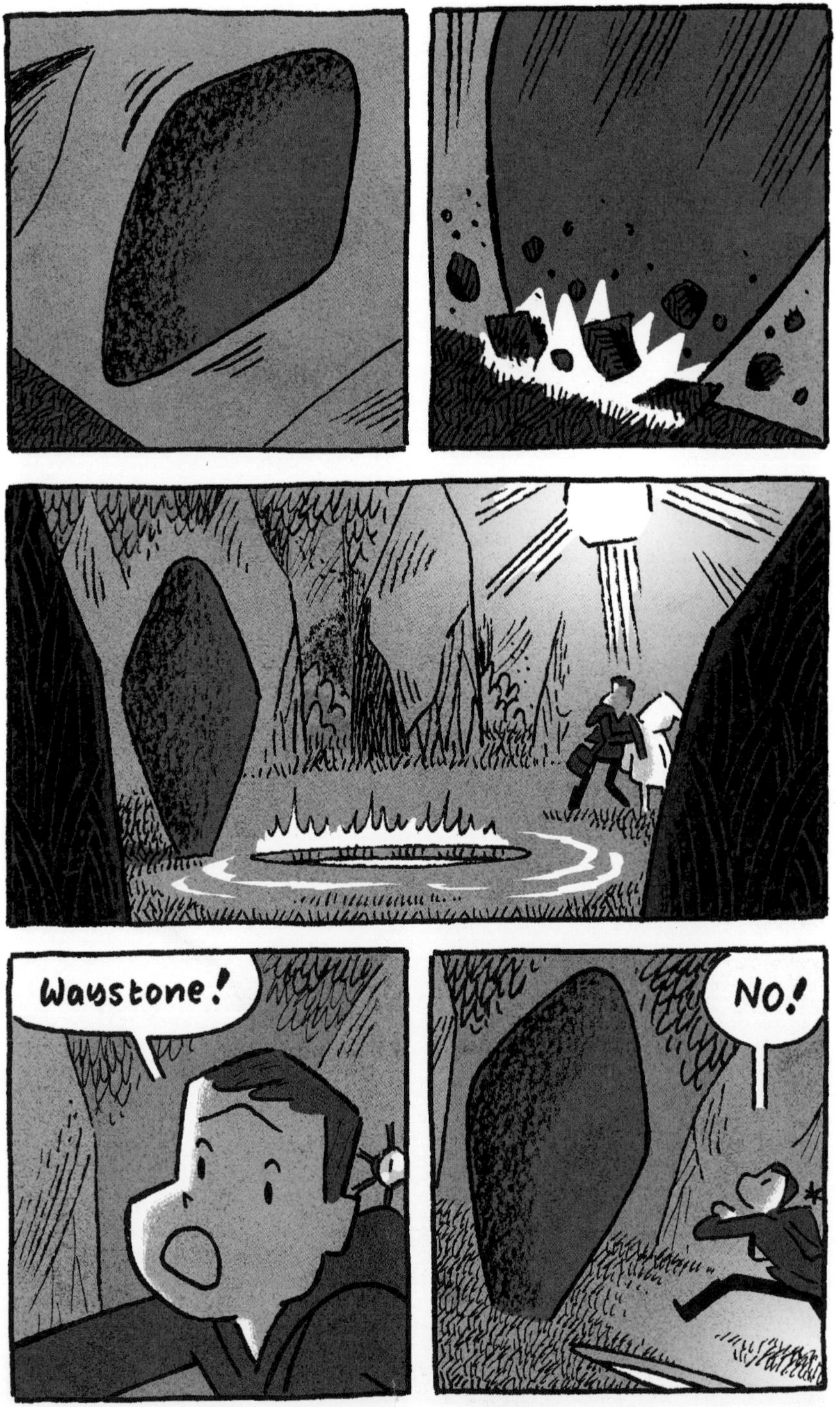
Waystone!
NO!

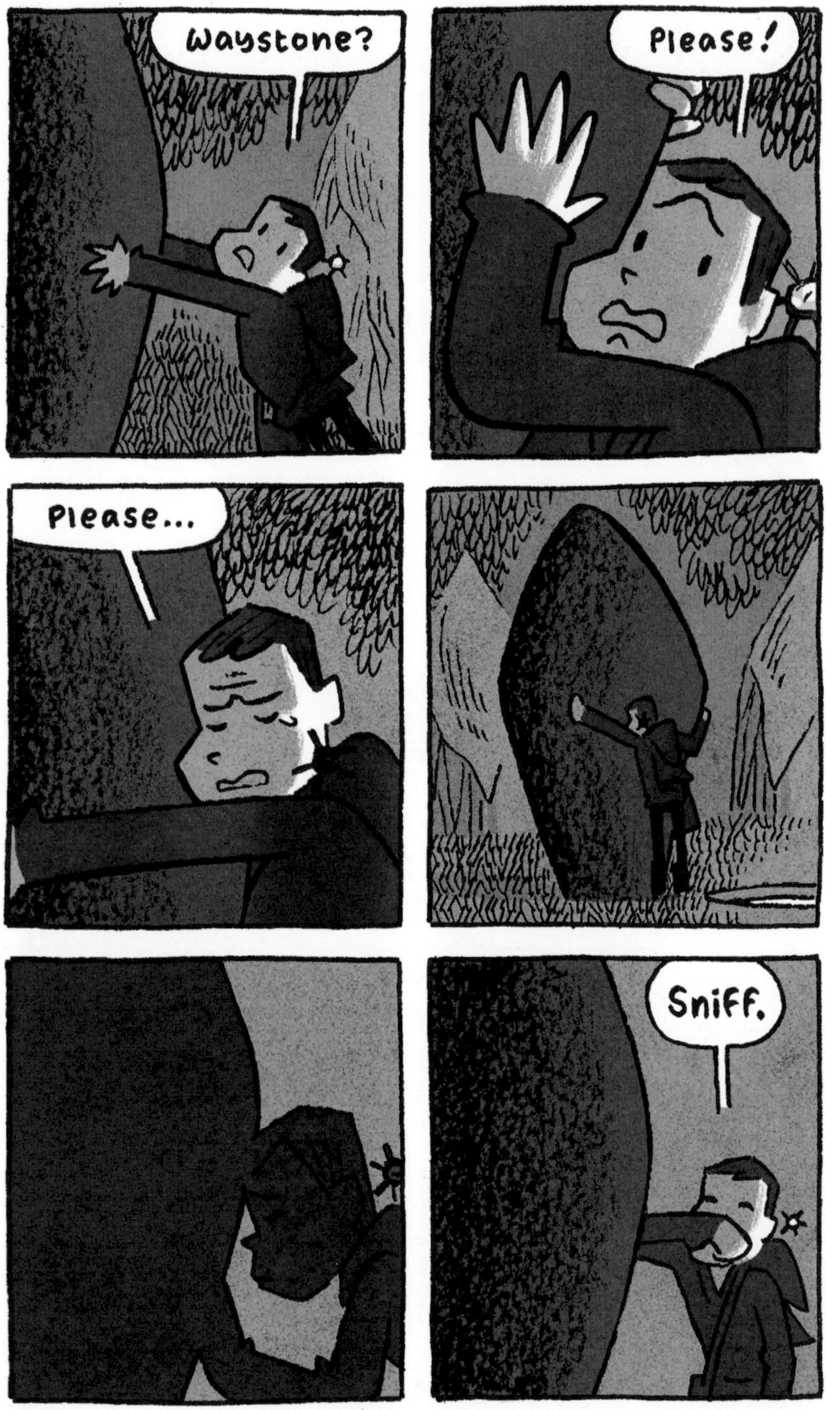
Waystone?
Please!
Please...
Sniff.

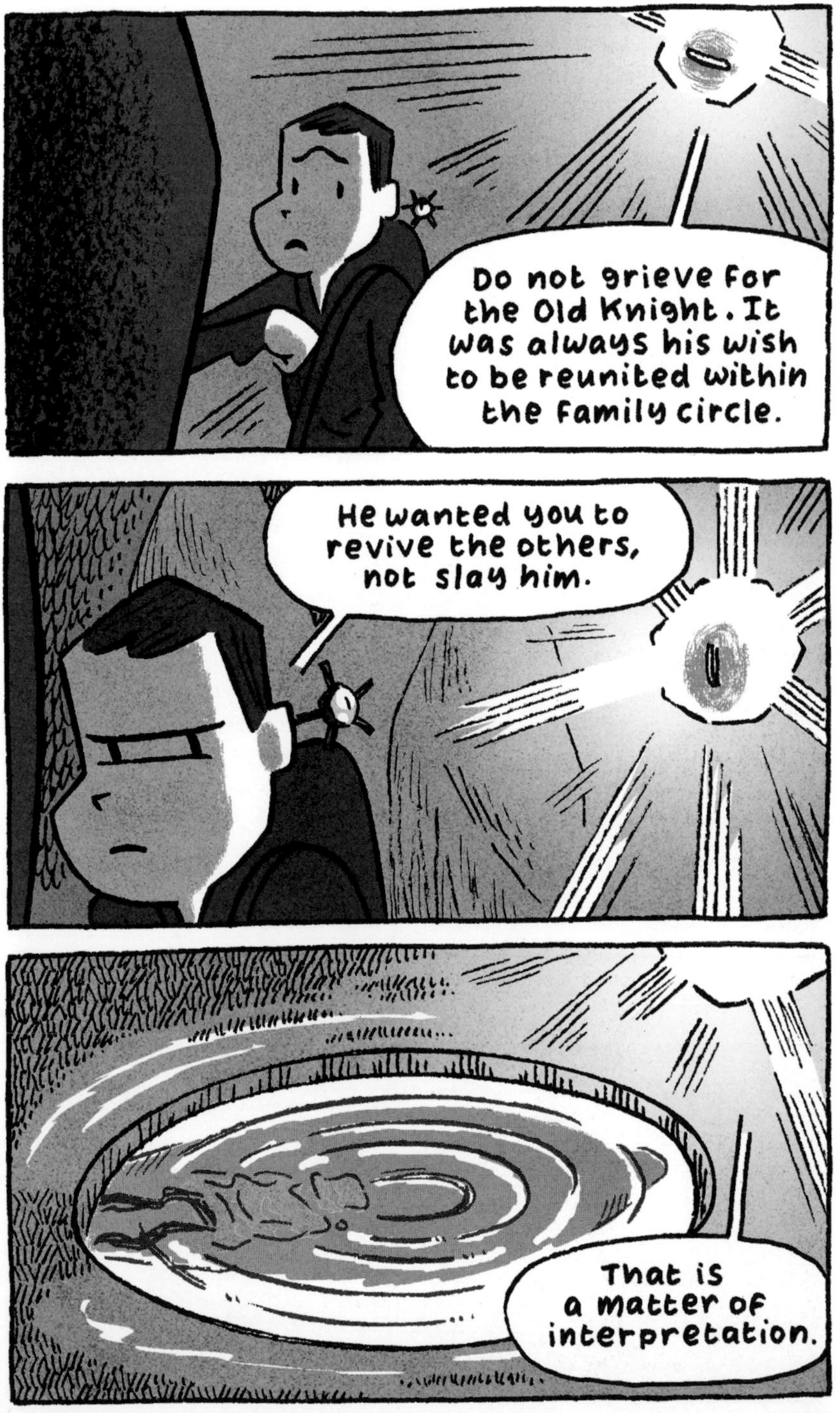
Do not grieve for the Old Knight. It was always his wish to be reunited within the family circle.
He wanted you to revive the others, not slay him.
That is a matter of interpretation.

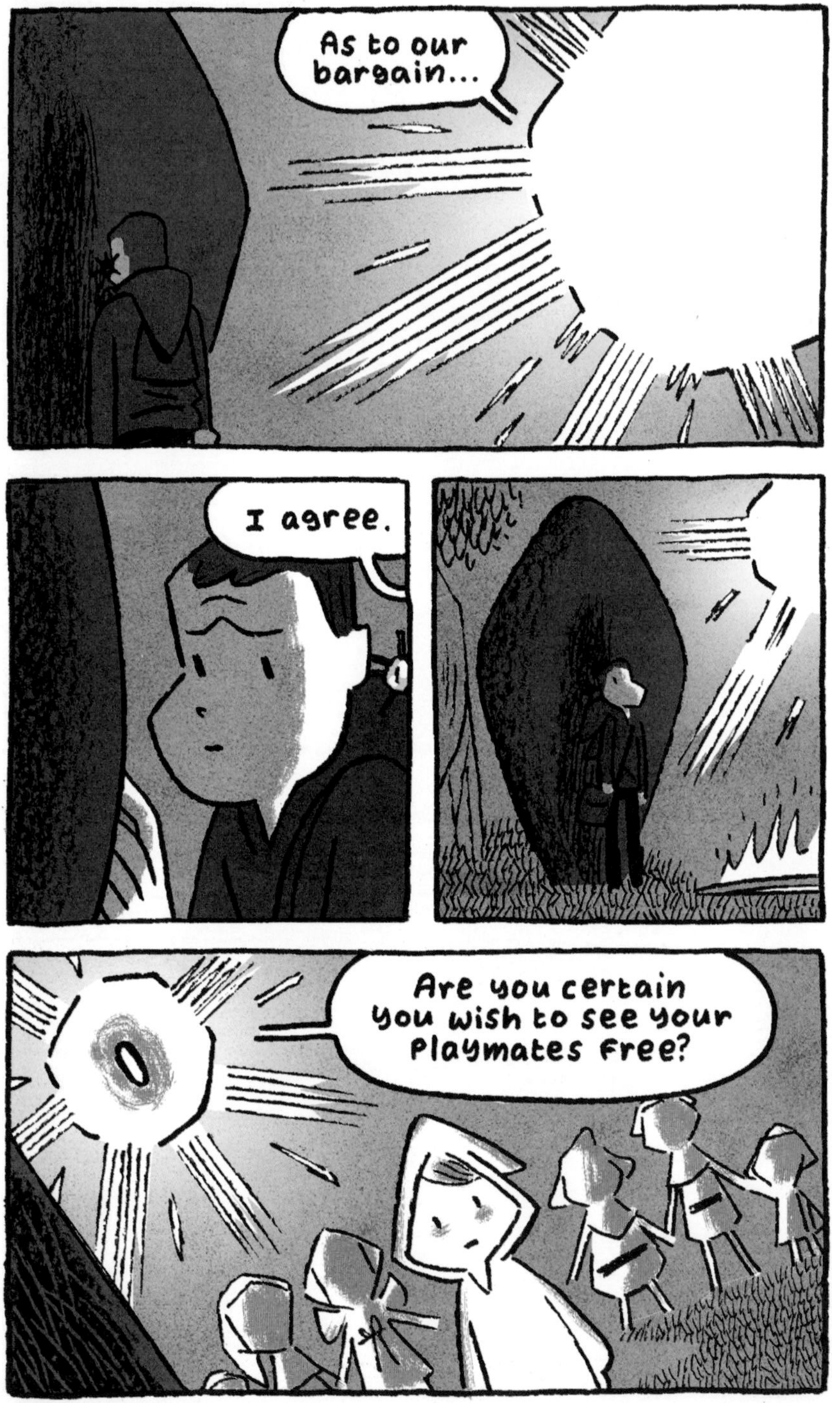
As to our bargain...
I agree.
Are you certain you wish to see your playmates free?

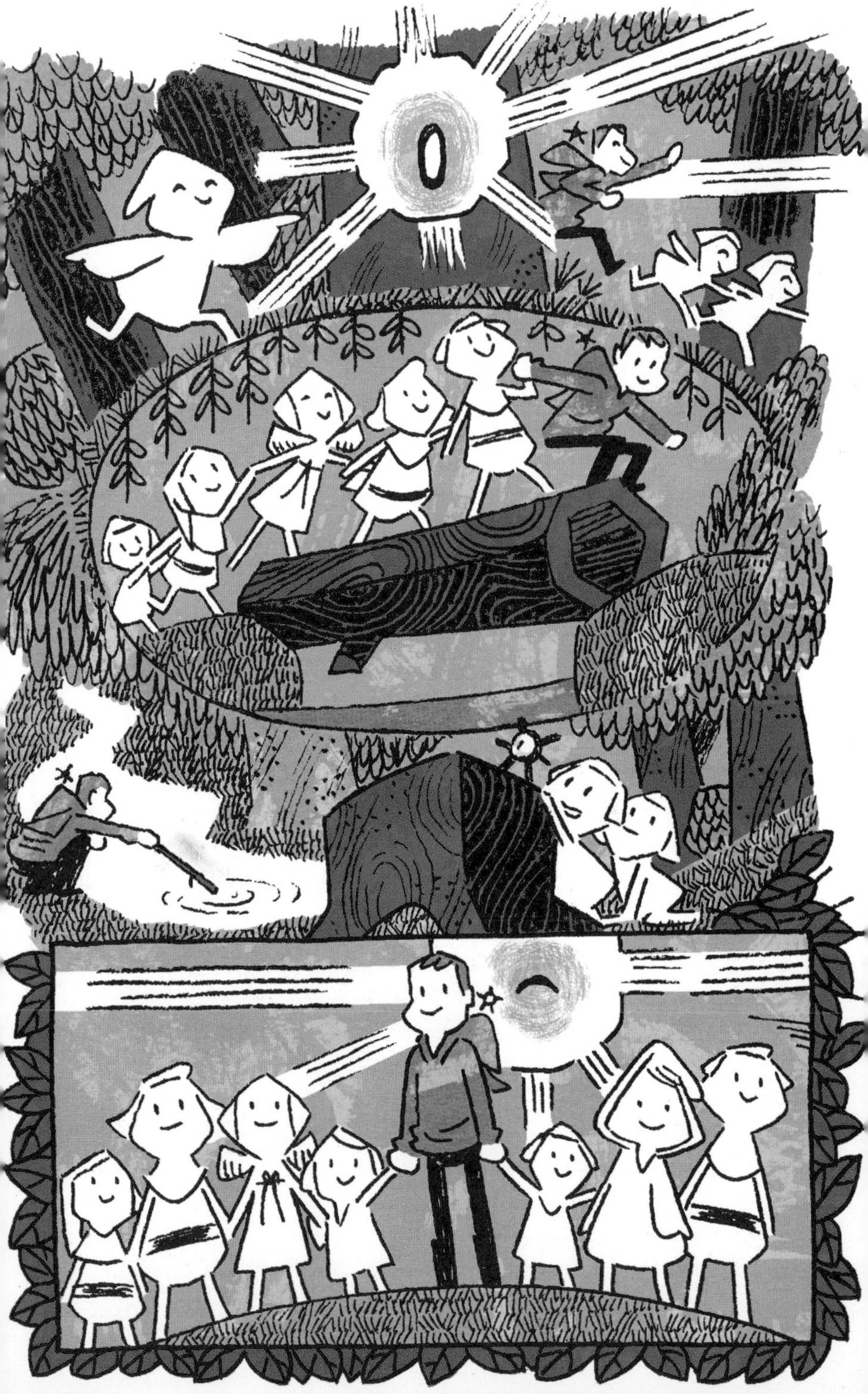

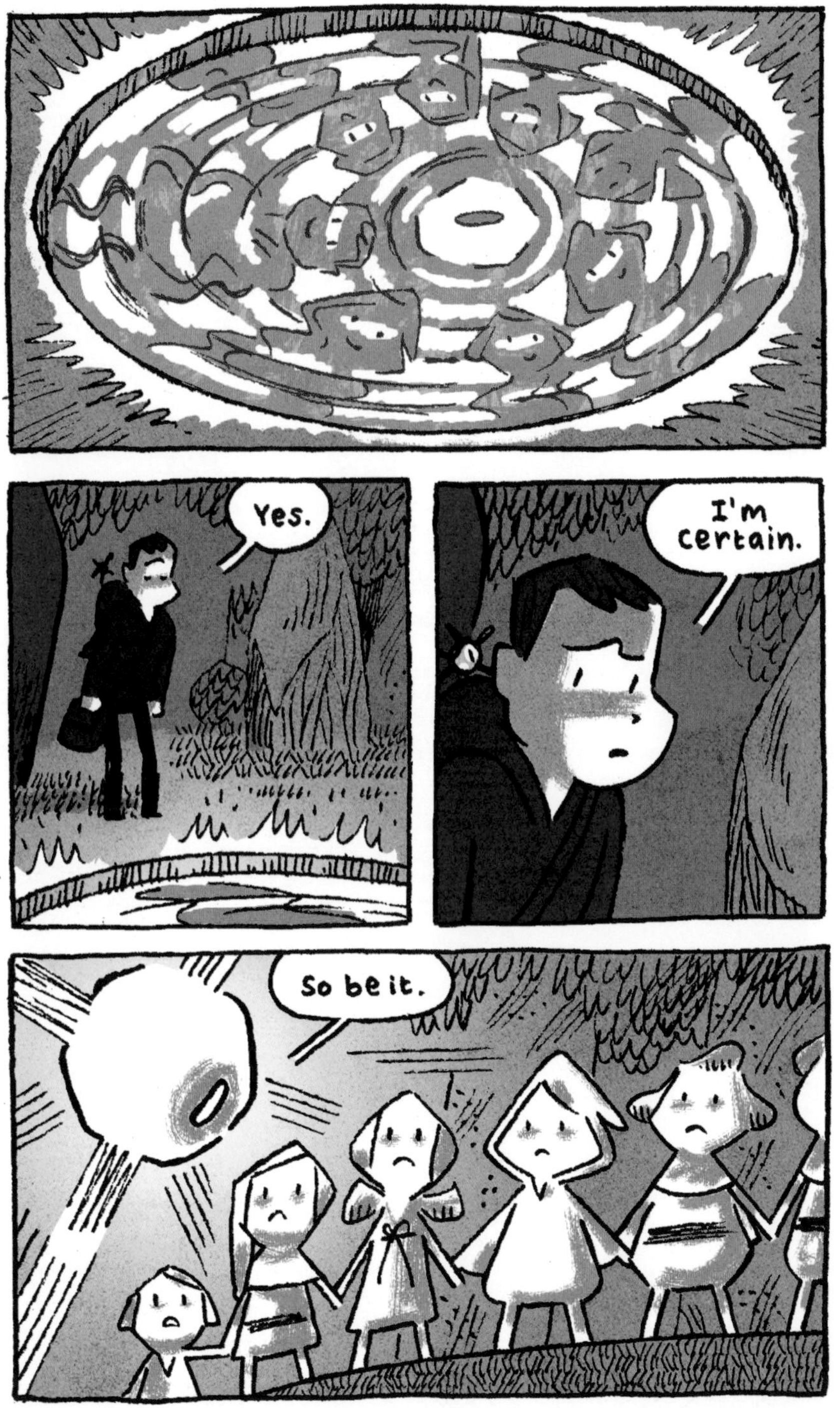
Yes.
I'm certain.
So be it.

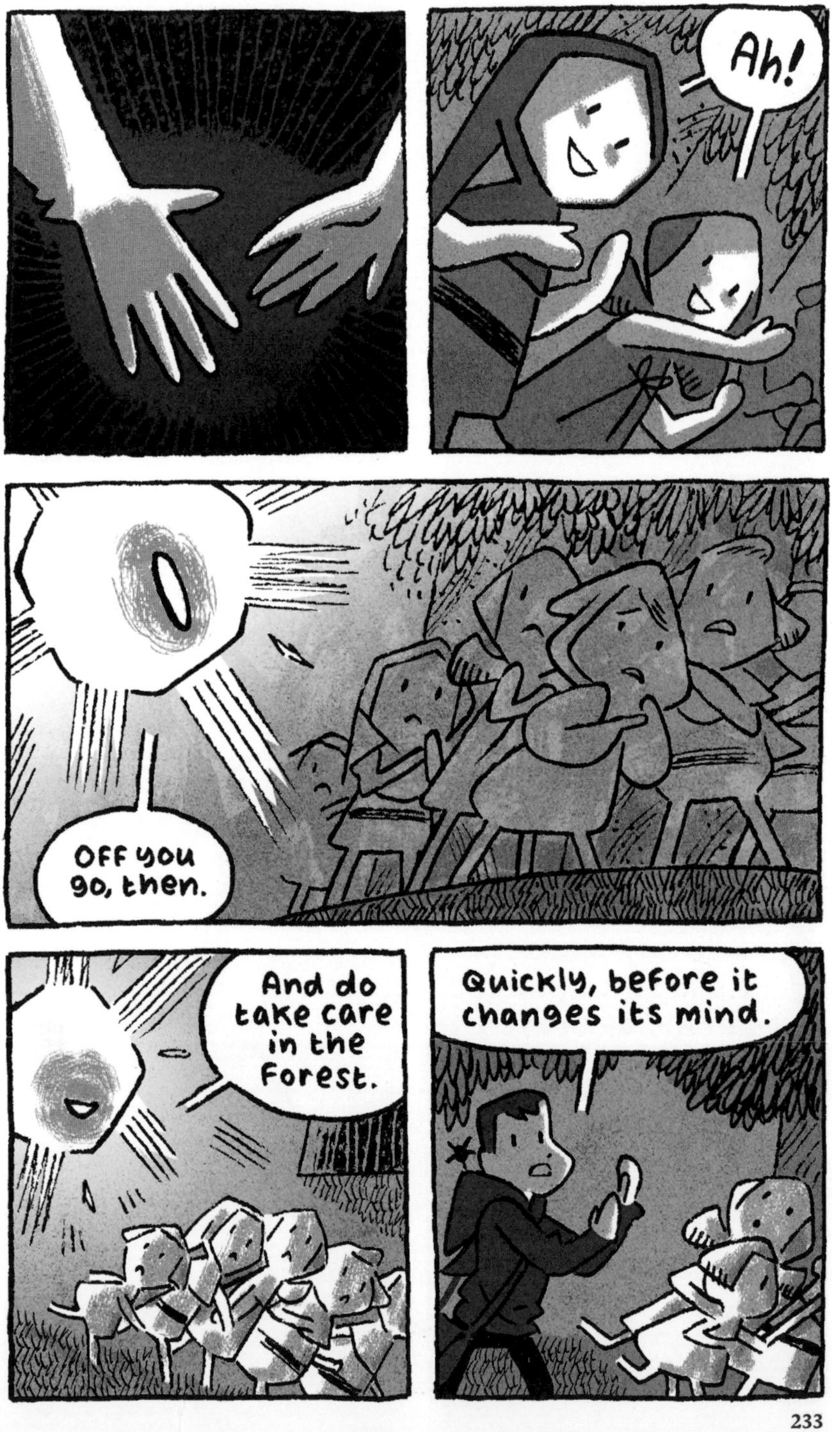
Ah!
Off you go, then.
And do take care in the forest.
Quickly, before it changes its mind.

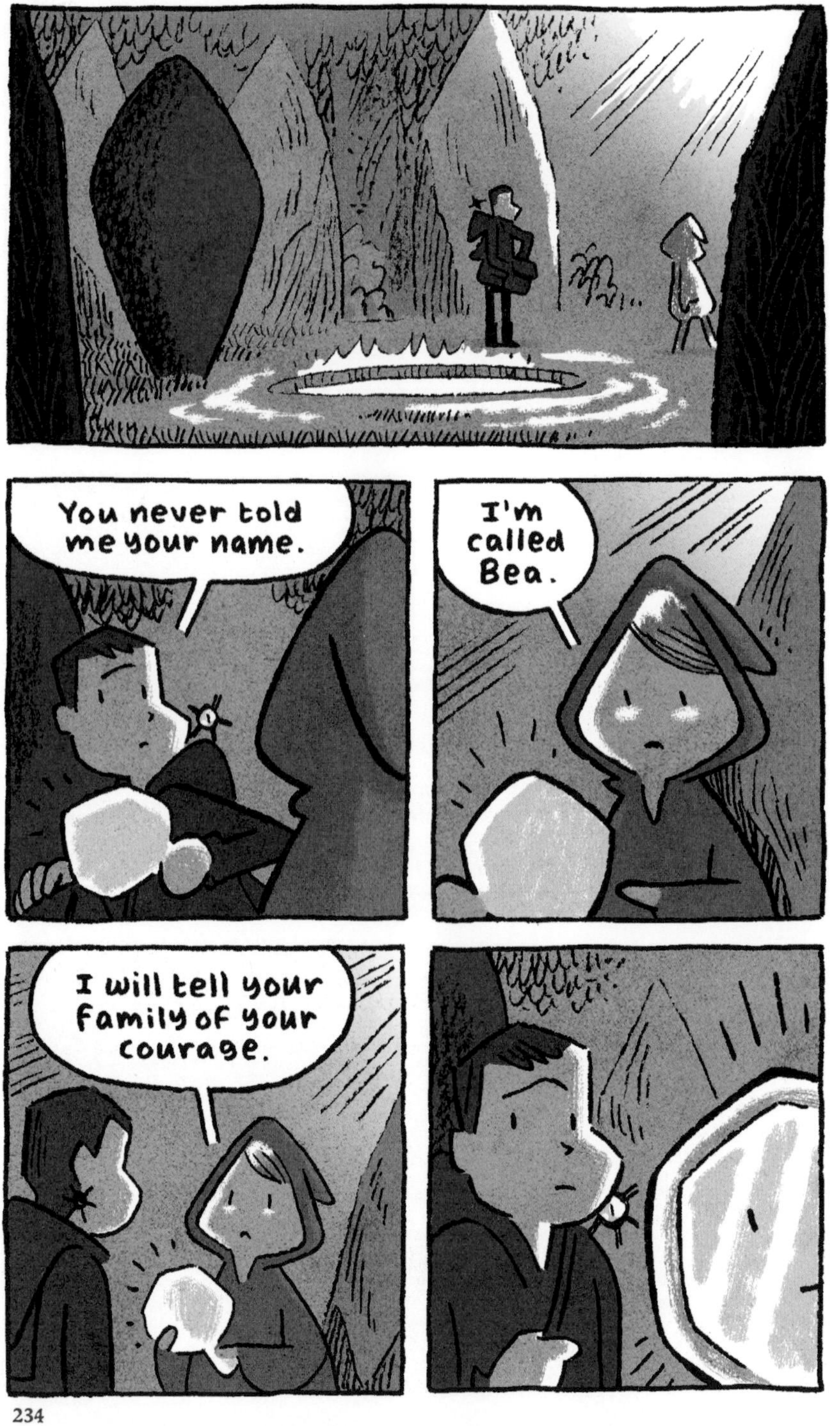
You never told me your name.
I'm called Bea.
I will tell your family of your courage.

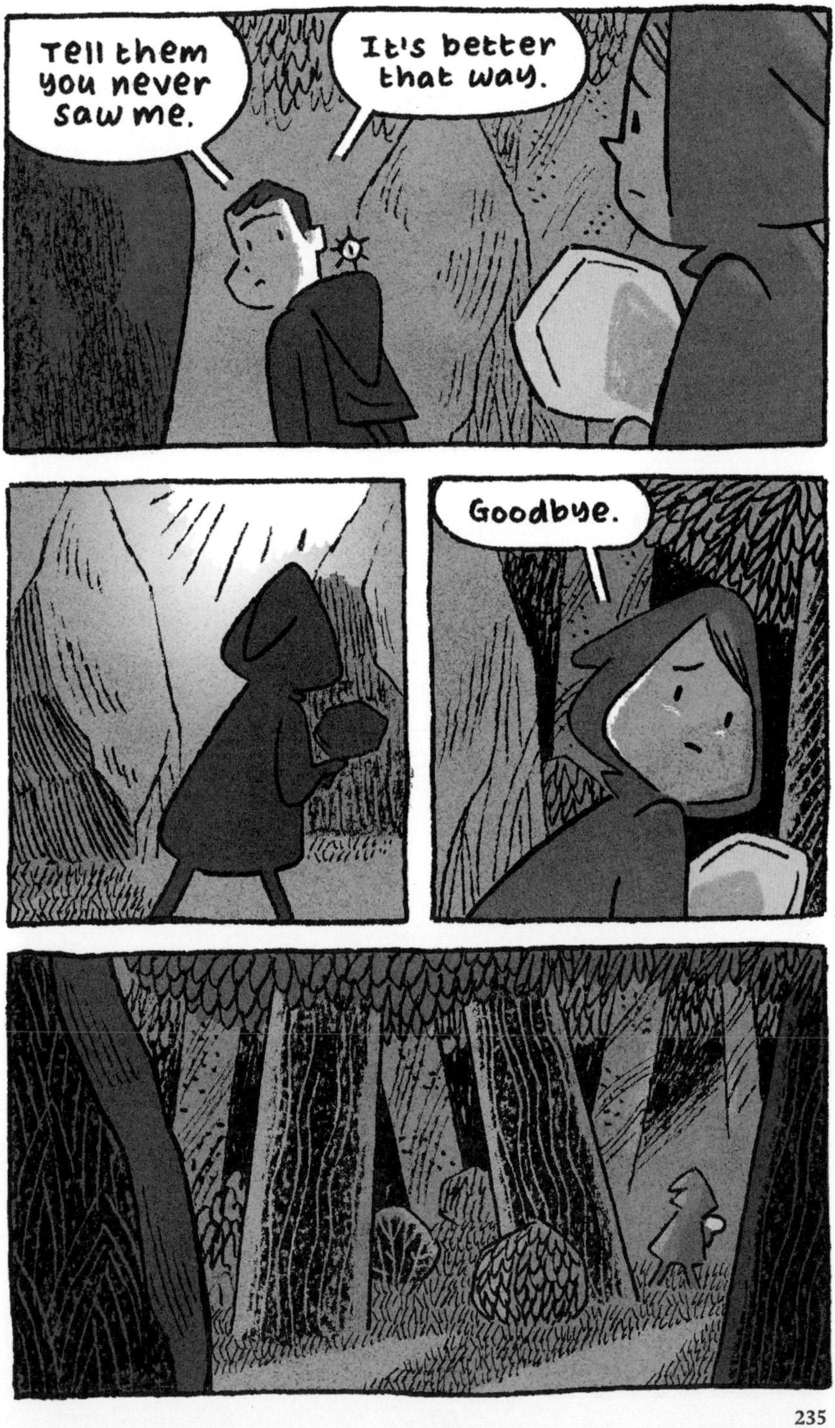
Tell them you never saw me.
It's better that way.
Goodbye.

Alas, it is bittersweet when the fledglings leave the nest.

Do not envy them, little one. Their fates are certain.

See.

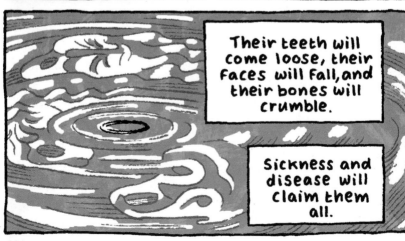

Their teeth will come loose, their faces will fall, and their bones will crumble.

Sickness and disease will claim them all.

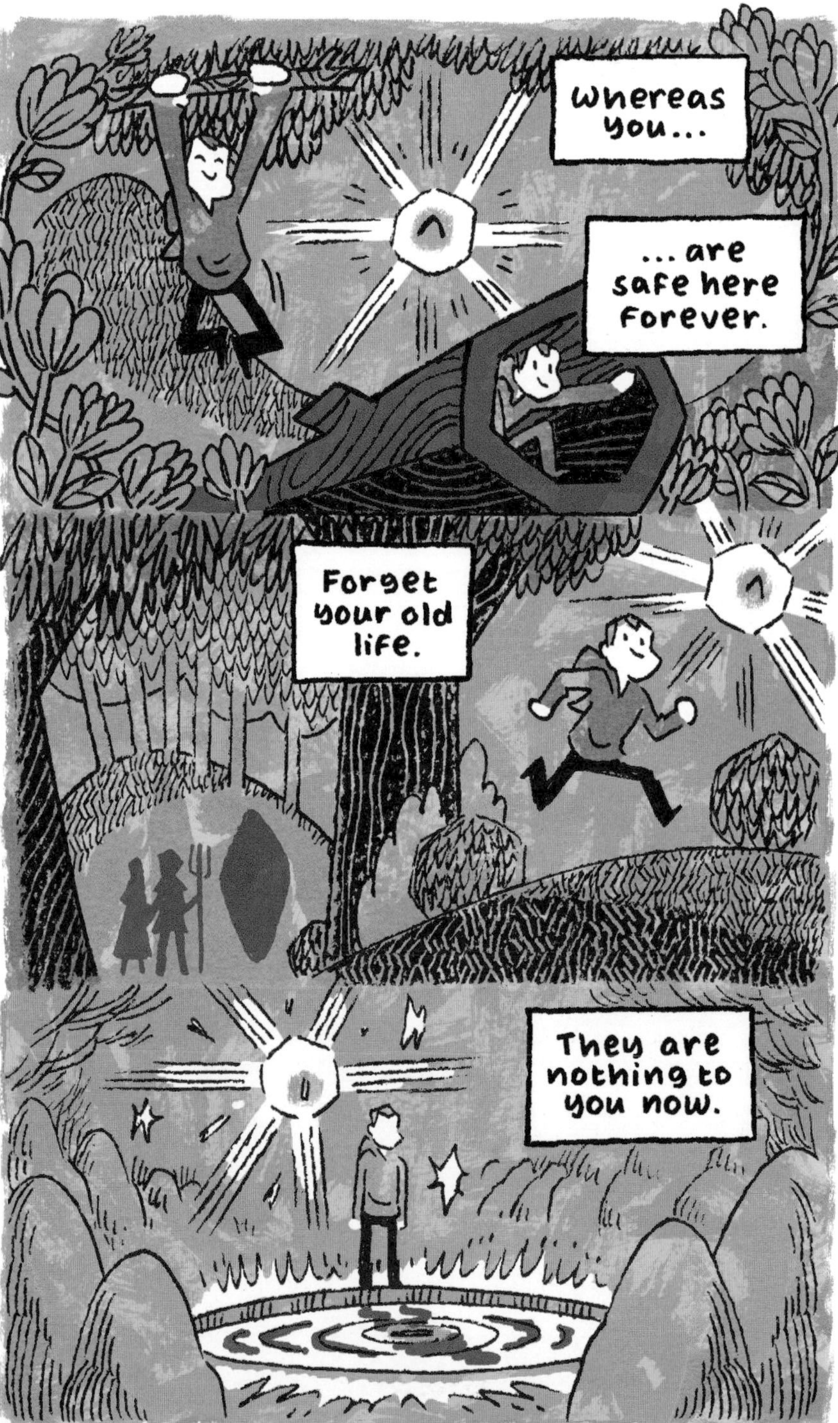
Whereas you...
...are safe here forever.
Forget your old life.
They are nothing to you now.

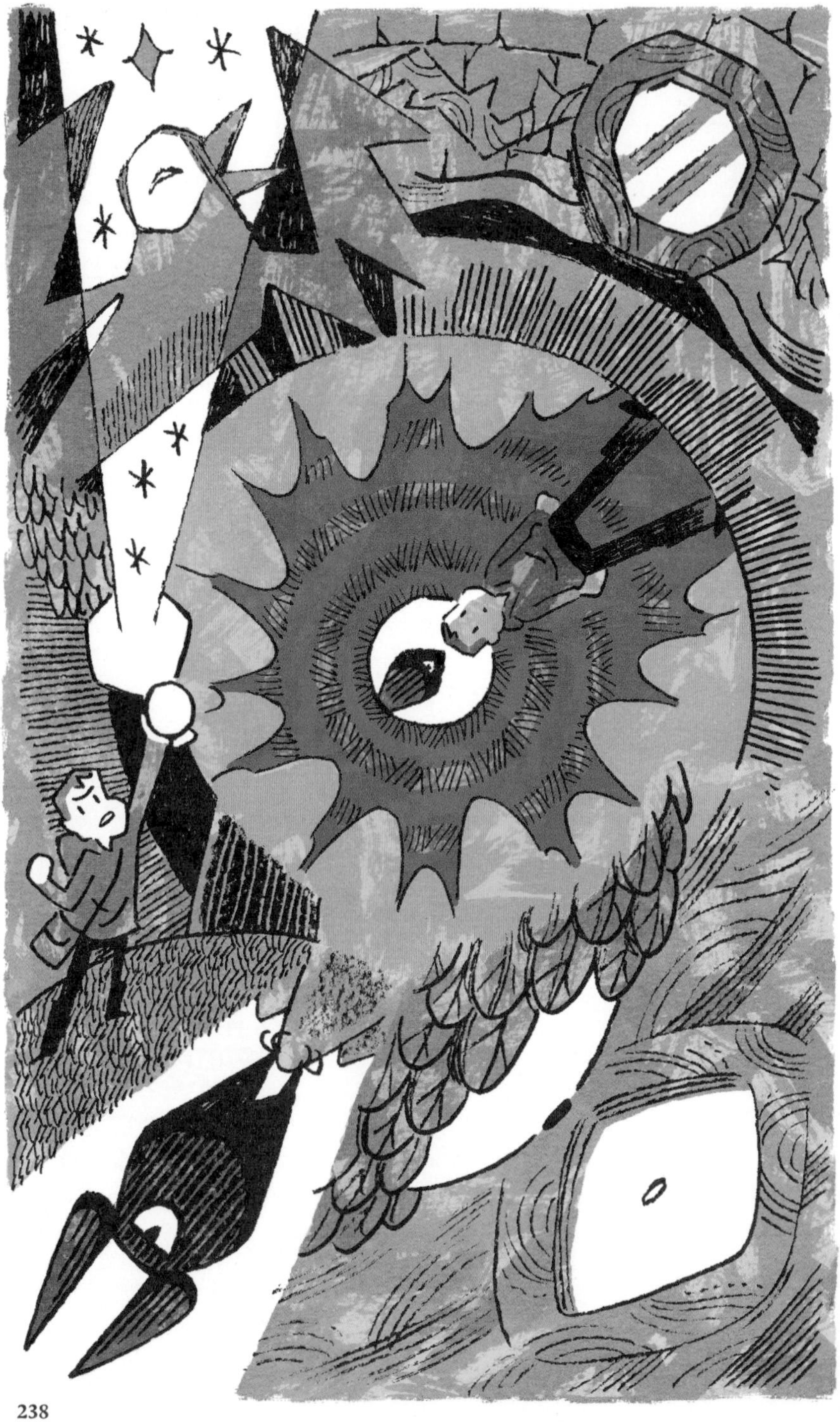

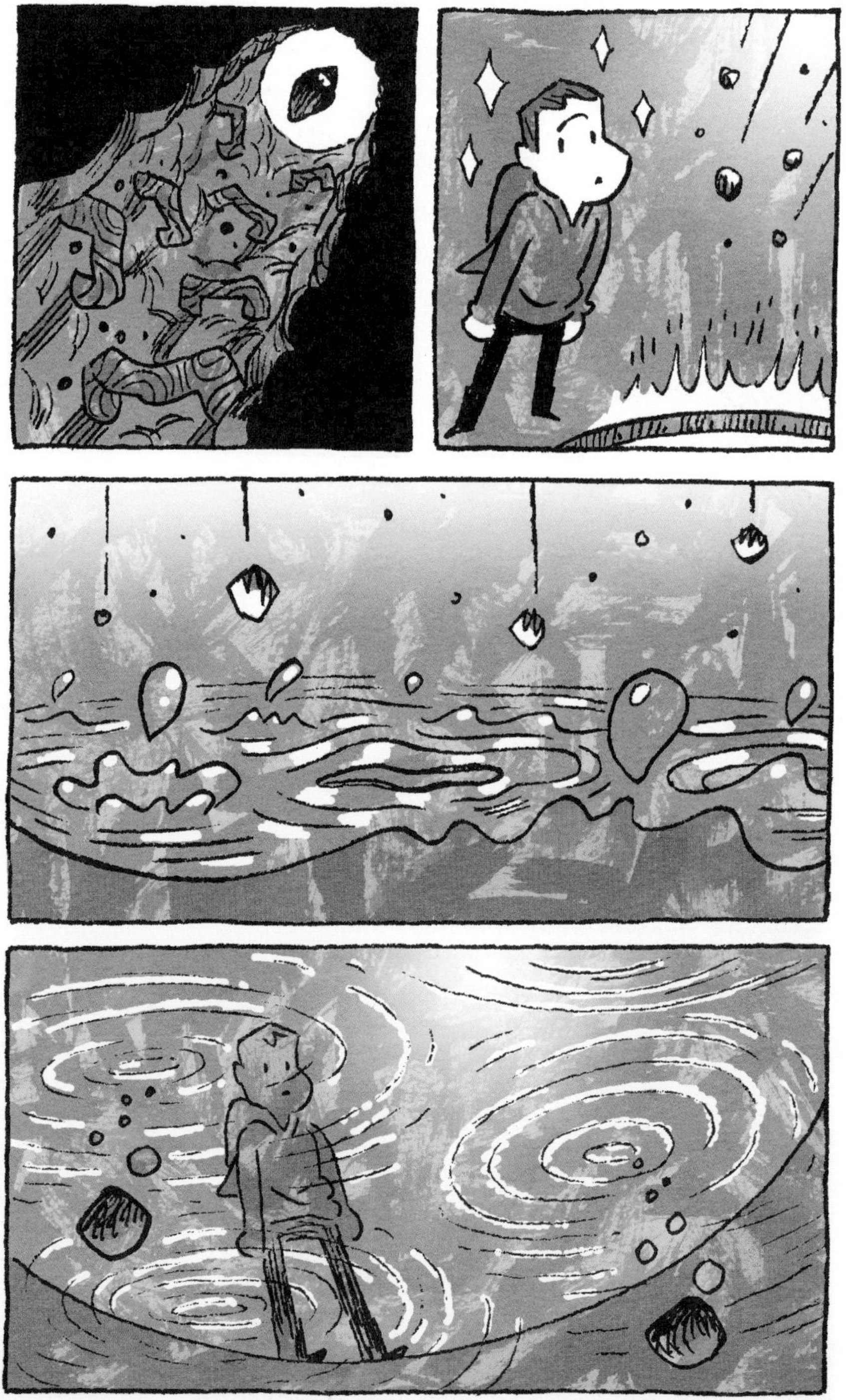

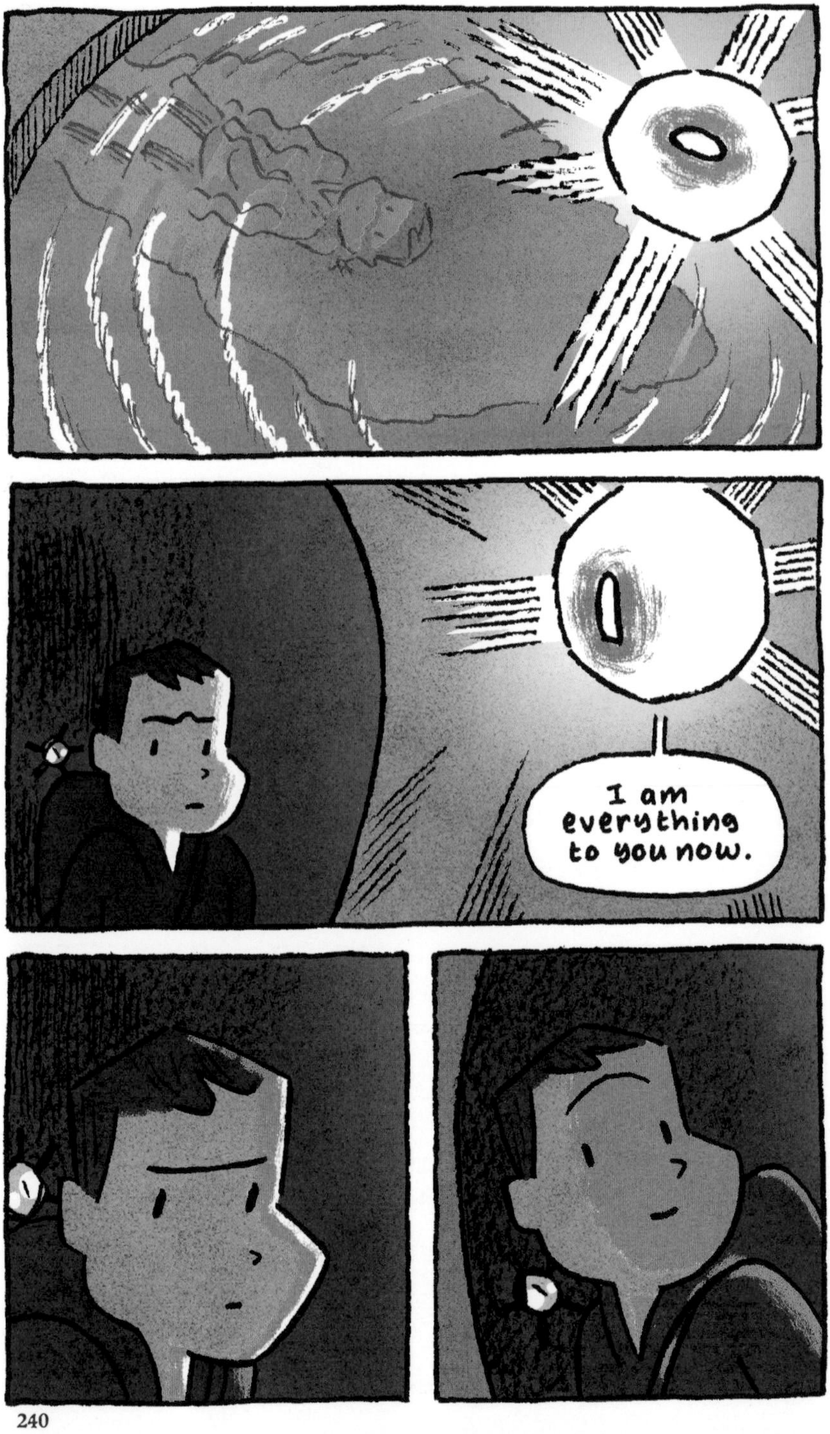
I am everything to you now.

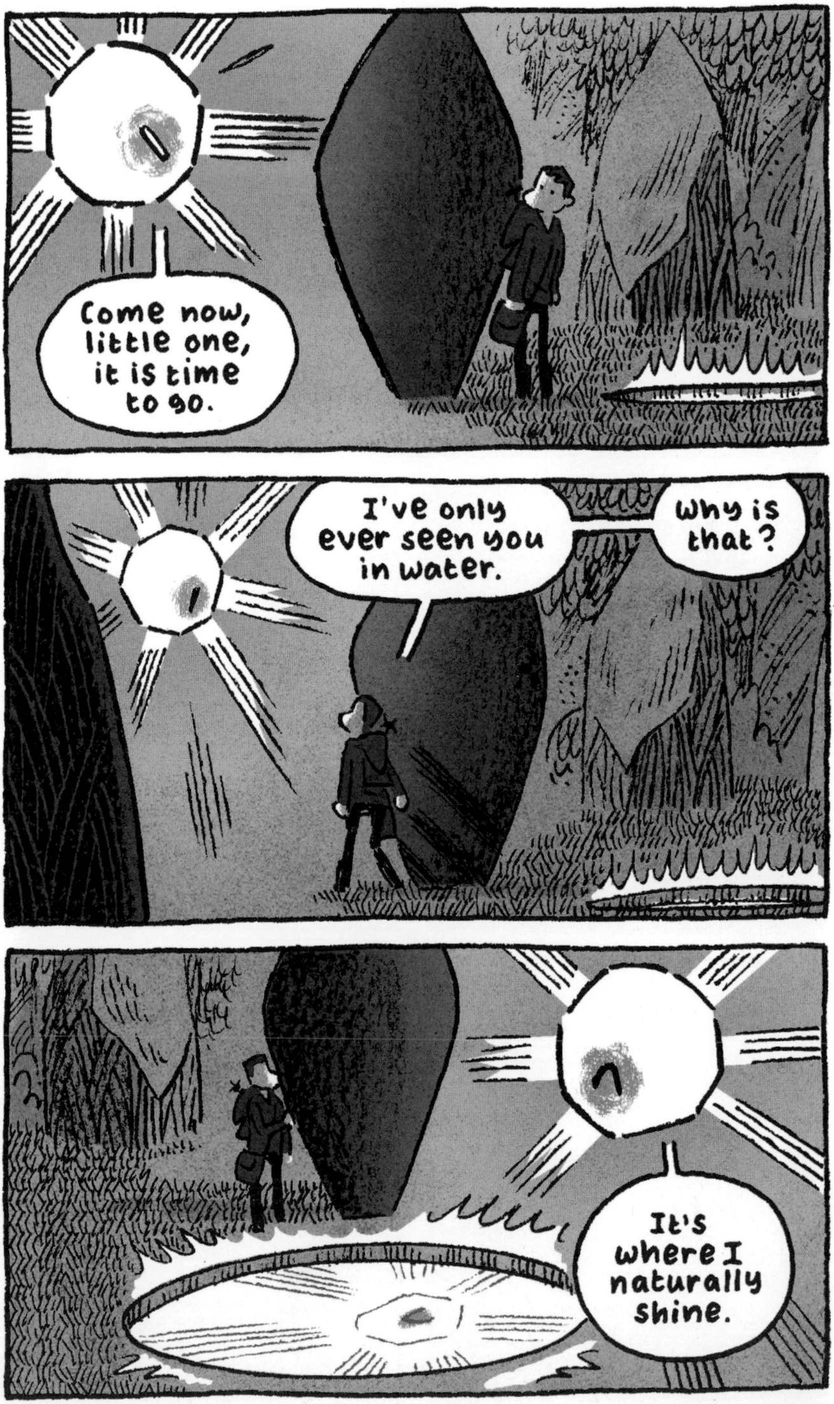
Come now, little one, it is time to go.
I've only ever seen you in water.
Why is that?
It's where I naturally shine.

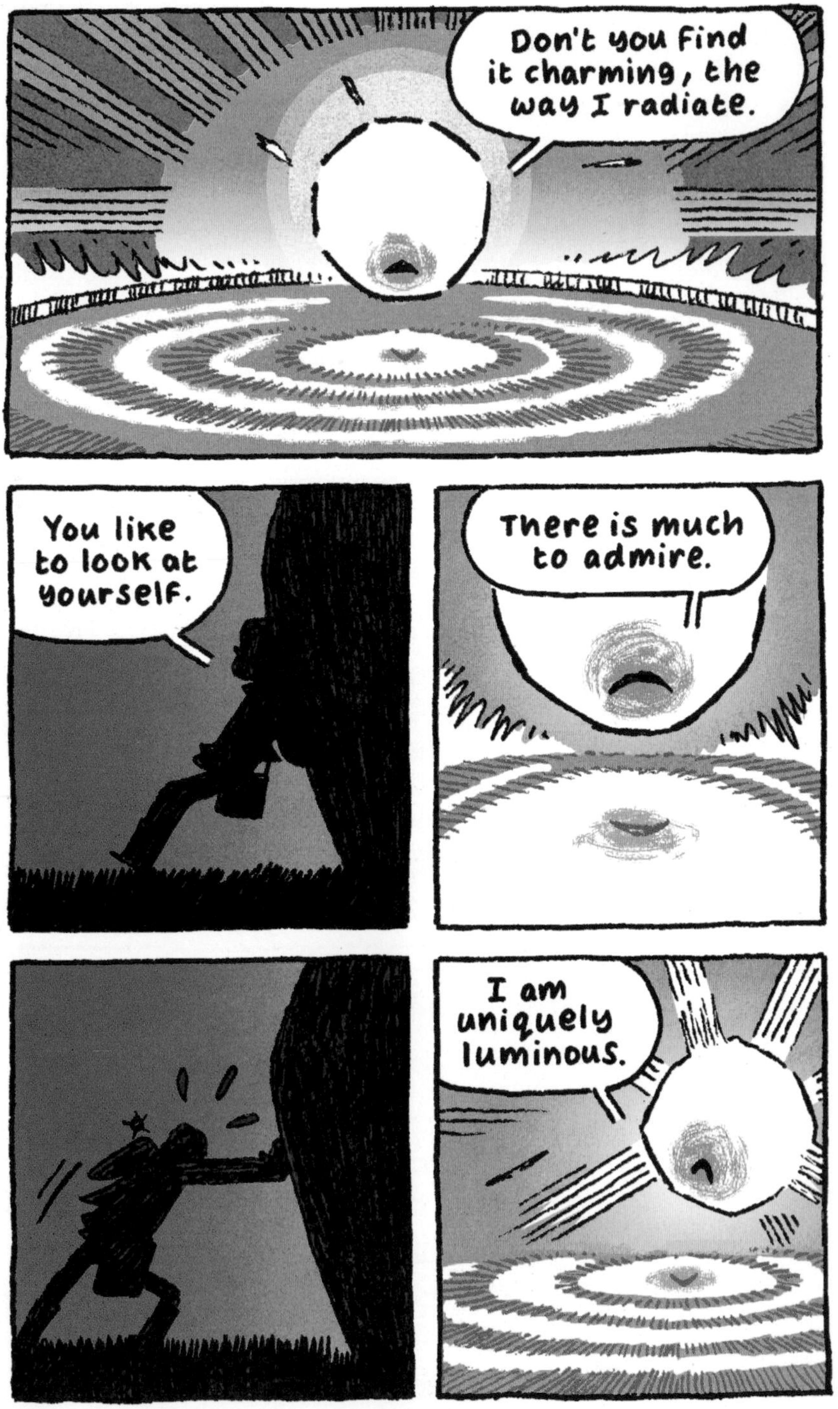
Don't you find it charming, the way I radiate.
You like to look at yourself.
There is much to admire.
I am uniquely luminous.

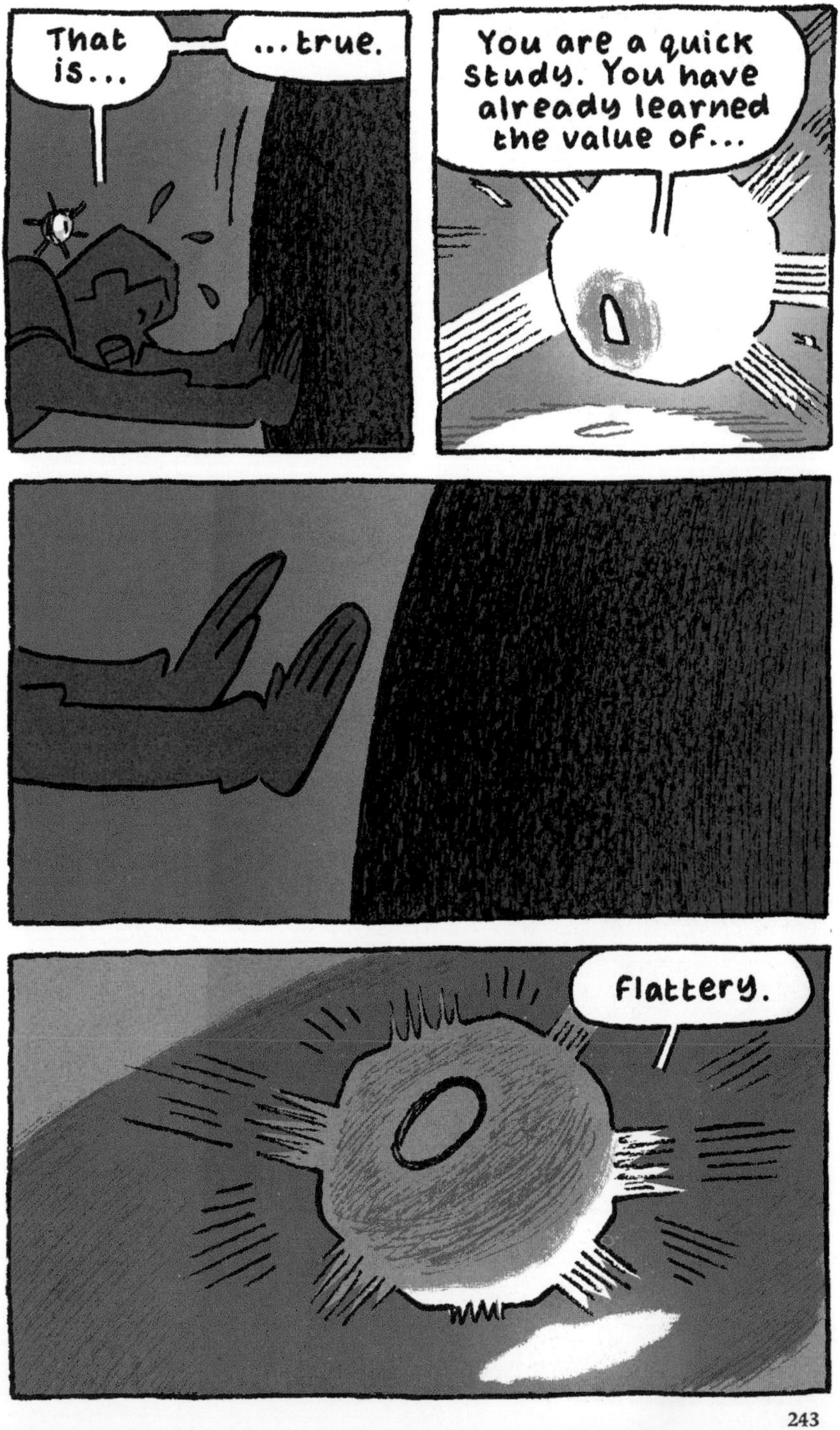
That is...
...true.
You are a quick study. You have already learned the value of...
Flattery.

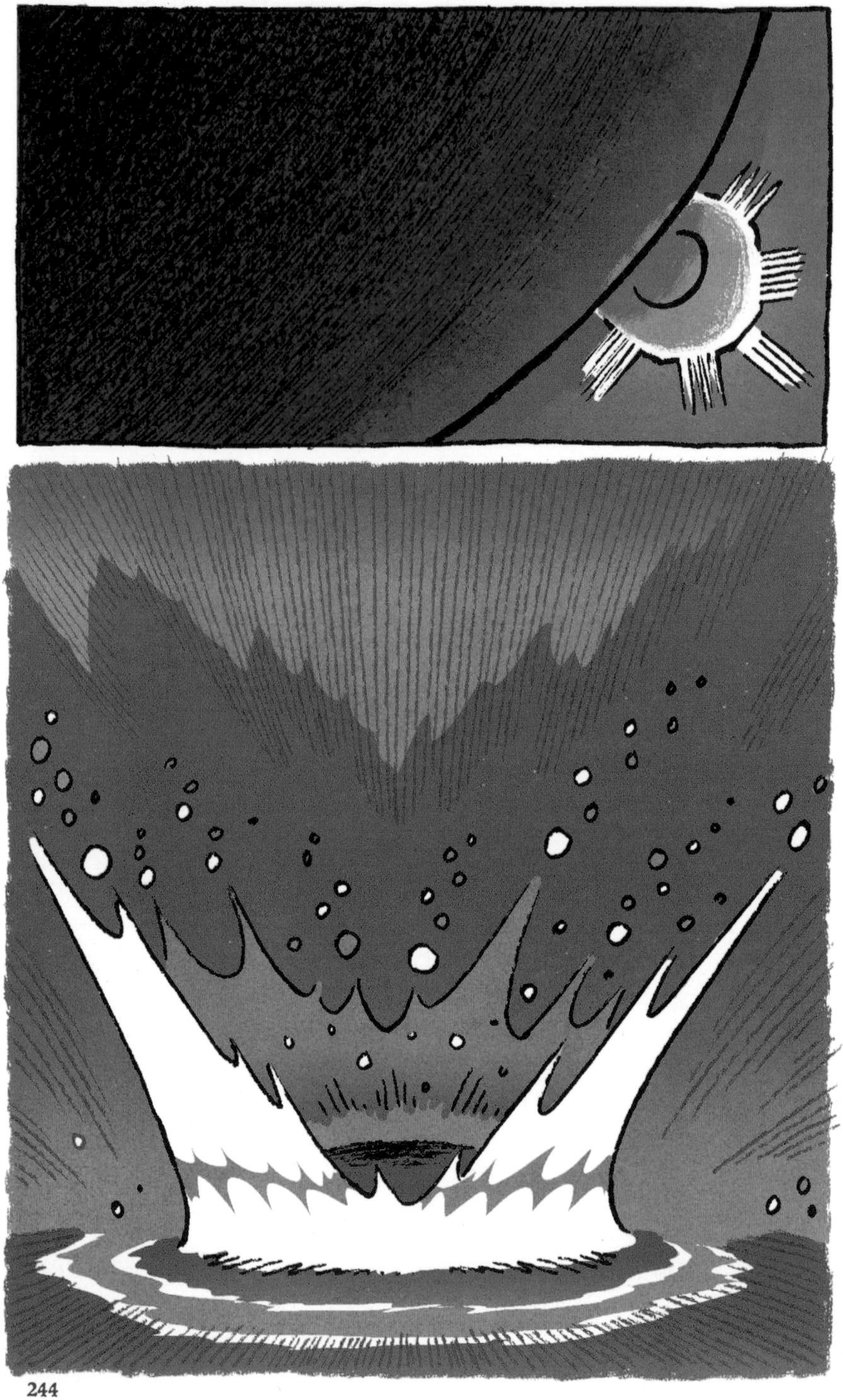

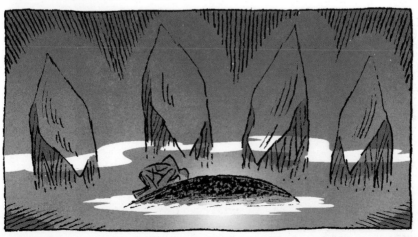

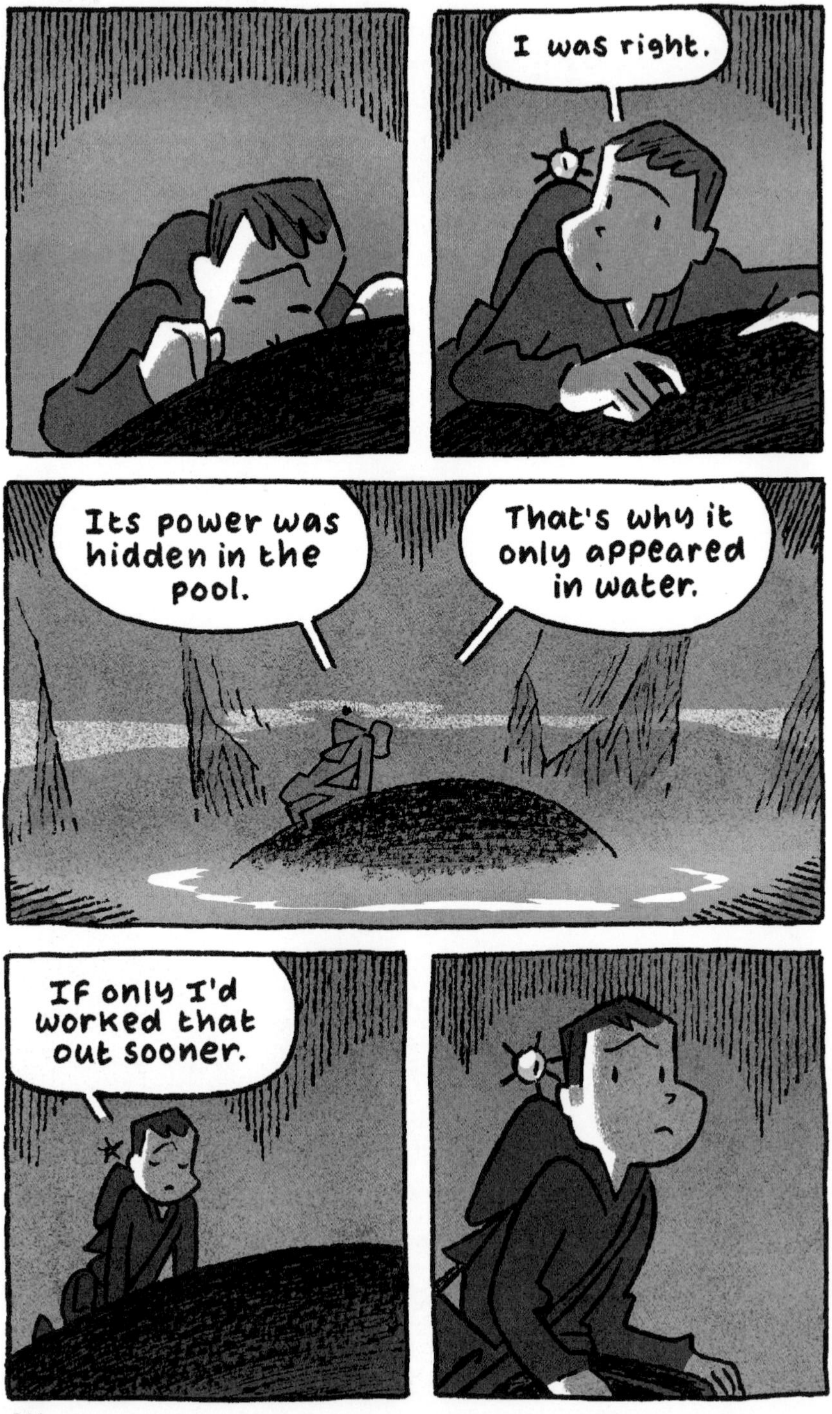
I was right.
Its power was hidden in the pool.
That's why it only appeared in water.
If only I'd worked that out sooner.

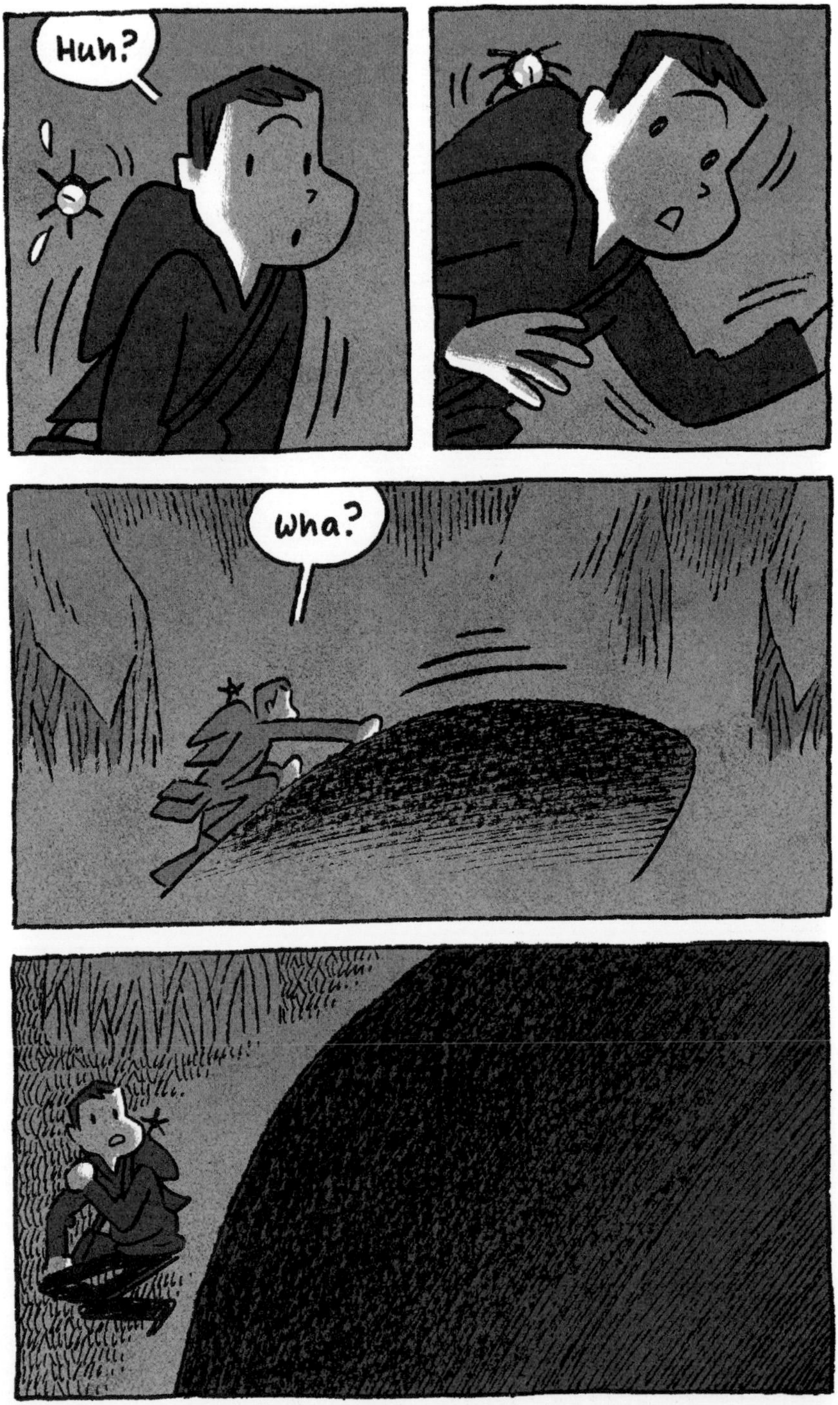
Huh?
Wha?

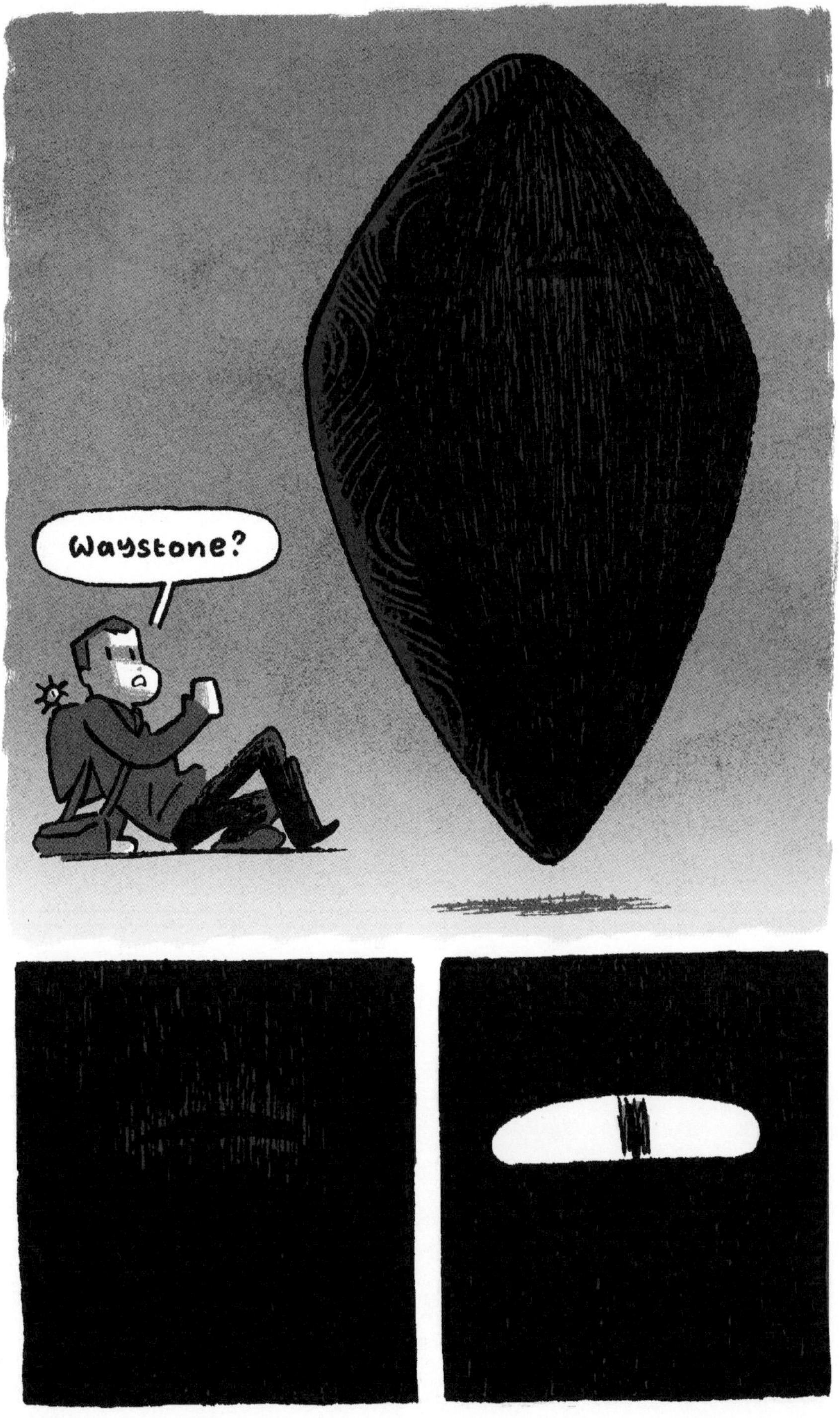
Waystone?

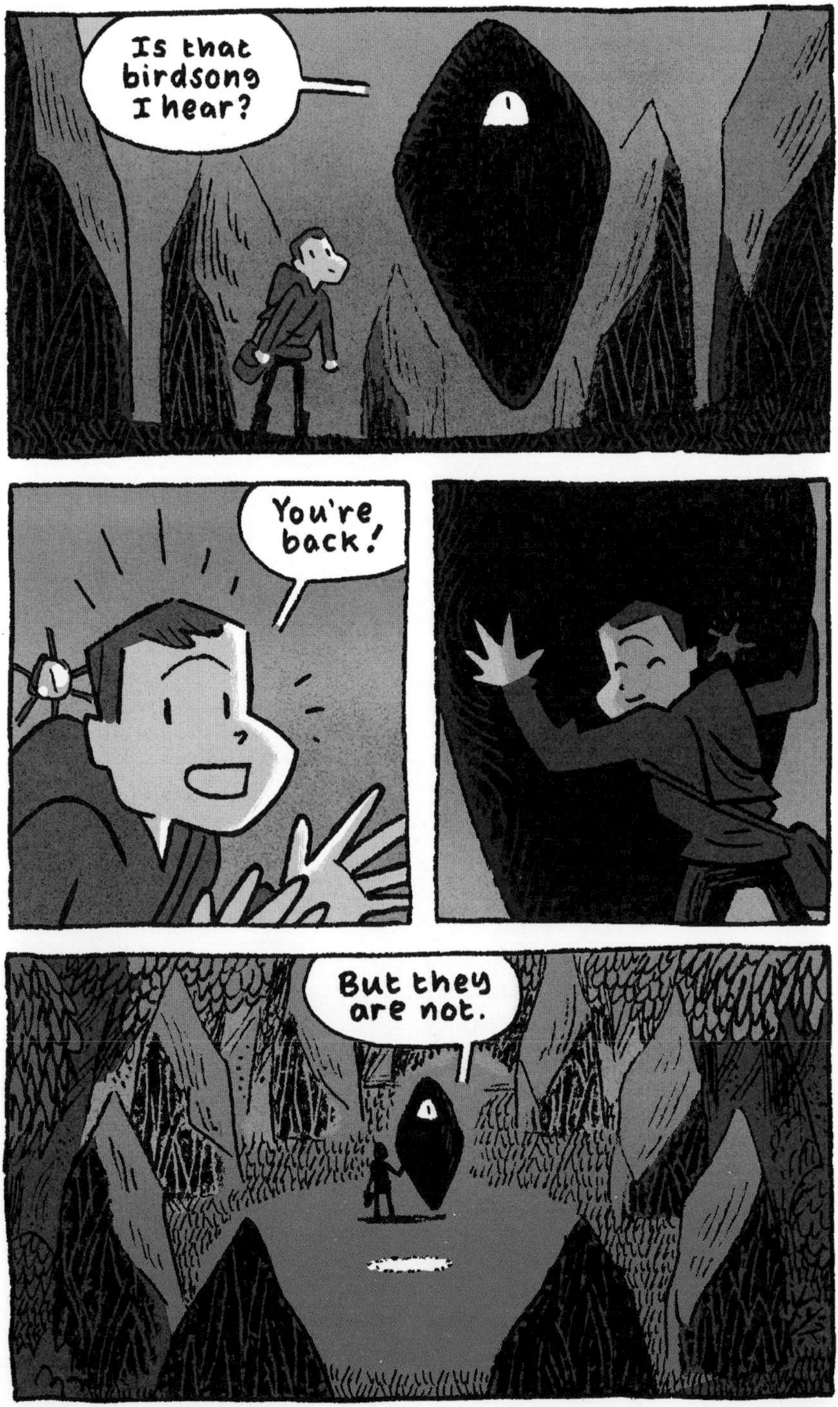
Is that birdsong I hear?
You're back!
But they are not.

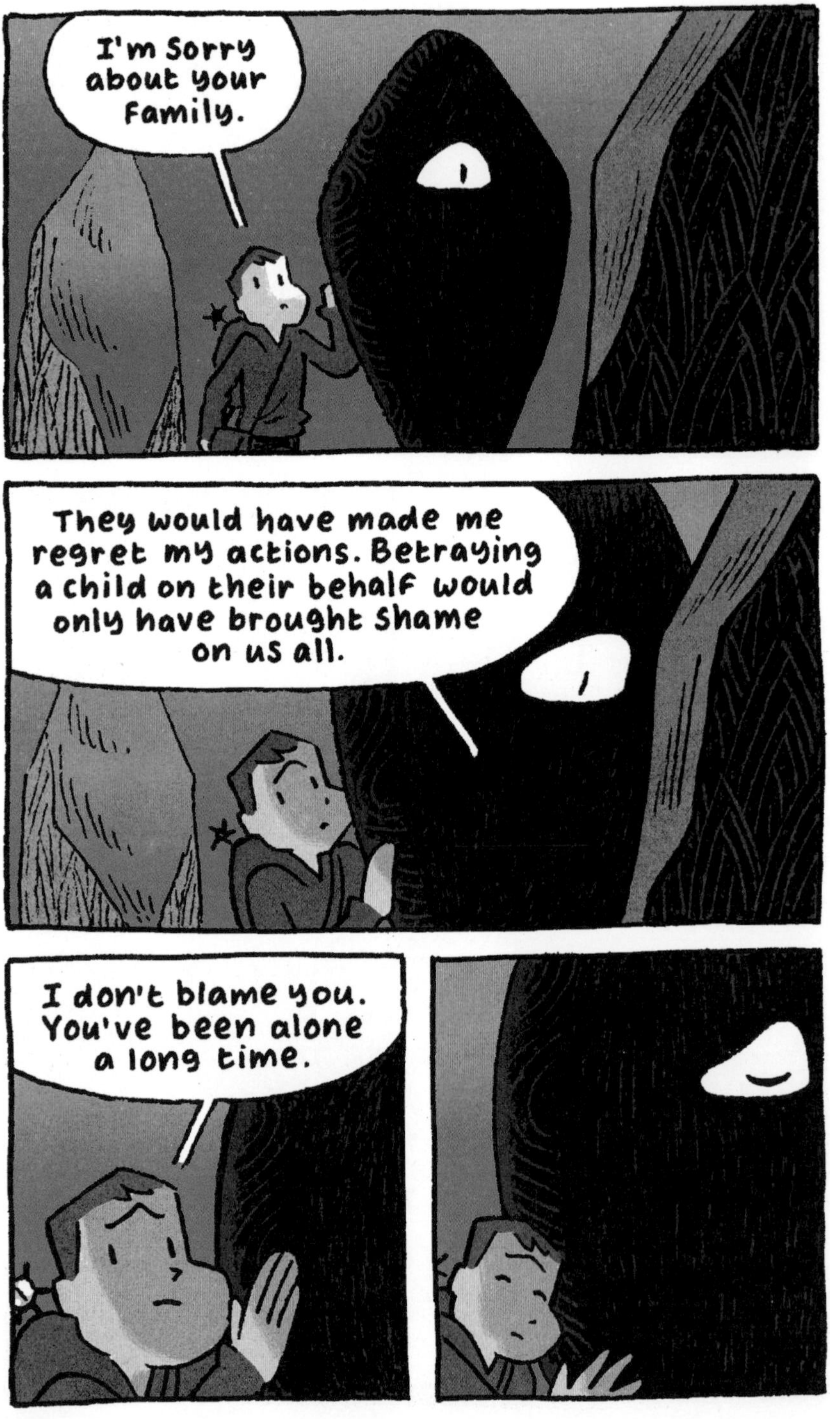
I'm Sorry about your Family.
They would have made me regret my actions. Betraying a child on their behalf would only have brought shame on us all.
I don't blame you. You've been alone a long time.

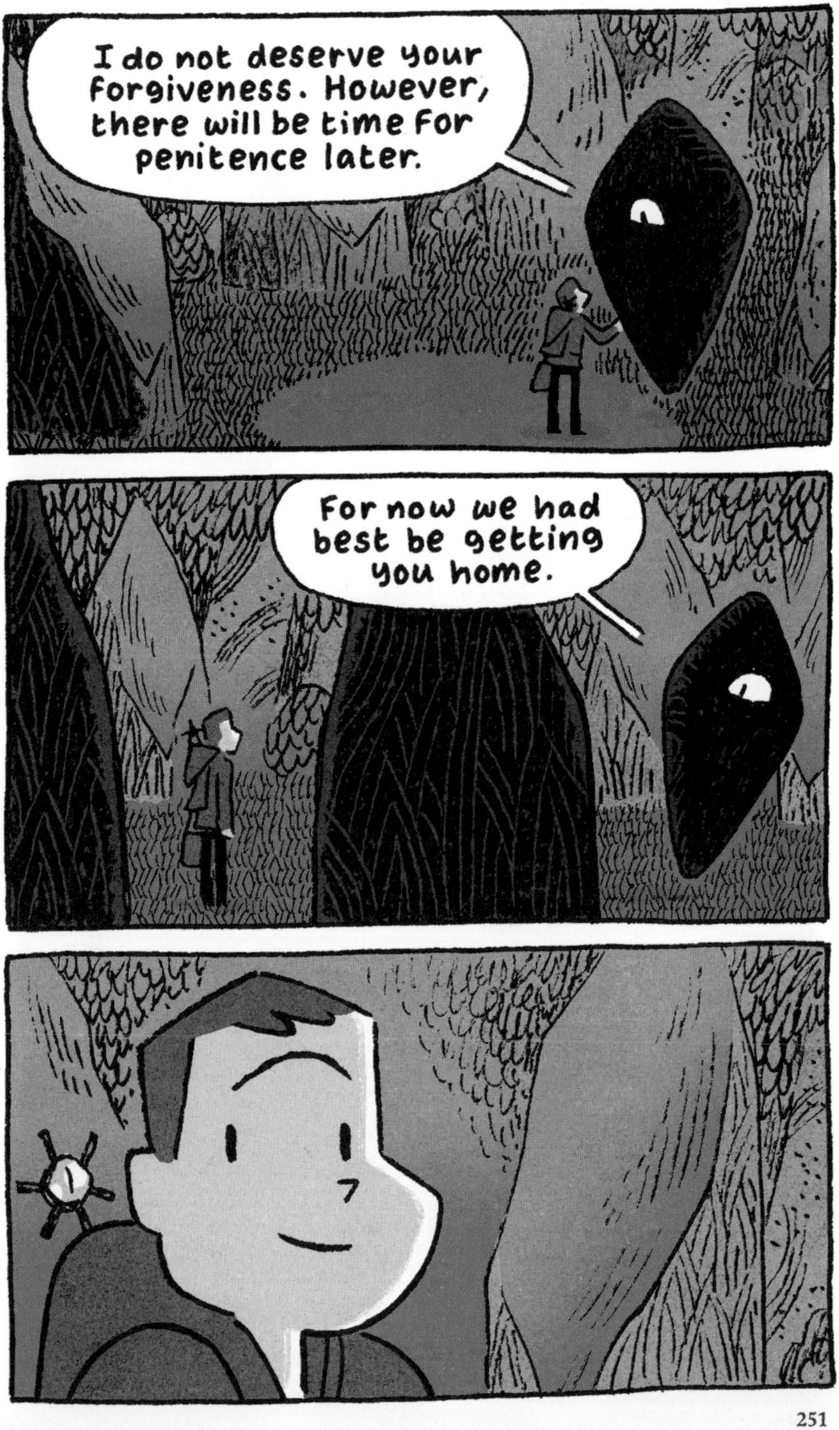
I do not deserve your forgiveness. However, there will be time for penitence later.
For now we had best be getting you home.

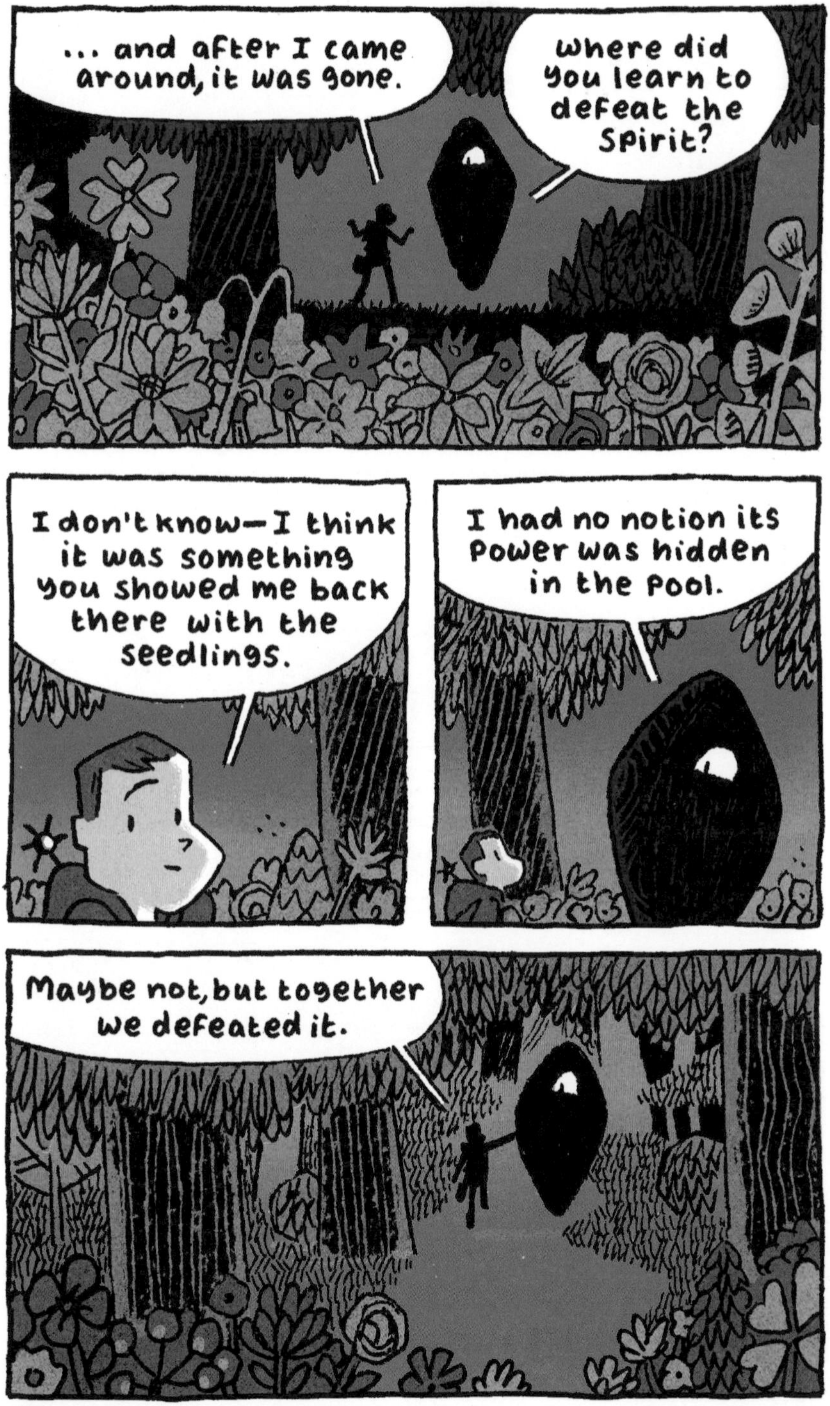
... and after I came around, it was gone.
Where did you learn to defeat the Spirit?
I don't know—I think it was something you showed me back there with the seedlings.
I had no notion its power was hidden in the pool.
Maybe not, but together we defeated it.

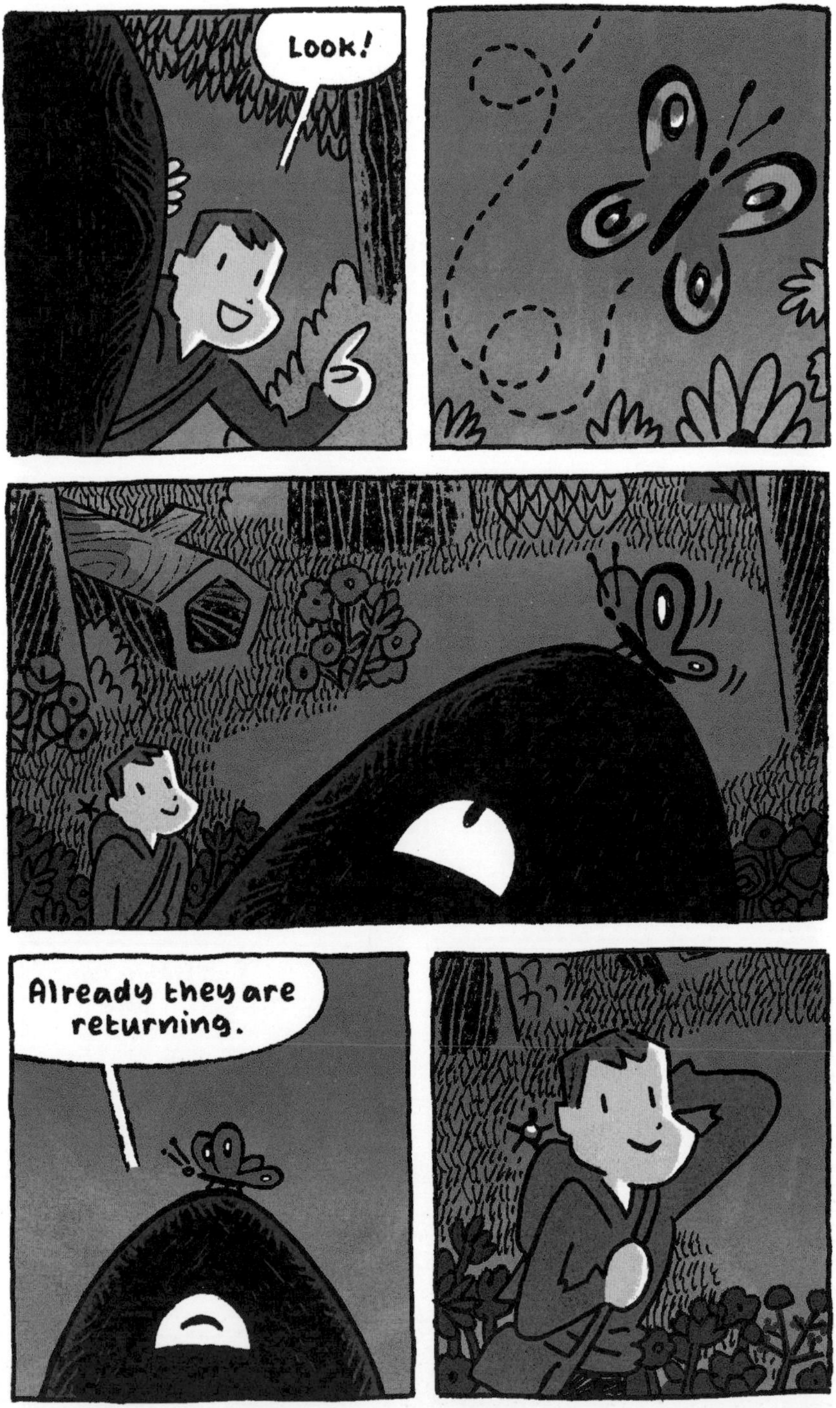
LOOK!
Already they are returning.

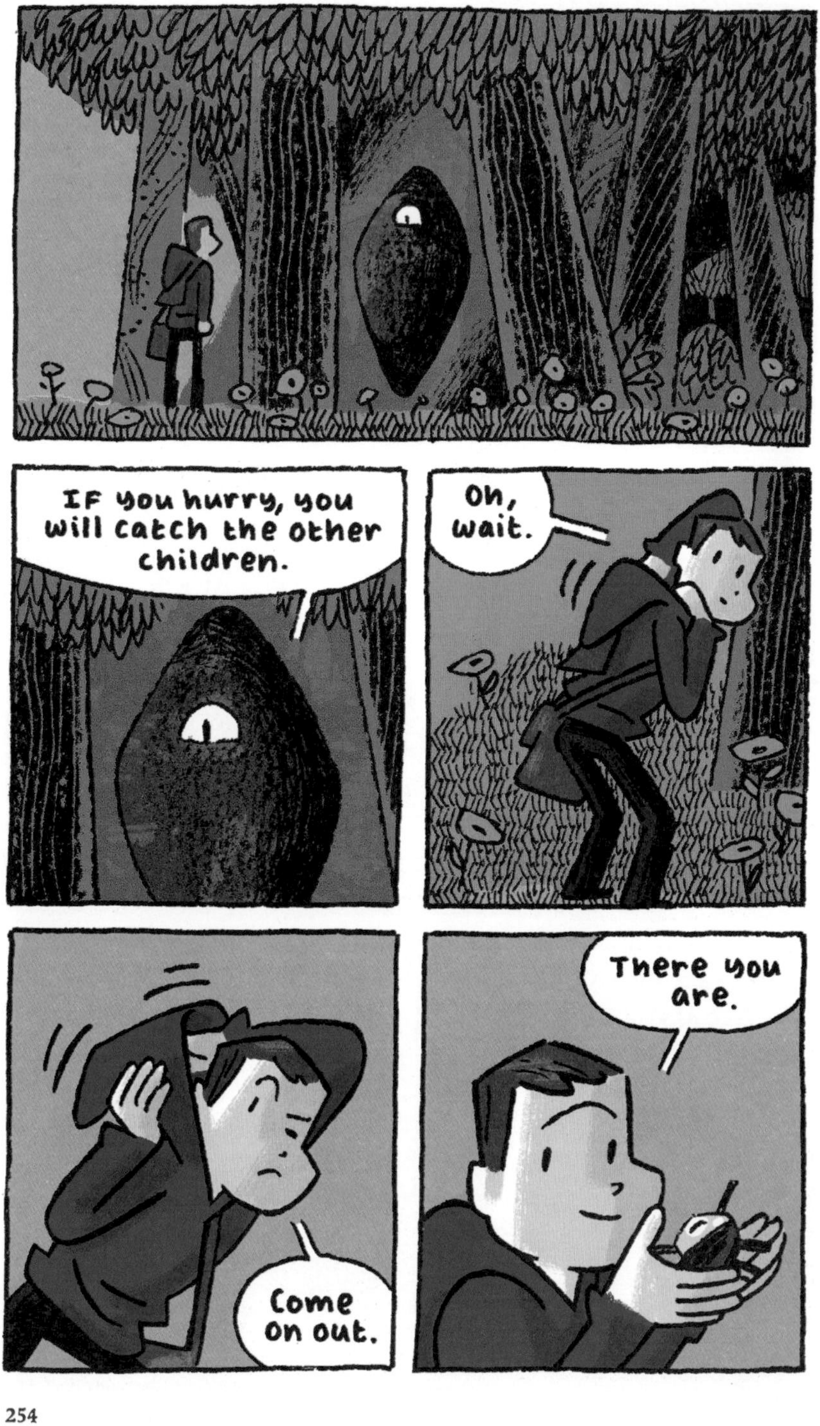
IF you hurry, you will catch the other children.
Oh, wait.
Come on out.
There you are.

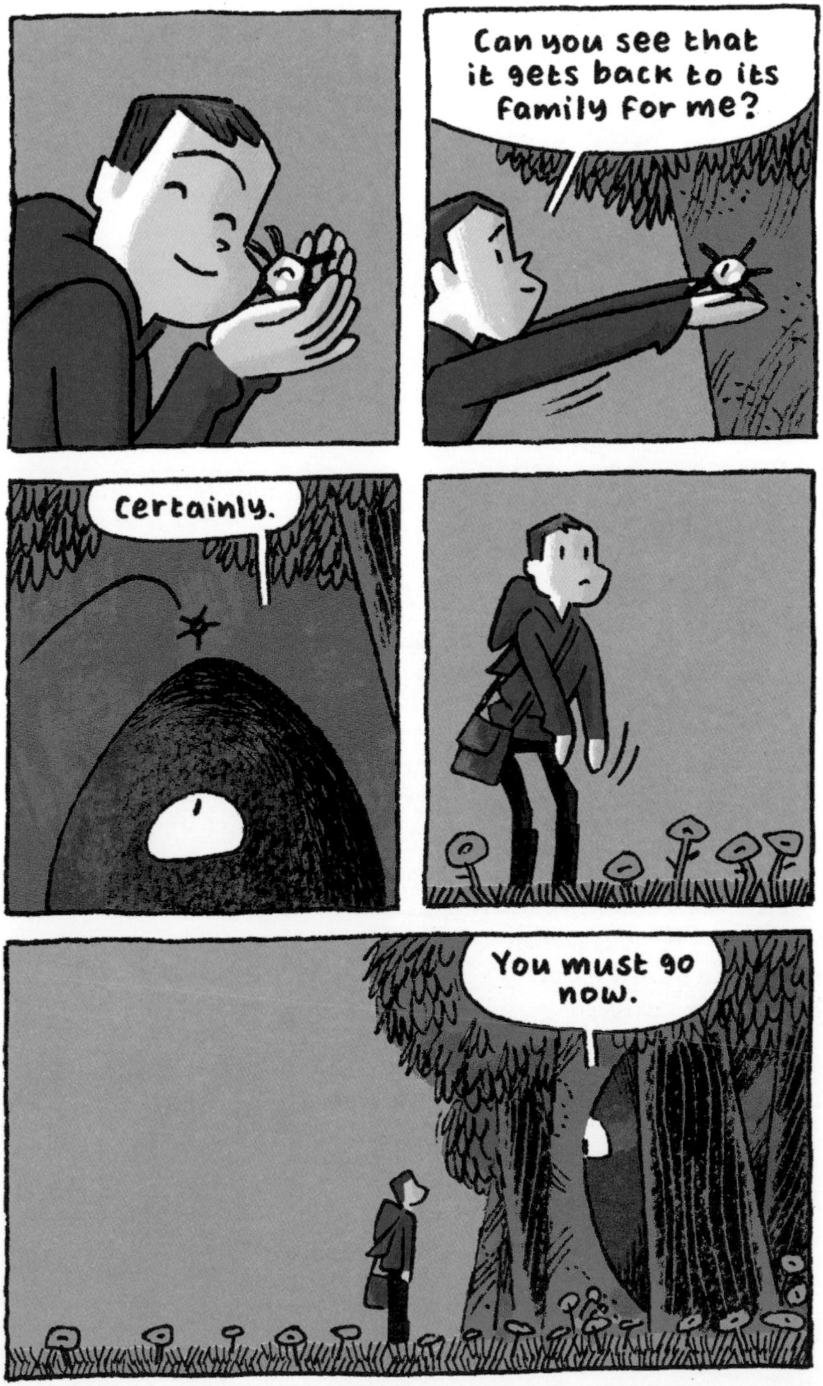
Can you see that it gets back to its family for me?
Certainly.
You must go now.

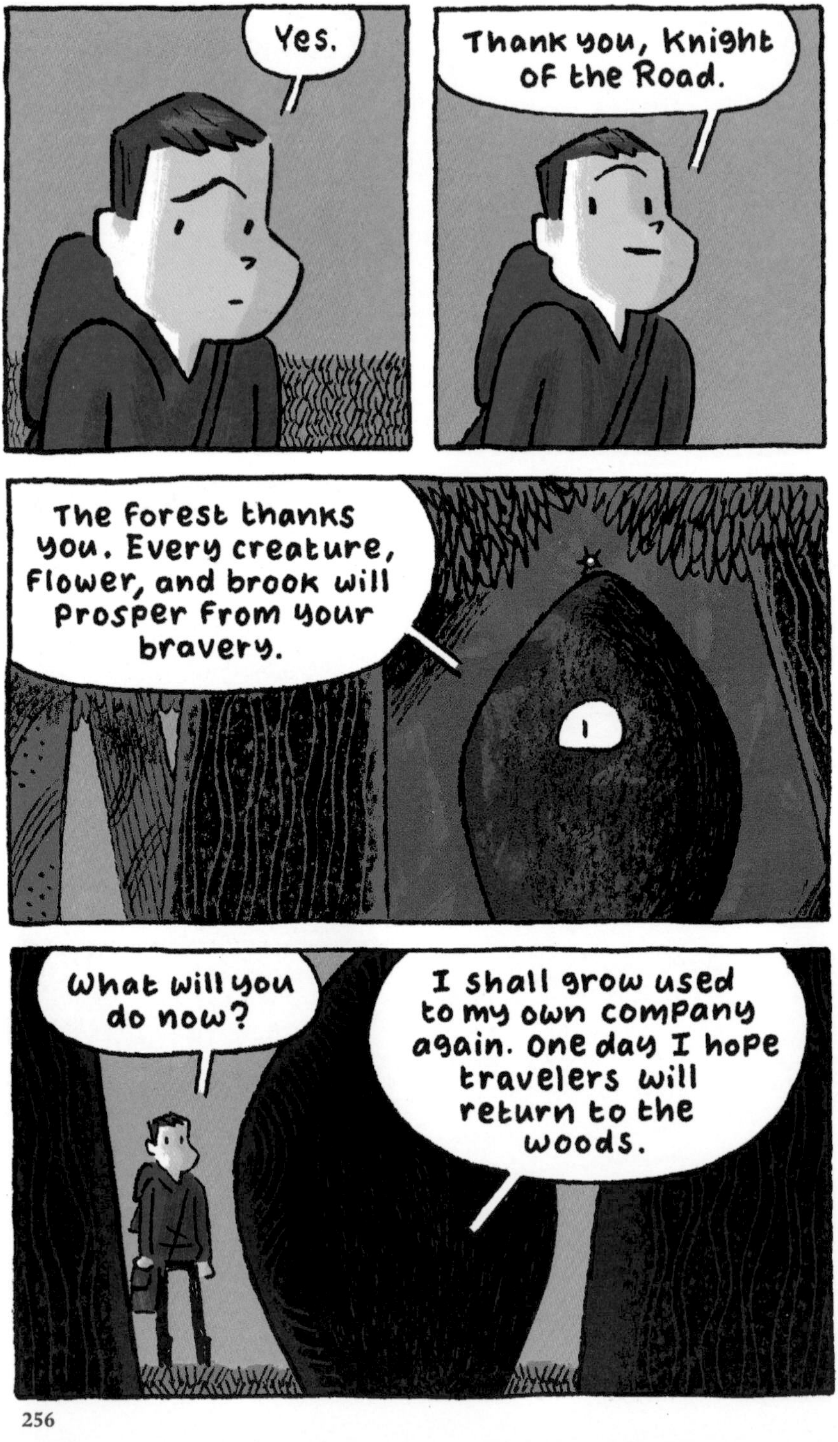
Yes.
Thank you, Knight of the Road.
The forest thanks you. Every creature, flower, and brook will prosper from your bravery.
What will you do now?
I shall grow used to my own company again. One day I hope travelers will return to the woods.

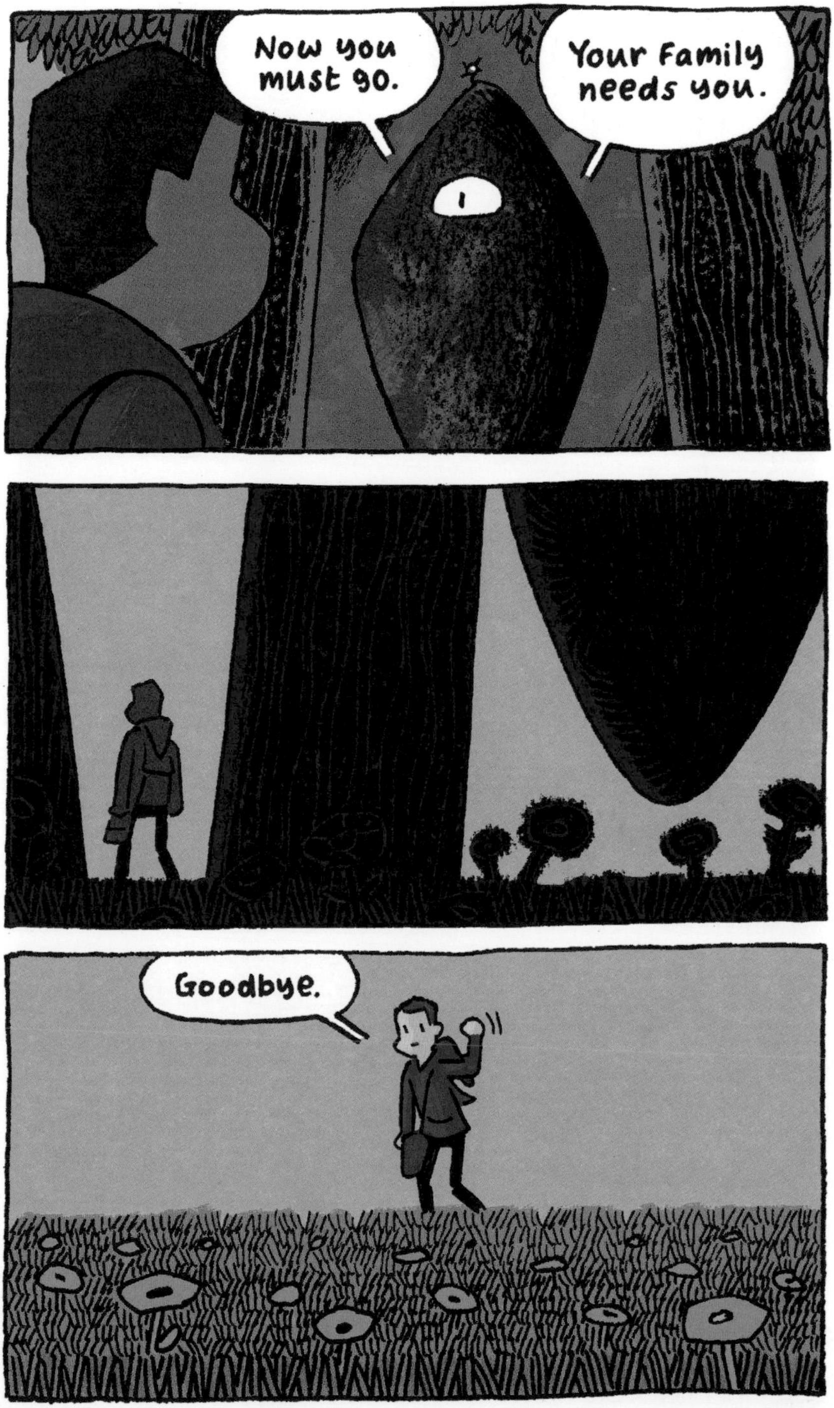
Now you must go.
Your family needs you.
Goodbye.

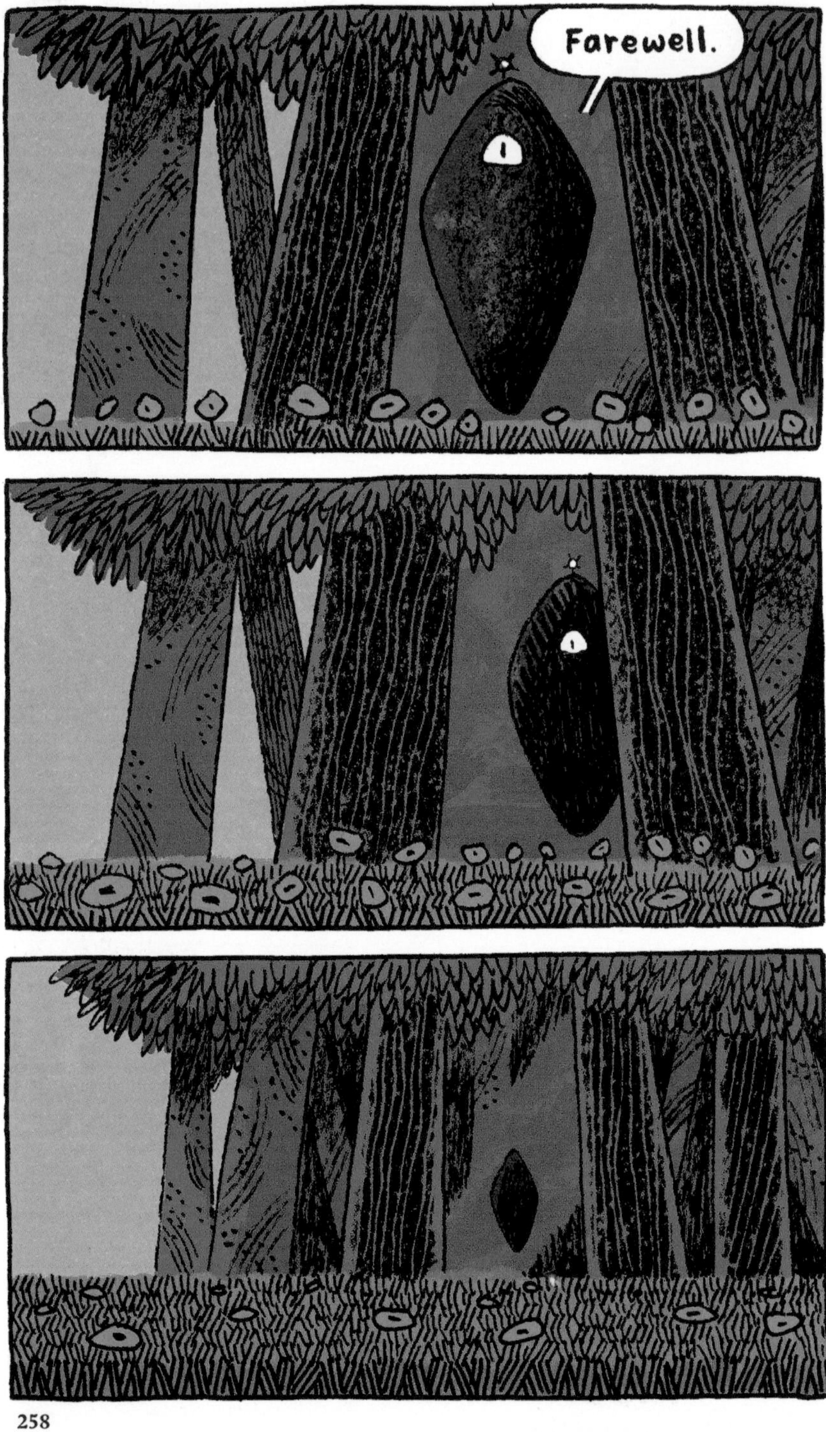
Farewell.

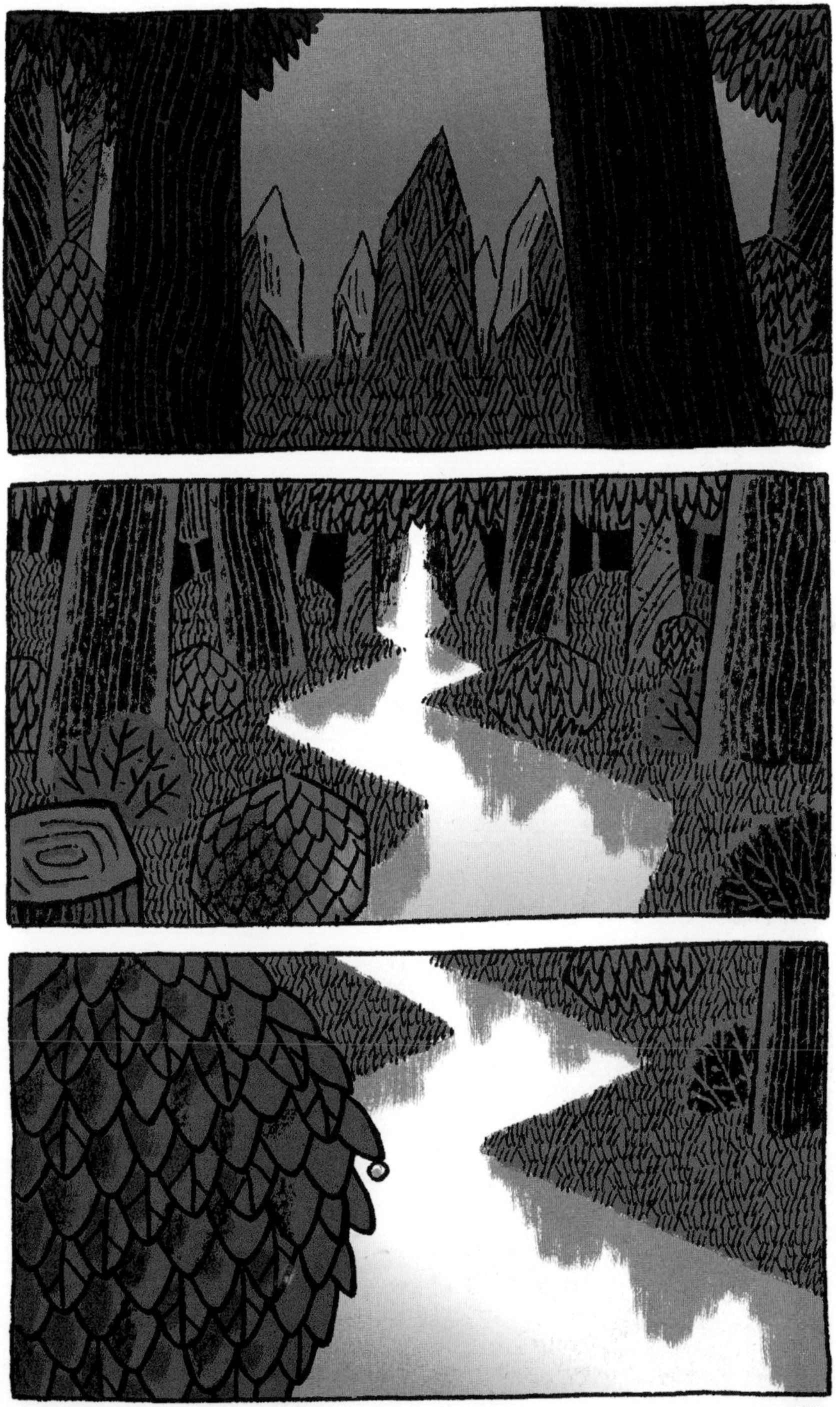

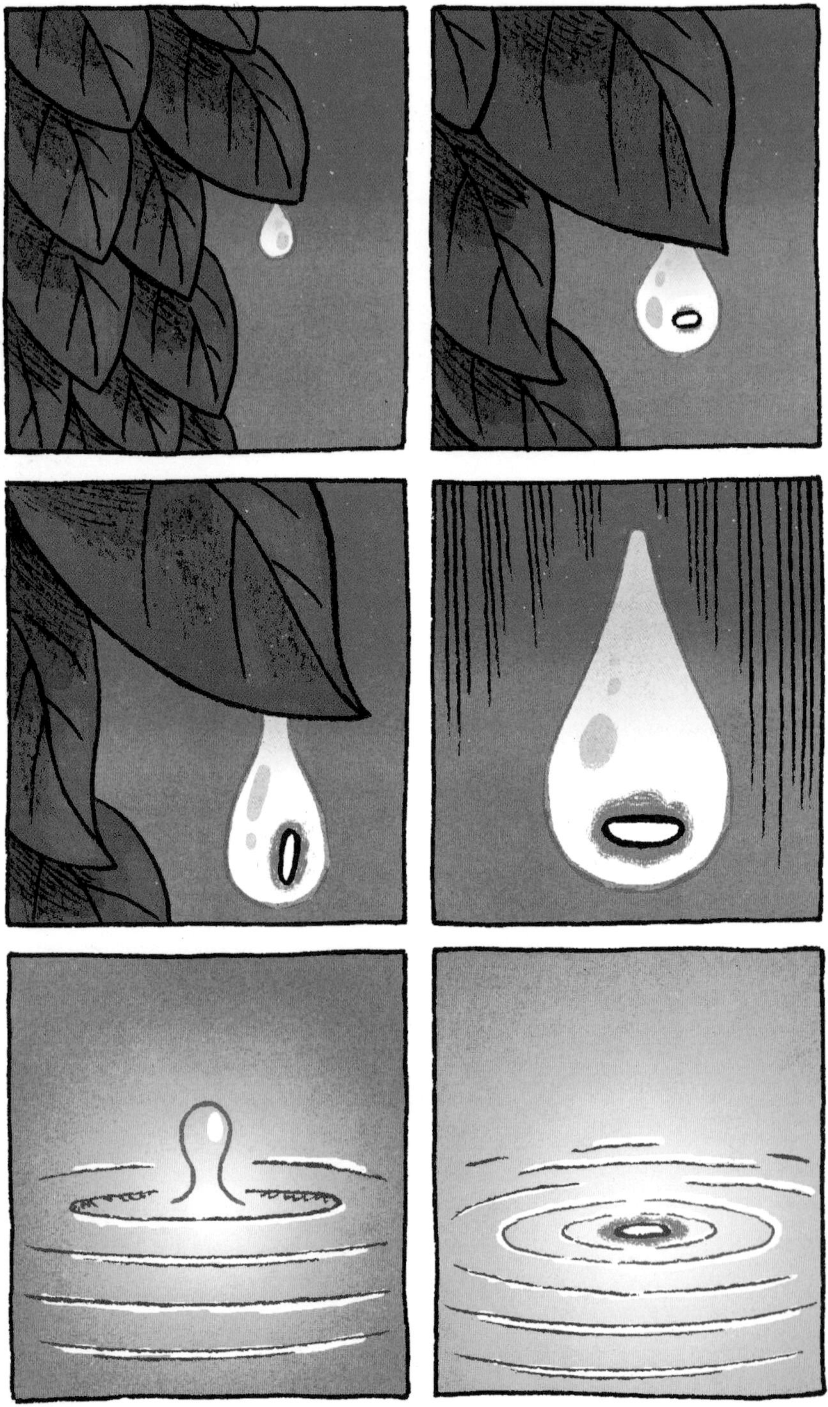

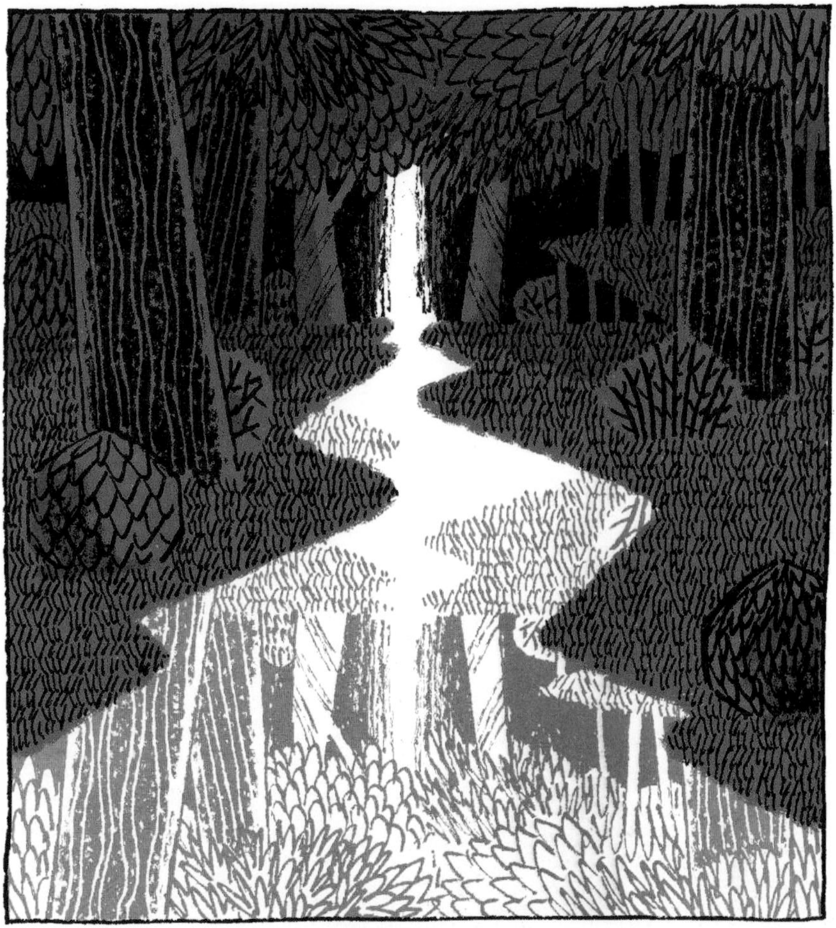

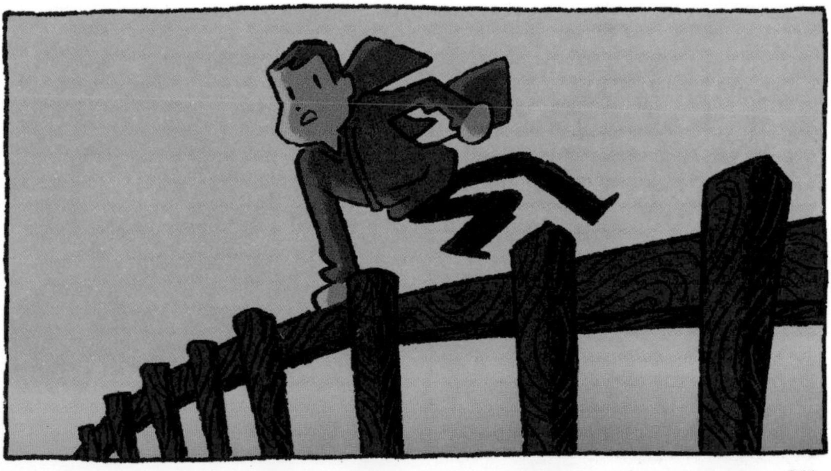

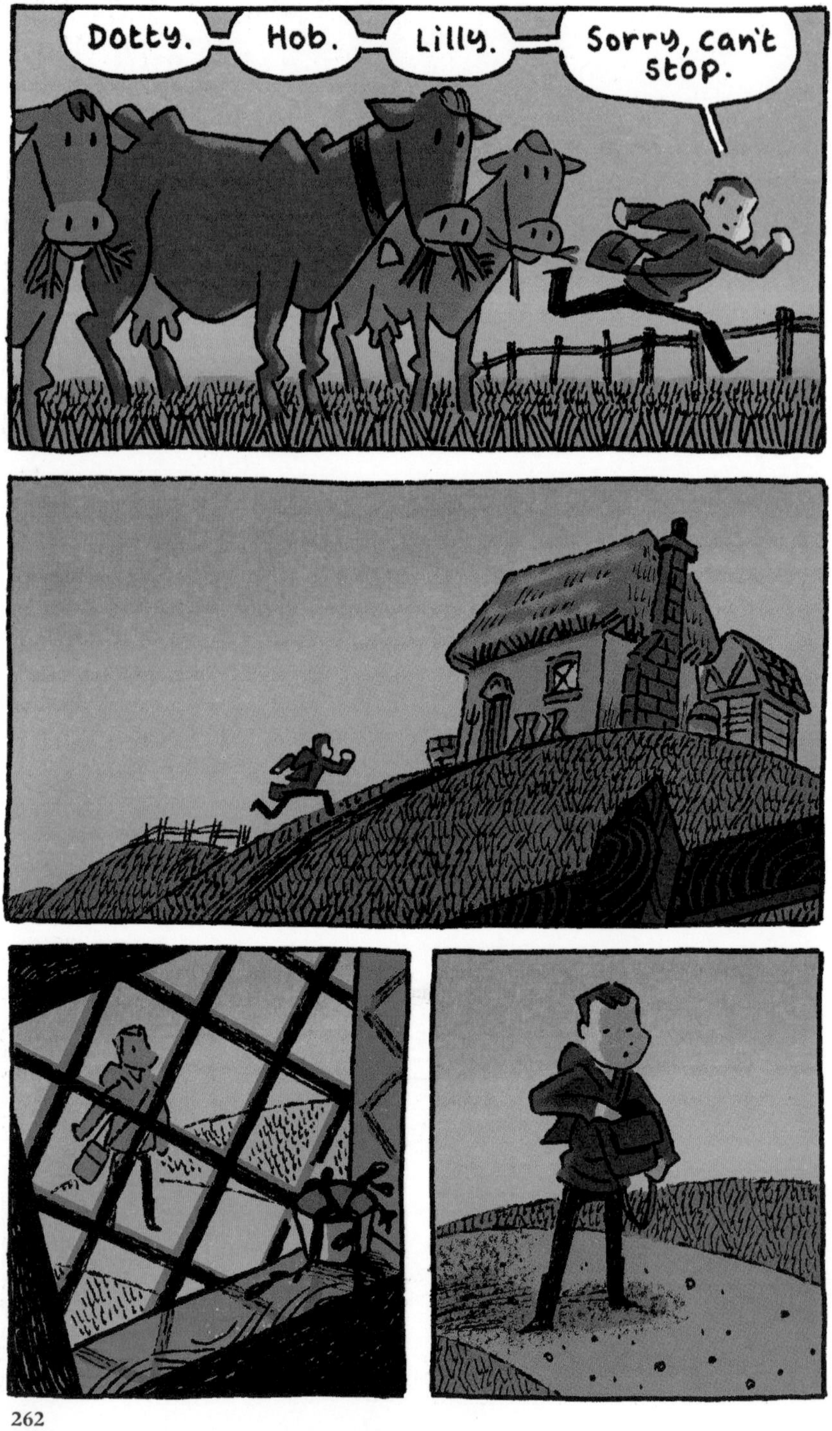
Dotty.
Hob.
Lilly.
Sorry, can't stop.

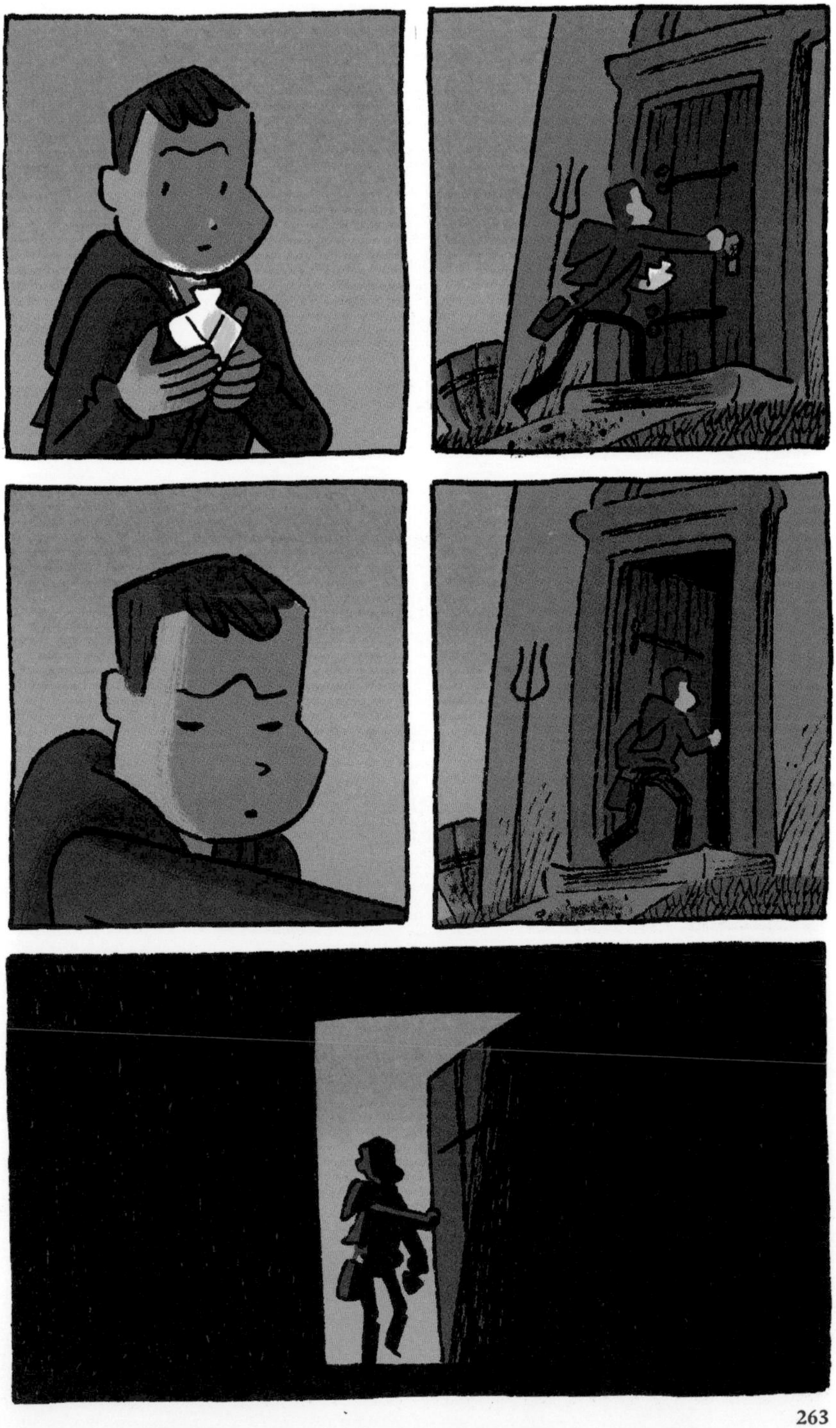

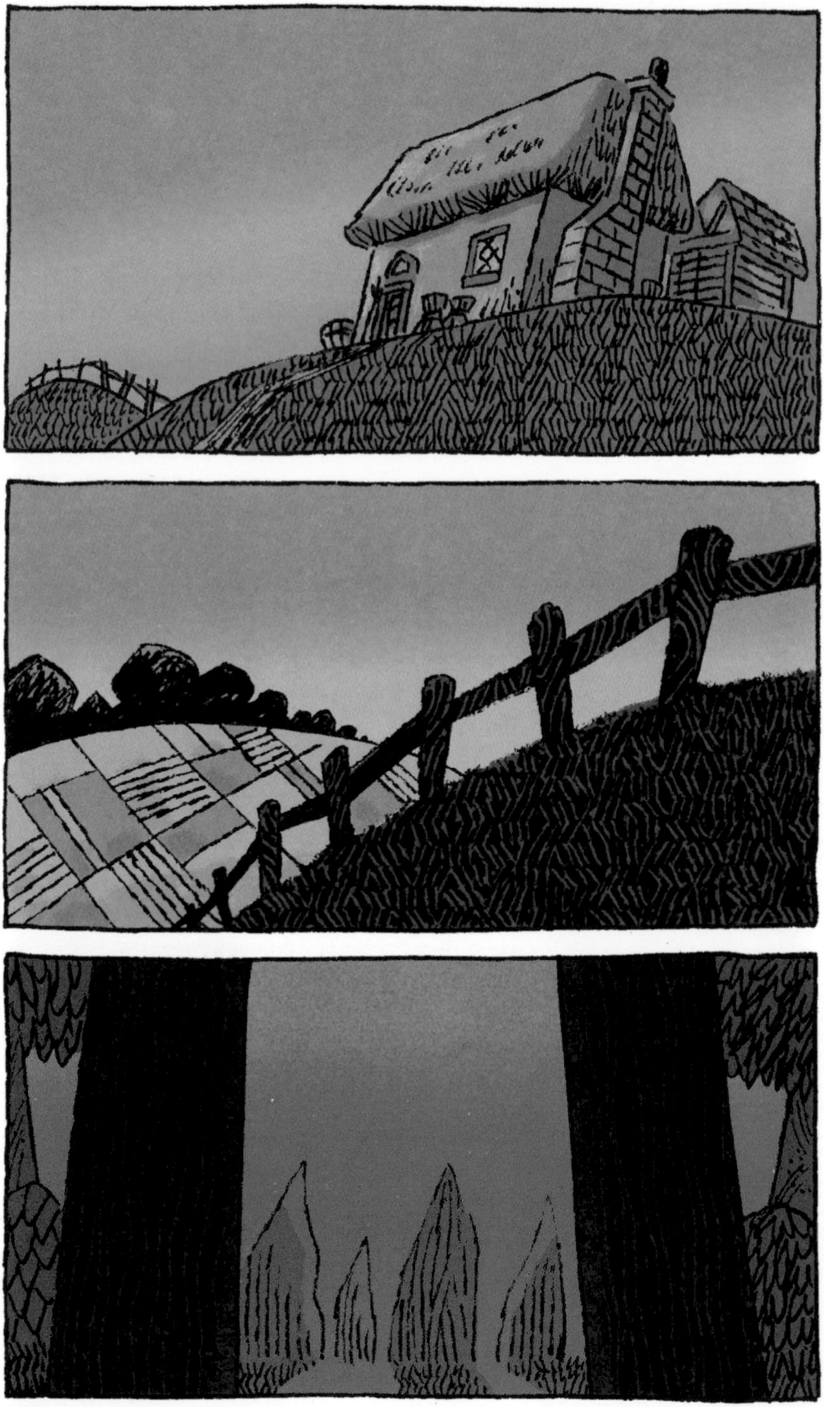

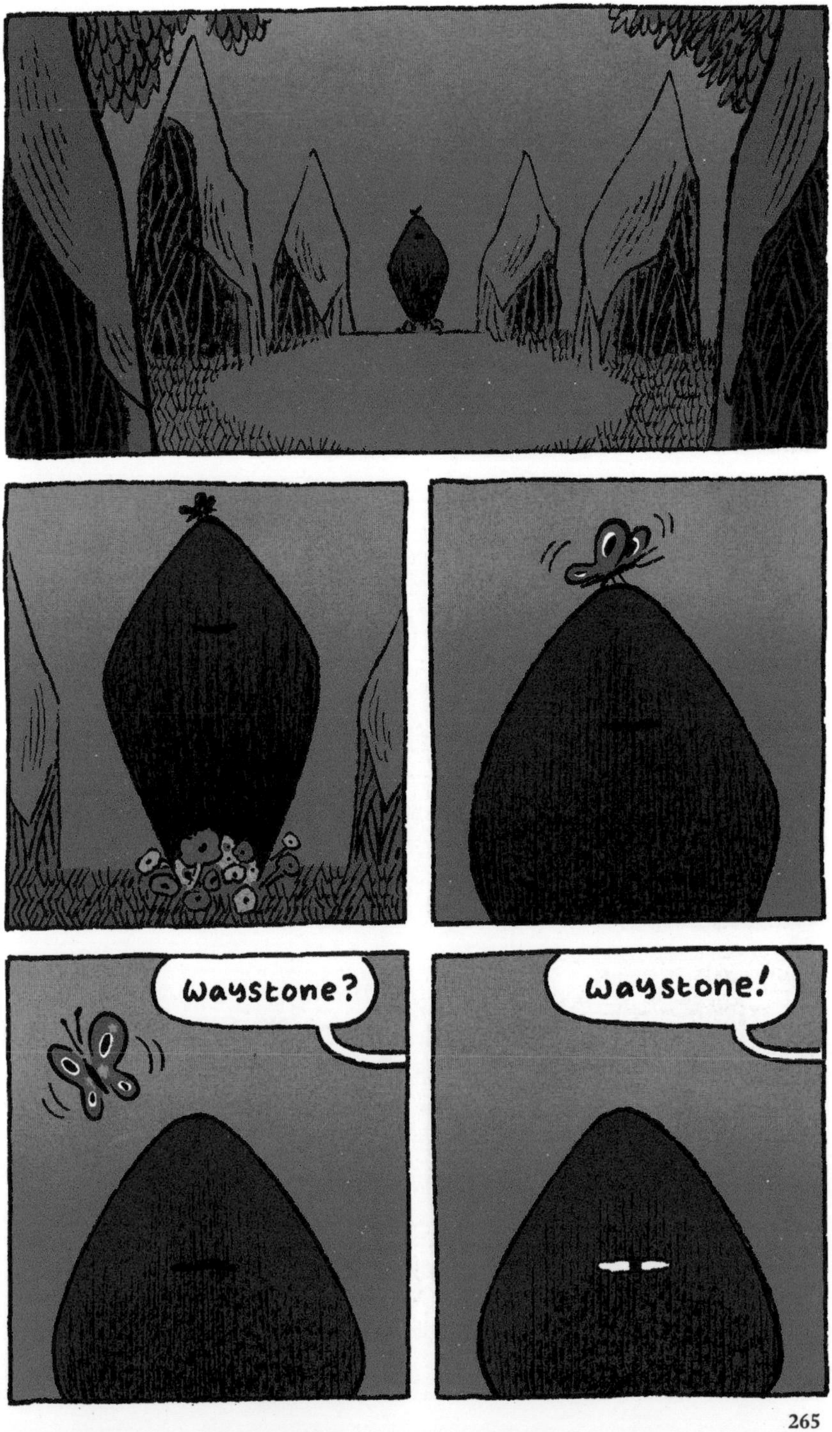
Waystone?
Waystone!

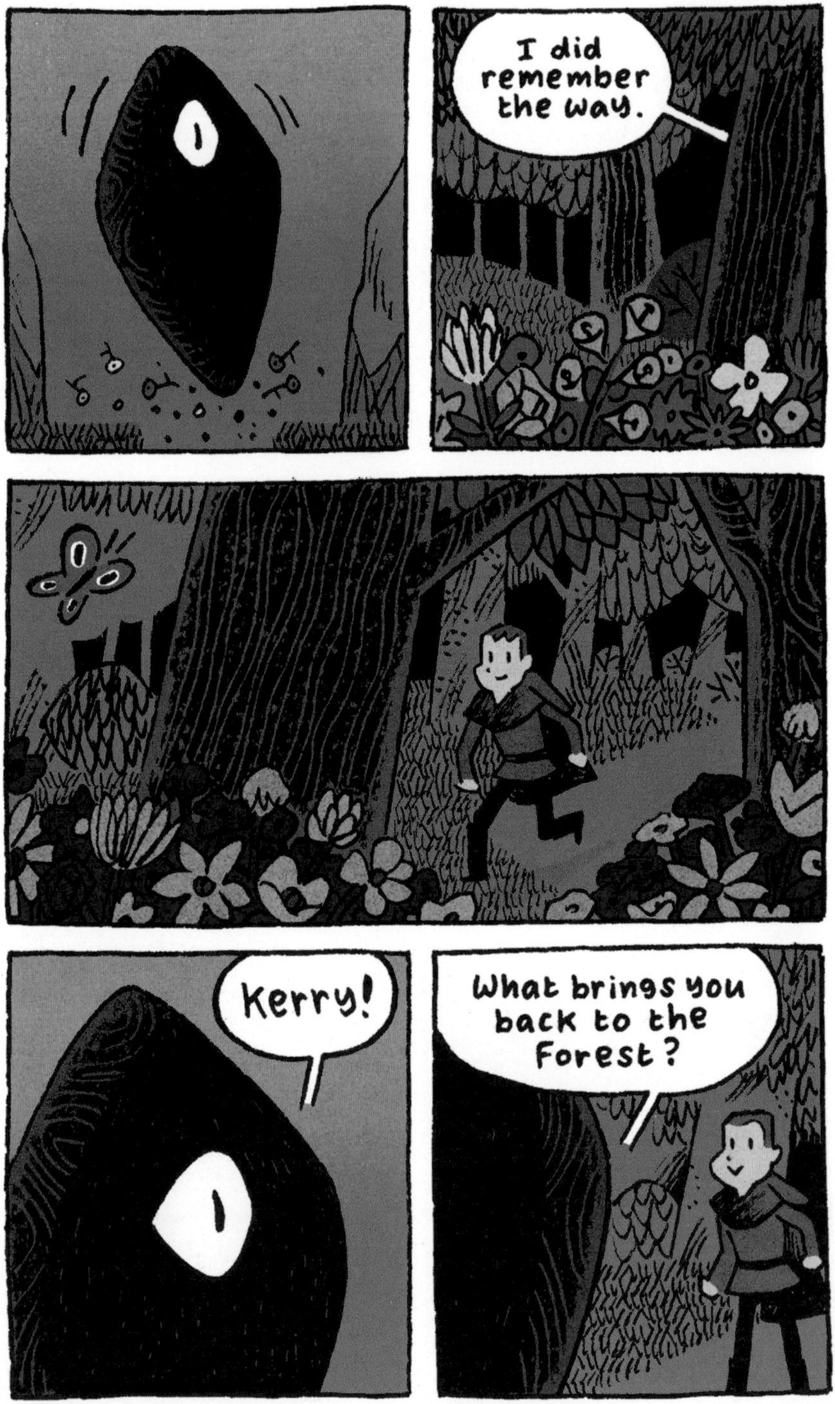
I did remember the way.
Kerry!
What brings you back to the Forest?

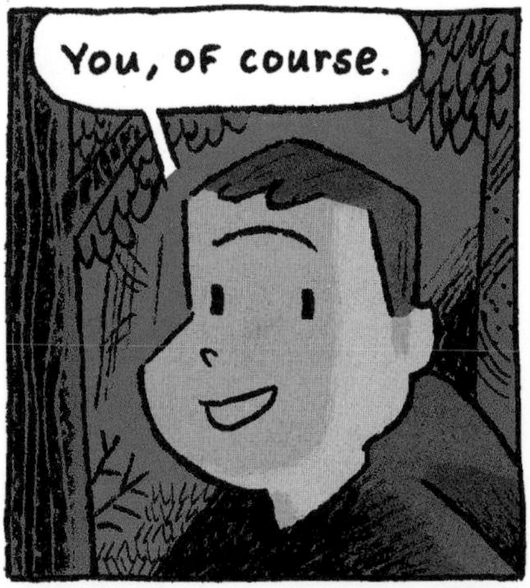
You, of course.

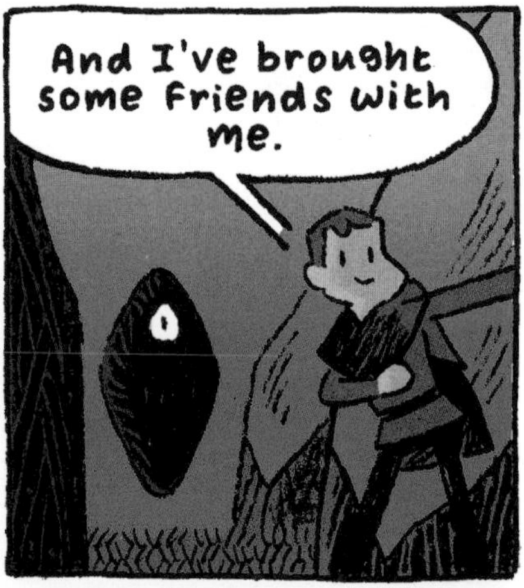
And I've brought some friends with me.

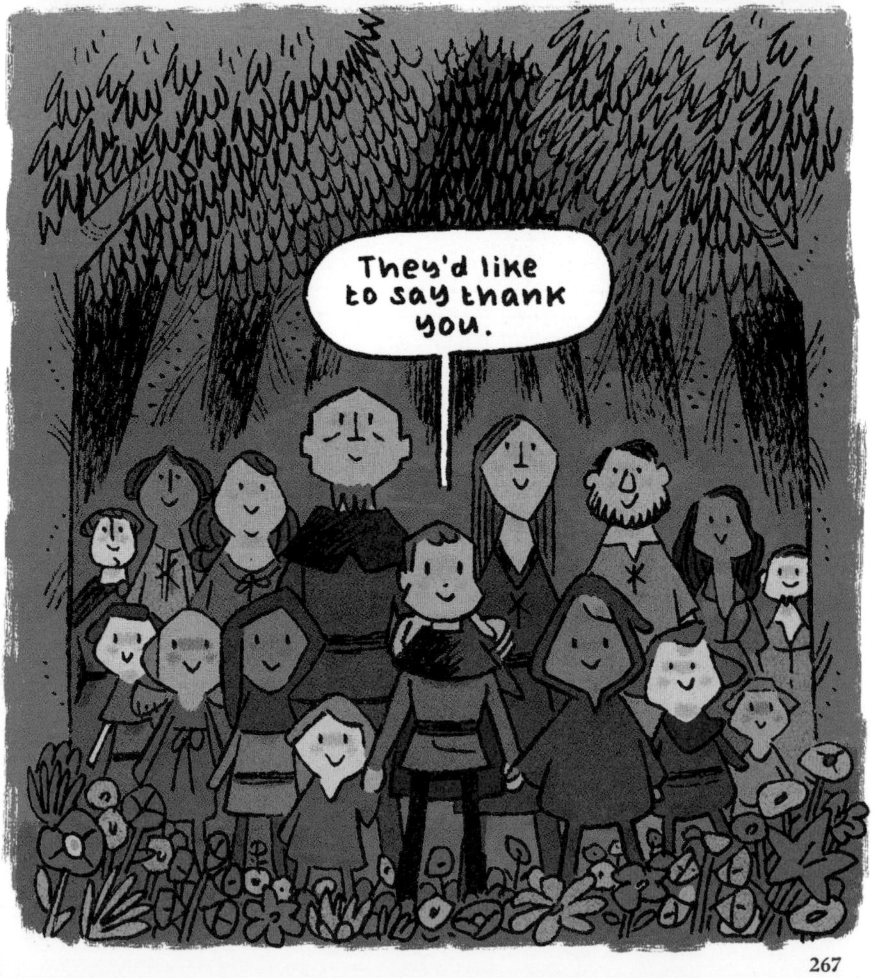
They'd like to say thank you.

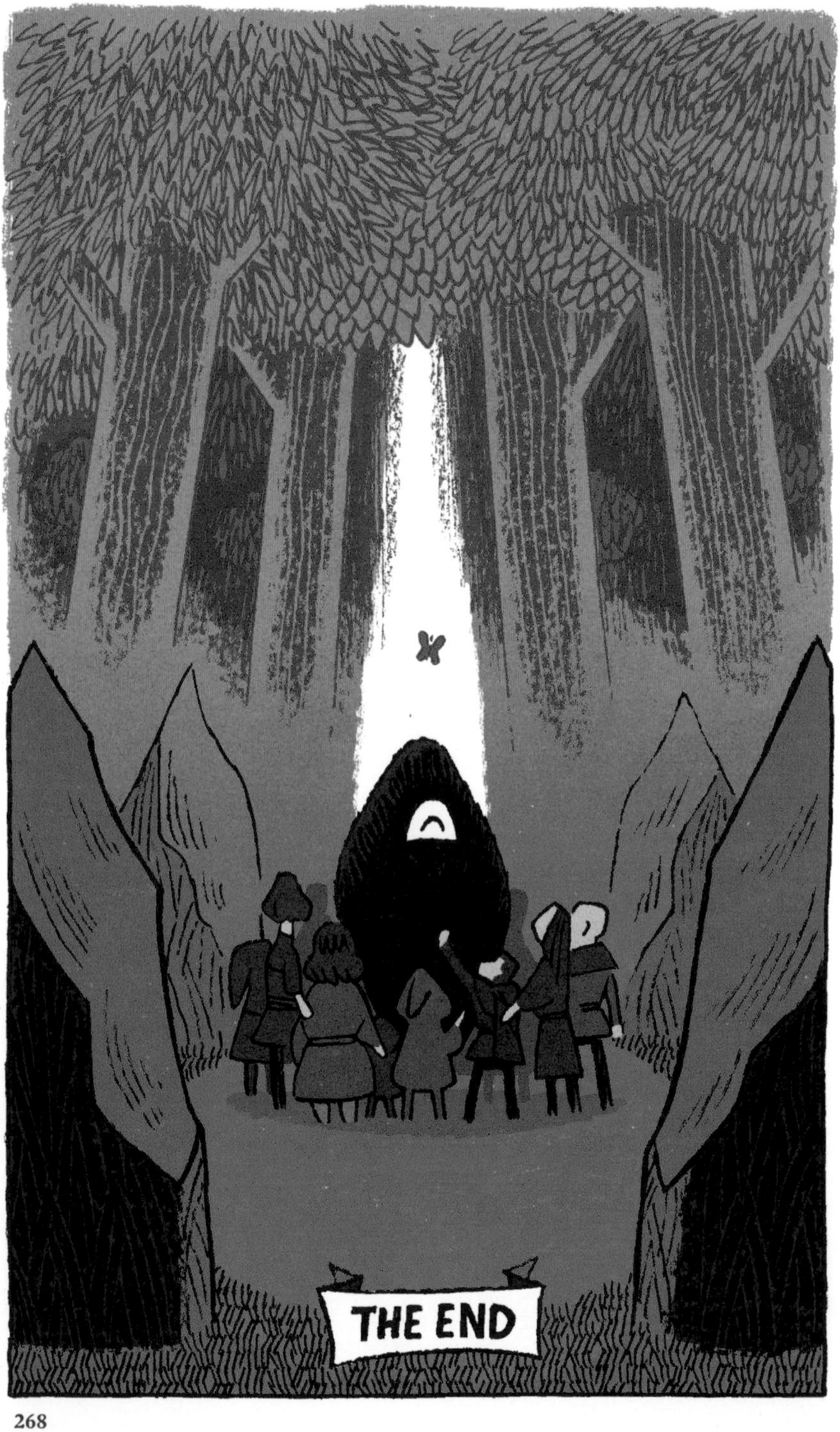
THE END

Kerry and the Knight of the Forest was drawn and lettered with Uni Pin pens, a blunt compass tip, and chinagraph pencils on 200g A5 sheets of fine grain paper. It was colored using Photoshop CS6 and a Wacom Bamboo tablet.

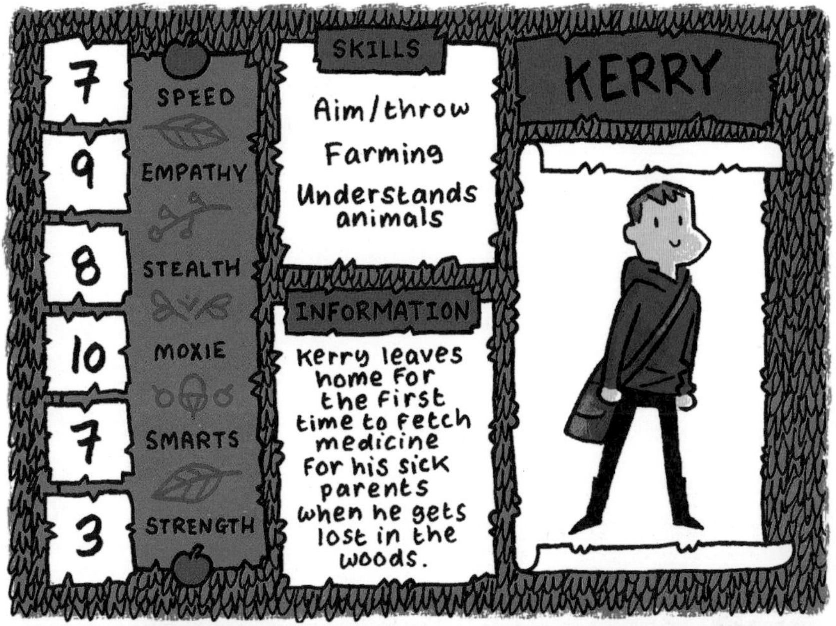
7
SPEED
9
EMPATHY
8
STEALTH
10
MOXIE
7
SMARTS
3
STRENGTH
SKILLS
Aim/throw
Farming
Understands animals
INFORMATION
Kerry leaves home for the first time to fetch medicine for his sick parents when he gets lost in the woods.
KERRY

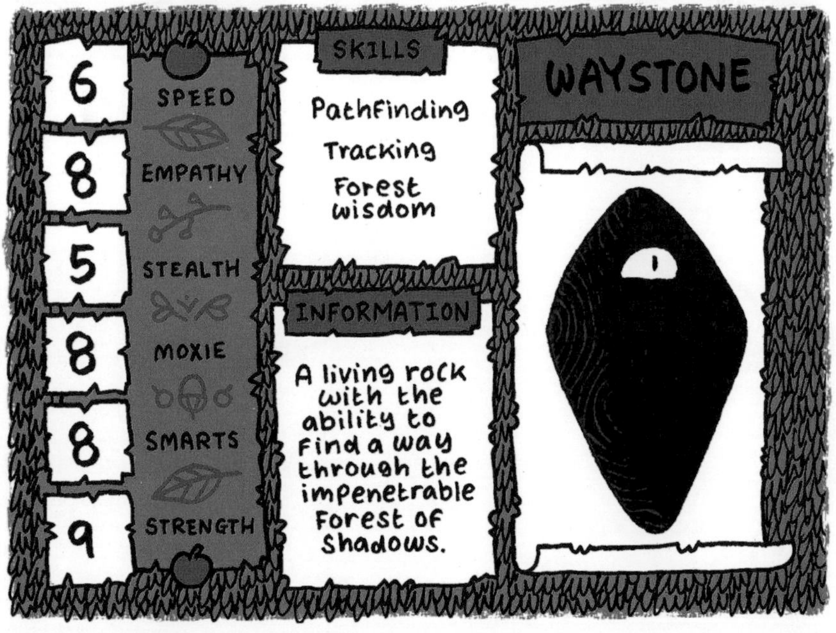
6
SPEED
8
EMPATHY
5
STEALTH
8
MOXIE
8
SMARTS
9
STRENGTH
SKILLS
Pathfinding
Tracking
Forest wisdom
INFORMATION
A living rock with the ability to find a way through the impenetrable Forest of Shadows.
WAYSTONE

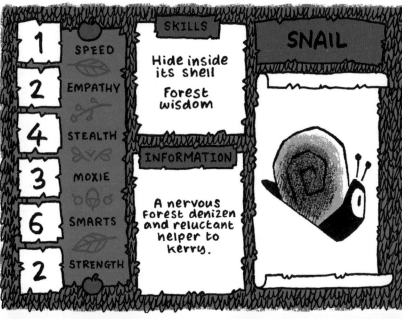

1	SPEED
2	EMPATHY
4	STEALTH
3	MOXIE
6	SMARTS
2	STRENGTH

SKILLS

Hide inside its shell

Forest wisdom

INFORMATION

A nervous forest denizen and reluctant helper to kerry.

SNAIL

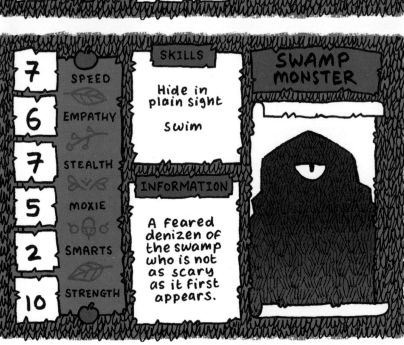

7	SPEED
6	EMPATHY
7	STEALTH
5	MOXIE
2	SMARTS
10	STRENGTH

SKILLS

Hide in plain sight

Swim

INFORMATION

A feared denizen of the swamp who is not as scary as it first appears.

SWAMP MONSTER

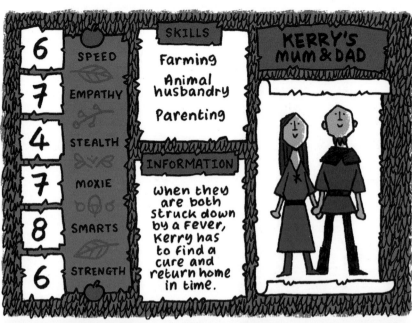

SKILLS

Farming

Animal husbandry

Parenting

INFORMATION

When they are both struck down by a fever, Kerry has to find a cure and return home in time.

6 SPEED
7 EMPATHY
4 STEALTH
7 MOXIE
8 SMARTS
6 STRENGTH

KERRY'S MUM & DAD

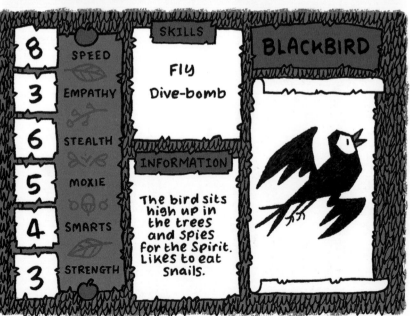

SKILLS

Fly

Dive-bomb

INFORMATION

The bird sits high up in the trees and spies for the Spirit. Likes to eat snails.

8 SPEED
3 EMPATHY
6 STEALTH
5 MOXIE
4 SMARTS
3 STRENGTH

BLACKBIRD

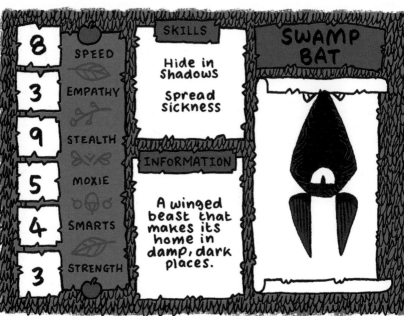

8	SPEED
3	EMPATHY
9	STEALTH
5	MOXIE
4	SMARTS
3	STRENGTH

SKILLS

Hide in Shadows

Spread Sickness

INFORMATION

A winged beast that makes its home in damp, dark places.

SWAMP BAT

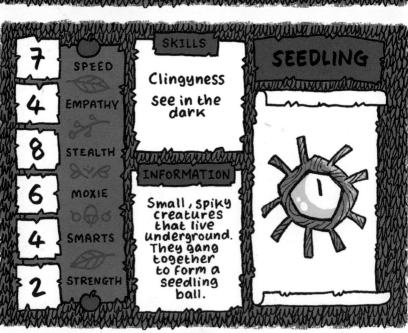

7	SPEED
4	EMPATHY
8	STEALTH
6	MOXIE
4	SMARTS
2	STRENGTH

SKILLS

Clingyness

See in the dark

INFORMATION

Small, spiky creatures that live underground. They gang together to form a seedling ball.

SEEDLING

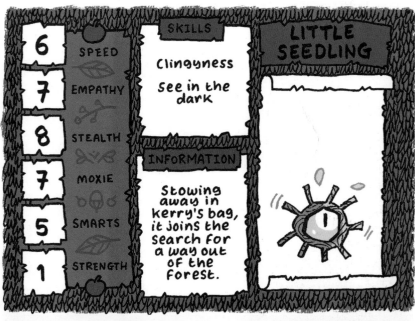

6	SPEED
7	EMPATHY
8	STEALTH
7	MOXIE
5	SMARTS
1	STRENGTH

SKILLS

Clingyness

See in the dark

INFORMATION

Stowing away in kerry's bag, it joins the search for a way out of the forest.

LITTLE SEEDLING

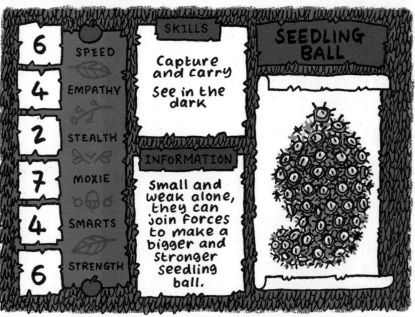

6	SPEED
4	EMPATHY
2	STEALTH
7	MOXIE
4	SMARTS
6	STRENGTH

SKILLS

Capture and carry

See in the dark

INFORMATION

Small and weak alone, they can join forces to make a bigger and stronger seedling ball.

SEEDLING BALL

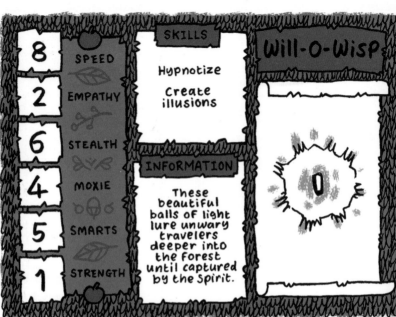

8	SPEED
2	EMPATHY
6	STEALTH
4	MOXIE
5	SMARTS
1	STRENGTH

SKILLS

Hypnotize

Create illusions

INFORMATION

These beautiful balls of light lure unwary travelers deeper into the forest until captured by the Spirit.

Will-O-Wisp

0

6	SPEED
3	EMPATHY
9	STEALTH
5	MOXIE
3	SMARTS
7	STRENGTH

SKILLS

Hide in plain sight

Tracking

INFORMATION

Disguising themselves as bushes, the Gorse Folk lie in wait to attack those who have lost their way.

GORSE FOLK

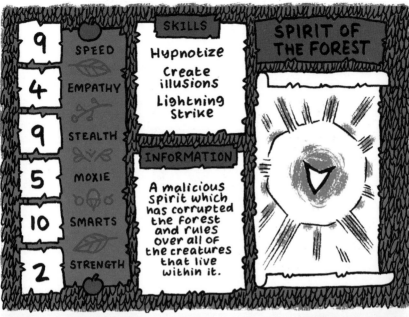

SPIRIT OF THE FOREST

9 SPEED
4 EMPATHY
9 STEALTH
5 MOXIE
10 SMARTS
2 STRENGTH

SKILLS

Hypnotize

Create illusions

Lightning Strike

INFORMATION

A malicious spirit which has corrupted the forest and rules over all of the creatures that live within it.

FOREST CHILDREN

6 SPEED
7 EMPATHY
8 STEALTH
3 MOXIE
6 SMARTS
2 STRENGTH

SKILLS

Mislead

Hide in plain sight

INFORMATION

Children lured into the forest by the Spirit and held there at the whim of their captor.

CREATE YOUR OWN CHARACTER

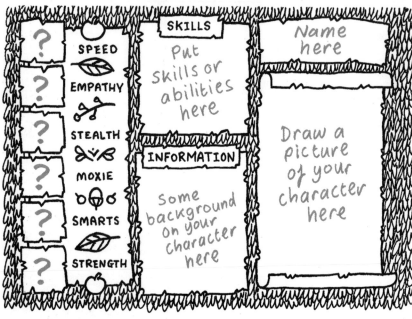

SPEED
EMPATHY
STEALTH
MOXIE
SMARTS
STRENGTH

? ? ? ? ? ?

SKILLS
Put skills or abilities here

INFORMATION
Some background on your character here

Name here

Draw a picture of your character here

Trace onto a separate sheet

- Assign your character a number between one and ten for each characteristic.

- Are they an animal, a creature or a person? Are they you?

- Give at least one characteristic a low number. If they are very strong, then they might have low stealth or speed.

- Note down their skills and a little bit about them in the information box.

- Draw a picture of your character.

10	SPEED
0	EMPATHY
10	STEALTH
5	MOXIE
6	SMARTS
10	STRENGTH

?

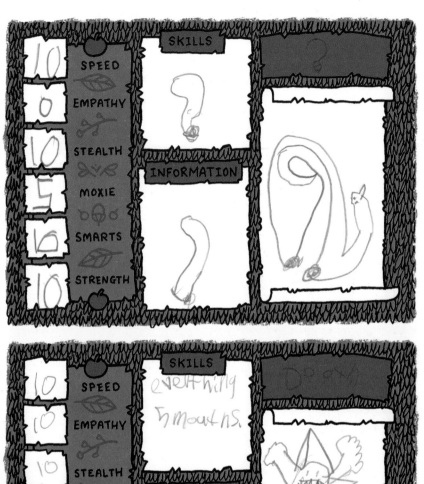

SKILLS

?

INFORMATION

?

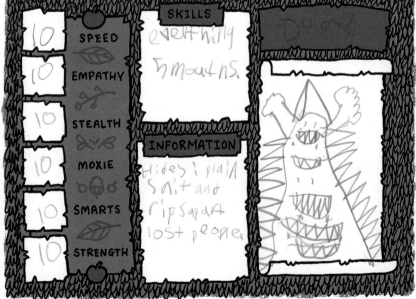

10	SPEED
10	EMPATHY
10	STEALTH
10	MOXIE
10	SMARTS
10	STRENGTH

Death

SKILLS

everything
5 mouths.

INFORMATION

Hides i plain
Sait and
rips apart
lost people.

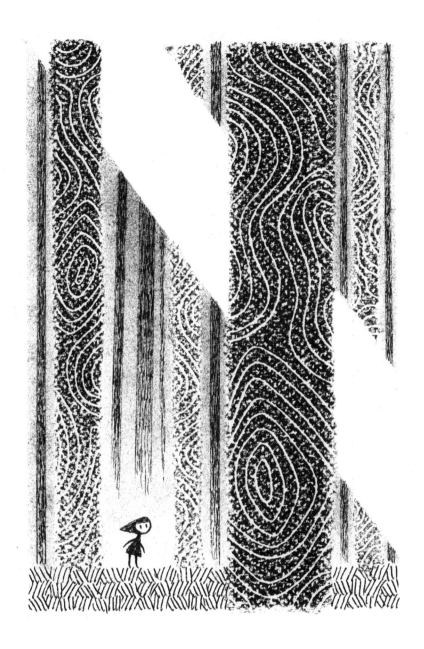

These are pages from an early attempt at this story a number of years ago. I'd picked it up and put it aside several times, including thumbnailing out an entire graphic novel before abandoning it.

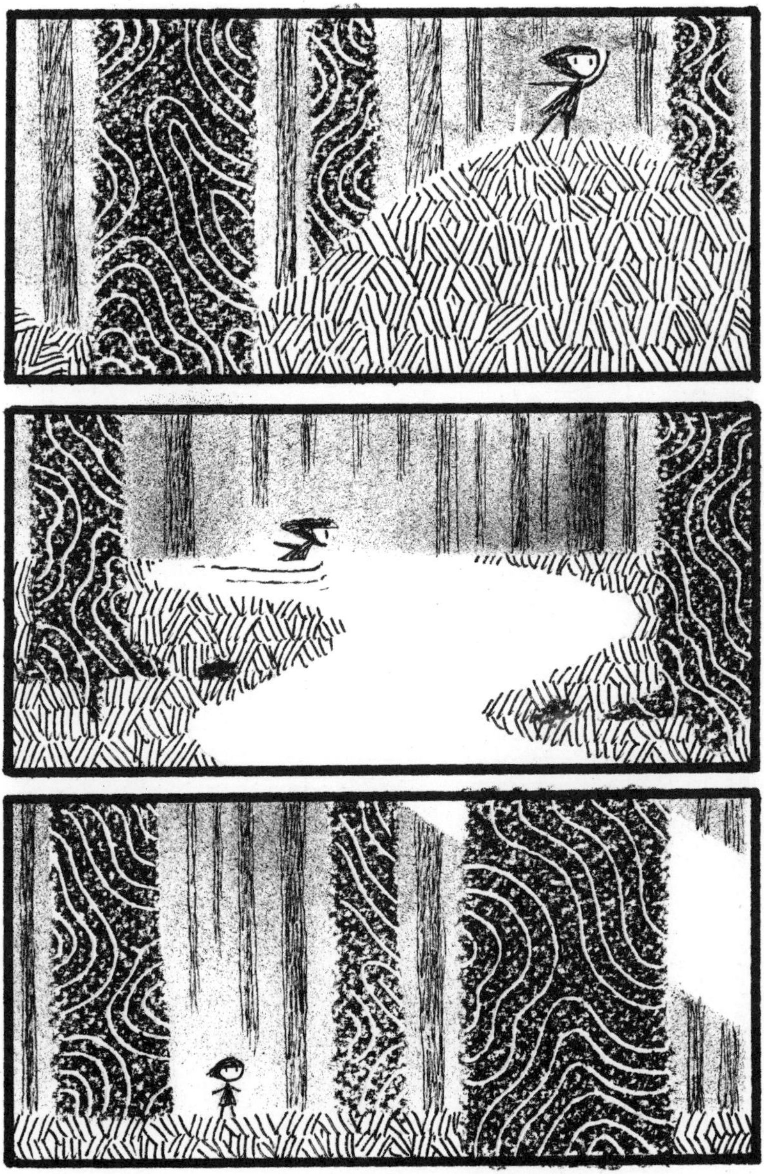

The fairy tale idea of the child lost in the woods wouldn't go away, though. Eventually I took it up again with the idea of the Waystone and it finally came together. Sometimes a story has to sit and stew a long time before it's ready.

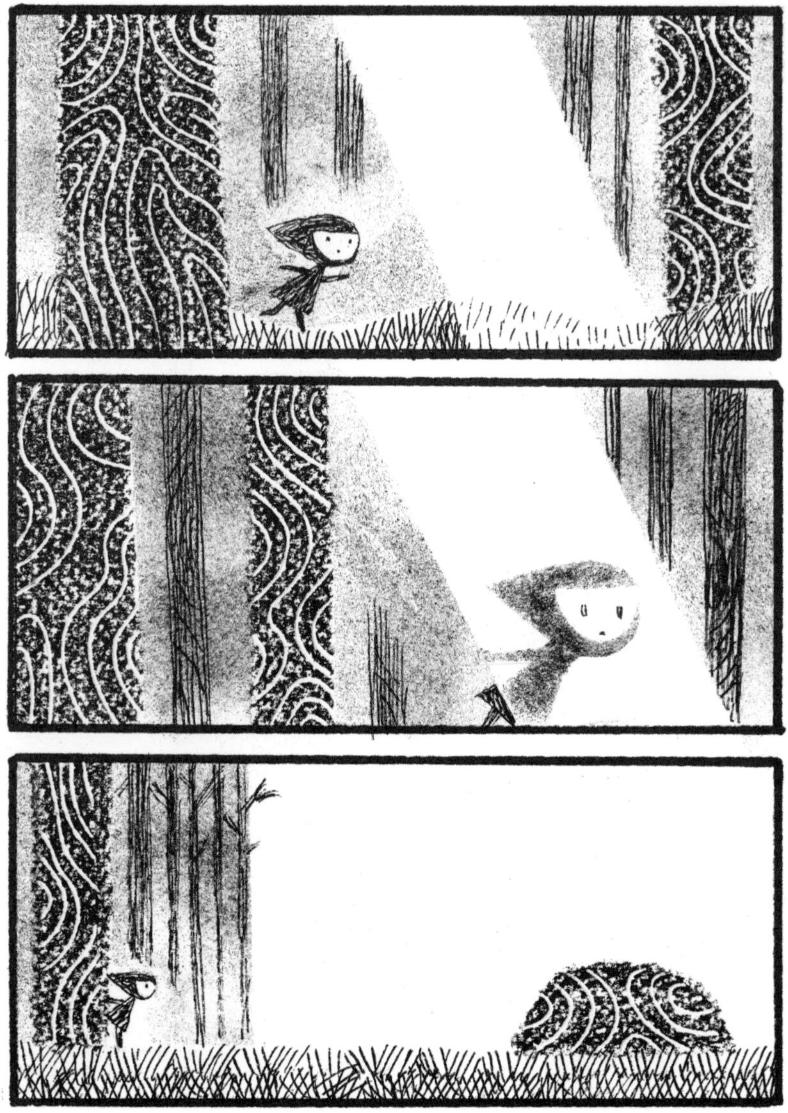

One thing that remained consistent throughout the development of the book was a way of drawing that would incorporate texture and pattern.

Kerry began as a very simple design, more of a symbol, like a pawn on a chessboard, than a person. I needed to add detail and bring him to life.

This is my first book to be in full color, and so I experimented with different ways to use it and what kind of color palette I was going to employ. Here I used an inkpad and sponge to get the murky effect.

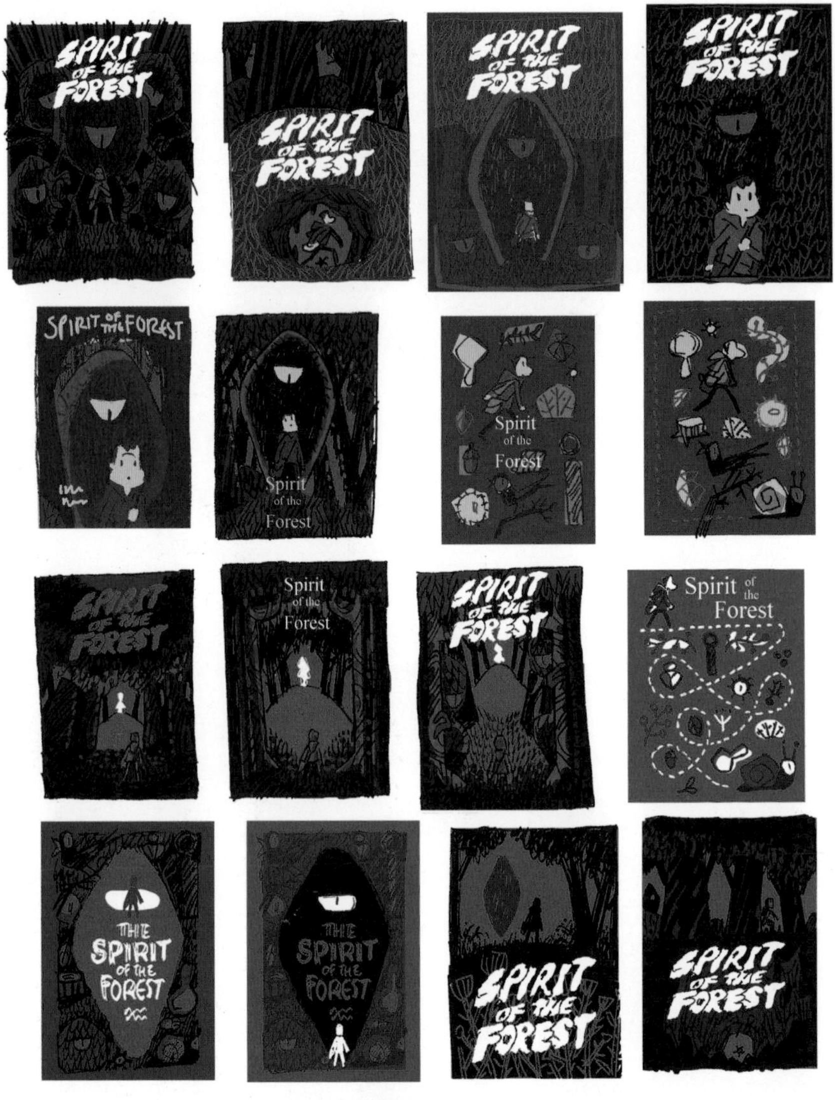
SPIRIT OF THE FOREST
SPIRIT OF THE FOREST
SPIRIT OF THE FOREST
SPIRIT OF THE FOREST
SPIRIT OF THE FOREST
Spirit of the Forest
Spirit of the Forest
SPIRIT OF THE FOREST
Spirit of the Forest
SPIRIT OF THE FOREST
Spirit of the Forest
THE SPIRIT OF THE FOREST
THE SPIRIT OF THE FOREST
SPIRIT OF THE FOREST
SPIRIT OF THE FOREST

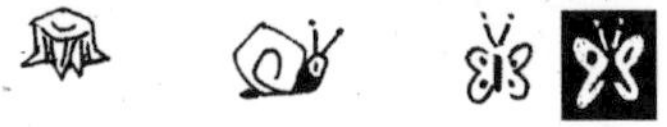

I studied graphic design and illustration at college and love the process of designing book covers. I tend to do lots of little thumbnail sketches to work out the best combinations of words and image. I find a cover that works well as a tiny sketch will often make an eye-catching cover design that will stand out on the bookshelves. Patrick (the designer) and I tried lots of different ideas before settling on the right one.

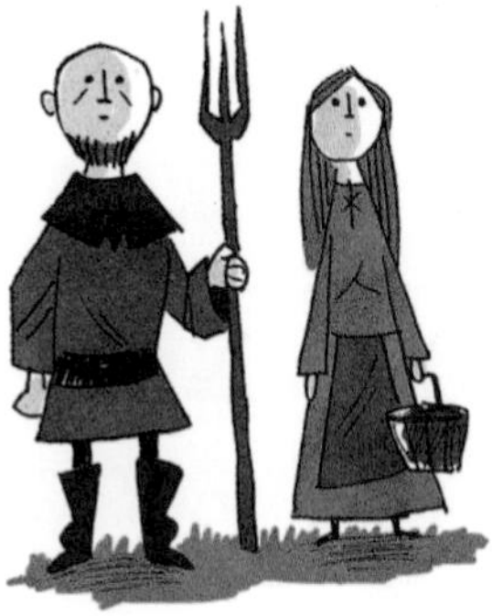

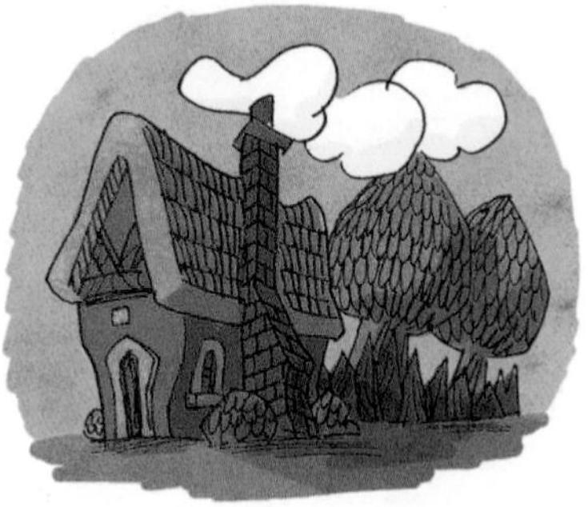

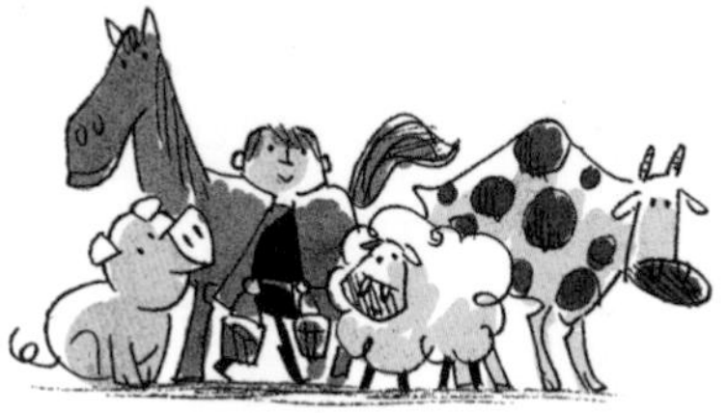

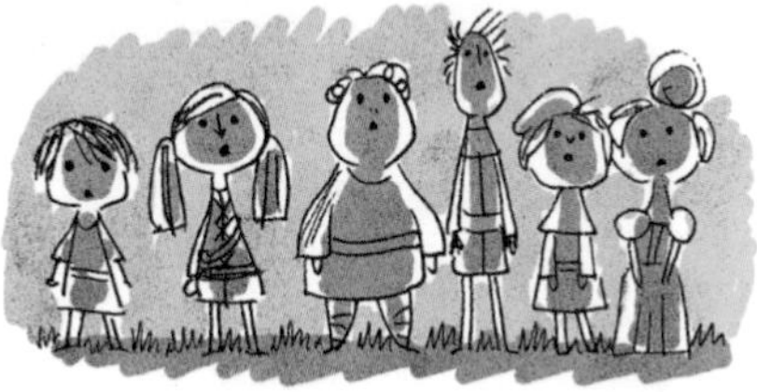

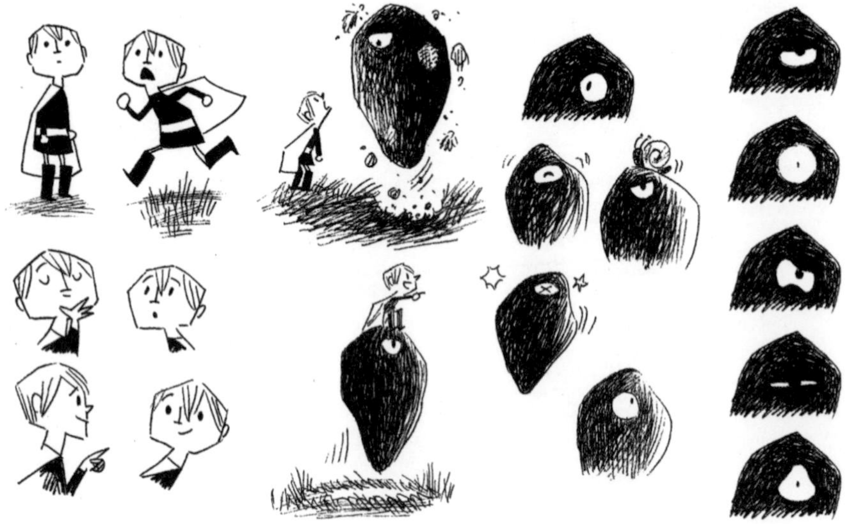

These are some of the development sketches I drew up in order to help visualize what the other characters and settings in the story would look like. I worked on giving Kerry more individuality and figured out how to bring a rock personality. They were stepping-stones on the way to the final designs. A finished book is only the visible tip of a mountain of sketches, scripts, and wrong turns.

Thank you to Gina, Whitney, Patrick, and the whole team at RHG for helping make this book happen.

Andi Watson was born and raised in a small town in the north of England, where he loved to draw and read books. As a kid, he read the Star Wars and Beano comic books. As a teenager, he read fantasy trilogies and obsessed over Dungeons & Dragons. He rediscovered comics while at art school, amazed by series like Akira and Love and Rockets. At the very end of his degree, he decided to make his own comic, as this would be his only opportunity before taking up a career in illustration. It didn't quite work out that way, as many years later he is still telling stories with words and pictures, this being his thirtieth book. He has created comics for grown-ups and children and those somewhere in between. These include stand-alone graphic novels for adults such as *Breakfast After Noon* and *Slow News Day*, series for teenagers like Skeleton Key, and series for children like Glister and Gum Girl. He's occasionally been nominated for awards and has had books translated into French, Spanish, German, and Italian. He still enjoys reading and drawing. He lives in Worcester, England, with his wife and daughter, where he drinks tea and is trying to learn French (again).

@andicomics
andiwatson.info

RH GRAPHIC

THE SUMMER 2020 LIST

CRABAPPLE TROUBLE
Kaeti Vandorn

CRABAPPLE TROUBLE

By Kaeti Vandorn

Life isn't easy when you're an apple.

Callaway and Thistle must figure out how to work together—with delicious and magical results.

Young Chapter Book

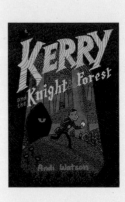

KERRY
and the Knight of the Forest
Andi Watson

KERRY AND THE KNIGHT OF THE FOREST

By Andi Watson

Kerry needs to get home!

To get back to his parents Kerry gets lost in a shortc He will have to make toug choices and figure out wh to trust—or remain lost in the forest . . . forever.

Middle Grade

STEPPING STONES

By Lucy Knisley

Jen did not want to leave the city.

She did not want to move to a farm.

And Jen definitely did not want to get two new "sisters."

Middle Grade

NEW YORK TIMES BESTSELLING AUTHOR
LUCY KNISLEY
STEPPING STONES
Peapod Farm
Berries
Flowers
Granola

SUNCATCHER

By Jose Pimienta

Beatriz loves music—more than her school, more than her friends—and she won't let anything stop her from achieving her dreams.

Even if it means losing everything else.

Young Adult

Suncatche
JOSE PIMIE

@RHKIDSGRAPHIC AND RHKIDSGRAPHIC.COM